D1326407

The Malory Towers Omnibus

ENID BLYTON

The Malory Towers Omnibus

containing

First Term at Malory Towers
Second Form at Malory Towers
Third Year at Malory Towers
Upper Fourth at Malory Towers

WHSMITH
EXCLUSIVE
· BOOKS ·

This edition published in 1987 by W. H. Smith & Son Ltd
by arrangement with Methuen Children's Books Ltd,
11 New Fetter Lane, London EC4P 4EE
Printed in Finland by Werner Söderström Oy
ISBN 0 416 97040 0

FIRST TERM AT MALORY TOWERS

Up the steps went Darrell, feeling lost and lonely

FIRST TERM
AT MALORY TOWERS

The First Book of Malory Towers

by

ENID BLYTON

ILLUSTRATED BY

JENNY CHAPPLE

This is the first book of the series about Malory Towers. The others are:

The series follows Darrell Rivers and her friends through their school life. Each book is complete in itself.

CONTENTS

1   OFF TO BOARDING SCHOOL

DARRELL RIVERS looked at herself in the glass. It was almost time to start for the train, but there was just a minute to see how she looked in her new school uniform.

'It's jolly nice,' said Darrell, turning herself about. 'Brown coat, brown hat, orange ribbon, and a brown tunic underneath with an orange belt. I like it.'

Her mother looked into Darrell's room, and smiled. 'Admiring yourself?' she said. 'Well, I like it all too. I must say Malory Towers has a lovely school uniform. Come along, Darrell. We don't want to miss the train your very first term!'

Darrell felt excited. She was going to boarding school for the first time. Malory Towers did not take children younger than twelve, so Darrell would be one of the youngest there. She looked forward to many terms of fun and friendship, work and play.

'What will it be like?' she kept wondering. 'I've read lots of school stories, but I expect it won't be quite the same at Malory Towers. Every school is different. I do hope I make some friends there.'

Darrell was sad at leaving her own friends behind her. None of them was going to Malory Towers. She had been to a day-school with them, and most of them were either staying on there or going to different boarding schools.

Her trunk was packed full. On the side was painted in big black letters DARRELL RIVERS. On the labels were the letters M.T. for Malory Towers. Darrell had only to carry her tennis racket in its press, and her small bag in which her mother had packed her things for the first night.

'Your trunks won't be unpacked the first evening,' she said. 'So each girl has to take a small hand-bag with her nighty and tooth-brush and things like that. Here is your ten-shilling note. You must make that last a whole term, because no girl in your form is allowed to have more pocket-money than that.'

'I shall make it do!' said Darrell, putting it into her purse. 'There won't be much I have to buy at school! There's the taxi waiting, Mother. Let's go!'

She had already said good-bye to her father, who had driven off to his work that morning. He had squeezed her hard and said 'Good-bye and good luck, Darrell. You'll get a lot out of Malory Towers, because it's a fine school. Be sure you give them a lot back!'

Now they were off at last, the trunk in the taxi too, beside the driver. Darrell put her head out to take a last look at her home. 'I'll be back soon!' she called, to the big black cat who sat on the wall, washing himself. 'I'll miss you all at first but I'll soon settle down. Shan't I, Mother?'

'Of course,' said her mother. 'You'll have a lovely time! You won't want to come home for the summer holidays!'

They had to go up to London to catch the train for Cornwall, where Malory Towers was. 'There's a special train always, for Malory Towers,' said Mrs. Rivers. 'Look, there's a notice up. Malory Towers. Platform 7. Come along. We're in nice time. I'll stay with you a few minutes and see you safely with your house-mistress, and her girls, then I'll go.'

They went on to the platform. A long train was drawn up there, labelled Malory Towers. All the carriages were reserved for the girls of that school. The train had different labels stuck in the windows. The first lot said 'North Tower.' The second lot said 'South Tower.' Then came compartments labelled 'West Tower' and others labelled 'East Tower'.

'You're North Tower,' said her mother. 'Malory Towers has four different boarding houses for its girls, all topped by a tower. You'll be in North Tower, the Head Mistress said, and your house-mistress is Miss Potts. We must find her.'

Darrell stared about her at the girls on the crowded platform. They all seemed to be Malory girls, for she saw the brown coats and hats, with the orange ribbons, everywhere. They all seemed to know one another, and laughed and chattered at the tops of their voices. Darrell felt suddenly shy.

'I shall never never know all these girls!' she thought, as she stared round. 'Gracious, what big ones some of them are! They look quite grown-up. I shall be terrified of them.'

Certainly the girls in the top forms seemed very grown-up to Darrell. They took no notice at all of the little ones. The younger girls made way for them, and they climbed into their carriages in a rather lordly manner.

'Hallo, Lottie! Hallo, Mary! I say, there's Penelope! Hie, Penny, come over here. Hilda, you never wrote to me in the hols., you mean pig! Jean, come into our carriage!'

The gay voices sounded all up and down the platform. Darrell looked for her mother. Ah, there she was, talking to a keen-faced mistress. That must be Miss Potts. Darrell stared at her. Yes, she liked her—she liked the way her eyes twinkled—but there was something very determined about her mouth. It wouldn't do to get into her bad books.

Miss Potts came over and smiled down at Darrell. 'Well, new girl!' she said. 'You'll be in my carriage going down—look, that one over there. The new girls always go with me.'

'Oh, are there new girls besides me—in my form, I mean ? ' asked Darrell.

'Oh, yes. Two more. They haven't arrived yet. Mrs. Rivers, here is a girl in Darrell's form—Alicia Johns. She will look after Darrell for you, when you've said good-bye.'

'Hallo,' said Alicia, and two bright eyes twinkled at Darrell. 'I'm in your form. Do you want to get a corner-seat ? If so, you'd better come now.'

'Then I'll say good-bye, dear,' said Mrs. Rivers, cheerfully, and she kissed Darrell and gave her a hug. 'I'll write as soon as I get your letter. Have a lovely time ! '

'Yes, I will,' said Darrell, and watched her mother go down the platform. She didn't have time to feel lonely because Alicia took complete charge of her at once, pushed her to Miss Potts's carriage, and shoved her up the step. 'Put your bag in one corner and I'll put mine opposite,' said Alicia. ' Then we can stand at the door and see what's happening. I say—look over there. Picture of How Not to Say Good-bye to your Darling Daughter ! '

Darrell looked to where Alicia nodded. She saw a girl about her own age, dressed in the same school uniform, but with her hair long and loose down her back. She was clinging to her mother and wailing.

' Now what that mother should do would be to grin, shove some chocolate at her and go ! ' said Alicia. ' If you've got a kid like that, it's hopeless to do anything else. Poor little mother's darling ! '

The mother was almost as bad as the girl. Tears were running down her face too. Miss Potts walked firmly up to them.

' Now you watch Potty,' said Alicia. Darrell felt rather shocked. Potty ! What a name to give your house-mistress. Anyway, Miss Potts didn't look in the least potty. She looked thoroughly all-there.

' I'll take Gwendoline,' she said to the girl's mother.

'It's time she went to her carriage. She'll soon settle down there, Mrs. Lacey.'

Gwendoline appeared ready to go, but her mother clung to her still. Alicia snorted. 'See what's made Gwendoline such an idiot?' she said. 'Her mother! Well, I'm glad mine is sensible. Yours looked jolly nice too—cheerful and jolly.'

Darrell was pleased at this praise of her mother. She watched Miss Potts firmly disentangle Gwendoline from her mother and lead her towards them.

'Alicia! Here's another one,' she said, and Alicia pulled Gwendoline up into the carriage.

Gwendoline's mother came to the carriage too and looked in. 'Take a corner-seat, darling,' she said. 'And don't sit with your back to the engine. You know how sick it makes you. And . . .'

Another girl came up to the carriage, a small, sturdy girl, with a plain face and hair tightly plaited back. 'Is this Miss Potts's carriage?' she asked.

'Yes,' said Alicia. 'Are you the third new girl? North Tower?'

'Yes. I'm Sally Hope,' said the girl.

'Where's your mother?' asked Alicia. 'She ought to go and deliver you to Miss Potts first, so that you can be crossed off her list.'

'Oh, Mother didn't bother to come up with me,' said Sally. 'I came by myself.'

'Gracious!' said Alicia. 'Well, mothers are all different. Some come along and smile and say good-bye, and some come along and weep and wail—and some just don't come at all.'

'Alicia—don't talk so much,' came Miss Potts's voice. She knew Alicia's wild tongue. Mrs. Lacey suddenly looked annoyed, and forgot to give any more instructions to Gwendoline. She stared at Alicia angrily. Fortunately

the guard blew his whistle just then and there was a wild
scramble for seats.

Miss Potts jumped in with two or three more girls. The
door slammed. Gwendoline's mother peered in, but alas,
Gwendoline was on the floor, hunting for something she
had dropped.

'Where's Gwendoline!' came Mrs. Lacey's voice. 'I
must say good-bye. Where's . . .'

But the train was now puffing out. Gwendoline sat up
and howled.

'I didn't say good-bye!' she wailed.

'Well, how many times did you want to?' demanded
Alicia. 'You'd already said it about twenty times.'

Miss Potts looked at Gwendoline. She had already
sized her up and knew her to be a spoilt, only child, selfish,
and difficult to handle at first.

She looked at quiet little Sally Hope. Funny little girl,
with her tight plaits and prim, closed-up face. No mother
had come to see her off. Did Sally care? Miss Potts
couldn't tell.

Then she looked at Darrell. It was quite easy to read
Darrell. She never hid anything, and she said what she
thought, though not so bluntly as Alicia did.

'A nice, straightforward, trustable girl,' thought Miss
Potts. 'Can be a bit of a monkey, I should think. She
looks as if she has good brains. I'll see that she uses
them! I can do with a girl like Darrell in North Tower!'

The girls began to talk. 'What's Malory Towers like?'
asked Darrell. 'I've seen a photograph of it, of course.
It looked awfully big.'

'It is. It's got the most gorgeous view over the sea, too,'
said Alicia. 'It's built on the cliff, you know. It's lucky
you're in North Tower—that's got the best view of all!'

'Does each Tower have its own schoolrooms?' asked
Darrell. Alicia shook her head.

'Oh, no! All the girls from each of the four Tower houses go to the same classrooms. There are about sixty girls in each house. Pamela is head of ours. There she is over there!'

Pamela was a tall, quiet girl, who had got into the carriage with another girl about her own age. They seemed very friendly with Miss Potts, and were eagerly discussing with her the happenings planned for the term.

Alicia, another girl called Tessie, Sally and Darrell chattered too. Gwendoline sat in her corner and looked gloomy. Nobody paid her any attention at all, and she wasn't used to that!

She gave a little sob, and looked at the others out of the corner of her eye. Sharp Alicia saw the look and grinned. 'Just putting it on!' she whispered to Darrell. 'People who really do feel miserable always turn away and hide it somehow. Don't take any notice of our darling Gwendoline.'

Poor Gwendoline! If she had only known it, Alicia's lack of sympathy was the best thing for her. She had always had far too much of it, and life at Malory Towers was not going to be easy for her.

'Cheer up, Gwendoline,' said Miss Potts, in a cheerful tone, and immediately turned to talk to the big girls again.

'I feel sick,' announced Gwendoline at last, quite determined to be in the limelight and get sympathy somehow.

'You don't look it,' said the downright Alicia. 'Does she, Miss Potts? I always go green when I feel sick.'

Gwendoline wished she could really be sick! That would serve this sharp-tongued girl right. She leaned back against the back of the seat, and murmured faintly. 'I really do feel sick! Oh, dear, what shall I do?'

'Here, wait a bit—I've got a paper bag,' said Alicia, and fished a big one out of her bag. 'I've got a brother who's always sick in a car, so Mother takes paper bags with her wherever she goes, for Sam. I always think it's funny to see him stick his nose in it, poor Sam—like a horse with a nose-bag!'

Nobody could help laughing at Alicia's story. Gwendoline didn't, of course, but looked angry. That horrid girl, poking fun at her again. She wasn't going to like her at all.

After that Gwendoline sat quiet, and made no further attempt to get the attention of the others. She was afraid of what Alicia might say next.

But Darrell looked at Alicia with amusement and liking. How she would like her for a friend! What fun they could have together!

2   MALORY TOWERS

IT was a long journey to Malory Towers, but as there was a dining-car on the train, and the girls took it in turns to go and have their midday meal, that made a good break. They had tea on the train too. At first all the girls were gay and chattery, but as the day wore on they fell silent. Some of them slept. It was such a long journey!

It was exciting to reach the station for Malory Towers. The school lay a mile or two away, and there were big motor coaches standing outside the station to take the girls to the school.

'Come on,' said Alicia, clutching hold of Darrell's arm. 'If we're quick we can get one of the front seats in a coach, beside the driver. Hurry! Got your bag?'

'I'll come too,' said Gwendoline. But the others were gone long before she had collected her belongings. They

climbed up into front seats. The other girls came out in
twos and threes, and the station's one and only porter helped
the drivers to load the many trunks on to the coaches.

'Can we see Malory Towers from here?' asked Darrell,
looking all round.

'No. I'll tell you when we can. There's a corner
where we suddenly get a glimpse of it,' said Alicia.

'Yes. It's lovely to get that sudden view of it,' said
Pamela, the quiet head-girl of North Tower, who had got
into the coach just behind Alicia and Darrell. Her eyes
shone as she spoke. 'I think Malory Towers shows at its
best when we come to that corner, especially if the sun is
behind it.'

Darrell could feel the warmth in Pamela's voice as she spoke
of the school she loved. She looked at her and liked her.

Pamela saw her look and laughed. 'You're lucky,
Darrell,' she said. 'You're just beginning at Malory
Towers! You've got terms and terms before you. I'm
just ending. Another term or two, and I shan't be coming
to Malory Towers any more—except as an old girl. You
make the most of it while you can.'

'I shall,' said Darrell, and stared ahead, waiting for her first
glimpse of the school she was to go to for at least six years.

They rounded a corner. Alicia nudged her arm. 'There
you are, look! Over there, on that hill! The sea is
behind, far down the cliff, but you can't see that, of course.'

Darrell looked. She saw a big, square-looking building
of soft grey stone standing high up on a hill. The hill was
really a cliff, that fell steeply down to the sea. At each
end of the gracious building stood rounded towers. Darrell
could glimpse two other towers behind as well, making
four in all. North Tower, South, East and West.

The windows shone. The green creeper that covered
parts of the wall climbed almost to the roof in places.
It looked like an old-time castle.

' My school ! ' thought Darrell, and a little warm feeling came into her heart. ' It's fine. How lucky I am to be having Malory Towers as my school-home for so many years. I shall love it.'

' Do you like it ? ' asked Alicia, impatiently.

' Yes. Very much,' said Darrell. ' But I shall never never know my way about it ! It's so big.'

' Oh, I'll soon show you,' said Alicia. ' It's surprising how quickly you get to know your way round.'

The coach turned another corner and Malory Towers was lost to sight. It came into view again, nearer still, round the next corner, and it wasn't very long before all the coaches roared up to the flight of steps that led to the great front door.

' It's just like a castle entrance ! ' said Darrell.

' Yes,' said Gwendoline, unexpectedly, from behind them. ' I shall feel like a fairy princess, going up those steps ! ' She tossed her loose golden hair back over her shoulders.

' You would ! ' said Alicia, scornfully. ' But you'll soon get ideas like that out of your head when Potty gets going on you.'

Darrell got down and was immediately lost in a crowd of girls, all swarming up the steps. She looked round for Alicia, but she seemed to have disappeared. So up the steps went Darrell, clutching her small bag and racket, feeling rather lost and lonely in the chattering crowd of girls. She felt in quite a panic without the friendly Alicia !

After that things were rather a blur. Darrell didn't know where to go and she didn't know what to do. She looked vainly for Alicia, or Pamela, the head-girl. Was she supposed to go straight to North Tower ? Everyone seemed to know exactly what to do and where to go, except poor Darrell !

Then she saw Miss Potts, and felt a wave of relief. She went up to her, and Miss Potts looked down, smiling.

'Hallo! Feeling lost? Where's that rascal of an Alicia?
She ought to look after you. All North Tower girls are
to go there and unpack their night-bags. Matron is waiting
for you all.'

Darrell had no idea which way to go for North Tower,
so she stood by Miss Potts, waiting. Alicia soon re-
appeared again, accompanied by a crowd of girls.

'Hallo!' she said to Darrell. 'I lost you. These are all
girls in our form, but I won't tell you their names just now.
You'll only get muddled. Some are North Tower girls, but
some belong to the other houses. Come on, let's go to North
Tower and see Matron. Where's darling Gwendoline?'

'Alicia,' said Miss Potts, her voice stern, but her eyes
twinkling. 'Give Gwendoline a chance!'

'And Sally Hope? Where's she?' said Alicia. 'Come
on, Sally. All right, Miss Potts, I'll take them along to
North Tower, and nurse them a bit!'

Sally, Gwendoline and Darrell followed Alicia. They
were in a big hall, that had doors leading off on either
side, and a wide staircase curving upwards.

'The assembly hall, the gyms., the lab., the art-rooms,
and the needlework room are all on this side,' said Alicia.
'Come on, we'll cross the Court to get to our tower.'

Darrell wondered what the Court was. She soon found
out. Malory Towers was built round a large oblong space,
called the Court. Alicia took her and the others out of a
door opposite the entrance they had come in by, and there
lay the Court surrounded on all sides by the buildings.

'What a lovely place!' said Darrell. 'What's that sunk
piece in the middle?'

She pointed to a great circle of green grass sunk a good
way below the level of the Court. Round the sloping sides
of the circle were stone seats. It looked like an open-air
circus ring, the ring sunk low, and the stone seats rising
upwards around it, Darrell thought.

' That's where we act plays in the summer,' said Alicia.
' The players perform in the ring, and the audience sit
round on those stone seats. We have good fun.'

Round the sunk circle, on the level, was a beautifully
set out garden, with roses and all kinds of flowers planted
there.   Green lawns, not yet cut by the gardeners, were
set between the beds.

' It's warm and sheltered in the Court,' said Darrell.

' It's too hot in the summer,' said Alicia, steering them
all across the Court to the opposite side.   ' But you should
see it in the Easter term !   When we come back, in January,
leaving our own homes in frost and maybe snow, we find
snowdrops and aconites and primroses blooming in all the
beds here, in the sheltered Court.   It's gorgeous.   Well,
look at the tulips coming out here already, and it's only
April ! '

At each end of the hollow oblong of buildings was ⸂
tower. Alicia was making for North Tower.   It was
exactly like the other three.   Darrell looked at it.   It was
four storeys high.   Alicia stopped short just outside.

' On the ground floor there's our dining-hall, our common
rooms, where we go when we're not in class, and the kitchens.
On the second floor are the dormies, where we sleep—
dormitories, you know.   On the third floor are more dormies.   On the top floor are the bedrooms of the staff, and
the box rooms for our luggage.'

' And each house is the same, I suppose ? ' said Darrell,
and she looked up at her tower.   ' I wish I slept right at
the top there, in the tower itself.   What a lovely view I'd
have ! '

Girls were going in and out of the open door at the
bottom of North Tower.   ' Buck up ! ' they called to
Alicia.   ' Supper's in a few minutes' time—something good
by the smell of it ! '

' We always get a jolly good supper the day we arrive,'

said Alicia. 'After that—not so good! Cocoa and biscuits, something like that. Come on, let's find Matron.'

Each of the Tower houses had its own matron, responsible for the girls' health and well-being. The matron of North Tower was a plump, bustling woman, dressed in starched apron and print frock, very neat and spotless.

Alicia took the new girls to her. 'Three more for you to dose and scold and run after!' said Alicia, with a grin.

Darrell looked at Matron, frowning over the long lists in her hand. Her hair was neatly tucked under a pretty cap, tied in a bow under her chin. She looked so spotless that Darrell began to feel very dirty and untidy. She felt a little scared of Matron, and hoped she wouldn't make her take nasty medicine too often.

Then Matron looked up and smiled, and at once Darrell's fears fell away. She couldn't be afraid of a person who smiled like that, with her eyes and her mouth and even her nose too!

'Now let me see—you're Darrell Rivers,' said Matron, ticking off her name on a list. 'Got your health certificate with you? Give it to me, please. And you're Sally Hope.'

'No, I'm Gwendoline Mary Lacey,' said Gwendoline.

'And don't forget the Mary,' said Alicia, pertly. 'Dear Gwendoline Mary.'

'That's enough, Alicia,' said Matron, ticking away down her list. 'You're as bad as your mother used to be. No. worse, I think.'

Alicia grinned. 'Mother came to Malory Towers when she was a girl,' she told the others. 'She was in North Tower too, and Matron had her for years. She sent you her best love, Matron. She says she wishes she could send all my brothers to you too. She's sure you're the only person who can manage them.'

'If they're anything like you, I'm very glad they're not here,' said Matron. 'One of the Johns family at a time

is quite enough for me. Your mother put some grey hairs
into my head, and you've certainly done your bit in adding
a few more.'

She smiled again. She had a wise, kindly face, and any
girl who fell ill felt safe in Matron's care. But woe betide
any pretender, or any lazy girl or careless one ! Then
Matron's smile snapped off, her face closed up, and her
eyes glinted dangerously !

A big gong boomed through North Tower. 'Supper,' said
Matron. 'Unpack your things afterwards, Alicia. Your
train was late and you must all be very tired. All first-
formers are to go to bed immediately after supper tonight.'

'Oh, *Ma*tron !' began Alicia, groaning. 'Can't we just
have ten minutes after . . .'

'I said im*mediate*ly, Alicia,' said Matron. 'Go along
now. Wash your hands quickly and go down. Hurry !'

And in five minutes time Alicia and the others were
sitting down, enjoying a good supper. They were hungry.
Darrell looked round at the tables. She was sure she would
never know all the girls in her house! And she was sure she
would never dare to join in their laugh and chatter either.

But she would, of course—and very soon too !

3   FIRST NIGHT AND MORNING

AFTER supper, obeying Matron's command, all the first-
formers went up to their dormitory. Darrell was delighted
with the room. It was long, and had windows all down
the length of it, which, to Darrell's joy, overlooked the sea.
She stood there, hearing the faraway sound of waves on
the beach, watching the slowly moving blue sea. What a
lovely place this was !

'Buck up, Dreamy!' said Alicia's voice. 'Matron will be along in two ticks.'

Darrell turned. She looked at the room. It had ten beds in it, each divided from the next by a white curtain which could be drawn or pulled back as the girls wished.

Each girl had a white bed with a coloured eiderdown. The eiderdowns were different colours and made a pretty show as Darrell looked down the row of beds. In each cubicle there was a cupboard to hang things, and a chest of drawers with a mirror on top. There were wash-basins with hot and cold water at each end of the room.

The girls were busy unpacking their small bags. Darrell opened hers. She shook out her night-dress. She took her face-flannel, her tooth-brush and paste. A clean towel hung ready for her on a rail at the side of her chest of drawers.

'It will be fun to sleep here, with all the others,' thought Darrell. 'What fun we shall have talking at night. We could have dormy games too, I should think.'

All the first-formers were in the same dormy. Alicia was there, Darrell, Sally and Gwendoline. There were six other girls besides. They stared at the three new girls as they ran to and from the wash-basins, washing, and cleaning their teeth.

One of the girls looked at her watch. 'Get into bed, everyone!' she ordered. She was a tall, dark girl, quiet in her manner. Everyone but Gwendoline scrambled into bed. Gwendoline was still brushing out her fine golden hair. She was counting as she brushed it.

'Fifty-four, fifty-five, fifty-six . . .'

'Hey, you new girl—what's your name—get into bed!' ordered the tall dark girl again.

'I've got to brush my hair a hundred times each night,' protested Gwendoline. 'Now I've forgotten what number I got to!'

'Shut up and get into bed, Gwendoline Mary,' said Alicia, who was next to Gwendoline. 'Katherine is the head of our dormy. You've got to do what she says.'

'But I promised M-M-Mo . . .' began Gwendoline, tears welling up. 'I promised Mother to b-b-b-brush my hair a hundred times each night!'

'You can add the number of brushings you leave out tonight on to tomorrow night,' came the head-girl's cool voice. 'Get into bed, please.'

'Oh, just let me finish!' said Gwendoline and began frantically brushing again. 'Fifty-seven, fifty . . .'

'Shall I spank her with my brush, Katherine?' said Alicia, sitting up. Gwendoline gave a squeal and leapt into bed. The girls laughed. They all knew that Alicia had no intention of spanking Gwendoline.

Gwendoline lay down, angry. She determined to make herself miserable and cry. She thought of her mother, and her faraway home, and she began to sniff.

'Do blow your nose, Gwendoline,' said Alicia, sleepily.

'Stop talking,' said Katherine. There was silence in the room. Sally Hope gave a little sigh. Darrell wondered if she was asleep. The curtains between her bed and Sally's were pulled back. No, Sally was not asleep. She lay with her eyes wide open. There were no tears in them, but her face looked sad.

'Perhaps she's homesick,' thought Darrell, and thought of her home too. But she was too sensible to be silly about it, and too excited to be at Malory Towers to miss her home. After all, she had badly wanted to come, and here she was— and she meant to be very happy and have a lot of fun.

Matron arrived. She took a look down the beds. One or two of the girls were already fast asleep, tired out. Matron walked down the long room, twitched an eiderdown into place, turned off a dripping tap, and pulled the curtains across the windows, for it was still very light outside.

'Good night,' she said, in a low voice. 'And no talking, please!'

'Good night, Matron,' murmured those girls who were not yet asleep. Darrell peeped to see if Matron's nice smile was on her face. She caught sight of Darrell's peeping eyes and nodded, smiling. 'Sleep well!' she said, and went out quietly.

Gwendoline was the only one who tried to keep awake. What had Mother said to her? 'You'll feel dreadful tonight, I know, darling, but be brave, won't you?'

So Gwendoline was determined to lie awake and feel dreadful. But her eyes wouldn't keep open! They shut and soon Gwendoline was as fast asleep as the others. And at home her mother was dabbing her eyes, and saying 'Poor little Gwen! I shouldn't have sent her away from me! I feel she's awake and crying her heart out!'

But Gwendoline was giving little contented snores, dreaming happily of how she would queen it over the girls here, be top of her form, and best at all games.

A loud bell awoke all the girls the next morning. At first Darrell couldn't imagine where she was. Then she heard Alicia's voice. 'Get up, lazy-bones! You've got to make your bed before breakfast!'

Darrell leapt out of bed. The sun poured into the room, for Katherine had drawn the curtains back. A loud chattering began. Girls hopped across the room to the wash-basins. Darrell dressed quickly, proud to put on her brown tunic with its brown orange belt, just like all the other girls wore. She brushed her hair back and put in two slides to keep it tidy. Gwendoline left her hair loose over her shoulders.

'You can't have it like that,' said Alicia. 'Not in *school*, Gwendoline!'

'I've always had it like this,' said Gwendoline, an obstinate look coming over her pretty, silly little face.

'Well, it looks awful,' said Alicia.

'It does not!' said Gwendoline. 'You only say that because your hair is short and coarse.'

Alicia winked at Katherine, who was coming up. 'Better let dear Gwendoline show off her long, fine-as-silk hair, don't you think so?' she said, in a bland voice. 'Miss Potts might be delighted to see it like that.'

'My governess, Miss Winter, always liked it like this,' said Gwendoline, looking pleased.

'Oh—haven't you been to a school before? Have you just had a governess?' asked Alicia. 'That explains a lot.'

'What does it explain?' asked Gwendoline, haughtily.

'Never mind. You'll find out,' said Alicia. 'Ready, Darrell? That's the breakfast gong. Tuck your sheet in well. That's right. Gwendoline, fold up your nighty. Look at Sally—there's a new girl for you! Everything done to time, nobody's got to chivvy her round!'

Sally gave a little smile. She hardly said a word. She did not seem in the least shy, but she was so quiet and self-possessed that Darrell could hardly believe she was a new girl. She always seemed to know exactly what to do.

They all went down to the dining-hall. The long tables were ready, and girls were already seating themselves, greeting their house-mistress politely. Matron was there too, and a third grown-up, whom Darrell had not seen before.

'That's Mam'zelle Dupont,' whispered Alicia. 'We've got two French mistresses at Malory Towers. One's fat and jolly and the other's thin and sour. We've got the fat and jolly one this term. They've both got simply awful tempers, so I hope you're pretty good at French.'

'Well, no, I'm not really,' said Darrell, wishing she was.

'Mam'zelle Dupont hates Mam'zelle Rougier and Mam'zelle Rougier hates Mam'zelle Dupont,' went on Alicia. 'You should see the fur fly sometimes. Matron has to be sent for to calm them down when they get too bad !'

Darrell's eyes opened wide. Katherine, across the table, laughed. 'Don't believe all that Alicia says,' she said. 'Her tongue runs away with her sometimes. Nobody has ever seen our two Mam'zelles fly at each other's throats yet.'

'Ah, but they will one day—and I hope I'll be there to see it,' said Alicia.

Mam'zelle Dupont was short, fat and round. She wore her hair in a little bun on top. Her eyes, black and beady, were never still. She wore a black frock that fitted her perfectly, and well-fitting black shoes on her tiny feet.

She was short-sighted but she would not wear glasses. She had instead a pair of long-handled glasses, called lorgnettes, which she wore dangling on a long black ribbon. These she used when she wanted to see anything at close quarters, holding them to her eyes with her hand.

Alicia, who was a good mimic, could keep her class in fits of laughter, blinking like poor Mam'zelle, and holding imaginary glasses up to her nose. But she was just as much in awe of Mam'zelle Dupont as anyone else, and did not rouse her hot temper if she could help it.

'New girls must go to see the Head Mistress after breakfast,' announced Miss Potts. 'There are three in the first form, two in the second form, and one in the fourth. You can all go together. Join us in the assembly room for Prayers later. Pamela, will you take the new girls to the Head, please ?'

Pamela, head-girl of North Tower House, rose. The new girls stood up, Darrell among them. They followed Pamela. She took them out of the door that let into the Court, and then in through another door set in the building that ran between East and North Tower. The Head Mistress's rooms were there, and so was the San. or sanatorium, where any sick girl went.

They came to a door painted a deep cream colour. Pamela knocked. A low voice said 'Come in!'

Pamela opened the door. 'I've brought the new girls to you, Miss Grayling,' she said.

'Thank you, Pamela,' said the low voice again, and Darrell saw a grey-haired woman sitting at a desk, writing. She had a calm, unwrinkled face, eyes that were startlingly blue, and a very firm mouth. Darrell felt frightened of this calm, low-voiced Head Mistress, and hoped she would never have to be sent to her for misbehaviour!

The new girls stood in a row before the Head, and Miss Grayling looked at them all closely. Darrell felt herself going red, she couldn't imagine why. Her knees felt a bit wobbly too. She hoped Miss Grayling wouldn't ask her any questions, for she was sure she wouldn't be able to say a word!

Miss Grayling asked them their names, and spoke a few words to each girl. Then she addressed them all solemnly.

'One day you will leave school and go out into the world as young women. You should take with you eager minds, kind hearts, and a will to help. You should take with you a good understanding of many things, and a willingness to accept responsibility and show yourselves as women to be loved and trusted. All these things you will be able to learn at Malory Towers—if you *will*. I do not count as our successes those who have won scholarships and passed exams., though these are good things to do. I count as our successes those who learn to be good-hearted and kind, sensible and trustable, good, sound women the world can lean on. Our failures are those who do not learn these things in the years they are here.'

These words were spoken so gravely and solemnly that Darrell hardly breathed. She immediately longed to be one of Malory Towers' successes.

'It is easy for some of you to learn these things, and hard for others. But easy or hard, they must be learnt if you are to be happy, after you leave here, and if you are to bring happiness to others.'

There was a pause. Then Miss Grayling spoke again, in a lighter tone. 'You will all get a tremendous lot out of your time at Malory Towers. See that you give a lot back!'

'Oh!' said Darrell, surprised and pleased, quite forgetting that she had thought she wouldn't be able to speak a word, 'that's *exactly* what my father said to me when he said good-bye, Miss Grayling!'

'Did he?' said Miss Grayling, looking with smiling eyes at the eager little girl. 'Well, as you have parents who think in that way, I imagine you will be one of the lucky ones, and will find that the things I have been speaking of will be easy to learn. Perhaps one day Malory Towers will be proud of you.'

A few more words and the girls were told to go. Very much impressed they walked out of the room. Not even Gwendoline said a word. Whatever they might do, in the years to come at Malory Towers, each girl wanted, at that moment, to do her best. Whether or not that wish would last, depended on the girl.

Then they went to the Assembly Hall for Prayers, found their places, and waited for Miss Grayling to come to the platform.

Soon the words of a hymn sounded in the big hall. The first day of term had begun. Darrell sang with all her might, happy and excited. What a lot she would have to tell her mother when she wrote!

ALL the school met each morning for prayers. The girls
stood together in their classes—first-formers of North
Tower, South, East, and West Tower, all together, and so on.

Darrell took a nervous look at her class.   What a big one
it seemed! About twenty-five or thirty girls, surely.
Miss Potts, her house-mistress, was also the first-form mistress.   There was Mam'zelle Dupont, singing lustily, and
the teacher beside her must be the other French mistress.
But how different!   She was skinny, tall and bony.   Her
hair too was done up in a little bun, but at the back instead
of on top.   Darrell thought she looked bad-tempered.

Alicia told her which the other mistresses were.   'That's
the history mistress, Miss Carton over there—see her—the
one with the high collar and pince-nez glasses on her nose.
She's frightfully clever, and awfully sarcastic if you don't like
history.   And that's the art mistress, Miss Linnie—she's
awfully nice.   Very easy-going.'

Darrell hoped she would have a lot to do with Miss
Linnie, if she was easy-going.   She looked nice.   She was
young and had red hair done in little curls.

'That's the music-master—Mr. Young—see him?   He's
always either in a very good temper or a very bad one.   We
always try and find out which, when he takes us for music
or singing.'

The matrons of the four houses were at Prayers too.
Darrell saw her own Matron, looking a little stern, as she
always did when she was thinking hard of what she was
doing.   Alicia began whispering again.

'And that's . . .'

Miss Potts eye swung round to her, and Alicia immediately stopped whispering and studied her hymn-book.   Miss

Potts did not look kindly on people who whispered at any time, least of all in Prayers.

Prayers over, the girls filed off to their various classrooms. These ran all along the west side of Malory Towers, and soon that building was filled with the sound of hurrying feet, laughter and chattering. There was no rule about silence in the corridors in the part of the building where the classrooms were.

The first-formers filed into their own classroom, a room with a lovely view over the sea. It was a big room, with the mistress's desk at one end, and cupboards at the other. Desks and chairs were arranged in orderly rows.

' Bags I one by the window ! ' said a fat girl and plumped herself down there.

' Bags I one too,' said Gwendoline. But the fat girl stared in surprise.

' You're new aren't you ? Well, you can't choose your own seat, then. New girls have to take the desks left over when the old girls have chosen the ones they want.'

Gwendoline went red. She tossed her golden hair back over her shoulders and looked sulky.

She stood close by the desk she had chosen, not quite daring to take it, but too obstinate to leave it. A small wiry girl pushed her away.

' Bags I this desk ! Hallo, Rita ! Did you have nice hols. ? Awful to be back with old Potty, isn't it ? '

Darrell stood and waited till she saw that all the girls except herself, Sally and Gwendoline and one or two others, had desks. Then she slipped into one beside Alicia, glad of her good luck. Alicia was exchanging news with a girl on the other side of her. She seemed to be very friendly indeed with her.

She turned to Darrell. ' Darrell, this is my friend, Betty Hill. We always sit next to each other. But Betty is in West House, worse luck.'

Darrell smiled at Betty, who was a lively-looking girl, with wicked brown eyes and hair that fell over her forehead. She liked Betty but she was sorry to hear that Alicia had a friend already. She had rather hoped that Alicia would be *her* friend. She didn't particularly want either Sally or Gwendoline.

'Sh!' said the girl at the door. 'Here comes Potty!'

There was silence at once. The girls stood up, and looked straight before them as they heard the quick, light steps of their form-mistress coming down the corridor outside. She swept into the room, nodded to the girls and said, 'You can sit!'

They sat down and waited in silence. Miss Potts took out her list of names and checked them all, tracking down a few more new girls in the other houses. Then she turned to the expectant faces before her.

'Well!' she said, 'the summer term is always the best of the lot, with swimming and tennis, picnics and rambles. But please don't make the mistake of thinking that the summer term is nothing *but* a picnic. It isn't. It's good hard work too. Some of you are taking exams. next term. Well, work hard this term, and you'll find the exams. easy next term. But slack this term, and I promise you I shall hear some groans and grumbles *next* term!'

She paused. Then she looked hard at two or three girls. 'Last term there were one or two girls who seemed to like to be bottom every week,' she said. 'Leave that place to the new girls, please, and go up a few places! I never expect much of new girls their first term—but I *shall* expect quite a lot of you.'

A few girls went red. Miss Potts went on talking. 'I don't really think I've any brainless girls this term,' she said, 'though I don't know much about the new girls, of course. If you are brainless and near the bottom, we shan't blame you, of course—but if you've got good brains

and are down at the bottom, I shall have a lot to say. And
you know what *that* means, don't you ? '

' Yes,' answered most of the girls, fervently. Miss Potts
smiled, and her keen face lit up for a moment. ' Well,
now, after all those threats, let's get on. Here's a list of
things each girl must have. If anyone lacks any of them,
she must go to Katherine, head-girl of the form, and get
them from her at the end of the lesson. I will give ten
minutes for that.'

Soon a lesson was in full swing. It was maths., and Miss
Potts was giving a quick test-paper to see what standard
the new girls were up to, and whether the whole form could
work together or not. Darrell found the paper quite easy,
but Gwendoline groaned and grunted terribly, her golden
hair all over the desk.

' What's the matter, Gwendoline ? ' enquired Miss Potts,
unsympathetically.

' Well, my governess, Miss Winter, never showed me
how to do sums like this,' wailed Gwendoline. ' She put
them down quite differently.'

' You'll have to learn *my* way now,' said Miss Potts.
And Gwendoline—why haven't you done your hair this
morning ? '

' I *did*,' said Gwendoline, raising her big pale blue eyes.
' I brushed it well. I gave it forty . . .'

' All right, I don't want details,' said Miss Potts. ' You
can't come to class with it like that. Plait it after Break.'

' *Plait* it ! ' mourned poor Gwendoline, whilst the rest
of the class began to giggle. ' But I've never . . .'

' That's enough,' said Miss Potts. ' If you can't plait
it and keep it tidy, perhaps your mother could have it cut
short next holidays.'

Gwendoline looked so horrified that it was all Darrell
could do to keep from laughing out loud.

' I told you so ! ' whispered Alicia, as soon as Miss Potts

turned to write something on the blackboard.   Gwendoline
glared angrily at her and made a face.   As if Mother would
dream of cutting off her beautiful fine sheet of hair.   And
now to think she'd got to plait it.   Why, she didn't even
know *how* to plait!   Gwendoline was so lost in sulky thought
that she hardly answered any of the maths. questions.

The morning went on.   Break came and the girls rushed
out to play where they liked.   Some went for a quick game
on one of the many tennis-courts.   Some went for a ramble
in the grounds.   Others lay about in the Court, talking.
Darrell would have liked to go with Alicia, but she was with
Betty, and Darrell felt sure they wouldn't want a third
person.   She looked at the other new girls.   Two of them,
whom she didn't know, had made friends already.   Another
girl, who had a cousin in the same form, went off with her.
Gwendoline was not to be seen.   Perhaps she had gone to
plait her hair !

Sally Hope was sitting on the grass alone, no expression
at all on her closed-up face.   Darrell went over to her.
' What do you think of Malory Towers ? ' she said.   ' I
think it's fine.'

Sally looked up primly.   ' It's not bad,' she said.

' Were you sorry to leave your other school ? ' asked
Darrell.   ' I wanted to come to Malory, of course, but I
hated leaving all my friends.   Didn't you hate leaving all
your friends too ? '

' I don't think I had any, really,' said Sally, considering.
Darrell thought that was queer.   It was hard to get anything out of Sally.   She was polite and answered questions,
but she didn't ask any in return.

' Well, I hope I don't have to make *her* my friend ! '
thought Darrell, at last.   ' Gracious, here's Gwendoline !
Does she think she's plaited her hair ?   It's all undone
already ! '

' Is my hair all right ? ' said Gwendoline, in a plaintive

Sally was sitting on the grass alone

voice. 'I've tried and tried to plait it. It was beastly of Miss Potts not to let me wear it as I've always worn it. I don't like her.'

'Let *me* plait it for you,' said Darrell, jumping up. 'It doesn't look to me as if you know *how* to plait, Gwendoline!'

She plaited the golden hair deftly and quickly into long braids and tied the ends with bits of narrow ribbon. 'There!' she said, swinging Gwendoline round to look at her. 'You look *much* nicer!'

Gwendoline scowled, and forgot to thank Darrell for her help. Actually, she did look much nicer now. 'How spoilt she is!' thought Darrell. 'Well, little as I want Sally for a friend, I want Gwendoline even less. I should want to slap her for all her silly airs and graces!'

The bell went, and scores of girls raced in to their class-rooms. Darrell raced too. She knew where her classroom was. She knew the names of a lot of her form. She would soon be quite at home at Malory Towers!

CHAPTER V

THE FIRST WEEK GOES BY

DARRELL soon began to settle down. She learnt the names not only of the girls in her form at North Tower, but of every girl there, from the head-girl Pamela, down to Mary-Lou, the youngest but one in the first form. Darrell herself was the youngest girl in North Tower, she found, but she felt that Mary-Lou was very much younger.

Mary-Lou was a scared mouse of a girl. She was fright-ened of mice, beetles, thunderstorms, noises at night, the dark, and a hundred other things. Poor Mary-Lou, no wonder she had big scared eyes. Darrell, not easily scared of anything, laughed when she saw poor Mary-Lou rush to the other side of the dormy because she saw an earwig on the floor.

There were ten girls in the first-form dormy at North Tower. Katherine, the quiet head-girl. Alicia, the talkative, unruly-tongued monkey. The three new girls, Darrell, Gwendoline, and Sally. Mary-Lou, with her big scared eyes, always ready to shy back like a nervous horse, at anything unexpected.

Then there was clever Irene, a marvel at maths. and music, usually top of the form—but oh, how stupid in the ordinary things of life. If anyone lost her book it was Irene. If anyone went to the wrong classroom at the wrong time it was Irene. It was said that once she had gone to the art-room, thinking that a painting lesson was to be taken there, and had actually sat there for half-an-hour, apparently waiting for Miss Linnie to come. What she thought had happened to the rest of the class, no one knew.

' But *how* could you sit there all that time and not even *wonder* why nobody came ! ' said Katherine, in amazement. ' What were you thinking of, Irene ? '

' I was just thinking of a maths. problem that Potty set us, that's all,' said Irene, her eyes shining through her big glasses. ' It was rather an interesting one, and there were two or three ways of getting it right. You see . . .'

' Oh, spare us maths. out of school ! ' groaned Alicia. ' Irene, I think you're bats ! '

But Irene wasn't. She was a most intelligent girl, who, because her mind was always so deeply at work at something, seemed to forget the smaller, everyday things of life. She had a sense of fun too, and when she was really tickled she came out with a tremendous explosive giggle that startled the class and made Miss Potts jump. It was Alicia's delight to provoke this explosion sometimes, and upset the class.

The other three girls in the form were Jean, a jolly, shrewd girl from Scotland, very able at handling money for various school societies and charities; Emily, a quiet studious girl, clever with her needle, and one of Mam'zelle's favourites because of this; and Violet, a shy, colourless child, very much left out of things because she never seemed to take any interest in them. Half the form never even noticed whether Violet was with them or not.

That made up the ten girls. Darrell felt that she had known them for years after she had lived with them only a few days. She knew the way Irene's stockings always fell down in wrinkles. She knew the way Jean spoke, clipped and sharp, in her Scots accent. She knew that Mam'zelle disliked Jean because Jean was scornful of Mam'zelle's enthusiasms and emotions. Jean herself never went into ecstasies about anything.

Darrell knew Gwendoline's sighs and moans over everything, and Mary-Lou's scared exclamations of fear at any insect or reptile. She liked Katherine's low, firm voice, and air of being able to cope with anything. She knew a great deal about Alicia, but then, so did everyone, for Alicia poured out everything that came into her head, she chattered about her brothers, her mother and father, her dogs, her work, her play, her knitting, her opinion of everything and everybody under the sun.

Alicia had no time at all for airs and graces, pretences, sighs, moans or affectations. She was as downright as Darrell, but not so kind. She was scornful and biting when it pleased her, so that girls like Gwendoline hated her, and those like scared Mary-Lou feared her. Darrell liked her immensely.

'She's so lively,' she thought to herself. 'Nobody could be dull with Alicia. I wish I was as interesting as she is. Everyone listens when Alicia speaks, even when she says something unkind. But nobody pays much attention when I want to say something. I do really like Alicia, and I wish she hadn't got Betty for a friend. She's just the one I would have chosen.'

It took Darrell longer to know the first-formers who came from the other Towers. She saw them in class, but not in the common room or dormies, for the first-formers of the other Towers had their own rooms, of course, in their own Towers. Still, it was enough to know her own Tower girls for a start, Darrell thought.

She didn't know very much about the older girls in her Tower, for she didn't even meet them in the classroom. She saw them at Prayers in the morning, sometimes during the singing-lesson, when Mr. Young took more than one class at a time, and sometimes on the tennis-courts and in the swimming-pool.

She heard a few things about some of them, of course. Marilyn, sixth-former, was captain of the games, and most of the girls liked her immensely. ' She's fair and really takes a lot of trouble to coach even the first-formers,' said Alicia. ' She's as good as old Remmington, the games-mistress, any day. *She* won't bother with the duds, but Marilyn *does*.'

Everyone appeared to look up to Pamela, the head-girl, too. She was clever, and rather literary. It was said that she was already writing a book. This impressed the first-formers very much. It was hard enough to write a decent composition, let alone a book.

No one seemed to like two girls called Doris and Fanny. ' Too spiteful for words,' said Alicia, who, of course, could always give an opinion immediately about anyone or any-thing, from Winston Churchill down to the little boy belonging to the Tower House cook. ' They're frightfully pi.'

' What do you mean—pi ? ' said Gwendoline, who hadn't apparently heard that word before.

' Golly—what an ignoramus you are ! ' said Alicia. ' Pi

means pious. Religious in the wrong way. Thinking they're wonderful and nobody else is. Trying to stop people's pleasure. They're a sickening pair. Always on the prowl and on the snoop. Once, when I slipped across the Court in the middle of the night to join Betty Hill, in West Tower for a midnight feast, Doris saw me out of the window, and lay in wait for me to come back. Beast.'

'Did she catch you?' asked Mary-Lou, her eyes wide with alarm.

''Course she didn't! You don't think I'd let myself be caught by the Pi Sisters, do you?' said Alicia, scornfully. 'I spotted her when I came back, and shut her in the boot-cupboard.'

Irene gave one of her loud explosive giggles and made them all jump. 'I'd never think of the things *you* think of, Alicia!' she said. 'No wonder the Pi Sisters glare at you in Prayers each morning. I bet they'll watch out for you to do something you shouldn't, and tell on you.'

'And I bet I'll get the better of them!' said Alicia, grimly. 'If they try any tricks on me, I'll try a few on them!'

'Oh, do, do,' begged Darrell, who had a great weakness for jokes and tricks. She didn't always dare to do them herself, but she was always ready to back up any one else who did.

Darrell soon got to know all the different classrooms too. She knew the art-room, with its clear north light. She hadn't yet had a lesson in the lab. or laboratory, which looked a bit frightening. She loved the great gym. with all its apparatus of swings, ropes, vaulting-horses and mattresses. She was good at gym. So was Alicia, who could climb like a monkey, and was as strong as a horse. Mary-Lou, of course, was too scared to do anything unless she was made to.

It was fun, the way all the girls slept in the Towers, and had their lessons in the other parts of the great building.

Darrell knew where the teachers lived now in the building facing south, except those who, like Miss Potts, and Mam'zelle, lived in with the girls, to keep an eye on them. She began to wonder how she could have felt so lost and over-awed when she first arrived. She didn't feel a bit like a new girl now.

One of the things that Darrell liked best of all was the big swimming-pool down by the sea. This had been hollowed out of a stretch of rocks, so that it had a nice rocky, uneven bottom. Seaweed grew at the sides, and sometimes the rocky bed of the pool felt a little slimy. But the sea swept into the big natural pool each day, filled it, and made lovely waves all across it. It was a sheer delight to bathe there.

The coast itself was too dangerous for bathing. The tides were so strong, and no girl was allowed to swim in the open sea. But anyone was safe in the pool. One end was quite deep, and here there were diving-boards and a chute, and a fine spring-board for running dives.

Mary-Lou and Gwendoline were terrified of the pool, Mary-Lou because she was afraid of water, anyhow, and Gwendoline because she hated the first cold plunge. Alicia's eyes always gleamed when she spied the shivering Gwendoline, and the poor girl so often had an unexpected push into the water that she soon began to step in hurriedly whenever she saw Alicia or Betty coming near.

The first week went very slowly. There was a lot to learn and know, things were so new and exciting. Darrell loved every minute, and soon got into the way of things. She was naturally quick and responsive, and the girls soon accepted her and liked her.

But they neither accepted nor liked poor Gwendoline, and as for Sally Hope, after trying in vain to draw her out a little, and get her to talk of her family and home, the girls let her live in her shell, and not come out of it at all.

' First week gone ! ' announced Alicia, some days later.
' The first week always crawls. After that the days fly,
and it's half-term in no time, and when that's gone we're
looking forward to the hols. You've soon settled in,
haven't you, Darrell ? '

' Oh, *yes*,' said Darrell. ' I love it. If every term is as
nice as this, I shall be thrilled ! '

' Ah, you wait,' said Alicia. ' Everything's always all
right at first—but when you've had a wigging or two from
Mam'zelle, and been dosed by Matron, and kept in by
Potty, and slated by Miss Remmington, and ticked off by
one of the older girls, and . . . ! '

' Oh, stop ! ' cried Darrell. ' Nothing like that will
happen, Alicia. Don't try and frighten me ! '

But Alicia was right, of course. Things were not going
to be quite so smooth and easy as Darrell thought !

6   ALICIA'S LITTLE JOKE

DARRELL had good brains and she had been taught how
to use them. She soon found that she could easily do the
work of her class, and in such things as composition was
ahead of most of the others. She felt pleased.

' I thought I'd have to work much much harder than at
my old school,' she thought to herself. ' But I shan't !
It's only maths. I'm not so good at. I wish I was as good
as Irene at maths. She does things in her head that I
can't even do on paper.'

So, after the first week or two, Darrell relaxed a little, and
did not worry herself too much about her work. She began
to enjoy amusing the class a little, just as Alicia did. Alicia
was thrilled to have someone to help her in her mischief.

Betty Hill went much further than Alicia. Darrell
sometimes wondered if there was anything she would stop
at. There were two mistresses that Betty and Alicia played
up to. One was Mam'zelle Dupont, the other was a quiet,
gentle mistress who took needlework, and sometimes took
prep. time at night. Miss Davies never seemed to realize
that Alicia and Betty could play tricks on her. Mam'zelle
did realize it, but was taken in all the same.

'Did you ever hear how Betty put a white mouse into
Mam'zelle's desk one day ? ' said Alicia. ' Poor little thing,
it couldn't get out, and suddenly, in despair, it pushed up
the little ink-pot, and stuck its nose out of the ink-pot hole.
Mam'zelle nearly had a fit.'

'What did she do ? ' asked Darrell, with great interest.

'Flew out of the room as if a hundred dogs were after
her ! ' said Alicia. ' When she was gone we took the mouse
out quickly, and Betty hid it down her neck. So, when
Mam'zelle ventured back, and ordered one of us to turn her
desk out and get the mouse, there was none to be found.
Mam'zelle thought her eyes had gone wrong ! '

'Oh, I *do* wish I'd been there ! ' sighed Darrell. 'Alicia,
do do something funny like that. Do something in maths.,
can't you ? I know Miss Potts is going to go for me over
my maths. prep., and something like that would take her
mind away from me ! '

'What ! Play a trick like that in Potty's class ! ' said
Alicia, scornfully. ' Don't be silly. Potty's up to everything. You can't fool *her* ! '

'Well—in Mam'zelle's class, then,' begged Darrell.
'I like Mam'zelle, but I haven't seen her in a temper yet
and I'd like to. *Do*, do play a trick in her class.'

Alicia felt that she would have a most admiring spectator
in Darrell, if only she could think of something. She
screwed her forehead into wrinkles and thought hard.

Betty prompted her. 'Can't you think of something

Sam or Roger or Dick did last term?' she asked. She turned to Darrell. 'Alicia's three brothers all go to the same school,' she said. 'And there's a master there called Toggles—at least that's what the boys call him—and he's such a dud the boys can play any trick they like on him and get away with it.'

Darrell thought Roger, Sam, and Dick sounded fine brothers to have. She wished she had a brother too. But she had only a younger sister.

'There's one thing Roger did last term that was quite funny,' said Alicia, suddenly. 'I believe we could do it. But you and Betty will have to help, Darrell.'

'Oh, I'd *love* to,' said Darrell. 'What is it?'

'Well, Roger pretended to be deaf,' said Alicia. 'And everything old Toggles asked him he pretended to hear wrong. When Toggles said 'Johns, sit still in your chair!' Roger said 'Give you a cheer, sir? Certainly! Hip, hip, hip, hurrah!''

Darrell laughed. 'Oh, Alicia! That would be fun! Do, do pretend to be deaf, please do. We'll play up to you like anything. We will really. Do it in Mam'zelle's class.'

The first form soon heard that Alicia was going to pull Mam'zelle's leg, and were thrilled. The first excitement of coming back to school had worn off. The girls were restless and ready for a bit of excitement.

'Now,' said Alicia, 'I'll pretend to misunderstand what Mam'zelle says—and then you can repeat it very loudly, Darrell, and then you, Betty, and then the rest of the class. See? We'll have some sport.'

Mam'zelle, all unsuspicious of this deep-laid plot, entered the first-form classroom smiling brightly the next morning. It was a beautiful summer day. She had had two letters from home, giving her the news that she had a new little nephew. She had on a new brooch, and had washed her hair the night before. She was feeling in a very good temper.

She beamed round at the class. ' Ah, my dear girls ! '
she said. ' We are going to do some very very good
French today, *n'est ce pas* ? We are going to be better
than the second form ! Even Gwendoline will be
able to say her verbs to me without one, single, mistake ! '

Gwendoline looked doubtful. Since she had been at
Malory Towers her opinion of her governess at home had
gone down. Miss Winter didn't seem to have taught her half
the things she ought to have known ! On the other hand,
thought Gwendoline, she had raved over her hair and blue
eyes, she had praised the sweetness of Gwendoline's temper,
and said how graceful she was in all she did. That kind
of thing was most enjoyable to a person like Gwendoline.
But a little more learning would have been very useful to
her at Malory Towers.

She wished she had learnt a lot more French. Mam'zelle
had exclaimed at the little she knew, and had even suggested
extra French lessons in order to get her up to the average
standard of the form. But so far Gwendoline had been
able to avoid extra lessons, and she was quite determined to
go *on* avoiding them ! French five times a week was bad
enough without extra time tagged on.

She smiled back rather doubtfully at Mam'zelle, hoping
that Alicia would soon begin her performance, so that
Mam'zelle's attention would not be directed at her.
Mam'zelle beamed round again. She thought the girls
looked eager and responsive this morning. The dear girls !
She would tell them about her new little nephew. That
would please them, no doubt !

Mam'zelle could never stop herself from talking about
her beloved family in France, if she had had news of them.
Usually the girls encouraged her, because the more they
heard about *la chère* Josephine, and *la mignonne* Yvonne,
and *la méchante* Louise, the less they heard about verbs and

genders. So they were delighted when Mam'zelle informed them of her new nephew.

'*Il est appelé, Jean*—he is called John. *Il est tout petit, oh, tout petit!*' Mam'zelle held up her two hands and measured a small distance between them to show how little her new nephew John was. 'Now, what does that mean? *Il—est—tout—petit.* Who will tell me?'

Alicia was sitting in an attitude of strained attention, leaning forward as far as possible over her desk, one of her hands behind her ear. Mam'zelle noticed her.

'Ah, Alicia, you did not hear me very well? I will repeat. *Il—est—tout—petit.* Repeat to me, please.'

'Pardon?' said Alicia, politely, and put both hands behind her ears.

Darrell wanted to giggle already. She tried to keep her face straight.

'Alicia! What is wrong with you?' cried Mam'zelle. 'Can you not hear?'

'What do I fear? Why, nothing, Mam'zelle,' said Alicia, looking slightly surprised. Somebody giggled and then smothered it quickly.

'Mam'zelle said "Can you not *hear*?"' repeated Betty in a loud voice to Alicia.

'Beer?' said Alicia, more astonished, apparently, than ever.

'CAN YOU NOT HEAR?' shouted Darrell, joining in the game. And the class joined in too. 'CAN YOU NOT HEAR?'

Mam'zelle banged on her desk. 'Girls! You forget yourselves. What a noise to make in class.'

'Mam'zelle, perhaps Alicia is DEAF,' said Darrell, speaking as if Mam'zelle herself were deaf. 'Maybe she has ear-ache.'

'Ah, *la pauvre petite!*' cried Mam'zelle, who suffered from ear-ache herself at times, and was always very sympathetic towards anyone else who did. She bellowed at Alicia.

'Have you ear-ache?'

'A rake? I don't want a rake, thank you, Mam'zelle,' replied Alicia. 'I'm not gardening today.'

This was too much for Irene, who let out one of her explosive laughs, making the girls in front of her jump.

'*Tiens!*' cried Mam'zelle, jumping too, 'what was that? Ah, you Irene—why do you make that extraordinary noise? I will not have it.'

'Can't help sneezing sometimes, Mam'zelle,' stuttered Irene, burying her nose in her handkerchief as if she was about to sneeze again. Curious noises came from her as she tried to choke back her giggles.

'Alicia,' said Mam'zelle, turning back to the mischief-maker, who at once put both hands behind her ears, and frowned as if trying her best to hear. 'Alicia, do not talk to me of rakes. Tell me, have you a cold?'

'No, I've no gold, only a ten-shilling note,' answered Alicia, much to Mam'zelle's mystification.

'Mam'zelle said COLD not GOLD,' explained Darrell at the top of her voice.

'You know—COLD, the opposite of HOT,' went on Betty, helpfully. 'Have you a COLD?'

'HAVE YOU A COLD?' roared the class, coming in like a well-trained chorus.

'Oh, *cold!* Why don't you speak clearly, then I should hear you,' said Alicia. 'Yes—I've had a cold, of course.'

'Ah—then it has affected your poor ears,' said Mam'zelle. 'How long ago was this cold, Alicia?'

Darrell repeated this question at the top of her voice, followed by Betty.

'Oh—when did I have it? About two years ago,' said Alicia. Irene buried her nose in her hanky again. Mam'zelle looked a little blank.

'It is of no use the poor child trying to follow the French lesson,' said Mam'zelle. 'Alicia, sit by the window in the sun and read your French book to yourself. You cannot hear a word we say.'

Alicia looked enquiringly at Darrell, as if she hadn't heard. Darrell obligingly repeated it all at the top of her voice. Betty unfortunately was too overcome by a desire to laugh to be able to repeat it too. But the rest of the class obliged with a will.

'YOU CANNOT HEAR A WORD WE SAY!' they chorused.

The door opened suddenly and a most irate Miss Potts looked in. She had been taking Form 2 next door, and could not imagine what the shouting was in Form 1.

'Mam'zelle, excuse my interrupting you, but is it necessary for the girls to repeat their French lesson so very loudly?' she asked.

'Ah, Miss Potts, I am so sorry. But it is not for me the girls repeat words so loudly, it is for the poor Alicia,' explained Mam'zelle.

Miss Potts looked most surprised. She looked at Alicia. Alicia felt uncomfortable. She also looked as innocent as she could. But Miss Potts was always on the alert when Betty or Alicia looked innocent.

'What do you mean, Mam'zelle?' she snapped. 'Has Alicia suddenly gone deaf? She was all right this morning.'

'She is quite, quite deaf now,' Mam'zelle assured her. Miss Potts looked sharply at Alicia.

'Come to me at Break, Alicia,' she said. 'I would like a few words with you.'

Nobody dared repeat these words to Alicia, but Mam'zelle herself obliged. She shouted across to Alicia.

'Miss Potts says, will you . . .'

'Don't bother to repeat what I said, Mam'zelle,' said Miss Potts. 'Alicia will come all right. I shall expect you at eleven, Alicia. And please stand up when I speak to you.'

Alicia stood up, her face a flaming red. Miss Potts

went out of the room, and she did not shut the door very
quietly. Mam'zelle disliked people who banged doors.

'Ah, this door, it goes through my poor head!' she
said. 'Miss Potts, she is very good and clever, but she
does not have the head-ache, as I do...'

'Nor the ear-ache,' put in Darrell, but no one raised a
giggle. Miss Potts's entry and fierceness had damped the
cheerfulness of the class considerably.

Alicia said no more about her ear-ache. She took a
book and sat down by the window in the sunshine, feeling
sure that Miss Potts would not appear again. She thought
she might as well get something out of her performance!
Mam'zelle took no further notice of her, and devoted herself to a whole-hearted search for someone in Form 1
who could and would conjugate a whole French verb
properly. Not finding anyone really good, she lost the
good temper she had entered with that morning, and gave
the class a bad time.

She stalked out when the bell for Break went. The
girls crowded round Alicia. 'Oh, Alicia! I nearly died
when you said " beer ".'—'Wasn't it a shame Potty coming
in like that?'—'Will you get into a fearful row, Alicia?'

'Darrell nearly yelled the roof off!' said Irene. 'I
almost burst with trying not to laugh.'

'I must go and hear what Potty has to say,' said Alicia. 'Pity
I forgot she was taking Form 2 next door! So long, girls!'

7   DARRELL LOSES HER TEMPER

ALICIA got a good scolding, and extra prep. She came
out from Miss Potts's room, and ran straight into Mam'zelle.
'Have you been to see Miss Potts, Alicia?' asked Mam'zelle,

thinking that perhaps Alicia hadn't heard what Miss Potts had said.

'Oh, yes, thank you, Mam'zelle,' said Alicia, and walked off. Mam'zelle stared after her. How queer! Alicia had heard perfectly what she had said. Could ears get better so quickly then? Mam'zelle stood still and frowned. Miss Potts came out of her room and saw her.

'If Alicia shows any further signs of deafness, send her to me,' said Miss Potts, coldly. 'I can always cure it at once.'

She walked off. Mam'zelle began to breathe quickly. 'The bad girl, Alicia!—She has pulled my foot,' said Mam'zelle, who sometimes got a little mixed! 'She has hoodle-winked me! Never again will I believe her, the bad girl.'

Darrell had thoroughly enjoyed the absurd affair. How cleverly Alicia had pulled it off! She looked at her admiringly, and Alicia liked the admiration. It always egged her on to further misbehaviour. Mary-Lou stared at her too, as if she was somebody most remarkable. Alicia went up and took Darrell's arm.

'We'll think of something else soon,' she said. 'You and I and Betty. We'll be the Bold Bad Three, or something like that!'

'Oh, *yes*!' said Darrell, thrilled at the idea of being one of a gang with Betty and Alicia. 'Do let's! Maybe I could think of something, too.'

It was decided, however, that it would be best not to try anything further until a little time had gone by. Perhaps something could be tried on Miss Linnie next.

Gwendoline was jealous of the way Alicia and Betty, recognized leaders in the first form, had made friends with Darrell. After all, Darrell was as new as she herself was. And she, Gwendoline, was much prettier, and had, she was sure, much more charm of manner.

She took Sally Hope into her confidence. 'I don't like the way Darrell Rivers pushes herself forward all the time,

do you ? ' she said to Sally.   ' Thinking she's so marvellous !
Chumming up with Alicia and Betty.   Not that I would if
they asked me.'

Sally didn't look very interested, but Gwendoline didn't
mind.   She went on grumbling about Darrell.   ' She
thinks she's got such good brains, she thinks she plays such
a marvellous game of tennis, she thinks she's so good at
swimming !   I've a good mind to show her that I'm *twice*
as good as she is ! '

' Well, why don't you ? ' said Sally, bored.   ' Instead of
showing everyone you're twice as bad ! '

Gwendoline was annoyed.   To think that the quiet little
Sally Hope should say such a thing to her !   She looked
at Sally as if she would like to wither her up.

' All right,' said Gwendoline, grandly.   ' I *will* just show
you, Sally.   I haven't really tried before, because it didn't
seem worth it.   *I* didn't want to come to Malory Towers,
and Mother didn't want me to either.   It was Daddy that
made me come.   I did marvellously with my governess,
Miss Winter, and I could do marvellously now, if only I
thought it was worth while ! '

Alicia came up and heard this curious speech.   She
laughed loudly.

' You can't play tennis, you can't swim, you squeal when
your toe touches the cold water, you don't even know all
your twelve times table, baby !   And then you talk of it not
being worth while to show what you can do !   You can't
do a thing and never will, whilst you have such a wonderful
opinion of yourself ! '

Sally laughed too, and that made Gwendoline angry.
How she would like to slap them both !   But Miss Winter
had always said that a little lady kept her hands to herself.
Anyway, it would be decidedly dangerous to slap Alicia.

Gwendoline walked off, her nose in the air.   ' Dear
Gwendoline Mary,' remarked Alicia, in a loud voice.

'Mummy's pet, Daddy's darling, Miss Winter's prize pupil. And can't do fractions properly yet!'

That evening the girls were in the swimming-pool, having a lovely time. Alicia swam under water the whole width of the pool, and then back again. Everyone applauded her.

'How *can* you hold your breath all that time?' cried Darrell. 'I wish I could! Do it again, Alicia, when you've got your breath.'

'The water's got properly into my ears this time!' said Alicia, shaking her head violently. 'They feel all bunged up. I'll wait till they're clear. I'll do a spot of diving.'

She was just as good a diver as a swimmer. Gwendoline, paddling about in the shallow end, envied her. She was certain *she* could swim and dive better than Alicia—if only she could get over the unpleasant beginnings. She did hate the first cold plunge. She couldn't bear going under the water. She spluttered and gasped if she got water up her nose, and felt as if she was drowning.

There was only one person worse than she was, and that was poor Mary-Lou. No one teased Mary-Lou too much. It was too like teasing a small, bewildered kitten. Gwendoline saw her floundering about near her, and, because she knew Mary-Lou was even more afraid of the pool than she was, she felt a sense of power.

She waded over to Mary-Lou, jumped on her suddenly and got her under the water. Mary-Lou had no time to scream. She opened her mouth and the water poured in. She began to struggle desperately. Gwendoline, feeling the struggles, spitefully held her under longer than she had intended to. She only let her go when she felt a sharp slap on her bare shoulder.

She turned. It was Darrell, trembling with rage, looking as if she was shivering, so great was her anger. 'You beast!' shouted Darrell. '*I* saw you duck poor Mary-Lou—and you know how scared she is. You nearly drowned her!

She pulled Mary-Lou to the surface, and held her there, gasping and choking, blue in the face, almost sick with the amount of salt water she had swallowed.

Girls began to swim across to the scene of excitement. Darrell, her voice shaking with rage, addressed Gwendoline again. 'You just wait a minute! I'll duck *you* under, Gwendoline, and see how *you* like it!'

Mary-Lou was clinging with all her might to Darrell. Gwendoline, rather scared by the anger in Darrell's voice, thought it would be just as well if she got out of the pool before Darrell or somebody else carried out the threat. She began to wade towards the steps that led down into the pool.

Just as she was climbing up them, Darrell, who had given the weeping Mary-Lou to Alicia, caught her up.

'I'm not going to duck you, you little coward!' she cried. 'But I *am* going to show you what happens to people like you!'

There came the sound of four stinging slaps and Gwendoline squealed with pain. Darrell's hand was strong and hard, and she had slapped with all her might, anywhere she could reach as Gwendoline hastily tried to drag herself out of the water. The slaps sounded like pistol-shots.

'Hey, Darrell!' came the voice of the head-girl of her dormy, Katherine. 'Stop that! What are you thinking of? Leave Gwendoline alone!'

Still blazing, Darrell rounded on Katherine. 'Somebody's got to teach that cowardly Gwendoline, haven't they?'

'Yes. But not *you*,' said Katherine, coolly. 'You put yourself in the wrong, slapping about like that. I'm ashamed of you!'

'And *I'm* ashamed of *you*!' burst out Darrell, much to everyone's amazement. 'If *I* were head-girl of the first form I'd jolly well see that girls like Gwendoline learnt to swim and dive and everything, and left people like Mary-Lou alone. See?'

No one had ever seen Darrell in a temper before. They stared. 'Get out of the pool,' ordered Katherine. 'Go on, get out. It's a good thing no mistress saw you doing that.'

Darrell got out, still trembling. She went to where she had flung down her towel-cloak and put it round her. She climbed up the cliff slowly, her heart pounding.

Hateful Gwendoline! Horrid Katherine! Beastly Malory Towers!

But before she reached the top of the cliff and came to the little gate that led into the grounds of Malory Towers, Darrell's anger had all gone. She was dismayed. How *could* she have acted like that? And she had absolutely *meant* always to keep her temper now, and never let that white-hot flame of rage flare up as it used to do when she was smaller.

Very much subdued, Darrell went back to the school, dried herself and changed. She had been publicly scolded by Katherine. Nobody had backed her up at all, not even Alicia. She had shouted at the head-girl of her form. She had behaved just as badly to Gwendoline as Gwendoline had behaved to Mary-Lou—except that it must have been sheer cruelty that made Gwendoline almost drown Mary-Lou, and it was anger, not cruelty, that made her slap Gwendoline so hard. Still—anger was cruel, so maybe she *was* just as bad as Gwendoline.

She felt sorry she had slapped Gwendoline now. That was the worst of having such a hot temper. You did things all in a hurry, without thinking, and then, when your temper had gone, you were terribly ashamed, and couldn't manage to feel better until you had gone to say you were sorry to the person you had hurt, and whom you still disliked heartily.

Darrell heard somebody sniffling in the changing-room. She looked to see who it was. It was Gwendoline, dolefully examining the brilliant red streaks down her thighs. That was where Darrell had slapped her. Gwendoline sniffed loudly.

'I shall write and tell Mother,' she thought. 'If only she could see those red streaks—why, you can see all Darrell's fingers in this one!'

Darrell came up behind her and made her jump. 'Gwendoline! I'm sorry I did that. I really am. I was just so awfully angry I couldn't stop myself.'

Gwendoline was neither generous nor gracious enough to accept such a natural apology. She drew herself up and looked at Darrell as if she smelt nasty.

'I should hope you *are* sorry!' she said contemptuously. 'I shall write and tell my mother. If she thought girls at Malory Towers would behave like you do, she'd never have sent me here!'

8   DARREL—AND GWENDOLINE

THE girls left in the pool discussed the sudden happenings with interest and much surprise.

'Who would have *thought* quiet old Darrell would have lashed out like that!'

'She can't be allowed to cheek Katherine. That was jolly rude of her.'

'Katherine, are you going to do anything about it?'

Katherine was now out of the pool, her usually calm face red and disturbed. She had liked Darrell so much—and now in one minute she had quite a different idea of her! Alicia was puzzled too. She shook her head from side to side, trying to get the water out of her ears. Who would have thought Darrell had such a temper?

'Come into the common room, North Tower girls, as soon as you are dressed,' said Katherine at last, in her usual cool voice. The girls looked at one another. A first-form meeting! About Gwendoline and Darrell, they supposed. They tore off up the cliff, and poured into the changing-room, chattering loudly. Neither Gwendoline nor Darrell was there.

Gwendoline had gone up to her dormy, to get some cold cream for her red-streaked legs. They didn't need cold cream, of course—but she meant to make as much fuss as she could! She had always been jealous of Darrell, and she was jolly glad she had got something against her. Coming up and apologizing like that—she didn't mean a word of it, Gwendoline was sure!

The rest of the first-form North Tower girls, eight of them, met in the common room. Katherine sat herself on a desk and looked round.

'I am sure you are all agreed that, much as we like Darrell, we can't pass behaviour of that sort,' she began.

'Oh, Katherine—don't row her!' begged Mary-Lou's small voice. 'She saved me from drowning, she really did.'

'She didn't,' said Katherine. 'Gwendoline isn't such an idiot as to drown anyone. I suppose she just suddenly felt spiteful after being teased by the others for not trying to swim properly.'

Mary-Lou was firmly convinced that Darrell was a heroine. She had suffered such agonies under the water, and had really and truly thought she was drowning—and then along had come strong, angry Darrell. How could Katherine judge her anyhow but kindly? Mary-Lou didn't dare to say any more, but she sat with a worried, anxious look on her face, wishing she could speak up for Darrell bravely and fearlessly. But she couldn't.

'I think,' said Irene, 'that Darrell should certainly

apologize to Katherine for being cheeky to her. And if she won't, we'll send her to Coventry. We won't speak to her for a week. I must say I'm surprised at Darrell.'

' Well, *I* think she must apologize to Gwendoline too,' said Katherine. ' I heard those slaps right at the other end of the pool ! That's much more important than apologizing to me.'

' But how *much* more unpleasant ! ' murmured Alicia. ' How I should hate to have to say I was sorry for anything to darling Gwendoline Mary ! '

' Aren't you going to address a few words to Gwendoline too ? ' asked Jean.

' Yes,' said Katherine. ' Of course. Now, I wonder where Darrell is. Oh, dear, I do hope she won't kick up a fuss about apologizing to Gwendoline. If she's still in a flaming temper she won't be easy to deal with. I don't *want* to report her, or to send her to Coventry. I never imagined she could be such a little spitfire.'

Just as she finished this speech, the door opened and Darrell herself walked in. She looked surprised to see the girls sitting about, silent and serious. Katherine opened her mouth to speak to her, astonished to see Darrell looking so calm.

But before she could say a word, Darrell walked right up to her. ' Katherine, I'm most awfully sorry I spoke to you like that. I can't think how I could. I was in such a temper, I suppose.'

The wind was completely taken out of Katherine's sails. Instead of glaring at Darrell, she smiled. ' That's all right,' she said, rather awkwardly. ' I saw you were in a rage. But, Darrell . . .'

' That's an awful fault of mine,' said Darrell, rubbing her nose as she always did when she felt ashamed of herself. ' My temper, I mean. I've always had it. I get it from Daddy, but he keeps his temper for something worth while

—I mean he only loses it when there's some really big reason. I don't. I go and lose it for silly little things. I'm awful, Katherine! But honestly I had made up my mind when I came to Malory Towers that I wouldn't lose it any more.'

The girls, who had looked coldly at Darrell when she had marched into the room, now regarded her with warm liking. Here was a person who had a fault, and who said so, and was sorry about it, and didn't attempt to excuse herself. Who could help warming to a person like that?

'Well,' said Katherine, 'you managed to lose it all right this evening! I think Gwendoline deserved all she got, Darrell—but you shouldn't have been the one to give it to her. I'm the one to tick her off, or Pamela, or even Miss Potts. Not you. Just imagine what the school would be like if we could all lose our tempers and go about slapping people when we felt like it!'

'I know,' said Darrell. 'I've thought all that out myself. I'm much more ashamed of myself, Katherine, than you are of me. I wish you'd believe me.'

'I do,' said Katherine. 'But I'm afraid, Darrell, you'll have to do something unpleasant, that you'll hate doing, before we can regard this matter as finished.'

'Oh—what's that?' asked Darrell, looking really alarmed.

'Well, you'll have to apologize to Gwendoline,' said Katherine, expecting an outburst from Darrell at once.

'Apologize to Gwendoline? Oh, I've done *that*,' said Darrell, with relief. 'I thought you meant I had to do something really awful. I'm always sorry very soon after I've lost my temper. I told you that. And that means I have to go and *say* I'm sorry!'

The girls stared at Darrell, who shook back her black curls and gazed with clear eyes at Katherine. Why, they hadn't needed to have a meeting at all! They hadn't needed to judge Darrell and set her to make amends. She

had judged herself and made amends herself. The girls
looked at her with admiration and Mary-Lou could hardly
keep still. What a wonderful person Darrell was, she
thought !

' Of course,' went on Darrell, ' I still think that Gwendoline did a beastly thing to Mary-Lou—and I think it's a pity
too that Mary-Lou doesn't pull herself together so that
spiteful people like Gwendoline can't tease her.'

Mary-Lou crumpled up. Oh ! Darrell thought her
feeble and weak and frightened. And she was too. She
knew she was. She knew that a strong person like Darrell
could never really like a stupid person like Mary-Lou.
But how she wished she would !

Gwendoline opened the door and came in, looking like
a martyr. She had undone her hair so that it lay in a
golden sheet over her shoulders again. She evidently
fancied herself as an ill-used angel or something of the kind.

She heard the last few words that Darrell spoke, and
flushed red. ' Spiteful people like Gwendoline can't tease
her ! ' That was what she heard.

' Oh—Gwendoline. The next time you want to give
anyone a nasty fright, choose someone able to stand up to
you,' said Katherine, her voice sounding rather hard. ' And
please tell Mary-Lou you're sorry you were such a beast.
You gave her an awful fright. Darrell has apologized to
you, and you can jolly well do *your* bit, now ! '

' Oh—so Darrell said she apologized to me, did she ? '
said Gwendoline. ' Well, *I* don't call it an apology ! '

' You fibber ! ' said Darrell, in amazement. She swung
round to the girls. ' I *did* ! ' she said. ' You can believe
which you like, me or Gwendoline. But I *did* apologize—
straightaway too.'

Katherine glanced from Darrell's hot face to Gwendoline's
sneering one. ' We believe *you*,' she said, quietly. Her
voice hardened again. ' And now, Gwendoline, in front of

us all, please, so that we can hear—what have you got to say to Mary-Lou ? '

Gwendoline was forced to say she was sorry. She stammered and stuttered, so little did she want to say the words, but, with everyone's eyes on her, she had to. She had never said she was sorry for anything before in her life, and she didn't like it. She hated Darrell at that moment— yes, and she hated that silly Mary-Lou too·!

She went out of the room almost in tears. There was a sigh of relief as she left. 'Well, it's a good thing *that's* over!' said Irene, who hated scenes. ' I'm off to one of the practice rooms. I feel a little music will be good after this upset ! '

She went off to play the piano to herself in one of the many practice rooms. She would soon forget about everything but the melody she was playing. But the others didn't forget so easily. It hadn't been nice to see Darrell lose control of herself, but everyone agreed that it served Gwendoline right to get a slapping.

The girls compared the natural, generous way in which Darrell had said she was sorry with the grudging, stammering words that Gwendoline had spoken to the embarrassed Mary-Lou. Gwendoline certainly hadn't come out of the affair at all well. And she knew it too. She felt humiliated. What a fuss to make over a joke ! Why, the girls often ducked one another ! Anyway, she *would* write to her mother about being slapped by that beast of a Darrell ! That would make all the girls sit up.

She went back to the common room, and opened her locker. Her writing-paper was in there. She took out a pad and sat down. She did not usually enjoy writing to her mother. She thought it a bore ! She had not written to Miss Winter at all since she had come to Malory Towers, though the governess had written to her three times a week. Gwendoline rather despised the people who liked her, and was spiteful towards those that didn't.

' I'm writing to my mother,' she announced to the girls around. Some were sewing, some were reading. It was a free hour for them before supper-time. Nobody took any notice of Gwendoline's remark except Jean.

' Not the day for writing home, is it now ? ' she said. ' What's come over you, Gwendoline, to be sending home in the middle of the week, when you sigh and groan over your Sunday letter fit to make us all hold our hands over our ears ! '

' I'm writing to tell Mother how Darrell slapped me,' said Gwendoline, clearly, so that everyone could hear. ' I'm not going to stand that sort of thing. Mother won't, either.'

Katherine got up. ' I'm glad you told me what you were going to do,' she said. ' I'll go and get *my* writing-pad too. I am sure you won't tell your mother what led up to your slapping ! But *I* will ! '

Gwendoline flung down her pen in a fury. She tore the sheet she had begun, right off the pad and crumpled it up. ' All right,' she said. ' I won't write. I'm not going to have you telling tales of me to my people. What a beastly school this is ! No wonder Mother didn't want to send me away from home.'

' Poor dariing Gwendoline,' said Alicia, as the angry girl flung out of the room. ' She just can't do *any*thing she wants ! I must say I think Malory Towers is going to be jolly good for her ! ' She shook her head violently again, and Darrell looked at her in surprise.

' Why do you keep doing that ? ' she asked.

' I told you. I can't seem to get the water out of my ears,' said Alicia. ' They feel blocked. I *say*—I do hope I shan't be deaf tomorrow ! I did go deaf once before when I swam under water for ages ! '

' Oh, Alicia ! How funny it would be if you really did go deaf tomorrow in Mam'zelle's class ! ' said Darrell heartlessly. 'Oh, dear. I can't imagine what would happen!'

'Well, *I* can!' said Alicia. 'Let's hope my ears get right before the morning!'

9　ALICIA IN TROUBLE

THE affair at the Pool had a good many results. First, it made Mary-Lou follow Darrell about like a dog that has found its master and doesn't mean to leave it! She was always there to fetch and carry for Darrell. She tidied her desk for her. She even tidied the drawers in her dressing-table, and offered to make her bed each day.

But Darrell didn't like that sort of thing. 'Don't,' she said to Mary-Lou. 'I can do things for myself. Why should you make my bed? You know we're all supposed to make our own, Mary-Lou. Don't be daft.'

'I'm not,' said Mary-Lou gazing at Darrell out of her big, wide eyes. 'I'm only just trying to make a—a little return to you, Darrell—for—for saving me from drowning.'

'Don't be silly,' said Darrell. 'You wouldn't have drowned, really. I know that now. And anyway I only slapped Gwendoline hard! That was nothing.'

But it didn't in the least matter what Darrell said, Mary-Lou persisted in adoring her, and being on the watch for anything she could do. Darrell found chocolates put inside her desk. She found a little vase of flowers always on her dressing-table. But it irritated her and made her cross. She could not see Mary-Lou's timid reaching-out for a friendship that might help her. Mary-Lou was so weak. She needed someone strong, and to her Darrell was the finest girl she had ever met.

The others teased Darrell about Mary-Lou's attentions.
'Has the little dog wagged its tail for you today?' asked
Alicia.

'I wish *I* had some one to put bee-yoo-tiful flowers on
my dressing-table!' said Irene.

'Just like Darrell to encourage silly nonsense like that!'
said Gwendoline, who was jealous of all Mary-Lou's friendly
little attentions to Darrell.

'She doesn't encourage it,' said Katherine. 'You can
see she doesn't.'

Another result of the Pool affair was that Gwendoline
really did feel bitter towards Darrell now. She had never
in her life been slapped by anyone, and she couldn't forget
it. Not even her mother had slapped her! It would have
been very much better for spoilt, selfish Gwendoline if a
few smacks had come her way when she was small. But
they hadn't, and now the four or five slaps she had received
from Darrell seemed to her, not a sudden flash of temper,
soon to be forgotten, but a great insult somehow to be
avenged.

'And one day I'll pay her back, see if I don't!' thought
Gwendoline to herself. 'I don't care how long I wait.'

The third result of the Pool affair was that Alicia really
did go deaf through swimming under water so long. It
was not a deafness that would last very long, Alicia knew.
Suddenly her ears would go 'pop' inside, and she would be
able to hear as well as ever. But in the meantime it was
really very annoying to think that just after she had *pretended*
to be deaf, she really had become deaf. Whatever would
Mam'zelle say this time?

It was unfortunate for Alicia that she sat at the back of
the room, in the last row but one. Anyone with normal
hearing could hear perfectly well, even in the back row, but
Alicia with both ears 'blocked,' as she called it, found it
extremely difficult to catch every word that was said.

To make matters worse, it was not Mam'zelle Dupont who took French that day, but Mam'zelle Rougier, thin, tall and bony. She was rarely in a good humour, as her thin lips, always tightly pressed together, showed. It was funny, Alicia thought, how bad-tempered people nearly always had thin lips.

Mam'zelle Rougier had a soft voice, which, however could become extremely loud when she was angry. Then it became raucous, like a rook's, and the girls hated it.

Today she was taking the beginnings of a French play with the girls. They nearly always had to learn one each term, taking different parts. Sometimes they performed it at school concerts, but often they didn't perform it at all, merely taking it in class.

'Now,' said Mam'zelle Rougier, 'today we will discuss the play, and perhaps give out the parts. Maybe one or two of the new girls are good at French, and can take the leading parts. That would be so nice! I cannot think any of the old girls would mind that!'

They wouldn't! The less learning they had to do, the better! The new girls smiled in a sickly fashion. They thought Mam'zelle Rougier's little jokes were feeble.

'Now, first we will see who took the chief parts in last term's play,' said Mam'zelle. 'You, Alicia, what part did you play?'

Alicia didn't hear, so she didn't answer. Betty nudged her. 'What part did you take in last term's play?' she said, loudly.

'Oh! Sorry, Mam'zelle, I didn't catch what you said,' said Alicia. 'I took the part of the shepherd.'

'I thought that was in the term before,' said Mam'zelle. Alicia again couldn't catch what she said. Betty repeated it loudly. 'MAM'ZELLE SAID SHE THOUGHT THAT WAS IN THE TERM BEFORE,' said Betty.

Mam'zelle was astonished. Why should Betty repeat

everything she said like that ? Then suddenly she remembered something Mam'zelle Dupont had told her about
Alicia—ah, yes, the bad naughty girl ! She had pretended
to be deaf, hadn't she—and here she was again, playing the
same trick on Mam'zelle Rougier.

' Ah non, non ! ' said Mam'zelle Rougier to herself angrily.
' It is too much ! I will not have it.'

' Alicia,' she said, patting the little bun at the back of
her head, ' you are a funny girl and you do funny things,
n'est ce pas ? But I also, I am funny and I do funny things.
I would like you to write out for me in French, fifty times in
your best handwriting, " I must not be deaf in Mam'zelle
Rougier's class." '

' What did you say, Mam'zelle ? ' asked Alicia, having
caught her own name at the beginning, but very little else.
' I couldn't quite hear.'

' Ah, *cette méchante fille !* ' cried Mam'zelle, losing her
temper as suddenly as she always did. ' Alicia, *écoutez
bien !* Listen well ! You shall write me out " I must not
be deaf in Mam'zelle Rougier's class " ONE HUNDRED TIMES ! '

' But you said fifty just now,' said Betty, indignantly.

' And you too, you shall write out "I must not interrupt,"
one hundred times ! ' stormed Mam'zelle. The class was
silent. They knew Mam'zelle Rougier in this mood. She
would be handing out a thousand lines soon to somebody.
She was the most irritable teacher in the whole school.

Betty whispered to Alicia as soon as Mam'zelle was writing
something on the board, but, seeing that poor Alicia couldn't
hear her whisper, she scribbled a message on a bit of paper.

' You've got to write out a hundred lines for M. For
goodness' sake don't say you can't hear anything else, or
you'll get a thousand ! She's in a real paddy ! '

Alicia nodded. And whenever Mam'zelle asked her if she
had heard what was said, she answered politely, ' Yes, thank
you, Mam'zelle,' hoping she would be forgiven for the story !

Miss Potts came for the next lesson. Mam'zelle stopped and spoke to her, with a gleam in her eye. 'Alas, Miss Potts, one of your girls, Alicia, has again got a deafness in her ear. It is sad, is it not? Such a young and healthy girl!'

With this parting shot Mam'zelle Rougier disappeared. Miss Potts looked at Alicia coldly.

'I shouldn't have thought that even *you* were foolish enough to try the same trick twice, Alicia,' she said. Poor Alicia! She didn't hear what Miss Potts said, but gazed at her enquiringly.

'You can leave your desk and come to one of the front ones,' said Miss Potts. 'Jean, change places with Alicia, please. You can change over the contents of your desk later.'

Jean stood up, very pleased to think that she could leave the front row, which was always under Miss Potts's eye, and go to one of the much-sought-after back rows. It was easy to whisper in the back row, and easy to play tricks or pass notes there. Alicia didn't move because she really hadn't heard. There was suddenly a curious buzzing noise in her ears.

'You've got to move, idiot!' said Betty in a loud whisper. 'Go on—go to Jean's place.'

Alicia realised what was happening. She was full of dismay! What, leave the back seat she liked so much, leave her seat beside Betty—and go to the front row, under every teacher's eagle eye. Everyone knew that the front row had no fun at all!

'Oh, Miss Potts,' she began, in dismay. 'Honestly. I *am* deaf! It's all that under-water swimming!'

'You thought—or pretended you were deaf the other day,' said Miss Potts, unfeelingly. 'How in the world am I supposed to know when you are and when you aren't, Alicia?'

'Well, I really *am* this time,' said Alicia, wishing her ears wouldn't buzz so. 'Please, Miss Potts, let me stay here!'

'Now Alicia,' said Miss Potts, speaking in loud, clear tones so that, deaf or not, Alicia would be sure to hear, 'listen to me, and tell me if you agree with me or not. If you are *not* deaf, but playing a trick, it would be best to have you out here under my eye. If you *are* deaf and can't hear in the back row, then it is only common sense that you should be placed out here where you can. What do you think about it ? '

Alicia, of course, could not do anything but agree. She sat rather sulkily down in Jean's place. She could, of course, hear much better there. Then a funny thing happened. First one of her ears went 'pop' and then the other. She shook her head. Goody, goody ! Her ears had gone pop and were all right again. She could hear as well as ever.

She was so pleased that she whispered to Mary-Lou, next to her. 'My ears have gone pop. I can hear !'

Miss Potts had extremely sharp hearing. She caught the whisper and turned round from the board. 'Will you kindly repeat what you said, Alicia ? ' she said.

'I said "My ears have gone pop. I can hear ! "' said Alicia.

'Good,' said Miss Potts. 'I thought you would probably find you could hear all right in the front there.'

'But Miss Potts, I . . .' began Alicia.

'That's enough,' said Miss Potts. 'Let us begin this lesson please without wasting any more time on your ears, deaf or not.'

Alicia was cross because Jean and she had to change over the contents of their desks in Break. She hated being out in the front. Jean was very cheerful about the change.

'I wished hard enough I could be at the back,' she said. 'And now I am.'

'It's not fair,' grumbled Alicia. 'I really *was* deaf this morning—and then my ears suddenly got right. Miss Potts ought to have believed me.'

Darrell, who was helping, couldn't help laughing. Alicia was not in a mood to be teased, and she scowled.

'Oh, Alicia, I know it's unkind of me to laugh,' said Darrell, 'but honestly it's funny! First you pretend to be deaf, and pull Mam'zelle's leg well. Then you really *do* get deaf, and nobody believes it! It's just like that fable of the shepherd boy who called " wolf wolf!" when there wasn't a wolf, and then, when there really was, and he called for help, nobody came because nobody believed him!'

'I thought you were my friend,' said Alicia, stiffly. 'I don't like being preached at.'

'Oh, I'm not preaching, really I'm not!' said Darrell. 'Listen, Alicia, I'll write out half your lines for you, I will really! It would take you ages to write out a hundred, and I know you hate writing. I love it.'

'All right. Thanks very much,' said Alicia, cheering up. So Mam'zelle Rougier was presented with one hundred lines that evening, half of them rather badly written and the other half quite nicely written. 'Strange that a child should write so badly on one side of the paper and so well on the other!' said Mam'zelle wonderingly. But fortunately for Alicia Mam'zelle got no further than wondering about it!

10   A QUEER FRIENDSHIP

IT was very hot. The girls simply lived for their time in the swimming-pool. They groaned when the tide was out and they couldn't bathe. Fortunately the pool was an enormous one, and would take practically the whole school when the tide was in.

Darrell loved to have a game of tennis and then sprint down to the pool to bathe. Oh, the delicious coolness of

the water then ! She couldn't understand how Gwendoline
or Mary-Lou could possibly shrink from getting in. But
they insisted that the hotter the day, the colder the water
felt, and they didn't like it.

' But that's what's so *lovely* about the water,' said Darrell.
' Feeling so cold on such a blazing hot day as this ! If
you could only make up your minds to plunge in instead
of going in inch by inch, you'd love it. You're awful
cowards, both of you.'

Neither Mary-Lou nor Gwendoline liked being called
cowards. Mary-Lou always felt very hurt when Darrell
so carelessly lined her up with Gwendoline, and scorned
her, too, for her timidity. She tried her hardest to make
Darrell pleased with her by running after her more than
ever, even to tidying her locker in the common room, which
exasperated Darrell because Mary-Lou always altered her
arrangement of things.

' *What's* happened to my sweets ? I *know* I put them in
the front here. And where's my writing-pad ? Blow, and
I'm in such a hurry, too ! '

And out would come every single thing in the locker,
higgledy-piggledy on the floor ! Mary-Lou would look on
mournfully.

' Oh—I tidied them all so nicely for you,' she would say.

' Well, *don't* ! ' Darrell would order. ' Why don't you
go and bother with somebody else's things ? You always
seem to make a bee-line for mine. You seem to have got
a craze for tidying things and putting them away. You go
and do Alicia's—they're much untidier than mine ! Just
leave mine alone ! '

' I only do it to help you,' Mary-Lou would murmur.
It was awful to have such an admiration for somebody and
for them to find it a nuisance. Perhaps Darrell *would* like
her to tidy Alicia's things. She knew Darrell liked Alicia
very much. Very well, then, she would help Alicia too.

But Alicia could not bear it any more than Darrell, and when poor Mary-Lou succeeded in breaking the glass of her mother's photograph, Alicia forbade her ever to touch any of her things again.

'Can't you *see* when you're a nuisance?' she said. 'Can't you see we don't want a little ninny like you always flapping round us? Look at that photograph! Smashed to bits just because you started messing around.'

Mary-Lou wept. She was always scared when anyone ticked her off. She went out of the room and bumped into Gwendoline in the passage.

'Hallo! Crying again! Whatever's up now?' asked Gwendoline, who was always interested in other people's rows, though never sympathetic.

'Nothing. It's only that Alicia and Darrell are always so hard on me when I want to help them,' wept poor Mary-Lou, feeling very sorry for herself.

'Oh, what do you expect from people like Alicia and Darrell—yes and Betty too?' asked Gwendoline, delighted to get in a few hard words about her enemies. 'Always so cocksure of themselves, and so ready with their tongues. I can't imagine why you want to make friends with them.'

'I've just broken the photograph of Alicia's mother,' said Mary-Lou, wiping her eyes. 'That's what the trouble was really about.'

'Well, you may be sure Alicia won't forgive you for *that*,' said Gwendoline. 'She'll have her knife into you now. She just adores her mother, and nobody is ever allowed to handle that photograph. You've done it now, Mary-Lou!'

As she spoke, a perfectly wonderful idea came into Gwendoline's head. She stopped and thought a moment, her eyes shining. In one moment she saw how she could get even with Alicia and Darrell, yes, and give that stupid little Mary-Lou a few bad moments too. Mary-Lou looked at her curiously.

' What's the matter, Gwendoline ? ' she asked.

' Nothing. Just an idea,' said Gwendoline. To Mary-Lou's intense surprise she suddenly slipped her arm through the younger girl's.

' You be friends with *me*,' she said, in a honeyed voice. ' *I* shan't treat you like Darrell does, and Alicia. I haven't a wicked tongue like Alicia, or scornful eyes like Darrell. Why don't you make friends with me ? *I* shouldn't jeer at you for any little kindnesses, I can tell you.'

Mary-Lou looked at Gwendoline doubtfully. She really didn't like her, but Gwendoline smiled at her so sweetly that she felt grateful. And Alicia and Darrell really *had* been horrid to her when she had tried to do things for them. Then she remembered how Gwendoline had held her under the water.

She took her arm away from Gwendoline's. ' No,' she said, ' I can't be friends with you, Gwendoline. You were very cruel to me that day in the pool. I've had dreams about it ever since.'

Gwendoline was angry to think that the stupid, feeble little Mary-Lou should refuse to be friends with her. But she still went on smiling sweetly. She took Mary-Lou's arm again.

' You know I didn't mean anything that time in the pool,' she said. ' It was just a joke. You've often seen the others being ducked. I'm sorry I ducked you so hard. I didn't realize you were so frightened.'

There was something very determined about Gwendoline, when she had made up her mind about anything. Mary-Lou didn't know how to get away. So, as usual, she surrendered.

' Well,' she said, hesitatingly, ' well—if you *really* didn't mean to hurt me, that time in the pool, Gwendoline, I'll be friends. But I'm not going to talk against Darrell or Alicia.'

Gwendoline gave her arm a squeeze, bestowed another honeyed smile on the perplexed Mary-Lou and walked off to think out her suddenly conceived plan in peace.

'It's marvellous!' she thought. 'Everyone knows how fed-up Darrell is with Mary-Lou, because she's always tagging after her, and soon everyone will know how cross Alicia is because she has broken her mother's photograph. So, if *I* start playing a few tricks on Mary-Lou, everyone will think it is Darrell or Alicia getting back at her! And oh, goody, goody, Alicia has to sit by Mary-Lou now! That makes it easier still.'

She sat down in the Court and thought out her plan. She meant to revenge herself on the three people she disliked. She would scare Mary-Lou to death—but she would make everyone think it was Alicia and Darrell! Then they would be blamed, and punished.

'And if I make close friends with Mary-Lou nobody would ever *think* I had anything to do with things,' thought Gwendoline, in delight. 'Really, I'm very clever. I bet no one else in the whole of the first form could think of a plan like this.'

She was right. They couldn't—but not because they weren't clever enough—but just because they weren't mean enough. Gwendoline couldn't see that. She couldn't even see that she was doing a mean thing. She called it 'giving them all a lesson!'

She laid her plans very carefully. She would wait her time, till Alicia or Darrell were carrying out the duty of tidying the classroom and filling the vases with water. Then everyone would know they and they only had been in the classroom and so had the opportunity of slipping anything into anyone's desk, or taking something out.

She would pop a blackbeetle into Mary-Lou's desk—or

a few worms—or even a mouse if she could get hold of it. But no—Gwendoline quickly ruled out mice because she was so scared of them herself. She didn't much like black-beetles or worms either, but she could manage to scoop those up into a match-box or something.

She could do that. And she could remove Mary-Lou's favourite pencils and hide them in Alicia's locker. That would be a cunning thing to do! She might put one or two of Mary-Lou's books in Darrell's locker too. And how sympathetic she would be with Mary-Lou when she found out these tricks!

Gwendoline began poking round the garden to see what insects she could find. Jean, who was a good gardener, and liked to give a hand with the school garden at times, was most amazed to see Gwendoline poking about in the beds with a trowel.

'What *are* you doing?' she asked. 'Looking for a bone you've buried?'

'Don't be silly,' said Gwendoline, angry that Jean should have come across her. 'Can't I do a little gardening? Are you to be the only one?'

'Well, what gardening are you doing?' demanded Jean, who always liked to know the ins and outs of everything that aroused her curiosity.

'Just digging,' said Gwendoline. 'Making the earth a bit loose. It's so dry.'

Jean gave a snort. She had a wonderful variety of snorts, which she kept mainly for Gwendoline, Sally and Mary-Lou. Gwendoline dug viciously with her trowel, wishing she could put a worm down Jean's neck. But probably Jean wouldn't mind, anyway.

Gwendoline didn't like to look for worms after that. She decided to look for spiders. But when she saw a large one in the wood-shed she almost ran out helter-skelter herself! Still, it was *such* a large one, it would be just the thing for Mary-Lou's desk. It would come running out marvellously!

Somehow Gwendoline caught it, though she shivered as she clapped a flower-pot over it. She managed to get it into a little cardboard box. Then, feeling very clever, she slipped away to the common room, meaning to hide the spider in its box away in her locker until the right moment came.

She led the conversation round to spiders that evening. ' I got my head caught in a web in the shed today,' she said. ' Oooh, it did feel horrid. I don't like spiders.'

' My brother Sam once had a tame spider,' began Alicia, who could always be relied on to produce a bit of family history at any moment. ' It lived under a fern in our green-house, and it came out every evening for a drink of water, when Mother watered the ferns.'

' Oooh! I should have hated to see it!' said Mary-Lou, with a shudder. ' I'm terrified of spiders.'

' You're an idiot,' said Alicia, still cross over the broken photograph. ' Terrified of this, scared of that—what a life you lead, Mary-Lou. I've a good mind to catch a large spider and put it down your neck!'

Mary-Lou turned pale. The very thought made her heart jump in fright. ' I should die if you did that!' she said, in a low voice.

' Cowardy custard,' said Alicia, lazily. ' Well—wait till I get a spider!'

Gwendoline said nothing—but how she rejoiced! Could anything be better! Alicia had said more than she could possibly have hoped she would say—and what was more, every North Tower first-former had heard it. It was marvellous!

' I'll wait till Monday, when Alicia and Darrell are on duty in the classroom,' she thought. ' Then I'll do the trick. It will teach them all a lesson!'

So, when Monday came, Gwendoline watched for her moment. She and Mary-Lou went about everywhere together now, much to the surprise and amazement of Darrell and Alicia and Betty. How could Mary-Lou chum up with that awful Gwendoline, especially after that cruel ducking ? And why was Gwendoline sucking up to Mary-Lou ? It seemed very queer to the first-formers.

Gwendoline's chance came, and she took it. She was told to go and fetch something from her common room, ten minutes before afternoon school. She tore there to get it, then raced to the first-form classroom with the cardboard box. She opened it and let the great, long-legged spider run into the desk. It ran to a dark corner and crouched there, quite still.

Gwendoline hurried away, certain that no one had seen her. Two minutes later Darrell and Alicia strolled in to fill the flower-vases with water. Ah, luck was with Gwendoline just then !

11   THE SPIDER AFFAIR

THE first lesson that afternoon was mental arithmetic. The girls groaned over this, except the quick ones, like Irene, who delighted in it. But it meant that there was no need for anyone to open a desk, because it was all oral work.

Miss Potts was lenient with the girls, for it was a very hot afternoon. Darrell was glad that Miss Potts was not as exacting as usual, for arithmetic was not her strong point, especially mental arithmetic.

The next lesson was to be taken by Mam'zelle Dupont. It was to be a French conversation lesson, in which the girls would endeavour to answer all Mam'zelle's simple questions in French. Miss Potts left, and Mam'zelle arrived, not quite so beaming as usual, because of the heat. She was too plump to enjoy the hot weather, and little beads of perspiration shone on her forehead as she sat down at the big desk, opposite the rows of girls.

' *Asseyez-vous*,' she said, and the girls sat down thankfully, feeling that the only lesson they would really enjoy that weather would be a swimming lesson.

The lesson proceeded slowly and haltingly. The flow of French conversation was not at all brisk on the girls' part, and the constant pauses began to irritate Mam'zelle.

' Ah ! ' she cried at last, ' it is too hot to make conversation with such stupid ones as you are this afternoon ! Get out your grammar books and I will explain a few things to you that will help your conversation if you can get them into your so-stupid heads ! '

The girls opened their desks to get out their grammar books. Gwendoline watched eagerly to see what would happen when Mary-Lou opened hers. But nothing did happen. Mary-Lou had neither seen the spider nor disturbed it. She shut her desk.

All the girls opened their grammar books at the page Mam'zelle commanded. Then Mary-Lou found that she had her English grammar instead of her French one. So she re-opened her desk to get the right book.

' *Que faites vous*, Mary-Lou ? ' demanded Mam'zelle, who hated desks being opened and shut too often. ' What are you doing ? '

Mary-Lou stuffed her English grammar into the back of her desk and pulled out the French one. The spider, feeling itself dislodged by the book, ran out in a fright. It ran almost up to Mary-Lou before she saw it. She let the desk-lid drop with a terrific bang and gave a heart-rending scream.

Everyone jumped in alarm. Mam'zelle leapt to her

feet, sending a pile of books clattering from her desk to the floor. She glared at Mary-Lou.

' *Tiens !* What is this noise ! Mary-Lou, have you gone mad ? '

Mary-Lou couldn't speak. The sight of the enormous spider apparently running straight at her had completely undone her. She scraped her chair away from her desk, and stared at it as if she expected the spider to jump through the lid.

' Mary-Lou ! ' thundered Mam'zelle. ' Tell me what is the matter with you ? I demand it ! '

' Oh, Mam'zelle—there's a—there's a simply enormous —giant—spider in my desk ! ' stammered Mary-Lou, quite pale.

' A spider ? ' said Mam'zelle. ' And you make this fuss, and call out so loudly that we all jump in fear ! Mary-Lou, be ashamed of yourself ! I am angry with you. Sit down.'

' Oh—I—I daren't,' said Mary-Lou, trembling. ' It might come out. Mam'zelle, it's enormous.'

Mam'zelle wasn't quite sure whether she really believed in this spider or not. What with Alicia's deafness last week and one thing and another. . . .

Irene giggled. Mam'zelle fixed her with a glare. ' We will see if this spider exists or not,' she said, firmly. ' And I warn you, Mary-Lou, if this is again a trick, and there is no spider, you will go to Miss Potts for punishment. I wash my hands of you.'

She advanced to the desk. She threw open the lid dramatically. Mary-Lou drew in her breath and got away as far as she could, looking at the inside of the desk with scared eyes.

There was no spider to be seen. It had, of course, retreated to the darkest corner it could find again. Mam'zelle swept the desk with a searching glance and then turned on poor Mary-Lou.

'Bad girl,' she said, and stamped her foot. 'You, so quiet and good, you too deceive me, the poor Mam'zelle! I will not have it.'

'Mam'zelle, *do* believe me,' begged Mary-Lou, in despair, for she could not bear to be scolded like that. 'It *was* there—an enormous one.'

Mam'zelle rummaged violently among the books in the desk. 'No spider! Not one!' she said. 'Tell me, where has it gone, if it is still in there?'

The spider was alarmed by the violent rummaging. It suddenly hurried out from its hiding-place, and ran on to Mam'zelle's hand and up her arm.

Mam'zelle stared at the enormous thing as if she really could not believe her eyes. She gave a shriek even louder than Mary-Lou had given! She too was scared of spiders, and here was a giant specimen running over her person!

Irene exploded. That was the signal for the class to enter into the fun, and one and all scrambled over to Mam'zelle.

'Ah, where is it, the monster? Girls, girls, can you see it?' wailed Mam'zelle.

'It's here,' said wicked Alicia and ran a light finger down Mam'zelle's spine. She gave a scream, thinking that it was the spider running there. 'Take it off! I beg you, Alicia, remove it from me!'

'I think it must have gone down your neck, Mam'zelle,' said Betty, which nearly made Mam'zelle have a fit. She immediately felt sure that it was all over her, and began to shiver and tremble.

Alicia tickled the back of her neck and she leapt in the air. 'Oh, la la! Oh, la la! What a miserable woman I am! Where is this monster? Girls, girls, tell me it is gone!'

There was now a complete uproar in the first-form room. Miss Potts, again in the second-form room, was amazed and exasperated. What *could* her form be doing now ? Had Mam'zelle left them alone, and had they all gone mad ?

'Go on with your maps for a minute,' she said to the second form, who were glancing at one another in astonishment, as they heard the noise from the first-form room. She left the room and went rapidly to the door of the first form.

She opened it and the noise hit her like something solid. Worse than Break, she thought grimly. At first she could not see any mistress there at all, and thought that the girls were alone. Then she caught sight of Mam'zelle's head in the middle of a crowd of girls. What *was* happening !

'Girls !' she said, but her voice went unheard. 'GIRLS !' Irene suddenly saw her and started to nudge everyone. 'Look out—here's Potty,' she hissed.

The girls flowed back from Mam'zelle as if they were water ! In a trice every one was by her desk. Mam'zelle stood alone, trembling, wondering what was happening. Where had that monster of a spider gone ?

'Mam'zelle, really !' said Miss Potts, almost forgetting the rule the staff had of never finding fault with one another before the girls. 'I simply cannot think what happens to this class when you take it !'

Mam'zelle blinked at Miss Potts. 'It was a spider,' she explained, looking up and down herself. 'Ah, Miss Potts, but a MONSTER of a spider. It ran up my arm and disappeared. Ah-h-h-h-h ! I seem to feel it everywhere.'

'A spider won't hurt you,' said Miss Potts, coldly and unfeelingly. 'Would you like to go and recover yourself, Mam'zelle, and let me deal with the first form ?'

'Ah non !' said Mam'zelle, indignantly. 'The class, it is good—the girls, they came to help me to get this monster of a spider. So big it was, Miss Potts !'

Miss Potts looked so disbelieving that Mam'zelle exaggerated the size of the spider, and held out her hands to show Miss Potts that it was at least as big as a fair-sized frog.

The girls had enjoyed everything immensely. What a
French lesson! Gwendoline had enjoyed it too, especially
as she was the cause of it, though nobody knew that, of
course. She sat demurely in her desk, watching the two
mistresses closely.

And then suddenly she felt something running up her
leg! She looked down. It was the spider! It had left
Mam'zelle a long time ago, and had secreted itself under
a desk, afraid of all the trampling feet around. Now, when
peace seemed restored, the spider wanted to seek a better
hiding-place. It ran over Gwendoline's shoe, up her
stocking and above her knee. She gave a piercing scream.
Everyone jumped again. Miss Potts turned fiercely.

'Gwendoline! Go out of the room! How dare you
squeal like that! No, don't tell me you've seen the spider.
I'm tired of the spider. I'm ashamed of you all!'

Gwendoline shook herself violently, not daring to scream
again, but filled with the utmost horror at the thought of
the spider creeping over her.

'It *was* the spider!' she began. 'It . . .'

'GWENDOLINE! What did I tell you! I will NOT hear
another word of the wretched spider!' said Miss Potts,
raising her voice angrily. 'Go out of the room. The whole
class can go to bed one hour earlier tonight as a punishment
for this shameful behaviour, and you, Gwendoline, can go
two hours earlier!'

Weeping, Gwendoline ran from the room. As soon as
she got outside she examined herself carefully and trem-
blingly to see if the spider was still anywhere about her. To
her enormous relief she suddenly saw it running down the
passage.

She leant against the wall. How tiresome of that spider
to come to her, when it might have gone to anyone else!
Now she had got to have double punishment. Still, she
would soon put it about that Alicia and Darrell had planted

A spider was running up her leg!

the spider in Mary-Lou's desk! How sickening of Miss
Potts to pounce on her like that. *She* couldn't help it if
the spider came to her.

But perhaps after all it was a good thing that Miss Potts
had come into the room and heard it all. Perhaps Gwen
doline might even drop a hint to Miss Potts about Alicia
and Darrell putting the spider in the desk.

Miss Potts came out of the room at this moment. She
eyed Gwendoline with dislike.

'Miss Potts, the spider ran away down there,' said
Gwendoline, pointing, anxious to get back into Miss Potts's
good books.

Miss Potts took not the slightest notice but swept into
the second-form classroom, and the door shut. Gwendoline felt very small. Now what was she to do? Stay out
here—or go back into the classroom? She didn't want to
be found out there if by any chance Miss Grayling, the
Head, came by. She decided to risk going back. She
opened the door and sidled in.

'Ha! You are back again! And who told you to come?'
demanded Mam'zelle, now ashamed of her part in the affair,
and ready to vent her humiliated feelings on anyone she could.
'You screamed and made Miss Potts white and angry!'

'Well, Mam'zelle, you screamed too,' protested Gwendoline, in an injured tone. 'Louder than I did, I should
think.'

Mam'zelle rose in her seat, and for all her smallness she
seemed enormous to Gwendoline just then. Her beady
black eyes flashed.

'You would be rude to *me*, Mam'zelle Dupont! You
would argue with *me*, who have taught here for twenty
years! You—you . . .'

Gwendoline turned and fled. She would rather stand
outside the door all day long than face Mam'zelle when
she looked like that!

THE Spider Affair, as it was called, went all over the school before the day was out. It caused a great deal of laughter. When Mam'zelle Rougier heard of it she sneered.

'To think that a Frenchwoman should be so foolish!' she said. 'Now *I* do not mind spiders or earwigs or moths or even snakes! Mam'zelle Dupont should be ashamed to make such an exhibition of herself!'

The first form talked about it more than anyone else, of course. They squealed with laughter whenever they thought of poor Mary-Lou, Mam'zelle, and Gwendoline all falling victims to the same spider.

'Jolly clever spider! said Irene. 'It knew the only three people in the form that would be scared of it. I take my hat off to that spider.'

'I can't think why it chose *my* desk,' said Mary-Lou.

'No. That was a shame,' said Gwendoline. 'Poor Mary-Lou! It must have been an awful shock for you when you saw it. I wonder who put it there?'

There was a silence. For the first time it occurred to the first form that the spider might have been put there on purpose. They looked at one another.

'It was a dirty trick to put it into poor Mary-Lou's desk,' said Jean. 'She can't *help* being scared of things, I suppose, and she almost jumped out of her skin when she saw it. I should have thought any joker in our form would have been decent enough to have popped it into, say, Alicia's desk!'

'Not if it happened to be *Alicia* who popped it in!' said a sly voice. 'You do so love playing tricks, don't you, Alicia? You and Darrell were in the first-form room before afternoon school. And I'm sure we all remember you saying you'd like to put a spider down Mary-Lou's neck ! '

It was Gwendoline speaking. Alicia glanced at her. ' Well, I didn't do it,' she said. ' Nor did Darrell. Sorry to disappoint you, darling Gwendoline Mary, but we just didn't. If it was anyone, I should think it was you ! '

' Mary-Lou is my friend,' said Gwendoline. ' I wouldn't do that to her.'

' Well, if you'd almost drown her one week, I should think you could quite well bring yourself to put a spider in her desk the next week,' said Darrell.

' It's pretty funny that you and Alicia were the only ones in the classroom before afternoon school,' persisted Gwendoline, angry that no one seemed to have agreed with her suggestion.

' Shut up,' said Katherine, shortly. ' We *know* it wasn't either Darrell or Alicia, because they *say* so ! The spider must have got in there by accident, and that's that.'

' Well, *I* think . . .' began Gwendoline, but the class took up a chant at once.

' Shut up, Gwendoline ; Gwendoline, shut up ! Shut *up*, Gwendoline ; Gwendoline, shut *up* ! '

There was nothing to do but shut up. Gwendoline was sulky and exasperated. It had been such a good idea, and all that had resulted from it was a double punishment for her, and a complete failure to make anyone believe that Alicia or Darrell had played the trick. True, the first formers had had to go to bed an hour earlier, but they had all voted it was worth it.

Gwendoline felt vicious about the whole affair. She determined not to be put off by her first failure but to go on doing things to Mary-Lou, so that in the end the class would have to put them down to tricks by Alicia and Darrell. She thought too she would also hint to Miss Potts that she thought Alicia and Darrell were at the bottom of things.

But she didn't get very far with this. She had to go
and see Miss Potts about some returned homework, and
stood very meekly beside her, in the little room that Miss
Potts shared with Mam'zelle Dupont at North Tower.

'Miss Potts, I was awfully sorry about that spider affair
the other day,' she began. 'Of course, Alicia and Darrell
were in the classroom beforehand, and I'm sure they know
something about it. I heard Alicia say . . .'

Miss Potts looked up. 'Are you trying to sneak?' she
said. 'Or in more polite language, to tell tales? Because
if so, don't try it on me. At the boarding school I went
to, Gwendoline, we had a very good punishment for sneaks.
All the girls in the sneak's dormy gave her one good spank
with the back of a hair-brush. You may have a lot of
interesting things to tell me but it's no use expecting me
to listen. I wonder if the girls here have the same punishment for sneaks. I must ask them.'

Gwendoline went flaming red. A sneak! Fancy Miss
Potts daring to call her, Gwendoline Mary Lacey, a sneak!
All because she had just wanted to drop a kindly hint.
Gwendoline didn't know what to say. She felt as if she
would like to burst into tears, but Miss Potts always got
very impatient with girls who did that. She went out of
the room, longing to slam the door as she often did at home.
But she didn't dare to here.

She felt very sorry for herself. If her mother knew what
an awful school she had come to she would take her away
at once. Miss Winter, too, would be horrified. But Gwendoline wasn't quite so sure about her father. He could
say things at times very like the things Miss Potts said.

The week went by. It was a very pleasant week, hot
with a cool breeze that made games and swimming even
more pleasure than usual. Alicia and Betty were practising hard for the school sports. Both were excellent
swimmers and divers. Darrell tried to imitate all they did.

She was good, too, but not quite so good as they were. But she was quite fearless, and dived off the highest diving-boards, and went down the chute in all kinds of peculiar positions.

The only unhappy person that week was Mary-Lou. She got into a lot of trouble over many little things. For instance, her clothes in the changing-room had been thrown down in a pool of water, and were soaking wet. She had to take them to Matron to be dried.

Matron was cross. 'Mary-Lou! Can't you hang your things up properly in that changing-room ? You know there are always puddles on the floor from the girls coming in and out from the pool.'

' I did hang them up, Matron,' said Mary-Lou, mildly. ' I know I did.'

Then Mary-Lou's tennis racket suddenly showed three broken strings. They were not frayed, but looked as if they had been cut. Mary-Lou was upset.

' My new racket ! ' she said. ' Look, Gwendoline, who would think a new racket could go like that ? '

' It couldn't,' said Gwendoline, pretending to examine it very closely. ' These strings have been cut, Mary-Lou. Someone's been playing a dirty trick on you.   What a shame.'

Mary-Lou was miserable. She couldn't believe that she had any enemies. But when she found buttons cut off her Sunday dress she knew that someone was being unkind and mean. Gwendoline comforted her.

' Never mind. *I'll* sew them on for you ! I hate sewing, but I'll do it for you, Mary-Lou.'

So, making a great show of it, Gwendoline sewed on the six blue buttons one night. The first-formers stared at her in surprise. They knew she never mended anything if she could help it.

' How did those buttons come off ? ' asked Jean.

' That's what *I'd* like to know,' said Gwendoline smugly.

'Six buttons, all ripped off! I'm putting them on for Mary-Lou, because I'm so sorry that anyone should play her such a dirty trick. And I'd like to know who cut the strings of her tennis racket, too.'

The first-formers looked at one another. It certainly was queer the way things had been happening to poor Mary-Lou lately. Even her prayer-book had disappeared. And some of her pencils had gone. True, they had been found in Alicia's desk—but everyone had thought that was just an accident. Now they began to wonder if some one had put them there. Not Alicia. Alicia wouldn't do a thing like that. But Somebody.

It was getting near half-term. Many of the girls were excited, because some of them were expecting visits from their parents. Any parent who lived not too far away would be sure to come. Darrell was thrilled because her father and mother were coming. They lived a long way away, but had decided to take a week's holiday in Cornwall, and come and see Darrell in the middle of it.

The girls began to talk about their families. 'I wish my three brothers could come,' said Alicia. 'We'd have some sport then.'

'I wish my little sister could come,' said Jean. 'I'd love to show her Malory Towers.'

'Is *your* mother coming, Sally?' asked Mary-Lou.

'No,' said Sally. 'She lives too far away.'

Darrell remembered something her mother had told her in a letter a week or two before. She had said that she had met Sally Hope's mother, and had liked her. She had said too that she had seen Mrs. Hope's baby, Sally's sister, a little girl of three months. Darrell had meant to tell Sally what her mother had said and had forgotten. Now she remembered it.

'Oh, Sally, I expect your mother won't come because of the baby,' she said.

Sally went stiff. She stared at Darrell as if she couldn't believe her ears. Her face went quite white, and when she spoke she sounded as if she were choking.

'You don't know what you're talking about,' she said. 'What baby? We haven't a baby! My mother won't be coming because it's so *far*, I tell you!'

Darrell was puzzled. 'But Sally—don't be silly—my mother said in a letter that she had *seen* your baby sister —she's three months old, she said.'

'I haven't *got* a baby sister!' said Sally, in a low, queer voice. 'I'm the only one. Mother and I have been everything to each other, because Daddy has had to be away such a lot. I haven't *got* a baby sister!'

The girls looked at Sally curiously. Whatever could be the matter with her? She sounded so queer.

'All right,' said Darrell, uneasily. '*You* ought to know, I suppose. Anyway, I expect you'd like a sister. It's nice having one.'

'I should hate a sister,' said Sally. 'I wouldn't share my mother with anyone!'

She walked out of the room, her face as wooden as ever. The girls were really puzzled. 'She's a funny one,' said Irene. 'Hardly ever says anything—all closed up, somehow. But sometimes those closed-up people burst open suddenly—and then, look out!'

'Well, I shall certainly write and tell Mother she's mistaken,' said Darrell, and she did so, then and there. She told Sally the next time she saw her.

'I'm sorry I made that mistake about your having a sister,' she said to Sally. 'I've written to tell Mother you said you hadn't one. She must have mistaken what your mother said.'

Sally stood still and glared at Darrell as if she suddenly hated her. 'What do you want to go interfering for?' she burst out. 'Leave me and my family alone! Little busybody, always sticking your nose into other people's affairs!'

Darrell's temper flared up. 'I don't,' she said. 'You guard your tongue, Sally. I never meant to interfere, and I can't think what all the fuss is about. Either you have a sister or you haven't. *I* don't care.'

'You tell your mother not to interfere either!' said Sally. 'Writing letters about my family!'

'Oh, don't be so *silly*!' flared back Darrell, really exasperated now. 'Anyone would think there was a deep, dark mystery, the way you go on! Anyway, I'll just see what my mother says when she next writes to me—and I'll tell you.'

'I don't want to know. I won't know!' said Sally, and she put out her hands as if she was fending Darrell off. 'I hate you, Darrell Rivers—you with your mother who comes to see you off, and sends you things and writes you long letters and comes to see you! And you boast about that to me; you do it all on purpose. You're mean, mean, mean!'

Darrell was utterly taken about. What in the wide world did Sally mean? She watched the girl go out of the room, and sank down on to a form, completely bewildered.

13 HALF-TERM AT LAST!

THE girls became very excited at the beginning of half-term week. Many of them would see their parents on the Saturday—and Miss Remmington, the games-mistress, had suddenly decided to have a small edition of the Swimming Sports for the benefit of the parents. Everyone who visited Malory Towers was struck with the beautiful natural pool, and loved to see it.

'So it would be nice this half-term, as it's so hot, for your people to go down to the breezy pool, and see not only the beauties of the water, but the way their girls can swim and dive!' said Miss Remmington. 'We will have a pleasant time down there and then come back for a strawberry and cream tea, with ices!'

What fun! Darrell hugged herself with joy whenever she thought of it. She had got on so well with her swimming and diving, and she knew her parents would be pleased. And strawberries and ice-cream afterwards. How simply wizard!

But she was rather taken aback on Wednesday when the half-term places were read out. Instead of being in the first three or four, as she had hoped, she was tenth from the bottom. She could hardly believe her ears! Katherine was top, Alicia was fifth, Betty was fourteenth, Gwendoline was bottom—Mary-Lou was sixth from the bottom, not very far below Darrell!

Darrell sat very quiet whilst the rest of the marks were read out. There were thirty or so girls in her form—and more than twenty of them had done better than she had. Surely, surely there must be some mistake?

She went to Miss Potts about it, looking worried. 'Miss Potts,' she began, rather timidly, for the mistress was correcting papers and looked very busy, 'Miss Potts, excuse my interrupting you, but can I ask you something?'

'What is it?' said Miss Potts, running her blue pencil across a line of writing.

'Well—it's about the form order,' said Darrell. 'Am I really so low down as that?'

'Let me see—what were you? Quite a long way down,' said Miss Potts, pulling the list to her and looking at it. 'Yes, that's right. I was surprised and disappointed, Darrell. You did so well in the first two weeks.'

'But Miss Potts,' said Darrell, and then stopped. She didn't know quite how to say what she wanted to say. She wanted to say that she had much better brains than at least half the form, so why was she so low ? But somehow that sounded conceited.

However Miss Potts, who was very quick-minded, saw her difficulty. 'You have come to ask me how it is you are nearer the bottom than the top when you could so easily be among the top ones ?' she said. 'Well, I'll tell you, Darrell. There are people like Alicia, who can play the fool in class and waste their time and everyone else's, and yet still come out well in their work. And there are people like you, who can also play the fool and waste their time—but unfortunately it affects their work and they slide down to the bottom. Do you understand ?'

Darrell flushed very red and looked as if she could sink through the floor. She nodded.

'Yes, thank you,' she said, in a small voice. She looked at Miss Potts out of her clear brown eyes. 'I wouldn't have been so silly if I'd known it was going to affect my place in the form,' she said. 'I—I just thought as I had good brains and a good memory I'd be all right, anyhow. Daddy and Mother will be disappointed.'

'They probably will,' said Miss Potts, taking up her pencil again. 'I shouldn't copy Alicia and Betty too much if I were you, Darrell. You will be a finer character if you go along on your own, than if you copy other people. You see, what *you* do, you do whole-heartedly—so if you play the fool, naturally other things will suffer. Alicia is able to do two or three things quite well at one and the same time. That certainly has its points—but the best people in this world are the whole-hearted ones, if they can only make for the right things.'

'I see,' said Darrell. 'Like my father. He's whole-hearted. He's a surgeon and he just goes in for giving back people their health and happiness with all his heart —so he's marvellous.'

' Exactly,' said Miss Potts. ' But if he split himself up, so to speak, and dabbled in half a dozen things, he would probably not be nearly such a remarkable surgeon. And when you choose something worth while like doctoring—or teaching—or writing or painting, it is best to be whole-hearted about it. It doesn't so much matter for a second-rate or third-rate person. But if you happen to have the makings of a first-rate person and you mean to choose a first-rate job when you grow up, then you must learn to be whole-hearted when you are young.'

Darrell didn't like to ask Miss Potts if she thought she had the makings of a first-rate person in her, but she couldn't help hoping that she had. She went away rather subdued. What a pity she hadn't been whole-hearted over her work and got up to the top, instead of being whole-hearted over playing the fool with Alicia and Betty, and sliding down towards the bottom.

Gwendoline's mother and her old governess, Miss Winter, were coming on Saturday too. Gwendoline was very much looking forward to showing off in front of them. How small she would make Miss Winter feel, when she talked of her lessons and how wonderful she was at everything !

Mary-Lou's people were not coming and she was disappointed. Gwendoline spoke kindly to her. ' Never mind, Mary-Lou. You can keep with me and my mother and Miss Winter all day. I won't let you feel lonely.'

Mary-Lou didn't much want to keep with Gwendoline. She was tired of being pawed about by Gwendoline, and tired of the never-ending stories of her family, in all of which Gwendoline herself shone out brightly as someone really too marvellous for words.

But Gwendoline thoroughly enjoyed such a quiet listener as Mary-Lou, though she despised her for being weak enough to put up with so much.

When Darrell heard that Mary-Lou's people could not
come on half-term Saturday she went to her. 'Would
you like to come and be with my mother and father and
me all day ?' she said. 'They are taking me out to lunch
in the car. We're having a gorgeous picnic.'

Mary-Lou's heart leapt. She gazed at Darrell in adora-
tion and delight. To be asked by *Darrell* to share the
half-term—could anything be nicer ? Darrell had ticked
her off so much lately, and found her such a nuisance—but
now she had been decent enough to give her this invitation.

Then she remembered Gwendoline's invitation, and her
face fell. 'Oh,' she said, 'Gwendoline's asked me to join
her—and I said I would.'

'Well, go and tell her *I've* asked you, and that my father
and mother would like to meet you,' said Darrell. 'I
shouldn't think she'd mind.'

'Well—I don't know if I dare say that,' said timid
Mary-Lou. 'She might be very angry—especially as she
doesn't like you, Darrell.'

'I suppose that means you'd rather go with Gwendoline
than with me,' said Darrell, unkindly. It always irritated
her when Mary-Lou put on her 'scared' look. 'Well,
go then.'

'*Darrell!* How can you say that ?' cried Mary-Lou,
almost in tears. 'Why—I'd—I'd—I'd give *anything* to
come with you.'

'Well, go and tell Gwendoline then,' said Darrell. 'If
you want a thing badly you can surely pluck up enough
courage to get it. You're a terrible little coward.'

'Oh, I know,' said Mary-Lou, in despair. 'Don't keep
on and on saying that ! It only makes me worse ! *You*
tell Gwendoline, Darrell.'

'Certainly not,' said Darrell. '*I'm* not going to do your
dirty work ! Anyway, I'm not sure I want such a silly
baby tagging on to me all half-term.'

She walked off, leaving Mary-Lou looking after her in despair. Jean, who was nearby and had overheard everything, felt a little sorry for Mary-Lou. She walked after Darrell.

'I think you're a bit hard on her,' she remarked, in her forthright Scots voice.

'Well, it's all for her good,' said Darrell. 'If I can *make* her have a little courage, she'll thank me for it. I said those things purposely, to shame her into going to Gwendoline and asking her.'

'You've shamed her all right, but not in the way that will make her pluck up her courage,' said Jean. 'You've given her the kind of shame that puts people into despair!'

Jean was right. Mary-Lou was quite in despair. The more she thought of going to Gwendoline and asking her if she minded her going with Darrell at half-term instead of with her, the more terrified she got. In the end she did go to find Gwendoline, but found that she didn't dare to ask her; which made it worse than ever! Poor Mary-Lou!

Gwendoline got to hear that Darrell had asked Mary-Lou for half-term, and she was pleased that Mary-Lou had not apparently wanted to go with her. She spoke to her about it.

'Fancy Darrell having the cheek to ask you, after *I'd* asked you!' she said. 'I'm glad you had the decency to refuse, Mary-Lou. You'd surely not want to go off with a girl like that, who thinks you're such a poor worm?'

'No,' said Mary-Lou, and couldn't say any more. If only she could have said yes, boldly, right out! But she couldn't.

The morning of half-term dawned bright and clear. It was going to be a super day. The sea glinted in the sunlight, as calm as a mirror. It would be high tide at two o'clock. The pool would be just right. What luck!

Girls took loads of camp-stools down to the pool and

set them up on the high rocky place above the pool, where the tide seldom reached. It was a fine place for watching. Darrell sang loudly as she went up and down, her heart leaping because she would see her parents that day. Mary-Lou did not sing. She looked sober and down-hearted. Sally Hope looked sober too—her face more ' closed-up ' than ever, thought Darrell.

Alicia was in high spirits. Her mother and father were coming and one of her brothers. Betty's parents were not coming, so she was, of course, going to be with Alicia.

Darrell, catching sight of Sally trudging up the cliff, after taking down some camp-stools, was struck by the sad expression on her face. Impulsively she hailed her.

' Hie, Sally ! Sally Hope ! Your people aren't coming, are they ? Wouldn't you like to join me and my parents today ? I can ask anyone I like.'

' I'd rather not, thank you,' said Sally, in a stiff little voice, and went on up the cliff without another word.

' Well, she *is* a funny girl,' thought Darrell, feeling rather annoyed that the two girls she had so far asked hadn't either of them agreed to come with her. She went off to find someone else whose people were not coming. She really must get *some*body, because her mother had said she would like to take another girl out too. ' Your own particular friend, if possible,' her mother had written.

But Darrell hadn't got a ' particular friend.' She would so much have liked Alicia, but Alicia was Betty's friend. She liked Irene, too, but Irene never seemed to feel the need of a friend. Her music made up to her for everything.

' Oh, well—what about asking Emily ? ' thought Darrell. She was not at all interested in the quiet, studious Emily, who always seemed to be sewing most industriously every evening. But Emily's people weren't coming, and no one had asked her to go out to lunch with them.

So she asked Emily, who blushed with pleasure and said

yes, she would be delighted to come. She seemed surprised that Darrell had asked her. Mary-Lou was almost in tears when she saw the two of them going off to get ready to meet Darrell's parents. She couldn't bear to think that Emily was going to have the treat she would so much have loved herself—but hadn't enough courage to get.

14   A REALLY LOVELY DAY

SOON the big drive in front of Malory Towers was crowded with cars of all shapes and sizes. Parents climbed out of them and looked for their girls. There were shrieks of delighted welcome all over the place.

'Mummy! Daddy! I'm so glad you've come early!'

'Mother! I didn't expect you so soon! Oh, it's lovely to see you again!'

Darrell was watching for her father and mother, too. She soon saw her father's plain black car, which he drove himself. And there was mother sitting beside him, looking pretty in a new dress, and excited because she would so soon see Darrell.

Darrell shot out of the doorway and down the drive like an arrow, nearly knocking over Gwendoline, who was waiting impatiently for her own mother. She flung herself on her parents. 'Mother! I've been waiting and waiting! Oh, it's lovely to see you again! Hallo, Daddy—did you drive all the way down?'

'Hallo, darling,' said her mother and looked at her in pleasure. Darrell was brown and glowing with colour. Her warm brown eyes were filled with delighted love. She looked happy and 'on top of the world' as her father put it to himself. Both her parents were pleased-

Darrell took them into the school, chattering at the top of her voice. 'You must see my dormy. You must see the very bed I sleep in—and I *must* show you the view out of our dormy window. It's super!'

In her intense excitement she had forgotten all about Emily, waiting patiently nearby. She suddenly saw her, and stopped.

'Oh—Emily! Mother, you said I could choose some one to come out with us—and here she is. This is Emily Lake, a girl in my form.'

Mrs. Rivers looked at Emily and was surprised. She had not expected a quiet sober little girl like this to be Darrell's chosen friend. She did not know that as yet Darrell had no definite friend. She shook hands with Emily, and said she was pleased she was coming out with them.

After that Emily tagged along behind them, listening to Darrell's excited chatter, and her parents' amused replies. She liked Darrell's parents. Her mother was pretty and amusing, and sensible too—and as for her father, well, any one would trust him at sight, thought Emily, gazing at his determined, good-looking face with its big dark eyes and intensely black eyebrows, just like Darrell's but bigger and shaggier.

Darrell was proud of her parents. She wanted to show them off. She saw Gwendoline with two women—one obviously her mother, with bright golden hair like Gwendoline's and a rather babyish, empty face. The other must be Miss Winter, the governess, thought Darrell. What an awful person!

Poor Miss Winter was not really awful. She was plain and poor and always eager to agree with everyone. She adored Gwendoline because she was pretty and graceful, and did not seem to see the selfishness and spoilt ways of the silly little girl.

Mary-Lou was with them, trying to smile, but really very unhappy. She didn't like either Mrs. Lacey or Miss Winter and she was beginning to feel horrified at some of the fibs that she had heard Gwendoline tell them.

'I'm almost the best at tennis in our form,' she heard Gwendoline say. 'I shouldn't be surprised if I'm put into a match-team, Mother!'

'Oh, darling—how clever you are!' said Mrs. Lacey, fondly. Mary-Lou stared at Gwendoline in surprise. Why, everyone knew Gwendoline was a real muff at all games!

'And Mam'zelle is very pleased with my French,' went on Gwendoline. 'I believe I might be top in that. She says I have a splendid accent.'

Miss Winter glowed. 'Oh, Gwen darling! Isn't that lovely now? I did my best with you, of course, but I was always afraid it was rather a *poor* best, because I've never been to France.'

Mary-Lou longed to say that Gwendoline was always bottom in the French class, but she did not dare to. How *could* Gwendoline stuff her people up with such a lot of lies? And how *could* they believe them?

'Are you going to go in for the swimming-match this afternoon?' asked Mrs. Lacey, looking fondly at Gwendoline, who today had her shining golden hair loose down her back, and looked, so her mother thought, like a real angel.

'No, I thought I wouldn't, Mother,' said Gwendoline. 'It's best to give the others a chance. After all, I've done well at so many things.'

'There's my sweet, unselfish girl!' said Mrs. Lacey, and squeezed Gwendoline's arm. Mary-Lou felt slightly sick.

Then Darrell spoilt it all! She passed by with her mother and father, and Mrs. Lacey was struck by her good looks and happy smile.

'*There's* a nice girl, dear!' she said to Gwendoline.
'Is she one of your friends? Let us speak to her.'

'Oh, no, she's not a friend of mine,' began Gwendoline,
but Mary-Lou, delighted at this praise of Darrell, was
calling to her. 'Darrell! Darrell! Mrs. Lacey wants to
speak to you.'

Darrell went over to Mrs. Lacey and was introduced
by a glowering Gwendoline. 'And are you going to go
in for the swimming-sports?' asked Mrs. Lacey, graciously.
'I hear dear Gwendoline is not, bless her.'

'Gwendoline! Oh, she can't swim a stroke!' said
Darrell. 'We always yell at her because she takes five
minutes putting one toe into the water. Don't we, Gwendoline?'

This was all said in good humour and fun—but Gwendoline could willingly have pushed Darrell over the cliff
at that moment! She went very red.

Mrs. Lacey really thought that Darrell was joking. She
laughed the tinkling laugh which she thought was so pretty.
'I suppose if Gwendoline entered she'd beat you all!' she
said. 'As she does at tennis—and lessons, I suppose.'

Darrell looked in astonishment at Gwendoline, who was
glaring at her, crimson in the face. 'Gwendoline's been
stuffing you up, I expect!' she said with a laugh, and went
off to join her own party.

'What a very outspoken, blunt sort of girl,' said Miss
Winter, puzzled and worried.

Gwendoline recovered herself. 'Oh, she's not a nice
girl,' she said. 'Nobody likes her. She hasn't got any
friend of her own at all—and you can see why. She's
always running other people down. Jealous, I suppose.
Don't you take any notice of her, Mother. Mary-Lou here
will tell you I'm first-rate at tennis and the rest!'

But that was beyond even timid Mary-Lou! She just
looked more scared than ever, and murmured something

about going to speak to Mam'zelle—and off she went, glad
to escape from the Lacey family for a few minutes.

On the way to the car, after Darrell had shown her
parents every single thing she could think of, from the
view up in North Tower, to the inside of her very well-
tidied desk, the Rivers' family saw Sally Hope.

'Why, isn't that Sally Hope?' said Mrs. Rivers, stopping. 'I'm sure it is. There was a very good photograph
of her in her mother's drawing-room, when I went to tea
there the other day.'

'Yes. That's Sally,' said Darrell. 'Do you want to
speak to her, Mother?'

'Well, I have a message for her from her mother,' said
Mrs. Rivers. So Darrell raised her clear voice and called.
'Sally! Sally Hope! Come here a minute, will you?'

Sally must have heard Darrell, for everyone around
did. But if so, she took no notice at all. She plunged
down into a path that led through some bushes in the drive
and disappeared.

'Blow her!' said Darrell. 'I should have thought she
would have heard my yell. I asked her to come out with
us, Mother, but she wouldn't.'

'Come along,' said her father, opening the door of the
car. 'We'll go along the cliff and then take an exciting
road I've found that leads right down to a lonely little cove.
We'll have our lunch there.'

Darrell and Emily got in. Emily was enjoying herself.
Mrs. Rivers was so nice, and asked her so many questions
about herself. Usually people found Emily dull, and left
her alone. But Mrs. Rivers, thinking that Emily was
Darrell's chosen friend, was very anxious to know her
well.

She soon learnt that Emily was very fond of sewing.
Darrell listened to her chattering in astonishment. She
had never heard Emily talk so much before! Gracious,

hark at her describing the cushion-cover she was making
—the colours, the stitches and everything !

' It's always been a disappointment to me that Darrell
never took any interest in embroidery,' said Mrs. Rivers
to Emily. ' I'm very fond of it too. I've done the seats
of six of our chairs at home, in tapestry work.'

' Oh, *have* you ! ' exclaimed Emily. ' I've done some
too—but only two so far. I loved that work.'

' Perhaps you will be able to interest Darrell in sewing ! '
said Mrs. Rivers, laughing. ' It's as much as I can do at
home to get her to do a simple darn ! '

' Well, I'll teach Darrell to darn, if she likes,' said Emily,
eager to please this nice Mrs. Rivers.

Darrell was horrified. Gracious, she hadn't brought
Emily out to have her planning with her mother to teach
her darning ! She changed the subject at once, and told
them about Gwendoline and how she had been boasting
to her mother and governess.

Soon they were down on the beach, eating the most
gorgeous lunch Darrell had had that term. Cold chicken
and pickles—*pickles* ! There was never a pickle to be seen
at school. Little cardboard containers full of fresh salad
and mayonnaise sauce. Delicious ! Jam-tarts and slabs
of chocolate ice-cream. What a lunch !

' And ginger-beer to wash it down,' said Mrs. Rivers,
filling up the glasses. ' More chicken, Darrell ? There's
plenty.'

After lunch it was time to go back for the sports. Emily
was not in the swimming, so she said she would find Darrell's
parents good places to watch from. Darrell left them in
her care when she got back to Malory Towers to change.

It was such a happy day. Everyone seemed in a good
temper, and jokes flew about everywhere. Even the two
Mam'zelles went about arm-in-arm, a thing that they had
not done at all that term.

The swimming-sports were exciting. Mrs. Rivers was delighted with Darrell's strong swimming, graceful diving, and fearlessness. She was one of the best of the small girls. Some of the big girls were extremely clever in their diving, especially Marilyn, the sixth-form games-captain. Everyone cheered her as she did a graceful swallow-dive from the topmost board.

'And can you do all these things, darling?' Darrell heard Mrs. Lacey ask Gwendoline. Gwendoline, who was near Darrell and a few others, looked round warily, wishing her mother wouldn't ask such awkward questions in public.

'Well—not quite all,' she said, and Miss Winter patted her fondly on the shoulder.

'Always so modest,' she said, and Darrell could hardly stop herself laughing outright at the thought of Gwendoline being called modest. She looked scornfully at little Mary-Lou sitting near Gwendoline, wondering how she could possibly listen to all the bigger girl's boasting and yet say nothing.

At tea-time Darrell and Emily kept the plates of the grown-ups (and their own!) well supplied with strawberries and cream, and fetched ice-creams in plenty. What a lunch they had had—and now, what a tea! Besides the strawberries and ice-creams, there were little buns and cakes and biscuits of every kind. Malory Towers knew how to do things well!

'Mother! There's Sally Hope again!' said Darrell suddenly, catching sight of Sally's head in the distance. 'I'll get her in a minute. By the way, you never told me how that mistake about Sally's baby sister happened— the one you said she had got, and hasn't.'

'But Darrell dear—she *has* got a baby sister!' said her mother in surprise. 'I've seen her!'

'Well—whatever *does* Sally mean!' said Darrell. 'I really must get her and find out!'

BUT Sally was not easy to find. She seemed to have completely disappeared again. It occurred to Darrell to wonder if Sally was avoiding her—but no, why should she ? There would be no reason for that.

She hunted everywhere for Sally. Nobody knew where she was. It was peculiar. Darrell went back to her parents, anxious not to lose any more of their company, for time was precious now.

'Well, *I* can't find Sally,' she said. 'She's completely vanished. Anyway, I'll give her her mother's message. What was it, Mother ? '

'Oh, her mother seemed a little worried about Sally, because it's her first term at boarding school, and Sally writes such funny wooden little letters,' said Mrs. Rivers. 'I showed Mrs. Hope some of *your* letters, darling. I knew you wouldn't mind ; and she said she did wish Sally would write more news to her, and send her letters like yours. She said she seemed to have lost touch with her completely. She was really very worried. She wanted me to speak to Sally and tell her she sent her fondest love, and was so sorry she couldn't come and see her this half-term. And she said her baby sister sent her hugs and kisses.'

'I'll tell her,' said Darrell, very puzzled. 'But Mother dear, Sally's awfully funny about things. She truly and honestly did tell me she hadn't got a sister, and she was furious with me for talking about her mother. She said I was interfering and all sorts of things.'

'Well—perhaps she was joking,' said Mrs. Rivers, also rather puzzled. 'Sally *does* know she's got a baby sister at home. For one thing, that was why she was sent to boarding school, so that the baby, who is rather delicate, could have all Mrs. Hope's care. It's a dear little thing.'

'Been losing your temper yet?' asked Darrell's father, with a twinkle in his eye. Darrell went red.

'Well—I did once,' she said. 'And after I'd made up my mind I wouldn't, too!'

'Oh, Darrell—you didn't lose it badly, I hope,' said her mother, anxiously.

Emily answered for Darrell. 'Oh, she just gave a most exasperating girl some jolly good slaps in the pool! You could almost hear them up at the Towers!'

'*Darrell!*' said her mother, shocked. Darrell grinned.

'I know. Awful of me, wasn't it. I shan't do it again. I've got my temper well in hand now.'

'We've all *wanted* to do a bit of slapping where that particular girl is concerned,' said Emily, 'so secretly we were rather pleased!'

They all laughed. Darrell felt so happy that she was sure she would never lose her temper again in her life! What a pity a day like this had to come to an end!

But it did come to an end. At about six o'clock the cars began to purr out of the big drive, and girls waved wildly. One by one their parents went, and the excited chattering died down. The girls went into their common rooms to talk over the events of the day.

After a while Darrell remembered the message she had for Sally Hope. She glanced round the common room. Sally wasn't there. Where was she? She seemed always to be disappearing!

'Where's Sally Hope?' asked Darrell.

'I believe she's in one of the music-rooms,' said Katherine. 'Goodness knows why she wants to practice today, when everyone is let off lessons!'

'I'll go and find her,' said Darrell, and walked off. She made her way to the music-rooms, where the girls did their practising each day. They were tiny rooms, containing only a piano, a stool, and a chair.

Music came from two of them. Darrell peeped into the first one. Irene was there, playing softly to herself. She didn't even see Darrell. Darrell smiled and shut the door. Irene was certainly mad on music!

She came to the other practice room, from which music was coming. It was not the entrancing melodies that Irene had been playing, though, but plain five-finger exercises, played over and over again, over and over again, in an almost angry manner.

Darrell opened the door. Yes—Sally was there all right. Good. Darrell went in and shut the door. Sally turned round and scowled.

'I'm practising,' she said. 'Get out.'

'What's the matter with you?' said Darrell, feeling annoyed immediately. 'You don't need to jump down my throat like that. I've been trying to find you all day. My mother wanted to speak to you.'

'Well, I didn't want to speak to her,' said Sally, and began to thump out the irritating exercise again, up and down, up and down.

'*Why* shouldn't you want to speak to my mother?' cried Darrell, angrily. 'She had a message for you from *your* mother.'

No answer. Up and down, up and down went Sally's fingers on the notes, more loudly than ever. Darrell lost her temper.

'Stop playing!' she shouted. 'Don't be so horribly rude! Whatever's the matter with you!'

Sally put the loud pedal down and crashed the notes more loudly than ever. Plainly she was not going to listen to a word.

Darrell went near to her and put her mouth to her ear.

'Why did you say you haven't got a sister? You *have*,

and that's why your mother couldn't come and see you! But she sent you her love and said . . .'

Sally swung round from the piano, her face looking queer and white. 'Shut up!' she said. 'Interfering little busybody! Leave me alone. Just because you've been with your mother all day long, and had her fussing round you, you think you can come and taunt me like this! I hate you!'

'You're mad!' cried Darrell, and she struck her hand on the piano, making a queer sound of clashing notes. 'You won't listen when I want to tell you things. But you *shall* listen! Your mother told mine that you only write her funny wooden letters. . . . She said . . .'

'I *won't* listen!' said Sally, in a choking voice, and got up from the stool. She pushed Darrell blindly away. But Darrell could not bear to be touched when she was in a temper, and she shoved back with all her might. She was strong, and she sent Sally flying across the little room. She fell across the chair, and lay there for a moment.

She put her hand on her stomach. 'Oh, it hurts,' she said. 'Oh, you wicked girl, Darrell!'

Darrell was still trembling with anger as Sally stumbled out of the room. But almost immediately her rage went, and she was overwhelmed with horror. How *could* she have been so awful? Sally was queer and silly and horrid, it was true—but she, Darrell, had used her strength against her to hurt her. She had lost her temper all over again, after boasting to her parents only a little while ago that she never would any more.

She ran to the door, eager to go after Sally and beg her pardon. But Sally was nowhere to be seen. Darrell ran back to the common room. No Sally there, either. She sat down in a chair and rubbed her hot forehead. What a scene! How disgusting! *Why* couldn't she manage her temper?

'What's up?' asked Alicia.

'Oh—nothing much. Sally was a bit difficult, that's all —and I lost my temper,' said Darrell.

'Idiot!' said Alicia. 'What did you do? Slap her? Give her some broth without any bread?'

Darrell couldn't smile. She felt near tears. What a horrid ending to such a lovely day! After all the excitement, and now this sudden row, she felt quite exhausted. She was not at all pleased when Emily came up with her sewing.

'I do think your people are nice,' began Emily, and started to chatter in a way she seldom did. How boring! Darrell wanted to tell Emily to be quiet. If she had been Alicia she would—but as a rule she was kinder than the sharp-tongued Alicia, and did not like to hurt people's feelings. So she bore with Emily as patiently as she could.

Mary-Lou watched her from the other side of the room. She wanted to come over and join Emily and Darrell. But Gwendoline was pouring out reams of family history to her, and she had to listen. Also she was a little afraid that Darrell might snub her if she went across.

Darrell watched for Sally to appear in the common room. Perhaps she could slip over to her then and tell her she was sorry. She was ashamed of herself now, and she could only put it right by telling Sally. Oh, dear! It was awful to have a temper that simply rose up out of the blue, before you even knew it was coming! What *could* you do with a temper like that?

Sally didn't come back to the common room. Soon the supper-bell went and the girls filed into the dining-room. Darrell looked about for Sally again. But still she wasn't there. This was really very queer.

Miss Potts noticed that there was an empty chair. 'Who's missing?' she said.

'Sally Hope,' said Darrell. 'I last saw her in one of the practice rooms—about an hour ago.'

'Well, go and fetch her, said Miss Potts, impatiently.

'Oh, she left when I was there,' said Darrell. 'I don't know where she went to.'

'We'll get on without her then,' said Miss Potts. 'She must have heard the supper-bell.'

The girls chattered about the day they had had. Only Darrell was silent. Was Sally somewhere, very upset? What could be the matter with her? Why was she so queer about things? Was she unhappy about something?

Mary-Lou sniffed loudly. 'Where's your hanky?' asked Miss Potts. 'Haven't you got one? Oh, Mary-Lou, you know you must always have one. Go and get one at once. I can't bear that sniff of yours.'

Mary-Lou slipped out of the room, and ran up to the dormy. She didn't come back for a little while and Miss Potts became impatient.

'Really! It seems to take Mary-Lou all evening to find a hanky!'

There came the sound of running steps and the door of the dining-room was flung open. Mary-Lou came in, looking even more scared than usual.

'Miss Potts! Oh, Miss Potts! I've found Sally. She's lying on her bed in the dormy, and she's making an awful noise!'

'What sort of noise?' said Miss Potts, hurriedly getting up.

'A groaning sort of noise and she keeps holding herself and saying, "Oh, my tummy!"' said poor Mary-Lou, bursting into tears. 'Oh, Miss Potts, do go to her. She wouldn't even speak to me!'

'Girls, get on with your supper,' said Miss Potts, briskly. 'It sounds as if Sally has eaten too many strawberries and too much ice-cream. Katherine, go and tell Matron, please, and ask her to go up to your dormy.'

She swept out of the room. The girls began talking at

once, asking scared Mary-Lou all kinds of questions. Only Darrell still sat silent, a cold fear creeping round her heart.

She had flung Sally across the room, and Sally had fallen over that chair ! She must have hurt herself in the stomach then. Darrell remembered how she had said, ' It hurts.' It wasn't too many strawberries and too much ice-cream. It was Darrell's temper that had caused the trouble !

Darrell couldn't eat any more supper. She slipped off to the common room to be by herself. Surely Sally wasn't *much* hurt ? Just bruised, perhaps. Surely Miss Potts would come in soon and say cheerfully, ' Well, well ! Nothing much wrong with Sally after all ! '

' Oh, I hope she does, I hope she does,' said poor Darrell, and waited impatiently and anxiously for the sound of Miss Potts's quick footsteps.

16   A BAD TIME FOR DARRELL

THE girls poured into the common room after their supper. They had half an hour before bedtime. They were tired after their exciting day, and some of them were sleepy already.

Alicia looked at Darrell in surprise. ' Why so gloomy ? ' she said.

' Well—I was just wondering about Sally,' said Darrell. ' Hoping she wasn't very ill.'

' Why ever should she be ? ' said Alicia.   ' Lots of people can't eat strawberries without getting a pain or a rash. One of my brothers is like that.'

Alicia plunged into one of her bits of family history and Darrell listened gratefully. Alicia did not relate stories that glorified herself, as Gwendoline always did—she simply poured out amusing tales of the life she and her brothers led in the holidays at home—and, if Alicia was to be believed, the pranks they got up to were enough to turn any mother's hair completely grey! However, Alicia's mother had not seemed to Darrell to have any grey hairs at all, when she had seen her that day.

The bed-time bell went for the first- and second-formers. They put away their things at once. Matron did not show much patience with laggards at bed-time. There were too many girls to hustle into bed for that!

Miss Potts had not come back. Darrell felt her anxiety creeping over her again. Perhaps Matron would know. She would ask her about Sally as soon as she saw her hovering around the bathrooms.

But Matron wasn't there. Mam'zelle was there instead, beaming placidly at everyone, still in a good temper because of the lovely day they had all had.

'Hallo, Mam'zelle! Where's Matron?' asked Alicia in surprise.

'Looking after Sally Hope,' said Mam'zelle. 'Ah, the poor child—she is in great pain.'

Darrell's heart sank. 'Is she—is she in the San. then?' she asked. Girls who were ill were always put in the San., which consisted of a good many nice rooms above the Head Mistress's own suite of rooms. There was also a special matron for the San. itself, a smiling, but strict hospital nurse, who was extremely efficient not only at dealing with any kind of school accident or illness, but also at dealing with any kind of girl!

'Yes. Of course she is in the San. She is very ill,' said Mam'zelle. Then, with her love of exaggerating, she added a sentence or two that sent Darrell's heart down into her boots. 'It is her poor tommy—no, tummy is what you say, n'est ce pas. She has a big pain there.'

'Oh,' said Darrell. 'Do they—do they know what has caused the pain, Mam'zelle? Has Sally hurt herself?'

Mam'zelle didn't know. 'All I know is that it is not the strawberries and the ice-cream,' she said. 'Because Sally did not have any. She has told Matron that.'

That made it all the more certain, then, that it must have been Darrell's rough push and the fall that followed! Poor Darrell! She felt so miserable that Mam'zelle's sharp eyes noticed her downcast face and she began to wonder if here was another girl about to be ill!

'You feel all right, my little Darrell?' she said, in a sympathetic voice.

'Oh, yes, thank you,' said Darrell, startled. 'I'm just—well, just tired, I suppose.'

Darrell hardly slept at all that night. She was so horrified at what had happened. How could she have lost her temper so thoroughly, how could she have yelled at Sally like that and how *could* she have sent her flying across the room? She, Darrell, was wicked! It was true that Sally was queer and annoying, but that was no excuse for Darrell's behaviour.

Now Sally was ill and in pain. Had she said anything about Darrell losing her temper? Darrell felt herself growing cold as she thought of what Miss Grayling might do if she heard.

'She would hear about my slapping Gwendoline too, and she would send for me and tell me I was a failure already,' thought Darrell. 'Oh, Sally, Sally, do get better by tomorrow! Then I'll tell you I'm terribly sorry, and I'll try to make it up to you all I can.'

She fell asleep at last, and was very tired when the dressing-bell rang for them all to get up. Her first thought was Sally. She saw the girl's empty bed and shivered. How she hoped Sally would be back there that night!

She ran downstairs before any one else. She saw Miss Potts and went to her. 'Please,' she said, 'how is Sally?'

Miss Potts thought what a kind child Darrell was. ' She's not at all well, I'm afraid,' she said. ' The doctor is still doubtful about what exactly is the matter. But she really seems rather ill, poor child. It was so sudden, too—she seemed all right yesterday.'

Darrell turned away, miserable. Yes, Sally had been all right till she had fallen across that chair. *She* knew what was the matter—but nobody else did ! It was plain that Sally hadn't told anyone of the quarrel.

It was Sunday. Darrell prayed hard for Sally all the time she was in church. She felt very guilty and ashamed. She also felt very much afraid. She felt that she ought to tell Miss Potts or Matron about the quarrel and how she had flung poor Sally across the room—but she was too frightened to tell !

Too frightened ! Darrell was so fearless in the usual way that it was something strange and queer to her to feel afraid. But she *was* afraid. Supposing Sally was very *very* ill ! Supposing—just supposing she didn't get better ! Supposing Darrell's temper caused all that !

She couldn't, couldn't tell anyone, because they would think her so wicked, and she would disgrace her mother and father. People would say ' That's the girl whose temper caused her to be expelled from Malory Towers ! You know she made another girl terribly ill ! '

It would be awful to be sent away from Malory Towers in disgrace. She would never get over it. But she was sure Miss Grayling wouldn't keep her another day if she knew that she had caused Sally's illness and pain.

' I can't tell anyone, I can't ! ' thought poor Darrell. ' I'm afraid of letting people know, because of what would happen to me, and how it would make Mother and Daddy feel. I'm a coward, but I daren't tell. I never knew I was a coward before ! '

She suddenly thought of Mary-Lou, whom she had so

often called a coward. Poor Mary-Lou—now she knew
how *she* felt when she was afraid of something. It was a
horrible feeling. You couldn't get away from it. How
could she have sneered at Mary-Lou and taunted her ? It
was bad enough to feel afraid of something without being
taunted about it.

Darrell felt very sad and very humble. She had started
the term in such high hopes and spirits. She was going
to be top ! She was going to shine in everything and
make her parents proud of her ! She was going to find a fine
girl for a friend. And she hadn't done any of those things.

She had got a low place in the form. She hadn't found
herself a friend. She had been hateful to little Mary-Lou
who had so shyly and eagerly offered her friendship—and
now she had done something wicked and didn't dare to
say anything about it !

Darrell was certainly down in the dumps that day and
nobody could rouse her out of them. Miss Potts wondered
if she was sickening for something and kept a sharp eye
on her. Mary-Lou was worried, and hovered round hoping
to be able to do something. And for once Darrell was
kind to her and did not snap at her to send her away. She
felt grateful for Mary-Lou's liking and sympathy.

Two doctors came to see Sally that day ! The news
went round North Tower House. ' She's *fearfully* ill !
But it's nothing infectious so we're not in quarantine.
Poor Sally. Tessie says she had to go and see the Head
this morning and she heard Sally groaning in the San.
rooms above ! '

How Darrell wished her mother was there that day !
But she couldn't remember where her parents had gone to,
though they had told her. She had forgotten in the excitement of yesterday. She sat down in a rocky corner by
the sea, and thought things out.

She couldn't be a coward any longer, because it would

be worse to stay at Malory Towers and know she was a coward than it would be to leave, knowing she had been brave enough to own up. But whom should she tell?
'I'd better write and tell Sally's mother,' she thought. 'She's the one that's nearest to Sally. I'll write and tell her all about the quarrel, and how it happened and everything. I'll have to tell her, too, how Sally says she hasn't got a sister. That's all very queer, but maybe Mrs. Hope will understand it. Then Mrs. Hope can do what she likes—tell the Head, I expect! Oh, dear! But I shall feel better when it's done.'

She left her seat by the sea and went back to North Tower. She got out her writing pad and began to write. It was not an easy letter to compose, but Darrell always found writing easy, and she poured out everything to Mrs. Hope—about the quarrel and what led up to it, and all about Sally not wanting to speak to Mrs. Rivers, and how unhappy she seemed to be. She was quite surprised to find how much she seemed to know about Sally!

She felt better immediately she had finished the letter. She didn't read it through, but stuck a stamp on the envelope and posted it at once. Mrs. Hope would get it the very next morning!

Then another rumour ran through North Tower. ' Sally's taken a turn for the worse ! A specialist is coming to see her ! Her people have been telegraphed for ! They're coming tomorrow ! '

Darrell could not eat anything at all that day. It was the longest day she had ever known. Mary-Lou, scared by Darrell's stricken face, kept close by her—and Darrell welcomed her and felt comforted. Mary-Lou had no idea why Darrell looked so miserable, and didn't dare to ask her. She forgot the many sneers and taunts that Darrell had thrown at her for her weakness and feebleness ; she only wanted to help.

The other girls did not notice anything much. They
went for walks, bathed, lay about in the sun, and had a
happy, lazy Sunday. Miss Potts still kept an eye on Darrell.
What *could* be the matter with her ? Was it Sally's illness
that was worrying her ? No, it couldn't be. She hadn't
been at all friendly with Sally. Nobody had, for that
matter.

Bed-time came at last. Matron had no more news of
Sally, except that she was no better. No one was allowed
to see her, of course. Matron had been quite shocked
because Darrell had begged to go and see her for a moment
or two !

Darrell lay in bed, thinking. The third- and fourth-
formers came up to bed. The fifth-formers came and
then the sixth. Then Matron, Mam'zelle and Miss Potts
retired too, and Darrell heard lights clicking out. It was
late. It was dark outside. Everyone was asleep except
Darrell.

' I simply can't lie here thinking and thinking ! ' said
Darrell to herself desperately, and she flung off her covers.
' I shall go mad ! I shall get up and go into the Court !
The roses will smell sweet there, and I shall get cool and
perhaps be able to go to sleep ! '

She slipped on her dressing-gown and went quietly out
of the room. Nobody stirred. She crept down the wide
stairs and out into the Court. And then, in the stillness
of the night, she heard the sound of a car purring up the
hill to Malory Towers ! It stopped outside. Whoever
could it be, so late at night ?

Darrell glanced up at the windows of the San. There
were bright lights there. Sally couldn't be asleep, or the
lights would be dimmed. What was going on now ? Oh,
dear, if only she knew !

Darrell slipped through the archway that led from the
Court to the drive. Yes, a car stood there, a dark shape,

silent now and empty. Whoever had come in it had gone
into Malory Towers. Darrell crept round to the door that
led into the Head's building. Someone had left it open!
She pushed it and went inside. Now she would find out
what was happening!

17   A WONDERFUL SURPRISE

THERE was a little light burning in the hall. The Head
Mistress's rooms were in darkness. She was evidently
upstairs in the San. Darrell crept upstairs. There were
bright lights everywhere, and a good deal of bustle. What
was happening to poor Sally?

Darrell couldn't understand what was going on. Sally
must be very ill to have so many people bothering about
her like this in the middle of the night! Darrell's heart
felt very heavy. She didn't dare to go any farther in case
someone saw her. But she felt she *must* stay where she
was. She must get to know *some*thing! She couldn't
possibly go back to bed without finding out what was
happening. If only, only she could help!

She sat down on a window-seat, and drew the heavy
curtains round her, straining her ears to catch a word from
any of the people bustling about from one of the San. rooms
to another. That was Matron's voice—the matron of
North Tower! And that was the other Matron's voice,
very crisp and sharp, giving an order. And that was a
man's voice. Darrell held her breath and listened to the
mysterious voices and noises, but she couldn't hear a word.

Oh, what would they all say if they knew that she, hot-
tempered, wicked little Darrell was at the bottom of all
this fuss and worry and bother? Darrell pulled the curtain

round her head and wept great tears that soaked into the heavy silk.

She sat there for about half an hour. Then, quite suddenly, and without meaning to, she fell fast asleep! Lost in the heavy curtains, she slept, tired out.

She did not know how long she slept. She awoke again later, hearing noises. She sat up, wondering where in the wide world she was! Then she remembered. Of course —she was near the San. She had come to find out what was happening to Sally.

At once all the fear and anxiety closed round her once again. She felt lonely and lost, and wanted her mother. She clutched the curtains round her as she heard voices coming near. Was it doctors? Nurses? Perhaps the Head Mistress herself?

And then Darrell's heart almost stopped beating! Some one was going by the window-seat where she sat, someone who spoke in a voice she knew and loved!

'She'll be all right,' said the voice. 'Just got her nicely in time! Now . . .'

Darrell sat as if she was turned to stone, listening to that well-known voice! It couldn't be! It couldn't be! It *couldn't be* her own father's voice!

She suddenly found herself able to move. She thrust the curtains aside and looked between them. She saw her father walking along with the Matron, talking earnestly. Yes, it was, it really was her father.

'DADDY!' squealed Darrell, forgetting absolutely everything except the fact that there was her father, whom she thought was miles away, walking along the passage just near her. 'Daddy! Oh, Daddy! Stop, here's Darrell!'

Her father stopped as if he was shot! He couldn't believe his ears! Darrell leapt down from the window-seat and flung herself on him like a small thunderbolt. She clung to him and began to cry.

She thrust the curtain aside and looked through

'What's the matter, darling?' said her father, amazed. 'Why are you here?'

Miss Grayling came up, astonished and rather disapproving. 'Darrell! What are you here for, child? Mr. Rivers, you had better come into my room downstairs, please.'

Carrying Darrell in his arms, her father followed Miss Grayling downstairs, with Matron clucking behind like an astonished hen. Darrell clung to her father as if she would never let him go. Was she dreaming? Could it be that this was really her own father, in the middle of the night? Darrell couldn't imagine how or why he was there, but it was enough that he was.

He sat down in a big armchair with Darrell on his knees. Matron disappeared. Only Miss Grayling was there, and she looked in a very puzzled manner at Darrell and her father. There was something here she didn't understand.

'You cry all you want to, then tell me what's the matter,' said Darrell's father. 'Why, we only saw you yesterday, and you were so happy! Never mind, I'm here, and I'll put everything right for you.'

'You can't!' wept Darrell. 'I've been wicked! It was my temper again. Oh, Daddy, it's all *my* fault that Sally is so ill!'

'My dear child, what *are* you talking about?' said her father, puzzled. Darrell snuggled her head into his chest and began to feel much better. Daddy could always put things right. So could Mother. What a blessing he was here tonight.

Then she raised her head, and spoke in surprise. 'But Daddy—*why* are you here? I thought you were miles away!'

'Well, I was,' said Mr. Rivers. 'But Miss Grayling telephoned to me to say that little Sally Hope had appendicitis and the surgeon they usually had was ill, so could I come straight along and do the operation. So of course

I did! I hopped into the car, drove here, found every-thing ready, did the little operation, and here I am! And Sally will be quite all right and back again in school in about two weeks' time!'

A great load fell away from Darrell's heart. She could almost feel it rolling away. Why, appendicitis was some-thing *any*one might have! Her father was always curing appendicitis! She spoke anxiously.

'Daddy—appendicitis couldn't be caused by a push—or a fall—could it?'

'Good gracious, no!' said her father. 'Sally's had this little affair coming on for some time, there's no doubt about that. All the term and before that, I should think. But what makes you ask that question?'

Then everything came pouring out—how funny and queer and rude Sally had been—how Darrell had lost her temper—the violent push, the fall—everything!

'And I worried and worried and worried,' said Darrell, with a sob. 'I thought if Miss Grayling knew, she would send me away from Malory Towers, and you and Mother would be ashamed of me, and I couldn't sleep, so I got up and . . .'

'What a silly little girl!' said her father, and kissed the top of her head. 'Perhaps we had better take you away from Malory Towers ourselves, and have you at home, if you are going to think such silly things, Darrell!'

'Oh, no—don't do that! I love being here!' said Darrell. 'Oh, Daddy—if you *knew* how different I feel now that I know Sally was going to be ill, anyhow—it wasn't anything to do with me, after all. But oh, dear—I wrote to Mrs. Hope about it! What *will* she think?'

Then she had to tell all about the letter and what she had said. Her father and Miss Grayling were puzzled to hear how Sally had said she hadn't a baby sister.

'Something queer there that must be sorted out,' said

Mr. Rivers to Miss Grayling. 'Might prevent her from getting better as quickly as she ought to. When did you say Mr. and Mrs. Hope were coming?'

'Tomorrow,' said Miss Grayling. 'I'll see them and explain. Now, Mr. Rivers—would you like us to give you a bed here tonight? It's so late.'

'Oh, no!' said Mr. Rivers. 'I'm used to driving out late at night. I'll go back, thank you. And Darrell must go to bed. Now don't worry any more, darling—things are all right—and your little push didn't do Sally any harm, though probably the fall made her feel her bad tummy a little bit more. I expect she felt ill all day, poor child.'

'It wasn't a little push I gave her. It was a big one,' said Darrell.

'It makes me sad to think I've handed on to you the temper I've got myself,' said her father. Darrell tightened her arms round his neck.

'Don't worry. I'll get on top of it!' she said. 'I'll soon do what you do—keep it for worth-while things!'

'Well, good night, darling,' said her father, and kissed her. 'Go and see Sally as soon as you're allowed to. I think you'll feel better then!'

'I feel better now!' said Darrell, and slipped off his knee. Her eyes were red but she was smiling. How different she felt! All her worry was gone.

Her father went off in the darkness in his car. Miss Grayling herself took Darrell to bed and tucked her in. Darrell fell asleep even before the Head Mistress was out of the room.

And, in the San. Sally slept too, her pain gone. Matron watched over her, pleased to hear her steady, regular breathing. What a deft, quick surgeon Darrell's father was—only thirteen minutes to do the operation! Matron thought how lucky it was that he had been near enough to come.

Next morning dawned fair and bright. Darrell awoke

when the dressing-bell went, tired but happy again. She
lay and thought for half a minute. Her heart was full of
thankfulness. Sally would be all right. Her father had
said so. And he had said that Darrell hadn't had anything
to do with her illness. All her worry had been for nothing.
No—not quite for nothing. It had made a deep impression
on her. It wouldn't be nearly so difficult to keep her
temper next time. She had had a jolly good lesson !

'I wish I could do something to show I'm grateful and
thankful it's all turned out like this,' thought Darrell,
jumping out of bed. 'But there's nothing I can do. I
wonder how Sally is today.'

Sally was getting on very well indeed. When she heard
that her mother and father were coming to see her she
could hardly believe her ears.

'But is *Mother* coming ? ' she asked, time and again.
'Are you sure *Mother's* coming ? But she couldn't come
last Saturday. Is she really coming ? '

Miss Grayling received Mr. and Mrs. Hope in her big
drawing-room. Mr. Hope was a big burly man, looking
anxious. Mrs. Hope was a delicate-looking woman with
a sweet face.

'Sally is not quite ready for you to see her yet,' said
Miss Grayling. 'I am so glad to be able to tell you that
the operation was very successful and she is getting along
wonderfully well. Mr. Rivers, the surgeon, happened to
be at a hotel not far off, and we got him to do it. He is
the father of one of our girls here, Darrell Rivers.'

'Oh—Darrell Rivers,' said Mrs. Hope, and she took out
a letter from her bag. 'I had such a *queer* letter from her
today, Miss Grayling. Please read it. She appears to
think she was the cause of Sally's illness, but of course she
wasn't. But the other things she says are very worrying
to me. Could we have Darrell in to speak to us, before
I see Sally, do you think ? '

Miss Grayling read the letter and looked grave. 'There *is* something puzzling here,' she said. 'Why should Sally keep saying she has no sister, when she knows she has?'

'I don't know,' said Mrs. Hope, sadly. 'But Sally has been queer ever since Baby Daphne came. She won't look at her or speak to her—and once, when she didn't know I was looking, I saw her pinch poor Daphne cruelly. And Sally is not a cruel child.'

'Have you any other children?' asked Miss Grayling. Mrs. Hope shook her head.

'No,' she said. 'Sally was twelve when Daphne was born. She had been the only child for all that time. I thought she would be so pleased to have a sister. We haven't spoilt Sally, you know—but she didn't have to share us with anyone till Daphne came—and sometimes I wondered if she was—well—jealous.'

'Of course she was!' said Miss Grayling at once. 'I should think, Mrs. Hope, that Sally is very much attached to you, and resented sharing your love when the baby came. She probably didn't like to tell you so, in case you thought badly of her.'

'Oh, she never said a word to me!' said Mrs. Hope. 'She just changed, that's all. She wasn't merry and gay any more, she didn't come to us and love us as she used to do, and she seemed to hate the baby. I thought it would blow over. And then, when it didn't, I and my husband thought it would be best if Sally came to boarding school, because I wasn't very well at the time, and it was all I could do to look after the baby, without having to cope with Sally too. We did it for the best.'

'Yes, I see,' said Miss Grayling, thoughtfully. 'But, from Sally's point of view it must have seemed that you didn't want her any more, but had sent her away to make room for a baby who was taking up all your care and attention. Mrs. Hope, this jealousy of a much younger child is very common and very natural, and you mustn't blame Sally for it. Neither must you let it grow. If only you can make Sally feel you love her as much as ever you did it will be quite all right. Now—shall we have Darrell in ? '

Darrell was sent for. She came in nervously, scared of what Mrs. Hope might say. But she was soon put at her ease, and she told all she knew.

Miss Grayling turned to Mrs. Hope. ' I think it would be a good idea if we let Darrell go in to see Sally for a few minutes before you do,' she said. ' We will let her tell Sally that you have come—and we will let her say that you have left the baby behind in order to hurry as fast as possible to Sally. Will you do that, Darrell ? '

Darrell nodded. She had suddenly seen all Sally's trouble ! Why, she was jealous of her little baby sister ! So jealous that she wouldn't even admit she had got one. Poor, funny Sally. It was so lovely to have a sister. Sally didn't know how lucky she was !

' I'll tell her,' she said, eagerly. ' I'll do what I can too, when you've gone, to make Sally think it's fun to have a sister. I wanted to do *some*thing—and I shall love to do that ! '

18   DARRELL AND SALLY

DARRELL went to the San. upstairs. She had a little note with her for Matron from Miss Grayling. ' Please allow Darrell to see Sally for a few minutes before her mother comes.'

Matron, surprised and not very pleased, opened the door to let Darrell in. Darrell tiptoed in. It was a pleasant room, with three white beds in it, and a lovely view from

the big windows. Everything was creamy white and spot-
lessly clean. In the end bed lay Sally, white but bright-eyed.

' Hallo, Sally,' said Darrell. ' I've been so worried about
you. Are you better ? Did my father make you better ? '

' Yes. I do like him. He was so kind,' said Sally. ' I
did feel so awful all Saturday, Darrell. But I couldn't
tell anyone, could I ? I couldn't spoil the day.'

' I think you're very brave,' said Darrell. ' I say—guess
who's here to see you ? '

' Not my mother ? ' said Sally, her eyes shining. Darrell
nodded. ' Yes. And your father too. And do you know,
Sally, your mother has left behind your little baby sister,
so that she could come more quickly to see you ? Fancy
that ! She must think an awful lot of you, because usually
mothers can't bear to leave babies when they're small.'

Sally seemed to have forgotten that she had told Darrell
she had no sister. She reached out for Darrell's hand.
' Hasn't she brought Baby ? ' she whispered. ' Did she
leave her behind ? Really and truly ? '

' Yes, poor little thing,' said Darrell. ' She must be
feeling lonely ! I've got a little sister, too. It's lovely to
have a sister. Mine looks up to me no end and thinks
I'm wonderful. I expect yours will, too.'

Sally's ideas of sisters underwent a sudden change.
Things seemed suddenly to fall into their proper places.
She smiled gratefully at Darrell. ' You'll come and see
me when you can, won't you ? ' she said. ' And don't say
anything about—about—all my silliness, will you ? To the
others, I mean.'

' Of course not. It wasn't silliness. It was just a mistake on your part,' said Darrell. ' Why, anyone could
see by giving one look at your mother that she's a *proper*
mother—I mean the kind that would always love you,
however many children she had, or whatever you did. I
think she's a darling.'

'So do I,' said Sally, with a sigh. 'I'm sorry I was such a beast to you, Darrell.'

'And I can't tell you *how* sorry I am for having shoved you like that when you had such a pain in your tummy,' said Darrell.

'Did you shove me?' said Sally. 'I've forgotten. Look, what's Matron saying?'

Matron was beckoning for Darrell to come away. Mr. and Mrs. Hope were outside the door. Darrell said a hurried good-bye and tiptoed out. Mr. and Mrs. Hope went in, and Darrell heard Sally's low cry of joy as she saw her mother.

Darrell skipped happily down the stairs and through the hall into the Court. She ran to the building in which her own classroom was. The bell was just going for the ending of a lesson.

Darrell slipped into the first-form classroom. The girls looked up at her.

'Where *have* you been? You've been ages! You've missed half of maths., lucky pig.'

'I've been to see Sally,' said Darrell, importantly.

'Fibber! No one is allowed to see her yet,' said Irene.

'Well, I *have*. And she says my father has cured her pain and made her much better,' said Darrell, proud to have such a father. 'He came in the night. I saw him.'

'Darrell Rivers, you're making it all up,' said Alicia.

'No, honestly I'm not. It's all true,' said Darrell. 'I saw Mr. and Mrs. Hope too, and they're seeing Sally now. They are staying the night with Miss Grayling and going back tomorrow.'

'And has dear Sally found out yet whether she has a baby sister or not?' drawled Gwendoline.

Darrell felt a hot flame of temper rise up but she choked it down at once. 'That's no business of yours—and it's a pity *you* didn't have about six older sisters to sit on you hard and squash you flat,' said Darrell. 'You'd have been a bit nicer then. But probably only a bit.'

'Shhhhh! Mam'zelle coming!' hissed the girl at the door, and in came Mam'zelle, rather cross this morning because the third form had just proved extraordinarily stupid. Darrell didn't mind how cross Mam'zelle or Miss Potts were that day. She kept thinking of Sally's happiness. She wondered how she was getting on.

Sally and her mother and father were happy together. The curious wall that Sally had built up between herself and her mother had fallen away, because suddenly the jealousy was gone. Her mother had left the baby alone to come to *her*—and Sally was content. Not that she wanted Baby Daphne to be left with strangers—but it was a sign to her that her mother thought of her and loved her. Funny little Sally!

'We'll come and see you tomorrow before we go home,' said her mother, when Matron said it was time for Mr. and Mrs. Hope to go. 'And, if you *badly* want me to, I'll stay an extra day, and let Daddy go home without me.'

'No,' said Sally, with a sigh. 'Don't let's leave Baby too long! And I know Daddy would rather you went with him. I'm getting better already, Mother. I'll soon be well—and I shall feel quite different.'

Then Mrs. Hope knew for certain that Sally was her own, unselfish little girl again, and she was glad. What a good thing Darrell Rivers had written to her as she did! Now everything was all cleared up.

Darrell was allowed to go and see Sally twice a day, long before anyone else was. Sally welcomed her eagerly. Sally was so different now—no longer a prim, closed-up little person, but a friendly, eager girl, ready to talk about her home and her dogs and her garden, asking Darrell about the lessons and the games, if Mam'zelle was cross, and what Miss Potts said, and whether Gwendoline and Mary-Lou were still friends.

'You know, Sally,' said Darrell, 'when I felt so awfully frightened because I thought I'd injured you and might be sent away from here, I suddenly knew how it must feel to be like Mary-Lou—always scared of everything! And I was sorry I'd teased her so.'

'Let's be nice to Mary-Lou,' said Sally, who, with her strength returning to her, and with Darrell's friendly visits each day, felt that she could be nice even to Gwendoline! 'Tell her I'd like her to come and see me.'

Mary-Lou was overwhelmed by this message. Fancy Sally choosing *her* for one of her first visitors! Armed with a big bottle of barley-sugar she went to the San. Sally looked rather pale, but very different. Her eyes were bright, and she smiled. She welcomed Mary-Lou graciously.

They talked, and Mary-Lou blossomed a little. She was not afraid of Sally. She told her all sorts of things. Then she looked worried.

'You know, Sally, I do wish Gwendoline wouldn't keep saying horrid things about Darrell. She keeps trying to make me think that Darrell is playing nasty tricks on me. Or that Alicia is. My ink-pot was spilt yesterday all over my atlas, and Gwendoline says she's sure Darrell did it, because she saw that Darrell's fingers were all inky that day.

'As if Darrell would do anything like *that*!' said Sally, indignantly. 'How *can* you listen to Gwendoline when she says things like that?'

'I can't stop her,' said Mary-Lou, the scared look coming into her face again. 'You see, she will keep saying that I'm her friend, and she can tell me anything.'

'*Are* you her friend?' demanded Sally.

'No. Not really. But I don't like telling her I don't want to be,' said Mary-Lou. 'Don't call me a coward. I know I am. But I can't help it.'

'Time to go, Mary-Lou,' said Matron, coming in. 'Tell Darrell she can come in half an hour's time, and bring a simple game with her—Happy Families or something. Not Snap.'

So Darrell came, armed with Happy Families. But the two girls didn't get beyond dealing out the cards. They talked about Mary-Lou and Gwendoline.

'Gwendoline's poisonous,' said Sally. 'She's always talking against you and Alicia, making out you play those rotten tricks on Mary-Lou.'

'I wonder who does them?' said Darrell. 'One of the other Tower girls, do you think? What about Evelyn from West Tower? She's always doing silly, teasing tricks.'

'No. I should think it might be Gwendoline herself!' said Sally, looking at the cards in her hand.

Darrell stared at her in surprise. 'Oh, *no*,' she said. 'Why, Gwendoline and Mary-Lou are *friends*.'

'So Gwendoline says. But Mary-Lou says different,' said Sally.

'Yes, but—*no* one could be so awful as to pretend to be friends with someone and then to play rotten tricks on them all the time!' said Darrell. 'It would be a disgusting thing to do.'

'I think Gwendoline *is* disgusting!' said Sally. 'I never could bear her. A real double-faced person, who doesn't care tuppence for anyone in the world but herself.'

Darrell looked at Sally. 'I think you're very clever,' she said. 'You seem to know all about people—much more than I do. I'm sure you know more about Mary-Lou than I do, already.'

'I like Mary-Lou,' said Sally. 'If only we could get her to be not so scared of everything, she'd be fun.'

'But how can we?' said Darrell, shuffling all the cards together absent-mindedly. 'Oh, dear—look what I've done. Never mind, it's more interesting to talk than play cards just now. How *can* we cure Mary-Lou? I've tried to buck her up and make her ashamed of herself, but it doesn't seem to do any good.'

'Can't you see that she *is* ashamed of herself already?' said Sally, unexpectedly. 'But being ashamed doesn't give her any courage. Nobody can give her pluck except her own self.'

'Well—think of a way to make her give herself pluck!' said Darrell. 'I bet you can't!'

'I'll think tonight, before I go to sleep,' said Sally. 'And when you come and see me in the morning, I'll have a plan—you see if I haven't!'

19   SALLY'S PLAN

DARRELL went to see Sally at Break as usual the next morning. Sally greeted her eagerly. 'Well, I've thought of something! It's not a *fright*fully good plan, but it will do as a beginning.'

'What is it?' asked Darrell, thinking how pretty the plain little Sally looked that morning, with colour in her cheeks, and twinkles in her eyes.

'Well, listen. What about you pretending to be in difficulties in the pool, when you get the chance, and yelling out to Mary-Lou to run and get the life-belt quickly and throw it to you?' said Sally. 'If she does that, and feels that she has saved you from going under, she'll be awfully bucked. We all know how to chuck the belt into the water. It would be quite easy for her to do.'

'Yes. It's a good idea,' said Darrell. 'I might try it out tomorrow. I'll give the tip to the others not to throw it to me, but to let Mary-Lou. At least, I'll tell the people

I can trust—not dear Gwendoline, for instance ! Do you really think it will help Mary-Lou not to be so scared of things if she does that ? '

' Well, it seems to me that Mary-Lou will never be able to face up to things unless she thinks she's got a bit of good sense and courage in her to start with ! ' said Sally, seriously. ' You can't possibly do anything if you *think* you can't. But you can do impossible things sometimes if you think you *can*.'

' How do you know things like that ? ' asked Darrell, in admiration. ' I wish *I* did ! '

' Oh, it's not very difficult really,' said Sally. ' All you do is put yourself into the place of the other person, and feel like them, and then think how you could cure yourself if you were them. That sounds muddled—but I can't very well say exactly what I mean. I haven't the words.'

' Oh, I know what you mean, all right ! ' said Darrell. ' You do what Mother is always telling *me* to do—get into somebody else's skin, and feel what *they're* feeling. But I'm too impatient to do that. I'm too tightly in my *own* skin ! You're not. I think you're clever and kind, Sally.'

Sally went red and looked pleased. She also looked rather shy. ' I'm not clever—and you know I'm not kind, by the way I behaved to Daphne,' she said. ' But it's nice that you think so, anyway ! Do you think you can work the idea out all right, Darrell ? '

' Oh, yes, I think so,' said Darrell. ' I'll try it tomorrow, when we're in the pool. Mary-Lou has got a bit of a cold and isn't allowed to bathe this week, so she'll be watching by the side. She can easily go and get the life-belt and fling it to me. Won't she be bucked ! '

' I guess she's glad she's got a cold this week,' said Sally, with a chuckle. ' She does so hate the water ! I bet she'll never learn to swim.'

' It was funny when Matron said Mary-Lou had a cold and wasn't to go in the water,' said Darrell, ' because dear

Gwendoline immediately began to sniff like anything in class, hoping Miss Potts would report it to Matron, and *she* would be told too that she mustn't bathe. She's even worse than Mary-Lou at getting into the water!'

'What happened?' asked Sally, with interest. 'Oh, I do wish I was back in school. I'd die of boredom if I hadn't got you to come and tell me things.'

'Well, Miss Potts got angry with Gwendoline's sniffs and sat on her properly,' said Darrell. 'And then Gwendoline said she was sure she had caught Mary-Lou's cold, so Miss Potts sent her to Matron—and Matron gave her a large dose of awful medicine, and was most unsympathetic —and she didn't say Gwendoline wasn't to go into the water, she said the salt in it would probably do her good. And I heard her tell Miss Potts that the only way to take Gwendoline's tales was with a pinch of salt, so she might as well swallow some in the pool!'

Sally laughed heartily. She could just picture Gwendoline's anger at having medicine for no real reason, and not getting her way after all. Darrell got up.

'There's the bell,' she said. 'I'll come back after lunch and tell you all the tit-bits. I haven't told you yet how Alicia and Betty tied thread to a pile of Mam'zelle's books on her desk, and Alicia pulled the thread and jerked off the books under Mam'zelle's very nose! I thought Irene would die of laughing. You know how she explodes.'

'Oh, yes, do come back and tell me everything,' said Sally, who looked forward to Darrell's visits more than to anything else. 'I do love hearing you talk.'

It was strange how completely different Sally seemed now. When Darrell looked back and remembered the quiet, self-contained, serious person Sally Hope had always appeared, it seemed impossible that she had turned into the laughing, eager, twinkling-eyed girl in the bed—a sensible, kindly girl with a real sense of fun.

'She's not such good fun as Alicia, of course,' said Darrell to herself, 'but she's more *trust*able, somehow. And she isn't as sharp-tongued, though she's just as clever in what she thinks about people.'

Darrell carefully thought out the plan for tricking Mary-Lou into sudden good sense and a bit of pluck. It should be quite easy. She would tell Alicia and Betty to take the others to the other end of the pool, so that she, Darrell, would be alone in the deep end. Then she would struggle and yell and pretend she had cramp.

'I'll yell out to Mary-Lou and shout, " Quick, quick, throw me the life-belt ! ",' she thought. 'Then surely Mary-Lou will do that, and I'll clutch it and pant and puff, and call out, " Oh, Mary-Lou, you've saved my life ! " And if after that Mary-Lou doesn't have a better opinion of herself, it'll be queer. Once she knows she can really do something like that, maybe she'll pull herself together and be able to face up to some of the silly things that scare her ! '

It really did seem a very good plan. Darrell let Alicia and Betty into the secret. 'It's really Sally's idea,' said Darrell. 'It's a very good one, don't you think so ? '

'Well—why ever should you want to bother yourselves with that silly little baby of a Mary-Lou ? ' said Alicia in surprise. 'You'll never make her any better. She's hopeless.'

'But we *might* make her better,' argued Darrell, rather disappointed with the way that Alicia took the idea.

'Not much chance,' said Alicia. 'I expect what *will* happen is that Mary-Lou will be too scared stiff to do a thing, and will simply stand blubbing by the pool and let somebody else run for the life-belt. And that will make her worse than ever, because everyone will despise her.'

'Oh,' said Darrell, feeling damped. 'That would be sickening. Oh, Alicia, I didn't think of that.'

Darrell told Sally what Alicia had said. 'I quite see what she means,' she said. 'And it might make Mary-Lou worse instead of better, because everyone would laugh at her. You see, Alicia is awfully smart, Sally—we never thought of that, did we?'

'Yes. Alicia *is* very smart,' said Sally, slowly. 'But sometimes she's a bit *too* smart, Darrell. She's forgotten something important.'

'What's that?' asked Darrell.

'She's forgotten that it's *you* who are going to struggle and yell for help,' said Sally. 'Everyone knows that Mary-Lou thinks you're wonderful and would do anything in the world for you—if you'd let her. Well, here is something she *can* do—and *will* do! You see if I'm not right. Give Mary-Lou a chance, Darrell. Alicia sees her as a weak little cry-baby. But she could be something more than that, for the sake of someone she loved.'

'All right, Sally. I'll give her a chance,' said Darrell. 'But I can't help thinking Alicia is right. She really is smart, you know, and can always size people up. I wish she wasn't friends with Betty. I wish she was *my* friend!'

Sally didn't say any more. She played dominoes with Darrell and was rather quiet. Matron came and shooed Darrell away soon after that, and she had to go off to her prep.

'I'm going to try out Sally's idea on Mary-Lou,' she told Alicia. 'So you and Betty will take the others off to the shallow end, won't you, when you see Mary-Lou standing by the deep end? Then I'll yell out, and we'll see if Mary-Lou has the nerve to throw me the belt. It's not much to do!'

'It'll be too much for *her*,' said Alicia, rather annoyed that Darrell should still think of going on with the idea after she had poured cold water on it. 'Still, we'll see.'

So, the next afternoon the plan was carried out. The

first-formers went chattering down to the pool in their
bathing costumes and beach-gowns. Gwendoline went too,
looking sulky because the form had teased her unmercifully
about her pretended cold !

Mary-Lou had not changed into her bathing-things, and
was pleased. She did so hate the water ! Darrell called
to her. 'You can throw pennies in for me, Mary-Lou,
and watch me dive for them in the deep end !'

'All right,' said Mary-Lou, pleased, and put some
pennies into her pocket. Her cold was almost better.
What a pity ! She had so much enjoyed not having to
bathe !

Into the water plunged the girls. Some jumped in,
some dived in. Only Gwendoline went cautiously down
the steps. But even she went in quickly for once, because
somebody gave her a push and down she went, spluttering
and gasping. And when she arose, angry and indignant,
not a single girl was near her, of course, so she had no idea
at all who had pushed her. Darrell or Alicia she supposed.
Beasts !

Mary-Lou was at the deep end, watching the others.
At least, she watched Darrell mostly, admiring the way
she swam, cutting the water so cleanly with her strong brown
arms, and thrusting through the waves like a small torpedo.
Mary-Lou put her hands into her pocket and felt the
pennies there. It was nice of Darrell to ask her to throw
them in for her. It was always nice to do anything for
Darrell, even if it was only a little thing.

'Come down to the other end and let's have a race !'
cried Alicia suddenly. 'Come on, everyone.'

'I'll just stay here for a bit and dive for pennies !' yelled
Darrell. 'I'm puffed for racing. I'll get out of your way
when you start. Hie, Mary-Lou, have you got the pennies ?'

Alicia and Betty, who were the only girls in the plan,
watched what would happen. Both girls felt certain that

Mary-Lou would weep and remain rooted to the rocks when Darrell called out. She wouldn't have the nerve to rush for the life-belt!

The other girls were splashing about, getting into position for the race. Mary-Lou threw a penny into the water and Darrell dived for it.

She brought it up in triumph. 'Throw another, Mary-Lou!' she cried. Splash! In went another penny. Darrell dived again, thinking that now was the time to pretend to be in difficulties. She came up, gasping.

'Help! Help!' she cried. 'I've got cramp! Quick, Mary-Lou, the life-belt, the life-belt! Help, help!'

She threw her arms about and struggled, letting herself sink under a little. Mary-Lou stared, absolutely petrified. Alicia nudged Betty.

'Just what I thought,' she said in a low voice. 'Too much of a ninny even to get the life-belt!'

'HELP!' yelled Darrell, and two or three of the other girls, thinking she was really in trouble, swam strongly up the pool.

But somebody else reached Darrell first! There was a resounding splash, and into the water, fully dressed, jumped the scared Mary-Lou, doing her best to remember the few swimming strokes she knew. She managed to reach Darrell, and put out her arms to her, to try and save her.

Darrell, popping her head out of the water for the second time, was filled with the utmost amazement to see Mary-Lou's wet head bobbing beside her! She stared as if she couldn't believe her eyes.

'Hold on to me, Darrell, hold on to me!' panted Mary-Lou. 'I'll save you.'

THEN up came the other two or three swimmers and called out sharply. 'What's up, Darrell ? Get out of the way, Mary-Lou.'

But Mary-Lou couldn't. She had made her great effort, jumped into the water and swum a few strokes—but now her strength was gone and her clothes were weighing her down. One of the swimmers took her safely to the side, where she clutched a bar, panting, looking anxiously over her shoulder to see if Darrell was safe.

She had apparently quite recovered from the cramp, for she was swimming over to Mary-Lou with strong, quick strokes, her eyes gleaming.

'Mary-Lou ! You jumped right into the water, and you hardly knew how to swim ! You're an idiot, but you're the pluckiest idiot ever I knew ! ' cried Darrell.

Somebody helped the shivering, astonished Mary-Lou out of the pool. Miss Potts came down the cliff at that moment and was amazed to see a fully-dressed and soaking Mary-Lou scrambling out, with girls crowding round her, clapping her on the shoulder and praising her.

'What's happened ? ' said Miss Potts, in wonder. ' Did Mary-Lou fall in ? '

Eager voices told her what had happened. ' She jumped in to save Darrell ! Darrell had the cramp and yelled for the life-belt. But Mary-Lou jumped straight in to save her—and she can hardly swim ! '

Miss Potts was as astonished as everyone else. *Mary-Lou !* But Mary-Lou screamed if she saw an earwig ! What an amazing thing.

'Why didn't she throw the life-belt ? ' asked Alicia.

'It w-w-w-wasn't there,' answered Mary-Lou, her teeth

Somebody helped the shivering Mary-Lou out of the pool

chattering partly from cold and partly from excitement and shock. 'It's g-g-g-gone to be m-m-m-mended. Didn't you know ?'

No. Nobody had noticed that it was gone from its place. So Mary-Lou had not been stupid. She had known the life-belt was not there to save Darrell, and she had done the next best thing—jumped in herself. Well, who would have thought it ?

Miss Potts hurried the shivering Mary-Lou up the cliff. Darrell turned to face Alicia, her eyes shining.

'Well—who was right ? Sally or you ? Why, Mary-Lou was *brave*. It isn't as if she liked the water or even knew how to swim properly ! She was as brave, no, braver than any of us, because she must have been so afraid ! '

Alicia could be generous even when she was proved to be in the wrong. She nodded. 'Yes. She was jolly brave. I never thought she had it in her. But I bet she wouldn't have done it for anyone else but *you* ! '

Darrell could hardly wait to tell Sally. She rushed to her after tea, her face glowing. 'Sally ! Your idea was *mar*vellous ! Simply wizard. Do you know, there wasn't a life-belt there this afternoon, so Mary-Lou jumped straight into the water with all her clothes on and everything, to try and save me ! '

'Gosh ! ' said Sally, and her face too began to glow. 'I never thought of *that*—did you ? Darrell, that's marvellous. You'll be able to tackle Mary-Lou properly now.'

'What do you mean ? ' asked Darrell.

'Well—tell her how brave she is, and how no one ever guessed it, and now she knows it herself she'll be able to be brave about lots of other things,' said Sally. 'Easy ! Once you can make anyone believe in themselves, they're all right.'

'You *are* a funny, wise person,' said Darrell, admiringly. 'I never think of things like that. All right. I'll do my

best, and when Mary-Lou comes to see you, you tell he
a few things, too ! '

So Mary-Lou, to her enormous surprise and delight,
became the heroine of the hour, for soon it had gone all up
and down the school how she had jumped into the pool,
fully-dressed, to try and save Darrell.

' It's no good you shrinking away into a corner any more,
or screaming yourself blue in the face because you've seen
a spider ! ' said Darrell. ' Now we know how brave you
are, we shall expect to see a bit more of your bravery ! '

' Oh, *yes*,' said Mary-Lou, beaming. ' I'll try. Now I
know I can be brave, it's different. It's when you know
you can't be, that things are awful. I never, never in my
life thought I would dare to jump into the deep end like
that—and yet I did ! I never even thought about it. I
just did it. It wasn't really brave, you know, because I
didn't have to screw up my courage or anything.'

The only person who had no word of praise for Mary-
Lou was Gwendoline. For one thing she was really jealous
of all the fuss made of Mary-Lou. Even the teachers made
quite a to-do about it, for one and all realized that this was
their one chance of making Mary-Lou realize that she
could do things if she wanted to. Gwendoline hated all the
fuss—especially as it was *Darrell* that Mary-Lou had jumped
in to save.

' Fancy anyone wanting to do *her* a good turn ! ' she
thought, remembering the hard slaps she had once had
from the angry girl. ' I'd have left her to struggle. Stupid
Mary-Lou ! I suppose she will get all conceited now.'

But Mary-Lou didn't. She remained her own rather
shy, quiet self, but now she had more confidence, and stood
up for herself better. She had been proved and had not been
found wanting. She was pleased and proud, though she did
not show it, as a girl like Gwendoline would have done.

For one thing she stood up to Gwendoline better, and

this annoyed and exasperated Gwendoline intensely. And when Sally came back into school again, as she did in two weeks' time, she too seemed changed, and would stand no nonsense from Gwendoline. She stood up for Mary-Lou, and ticked Gwendoline off in a way that irritated her and made her long to snap at Sally.

The term went on, more and more quickly now. Only three more weeks till the holidays ! Darrell could hardly believe the time had flown by so quickly.

She was working much better now, and twice she had been fifth from the top in her weekly marks. Gwendoline was the only one steadily at the bottom. Even Mary-Lou had crept up a place or two. Darrell wondered how Gwendoline was going to persuade her parents that she was top in everything at the end of the term, when she took home her report. Because her report would certainly show up Gwendoline's appalling work.

Darrell spoke to her one day about it. 'Gwendoline, what will your mother and father say when they see on your report how badly you've done in your form work ? ' she asked, curiously.

Gwendoline looked very startled. 'What do you mean —my report ? ' she asked.

'Golly, don't you know what reports are ? ' asked Darrell, in surprise. 'Look, I'll show you an old one of mine. I've got my last one here, from my old school. I had to bring it with me to show Miss Potts.'

She showed the report to Gwendoline who stared at it in the utmost horror. What ! A list of all the subjects taken, with their marks, and position in form, and comments on the work done ! Gwendoline could quite well imagine some of the comments that would be on hers !

'French. Very backward and lazy.

'Maths. Does not try in the least. Could do with some coaching in the holidays.

Games. Disgraceful. Has no sense of sportsmanship or team-work at all.'

And so on. Poor Gwendoline. It really had never occurred to her for one single moment that her bad and lazy work would be reported in this fashion to her parents. She sank down in a chair and stared at Darrell.

'But Gwendoline, did you *never* have a report on your work before?' asked Darrell, in surprise.

'No,' said the crest-fallen Gwendoline. 'Never. I told you I had never been to school before I came here. Only my governess, Miss Winter, taught me—and she never made out reports, of course. She just told Mother how well I was getting on, and Mother believed her. I didn't know I was so backward till I came here.'

'Well, I should think your parents will get a terrific shock when they see your report!' said Darrell, heartlessly. 'I should think it will be the worst one in the school. You'll be sorry you told so many fibs to your mother and Miss Winter at half-term, when you take your report home for the holidays!'

'I shall tear it up!' said Gwendoline, fiercely, feeling that she wouldn't be able to bear the astonishment, dismay and anger of her parents when they saw her report.

'You can't,' said Darrell. 'It goes by post. Ha ha! I'm jolly glad you'll be shown up at home. Mary-Lou told me some of the idiotic things you told your mother and Miss Winter at half-term. Fancy boasting like that, when you've no more brains than a mouse, and what you have you don't use!'

Gwendoline was speechless. How *dare* Darrell speak to her like that? And HOW DARE Mary-Lou repeat to the others the things she had overheard her say to her mother at half-term? Nasty, sly, disgusting little meanie! She would jolly well pay her out. She would take her fountain-pen and stamp on it! She would—she would . . . Oh, there was no end to the things she would do to that beastly, ungrateful Mary-Lou !

' After I've been friends with her, too ! ' thought Gwendoline, angrily. ' There's disloyalty for you ! I hate her.'

Then she began to think about her report. She felt afraid when she thought of her father reading it. That was why he had sent her away to school—because he had said she was lazy and vain and too pleased with herself. He had said some horrid things. Gwendoline tried to forget them, but they came back into her mind at odd times.

She could tell what untruths she pleased, she could boast all she liked—but if in her report there were the words ' lazy, unreliable, irresponsible, conceited, stupid '—words she knew she richly deserved—well, her boasts and fibs would all be wasted.

' Only two or three weeks more,' thought Gwendoline, frantically. ' Can I possibly make my report any better in those few weeks ? I shall *have* to try ! *Why* didn't I know there were school reports before ? I could have worked a bit harder. Now I shall simply have to SLAVE ! '

And, to the intense astonishment of Miss Potts, and the no less intense surprise of Mam'zelle, Gwendoline began to work ! How she worked ! She pored over her books. She wrote endless compositions and then rewrote them in her best writing. She was the most attentive one in the class.

' *What* has happened to Gwendoline ? ' asked Miss Potts of Mam'zelle. ' I begin to believe she has a few—just a few—brains at last ! '

' I too,' said Mam'zelle. ' See this French exercise ? Only one mistake ! Never has this happened before to Gwendoline. She is turning over a new stalk.'

' New *leaf*, you mean,' said Miss Potts. ' Well, well, surprising things happen. There's Darrell working much better too—and Sally Hope quite a new child. And Mary-

Lou has blossomed out tremendously since she jumped into
the pool.   But, Gwendoline is really the most surprising
one.   She wrote me quite a passable composition yesterday, with only six spelling mistakes.   Usually she makes at
least twenty.   I shall be able to put " *Can* use her brains "
on her report, instead of " *Never* uses her brains ! " '

Gwendoline did not enjoy working so hard.   Darrell
laughed at her, and told the others why there was such
a sudden change in the lazy Gwendoline.

' She doesn't want her people to know she told such fibs
to them at half-term,' she said.   ' Does she, Mary-Lou ?
That's what comes of boasting, Gwendoline.   Sooner or
later you have to eat your words.'

Mary-Lou laughed too.   She was much bolder nowadays,
though only when Darrell or Sally were there.   Gwendoline
scowled at her.   Horrid little turn-coat !

Gwendoline had her chance of paying Mary-Lou out
the next day.   She went into the common room when there
was no one else there—and in Mary-Lou's locker was her
precious fountain-pen !   Gwendoline saw it at once.

' That's the end of *that* ! ' she said, spitefully, and threw
it on the floor.   She stamped on it hard, and the pen
smashed, spilling ink all over the wooden floor !

21   A SHOCK FOR DARRELL

IT was Jean who saw the smashed pen first.   She came into
the common room to get a book, and stopped short when
she saw the ink on the floor, and the bits and pieces of the
blue pen.

' Golly ! ' said Jean.   ' Who's done that ?   What a mean
trick ! '

Emily and Katherine came in. Jean pointed to the pen.
'Look,' she said. 'There's a nice little bit of spite for you.'

'It's Mary-Lou's pen,' said Katherine, in distress.
'What a mess. Who *could* have smashed it? It's not an
accident.'

Mary-Lou came in with the quiet Violet. When she
saw her pen, she stood and wailed aloud. 'Oh! Who's
done that? I had it for my birthday from Mother. And
now it's all smashed!'

All the girls gathered round. Darrell and Sally and
Irene were astonished to see such a silent circle when they
came chattering in. They joined it, and were not surprised
when Mary-Lou's wails broke out again.

'What will Mother say? She told me to take great care
of it if I took it to school.'

Alicia came whistling in, and she too was amazed to see
the smashed pen, surrounded by its pool of deep violet ink.
What a hateful thing to do to anyone!

'Who did it?' she demanded. 'It ought to be reported
to Potty. I bet it's Gwendoline—spiteful little beast.'

'Where *is* Gwendoline?' asked Katherine. Nobody
knew. Actually she was just outside the door, about to come
in and pretend to be surprised and disgusted at the broken
pen too. But, hearing the angry voices of the girls, her
heart failed her. She stood hesitating and listening.

'Look here,' said Alicia, 'there's one certain way we can
find out who did this—and we will too.'

'What's that?' asked Katherine.

'Well, whoever stamped on this pen and smashed it must
have got violet ink on the underneath of their shoes,' said
Alicia grimly.

'Oh, yes,' said the others. 'Of course!'

'That's clever of you, Alicia,' said Katherine. 'We'll
examine every pair of shoes in our North Tower lockers—
and when we see violet ink we shall know who did this.'

' I know without looking ! ' said Darrell's scornful voice.
' Nobody could have done it but Gwendoline.   There's no
one mean or spiteful enough but her ! '

Gwendoline trembled with rage and fright.   She took a
hasty look at the underneath of her out-door shoes.   Yes,
they were stained with violet ink.   Hastily she ran down the
passage, ran into the little store-room, took up a bottle of
violet ink, and raced to the cloakroom where the shoe-
lockers were.   If only she got there in time !

She did, because the others were busy clearing up the
mess before going to examine the shoes.   Gwendoline
smeared some of the violet ink on to the under-sides of one
of Darrell's shoes, then threw the bottle into a nearby cupboard.   Then she hastily took off her own stained shoes,
and stuffed them into the cupboard too.   She pulled on a
pair of slippers.

She ran out into the Court, and re-appeared at the
door of the common room, apparently quite calm and
unruffled.   Oh, Gwendoline could act very well when it
suited her !

' Here's Gwendoline ! ' cried Alicia.   ' Gwendoline, do
you know anything about Mary-Lou's pen ? '

' Pen ? What about her pen ? ' asked Gwendoline,
innocently.

' Someone's jumped on it and smashed it,' said Sally.

' What a *beastly* thing to do ! ' said Gwendoline, putting
on a disgusted face.   ' Who did it ? '

' That's what *we* want to know,' said Darrell, feeling
infuriated with Gwendoline's smug expression.   ' And
we're going to find out, see ! '

' I hope you will,' said Gwendoline.   ' Don't glare at
me like that, Darrell.   *I* haven't done it !   Much more
likely *you* have !   I've noticed you've been jealous ever
since so much fuss was made of Mary-Lou for jumping into
the pool to rescue you ! '

Everyone gasped. How could Gwendoline have the cheek to say a thing like that ? Darrell began to boil. She felt the familiar red-hot flame rising up in her. Sally saw her face and put her hand on her arm.

' Go slow, old thing,' she said, gently, and Darrell simmered down. But she almost choked in the effort not to rage back at the smiling Gwendoline.

' Gwendoline,' said Katherine, keeping her eyes on the girl's face, ' we think that whoever stamped on this pen must have violet ink on her shoes. So we mean to examine everyone's shoes, and we are sure we shall find the culprit in that way.'

Gwendoline did not change her expression at all. ' That's a very good idea ! ' she said, warmly. ' A very good idea indeed. I wish I'd thought of it myself. It certainly *will* tell us who the hateful person is that smashed up poor Mary-Lou's pen.'

Everyone was astonished to hear these words. A little doubt crept into the minds of the girls. Would Gwendoline be so pleased with the idea if she *had* smashed the pen ? Perhaps she didn't do it after all ?

' You can look at my shoes first of all, if you like,' said Gwendoline, and she turned up first one foot and then another. There was no smear of ink on them, of course.

' We shall have to examine the shoes in the lockers too,' said Katherine. ' But first, will everyone please turn up their feet for us to see ? '

Everyone did, but no one had inky marks. Then, in a solemn group, the first-formers set off for the cloakroom in which their shoe-lockers were kept.

Gwendoline's shoes were examined first, because Katherine, like the rest, felt that her shoes were more likely to be marked with ink than anyone else's. But they were not.

It was one of Darrell's shoes that was smeared with the

bright-coloured ink! Katherine pulled it out, and then
stared at it in the greatest amazement and horror. She
held it out in silence to Darrell.

'It's—it's *your* shoe!' she said. 'Oh, Darrell!'

Darrell stared at the inky shoe speechlessly. She looked
round at the silent girls beside her. Some of them turned
away their eyes. Alicia met hers with a hard look.

'Well, well, who would have guessed it was our straight
forward Darrell?' said Alicia, flippantly. 'I wouldn't
have thought it of you, Darrell.'

She turned away with a look of disgust. Darrell caught
hold of her arm.

'Alicia! You surely don't think *I* smashed the pen!
I didn't, I tell you, I didn't! I would never dream of
doing such a hateful thing. Oh, Alicia—how *could* you
think I'd do it?'

'Well—you can't deny your shoe is inky,' said Alicia.
'You've got a dreadful temper, Darrell, and I've no doubt
that in a fit of spite you stamped on Mary-Lou's pen.
Don't ask me why! I haven't a temper like yours.'

'But Alicia—I'm not spiteful!' cried Darrell. 'You
know I'm not. Alicia, I thought you were my friend!
You and Betty always let me come with you. You can't
believe a thing like this about a friend of yours.'

'You're no friend of mine,' said Alicia, and swung out
of the room.

'There's some mistake!' said Darrell, wildly. 'Oh,
don't believe I did it, please, don't believe it!'

'*I* don't believe you did it!' said Mary-Lou, with tears
running down her cheeks. She slipped her arm through
Darrell's. 'I know you didn't. I'll stick by you, Darrell!'

'And so will I, of course,' said Sally's soft voice. 'I
can't believe you did it, Darrell, either.'

Darrell was so glad to have two friends out of the stony-
eyed girls around that she could almost have wept. Sally

took her out of the cloakroom. Katherine looked round at the others. Her face was puzzled and dismayed.

'I can't believe it's Darrell either,' she said. 'But—I suppose—until it's proved differently we'll have to think of her as the culprit. It's a pity, because we've all liked Darrell.'

'I never did,' said Gwendoline's malicious voice. 'I always thought she was capable of any mean trick, with that temper of hers.'

'Shut up,' said Jean, roughly, and Gwendoline shut up, well satisfied with what she had said and done.

Sally and Mary-Lou were good friends to Darrell then. They stuck by her, helped her, and stoutly defended her. Mary-Lou was openly defiant to Gwendoline. But it was all very unpleasant, and though no one had suggested a punishment for the smashing of the pen, it was punishment enough to have cool looks and cold voices always around.

Mary-Lou was very worried about the matter. It was all because of *her* pen that Darrell had got into this trouble. But she knew that it couldn't be Darrell. Like Sally, she had great faith in Darrell's natural honesty and kindness, and she was certain she could never do a mean trick to any one.

Well, then, who could have done it? It must have been someone with a spite against both Mary-Lou and Darrell, and that person must be Gwendoline. Therefore, Gwendoline must have smeared Darrell's shoes with the ink!

But it also followed that Gwendoline's own shoes must have been inky too—and yet, when she showed them to the girls, they had been quite free from ink.

Mary-Lou lay in bed one night and frowned over the problem. How could it have been done? Was Gwendoline there when they had planned to examine the shoes? No, she wasn't.

But she might have been listening outside ! And she would have had time to rush to the shoe-lockers, smear Darrell's shoes with ink, and take off her own, before sauntering back to the common room and joining in the conversation !

Mary-Lou sat up in excitement. She was suddenly sure that that was what had happened. She began to shake a little, as she always did when she was frightened or excited. Where could Gwendoline have hidden her shoes ? Somewhere near the shoe-lockers, anyway. Would she have taken them away and hidden them in a safer place ? Or might they still be there ?

It was very late and very dark. Everyone had gone to bed long ago. Mary-Lou wondered if she dared to go down to the cloakroom and have a look round. She so badly wanted this hateful affair to be cleared up.

But she was so afraid of the dark ! Still, she had been afraid of the water too, till she had jumped in to save Darrell. Perhaps she wouldn't be afraid of the dark either, if it was to help Darrell. She would try and see.

Mary-Lou crept out of bed. She didn't put on a dressing-gown. She simply didn't think of it. She crept down the room and out of the door. Thank goodness there was a dim light shining in the passage !

Down the passage she went, to the stairs, and down the stairs to the rooms below. She made her way to the cloak-rooms. Oh, dear, they were in pitch-darkness. Mary-Lou felt a cold shiver creeping down her back. She was frightened. In a moment she would scream. She knew she would !

' This is for Darrell ! I'm doing something for somebody else and it's very important,' she said to herself, as firmly as she could. ' I shan't scream. But oh, *where's* the switch ? '

She found it and pressed it down. At once the light

Mary-Lou crept down the stairs

came on and the cloakroom could be seen clearly. Mary-
Lou drew a deep breath. Now it was all right. She
wasn't in the dark any more. She felt very proud of herself for not screaming when she had so badly wanted to.

She looked at the lockers. That was Gwendoline's
over there. She went to it and took out all the shoes.
No—not one was inky. Now—where could the inky ones
be hidden ?

22   THE END OF THE TERM

MARY-LOU caught sight of the little cupboard nearby.
She knew what was kept there. Old balls, an old racket or
two, split gym shoes and all kinds of rubbish. Gwendoline's
shoes *might* be there ! She opened the cupboard door
cautiously, afraid that a spider or earwig might come out.

She peered into the dusty rubbish, and poked it about
with her finger. She pulled at an old racket—and something fell with a thud.

Mary-Lou wondered if the noise had awakened anyone
and she held her breath, shaking. But no one seemed to
have heard. She began to poke about again.

She found Gwendoline's shoes ! She found the bottle
of violet ink ! That was what had fallen down with a thud !
Mary-Lou looked at the bottle, and knew what Gwendoline
had used it for. She looked at the shoes—and there, on
the right-hand one was a broad violet mark !

With trembling hands Mary-Lou looked at the name
inside the shoe again, just to make sure. Yes—there was
the name, written in Miss Winter's small printing—Gwendoline Lacey.

'So it *was* Gwendoline ! It *was* ! I knew it wasn't

Darrell ! ' thought Mary-Lou, joyfully. ' I'll go straight back and wake the others. I'll tell them at once. Well— no, I won't. Perhaps Katherine would be cross if she knew I'd gone snooping round at night.'

Mary-Lou took the bottle of ink, and the shoes. She clicked off the light and stood in darkness. But did she mind ? Not a bit. She didn't once think of the black darkness as she sped upstairs. Her mind was full of her grand discovery. Darrell hadn't done it ! Darrell hadn't done it !

Mary-Lou was awake first in the morning. She went to Katherine's bed and shook the surprised head-girl. ' Wake up ! I've something important to tell you ! Wake all the others.'

The others awoke when they heard the disturbance, and sat up in bed, rubbing their eyes. Mary-Lou stood in front of the beds, and waved Gwendoline's shoes dramatically.

' Look ! I've found the *real* inky shoes ! And I've found with them a bottle of violet ink ! See ? The person who really smashed my pen hid her own shoes and smeared Darrell's with this ink to make it seem as if *she'd* done it ! '

' But *whose* shoes are they ? ' asked Katherine, in amaze- ment. ' And where did you get them ? '

' I crept downstairs in the dark last night, and hunted in the cloakroom,' said Mary-Lou triumphantly. Every- one gaped in surprise. Mary-Lou creeping down in the dark ! Why, she was terrified of the dark, everyone knew that !

' I found the shoes and the bottle in the cupboard there,' said Mary-Lou. ' And shall I tell you the name written inside ? No, I won't. Have a look round the room, all of you—and you'll see whose name is written in these shoes—you can tell by her face ! '

It was true. Gwendoline's face was red with shame and horror. She stared at Mary-Lou in misery and anger. So she had been found out after all! *Why* hadn't she taken those shoes and the bottle and thrown them into the sea!

'It's Gwendoline!' said the girls, in hushed voices, staring at the red-faced girl in disgust and horror. And this time Gwendoline did not attempt to deny anything. She lay down in bed with her face hidden in the pillow.

Katherine examined the shoes and the bottle. Then she walked up to Darrell's bed and held out her hand.

'Darrell, I apologize to you for thinking for one moment it was you. I didn't really—but there seemed nothing else to think. I do beg your pardon.'

'Oh—it's all right,' said Darrell, her face radiant. 'It's quite all right! I have felt pretty awful—but I did have Mary-Lou and Sally sticking up for me. Gwendoline won't have anyone!'

One by one the girls begged Darrell's pardon. Alicia was a little stiff about it, for she felt really ashamed of the hard words she had said. But then, Alicia *was* hard. She had a good many lessons to learn before she could lose her hardness and gain in sympathy and understanding of others.

'I'd like to be friends again,' she said, awkwardly. 'You come along with Betty and me as you did before, won't you?'

'Well,' said Darrell, looking round at Sally's steadfast little face beside her, 'well—I think if you don't mind, I'll stick to Sally and Mary-Lou. I wasn't always nice to them, but they did stick by me when I was in trouble—and they're my real friends now!'

'Oh!' said Mary-Lou, her face glowing. 'Thank you, Darrell!'

Sally said nothing, but Darrell felt a delighted pinch just above her elbow. She turned and smiled. She felt very happy. Now everything would be all right again till the end of the term. Good !

She saw Gwendoline lying face downwards on her bed. She was crying bitterly. In the gladness of her heart Darrell could not bear to see even her enemy in misery. She went over to Gwendoline and shook her, but not unkindly.

' Gwendoline ! I shan't say a word about this to any one and neither will the others if I ask them not to. But you've got to buy Mary-Lou a lovely pen in return for the one you smashed. See ? '

' Yes,' said Gwendoline's muffled voice. ' I will.'

And that was all that anyone got out of Gwendoline. She could not say she was sorry. She could not even say a few ashamed words when she gave Mary-Lou a really magnificent fountain-pen she had bought. She was weaker than Mary-Lou ever was, for she hadn't even the strength to conquer herself.

' She'll never be any good, Katherine, will she ? ' said Darrell one day. Katherine smiled.

' It depends how long she stays at Malory Towers,' she said. ' It's queer how the longer you stay here the decenter you get. That's what my aunt told me. She came here, too, and she told me all kinds of stories about awful girls who got all right ! '

' Not if they're like Gwendoline,' said Darrell. ' Nothing will ever alter *her*. I wish she was leaving ! '

Gwendoline wished she was, too. The last two weeks of the term were not pleasant ones for her. Nobody mentioned the affair of the fountain-pen again, but everyone thought of it whenever they saw Gwendoline, and they would not look at her, or speak to her if they could help it. They were certain, too, that it was she who had played so many horrid tricks on Mary-Lou the whole of the term.

Poor Gwendoline ! What with the girls' contempt, and

her own feeling that she must work like a slave for the rest of the term, she did not have at all an easy time. But she was only reaping what she had sowed, so she could not grumble !

Darrell was very happy for the rest of that term. She and Sally and Mary-Lou were always together. Darrell no longer wanted Alicia's friendship. Sally was her friend now, and a very satisfying friendship it was, for Sally was even-tempered and well-balanced, and Darrell was not likely to fly into tempers with Sally around !

Exams. came and went. Darrell did very well. Sally did not do so well, partly because she had missed two or three weeks of the term, and partly because she had not been allowed to take the full work of her form after her illness.

Gwendoline came out better than anyone expected. ' It just shows,' said Miss Potts, rather severely, ' it just shows, Gwendoline, what you can do if you try. Why you saved your efforts for the last two or three weeks of the term I can't imagine. Perhaps next term you will be obliging enough to work during the whole of the term ! '

Gwendoline did not tell Miss Potts what had made her work so hard the last few weeks ! She hoped fervently that Miss Potts would put a few nice things down on her report. What a horrid term it had been ! She wished she wasn't coming back. Next term she must try and make the girls forget all she had done this term.

Darrell thought it had been a lovely term—except for Sally's illness and the two or three days when the girls had thought she had played that horrid trick on Mary-Lou. But Darrell didn't often think of those times. She was sunny-natured and liked to think of the nice things. She was sorry the term was coming to an end—but still, the hols. would be lovely !

Sally was going to stay with her in the holidays, and she was going to stay a week with Sally, too.

' You'll see my little sister,' Darrell said.   ' You'll like her.
She's a sport.'

' And you'll see mine, too,' said Sally, half-shyly.   ' I
shall have to teach her to be a sport—like you ! '

Mary-Lou wished she lived nearer either Sally or Darrell,
then she might have been able to see them.   Never mind,
there was always next term, and the next—and the next . . .
Mary-Lou had the sense to know that Sally was Darrell's
real friend, and not herself—but she didn't mind.   Darrell
was fond of her and admired her.   That was all that
mattered to loyal little Mary-Lou.   How surprised her
mother was going to be when she found that Mary-Lou
was no longer afraid of the dark !

The last day came, with all its excitement of last-minute
strapping of trunks and hunting for lost keys.   The school
became a perfect circus, and North, South, East, and West
Tower girls became all mixed up everywhere.

' Always this last day is a madness ! ' panted Mam'zelle,
trying to force her way through a seething mass of excited
girls.   ' Darrell !   Sally !   *Will* you please let me through ?
Ah, these mad English girls ! '

Miss Potts, calm and efficient even in the midst of utter
confusion, handed out small bags, marked children off the
list when parents fetched them in cars, found lost keys and
generally remained the one sane person in North Tower.
Even Matron got flustered at times, and spent ages looking
for a clothes list she had carefully stuck into her belt.

The coaches came rolling up for the train-girls.   ' Come
on, Darrell ! ' cried Sally.   ' Let's get the front seats.
Where's Mary-Lou ? '

' She's going by car ! ' called Darrell.   ' Hie, Mary-Lou,
good-bye !   Write to me and tell me all your news.   Good-
bye ! '

' Come along, now ! ' cried Miss Potts, and the girls
were all hustled into the coaches.   ' Where's Alicia ?   If

she disappears again I shall really go mad. Alicia! Get in at once, and don't get out again. Good-bye, girls. Be good—or at least, as good as you can! And don't dare to face me next term without your health certificates!'

'Good-bye, Potty. Good-bye!' yelled the girls. 'Good-bye, dear old Potty!'

'Goodness!' said Darrell, who had never heard Miss Potts called Potty to her face before. 'How dare they!'

'It's the only time we do, just when we shout good-bye!' said Alicia with a grin. 'She never seems to mind then. Look at her grinning all over her face!'

Darrell leaned out of the coach. 'Good-bye, Potty!' she yelled. 'Good-bye—and good-bye Malory Towers!' she said, almost under her breath. 'I'll be glad to see you again.'

Good-bye! Good-bye till next time. Good-bye, Darrell and Sally and the rest. We'll meet you again soon. Good luck till then!

THE SECOND FORM AT MALORY TOWERS

'*Take charge of this new girl for me*'

THE SECOND FORM
AT MALORY TOWERS

by

ENID BLYTON

ILLUSTRATED BY
JENNY CHAPPLE

CONTENTS

'I'VE simply loved the hols.,' said Darrell, as she got into her father's car, ready to set off to school once more. 'But I'm glad it's time for school again. I've been eight weeks away from it!'

'Well, well, how simply terrible!' said her father. 'Is your mother ready, or must I hoot? It's an extraordinary thing that I'm always the first one ready. Ah, here comes Mother!'

Mrs. Rivers hurried down the steps. 'Oh dear, have I kept you waiting?' she said. 'The telephone went at the last minute. It was Sally Hope's mother, Darrell, asking what time we shall be along to pick up Sally and take her with us.'

Sally Hope was Darrell's best friend. Mr. Rivers, Darrell's father, was motoring them both down to Malory Towers, their school in Cornwall. They were setting off very early so that they would be there before dark, and Sally was going with them.

'I hate leaving home but I just can't help being excited at going back again,' said Darrell. 'This will be my fifth term at Malory Towers, Mother—and I'm to be in the Second Form. I *shall* feel grand!'

'Well, you're thirteen now, so it's time you went up,' said her mother, settling down in the car. 'You will quite look down on the first form, won't you?—think they are mere babies!'

'I suppose I shall,' said Darrell, with a laugh. 'Well, the third form look down on *us*—so we're all kept in our places!'

'There's your little sister waving to you,' said her father, as the car slid down the drive. 'She will miss you, Darrell.'

Darrell waved frantically. 'Good-bye, Felicity!' she yelled. ' *You'll* be coming to Malory Towers sometime, then we'll go together!'

The car purred out of the drive into the road. Darrell took a last look back at her home. She would not see it again for three months. She felt a little sad—but then, being a sensible girl, she cheered up at once and set her thoughts on Malory Towers. She had grown to love her school very much in the last year, and she was proud that she belonged to it. Four terms in the first form with Miss Potts lay behind her—now she had a year in the second form to look forward to.

They arrived at Sally Hope's house in an hour's time. Sally was ready for them, her school trunk and her night-case standing beside her on the steps. With her was her mother, and by them stood a toddler of about eighteen months, clutching at Sally's hand.

'Hallo, Sally! hallo, Daffy!' shouted Darrell, in excitement. 'Good, you're ready!'

The trunk was put in the boot at the back of the car, with Darrell's. The night-case was strapped on the grid. Sally's lacrosse stick was shoved in with the odds and ends, and then she got in herself.

'Want to come too!' called Daffy, her eyes full of tears as she saw her beloved Sally going away.

'Good-bye, Mother dear! I'll write as soon as I can!' called Sally. 'Good-bye, Daffy darling.'

The car slid off again, and Daffy began to howl. Sally looked a little upset. 'I hate leaving Mother,' she said, ' and now I hate leaving Daffy, too. She's lovely now—she can run everywhere, and she talks awfully well.'

'Do you remember how you hated her when she was a baby?' said Darrell. 'Now I bet you wouldn't be without her. It's fun to have a sister.'

'Yes, I was horrid to her,' said Sally, remembering.

'That was an awful first term I had at Malory Towers— I was so miserable, thinking I'd been sent away from home to make room for Daffy, the new baby. I hated you too, Darrell—isn't it queer to think of?'

'And now we're best friends,' said Darrell with a laugh. 'I say—who do you think will be head of the second form this term, Sally? Katherine's in the third form now, so she won't be. It'll be somebody else.'

'Alicia perhaps,' said Sally. 'She's about the oldest.'

'I know—but do you think she would make a good head?' said Darrell, doubtfully. 'I know she's awfully clever, and gets top marks in anything—but don't you think she's too fond of playing the fool?'

'She might stop that if she was head of the form,' said Sally. 'What Alicia wants is a bit of responsibility, *I* think. She just won't take any. You know she was asked to run the Nature Walks last term, and she wouldn't. But I can think of another reason why she wouldn't make a good head-girl.'

'What?' asked Darrell, enjoying this gossip about her school fellows.

'Well, she's rather hard,' said Sally. 'She wouldn't bother to help people if they were in trouble, she wouldn't bother herself to be kind, she'd just be head-of-the-form and give orders, and see that they were kept, and nothing else—and you do want something else in a head-girl, don't you think so?'

'Well, who do you think is fit to be head of the form?' demanded Darrell. 'What about *you*? You size people up awfully well, and you're fine when anybody's upset or in trouble. And you're so—well, so *steady*, somehow. You don't fly off the handle like I do, or get all worked up about things. I'd love you to be head.'

'I wouldn't want to be,' said Sally, 'and any way, there's no chance of it. I think *you* would be fine as head of the form, Darrell—you really would. Everyone likes you and trusts you.'

For a wild moment Darrell wondered if it was possible that she might be chosen ! It was true that all the girls, except one or two, really liked and trusted her.

' But there's my temper, still,' she said, regretfully. ' Look how I flared up last term when Marigold ticked me off at tennis, thinking I was somebody else. I didn't know she'd make a mistake, of course—but just think how I yelled at her and flung my racket down and stamped off. I can't think what came over me.'

' Oh, the sun was too much for you and lots of us that day,' said Sally, comfortingly. ' You don't usually lose your temper for silly things like that. You *are* learning to keep it for things it's useful for ! Like going for that ass of a Gwendoline Mary, for instance ! '

Darrell laughed. ' Yes, she really is an idiot, isn't she ? Do you remember how silly she was over Miss Terry, that singing mistress we had last term—the one that took Mr. Young's place for two months ? I thought Miss Terry was stupid to put up with it.'

' Oh, Gwendoline will always be silly over *some*body,' said Sally. ' She's that kind. I expect she'll pick on somebody this term too, to worship and follow round. Well, thank goodness it's not likely to be *me* ! '

' I hope there'll be some new girls,' said Darrell. ' It's fun sizing them up, isn't it ?—and seeing what they're like.'

' There are sure to be some,' said Sally. ' I say— wouldn't it be funny if Mary-Lou was told to be head-girl ! '

Both girls laughed. Mary-Lou was devoted to both Sally and Darrell, though Darrell was her heroine—and the girls liked little Mary-Lou very much. But she was such a timid little thing, shrinking away from all idea of responsibility, that it was quite funny to picture her face if she was ever told she was to be head of the form.

'She'd have a blue fit and go up in smoke,' said Darrell. 'But she's *much* better now, Sally. Do you remember how she used to shake at the knees when she was scared ? She hardly ever does that now. We've all been decent to her and not scared her, and we've made her believe in herself— so she's different. She'll never be so bad again.'

It was a long, long drive to Cornwall. The journey was broken by picnic meals, taken by the wayside, sitting on heather or grass. Mrs. Rivers took the wheel of the car once to relieve her husband. The girls sat at the back and talked or drowsed, as the journey lengthened out.

'Not very far now,' said Mr. Rivers, who was back at the wheel. 'We may see some other cars on their way to the school, too. Look out for them.'

They soon saw one—a low red car belonging to Irene's people. Irene was at the back and waved violently, almost knocking off her father's glasses, as he sat at the wheel. The car swerved.

'Isn't that just like Irene,' said Sally, with a grin. 'Hey, Irene ! Had good hols. ? '

The two cars kept more or less together, and the girls looked back at Irene's merry face. They liked her. She was a clever girl, especially at music, but a real scatter-brain otherwise, always forgetting things and losing them. But she was so good-humoured that nobody could be cross with her for long.

'There's another car ! Whose is it ? ' said Sally, as a third one came in from a side-road, complete with school trunk at the back. It swung away ahead of them.

'One of the bigger girls,' said Darrell. 'Looks like Georgina Thomas. I wonder who will be head of the whole school this year. Pamela's gone now. I hope Georgina won't. She's too bossy for anything.'

Now they were very near the school and it suddenly came into sight round a corner. The girls looked at it in silence.

They both liked their school immensely and were very proud
of it.   They saw the great grey building, with a rounded
tower at each end—North Tower, South Tower, East and
West.   A creeper, now turning red, climbed almost up to
the roof.

'Our castle!' said Darrell, proudly.   'Malory Towers.
Best school in the world.'

Soon the car swung up to the big flight of steps leading
to the great front door.   Other cars were in the drive, and
groups of chattering girls stood about.   Gay voices called
across the drive.

'Hallo, Lucy!   Look, there's Freda!   Isn't she brown?
Had good hols., Freda?   You look as if you'd lived in the
water, you're so brown.'

'Hallo, Jenny!   Did you get my letters?   You never
answered one, you pig.   Hey, Tessie.   Look out for my
night-case.   Take your great feet off it!'

'Good-bye, Mother!   Good-bye, Daddy!   I'll write as
soon as I've settled in.   Don't forget to feed my pet mice,
will you?'

'Get out of the way there!   You'll be run over by that
car!   Oh, it's Betty Hill.   Betty, Betty!   Have you
brought any tricks or jokes back with you?'

A pair of wicked eyes looked out of the window of the
car, and a tuft of hair fell over a brown forehead.   'I may
have!' said Betty, stepping out.   'You never know!
Anyone seen Alicia?   Or hasn't she come yet?'

'The train-girls haven't arrived!   The train is late, as
usual!'

'Darrell!   Darrell Rivers!   Hallo, there!   And Sally.
I say, let's go in and find our dormy.   Come on!'

What a noise!   What a tumult!   Darrell couldn't help
feeling thrilled.   It was good to be back at school again—
back at Malory Towers.

DARRELL said good-bye to her parents and they purred off in the car. Darrell was always glad that her father and mother were sensible when they said good-bye. They didn't burst into tears as Gwendoline's mother always did. They didn't expect her to stay close beside them and look mournful. They laughed and talked just as usual, promised to come down at half-term, then kissed her good-bye, and went, waving cheerfully.

Soon she and Sally were carrying their night-cases up the steps into the big hall. They had their lacrosse sticks too, which got entangled with people's legs as the other girls surged around and about.

Miss Potts was in the hall. She had been their form-mistress when they had been in the first form, and was still their house-mistress, for she was in charge of North Tower, in which they slept. All the girls' bedrooms or dormitories were in the four towers, and there was a house-mistress in charge of each one, and also a matron.

Miss Potts saw Sally and Darrell and called them. 'Sally! Darrell! Take charge of this new girl for me, will you? She will be in the second form with you, and will be in your dormy. Take her up to Matron.'

Darrell saw a tall, thin girl standing by Miss Potts, looking nervous and scared. Darrell remembered how lost she had felt when she had first come to Malory Towers, and she felt sorry for the girl. She went up to her, Sally behind her.

'Hallo! Come along with us and we'll look after you. What's your name?'

'Ellen Wilson,' said the girl. She had a very pale face and looked tired out. In the middle of her forehead was a deep line, cutting down between her eyebrows, making her look as if she was continually frowning. Darrell didn't much like the look of her, but she smiled at Ellen kindly.

' I expect you feel pretty muddled with all this row going on,' she said. ' I felt the same last year when I came. My name's Darrell Rivers. And this is my friend, Sally Hope.'

The girl gave polite little smiles and then followed silently behind them. They all made their way through the excited throng of girls.

' There's Mary-Lou ! ' said Darrell. ' Hallo, Mary-Lou ! You've grown ! '

Little Mary-Lou smiled. ' I hope so ! ' she said. ' I'm tired of being the smallest in the form. Who's this ? '

' Ellen Wilson. New girl. Second form,' said Darrell.

' In our dormy,' added Sally. ' We're taking her to Matron. Hallo, here's Irene. Irene, we saw you nearly knock off your father's glasses in the car, when you waved to us.'

Irene grinned. ' Yes, that was the third time I'd done it. He was just getting annoyed with me. Are you going to Matron ? I'll come along too.'

' Got your health certificate ? ' asked Sally, slyly. It was a standing joke with the girls that Irene always arrived without it, no matter how safely her mother had packed it in her night-case, or given it in an envelope to Irene to put in her pocket.

' Got yours ? ' said Darrell to Ellen Wilson. ' We have to hand them over at once. And woe betide you if you go down with measles or chicken pox or something if you've just handed in a certificate saying you haven't been near anyone ill ! Golly, Irene, you don't *really* mean to say you haven't got yours again ? '

Irene was feeling in all her pockets, with a humorous look of dismay on her face. ' Can't find it at the moment,' she said. ' Must be in my night-case. But no—Mother said

she wasn't going to put it in there any more because it always
disappeared. Blow ! '

'Matron said she'd isolate you next time you came
without a health certificate,' said Sally. 'You'll have to be
in the San. for two days till your mother sends another one.
You really are an idiot, Irene.'

Feeling frantically in all her pockets, Irene followed
Sally, Darrell and Ellen to North Tower, and went in with
them. The second-form dormy was not far from the first-
form dormy, where Darrell had slept for the last four terms.
It was on the second floor and was a lovely big room with
ten white beds in it, each covered with a pretty eiderdown.

The girls dumped their night-cases down in the dormy
and went to look for Matron. Ah, there she was, shepherd-
ing another new girl up to the dormy. Darrell looked at the
girl. She was about the same age as Darrell, and, like
Darrell, had black curly hair, but cut much shorter, more
like a boy. She looked rather dirty and untidy, but she had
a very attractive grin, and her eyes twinkled as she looked
at the other girls. She did not look nearly so lost or forlorn
as Ellen.

'Ah, Sally—Darrell—here's another new girl,' said
Matron, briskly. 'Take charge of her, will you ? Her
name is Belinda Morris. Now—have you all got your night-
cases ? And what about your health certificates ? '

'Our night-cases are there,' said Darrell, pointing to
where they had dumped them on the floor. 'And here's
my health certificate, Matron.'

'Where's *my* night-case ? ' said Belinda, suddenly.

'Surely you had it with you a minute ago ? ' said Matron,
looking all round. 'Well, give me your certificate and then
go and look for your case.'

'But it's in the case,' said Belinda, and looked vaguely
round.

'You probably left it down in the hall for everyone to

fall over,' said Matron. 'You girls! Thank you, Darrell. Is this your certificate, Sally?—and yours, Mary-Lou—and yours, Ellen. What about yours, Irene?'

'It's a most peculiar thing, Matron,' began Irene, hunting in all her pockets again. 'You know, I *had* it when I started off this morning. I remember Mother saying . . .'

Matron stared at Irene, really exasperated. 'Irene! Don't dare to tell me you've not brought it again. You know what I told you last term. There is a rule here that girls who forget their health certificates shall be isolated until one is produced. I've never had to enforce that rule yet—but in your case I really think . . .'

'Oh, Matron, don't isolate me!' begged Irene, taking her night-case, opening it and emptying all the contents higgledy-piggledy on the floor. 'I'll find it. I will!'

The girls stood by, laughing. Really, Irene was very funny when she had lost something. Matron looked on grimly. Irene bent low over the case, hunting hard—and suddenly she gave a cry and put her hand to her chest.

'Oooh! Something's pricking me! Whatever can it be? Gracious, something's run a sharp point right into me!'

She stood up, rubbing her chest. Then she opened the front of her coat—and the girls gave a scream of laughter.

'Irene! You donkey! You've got your health certificate pinned on to your front! You couldn't lose it if you wanted to.'

Irene looked down, pleased. 'Of course!' she said, unpinning it. 'I remember now. I *knew* I should lose it unless I really did hang on to it somehow—so I pinned it tightly to my front. Here it is, Matron. You won't have to isolate me after all!'

Matron took·it, and put it with the others she had. 'A narrow squeak for you, Irene!' she said, and her plump face broke into a smile. 'You put a grey hair into my head at the beginning of every term! Now, you girls—unpack your night-cases and put out your things. The trunks won't be unpacked till tomorrow—and then each of you will have to check the clothes' list you brought with you.'

She departed, rustling stiffly in her starched apron, looking out for more returning girls, collecting lists and names and certificates, bringing order out of confusion, and welcoming back all the sixty or so girls returning to North Tower. In the other towers, three more matrons were doing the same thing. It was a real task to welcome back about two hundred and fifty girls, with their trunks, night-cases and odds-and-ends!

Belinda had wandered off to look for her night-case. Whilst the others were still putting out their things, she sauntered back, a brown suit-case in her hand. She opened it and shook out a pair of pyjamas. She stared at them in surprise.

'Golly! I didn't know I had pyjamas like this,' she said. 'And what posh bedroom slippers Mother has put in for me. For a surprise, I suppose!'

Darrell looked over her shoulder. Then she grinned. 'You'll get into trouble if you unpack any more of those things,' she said. 'They belong to Georgina Thomas! She'll be jolly wild if she finds out you've got her night-case! She's probably hunting all over the place for it now. Can't you read, Belinda?'

Darrell pointed to the name marked on the collar of the pyjamas. 'Georgina Thomas'.

'Goodness, what an ass I am!' said Belinda, and stuffed all the things back untidily into the case. 'I thought it was *my* case!'

She went out of the room again, presumably to hunt once more for her lost case. Darrell grinned at Irene.

'I don't know what we're going to do if we have *two* people like you, Irene!' she said. 'One's bad enough—

but *two*! You'll drive Mam'zelle cracked between you. And as for Miss Parker, our form-mistress—well, you know what she is! She can't stand anything vague or careless. We shall have some fun this term with you and Belinda in the class together!'

Irene didn't in the least mind being teased. She was a clever, good-humoured girl, brilliant at music, but very thoughtless and vague over the ordinary little everyday things. If anyone lost a grammar book it was Irene. If anyone forgot to turn up at a special lesson, it was Irene. And now here was another girl, Belinda, who seemed to be just as bad. Irene very much liked the look of her, and had already made up her mind to be friends.

Belinda soon came back again, this time, fortunately, with her own case. She tipped everything out, and then proceeded to put her things in place, just as the others did— pyjamas under the pillow—tooth-brush, face-flannel, tooth-paste and sponge on a glass ledge at one end of the dormy, where the wash-basins were. Brush and comb in their bag inside the top drawer of the dressing-table. Then the empty night-case was put with the pile outside in the corridor, waiting to be taken to the box-room.

There came a great clatter up the stairs and the girls in the dormy raised their heads. 'The train-girls! They've come at last. Aren't they late!'

More girls clattered into the dormy. Alicia Johns came in, her eyes bright. Behind her came Jean, the straight-forward, sensible Scots girl. Then came Emily, a quiet girl whose only real interest was sewing, and the most elaborate embroidery.

'One, two, three, four, five, six, seven, eight of us,' said Darrell, counting. 'Two more to come. Who are they?'

'Gwendoline Mary for one, I suppose,' said Irene, with a grimace. 'Dear Gwendoline Mary! I expect her mother

is still sobbing over letting her darling lamb go away from
her! Who's the tenth?'

'Here comes Gwendoline,' said Darrell, and the girls
heard that familiar, rather whining voice. Gwendoline was
a spoilt only child, and although Malory Towers had done
her a lot of good, the holidays always seemed to make her
worse again.

She came in—and with her was the tenth girl.
Gwendoline Mary introduced her. 'Hallo, everyone!
This is Daphne Millicent Turner, a new girl. She's in our
form and in our dormy. She travelled down in my carriage
and I'm sure she's going to be a favourite with all of us
in no time!'

3   FIRST DAY OF TERM

THIS, of course, was a silly way to introduce any new girl,
especially as every listening girl immediately felt that anyone
likely to be Gwendoline's favourite was not at all likely to be
theirs! They smiled politely at the new girl, taking her in
from top to bottom.

She was very pretty. Her golden hair curled about her
forehead, and her eyes were much bluer than Gwendoline's
large pale ones, but they were set nearer together than
Gwendoline's, giving her rather a sly look. She had beautiful white teeth, and a very charming smile.

She used it now. 'I'm so pleased to come to Malory
Towers,' she said. 'I've never been to a school before.'

'That's one thing we had in common!' said Gwendoline,
in a pleased voice. 'I didn't go to school before I came here
either.'

'It would have been better for you if you had,' said

Alicia. 'You wanted a lot of licking into shape, Gwendoline. I suppose, as usual, you were waited on hand and foot at home these hols., with your old governess and your mother telling you that you were the most wonderful girl in the world!'

Gwendoline looked annoyed. 'You don't need to be rude immediately you see me, Alicia,' she said. 'Come along, Daphne, I'll show you what to do. You are in our dormy, which will be very nice. I can show you round quite a lot. I know how I felt when I first got here and didn't know anyone.'

Daphne seemed very grateful. She had very good manners, and thanked everyone nicely whenever they showed her or told her anything. She certainly was very pretty and graceful. It was clear that for some reason Gwendoline had quite made up her mind to be her friend and helper.

'I told you she'd have to be silly about *some*body,' said Sally to Darrell, as they went downstairs to their supper. 'Well, she's welcome to Daphne. She's got too many airs and graces for me!'

'Gwendoline says that Daphne's father is practically a millionaire,' said Darrell. 'She had a nurse, a governess and her own maid before she came here!'

'Oh—so that's why dear Gwendoline is sucking up to her!' said Sally. 'I thought there must be *some*thing. Hey, Irene—you've still got your hat on! Do you particularly want to wear it at supper?'

'Oh, gosh!' said Irene, putting her hand up to her head. 'Have I forgotten to take it off? Belinda, you might have told me!'

Belinda grinned. 'I don't know that I noticed it,' she said. 'So many things strike me as odd here, at the moment. Wearing a hat to supper didn't seem to be anything out of the ordinary.'

'What a pair you'll make!' said Sally. 'Come on, Darrell, come on, Mary-Lou. We shan't get any supper if we don't hurry.'

All the girls were tired that night, and the second-formers were very glad to tumble into bed. Gwendoline had chosen the bed next to Daphne. 'If you feel homesick, just tell me,' she said to Daphne, who looked really charming in blue pyjamas, her curly hair all about her shoulders in a golden mass. Gwendoline's hair, too, was golden, but it was straight. She envied Daphne her curls.

'I expect I shall feel rather queer,' said Daphne, getting into bed. 'You see, I'm so used to lots of people round me —Mummy coming to kiss me good night—and my governess popping in to see if I'm all right—and my maid folding all my things. I shall . . .'

'No more talking,' said Sally, suddenly.

Gwendoline sat up. 'You're not head of form *or* dormy, Sally,' she said. 'Don't give orders, then!'

'I'm not,' said Sally. 'You know the rules, Gwendoline. I'm just reminding you of them, that's all.'

Gwendoline lay down. Presently the whispering began again. Sally got cross.

'Shut up, Gwendoline. It's long past time to stop talking. We all want to go to sleep.'

'Wait till you're head and I'll obey you, but not till then!' said Gwendoline, rather anxious to show off in front of her grand new friend. 'We'll know tomorrow who's head.'

'Well, it won't be *you*,' said Alicia's malicious voice from down the room.

'Shhhh!' said Darrell, hearing a footstep. It was Matron. She came in quietly, saw the wakeful girls, and spoke kindly to them. 'Not asleep yet? Hurry up! No more talking now, of course. Good night.'

She went out. Gwendoline debated whether or not to begin whispering to Daphne again. But a tiny snore from

Daphne showed that she was asleep.   So it wouldn't be any good to defy Sally—Daphne wouldn't be able to whisper back !

Soon all the girls were fast asleep.   They didn't hear Miss Potts peep into the room and shut the door quietly. They didn't even hear the sixth-formers trooping upstairs later on.   They were all tired out.

The dressing-bell awoke everyone with a jump.   Sally sat straight up, startled.   ' Oh—it's only the school bell,' she said, and laughed.   ' I couldn't think what it was for a moment.'

The first day was always fun.   No real lessons were done, though classes were held.   Tests were given to see what the new girls knew.   New books, pencils and so on were given out.   A list of various duties was compiled, each girl taking her turn at them, week by week.

The new girls all had to go to see Miss Grayling, the quiet, low-voiced Head Mistress.   She told the girls exactly the same as she had told Darrell the year before.   ' You will all get a lot out of your years at Malory Towers.   See that you give a lot back !   Be just and responsible, kind and hardworking.   I count as our successes those who leave here as young women good-hearted and kind, sensible and trustable, good sound people that the world can lean on. Our failures are those who do not learn these things in the years they are here.'

Daphne, Ellen, Belinda and all the other new girls in various forms, heard these words that morning.   All of them listened, impressed.   Some remembered the words and never forgot them.   They would be the successes.   All three new girls in the second form seemed to be listening earnestly and sincerely, especially Daphne.   Miss Grayling glanced at her, looking at her closely without appearing to. She knew quite a lot about Daphne Millicent Turner.

Daphne looked back, putting all her soul into her eyes.

She wanted badly to make a good impression on Miss Grayling. She smiled her charming smile, but the Head Mistress did not return it. She spoke a few more serious words and then dismissed the girls. They went silently out of the room.

'Isn't she wonderful?' said Daphne, fervently. 'Gwendoline said she'd make a real impression on me, and she has.'

Nobody appeared to care whether any impression had been made on Daphne or not. They separated and went their different ways.

This term Darrell and Sally made their way to the second-form room. They passed the door of the first-formers, the room where they themselves had sat for many terms. The door was open. A tangled crowd of small girls were choosing desks and bagging seats.

'Babies!' said Darrell, loftily. 'Just inky-fingered kids who probably don't know their twelve-times table yet.'

Two old second-formers, now third-formers, passed them in the passage. 'Hallo, kinds!' said one of the third-formers, condescendingly. 'Look out for old Nosey! She's hard on people who make too many spelling mistakes!'

Nosey was the popular name for Miss Parker, the second-form mistress. She had rather a large nose, which, so the girls said, she kept putting into things that were no concern of hers. Certainly she was a most inquisitive person when she suspected any mischief was going on, and did not rest till she had got to the bottom of it.

She was strict but sometimes she had dreamy fits when she seemed to forget the class and sit gazing into the distance. The class lived for these rare moments and then made the most of them. Darrell was sure she would not like Miss Parker nearly as much as she had liked Potty, the mistress who had taught her in the first form.

Belinda and Ellen seemed to be very keen to know all the

details about the various teachers. Darrell and Sally were pleased to supply them. Daphne, of course, went to Gwendoline for information.

' You've got to be careful of both Mam'zelles,' said Darrell. ' But most of all of Mam'zelle Rougier, the tall thin one. They've both got tempers—but Mam'zelle Dupont's temper is just a short, hot one, and Mam'zelle Rougier's is a real *bad* one ! '

' And look out for Miss Carton, the history mistress, because, if you don't like history, she'll sharpen her tongue on you ! ' said Alicia. ' I do like it, so I'm all right. But if you don't, look out ! '

The first day passed pleasantly and interestingly. The new girls were taken to see the various parts of the big school buildings, the tennis courts, and the gardens. They marvelled at the great swimming-pool hollowed out from the rocks continually filled with fresh water each tide.

' I suppose you can swim very well,' said Daphne to Gwendoline. Gwendoline hesitated and looked round. She had been boasting quite a lot to Daphne, but not in the hearing of the others. Now Darrell was too near for her to make any untruthful statement about her swimming.

' Well—not so well as the others,' she said.

' I bet you swim the best,' said Daphne, warmly. ' You're too modest ! '

Darrell giggled. No one could call Gwendoline modest, surely ! She was the worst boaster in the school, and sometimes could not draw the line between stupid boasting and real untruth.

Ellen said she could not swim. ' I've never had much time for games,' she said. ' But I'd like to play them well. I've had to work so hard always.'

' You must be jolly clever,' said Mary-Lou. ' You won the only scholarship offered that would take you to Malory Towers, didn't you ? '

'Yes. But I don't believe I'm *really* clever,' said
Ellen, the little line deepening on her forehead and giving
her a worried look. 'I mean—I can work and work and
work, and remember things all right—but I'm not brilliant
like some girls. Some don't need to work hard at all—
they're top because they're so clever, and they can't help
it. I have had to work for everything. Still—I badly
wanted to come to Malory Towers, and here I am, so the
hard work was worth it!'

'Well, you try being good at games as well as at work,'
said Sally, who was very keen on all games herself. 'You
know what they say " All work and no play . . ." '

'Makes Jack a dull boy—and Ellen a dull girl!' said
Ellen, with a small laugh. 'I'm afraid that's what I am,
too—dull!'

Belinda loved everything about Malory Towers. Irene,
who seemed to have taken her as much in tow as Gwendoline
had taken Daphne, was delighted with Belinda's rapturous
admiration of everything.

'Oh, the views!' cried Belinda. 'Look at that sea!
Look at the colours in that swimming-pool! Where's my
paint-box, quick!'

It was then that for the first time the girls discovered
Belinda's talent. She could draw and paint marvellously
well. Best of all, or so the girls thought, she could carica-
ture anyone in a bold pencil or charcoal drawing, producing
a comic exaggerated likeness that sent everyone into peals
of laughter.

'We'll have some fun with you, Belinda!' said Irene.
'You can draw Nosey Parker—and Mam'zelle—both
Mam'zelles, in fact—and Matron—and everyone. I'm glad
you came. We'll certainly have some fun with you!'

ON the first day of the term Miss Parker announced who the head-girl of the form was to be. The class were all agog to hear her, and sat like mice whilst she rustled her papers and looked for her pencil.

'I am sure you all want to know who has been chosen for head-girl this term,' she said. 'Well, I will not keep you in suspense long. After a short discussion at the staff meeting we decided on—Sally Hope.'

The girls clapped and Sally blushed red. She was very pleased indeed. Miss Parker went on, glancing at her notes as she spoke.

'You may perhaps like to know what girls were in the running for the position. Darrell Rivers was, Jean Mac-Donald was another. Winnie Toms was a third.'

Everyone expected to hear Alicia's name mentioned, or Irene's. But Miss Parker did not give any more names at all. Irene didn't mind. She knew she was a scatter-brain and she didn't in the least want to be head of the form. So long as she had her music she was happy. Being head of the form might rob her of some of her practice time!

But Alicia did mind. She had been top of the form last term. She had a fine brain and an excellent memory, and although she never needed to work hard because she had these to help her, still she certainly had done well last term.

And yet she wasn't even in the running for the position of head-girl! She bit her lips and wished she could stop herself going red.

'There's too much favouritism!' she told herself, fiercely. 'Just because I play the fool sometimes and upset the mistresses, they won't even consider me as head!'

But Alicia was not altogether right. It was not playing the fool that made the staff pass over her name, but something else. It was Alicia's hardness to those she didn't like, her sneers at those less clever than herself, who needed help, not taunts. Often the staff laughed privately over Alicia's ridiculous tricks, and enjoyed them—but nobody liked her wild and unruly tongue, and the sharp things it could say.

'She'll get a lot of admiration and envy but she won't get much love or real friendship from others,' Miss Grayling had said at the staff meeting. 'As for Betty, her friend, she is clever too, but a little empty-head, compared with Alicia, who really has it in her to make good if she tried. It isn't Alicia's brain that is at fault, it's her heart!'

And so the choice had been made—Sally Hope, the steady, loyal, kindly, sensible Sally, Darrell's best friend. Sally might not be top of the form, but she would always listen to anyone in a difficulty. Sally would not do brilliantly in exams, as Alicia would—but she would always help a younger girl at games or lessons. She would be completely fair and just as head-girl of the form, and she wouldn't stand any nonsense.

Everyone in the form knew that a good choice had been made, although some of them would have welcomed a bad choice, for they didn't like Sally! Gwendoline was furious. So was Betty, who had hoped that Alicia would have been chosen. So were one or two of Betty's friends, not in Sally's dormy.

Darrell squeezed Sally's arm. 'Jolly good!' she said. 'I'm glad. Won't your mother be pleased? You'll be head of our dormy too, Sally. Sucks for Gwendoline!'

It certainly was most annoying for Gwendoline that night in bed, when Sally took command. Sally did not mean to use her new power too much or too soon, but she knew that if Gwendoline began to be silly again, she would have to make a stand at once. Gwendoline didn't understand leniency, but took advantage of it.

So, as soon as the whispering began again, after lights out, Sally spoke up.

' Shut up, Gwendoline. I told you that last night. I wasn't head of dormy then. But I am now. So shut up when I tell you.'

' Poor Daphne's homesick ' began Gwendoline.

' It won't make her any better if you whisper stuff and nonsense into her ear,' said Sally.

There was a short silence. Then Belinda's voice cut through the darkness, asking a question.

' Sally ! What happens if we disobey and go on whispering when the head-girl has said we're not to ? '

' Nobody ever does,' said Sally, grimly. ' But I believe there is an unwritten law at Malory Towers that if anyone makes herself a nuisance at night a nice big hair-brush is chosen and a few slaps given.'

' Oh ! ' said Belinda, and snuggled down in bed, grinning to think of what Gwendoline would feel now. Would she whisper again or not ?

Gwendoline had opened her mouth to continue her conversation with Daphne, but when she heard Belinda's question and its answer, she shut it again, shocked. How dare Sally hint such a thing to a second-former ! She debated whether or not Sally was just saying it to scare her. But, remembering Sally's grim voice, she decided she wouldn't risk it. It would be too humiliating if Sally really did carry out her threat. Daphne would never respect her again !

So there was peace in the dormy, and when Matron came silently to the door, there was only the regular breathing of ten girls to be heard. Eight were fast asleep. But two were awake.

They were Gwendoline and Ellen. Gwendoline was

cross, and that always made her wakeful. Ellen was
thinking about her work. She had done fairly well in the
test-papers that morning, but not brilliantly. Was she
really up to the second-form work here? Oh yes, she had
won that scholarship, but it wasn't brains that had done it,
only hard, hard work. Was it going to be terribly hard
work here to keep up with the others? Her brain didn't
seem to work so easily as it used to. Ellen was worried,
and did not fall asleep till long after Gwendoline.

It took the new girls a few days to get into the way of
things. Ellen and Daphne learnt their way about more
quickly than Belinda, who kept turning up in the wrong
classroom continually. She would go into the first-form
classroom instead of in the second form, and Miss Potts
got quite annoyed with her.

'Belinda! Don't tell me you're here *again*!' she
would say. 'Do you particularly want to work with the
first form? Of course, if you really feel that the work of
the second form is . . .'

But by that time Belinda had fled, muttering hurried
apologies. She would appear in her own form-room a
minute or two late, giggling.

'I'm so sorry, I got lost, Miss Parker,' she would say,
and subside into her seat.

'I'll look after her a bit, Miss Parker,' said Irene. But
Miss Parker forbade that immediately.

'That would mean the two of you getting lost,' she said.
'You'd probably be down in the swimming-pool waiting
for a diving lesson whilst we were all up here doing maths.
It's time Belinda learnt to look after herself. After all,
she's been here three days now!'

'Yes, Miss Parker,' said Belinda, meekly, and began to
make a little sketch of the teacher on her blotting-pad. She
was always drawing, wherever she was. She kept a little
sketch book in her pocket and filled it with odd drawings

of the girls, the flowers on the window-sill, the view from the window, anything that caught her observant eye.

Mam'zelle Dupont, plump, short and beady-eyed, holding her lorgnettes close to her eyes, was a source of delight to Belinda, for she was so easy to draw. Nearly every girl in the class now had a neat little sketch of Mam'zelle marking her place in her French grammar. It was the ambition of the class to have, as a marker, caricatures of all the mistresses taking their different classes—Miss Carton for their history books, Miss Grayling for the scripture exercise books, Mr. Young for the school song book and so on.

Belinda had promised to do one for each girl as a marker, providing that they would tidy her drawers for her, keep her desk spick and span, and generally see that whatever she forgot, was done before she got into trouble.

'I simply can't help forgetting things,' she explained. 'I'm even worse than Irene. If I get into too many rows I get upset and can't draw. That's awful.'

'Don't worry! We'll run round you all right!' said Alicia, looking in delight at the sly drawing Belinda had done of Mr. Young the singing-master. There he was, with his funny little moustache twisted up at the ends, his bald head with the three or four hairs plastered down the middle, his too-high collar, and his eyes large behind their glasses.

'You really are a marvel, Belinda,' said Betty, looking over Alicia's shoulder at the drawing. 'What will you draw for me if I promise to take over your week of class-room duties when your turn comes?'

Thus Belinda made her bargains, and got out of all the jobs she didn't want to do! Miss Parker was amazed to find the girls doing so much for Belinda. Belinda exasperated her, with her irresponsible ways, and she couldn't think why the girls ran round her so much.

'It's queer,' she said to Mam'zelle. 'They never do

that for Irene, who is almost as bad. Do they like Belinda
so much then ? I can't see what there is in that silly child
to make them fuss round her so much ! Why, I even saw
Gwendoline tidying out her desk for her this morning,
instead of going off at Break ! '

'Ah, Belinda has the artistic temperament ! ' said
Mam'zelle. 'She has no time for such things as tidying
desks and making beds. I myself have an artistic temperament, but in this so-English school, it gets no sympathy.
You English, you do not like such things.'

'No, we don't,' said Miss Parker, who had heard a
good many times before about Mam'zelle Dupont's artistic
temperament. It usually took the form of groaning over
such laborious jobs as marking papers, making out long lists
and so on. Mam'zelle's artistic temperament was always
at war with such tasks, and she tried in vain to hand them
over to more practical people, such as Miss Potts or Miss
Parker.

'We must be patient with such as Belinda,' went on
Mam'zelle. 'How I have suffered because people . . .'

'Well, believe me, Belinda will suffer too, if she doesn't
get rid of some of her ways,' said Miss Parker, grimly.
'I know what Miss Potts had to put up with, in Irene, the
last year. She put a bit of sense into her, thank goodness,
and I can deal with her. Belinda's got to toe the line too.
It's a pity all the girls seem bent on doing so much for her.'

Nobody told Miss Parker the real reason, and although
she tried hard to find out, she couldn't. Nobody showed
Miss Parker any of the drawings either. Belinda had a
malicious pencil sometimes, and just hit off the weak points
in her subjects. Miss Parker's big nose always appeared
in her drawings just a *little* bit bigger than life ! Mam'zelle
Rougier was always bonier than she really was. Mam'zelle
Dupont was rounder and fatter. No, the girls certainly
didn't want to show those clever caricatures to their teachers !

The only teacher who was really delighted with Belinda was Miss Linnie, the art mistress. She was young and light-hearted with a great sense of fun. She soon found out Belinda's gift for art, and encouraged her all she could.

'I'm going to enjoy myself here!' said Belinda to Irene. 'Miss Linnie's thrilled with me and is helping me no end. And I've got out of all the silly jobs I hate. Emily's even going to darn my stockings for me!'

'You're lucky,' said Irene, enviously. 'I wouldn't mind swopping some of my music compositions if somebody would do jobs for *me*—but nobody wants the music I write! But they all want your funny drawings, Belinda!'

5   SORTING THEMSELVES OUT

THE first week went slowly by. It always did go slowly, and then after that the weeks went faster and faster. All the girls had now settled in well, and were enjoying themselves.

The weather kept fine and warm and there was still bathing to be had for those who wanted it. The tennis courts were still in use too, although the winter game of lacrosse was now being played. So there was plenty to do in spare time.

Gwendoline and Daphne had become firm friends. Gwendoline had not had a proper friend during the four terms she had been at Malory Towers and she was thrilled to have Daphne. She admired the girl's prettiness and her charming ways, and loved to hear the stories of her wealthy home.

The two girls had much in common. Neither of them

liked the water and nothing would persuade them to take a dip in the Pool.

'We have to do enough of that each summer,' objected Gwendoline, one hot day, when her form tried to get her to come along and bathe. 'We don't *have* to swim this term, so I'm jolly well not going to. Anyway, you don't really want me to come—all you want me for is to creep behind me and push me in!'

'No—we want Belinda to see you shivering in your bathing suit, putting one toe gingerly into the water!' said Alicia. 'It would make such a comical picture for our classroom wall, Gwendoline!'

'Beast!' said Gwendoline, who hated to be made fun of. She walked off with Daphne. 'Just because they like violent things like swimming and tennis and rough games, they think everyone ought to,' she said to Daphne. 'After all, you and I have never been to school before we came here, and we'll never get used to all their stupid ideas. I wish I had been born French. Then I shouldn't have had to swim if I didn't want to, or tire myself out trying to hit a silly ball over a net.'

'We have three courts at home,' said Daphne. 'Two are hard and one is soft. You see, Mother is a marvellous hostess, and she likes to give tennis parties as well as other kinds. But, of course, the ones people really love are the ones she gives on board Daddy's yacht.'

Gwendoline hadn't heard about the yacht before. She gazed enviously at her friend. Perhaps Daphne would invite her to stay one summer holidays and then she too could go on this wonderful yacht. How pleased her mother would be to know she had made such a fine friend at last!

'You must have hated coming away to school, Daphne,' she said. 'Leaving all your luxury, and having to pig it here. I don't expect you ever made your bed in your life before you came here.'

'Of course I didn't,' said Daphne, shaking back her pretty hair. 'And I bet you didn't either!'

'No, I didn't,' said Gwendoline. 'My governess Miss Winter always did things like that for me. She still does in the holidays. She's a stupid old thing but she's useful in those ways. She wasn't much good at teaching me, though. I was awfully backward when I first came here.'

Gwendoline still was! Instead of getting down to things and trying to work really hard all the term to catch up with the others, she made a great show and did very little. Her parents were almost resigned to the fact that her reports always contained the words 'Fair. Could work harder.' 'Weak. Does not use her brains enough.' 'Poor—has not tried her best.'

Her father made plenty of cutting remarks about her reports, but as her mother always sympathized with Gwendoline, and spoilt her, his remarks did no good at all, except to make Gwendoline cross. Then she would burst into tears and it would be all that Miss Winter and her mother could do to comfort her. Gwendoline knew how to turn on her tears all right.

And Daphne knew how to turn on her charming smile! It got her out of a good deal of trouble, especially with Mam'zelle Dupont, Miss Linnie the art mistress, and Mr. Young the singing master.

Mam'zelle could not resist that smile. Daphne could make it sweet, pathetic, brave, affectionate—it was extraordinary what a smile could be!

When Daphne presented a badly written French exercise to Mam'zelle, she would turn on her smile, and Mam'zelle would gaze warmly at her. Ah, the pretty child!

'I've done my best, Mam'zelle,' Daphne would say, still keeping on her smile. 'But I'm afraid it's not very good yet. You see—it's so difficult my not having been to school before.'

Then the smile would become rather pathetic, and Mam'zelle, quite overcome, would pat Daphne's arm.

'You do your best, *mon enfant*! You cannot do more! See, I will help you if you like to come to me in the evenings for extra work!'

Mam'zelle would make this generous offer, beaming all over her face. But Daphne was quick enough to deal with it at once. She would shake her head regretfully and say how sorry she was, but already she had extra work with another mistress.

Then on would come that smile again, and the blue eyes would look beseechingly at Mam'zelle.

'Do not make me do all this French work again, please, Mam'zelle,' she would say. 'I have so much to do, to catch up with the others my first term.'

And, no matter who had their French exercises to do all over again, Daphne never did. She could do anything with Mam'zelle, if only she exerted her charm and put on that ravishing smile!

Unfortunately it worked the other way with Miss Parker, Miss Potts and Mam'zelle Rougier—especially with Mam'-zelle Rougier, who, as a rule, made it a habit to dislike those girls that the other Mam'zelle liked, and to like those she didn't.

She was hard on Daphne, and soon it became impossible for the girl even to try to smile at her. They both disliked one another intensely. If it had not been for the unexpected help of somebody else in the class, Daphne would have had a very bad time, and have had all her work returned from Mam'zelle Rougier.

That somebody was, surprisingly enough, Mary-Lou! Mary-Lou had become exceedingly good at French, for her mother had had a French girl to look after her in the holidays for the past year, and Mary-Lou could chatter almost as

well in French now, as she could in English, pleasing both
Mam'zelles immensely.

Mary-Lou thought Daphne was lovely. She couldn't
help gazing and gazing at her. She would never, never like
her as much as she liked Darrell and Sally, of course, but
she couldn't help warming to her prettiness and nice manners.

One day she saw Daphne almost in tears over some
returned work from Mam'zelle Rougier, who had told
Daphne that she would return it yet again if it was not
given in perfect this time. Mary-Lou went to her.

' Can't Gwendoline help you ? ' she asked timidly.
' She's not doing anything in particular. Shall I ask her
to come and help you ? '

Daphne dabbed her eyes and turned a watery but still
charming smile on Mary-Lou. ' No, it's no good asking
Gwen. She'd help if she could. But she's not much better
than I am at French ! '

' Well—I suppose you wouldn't like *me* to help you,
would you ? ' asked Mary-Lou, eagerly. ' I'd like to.'

' Oh, thanks awfully,' said Daphne, thrilled. ' You're
frightfully good at it, I know. Simply wizard. Look,
what have I done wrong here ? '

Mary-Lou slipped happily into a seat beside Daphne and
began to explain a few things to her. Without realizing it
she had soon done the whole of the work, and Daphne
smiled to herself, and thanked Mary-Lou warmly.

' That's all right,' said Mary-Lou, shyly. She gazed at
Daphne's curling golden hair. ' You've got beautiful hair,'
she said.

Daphne was like Gwen. She loved people to admire her
and say nice things. She looked at little Mary-Lou and
quite liked her. Also she thought it would be extremely
useful if Mary-Lou would always help her with her French.

' I suppose you wouldn't give me a hand with my French
sometimes, would you ? ' she asked. ' I don't want any

extra coaching from either of the Mam'zelles, but I'd love
to let you explain things to me. You explain very well.'

Nobody had ever asked Mary-Lou for help before in that
way. She went brilliant red, and swallowed hard.

'I'd love to,' she said at last. 'Fancy *me* helping *you*!
I'm the one that's usually always rushing round for help.
I'd love to, Daphne.'

So, to the astonishment of the second-formers, they saw
the curious sight of little Mary-Lou sitting by Daphne in
the evenings at the end of the common-room, carefully
explaining the mistakes made in the French exercise of the
day before!

'*And* doing all the next day's work for her too!' said
Darrell, in disgust. She didn't like to see the faithful
Mary-Lou sitting so long with somebody else. Why,
Mary-Lou had tagged along behind Darrell and Sally for
terms and terms! Surely she wasn't going to make that
awful Daphne her friend.

'Let her be,' said the sensible Sally. 'If she wants
to help her, why not? Daphne is awful at French, but I
don't blame her for not taking extra coaching from the
Mam-zelles. You know how irritable Mam'zelle Rougier
gets in the evening, and you know how long Mam-zelle
Dupont keeps you if you do go for extra work. You're
supposed to go for half an hour and she keeps you two
hours!'

'I hope Daphne won't put any of her silly ideas into
Mary-Lou's head,' said Darrell.

'Maybe Mary-Lou will put a few *sensible* ideas into
Daphne's head,' said Sally. 'I know you're longing to
interfere, Darrell. Well, don't!'

The girls soon sorted themselves out in the form, making
their own friends, choosing people to sit next to and go
walks with. It was nice to have a particular friend, and to
have someone to confide in.

Sally had Darrell and Darrell had Sally. Irene had Belinda. The two became quite inseparable, and did one another no good. What one forgot the other certainly didn't remember! They seemed to make one another worse.

Alicia, of course, had Betty. Alicia was not as good-tempered as usual. She still smarted because she had not been made head-girl, and she was not at all nice to Sally nor as loyal to her as she should have been. Sally took no notice, but she was not very happy about it.

Gwen had Daphne, of course—and now Mary-Lou seemed to want Daphne too! How was Gwen going to feel about that?

'You needn't worry,' said Daphne to Gwen. 'I'm only using her, silly little thing! I'll let her come out with me sometimes, when you're busy, because I don't want her to think I only want her help for my French. You can use her too, Gwen. Copy my work when I've done it!'

So Gwendoline put up with Mary-Lou's company at times, and even said nothing when she went off alone with Daphne. What did it matter? Daphne was only using her!

But all the same Daphne couldn't help liking little Mary-Lou—and it was certainly a change from the silly Gwen to have good-hearted Mary-Lou trotting by her side once or twice a week!

6   THE INVISIBLE CHALK

AFTER a few weeks Alicia got restless. 'It's time we livened things up a bit!' she said to Betty. 'I know we're second-formers now and all that—but there's no reason why we shouldn't have a bit of fun. Sally's such a bore—never a joke, never a trick!'

'What shall we do?' said Betty, her wicked dark eyes gleaming. 'I've got some invisible chalk. Have you got anything?'

'Invisible chalk! You never told me!' said Alicia, her face brightening. 'What is it? Show me!'

'I've got it in my locker, in a box,' said Betty. 'The common-room will be empty now. Come along and I'll show you. It's queer stuff.'

The two girls went to their common-room. Betty opened her locker and took out a tin box. Inside, wrapped carefully in paper, was a thick slab of curious pink chalk.

'It doesn't look invisible!' said Alicia. 'What does it do?'

'Well, if you rub it on to a chair, it can't possibly be seen,' said Betty. 'And whoever sits down on it makes it warm and it leaves a bright pink patch on a dress or skirt.'

'I see,' said Alicia. 'Golly—we could rub it on the mistress's chair in our form-room—when Mam'zelle Rougier is coming perhaps.'

'I know! Let's rub it on to Mr. Young's chair, when he comes to take singing!' said Betty. 'On his piano stool! Then he'll sit down hard on it when he plays the accompaniment for our songs—and when he gets up and turns round to write on the blackboard—golly, what a scream!'

Alicia laughed loudly. 'It would be better to play it on Mr. Young than on Nosey or Mam'zelle—he won't suspect a thing—and the first form will have a share in the joke too, because they take singing with us!'

Alicia cheered up considerably after this. She and Betty

tried out the invisible chalk very carefully, and it was a great success.

Betty took a wooden-bottomed chair and rubbed the curious pink chalk all over it. 'Look,' she said, 'it doesn't show at all, Alicia. Can you see anything of it?'

Alicia looked carefully at the chair, tipping it this way and that. 'It's perfect,' she said. 'Not a thing to be seen! Funny how you can rub it on and it seems to disappear, Betty. It really is invisible. Now, you sit down on it and let me see what happens.'

Betty sat down, and remained there for a minute or two. The chalk would not work unless it was slightly warmed. As Betty was sitting solemnly there with Alicia watching her, Gwendoline popped her head in to look for Daphne. She was astonished to see Betty sitting solemnly by herself on a chair, with Alicia a little way off.

'What are you doing?' she asked curiously. 'What's happening?'

'Nothing,' said Alicia. 'Buzz off! Daphne's not here.'

'But what are you *doing*?' persisted Gwendoline, suspecting something, though she didn't know what. 'Why is Betty sitting on that uncomfortable chair in the middle of the room like that?'

'Alicia! Nosey wants you!' suddenly cried a voice, and Jean's head came round the door. 'Hurry! She's in a stew about something. Your maths paper, I should think.'

'Blow!' said Alicia, and shot off. 'Be back in a minute, Betty,' she said, and ran down the passage. Jean looked with interest at Betty sitting all alone in the middle of the common-room.

'Tired?' she asked. Betty scowled. She felt foolish. She wanted to hurl a book at Gwendoline's silly golden head, but she didn't dare to get up in case she had a nice

chalky pattern on her back.   She didn't want to let anyone
else into the trick at the moment.

'Paralysed or something, poor thing,' said Gwendoline.
'Can't get up.   Or perhaps it's rheumatism!'

To Betty's great relief Gwendoline became tired of teasing
her and went out to find Daphne.   Jean gave a grin and
left too.   Betty got up and looked round at herself.   She
gave a chuckle of delight.   She had a brilliant pink pattern
on the skirt of her tunic.   How extraordinary that the
invisible chalk should act like that when it was warmed up!

Alicia came flying in.   'Does it work?' she cried, and
giggled when Betty swung round and showed her the bright
pink marks.   'Golly, it's fine!   We'll try it on old Mr.
Young tomorrow!'

'Shall we tell anyone?' asked Betty.

'Not a soul,' said Alicia.   'Someone's sure to give it
away by giggling if we do.   No—we'll let dear Mr. Young
spring this surprise himself on an astonished audience!'

Neither Betty nor Alicia did much prep that night.
Potty, who was taking prep, looked with suspicion at the
two plotters and wondered what was up.   It was obvious
that their thoughts were pleasantly and humorously engaged
far elsewhere.

Potty knew the signs.   She warned Miss Parker.   'Those
two in your form, Alicia and Betty, are up to something,
Miss Parker.   Look out tomorrow.   You'll have an un-
accountable smell, or a curious noise, or an orgy of book-
dropping or something.'

'Thanks,' said Miss Parker, grimly.   'I'll watch out.'

But she could see nothing out of the way in her first
lesson, or in her second one either.   The girls worked
much as usual.   Only Alicia and Betty seemed restless.
But then they often were, especially Alicia, whose quick
mind often chafed at the slower rate of the others.

The lesson before Break was singing.   Just before the

second lesson was finished Betty put up her hand. 'Please, Miss Parker, it's my turn to get things ready for Mr. Young in the singing-room. May I go?'

Miss Parker glanced at the clock. 'Yes. You have about four minutes.'

Betty flashed a quick grin at Alicia and went demurely to the door. Once outside she raced down the corridor and made her way to the singing-room. No one was there. Mr. Young was always a minute or two late, thank goodness!

Betty flew to the piano stool. It was the round leather-topped kind, that could be screwed round and round. Betty took out her piece of pink chalk and rubbed it vigorously all over the top of the round stool.

She was sure there was not a single spot unchalked, though, of course, she could not see anything of what she had done at all. It certainly was invisible chalk!

Then she quickly sent the stool spinning round till it was too low for Mr. Young. If ever it was too low or too high he had a little habit of sitting on the stool and going round and round with it till it had reached the height he liked. If only he did that today it would give the chalk a wonderful chance of getting properly on to him!

Betty stacked the music ready and cleaned the blackboard. Then there came the sound of feet and the first form marched into the room under the sharp eye of Miss Potts.

Then came the second form. Alicia's eyes were bright. Betty grinned at her and winked. Then she went to hold the door for the two mistresses to go out and for Mr. Young to come in.

In he trotted, a dapper little man in a well-brushed black suit and a too-high collar. He smoothed his pointed moustache and bowed politely to the girls.

'Good morning, young ladies.'

'Good morning, Mr. Young,' they chorused, and rustled

their song-sheets. The lesson began. Mr. Young took some blackboard drill for five minutes, explaining various notes and signs. Then he went to the piano.

Betty nudged Alicia and held her breath. But, most annoyingly, Mr. Young did not sit down. He struck a few notes with one hand, standing facing the girls as he did so, his baton raised.

'Exercises, please,' he said. 'I wish to see your mouths well open, and to hear the sound coming from the Back of the Throat.'

Mr. Young set great store on the 'Back of the Throat'. It was always coming into everything, exercises, songs and sight-reading. 'Back of the Throat' was his one unfailing motto.

Now he stood, instead of sitting, and conducted the exercises. Alicia was in agonies of disappointment. Suppose he didn't sit down at all? Probably the next person then to sit down would be the accompanist of the mistress who taught dancing—and she always wore a brightly coloured frock so that the chalk wouldn't show at all! What a waste!

But Mr. Young did sit down eventually, of course. He had a new song to teach to the girls, and, as always, he wanted to play the whole thing through two or three times before he taught it, so that the girls could catch the lilt and swing and tune of it.

So down he sat. Aha! That stool was once more too low! Mr. Young twirled himself vigorously round on it till it was the right height. The girls giggled. Mr. Young could never realize how funny he was, twirling round lightly on that little stool.

'Now I will play you your new song,' said Mr. Young. 'You may sit to listen to it. You will hear when the chorus comes, for I will sing it to you.'

Off he started, tumty-tum-ti-tum, his hands flying up

and down, and then his voice booming out at the chorus.
Alicia and Betty winked at one another. The chalk ought
to be working now!

Three times Mr. Young played the song and then he got
up. 'Did you like it?' he asked, and the girls chorused
loudly. 'Oh, *yes*, Mr. Young!'

Mr. Young turned towards the blackboard and picked
up a piece of white chalk. At once the girls saw that he
was smeared with the brightest imaginable pink at the back!
They stared in delight.

'Look at Mr. Young! What's he rubbed against? Oh,
do look!'

Soon the class was in a state of giggle and Mr. Young
glared round.

'Silence, please! What behaviour is this today?'

There was a momentary silence, but as soon as the
unfortunate singing-master turned back to the board again
more giggles broke out. Then Irene gave one of her
terrific explosions.

Mr. Young flung the chalk down on the floor. He
looked as if he was about to stamp on it, and probably
he would have done so if the door hadn't suddenly opened,
and Miss Grayling appeared. She had someone with
her.

'Oh, excuse me for interrupting your class, Mr. Young,'
she said. 'But could you just have a word with Mr.
Lemming about the piano here?'

Mr. Young had to swallow his annoyance and explain
what was wrong with the piano. In doing so he turned
his back to Miss Grayling who eyed his patch of brilliant
pink with the utmost astonishment. The girls were as
quiet as mice now, and Alicia and Betty felt distinctly
anxious.

Miss Grayling turned to Sally, the head of the second
form. 'Will you go to the hall and fetch the clothes brush

there ? ' she said.   'Poor Mr. Young has brushed against something.'

Sally flew off and fetched the brush.   Mr. Young was surprised to hear Miss Grayling's remark.   He looked over his shoulder trying to see himself.

'Is it paint ? ' he asked in alarm.   'I do hope not ! Oh—only chalk !   How in the world did it get there ? '

7   'OY!'

SOON the offending pink chalk had been vigorously brushed away by Mr. Lemming, who then proceeded to sit down on the piano stool himself to try out some of the bass notes, which had gone wrong.   Alicia and Betty watched breathlessly.   Most of the girls, guessing that some trick was being played, watched eagerly too.

They were well rewarded when Mr. Lemming rose from the stool.   He was wearing a long black overcoat and on it was a wonderful pattern of bright pink.   Mr. Young stared at it in amazement.

'Ah, you have it too ! ' he cried.   'See, Miss Grayling, Mr. Lemming has brushed up against something also.   I will soon put him right.'

In spite of being under Miss Grayling's eye the girls began to giggle.   Miss Grayling looked very puzzled.

'Your coat was quite all right when we came along here,' she said to Mr. Lemming.   'I am sure I should have noticed it if you had brushed against anything so violently pink as this.   In any case there is no wall as pink as this chalk !   Whatever can have happened ? '

She walked to the stool and looked at it very closely. Alicia and Betty hardly dared to breathe. But the invisible chalk lived up to its name and Miss Grayling did not see a sign of it. It did not occur to her to sit down and see if the same thing happened to her. Still feeling puzzled she took Mr. Lemming out of the room, and the lesson proceeded again.

Not until the end of it did poor Mr. Young sit down on that stool again. When he got up, behold! He was as pretty a sight as before, and the girls stuffed their hankies into their mouths trying not to explode with mirth. Mr. Young noticed nothing this time. He walked pompously to the door and gave the girls the quick little bow he always kept for them.

'Good morning, young ladies!' And out he went, showing his patch of brilliant colour. As he went the bell for Break rang, and the girls tore into the Court, longing to give way to their pent-up laughter.

'Alicia! You had something to do with it! *What* was it?'

'Oh, it was marvellous! When he turned round to the blackboard I thought I should die!'

'Betty! Do tell! Was it your trick? How did you do it? I looked at the stool and there wasn't a thing to be seen!'

'That reminds me,' said Betty to Alicia with a grin. 'I must get a wet cloth and rub it over the stool.' She disappeared, and the girls surged round Alicia, begging her to tell them the secret.

Meanwhile Mr. Young was walking down one of the long corridors, quite unaware of his beautiful decoration. Mam'zelle Dupont happened to come out of a room just behind him, and stared disbelievingly at the extraordinary sight. She raced after him.

'Monsieur Young! Ha, Monsieur Young!'

' The chalk ought to be working now! '

Mr. Young was scared of both Mam'zelles. He hastened his steps. Mam'zelle ran more quickly.

'Monsieur, Monsieur, attendez, je vous prie! Wait, wait. You cannot go out like that! It is terrible!'

Mr. Young swung round, annoyed. 'What is it? What's terrible?'

'This! This!' said Mam'zelle, and tapped him smartly on the chalk. A cloud of it flew off at once. Mr. Young was horrified at being tapped so familiarly by Mam'zelle and amazed at the cloud of chalk that flew from his person. He wriggled himself round to try and see it, remembering what Mr. Lemming's coat had been like.

' I will attend to you,' said Mam'zelle, out of the kindness of her heart, and caught hold of his arm. She hurried him to a hall-stand, took up a brush there, and with extremely vigorous strokes she removed the chalk from his clothes.

He was angry and not at all grateful. 'Twice it has happened this morning,' he said angrily to Mam'zelle and actually shook his fist in her face as if she was the culprit. She backed away, alarmed. Mr. Young snatched up his hat and went off, muttering to himself.

'He is not polite, that man,' said Mam'zelle to herself. ' I do him a kindness, and he puts his fist into my face. I will never speak to him again.'

The only girl who had seen this episode in the hall was Darrell, and she hurried to the others with the tit-bit. ' I was going past the end of the hall and I saw Mam'zelle banging at Mr. Young for all she was worth with the clothes brush,' she panted. 'He was so angry! Oh, do let's do it again, Alicia. It's a gorgeous trick!'

It is always a mistake to play the same trick twice running, and Alicia knew it. But she could not resist the temptation to try it on Mam'zelle Dupont.

'Shall we?' she asked Betty, and Betty nodded in glee. The girls crowded round to see the queer invisible chalk.

They chuckled and laughed when they thought of the singing-lesson, and they let the first-formers into the secret too.

Altogether the trick cheered up everyone considerably, and the thought that they would play it once more gave them something to look forward to.

'Who can rub it on the mistress's chair before the French lesson this afternoon?' demanded Betty. 'Alicia and I can't. We've no chance of being in the room. Who is room monitor?'

'I am,' said Darrell. 'I'll do it! Give me the chalk! What do you do? Just rub it over the chair?'

Ten minutes before afternoon school Darrell slipped into the second-form classroom. It was her job that week to tidy the bookshelves, clean the blackboard and see that the chalk was handy and the duster there.

It took her only a minute to do these things. Then she went to the chair that stood behind the desk and took the chalk from her pocket. She was about to rub it over the seat of the chair when a mischievous idea struck her.

Couldn't she write something short so that a word would appear on Mam'zelle's skirt, and send everyone into fits? It would have to be a short word.

'I'll write " OY ! " ' said Darrell to herself, in glee. 'I'll have to write it backwards, so that it will come off on Mam'zelle the right way round.'

So, very painstakingly she rubbed the chalk on the seat of the chair in the form of the two letters O and Y. Oy! Fancy going about with that written on you! How all the girls would yell.

The bell went for lessons. Darrell slipped the chalk into her pocket and went to her place. She giggled when the rest of the form came in.

'Did you do it? Did you have time?' whispered

the girls. Darrell nodded. Then in came Mam'zelle, appearing to be in quite a good temper, and the door was shut.

Mam'zelle sat down at once. She had very tiny feet and did not like standing. The girls watched eagerly. When would she stand up ? Darrell could hardly wait for her to turn her back to the class. What would they say when they saw what she had written on the chair !

Jean was called to the blackboard to write something. ' Do it all wrong ! ' hissed Darrell. ' Then Mam'zelle will get up to correct it.'

So, much to Mam'zelle's surprise, the usually careful Jean made ridiculous mistakes in the French words she wrote down, and appeared to be quite unable to put them right, despite Mam'zelle's exasperated instructions. At last, thoroughly annoyed, she dismissed Jean to her seat, and got up to put the mistakes right herself.

The class saw her back view at once, and gasped. Written across her tight-fitting skirt in bright pink letters was the word ' OY ! ' Even Darrell was surprised to see it so clearly, and suddenly felt very uncomfortable. It was one thing to make a patch of pink appear on somebody's clothes —it could easily be explained away—but how could the word ' OY ! ' be explained ? It was quite impossible.

The class gaped at Mam'zelle's back view. They were absolutely taken aback. They didn't know whether to giggle or to be alarmed.

' Darrell ! You idiot ! Suppose she goes walking up the corridor in front of all the other mistresses with that written on her skirt ! ' hissed Alicia. ' Really, you might have more sense.'

The thought of the other mistresses seeing Mam'zelle's ' OY ! ' really alarmed the form. Miss Parker would certainly not approve. She would consider it most disrespectful.

But how to get it off ? That dreadful pink ' OY ! ' flashed

back and forth as Mam'zelle wrote on the board, turned
to the class to explain, and wrote again.

' I'll tell Mam'zelle she's got some dust or something **on**
her skirt and I'll brush it off,' promised Darrell, in a whisper.
' At the end of the lesson.'

But she had no chance to, for Mam'zelle walked off in
a hurry, remembering that she was late for the first form,
next door. And the first-formers had the surprise of their
lives when they saw Mam'zelle's pink ' OY ! ' flashing at
them every other minute !

They couldn't keep back their giggles and Mam'zelle
grew more and more furious. ' What is there so funny
about me this afternoon ? ' she demanded. ' Is my hair
untidy ? Is my face black ? Are my shoes not a pair ? '

' No, Mam'zelle,' said the first form, almost helpless with
trying to stop their laughter.

' I am not funny and I do not feel funny,' said Mam'zelle,
severely. ' But I shall soon do some funny things. Ah,
yes ! I shall soon say " One hundred lines of French
poetry from you, please, and from you and you ! " Aha !
I shall soon be very funny ! '

With that she swung round to the blackboard and the
' OY ! ' flashed again. The first form clutched one another
in agonies of suppressed laughter.

But all the same they had the sense to grab Mam'zelle
before she went out of the room. ' We'll have to get that
off her before she goes,' said Hilda. ' Or else the second-
formers will get into awful trouble. I expect they meant
to brush it off somehow and didn't have the chance.'

So, before Mam'zelle left the first-form room, Hilda
politely offered to brush down her skirt, as it was all dusty
with chalk.

' Tiens ! ' said Mam'zelle, looking down at it. ' This
blackboard chalk ! It is not good for dresses. Thank you,
Hilda, *vous êtes gentille !* You are kind.'

She stood like a lamb whilst Hilda assiduously brushed her skirt back and front, and got rid of the pink ' OY ! ' Then she walked out of the room. The second-formers, who had finished their lesson, were watching for her, hoping to brush her down themselves before she went off to the little room she shared with Miss Potts.

With great relief they saw that Mam'zelle's skirt was now spotless. They went back into their form-room and sank down into their chairs.

' Thank goodness ! ' said Alicia. ' We might have got into a first-class row over that. Potty or Nosey would certainly have reported it if they'd seen that " OY ! " You know how annoyed the mistresses get if they think we've been really disrespectful, Darrell. You were an idiot. I suppose Sally put you up to it. Fine head of form she is ! '

' Shut up ! ' said Darrell, annoyed with herself and everyone else too. ' Sally had nothing to do with it. I just didn't think, that's all ! '

8   THE TERM GOES ON

THE affair of the invisible chalk was talked about for days afterwards. Some of the upper school got to hear about it, and secretly wished they too could have seen Mam'zelle's ' Oy ! ' Those in the know grinned at Darrell when they met her, and whispered ' Oy ! ' into her ear !

It seemed as if everyone thought that the whole idea was Darrell's, and Alicia and Betty were annoyed about it. Why should Darrell get all the credit, when all she had done was to make that word appear on Mam'zelle's skirt, and risk getting the whole of the form into very serious trouble ?

The two of them cold-shouldered Darrell, and Darrell retaliated by ignoring them as much as she could. She knew that Alicia was still sore about not being head-girl, and was not being nice to Sally. Darrell was loyal, and she was not going to have that if she could help it !

Alicia's tongue grew wild and sharp again. Darrell, knowing that Alicia was trying to make her lose her temper, grew red with suppressed rage, but said nothing. She mustn't lose her temper, she mustn't ! If she did she would begin to shout, she might even throw something at Alicia—and then she would put herself in the wrong immediately. So she looked as if she was going to burst, but didn't.

And it was very bad for her. Sally tried to calm her down, but that made Darrell worse.

' Don't you see that it's because you're my friend that I get so wild with Alicia ? ' Darrell would say. ' She could say all she liked about me, I wouldn't care—but it's hard to sit and listen to things about *you*, Sally. All because she's jealous. She just says them because she knows I've got a temper and want to stick up for you.'

' Well, for goodness' sake don't go and fall into her trap,' said the sensible Sally. ' That would be idiotic. She and Betty would have the laugh over you easily.'

So poor Darrell had to grit her teeth and say nothing when Alicia and Betty had one of their cross-talk conversations to bait her.

' *Dear* Sally ! ' Alicia would say. ' Always so good— and yet so dull. The Perfect Head-Girl. Don't you think so, Betty ? '

' Oh, I do so agree with you,' Betty would say, with a smile that infuriated Darrell. ' Think what a good example she is to us all—dear, conscientious Sally. Really, I feel overcome with shame at my faults when I see Sally sitting so prim and good in class. Not a joke, not a smile. *Such* a model for all of us!'

'What *should* we do without her?' Alicia would go on, glancing slyly at Darrell to see if she was at bursting-point yet. If Darrell got up and went away, the two counted it as a victory for them—but poor Darrell knew quite well that if she stayed much longer, her mouth would open and she would say things she would regret bitterly afterwards.

So Darrell's temper was not too good those days. And there was someone else whose temper was not good either. And that was Ellen's.

She had been quite even-tempered, though rather worried-looking for the first few weeks. And then suddenly she became really irritable. She snapped at the girls, and the little cleft in her forehead deepened until it seemed as if she was always frowning.

Jean tried to find out if anything was the matter. Sally had tried, but Ellen seemed to think that Sally was just being a good head-girl, trying to set her right and stop her being so irritable. So she snapped at Sally, and the head-girl, surprised and hurt, said no more.

'Funny girl!' she said to Darrell. 'I don't understand her. She's won a scholarship to Malory Towers which must mean she's terribly clever—and she works as hard or harder than any of us do—and yet she's never top, or even in the first three or four! I suppose she's cross about that and gets bad-tempered. I don't like her.'

'Neither do I,' said Darrell. 'She's not worth bothering about, Sally. Leave her alone.'

'Oh, I think she's worth bothering about,' said Sally. 'Everybody is. I'll ask Jean to have a word with her. She sits next to her in class.'

Jean was a very forthright girl, with little imagination, and usually went at things in the way a tank might, crushing all resistance, insisting on knowing what she wanted to know. But for some reason she did not tackle Ellen quite in this way. She sat next to her in class and she slept next to her in the dormy—so she had had plenty of opportunity of hearing Ellen's unconscious sighs and little groans when she was hard at work—or when she was trying to go to sleep!

She knew that Ellen often lay awake at night, and she guessed that Ellen was worrying about something. It couldn't be her work, surely—no scholarship girl needed to worry about work! As far as she had seen, all scholarship girls found work very easy indeed.

Jean was a kindly girl, though sometimes much too blunt in her speech and ways. She tried to think how to get at Ellen. There didn't seem any way except by asking her straight out what was the matter, and couldn't it be put right ?

But that just wouldn't do. Ellen would snap at once, as she did to Sally. So, for once, Jean gave the matter some thought, and did not act as clumsily as she usually did.

Ellen had no friend. She did not encourage anyone at all, not even the quiet Emily. Jean set herself out to be friendly in unobtrusive ways. She would never be able to force out of Ellen what was the matter—but perhaps she could persuade the girl to trust her enough to want to tell her! This was really a very praiseworthy idea on Jean's part, for it was seldom that the blunt Scots girl bothered herself to go to a lot of trouble in her dealings with people.

But she was rather proud that Sally had asked her to try her hand at Ellen, as she herself had failed. So, although Ellen did not realize it at the time, Jean set herself out to be kind and helpful in all kinds of little ways.

She helped Ellen to hunt for ages for her gym shoes which were lost. She sympathized when the photograph

of Ellen's parents got broken, and offered to get some glass
cut for the frame, when next she went to the shops.   She
helped her to dry her hair when she washed it.   Just little
things that nobody, not even Ellen at first, noticed very
much.

But gradually Ellen grew to trust this shrewd Scots girl.
She told her when she had a very bad headache, although
she refused to go to Matron and tell her too.   She stopped
snapping at Jean, though she still snapped at everyone else
—except Mary-Lou.   It would need a very hard-hearted,
bad-tempered person to snap at little Mary-Lou !

There were some evenings when Ellen was quite unbearable.   ' Really, anyone would think she suffered from what
my mother calls " Nerves ",' said Alicia, one evening.
' Jumps at any little thing, takes things the wrong way,
snaps like a bad dog—look at her now, scowling at her
work-basket as if it had bitten her ! '

If anyone passed too close to Ellen and knocked her
elbow, she would jump and snap ' Look out !   Can't you
see where you're going ? '

If anyone interrupted her reading, she would slam her
book down on the table and glare at the offender.   ' Can't
you see I'm reading ?   There isn't a quiet place in the
whole of this beastly house ! '

' You're not reading,' Darrell would say.   ' You haven't
turned a page since you took up your book ! '

' Oh—so you've been watching me, have you ? ' Ellen
would say, and her eyes would suddenly fill with tears.
Then she would go out of the room and slam the door.

' Isn't she awful !   Scratches like a cat ! '

' I wish she'd won a scholarship to somewhere else ! '

' Always pretending to read and study and yet she slides
down lower every week !   Hypocrite, I call her ! '

' Och, she's not a happy girl !   Maybe she hasn't settled
down here yet ! '   That was Jean, of course, and Sally

would flash her a glance of approval. Jean certainly had an uphill task with Ellen, but she was persevering with it !

The weather was bad just then, and there was no lacrosse, and not even a walk, for the country round about was deep in mud. The girls grew restless, penned up indoors, and the teachers decided that, bad weather or not, there had better be a School Walk the next day.

Everyone groaned. The rain poured down. The sky was black and lowering. The lacrosse fields were half under water. Whatever would the country lanes be like ? The sea was an angry grey-green, and the wind was so high on the cliff that no girl was allowed up there in case she was blown over.

Gwendoline and Daphne grumbled the loudest of all. Gwendoline developed a persistent sniff in class, hoping that Miss Parker would think she had a cold and let her off the walk. But Miss Parker had been warned by Potty of Gwendoline's sniffs, and was not sympathetic.

' If you sniff any more, you can go and do it outside the door,' she said. ' If there's one thing I cannot bear, it's somebody sniffing. It's disgusting, it's unnecessary, and in your case, it is probably put on, Gwendoline.'

Gwendoline glared. Why were there no school teachers like her old governess at home, Miss Winter ? She always rushed for a thermometer at once, if Gwendoline so much as cleared her throat, and would never, never dream of making her go out for a walk in such terrible weather !

She did not dare to sniff again, and was annoyed at Darrell's grins. Daphne looked at her sympathetically. Not that she cared whether Gwendoline had a cold or not, but it was the thing to do—Gwendoline simply lapped up sympathy.

Daphne herself tried other tactics to get out of the walk. She had no intention at all of wading through miles of mud. She went to Mam'zelle Dupont with her exercise book that evening. She put on her sweetest smile and knocked at the door of the little room which Miss Potts shared with Mam'zelle. She hoped fervently that Potty wasn't there. Potty always seemed to be irritated by Daphne's presence.

Fortunately Potty wasn't there. ' Ah, it is you, *ma petite* Daphne ! ' cried Mam'zelle, welcoming her favourite with a smile almost as charming as Daphne's. ' You have something to say to me ? You do not understand something, is it not ? '

' Oh, Mam'zelle, I'm in such a muddle over these tenses,' said Daphne. ' I really do feel that I ought to have a little extra coaching in them, if you could possibly spare the time. I do so badly want to get my French better.'

' But it has been much better lately, my dear child ! ' cried Mam'zelle, beaming, not knowing that little Mary-Lou had been doing most of Daphne's French for her. ' I am pleased with you.'

Daphne turned on her smile again and Mam'zelle's heart melted still further. Ah, this pretty Daphne ! She put her arm round her. ' Yes, yes, of course I will give you a little extra coaching,' she said. ' We shall soon put these tenses right. You can stay now, *ma petite* ? '

' No, not now, Mam'zelle,' said Daphne. ' But I could give up that lovely country walk tomorrow, if you would be good enough to take me then. It's the only spare time I have.'

' The good child—to give up the walk that you English girls so dearly love ! ' cried Mam'zelle, who thought that all walks were an extremely silly invention. ' Yes, I can take you then. I will tell Miss Parker. You are a good girl, Daphne. I am pleased with you ! '

' Thank you, Mam'zelle,' said Daphne, delighted, and gave Mam'zelle a ravishing smile as she went triumphantly out of the room.

MISS PARKER was surprised and annoyed when she heard that Daphne was not to go with the class on their long walk. She looked crossly at Mam'zelle.

'But why this sudden desire for French on Daphne's part?' she said. 'She's just the type of girl that needs a jolly good long walk—yes, and a muddy one too. Shake some of her airs and graces off her! Give her the extra lesson another time, Mam'zelle.'

But Mam'zelle was obstinate. She did not like Miss Parker, with her big nose. She pursed up her small mouth and shook her head. 'I cannot take Daphne any other time. It is good of the girl to give up a nice walk to improve her French.'

Miss Parker made a disbelieving noise that irritated Mam'zelle at once. 'She wants to get out of the walk, you know that perfectly well, Mam'zelle. It's foolish to give her her way like that! Daphne gets her way too easily, and I don't like some of her methods. Too underhand for me!'

Mam'zelle stood up for her favourite, and began to exaggerate. 'Miss Parker! If you knew how much that girl wanted to go for her walk! Ah, to splash through the autumn lanes! Ah, to sniff the sea air after being cooped up so long! Daphne has sacrificed her pleasure, and she should be praised for that, not blamed. She will be hard at work with me whilst you are all enjoying yourselves out in the lovely air.'

'Well, she wouldn't take Mam'zelle Rougier in quite so easily as she takes *you*,' said Miss Parker, beginning to lose her temper. '*She* sees through her all right!'

Mam'zelle began to bristle. ' I will have a word with Mam'zelle Rougier,' she began. ' I will have two, three, four words. She shall not say things about Daphne, who is getting so much better at French ! '

' Let's drop the subject,' said Miss Parker, feeling heartily tired of Daphne. ' Go and have it out with Mam'zelle Rougier if you like. I don't care ! Except that I feel Daphne has got the better of us, I'm glad not to have her with us on the walk, moaning and groaning, dragging her feet along ! '

Daphne could not resist telling everyone of the way she had managed to get out of the walk. Gwendoline wished she had been sharp enough to do the same. The others were frankly disgusted with the hypocritical little trick.

' Fancy doing all that just to get out of going for a walk ! ' said Darrell. ' It'll be fun, splashing through the puddles in our Wellingtons. Well—if you *want* to spend the afternoon doing French verbs, good luck to you ! That's just like you, somehow, Daphne.'

But, the walk didn't come off after all ! The wind blew itself into a gale, and Miss Parker decided that it must be put off. The girls were just putting on their macs and Wellingtons when she came to the cloakroom to tell them. Daphne had already taken her French book to Mam'zelle.

' Girls ! I'm sorry ! But the wind has become a perfect gale ! ' said Miss Parker, appearing suddenly in the cloakroom. ' The walk is off. But to make up, we'll all go into the gym and have an afternoon of riotous games, shall we ? And I'll get Matron to let us have a picnic tea in there, to make a change, if some of you will carry in the stuff.'

The girls cheered. An afternoon of jolly games—racing round, competing with one another, laughing, yelling—and ending up with a picnic tea on the floor. That certainly would be a change !

Matron came up to scratch too—she provided four super chocolate cakes for a treat, as well as two pots of golden honey. The girls were thrilled.

'What about Daphne, Miss Parker?' said Mary-Lou, remembering that Daphne was with Mam'zelle. 'Shall I go and fetch her?'

'Idiot!' said Alicia, under her breath. 'Fancy reminding Miss Parker of Daphne! Serve her right to miss all this! I'll tell Mary-Lou what I think of her in a minute!'

Miss Parker looked down at Mary-Lou's anxious face, and wondered for the twentieth time why Mary-Lou bothered about Daphne when she had Darrell and Sally for friends.

'Oh, Mary-Lou, no, you mustn't disturb Daphne!' said Miss Parker, clearly, so that all the listening girls heard quite well. 'She badly wanted to have this extra coaching, Mam'zelle tells me, and was quite willing to forgo the walk. She would be willing to forgo the games and picnic too, I am sure. We mustn't disturb her. When a girl shows herself to be as studious as that it would be a pity to spoil it all.'

Mary-Lou was the only one who did not see the sly humour of Miss Parker's words. The others did immediately, and a roar of laughter broke out. Miss Parker smiled too.

'Sucks for Daphne!' said Alicia. 'Serves her jolly well right!'

They had a gay and riotous afternoon, and got thoroughly tired and dusty. Then they sat down to an enormous tea, demolishing bread and butter and honey and the four chocolate cakes in no time.

Daphne appeared just as the last piece of cake was eaten. She had had an extremely boring afternoon, for Mam'zelle Dupont had taken her at her word and had given her some very, very thorough coaching in the French verbs. She had made poor Daphne repeat them after her scores of times, she had corrected her pronunciation conscientiously, she had even made her write them out.

Daphne wished heartily she had never suggested such a thing. She had thought that she would have had a nice cosy time with Mam'zelle, talking about herself. But although Mam'zelle was fond of Daphne and quite taken in by her, she was determined to do her duty as regards coaching the girl. So she kept poor Daphne's nose to the grindstone, and when Daphne faintly protested, saying that she thought she had bothered Mam'zelle enough and the girls would be back from their walk now, surely, Mam'zelle pooh-poohed the idea at once.

'We shall hear the girls come back,' she said, not knowing that they had never gone out. 'As soon as we hear them, you shall go down to join them, *ma petite*, and you will enjoy your tea, I am sure. A good conscience makes us enjoy our food well.'

When Mam'zelle, puzzled by the non-appearance of the girls back from their walk, sent Daphne down to see what had happened, the girl could have burst into tears when she saw the empty plates, the cake all gone, and the happy faces of the second-formers in the gym.

'You mean pigs!' she cried. 'You didn't go out after all! And you've had tea without me!'

'We couldn't disturb you at your extra French lesson,' grinned Alicia. 'Dear Miss Parker quite agreed it would be a pity to spoil it for you, as you were so anxious to have it.'

Daphne glared at Gwendoline. '*You* might have come for me,' she said. 'You could easily have slipped off and fetched me!'

'The only person who tried to get you was Mary-Lou,' said Sally. 'She actually went up to Miss Parker and suggested that she should go and get you. Mary-Lou doesn't think that extra French is preferable to walks or games.'

Daphne looked at Mary-Lou and felt warm towards her. Not even Gwendoline, her friend, had tried to get her out of that awful French lesson to join the games. But Mary-Lou had. Mary-Lou had thought loyally of her.

'Thanks, Mary-Lou,' said Daphne, and turned a rather watery smile on her. 'I won't forget that. That was decent of you.'

From that time the selfish, boastful, untrustworthy Daphne was nice to Mary-Lou, not only because the smaller girl helped her so much with her French but because she really liked her and admired her. Perhaps never before had Daphne really liked anyone for themselves.

Mary-Lou, of course, was delighted. She had quite fallen under Daphne's spell, and was too simple to see the faults in the girl's character. She was very happy to be with her, and delighted to help her whenever she could. She did not even see that the help she gave almost amounted to making Daphne cheat, for many an evening she did practically the whole of Daphne's prep for her.

Gwendoline began to be jealous of Mary-Lou, for she sensed that Daphne was really beginning to like her very much. But Daphne always laughed when Gwendoline spoke to her about it.

'You *know* I'm only using her!' she said. 'Don't be a mutt, Gwen. You're my friend and I don't want anybody else. I've nothing whatever in common with Mary-Lou—— She's a silly little simpleton, a stupid little mouse!'

It was a good thing that Mary-Lou did not hear these remarks, for she would have been shocked and hurt. She was very glad to feel that Daphne really did like her. She often lay in bed thinking of the girl's beautiful hair and lovely smile. She wished she was as charming as that. But she wasn't, and never would be.

Daphne did not forgive the others for being mean enough not to warn her, when they knew the walk was off. She was even a little cold to Gwendoline about it, and Gwendoline, fearful of losing her grand friend's liking, made haste to lick her boots again, listening to all Daphne's tales with most satisfactory attention.

Sally heard Daphne one evening. She was sitting near the curtain in the common-room and the two girls, Gwen and Daphne, did not see her.

' Didn't I ever tell you about the time my mother gave a party on board our yacht, and I sat next to the Prince at supper ? ' began Daphne.

' Were you allowed to sit up to supper ? ' said Gwendoline. ' And whatever did you find to say to a prince ? '

' Oh, well—he seemed to admire my hair and talked to me awfully nicely,' said Daphne, beginning to embroider her tale as usual. ' I stayed up till one o'clock that night. The yacht was lovely. It had little lights all over it, and people on land said it looked beautiful—like a ship in a fairy-tale.'

' What were you dressed in ? ' asked Gwendoline.

' Oh—a frilly frock with little pearls all over it and my pearl necklace. It's worth hundreds of pounds,' said Daphne.

Gwendoline gasped. ' Where is it ? ' she said.

' Oh, I'm not allowed to bring anything like that to school,' said Daphne. ' Mother's very strict about things of that sort, you know. I haven't any jewellery here—or grand dresses—or anything you haven't got.'

' No. I've noticed that—I think it's very sensible of your mother,' said Gwendoline.

Sally had got tired of all this grand talk. She slipped off the window-sill. ' It's a pity your mother didn't supply you with your own lacrosse stick, and another pair of shoes, and plenty of writing-paper,' she remarked. ' Then you wouldn't have to keep borrowing from everyone else! A little less yacht, and fewer cars—and more envelopes and a book of stamps would be better for you, Daphne!'

Daphne looked haughtily at Sally. 'Mind your own business!' she said. 'I was talking to Gwen.'

'It *is* my business!' persisted Sally. 'You are always borrowing from one or other of us—and you never pay back! As you're so rich, you ought to use some of your plentiful pocket-money to buy the things you lack!'

'Beast!' said Daphne, as Sally went out of the room. 'She's jealous of me, I suppose—just because *her* people aren't as well-off as mine!'

10 THE TWO MAM'ZELLES

HALF-TERM came and went. Sally and Darrell went out together with Darrell's parents and had a lovely time. To Gwendoline's disappointment Daphne's parents did not visit her, so there was no chance of being asked out to meals with Daphne, or going off in a magnificent car.

'I wanted to see your mother,' said Gwendoline. 'She looks so lovely in her photo.'

On Daphne's dressing-table stood a photograph of a very beautiful woman, in a flowing evening gown, with gleaming jewels round her lovely neck. Everyone had admired it.

'You aren't much like your mother, all the same,' said Darrell, critically, to Daphne. 'She's got wide-set eyes—and yours are rather near together. And your nose isn't the same.'

'Everybody isn't always like their mother,' said Daphne. 'I take after my father's family, I suppose. I have an aunt who is very, very beautiful.'

'And I suppose you are considered to resemble her, Daphne?' said Jean, in her quiet, amused voice. 'What it is to have beautiful and distinguished relatives! I have a plain mother, who's the kindest darling on earth—and quite an ugly father—and all my aunts are as plain as I am! But I don't care a bit. They're jolly good fun, and I like the whole lot.'

Gwendoline asked Daphne if she would like to go out with her at half-term, and Daphne accepted graciously. Mrs. Lacey, Gwendoline's mother, was very struck with the beautiful girl and her charming smile. As for Miss Winter, the governess, who always most faithfully came to see her darling Gwen every half-term, she could hardly take her eyes off her, which annoyed Gwendoline very much.

'*Such* a nice friend for you, dear,' said Mrs. Lacey to Gwendoline. 'Such beautiful manners! And how rich her people must be to own a yacht and all those cars. Wouldn't it be nice if you could go and stay with them?'

'Ssh, Mother,' said Gwendoline, afraid that Daphne would hear. But Daphne was far too busy charming poor Miss Winter. She played up to Gwendoline very well too, remarking on her friend's brilliance, her clever comments in class, and what a favourite she was with the teachers.

Mrs. Lacey listened with pride and pleasure. 'Well, you never told me these things in your letters, Gwen darling,' she said, fondly. 'You're too modest!'

Gwendoline felt a little embarrassed and began to hope that Daphne wouldn't lay it on too thickly—if she did, her mother would expect a wonderful report, and Gwendoline knew perfectly well there was no hope of that.

Belinda and Irene went out together, both forgetting their hats, and both returning without their gloves. They went with Belinda's parents, who appeared to be as bad as Belinda herself, for they lost the way when bringing the girls back to Malory Towers, and turned up over an hour late, much to Miss Parker's annoyance. She could not bear the time-table to be played about with. But neither Belinda nor Irene noticed her cold manner as they went noisily into the room to report their return to her.

Alicia and Betty had gone out together, of course, and had come back full of giggles. Apparently one of Alicia's brothers had been in the party, and had related with much gusto all the tricks that he and his class had been up to that term.

To everyone's surprise Jean had asked the bad-tempered, irritable Ellen to come out with her! Ellen had refused at first, rather ungraciously—and then had unexpectedly said she would. But it had not been a very pleasant outing, for Ellen had been rather silent and had not tried in any way to be pleasant to her hosts. She seemed sunk into herself, and Jean was sorry she had asked her.

'You might have been a bit more cheerful, Ellen,' she said, as they came into the school again. 'You hardly spoke and you didn't laugh once, even when my father made some quite good jokes!'

'Well, don't ask me out again then,' said Ellen, snappily, and turned away. Jean caught the gleam of tears in her eyes. Funny girl! So touchy that nobody could say a word to her without getting their head bitten off! Jean was beginning to be tired of her efforts to be nice to Ellen.

'Now we can look forward to Christmas!' said Darrell, with satisfaction. 'Half-term's over.'

'We've got those awful French plays to mug up now,' groaned Alicia. 'Whatever possessed the two Mam'zelles to think up such a horrible thing for the second form to do? Who wants to see us perform French plays?'

Each form had to produce some sort of entertainment at the end of the term. It was the lot of the second form to learn two French plays, one chosen by Mam'zelle Dupont, the other by Mam'zelle Rougier.

It was over the choosing of the girls to play the different characters in these plays that the two Mam'zelles almost came to blows.

In one play there was a Princess—the Princess True-Heart. In the other there was an angel—the Angel of Goodness. Mam'zelle Dupont wanted her favourite, Daphne, to play both parts. She pictured the pretty, golden-haired girl as the Princess—ah, how wonderful she would look ! And as an angel ! Truly Daphne was made for the part of an angel !

But Mam'zelle Rougier unfortunately had quite different ideas. 'What ! You would choose that imbecile of a Daphne to play two good parts like that ! ' scoffed Mam'zelle Rougier. ' She could never learn half the words—and her pronunciation is AB—OM—IN—ABLE ! You know it. I will not have that girl in a good part.'

' Ah, but she will look the parts to perfection ! ' cried Mam'zelle Dupont, sweeping her arms wide part to emphasize her words. ' She looks a real Princess—and when she smiles, it is truly the smile of an angel.'

' Bah ! ' said Mam'zelle Rougier, rudely. ' She is one of your favourites, your little pets. Now Sally would do well in one of those parts—she would learn well and her pronunciation is good. Or Darrell. Or even Mary-Lou would be better than Daphne, for she at least speaks French as it should be spoken.'

' You are mad ! ' cried Mam'zelle Dupont. ' As if any of those girls could play such parts as these. I insist on Daphne playing the parts.'

' Then I shall not have anything to do with the plays,' said Mam'zelle Rougier, stiffly. ' It is always a mistake to

do as you do, Mamzelle Dupont, and have favourites—and
when it comes to forcing them on me, it is finished ! '

' I do not have favourites ! ' said Mam'zelle Dupont,
untruthfully, tapping her foot on the ground. ' I like all
the girls just the same.'

Mam'zelle Rougier snorted disbelievingly. ' Then you
are the only one who thinks so,' she said. ' Good day,
Mam'zelle. I cannot stand arguing here, talking nonsense
about such girls as Daphne.'

She swung round and walked off stiffly, holding her thin
bony body like a stick. Plump little Mam'zelle Dupont
stared after her angrily. Favourites, indeed ! How dared
Mam'zelle say things like that to her ? Never would she
speak to Mam'zelle Rougier again. Never, never, never !
She would leave Malory Towers. She would go back to
her beloved France. She would write to the newspapers
about it. Mam'zelle Dupont made a noise like the growling
of a dog, and startled Miss Potts considerably as she came
in at the door.

' Don't you feel well, Mam'zelle ? ' she said, rather
alarmed at Mam'zelle's red face and glaring eyes.

' I do not feel at all well. I have been insulted,' said
Mam'zelle Dupont. ' I am not to be allowed to choose the
girls in my own plays. Mam'zelle Rougier objects to my
choosing the pretty, charming Daphne for the Princess.
She will not even allow me—me, Mam'zelle Dupont—to give
her the part of the Angel of Goodness ! '

' Well, I must say I agree with her,' said Miss Potts,
sitting down and arranging her papers. ' Daphne always
seems a double-faced little creature to me.'

' You too are in the plot against me ! ' said Mam'zelle,
going all dramatic, and working herself up into a tearful
rage. ' You too ! Ah, these cold English people ! Ah,
these . . .'

Miss Potts was very glad indeed to hear a knock at the

door at that moment. She didn't like dealing with Mam'-
zelle in these moods. Matron came in, smiling. 'Can I
have a word with you, Mam'zelle ? ' she asked.

'No, you cannot,' said Mam'zelle, fiercely. 'I am
upset. My heart it beats so—and so—and so. But I
tell you this—I will choose what girl I wish for my plays.
Ah-h-h-h ! '

And, making a noise like a dog again, Mam'zelle walked
angrily from the room, leaving Matron quite stupefied.
'Whatever is she talking about ? ' she asked Miss Potts.

'Oh, she's had some sort of upset with the other Mam'-
zelle,' said Miss Potts, beginning to add up marks. 'They
get across one another at times, you know. But this appears
to be more serious than usual. Well, they'll have to sort
out their own tangles ! '

Mam'zelle Dupont and Mam'zelle Rougier took it in
turns to train the girls in the two French plays. Mam'zelle
Dupont put Daphne into the two principal parts each time
she took the play, much to the girl's gratification. But,
equally promptly, Mam'zelle Rougier relegated her to a
minor part the next day and put Sally and Darrell into the
principal ones. It was most muddling.

Neither Mam'zelle would give way. The quarrel
appeared to be deadly and serious. They looked the other
way when they met. They never spoke to one another.
The girls thought it was a great joke, but on the whole they
took Mam'zelle Dupont's part, for they liked her much the
better of the two. They did not approve of her choice of
Daphne for the principal parts, but that couldn't be helped.

Belinda, intrigued by the quarrel, did a masterly set of
caricatures of Mam'zelle Rougier, taller and bonier than
ever. She drew her with a dagger in her hand, stalking
poor Mam'zelle Dupont. She drew her hiding behind a
bush with a gun. She drew her pouring poison into a tea-
cup to present to her enemy.

The girls giggled over the pictures. Alicia was very struck by them. A wicked idea came into her head.

' Belinda ! Mam'zelle Dupont would adore these pictures ! You know what a sense of humour she has. She ought to see them. Put them on her desk tomorrow afternoon, just before she takes French translation—and watch her face when she opens the book ! '

' I bet we shan't have any French translation tomorrow afternoon once she sees the pictures ! ' giggled Betty, and the others agreed.

Belinda bound the pictures neatly into a book. She had put no name to them, but they were so cleverly drawn that anyone could see at once that they were meant to represent the two Mam'zelles. ' I'll pop it on the desk just before the afternoon class, ' she said. ' And you can jolly well all of you do my prep for me tonight, to repay me for getting you off your French translation tomorrow ! '

Alicia whispered something to Betty. Betty looked startled and then grinned broadly. Alicia had just told her something interesting. ' It isn't Mam'zelle Dupont who's taking us tomorrow. It's Mam'zelle Rougier ! Watch out for fireworks ! '

11   A SHOCK FOR THE SECOND FORM

THE book of drawings was placed on the classroom desk in good time. The girls stood in their places, excited, waiting for Mam'zelle to come. How she would roar at the pictures ! How she would enjoy the joke against her enemy, Mam'zelle Rougier !

Alicia was holding the door.   It had been quite by chance
that she had heard that the lesson was to be taken by Mam'-
zelle Rougier instead of Mam'zelle Dupont.   She hugged
herself secretly when she thought of the bombshell she had
prepared.   It would pay back Mam'zelle Rougier for many
a sharp word she had given Alicia !

Quick footsteps came down the passage.   The girls
stiffened.   Somebody came in at the door and went to the
desk—but it wasn't the Mam'zelle they had been expecting.
It was, of course, the other one.   Mam'zelle Rougier seated
herself and addressed the class.

'Asseyez vous, s'il vous plait ! '

Some of the girls forgot to sit down, so overcome with
horror were they to think that Mam'zelle Rougier was
sitting there with that book of caricatures right under her
nose.   Mam'zelle rapped on her desk.

'Are you deaf ?   Sit ! '

They sat.   Belinda stared beseechingly round.   She
caught Alicia's satisfied grin and felt angry.   So Alicia had
known that Mam'zelle Rougier was coming instead of Mam'-
zelle Dupont—and had used her as a cat's paw to play a
very dangerous trick.   Everyone knew what Mam'zelle
Rougier's temper was like.   She would probably go straight
to the head !

Belinda didn't know what do do.   Darrell saw how
alarmed she was, and did a bold thing.   She got up and
walked to Mam'zelle's desk, and put her hand on the book.

'I'm sorry this was left here by mistake, Mam'zelle,' she
said, politely.   She almost got away with it.   But not quite.
The girls stared breathlessly.

'Wait a moment,' said Mam'zelle Rougier.   'Books left
on the desk must not be removed without permission.
What is this book ? '

'Oh—only a—a sketch-book,' said Darrell, desperately.
Mam'zelle glanced round the silent class.   Why were they

all looking and listening so intently? There was something curious here.

She took up the book and opened it. Her glance fell on the picture of herself stalking Mam'selle Dupont with a dagger. She stared at it incredulously. There she was in the picture, tall, thin, bony—positively evil-looking—and with a dagger too!

She turned over a page. What! Here she was again—with a gun. Ah, no, this was too much! She turned another page and another. Always she saw herself there, unkindly caricatured, pursuing poor Mam'zelle Dupont, who had been given a most amiable look, and was obviously the heroine, whilst she, Mam'zelle Rougier, was the villain!

'This is unbelievable!' said Mam'zelle, under her breath, almost forgetting Darrell, who stood petrified nearby, and all the other waiting girls. Belinda was very pale. What bad luck! Whatever would happen now? Oh, why had she been such an idiot as to let Alicia lead her into this silly trap—just to make Alicia and Betty enjoy seeing her well ticked-off.

Mam'zelle became aware of the girls again. She snapped at Darrell and made her jump. 'Go back to your place.'

Darrell fled thankfully. Mam'zelle looked round the class, raking them with cold, angry eyes.

'Who has done this? Who has committed the insult of placing this book beneath my eyes?'

Sally spoke up at once. 'We're all in it, Mam'zelle. But we didn't mean *you* to see the book. We meant it for Mam'zelle Dupont. We didn't know you had changed over lessons today.'

This was unfortunately the worst possible thing that Sally could have said. Mam'zelle shot to her feet at once, her eyes stony.

'What! You meant to give this to Mam'zelle Dupont! You meant her to laugh at me with you! Is that what she does behind my back ? Ah, how glad I am to know how she behaves, this shameful Frenchwoman ! She shall know of this ! I go to Miss Grayling at once—this very minute ! '

The class sat in horrified silence. It had not occurred to them that it might be insulting to Mam'zelle Rougier to show the book of comical drawings to Mam'zelle Dupont. Belinda felt faint.

' Mam'zelle ! Don't go to Miss Grayling. I . . .'

But the class were not going to let Belinda take the blame. Even Alicia looked scared now. Many of the girls spoke at once, drowning poor Belinda's faint voice.

' Mam'zelle, we're sorry. Don't report us ! '

But Mam'zelle, swept by a cold fury, was already departing out of the door. The girls looked at one another in real horror.

' Alicia—*you knew* Mam'zelle Rougier was coming this afternoon instead of Mam'zelle Dupont,' said Belinda. ' I saw you wink at Betty. You *knew*! And you used me to play one of your nasty tricks ! I'd never have shown those pictures to Mam'zelle Rougier, and you know it.'

Alicia was truthful, whatever her faults were. She did not deny it. ' I didn't know she'd make such a fuss,' she said, rather feebly.

' Alicia, you're a beast ! ' said Darrell, feeling a hot flame working up inside her. ' You might have thought what serious trouble you'd get Belinda into. You, you . . .'

' Leave me to deal with this,' said Sally's quiet voice behind her. ' Don't get all worked up, Darrell. I'll deal with Alicia.'

' Oh, will you ? ' said Alicia, spitefully. ' Well, you won't. If you think you're going to tick me off, you're not, Miss Head-of-the-Form, Good-Girl-of-the-School, Sally Hope.'

' Don't be silly,' said Sally, in disgust. ' I can't think what's come over you lately, Alicia. You are always trying

' This is unbelievable! ' said Mam'zelle

to make things difficult for me. I'm going down to the Head myself, this very minute—and you're to come too, Belinda. We'll try to get things put straight before they go too far.'

'You'll put the whole blame on to me, of course!' said Alicia, scornfully. 'I know you! Get Belinda out of trouble and me into it!'

'I shan't say anything about you,' said Sally. 'I'm not a sneak. But I'd think a lot better of you if you came along with us, and explained your part in the affair!'

'I don't care what you think of me,' said Alicia, getting angry. 'I'm not going to tag along at your heels and say "Please, I did it!" You're not going to make me do anything I don't want to do!'

'I'm not going to try,' said Sally. 'Come on, Belinda, let's go before it's too late.'

Poor Belinda, looking frightened out of her life, went along the passage and down the stairs and out into the Court. They made their way to the Head Mistress's rooms.

'Oh, Sally—it's awful!' said Belinda, all her high spirits and light-heartedness gone. 'Mam'zelle was so fierce. And those pictures were rather beastly, some of them.'

When the girls knocked on the door of the Head Mistress's drawing-room, they heard voices inside. Miss Grayling was there, and Mam'zelle Rougier—and Miss Linnie the art mistress. She had been called in to see if she could tell them who had done the clever and malicious drawings.

'Belinda Morris, of course!' she said, after a glance. 'There's no girl in the school as clever as she is at sketching. She'll be a first-class artist one of these days. My word— these *are* clever!'

'Clever!' snorted Mam'zelle. 'They are wicked, they

are disrespectful, they are bad, bad, bad ! I demand that you punish this girl, Miss Grayling. I demand that the whole class shall be severely punished too.'

Just at that moment Sally knocked at the door. 'Come in !' said Miss Grayling, and the two girls entered.

'Well ?' said Miss Grayling. Sally swallowed hard. It was all very difficult—especially as Mam'zelle was glaring at her so fiercely.

'Miss Grayling,' she began, 'we're very, very sorry about this.'

'What is it to do with you ?' asked Miss Grayling. 'I thought Belinda did the pictures ?'

'Yes, I did,' said Belinda, in a low voice.

'But it was the whole class who wanted to put them on the desk—and let Mam'zelle Dupont see them,' said Sally. 'But—Mam'zelle Rougier came instead, and she saw them. I'm very sorry about it.'

'But why should you picture Mam'zelle Rougier pursuing her friend in such a murderous manner ?' asked the Head, looking through the book. 'I don't see why that should interest or amuse Mam'zelle Dupont.'

There was a silence. Then Mam'zelle Rougier spoke stiffly. 'We are not friends, Mam'zelle Dupont and I.'

And before Miss Grayling could stop her, Mam'zelle had poured out her grievance over the plays. Miss Grayling listened gravely. Then she turned to the girls.

'Then do I understand that one day the chief characters are played by Sally and Darrell, and the next day by Daphne ?' she asked.

Sally said yes, that was what had happened. Mam'zelle Rougier suddenly looked rather ashamed. It occurred to her that she and Mam'zelle Dupont had been very silly, and had allowed their private quarrel to muddle up the play and make things awkward for the girls.

She wished she had thought twice about taking the book down to the Head. No wonder the girls had put the quarrel into those stupid drawings—but why did they make her the villain and Mam'zelle Dupont the heroine ? Ah, that was not nice !

'You didn't know, then, that Mam'zelle Rougier was going to take the class instead of Mam'zelle Dupont ? ' said the Head, suddenly. Sally hesitated a fraction of a second. Alicia had known—and Betty too. But she, Sally, hadn't known, nor had any of the others.

'I didn't know that, of course, Miss Grayling,' she said.

'Did anyone know ? ' persisted the Head. Sally did not know how to answer. She did not want to tell tales, but she could not very well say nothing. Belinda broke in.

'Yes, someone knew—and that someone used me for a cat's paw. I'd never, never have shown those drawings to Mam'zelle Rougier. I won't tell who it was—but do believe me when I say I wouldn't have hurt Mam'zelle Rougier's feelings for anything. It was just a joke.'

'Yes, I see that,' said Miss Grayling. 'An unfortunate joke, of course, but still a joke. A joke that was played on the wrong person and caused anger and distress. As I see it, quite a lot of people are to blame in this.' She glanced at Mam'zelle Rougier, who grew rather red. 'There was a quarrel, it seems, to start with. Without that, possibly all this would not have occurred. You two girls may go now. I will discuss with Mam'zelle what punishment is fitting for you all.'

In silence Belinda and Sally went out of the door. Miss Linnie came with them. Mam'zelle Rougier was left behind, as Miss Grayling had made her a sign to stop.

'Belinda, you're an idiot,' said Miss Linnie.

'I'll never draw anyone again ! ' said Belinda, dismally.

'Oh, yes you will ! ' said Miss Linnie. ' But you'll probably draw kinder pictures in future. Don't be too clever, Belinda—it always lands you into trouble sooner or later ! '

12   MAM'ZELLE DUPONT
PUTS THINGS RIGHT

UPSTAIRS something was happening.   Mam'zelle Dupont had come past the door of the second form, and had found it open.   On looking in, she had found, to her surprise, that Mam'zelle Rougier had apparently deserted her form and left the girls alone.   More surprising still, the girls were sitting as quiet as mice—and what long faces !

' What is the matter, *mes petites* ? ' cried Mam'zelle, her little beady eyes ranging over the silent class.   ' What has happened ? '

Mary-Lou, thoroughly upset by everything, gave an unexpected sob.   Mam'zelle turned to her.   Mary-Lou was one of her pets, for Mary-Lou could chatter French perfectly.

' What is wrong, then !   Tell me !   Am I not your friend !   What is this that has happened ? '

' Oh, Mam'zelle—an awful thing has happened ! ' burst out Mary-Lou.   ' Belinda did some pictures of you and Mam'zelle Rougier.   Nice ones of you but awful ones of Mam'zelle Rougier—and we didn't know Mam'zelle was coming instead of you this afternoon—and we put the book on the desk for *you* to see, and . . . and . . .'

' Ah !   Mam'zelle Rougier, she saw them instead, and she has gone blue in the face, and she has taken Belinda and poor Sally to Miss Grayling ! ' cried Mam'zelle. ' Ah, this bad-tempered woman !   She cannot see a joke.

I, I myself will go to see Miss Grayling. I will tell her one, two, three things about Mam'zelle Rougier! Ah-h-h!'

And off went Mam'zelle Dupont, scuttling along on her high heels like a harassed rabbit. The girls looked at one another. What an afternoon!

Mam'zelle did not meet Belinda and Sally, for they went different ways. Just at the moment that she knocked at Miss Grayling's door, Sally and Belinda walked into the classroom, looking rather gloomy. They reported what had happened.

'So you did split on me after all,' said Alicia, in disgust.

'We didn't even mention your name,' said Belinda. 'So you needn't be afraid, Alicia.'

'I'm not afraid!' said Alicia. But she was. She hadn't been in Miss Grayling's good books lately and she knew it. She didn't want to be hauled over the coals for this now. But she didn't like the girls' scornful glances.

'Mam'zelle Dupont's gone off to join the merry family now,' said Darrell. 'I wonder what is happening.'

Mam'zelle Dupont had swept into the Head's drawing-room, startling both Miss Grayling and Mam'zelle Rougier. Miss Grayling was just getting an account of the quarrel between the two French mistresses from a rather shame-faced Mam'zelle Rougier, when the other Mam'zelle swept in.

She saw the book of drawings at once and picked them up. She examined them. 'Ah, *là, là!* This Belinda is a genius! Ha ha!—look at me here, Miss Grayling—did you ever see such a plump rabbit as I look? And oh, Mam'zelle Rougier, what are you doing with that dagger? It is marvellous, wonderful! But see here! I am to be poisoned!'

Mam'zelle Dupont went off into peals of laughter. She wiped the tears from her eyes. 'You do not think it is funny?' she said in astonishment to the other mistresses.

' But look—look—here I am to be shot with this gun. As
if my good friend Mam'zelle Rougier would do such a
thing to me ! Ah, we quarrel sometimes, she and I, but
it matters nothing ! We are two Frenchwomen together,
n'est ce pas, Mam'zelle Rougier, and we have much to put
up with from these bad English girls ! '

Mam'zelle Rougier began to look a little less frigid.
Miss Grayling looked at one or two of the pictures and
allowed herself to smile. ' This one is really very funny,
Mam'zelle Dupont,' she said. ' And this one, too. Of
course, the whole thing is most disrespectful, and I want
you both to say what punishment we must give the class
—and especially, of course, Belinda.'

There was a silence. ' I feel,' began Mam'zelle Rougier,
at last, ' I feel, Miss Grayling, that perhaps Mam'zelle
Dupont and I are a little to blame for all this—our stupid
quarrel, you know—naturally it intrigues the girls—and . . .'

' Ah, yes, you are right ! ' cried Mam'zelle Dupont,
fervently. ' You are quite, quite right, my friend. It is
we who are to blame. Miss Grayling—we demand no
punishment for the bad, bad girls ! We will forgive them.'

Mam'zelle Rougier looked a little taken aback. Why
should Mam'zelle Dupont forgive them ? They hadn't
drawn *her* unkindly ! But Mam'zelle Dupont was rushing
on in her headlong way.

' These pictures, they are more funny than bad ! It is
a tease, a joke, is it not ? We do not mind ! It was our
stupid quarrel that started it. But now, now we are
friends, are we not, Mam'zelle Rougier ? '

Mam'zelle Rougier could not say no to that. Swept
away in spite of herself, she nodded. Mam'zelle Dupont
gave her two sudden and exuberant kisses, one on each
cheek. Miss Grayling was much amused.

' That Belinda ! ' said Mam'zelle Dupont, looking at the
drawings again. ' Ah, what a clever child. One day,

maybe, Miss Grayling, we shall be proud of these drawings ! When Belinda is famous, Mam'zelle Rougier and I, we shall look together with pride on these pictures, and we shall say, " Ah, the little Belinda did these for us when she was in our class ! " '

Mam'zelle Rougier said nothing to this. She was feeling that she had been made to do all kinds of things she hadn't meant to do. But she couldn't go back on what she had said now. That was certain.

' Well, perhaps you would go back to your classes now,' suggested Miss Grayling. ' And you will tell the girls, and set their minds at rest ? Belinda must apologize, of course. But I think you'll find she will do that without any prompting.'

The two Mam'zelles departed, arm-in-arm. The girls they met stared at them in surprise, for everyone knew that the two had been bitter enemies for the last week or so. They went up to the second form, who stood in silence, glad to see Mam'zelle Dupont looking so cheerful, and the other Mam'zelle not quite so sour as usual.

Mam'zelle Dupont set their minds at rest. ' You have been bad girls. Very bad girls. Belinda, you let your pencil run away with you. I am shocked ! '

She didn't look shocked. Her beady black eyes twinkled. Belinda stood up.

' I want to apologize,' she said, rather shakily, ' to both of you.'

Mam'zelle Rougier didn't see any necessity for Belinda to apologize to Mam'zelle Dupont, but she didn't say so. She accepted the apology as graciously as she could.

' And now for punishment,' said Mam'zelle Dupont, in a stern voice, but still with twinkling eyes, ' for punishment you will pay better attention to your French lessons than you have ever done before. You will learn well, you will translate marvellously, you will be my best pupils. Is that not so ? '

' Oh, *yes*, Mam'zelle,' promised the girls fervently, and, for the time being at any rate, even Gwendoline and Daphne meant it ! Mam'zelle Rougier went. Mam'zelle Dupont took over the five remaining minutes of the lesson.

' Please,' said Darrell, at the end, ' Mam'zelle, will you tell us who *is* to take the chief parts in the French plays we're doing ? It's so muddling not knowing. Perhaps you and Mam'zelle Rougier have settled it now.'

' We have not,' said Mam'zelle Dupont, ' but I, I am generous today. I will let the poor Mam'zelle Rougier have her way, to make up to her for the shock you have given her this morning. I will not take Daphne for the chief parts. You, Darrell and Sally, shall have them. That will please Mam'zelle Rougier and put her into such a good mood that she will smile on you all ! '

Daphne was not too pleased about this. She looked at Mam'zelle, rather hurt. All the same, it was a good thing, she thought, because how she was EVER going to learn all that French talk in the play she really didn't know ? Perhaps it would be just as well if she didn't have the chief parts, after all. She would look hurt, but be very sweet and generous about it !

So, looking rather stricken, she spoke to Mam'zelle. ' It's just as you like, Mam'zelle. I *had* been looking forward to swotting up my parts for you—but I hope I'm generous enough to give them up to others without a fuss ! '

' The kind girl ! ' said Mam'zelle, beaming. ' I will make it up to you, Daphne. You shall come to me and we will read together a French book I loved when I was a girl. Ah, that will be a treat for both of us ! '

The class wanted to laugh when they saw Daphne's horrified face. Read a French book with Mam'zelle ! How dreadful. She would have to get out of that somehow.

The affair of the drawings had three results. Alicia was sulky, because she felt she had come out very badly in the matter, and she knew that Sally and Darrell and some of the others didn't think very much of her because of it. The two Mam'zelles were firm friends now, instead of enemies. And Daphne was now given a very minor part indeed in the plays, where she would not appear as someone beautiful, but only as an old man in a hood. She was very much disgusted.

'Especially as I've written and told my people all about my fine parts,' she complained. 'It's a shame.'

'Yes, it is,' said Gwendoline. 'Never mind, Daphne— you won't have to do all that swotting now!'

Jean came up with a box at that moment. She jingled it under their noses. 'Have you got your games sub., you two? We're collecting it today. Five bob each.'

'Here's mine,' said Gwendoline, getting out her purse.

'Yours, please, Daphne,' said Jean. Daphne took out her purse. 'Blow!' she said. 'I thought I had ten shillings, but there's only a sixpence. Oh, yes—I had to buy a birthday present for my governess last week. Gwen, lend me the money till I get some from home, will you?'

'She lent you two bob last week,' said Jean, jingling the box again. 'I bet you didn't pay her back! And you borrowed sixpence off me for church collection, let me tell you. Why don't you keep a little book showing your debts?'

'What do little sums like that matter?' said Daphne, annoyed. 'I'll be getting pounds and pounds on my birth-day soon. Anyway, I can pay back this week. My uncle is sending me thirty shillings.'

'Well, I'll, I'll lend you five bob till then,' said Gwen-doline, and put a ten-shilling note into the box. Jean turned to Darrell and collected her money. She went to Ellen and jingled the box under her nose.

'Five bob, please, Ellen.'

'Don't do that under my nose!' said Ellen, jumping.
'What is it you want? Five shillings? Well, I haven't
got it on me just now. I'll give it to you later.'

'You said that last time,' said Jean, who was a most
persistent person when it came to collecting money. 'Go
on—get it, Ellen, and then the collection will be finished.'

'I'm working,' said Ellen, annoyed. 'Take the thing
away. I'll give you the five shillings soon.'

Jean went off, also annoyed. Daphne spoke in a low
voice to Gwendoline. 'I bet she hasn't got the five bob
to give! She won a scholarship here, but I don't believe
her people can really afford to keep her at a school like
this!'

Ellen didn't quite hear what was said but she knew it
was something nasty, by Daphne's sneering tone. She
flung down her book. 'Can't *any*body work in this place!'
she said. 'Stop your whispering, Daphne, and take that
smile off your silly face!'

13   POOR ELLEN!

'REALLY!' said Daphne, as Ellen walked out of the
room and banged the door. 'What awful manners that
girl's got! What's the matter with her?'

Nobody knew. Nobody guessed that Ellen was getting
more and more worried about her work. She knew that
the end of term tests were coming along, and she wanted
to come out well in them. She must! So she was working

hard every minute, and she had begun to feel at last that she would be able to face the tests and do well.

But that evening she did not feel very well. Her throat hurt her. Her eyes hurt her, especially when she moved them about. She coughed.

Surely she wasn't going to be ill! That would put her terribly behind in her work. It would never do. So Ellen dosed herself with cough lozenges, and gargled secretly in the bathroom, hoping that Matron would not notice anything wrong.

Her eyes were too bright that evening. Her usually pale cheeks were red. She coughed in prep. Miss Potts, who was taking prep, looked at her.

'Do you feel all right, Ellen?' she asked.

'Oh, quite all right, Miss Potts,' said Ellen, untruthfully, and bent her head over her book. She coughed again.

'I don't like that cough,' said Miss Potts. 'I think perhaps you had better go to . . .'

'Oh, Miss Potts, it's only a tickle in my throat,' said Ellen, desperately. 'Perhaps I'd better get a drink of water.'

'Well, go then,' said Miss Potts, still not quite satisfied. So Ellen went. She leaned her hot head against the cool wall of the cloakroom and wished miserably that she had someone she could confide in. But her snappiness and irritability had put everyone against her—even Jean. Jean had tried to be nice—and Ellen hadn't even bothered to go and get the games subscription for her.

'I don't know what's come over me lately,' thought the girl. 'I used not to be like this, surely. I had plenty of friends at my other school. I wish I'd never left there. I wish I'd never won a scholarship!'

She must go back. Her throat still hurt her and she slipped a lozenge into her mouth. Then she went back to the classroom, trying to walk firmly, though her legs felt rather wobbly.

She had a high temperature and should have been tucked up in bed. But she wasn't going to give in. She must do her work. She mustn't get behind. She must do well in the tests, whatever happened.

She tried to learn some French poetry, but it buzzed round and round in her head. She began to cough again.

'Oh, shut up,' said Alicia, in a whisper. 'You're putting it on to get Potty's sympathy!'

That was so like Alicia! She didn't like people who coughed or sniffed or groaned. She had no sympathy to spare for those who needed it. She was a healthy, strong, clever girl, who had never been ill in her life, and she scorned stupid people, or those who were delicate and ailing, or in trouble. She was hard, and it didn't seem as if she was getting any kinder. Darrell often wondered how she could so badly have wanted Alicia to be her friend when she had first come to Malory Towers!

Ellen looked at Alicia with dislike. 'I can't help it,' she said. 'I'm not putting it on.' She sneezed and Alicia gave an exclamation of disgust.

'Don't! Go to bed if you're as bad as all that!'

'Silence!' said Miss Potts, annoyed. Alicia said no more. Ellen sighed and tried to concentrate on her book again. But she couldn't. She was glad when the bell went and she could get up and go out into the cooler air. She was hot and yet she shivered. Oh, blow, she certainly was in for a cold. Perhaps it would be better tomorrow.

She tried to stuff some food down her throat at supper-time, in case Miss Parker noticed she wasn't eating any-thing. But Miss Parker did not often take any notice of Ellen. She was usually a quiet girl, with a name for bad temper, and Miss Parker was not at all interested in her, though sometimes surprised that her work was not better.

It was Sally who noticed that Ellen seemed ill that night. She heard her quick, rather hoarse breathing and looked

at her in concern.   She remembered how Ellen had coughed
in prep.   Poor Ellen—was she feeling simply awful, and
not wanting to make a fuss ?

Sally was both sensible and kind.   She went to Ellen
and took her hot hands.   ' Ellen !   You're not well !   Let
me go with you to Matron, silly ! '

The little act of kindness made the tears start to Ellen's
eyes.   But she shook her head impatiently.

' I'm all right.   Leave me alone !   Just got a headache,
that's all.'

' Poor old Ellen,' said Sally.   ' You've got more than a
headache.   Come along to Matron.   You ought to be in
bed ! '

But Ellen wouldn't go.   It was not until Jean came up
and sympathized with her that she broke down and confessed that yes, she really did feel awful, but she couldn't
possibly go to bed with all that work to do before the tests !
' I must do well, you see,' she kept saying.   ' I must.'
The tears ran down her cheeks as she spoke, and she
suddenly shivered.

' You won't do any good by keeping up when you should
be in bed,' said Jean.   ' Come along.   I'll keep you well
posted in what we do in lessons, I promise you !   I'll make
notes for you and everything ! '

' Oh, will you ? ' said poor Ellen, coughing.   ' All
right then.   If you'll help me to catch up, I'll go and see
Matron now.   Perhaps just one day in bed will put me
right.'

But one day was certainly not going to put Ellen right !
She was very ill and Matron put her to bed in the San.
at once.   Ellen was so thankful to be there that she couldn't
help crying.   She was ashamed of herself, but she couldn't
stop the tears.

' Now don't you worry,' said Matron, kindly.   ' You
should have been in bed days ago by the look of you !

Silly child! Now you just lie still and enjoy a week in bed.'

A week! Ellen started up in horror. She couldn't possibly miss a week's work. She stared at Matron in dismay. Matron pushed her back.

'Don't look so horrified. You'll enjoy it. And as soon as you feel like it, and your cold is not infectious, you can choose a visitor.'

'Poor Ellen's really ill,' said Jean, as she went back to the others. 'I don't know what her temperature is, but I saw Matron's face when she took it, and it must be pretty high.'

'She coughed like anything in prep tonight,' said Sally. 'I felt sorry for her.'

'Well, Alicia didn't,' said Gwen, maliciously. 'She told her to shut up! Dear, kind Alicia!'

Alicia glared. She was always making sharp remarks about Gwen—but this time Gwen had got one back at *her* —and Alicia didn't much like it.

'Oh, we all know that Alicia can't bear to give a little sympathy out,' said Darrell, unable to stop herself. She had felt annoyed with Alicia lately, because she had been so offhand with Sally. Also she had thought that Alicia should certainly have owned up that it was she who had known Mam'zelle Rougier was going to take the lesson instead of Mam'zelle Dupont. She had made Belinda get into a row, when she could have prevented it.

Alicia, too, was ashamed of this now. But it was too late to do anything about it. There was no point in owning up now that the matter was closed. But she kept kicking herself for not doing so at the right time. She had been too obstinate.

She was sorry too that she had been hard on Ellen that evening—but how could she know she was really ill? She hadn't any time for that silly Ellen, always snapping and snarling at everyone! Let her be ill! A good thing if she *was* away from the class for a while. *She* wouldn't miss her!

Ellen felt very ill for four days, then she felt a little better. Her temperature went down, and she began to take a little more interest in things. But alas! her old worry came back immediately she was well enough to think clearly!

Those tests! She knew that on the result of the tests depended her place in form. And it was very important that she should be top or nearly top. Her father and mother were so very proud that she had won the scholarship to such a fine school. They were not well-off, but they had told Ellen they would do anything they could to keep her at Malory Towers, now that she had won the right to be there by her own hard work.

The uniform had been so expensive. Even the train fare was expensive. It was a good thing she had been able to get a lift down in somebody's car. Mother had bought her a new trunk and a new suit-case. More expense. Oh, dear—was it really a good thing to win a scholarship to a school like Malory Towers if you had to count your pennies? Perhaps it wasn't.

Then another thought struck her. She had had to have the doctor. That would be another expense on the bill. And all the time she was losing her school work, and would do badly her first term. Her parents would be bitterly disappointed.

So Ellen worried and worried. The Matron and the Nurse couldn't think why she did not throw off her illness as quickly as she should. Every day she begged to be allowed to get up, but Matron shook her head. 'No, you can't, dear. You're not quite right yet. But would you like a visitor now? You can have one if you like.'

'Oh, yes. I'd like Jean, please,' said Ellen at once.

Jean had promised to take notes for her. Jean would tell her all about the lessons she had missed. Jean was dependable and reliable.

So Jean came to see her, bringing a pot of honey. But it was not honey that Ellen wanted. She hardly even glanced at it.

'Did you bring the notes you said you would make for me?' she asked, eagerly. 'Oh, Jean—didn't you?'

'Good gracious me—what do you want notes of lessons for already?' demanded Jean, in astonishment. 'You're not even up!'

'Oh, I do, I do,' said Ellen. 'You promised, Jean. Well, bring them next time. You tell me all the lessons you've had now.'

Jean screwed up her eyes and tried to remember. She thought Ellen queer to want to talk about lessons instead of games or fun. She began to tell Ellen.

'Well, in maths. we did those new sums again. I can bring you some to show you. And in French we learnt that long piece of poetry on page sixty-four. I can recite some of it if you like. And for geography we learnt . . .'

Matron bustled up. 'Jean! Ellen mustn't hear a word about lessons yet! She mustn't start worrying her head about work. She couldn't help missing it, and Miss Parker and Mam'zelle will quite understand that she will be a bit behind when she comes back.'

Ellen stared at her in consternation. 'But, Matron! I *must* know it all. I must! Oh, do let Jean tell me. And she's going to bring me some lesson notes she's made for me too.'

'Well, she certainly mustn't. I forbid it,' said Matron. So that was that. Ellen took no more interest in Jean's conversation. She lay back, desperate. She'd be near the bottom now! How unlucky she was!

NOBODY missed Ellen very much. She hadn't any of Darrell's high spirits or friendliness, none of Alicia's mischief or fun, she hadn't even the shyness and timidity of Mary-Lou, that made her missed when she wasn't there.

'You don't much notice Mary-Lou when she's there under your nose—but you do miss her when she's not,' said Darrell once. And that was true.

Darrell was missing Mary-Lou quite a lot these days, for Mary-Lou was attaching herself firmly to Daphne. Nobody could quite understand it. Nobody believed that Daphne wanted Mary-Lou's friendship—she only wanted her help in French. Even when Darrell pointed out that it was almost cheating for Mary-Lou to do such a lot for her, she would hardly listen.

'I can't do much to help anybody,' said Mary-Lou. 'It's only in French that I'm really good—and it's so nice to help somebody who wants it. And besides—Daphne does really like me, Darrell!'

'Well, so do I like you, and so does Sally,' said Darrell, really exasperated to think that Mary-Lou should attach herself to such a double-faced person as Daphne.

'Yes, I know. But you only put up with me out of the kindness of your heart!' said Mary-Lou. 'You've got Sally. You let me tag along behind you like a nice puppy —but you don't really want me, and I couldn't possibly help you in any way. But I *can* help Daphne—and though I know you think she's only using me for her French, she's not.'

Darrell was certain that Daphne only put up with Mary-Lou because of the French—but she wasn't quite right.

Daphne was very fond of Mary-Lou now. She couldn't quite think why, because it wasn't like her to be fond of anyone—but Mary-Lou was so unobtrusive, so shy, so willing to help in any way. ' She's like a pet mouse, that you want to protect and take care of ! ' thought Daphne. ' You can't help liking a mouse.'

She poured out her tales of wealth to Mary-Lou, and Mary-Lou listened in the most gratifying manner. The younger girl was proud that someone as grand as Daphne should bother to notice her and talk to her and tell her things.

Ellen was away from school eleven days and had worried terribly the last six or seven because Jean had not been allowed to bring her lesson-notes or to tell her about the lessons. Now she came back, pale, a little thinner, with an obstinate look in her eyes. She was going to catch up somehow ! If she had to get up at six in the morning, and learn her lessons under the sheets by means of a flashlight, she would !

She asked Miss Parker if she would be kind enough to give her extra coaching in what she had missed. Miss Parker refused in a kindly manner.

' No, Ellen. You're not up even to your ordinary work at the moment, let alone taking extra coaching. I shan't expect much from you, nor will anyone else. So don't worry.'

Ellen went to Mam'zelle Dupont and even to Mam'zelle Rougier. ' I do so want to know what I've missed so that I can make it up,' she said. ' Could you give me a little extra coaching ? '

But neither of the Mam'zelles would. ' You are not yet quite strong, *mon enfant* ! ' said Mam'zelle Dupont, kindly. ' No one will expect you to do brilliantly now this term. Take things more easily.'

So poor Ellen was quite in despair. Nobody would help

her! They all seemed to be in a league against her—Matron, Doctor, Miss Parker, the two Mam'zelles.

And in ten days' time the tests began! Ellen usually liked exams, but she was dreading these. She couldn't think how it was that the girls joked about them so light-heartedly.

Then an idea came to her—a bad idea, that at first she put away from her mind at once. But it came back again and again, whispering itself into her mind so that she had to listen to it.

' If you could perhaps see the test-papers before they were given out! If you could read the questions and know what you were going to be asked! '

Ellen had never cheated in her life. She had never needed to for she had good brains and she knew how to work hard. People didn't cheat if they could do as well or better without cheating! Ah, but when you couldn't, when something had gone wrong, and you didn't know your work—would you cheat then if it was the only way to gain a good place?

It is not often that a test like that comes to a person with good brains, who has always scorned cheating—but now it came to Ellen. It is easy not to cheat if you don't need to. Is it easy not to cheat if you *do* need to ? When that test comes, you will know your character for what it is, weak or strong, crooked or upright.

Ellen could no longer push the thought out of her mind. It was always there. Then one day she was in Miss Parker's room and saw what she thought was a test-paper on her desk. Miss Parker was not in the room. It needed only a moment to slip round and look at the paper.

Ellen read swiftly down the questions. How easy they were! Then, with a shock she saw that they were questions set for the first form, not the second. Her heart sank.

Before she could look for the second-form questions and

see if they were there she heard Miss Parker's footsteps
and slipped round to the other side of the desk. She
must never let anyone guess that she was thinking of doing
such a dreadful thing.

Ellen was always slipping into Miss Parker's room, or
Miss Potts' room after that. She chose times when she
knew they would not be there. She even went through
Miss Parker's desk in the second-form room one morning
after school hoping to find something there in the way of
test questions.

Alicia found her there and looked surprised. 'What *are*
you doing?' she said. 'You know we're not supposed to
go to that desk. Really, Ellen!'

'I've lost my fountain pen,' mumbled Ellen. 'I wondered if perhaps Miss Parker had . . .'

'Well, even if she *had* got it, you shouldn't go sneaking
in her desk,' said Alicia, scornfully.

Then another time Darrell found her in Miss Potts'
room, standing at Mam'zelle's empty desk, running her
fingers through the papers there. She stared in surprise.

'Oh—er—Mam'zelle sent me here to find a book for her,'
said Ellen, and was shocked at herself. She had always
heard that one sin leads to another, and she was finding
out that this was true. She was trying to cheat—and that
made her tell untruths. What next would it be!

'Well, I must say Ellen isn't much improved by being
away for nearly a fortnight,' said Betty, one evening in
the common-room, when Ellen had snapped someone's
head off, and gone out sulkily. 'She's just as snappy as
ever—and she doesn't look a bit well yet.'

'Bad temper's her trouble,' said Alicia. 'I'm fed up
with her. Always frowning and sighing and looking
miserable!'

Gwendoline came in, looking bothered. 'Anyone seen
my purse? I'm sure I put it into my desk, and now it's

gone. And I put a ten-shilling note in it only this morning, because I wanted to go out and buy something! Now I can't!'

'I'll help you to look for it,' said Daphne obligingly, and got up. 'I bet it's still in your desk somewhere!'

But it wasn't. It was most annoying. Gwendoline screwed up her forehead and tried in vain to think if she had put it anywhere else.

'I'm sure I didn't,' she said at last. 'Oh, how sickening it is. Can you lend me some money, Daphne?'

'Yes. I've got my purse in my pocket,' said Daphne. 'Anyway I owe you some. I meant to have paid you before. I got some money yesterday from my uncle.'

She felt in her pocket and then looked up, a dismayed expression on her face. 'It's gone! There's a hole in my pocket! Blow! Wherever can I have dropped it?'

'Well, I must say you're a pretty pair!' said Alicia. 'Both of you losing your purses—just when they are full of money too! You're as bad as Irene or Belinda!'

Belinda had lost a half-crown only the day before, and had crawled all over the form-room floor looking for it, much to Mam'zelle's amazement. She hadn't found it and had demanded her games subscription back from Jean. She hadn't got it, however, for Jean maintained that once the money had gone into her box, it was no longer the giver's—it belonged to the Games' secretary, or the school, or whatever fund it was meant for.

The two purses didn't turn up. It was annoying and rather mysterious. *Two* purses—full of money. Gwendoline looked at Daphne and lowered her voice. 'You don't think somebody's taken them, do you? Surely there couldn't be anyone in our form that would do a thing like that!'

Alicia was very curious about the purses. Into her mind slid the memory of seeing Ellen going through the mistress's

Ellen was rummaging through Miss Parker's desk

desk in the second-form room.　Why should she do that?
She had said she had lost her fountain pen—but she hadn't,
because Alicia had seen her using it at the very next lesson.
Well, then . . .

Alicia determined to keep an eye on Ellen.　If she was
doing anything dishonest or underhand it ought to be
reported to Sally.　It was tiresome to think that Sally would
have the right to hear about it and settle whether or not
it should go before Miss Parker.　Alicia felt the usual stab
of jealousy when she thought of Sally as head-girl.

Ellen didn't know that Alicia was keeping an eye on
her, but she did know that she was suddenly finding it
very difficult to be alone, or to go into either Miss Parker's
room, or Miss Potts' room, or even the form-room when
nobody else was there.　Alicia always seemed to pop up
and say:

'Hallo, Ellen!　Looking for somebody?　Can I help
you?'

Daphne borrowed as usual from somebody, but Gwendoline didn't.　Gwendoline had been taught not to borrow,
and she had written to ask her people to send her some
more money to get on with.　Daphne borrowed some from
Mary-Lou and then offered half of it to Gwendoline.

'Oh *no*,' said Gwendoline, a little shocked.　'You can't
lend other people's money to me, Daphne!　I know you
borrowed that from Mary-Lou.　Why don't you do as
I'm doing and wait till you get some more from your
people?　That's the worst of being as rich as you are—
I suppose you just simply don't understand the value of
money!'

Daphne looked a little surprised, for this was the first
time she had ever had any kind of criticism, even slight,
from her faithful Gwendoline.　Then she slipped her arm
through her friend's.

'I expect you're right!' she said.　'I've always had as

much money as I wanted—I don't really know the value of it. It's the way I've been brought up. Don't be cross, Gwen.'

'I don't know what would happen to you if you were ever in real need of money!' said Gwendoline. 'You *would* be miserable without your yacht and your cars and your servants and your beautiful house! How I wish I could see them all!'

But Daphne did not say, as Gwen always hoped she would, 'Well, come and stay with me for the holidays!' It rather looked as if Gwendoline would not be seeing her grand friend during the Christmas holidays, or attending parties and pantomimes with her. It rather looked as if she would have to put up with her own home and adoring mother and worshipping governess!

15   A DREADFUL EVENING

IT was the day before the tests were to begin. Some of the girls were swotting up hard, feeling rather guilty because they hadn't paid as much attention to their work as they ought to have done. Betty Hill was poring over her books. So was Gwendoline. And, as usual, poor Ellen had her nose between the pages of a book, trying to cram into a short time what could only be learnt slowly and in peace.

Miss Parker was quite worried about Ellen. The girl gave her a strained attention in class, and yet her work was only fair. It wasn't for lack of trying, Miss Parker knew. She supposed it must be that Ellen was not very fit after her illness.

Ellen knew that the test-papers were ready. She had heard Miss Parker talking about them. As for Mam'zelle, in her usual tantalizing manner she had shaken her test-paper in front of her class, and cried ' Ah, you would like to know what I have set you, would you not ! You would like to know what are these difficult questions ! Now the first one is . . .'

But she never did say what the first one was, and the class laughed. Anyway, Mam'zelle Dupont was never so strict over tests as Mam'zelle Rougier, who set the most difficult questions and expected them to be answered perfectly—and then groaned and grumbled because nearly all the girls failed to get high marks !

It was Ellen's last chance that day to try to see the papers. If only that irritating Alicia wouldn't always keep hanging around ! The thought occurred to Ellen that Alicia might be spying on her—but she dismissed it at once. Why should she ? Nobody in the world save Ellen herself knew that she wanted to see the test-papers.

She hung about in the passage outside Miss Parker's room for a long time that evening. But there was never any chance of going in without being seen. Somebody always seemed to be going by. It was astonishing how many girls went this way and that way past Miss Parker's door.

Then, most annoyingly, the only time that the passage was really empty was when Miss Parker herself was in the room. She was there with Miss Potts. Ellen could quite well hear what they were saying.

She bent down by the door as if she was re-tying her shoe-lace.

' The second form haven't done too badly this term,' she heard Miss Parker say to Miss Potts. ' They seem to have benefited by the year they spent with you ! Most of them can use their brains, which is something ! '

'Well, I hope they do well in the tests,' said Miss Potts.
'I always take an interest in their first tests when they go
up to the second form for the first time. Having had the
girls for three or four terms I can't lose my interest in them
quickly. I suppose Alicia or Irene or Darrell will be top.
They've all got good brains.'

'Have a look at the questions,' said Miss Parker, and
Ellen actually heard the rustling of the test-papers being
handed over to Miss Potts. How she longed to see
them!

There was a silence as Miss Potts read them. 'Yes. A
bit stiff, one or two of them—but if the girls have paid
attention, they ought to do them all quite well. What
about the French papers?'

'Mam'zelle's got them in her room,' said Miss Parker.
'I'll take these along to her and give them to her. She
takes the second form first thing tomorrow and can take
the papers there with her.'

Ellen's heart leapt. Now she knew where the papers
would be that night! In Mam'zelle's room. And that
was not very far from the dormy. Could she—dare she—
get up in the night.and go and peep at them?

A girl came round the corner and almost knocked Ellen
over. It was Alicia.

'Gracious, it's you, Ellen! You were lounging about
here when I came up—and now I come down and you're
still here! What on earth are you doing?'

It's no business of yours!' said Ellen, and walked off.
She went to the common-room and sat down. She had to
work things out. Dare she creep out in the middle of the
night and hunt for the papers? It was a very, very wrong
thing to do. But oh, if only she had been well all the term,
and had been able to work and use her brains properly, she
could easily have been top or near the top. It wasn't her
fault that she would be near the bottom.

So she sat and reasoned with herself, trying to persuade herself that what she was doing wasn't really so bad as it looked. She was doing it to save her parents from being so disappointed. She couldn't let them down. Poor Ellen! She didn't stop to think that her parents would much rather see her honestly at the bottom, than dishonestly at the top!

Alicia was growing quite certain that it was Ellen who had taken the money. If not, why in the world was she always sneaking about by herself, listening outside doors, and doing such peculiar things? Neither of the purses had turned up. Nor had Belinda's half-crown. Another purse and more missing money had not been traced either, and Emily had reported that her gold bar brooch, which her god-mother had given her the term before, had also gone.

Emily was very tidy and careful and never lost things like Belinda or Irene. When Alicia heard her talking about her lost brooch in the common-room, she made up her mind to tell the others what she thought. Ellen, as usual, was not there. 'Out sneaking round somebody's door, I expect!' thought Alicia.

'I say,' she said, raising her voice a little. 'Sally! I've got something to say about all these mysterious disappear-ances. I don't exactly want to accuse anyone—but I've been watching somebody lately, and they've been doing rather peculiar things.'

Everyone looked up in surprise. Sally looked round the common-room. 'Are we all here?' she said. 'Yes— wait though—Ellen isn't. We'll get her.'

'No, don't,' said Alicia. 'It would be as well not to.'

'What do you mean?' said Sally, puzzled. Then her eyes widened. 'Oh—you don't mean—no, Alicia, you don't mean that it's Ellen you've been watching! What has she been doing that's so peculiar?'

Alicia told how she had watched Ellen and seen her

sneaking about in the passages, apparently waiting for a room to be empty. She related how she had found her going through Miss Parker's desk. Everyone listened, amazed.

' I wouldn't have thought it of her ! ' said Daphne, in a disgusted voice. ' What a thing to do ! I never did like her. There's no doubt she took my purse and Gwen's—and Emily's brooch, and goodness knows how many things besides.'

' You're not to say that till we've proved something,' said Sally, sharply. ' We've no definite proof yet—and only Alicia, apparently, has seen Ellen sneaking about.'

' Well,' said Darrell, reluctantly, ' Sally, I noticed something once too. I found Ellen in Miss Potts' room, going through some things on her desk.'

' How dreadful ! ' said Daphne, and Gwen echoed her. Jean said nothing. She had been more friendly with Ellen than anyone else, though she had never been able to like her very much—but it seemed to her that Ellen was not quite the type of girl to become a thief. A thief ! How terrible it sounded. Jean frowned. Surely Ellen couldn't be that !

' I don't think I believe it,' she said, slowly, in her clear Scots voice. ' She's a queer girl—but I don't think she's queer in that way.'

' Well, I bet she never gave you her games subscription ! ' said Alicia, remembering how Ellen had refused to go and get it.

' She did, the next time I asked her,' said Jean.

' Yes—and I bet it was after one of the purses had disappeared ! ' exclaimed Betty. Jean was silent. Yes, that was true. Ellen had not given up her subscription until the purses had gone. Things looked very black for Ellen.

' What are we to do ? ' said Darrell, helplessly. ' Sally, you're head-girl. What are you going to do ? '

' I'll have to think about it,' said Sally.   ' I can't decide this very minute.'

' There's nothing to decide ! ' said Alicia, with scorn in her voice.   ' She's the thief.   Well, tackle her with it and make her confess !   If you don't, I shall ! '

' No, you mustn't,' said Sally at once.   ' I tell you, we've none of us got real proof—and it's a bad, wicked thing to do to accuse somebody without definite proof. You are not to say a word, Alicia.   As head-girl I forbid you.'

Alicia's eyes sparkled wickedly.   ' We'll see ! ' she said, and at that very moment who should come into the room but Ellen !   She sensed hostility as soon as she came in and looked round, half-scared.

The girls stared at her silently, rather taken-aback at her sudden appearance.   Then Sally began to talk to Darrell and Jean turned to Emily.   But Alicia was not going to change the subject, or to obey Sally either !

' Ellen,' she said, in a loud clear voice, ' What do you find when you go sneaking about in empty rooms and looking through desks ? '

Ellen went pale.   She stood perfectly still, her eyes glued on Alicia.   ' What—what do you mean ? ' she stammered at last.   Surely, surely nobody had guessed that she was looking for the exam papers !

' Shut up, Alicia ! ' said Sally, peremptorily.   ' You know what I said.'

Alicia took no notice.   ' You know jolly well what I mean, don't you ? ' she said to Ellen, in a hard voice.   ' You know what you take when you creep into an empty room or go through somebody's desk or locker or drawer !   Don't you ? '

' I've never taken anything ! ' cried Ellen, a hunted look on her face.   ' What should I take ? '

' Oh—perhaps purses with money in—or a gold brooch

or two,' drawled Alicia. 'Come on—own up, Ellen. You look as guilty as can be, so why deny it ?'

Ellen stared as if she could not believe her eyes. She looked round at the quiet girls. Some of them could not look at her. Mary-Lou was crying, for she hated scenes of this kind. Sally looked angrily and hopelessly at Alicia. It was no good stopping things now. They had gone too far. How dared Alicia defy her like that !

Darrell was angry, too, but her anger was partly directed at Ellen, whom she too thought looked exceedingly guilty. She was angry that Alicia had defied Sally, the head-girl— but after all—if Ellen was guilty, it was surely better that it should all be cleared up immediately ?

'Do you mean that—that you think I've been stealing your things ?' asked Ellen at last, with a great effort. 'You can't mean that !'

'We do,' said Alicia, grimly. 'Why else should you snoop round as you do ? And why go through Miss Parker's desk ? Can you give us a good explanation of that ?'

No. Ellen couldn't. How could she say that she was hunting for the exam papers because she wanted to cheat. Oh, if once you started doing something wrong there was no end to it ! She put her hands up to her face.

'I can't tell you anything,' she said, and tears made her fingers wet. 'But I didn't take your things. I didn't.'

'You *did*,' said Alicia. 'You're a coward as well as a thief. You can't even own up and give the things back !'

Ellen stumbled out of the room. The door shut behind her. Mary-Lou gave an unhappy sob. 'I'm so sorry for her !' she said. 'I can't help it ! I am !'

THERE was a silence, only broken by Mary-Lou's sniffs. Most of the girls were upset and horrified. Alicia looked rather pleased with herself. Sally was tight-lipped and angry. Alicia looked at her and smiled maliciously.

'Sorry if I've upset you, Sally,' she said, 'but it was time we had it out with Ellen. As head-girl you should have done it yourself. As it was, you left it to me!'

'I did not!' said Sally. 'I forbade you to say anything. We shouldn't have accused Ellen—I know it's not right till we've got proof. And I wanted to think of the best way of doing it—not in front of everyone, that's certain!'

Darrell felt uncomfortably that Sally was right. It would have been best to wait a little, and think about it and then perhaps for Sally to have spoken with Ellen alone. Now the fat was in the fire! Everyone knew. Whatever would Ellen do!

'Well, all I can say is I'm grateful to Alicia for bringing the matter to a head,' said Daphne, shaking back her shining curls from her forehead. 'Perhaps our belongings will be safe now.'

'You ought to be loyal to Sally, not to Alicia,' flared up Darrell.

'Don't let's argue any more,' said Sally. 'The thing's done now, more's the pity. There's the supper-bell. For goodness' sake, let's go.'

They went soberly down to the supper-table. Ellen was not there. Jean asked about her.

'Shall I go and fetch Ellen, Miss Parker?' she said.

'No. She's got one of her headaches and has gone early

to bed,' said Miss Parker. The girls exchanged looks. So Ellen couldn't even face them again that evening.

'Guilty conscience,' said Alicia to Betty, in a voice loud enough to reach Darrell and Sally.

Ellen was in bed when the form went up at their bed-time. She lay on her side, her face in the pillow, perfectly still. 'Pretending to be asleep,' said Alicia.

'Shut up,' said Jean, unexpectedly, in a low voice. 'You've done your bit already, Alicia Johns! We'll have no more jeering tonight, Hold your tongue.'

Alicia was taken-aback and glared at Jean. Jean glared back. Alicia said no more. Soon the girls were in bed and the lights were put out. They stopped talking at once. Sally had insisted that the rules were to be kept, and the girls respected her and kept them.

One by one they fell asleep. Daphne was one of the last to sleep, but long after she was asleep too, somebody else was wide awake. That was Ellen, of course.

She had gone to bed early for three reasons. One was that she really had got 'one of her headaches'. Another was that she didn't want to face the girls after their accusing faces. And the third was that she wanted to think.

She had hardly been able to believe her ears when the girls had accused her so unjustly. Ellen had not taken anything. She was completely honest in that way, however much she might have made up her mind to cheat over the exam. A thief! Alicia had called her that in front of everyone. It wasn't fair. It was most cruel and unjust!

But was it altogether unjust? After all, the girls, two of them at least, had seen her snooping round and had seen her going through Miss Parker's desk and looking through things on Miss Potts' desk too. It must seem to them as if such behaviour meant dishonesty—and it did mean dis-honesty, though not the kind they accused her of.

'What am I doing! How can I cheat like this! How

can I be such a sneak and do such dreadful things ! ' Ellen
suddenly cried in her mind. ' What would Mother think
of me ! But oh, Mother, it's all because of you and Daddy
that I want to do well. Not for myself. Surely it isn't so
wrong if I cheat to please my parents, and not to please
myself ? '

' It *is* wrong,' said her conscience. ' You know it is !
See what your foolishness has led you into ! You have been
accused of something terrible—all because you were trying
to do something wrong, and hadn't even done it ! '

' I shan't cheat. I won't think of it any more,' Ellen
decided suddenly. ' I'll do badly in the papers and explain
why to Mother. I will, I will ! '

Then the girls came up and she heard Alicia's spiteful
remark. ' Pretending to be asleep.' In a flash she remembered her unkind accusations, her sneering words, and she
remembered too how all the girls seemed to be against her
and to believe she was wicked and bad.

Anger crept through her. How dared they accuse her
wrongly, without any real proof at all ? They all thought
her bad, and nothing would convince them that she wasn't,
she was sure. Very well, then, she *would* be bad ! She
would cheat ! She'd get up in the middle of the night and
go and find those papers. She knew where they were—
in Mam'zelle's room.

Ellen lay there in the darkness, her mind going over
everything again and again. She felt defiant and obstinate
now. She was labelled ' Bad ' by the girls. Then she
would be bad. She'd enjoy it now ! She would read
those exam papers, and then she would look up all the
answers, and she would surprise everyone by coming out
top with practically perfect marks ! That would make
them all sit up !

She had no difficulty at all in lying awake until she was
sure that the staff had gone to bed. Her eyes looked

straight up into the darkness, and her head felt hot. She
clenched her fists when she thought of Alicia's scornful
face.

At last she thought it would be safe to get up. She sat
up in bed and looked round. The moon was up and a ray
pierced the darkness of the room. There was no move·
ment anywhere, and all she could hear was the regular
breathing of the other girls. She slid out of bed. She put
her feet into her bedroom slippers and pulled her dressing-
gown round her. Her heart was beating painfully.

She crept out of the room. She knocked against one of
the beds on the way and held her breath in case she awoke
the girl asleep there. But there was no movement.

She made her way down the moonlit passage, and down
the stairs to Mam'zelle's room, the one she shared with
Miss Potts. It was in darkness. Mam'zelle had gone to
bed long ago.

Ellen went to the window to make sure that the curtains
were tightly drawn. She did not want anyone to see even
a crack of light there at that time of night. They were
thick curtains and shut out the moonlight. Then she shut
the door and switched on the electric light.

She went to the desk. It was untidy as usual, for Mam'-
zelle Dupont, unlike Mam'zelle Rougier, could never keep
her books and papers in neat order. Ellen began to go
through the papers on top of the desk.

She went through them twice. The exam papers were
not there! Her heart stood still. Surely they must be
there. Perhaps they were *in* the desk. She hoped it was
not locked. She had seen Mam'zelle lock it sometimes.

She tried it. Yes—it *was* locked. What a blow!
Mam'zelle must have locked the test-papers up! Ellen
sat down, her knees shaking with the suspense. Then her
eyes caught sight of a key lying in the pen-tray. She
snatched it up. She fitted it into the desk—and it opened !

How like Mam'zelle to lock the desk carefully and leave the key in the pen-tray!

With trembling hands Ellen looked through the vast collection of papers there. In a corner, neatly banded together by Miss Parker, were the second-form test-papers!

With a thankful sigh Ellen took them up. She was just about to look carefully through them when she heard a sound. Her heart almost stopped! In a trice she slipped to the door and switched off the light. Then she shut the desk quietly and went over to the door to listen.

The sound came again. What was it? Was it somebody walking about? She would have to be very careful if so. She stuffed the papers into the big pocket of her dressing-gown and held them there. She had better get out of Mam'zelle's room if she could, because if anyone found her there she would get into very serious trouble.

Upstairs, in the dormy, just after Ellen had crept out, Darrell awoke. It was her bed that Ellen had bumped into, and she had not awakened immediately. But she sat up half a minute after Ellen had gone out of the room, wondering what had awakened her.

She was just about to settle down again when she noticed Ellen's empty bed. The moon was sending a bright ray down on it—and there was no lump there to show that Ellen was lying asleep. It was flat and empty!

Darrell stared at the empty bed. Where was Ellen? Was she ill again? Or—was she doing a bit more snooping to see if she could find anything valuable?

Darrell looked across at Sally. She ought to tell Sally and let her deal with it. Alicia had already interfered enough, and she, Darrell, ought to let Sally say what was to be done about the empty bed, if Ellen didn't come back very quickly.

Ellen didn't come back. Darrell waited impatiently for some minutes and then decided to try to find her. She wouldn't wake Sally. She was full of curiosity and wanted to follow Ellen herself. It seemed an exciting thing to do in the middle of the night!

She put on her slippers and dressing-gown. She went out of the room, treading quietly in her soft slippers. She stood in the passage and listened. She could hear nothing.

She padded down the passage and came to the stairs. Perhaps Ellen was going through the desks in the second-form room—or even in the first form! She went quietly down the stairs. She came to the first-form room, which had its door shut. Darrell opened it. The room was in darkness and she shut the door again. It made a little click.

She went to the second-form room and opened the door there. She thought she heard something and switched on the light quickly. She could see no one there. She switched off the light again and was about to shut the door when she thought she heard a sound. She quickly switched the light on again—and then, over by the cupboard she saw a movement! Just as if someone had pulled the door to very quickly.

Darrell's heart beat. Was it Ellen in there? Or somebody else? She wouldn't like it at all if it was a burglar. But it must be Ellen. She had gone from her bed and was nowhere to be seen. She must be there, in the cupboard, hiding.

Darrell went swiftly to the cupboard and gave the door a sharp tug. It came open—and there, crouching in the cupboard, scared and trembling, was Ellen! She had slipped out of Mam'zelle's room and gone into the second-form room when she had heard Darrell coming. She had hidden in the cupboard, as still as a mouse.

Darrell looked in amazement at her. 'Come out!' she said. 'You bad girl, Ellen! Have you been stealing something again?'

'No,' said Ellen, and came out.   She held on to the test-
papers in her pocket, and Darrell noticed the action.

'What have you got there ? ' she demanded.   'Show
me !   Quick !   You're hiding something.'

'I'm not !   I'm not ! ' cried Ellen, forgetting all about
being quiet.   Darrell tried to snatch Ellen's hand away
from her pocket, and Ellen, afraid, lashed out at Darrell
with her other hand.   It caught her on the face.

Then Darrell lost her temper !   She flew at Ellen, shook
her fiercely, and slapped her hard on the cheek !   Ellen
fell over the legs of a desk and dragged Darrell down with
her.   She struggled and Darrell pummelled her well.
'You wicked girl ! ' shouted Darrell.   'Coming out and
stealing things !   You give me what you've taken ! '

Ellen suddenly went limp.   She could not struggle any
longer.   Darrell was able to drag her up and make her take
her hand away from her pocket.   She pulled out the packet
of papers roughly.   The band broke and they scattered all
over the floor.   Ellen covered her face and began to sob
loudly.

Darrell stared at the papers and picked one or two up.
'So you cheat too, do you ? ' she said, in a scornful voice.
'Tomorrow's exam papers !   Ellen Wilson, what sort of a
girl are you ?   A thief and a cheat !   How dare you come
here to Malory Towers ? '

'Oh, put the papers back and don't let anyone know ! '
sobbed Ellen.   'Oh, don't tell anyone ! '

'I'll certainly put the papers back,' said Darrell, grimly.
'But as for not telling anyone, that's absurd ! '

She dragged Ellen to the door.   'Where did you find the
papers ?   In Mam'zelle's desk.   We'll put them back there
then.'

She put them back, and then, with trembling fingers,
Ellen locked the desk again.   They went up to the dormy.
All the girls were still asleep.

Crouching in the cupboard was Ellen

'Tomorrow,' said Darrell, 'I shall tell Sally, Ellen. And she will decide what is to be done about you. I expect you'll be expelled. Now get into bed and try to go to sleep!'

17   RUMOURS AND TALES

NOBODY heard the two girls coming back. No one guessed that Darrell and Ellen had been out of their beds and back again. Darrell, furious and excited, lay awake for some time, debating whether or not to wake Sally there and then and tell her what had happened.

'No, I won't,' she decided, reluctantly. 'It would only wake all the others, and I must get Sally alone and tell her.'

She suddenly fell asleep, and, tired out with excitement, slept very soundly indeed. But Ellen could not sleep at all. This was nothing new for her. Most nights she did not sleep until the early hours of the morning. Now she lay on her back in bed, quite stunned by all the night's happenings. But gradually she ceased to worry about them for a bigger trouble came upon her. Her headache grew so bad that she thought her head must surely burst! Red hot hammers seemed at work inside it and at last the girl grew really frightened.

What was happening to her? Was she going mad? Was this what it felt like? She lay perfectly still with her eyes closed, hoping that the pain would die down. But it didn't. It got worse.

At last it was so bad that she began to moan softly. The thought of kind, comforting Matron came to her. Matron!

Matron had been kind to her in the San. She would be kind now. Ellen felt that if she could only have one small bit of kindness from someone she would feel better.

She sat up painfully, her head spinning round. The moon was now shining fully into the dormy. She could see all the white beds with their eiderdowns slipping off, or neatly pulled up. The girls lay in various positions, fast asleep.

Ellen got out of bed slowly, because any quick movement made her head hurt unbearably. She forgot about her dressing-gown, she forgot about her slippers. She made her way slowly to the door as if she was walking in her sleep. She passed out of it like a little ghost in pyjamas.

How she found her way to Matron's room she never remembered. But Matron suddenly awoke from sleep to hear a soft knocking at her door that went on and on.

'Come in!' she cried, 'Who is it?' She switched on the light. But nobody came in. The soft knocking went on and on. Matron was puzzled and a little alarmed.

'Come in!' she called again. But nobody came. Matron leapt out of bed and went to the door, a sturdy figure in a voluminous nightdress. She flung the door open—and there stood poor Ellen, drooping like a weeping willow tree, her hand up as if she was still knocking at the door.

'Ellen! What's the matter, child? Are you ill?' cried Matron and pulled her gently into her room.

'My head,' said Ellen, in a tired whisper. 'It's bursting, Matron.'

It didn't take Matron long to deal with Ellen. Seeing that the girl was in great pain, and that she could hardly even open her eyes, Matron soon had her in a warm and comfortable bed in a little room opening off her own. She gave her medicine and a hot drink. She put a comforting hot-water bottle in beside her. She was kind and gentle and spoke in a very low voice so as not to jar Ellen's aching head.

'Now you go to sleep,' she said. 'You'll feel better in the morning.'

Ellen did fall asleep. Matron stood by the bed and looked down at her. She was puzzled. There was something wrong with this girl. She was worrying secretly about something, and she had been doing worrying before, when she was in the San. Perhaps it would be better for her to go home for a while.

In the morning Darrell woke up with the others when the dressing-bell went. She sat up, remembering all the excitement of the night. She glanced at Sally. She must somehow get her alone.

Then Sally gave an exclamation. 'Where's Ellen? Her bed's empty!'

Everyone looked at Ellen's empty bed. 'Perhaps she got up early,' suggested Emily. 'We'll see her at break-fast-time.'

Darrell felt a bit worried. Had Ellen got up early? Where was she?

Ellen was not at breakfast, of course. The girls looked at the empty place, and Darrell felt distinctly uncomfortable. Surely—surely Ellen hadn't run away in the night and not come back! Mam'zelle was taking breakfast that day and Darrell spoke to her.

'Where's Ellen, Mam'zelle?'

'She is not coming to breakfast,' said Mam'zelle, who knew nothing more than that. Miss Parker had told her hurriedly as she passed her in the corridor. 'I do not know why. Perhaps she is ill.'

Now Alicia began to feel uncomfortable too. She remembered how she had accused Ellen so bitterly the day before. Where *was* Ellen? She too began to wonder if

the girl had run away home.   She ate her porridge rather
silently.

The next piece of news came from a first-former, Katie.
She had heard Miss Parker talking to Miss Potts, and had
caught a few words.

' I say !   What's up with Ellen Wilson ? ' she demanded.
' I heard Nosey tell Potty that she was going to be sent home !
What's she done ? '

Sent home !   The second-formers looked at one another.
Did that mean that the staff had found out about Ellen—
had perhaps discovered she had been stealing ?   And she
was to be expelled !   Good gracious !

' She's either been found out by one of the mistresses,
or else she's gone and confessed,' said Alicia, at last.   ' We'd
better not say too much about what we know.   It's not
much to the credit of the school.   I expect it will be all
hushed up.'

' Do you mean that you really think Ellen is being sent
away—expelled from the school—because she stole those
things ? ' said Daphne, looking suddenly white.   ' Surely
she won't ! '

' She jolly well will,' said Betty, and there was such scorn
in her voice that Daphne looked quite startled.   ' And a
good thing too !   Fancy having that kind of girl at Malory
Towers ! '

Darrell was bewildered by the turn things had taken.
Now she didn't know whether to report the happenings of
last night or not.   If Ellen was to be sent home for stealing,
then there didn't seem much point in telling anyone that
she, Darrell, had caught her cheating—taking the test-
papers to look at before the test.   Because certainly Ellen
wouldn't take the tests now, and why blacken her name
even more, now that she was apparently being sent off in
disgrace ?

Darrell was a generous girl, even to those she considered

her enemies.   She thought over the night before.   She had
certainly given Ellen a good deal of punishment for cheating !
She felt rather hot when she remembered how she had
slapped Ellen's face, pummelled her and knocked her down.
That was her temper again, of course.   Sally wouldn't have
done a thing like that.   Sally would have dealt with the
whole thing in a dignified, calm way, and would have made
Ellen show her the test-papers without a lot of undignified
rough behaviour that ended in both girls rolling on the
floor !

' I don't manage things very well, somehow,' thought
Darrell, rubbing her nose with her hand.   ' I just go off the
deep end with a splash !   I fly off the handle, I go up in
smoke !   Well, what am I going to do ?   Tell Sally or
not ? '

She decided not to.   There didn't seem any point at
all in complaining about Ellen, and making her character
still worse if she was really going to be sent home.   So
Darrell held her tongue, a thing that not many of the second
form would have done in the circumstances, for most of them
dearly loved a gossip.

Still, there was plenty of gossip in the second form
about Ellen.   Everyone seemed to take it for granted that
somehow or other it had been found out by the staff that
Ellen had taken the purses, money and brooch and possibly
other things as well, and was being expelled for that.

Curiously enough, one of the girls who seemed most distressed about this was Daphne.   ' But surely they won't
expel her without some proof ? ' she kept saying.   ' Sally,
Darrell, you said to Alicia yesterday that there was no real
proof that Ellen had stolen anything.   What will happen
to Ellen ?   Will another school take her ? '

' I don't know.   I shouldn't think so,' said Alicia.   ' She's
finished !   Serve her right ! '

' Don't be so hard,' said Jean.   ' Don't think I'm standing up for her—I'm not. But you always sound so hard and unmerciful, Alicia.'

'Well, I was right yesterday when I accused Ellen, wasn't I?' demanded Alicia. 'You were all so soft you didn't want to have it out with her! Good thing I did.'

The second form decided to say nothing about Ellen to the staff. If Miss Grayling was going to expel the girl, she would want to keep it quiet. So the less said the better.

So, rather to Miss Parker's surprise, nobody asked about Ellen at all. 'Curious, this lack of interest,' she thought, and she said nothing either. The girls had no idea at all when or if Ellen had gone home, though somebody passed round a rumour that a car had been seen in the drive that morning. Perhaps it had come to fetch Ellen!

It hadn't. It was the doctor's car. He had been called in to examine the girl, and he had spoken gravely to Matron and Miss Grayling. 'There's something here I don't understand. Is the child worried about anything? Is there anything wrong at her home? Has anything upset her at school?'

Neither Matron nor the Head Mistress could give the doctor any information. As far as they knew there was nothing wrong at Ellen's home, and there had been no upset in her form. Miss Parker was called in and she too said that as far as she knew Ellen had not been in any trouble in any class, except for mild tickings-off for not doing work up to standard.

'We think, Ellen,' said Miss Grayling gently, when the doctor had gone, 'we think you should go home when you feel well enough. That would be the best place for you now.'

She was startled by Ellen's response to this suggestion. The girl sat up and pushed back her hair in a despairing way. 'Oh, no, Miss Grayling! Don't expel me! Please don't!'

'Expel you!' said the Head, in amazement. 'What do you mean?'

Ellen had broken into sobs and Matron came hurrying up at once, making signs to Miss Grayling to go. 'She mustn't be excited in any way,' she whispered. 'So sorry, Miss Grayling, but I think you'd better go. I'll deal with her now.'

Miss Grayling, very puzzled indeed, went quietly out of the room. Why should Ellen think she was going to be expelled? There was something here that needed looking into.

It took Ellen a long time to calm down. She really thought that Miss Grayling's suggestion of going home meant that she was telling her she was to be sent away from Malory Towers—expelled in disgrace. Perhaps Darrell had been to her and told her about the cheating? Or perhaps Alicia had told her that they all believed she had been stealing, and Miss Grayling had decided to expel her because of that. Ellen didn't know. She began to worry all over again and Matron was alarmed at the quick rise in her temperature.

Some of the second-formers were upset at the thought that Ellen might have been already expelled, and had been sent home without even saying goodbye. Mary-Lou especially was upset. She hadn't liked Ellen very much, but she was very sorry for her. She spoke to Daphne about it at Break.

'Daphne, isn't it awful? What will poor Ellen say to her parents when she gets home? Do you think she will have to tell them herself that she's been sent away for stealing?'

'Don't!' said Daphne. 'Don't let's talk about it, Mary-Lou. Look, we've got about ten minutes, haven't we? I've got a most important parcel to send off this morning, and I can't find any string anywhere. Be a dear and get me some. I've got the brown paper.'

Mary-Lou sped off, wondering what the important parcel was. She couldn't seem to find any string at all. It was astonishing, the total lack of any string that morning! When at last she got back to Daphne, the bell went for the next lesson.

'Haven't you got any string?' said Daphne, disappointed. 'Oh, blow! Well, I'll see if I can find some after the morning lessons, and then I'll slip down to the post with the parcel this afternoon. I've got half an hour in between two lessons, because my music mistress isn't here today.'

'Is it so very important?' asked Mary-Lou. 'I could run with it for you, if you like.'

'No. You'd never get there and back in time,' said Daphne. 'It's a long way by the inland road. You could manage it by the coast road, but there's such a gale again today you'd be blown over the top! I'll go in between lessons this afternoon.'

But she couldn't go after all, with her 'important parcel', whatever it was, for the music mistress turned up, and Daphne was called away to her lesson. She left the parcel in her desk.

'Oh dear!' she said at teatime, to Gwen and Mary-Lou. 'I did so badly want to take my parcel to the post—and I had to have my music-lesson after all—and now I've got to go to Miss Parker after tea for a returned lesson, and after that there's a rehearsal for that silly French play.'

'What's so urgent about the parcel?' asked Gwen. 'Somebody's birthday?'

Daphne hesitated. 'Yes,' she said. 'That's it. If it doesn't go today it won't get there in time!'

'Well, you'll have to post it tomorrow,' said Gwen. Mary-Lou looked at Daphne's worried face. What a pity she, Mary-Lou, couldn't take it for her. She always liked doing things for Daphne, and getting that charming smile in return.

She began to think how she might do it. 'I'm free at seven, after prep,' she thought. 'I'll have half an hour before supper. I could never get to the post-office and back if I take the inland road—but I could if I took the coast road. Would I dare to—in the dark and rain ?'

She thought about it as she sat in afternoon school. 'People don't mind what they do for their friends,' she thought. 'They dare anything. Daphne would be so thrilled if I went to the post and got her birthday parcel off for her. How kind she is to want it to get there on the day. Just like her. Well—if it isn't too dark and horrible, I might run along tonight for her. I mustn't tell anyone though, because it's against the rules. If Sally got to know, she'd forbid me !'

So timid little Mary-Lou planned to do something that even not one of the seniors would do on a dark, windy night—take the coast road on the cliff, whilst a gale blew wildly round !

18   MARY-LOU

AFTER prep that night Mary-Lou scuttled back to the second-form room, which was now empty except for Gwendoline, who was tidying up.

Mary-Lou went to Daphne's desk. Gwendoline looked at her jealously. 'What do you want in Daphne's desk ? I can take her anything she's forgotten. I wish you wouldn't suck up to her so much, Mary-Lou.'

'I don't,' said Mary-Lou. She opened the desk-lid and fished for the brown-paper parcel, now neatly tied up with string. 'I'm going to the post with this for Daphne. But don't go and split on me, Gwen. I know it's against the rules.'

Gwendoline stared at Mary-Lou in surprise. '*You* breaking the rules!' she said. 'I don't believe you ever did that before. You're mad to think you can get to the post and back in time.'

'I shall. I'm taking the coast road,' said Mary-Lou, valiantly, though her heart failed her when she said it. 'It's only ten minutes there and back by that road.'

'Mary-Lou! You must be daft!' said Gwendoline. 'There's a gale blowing and it's dark as pitch. You'll be blown over the cliff as sure as anything.'

'I shan't,' said Mary-Lou, stoutly, though again her heart sank inside her. 'And, anyway, it's only a small thing to do for a friend. I know Daphne particularly wants this parcel to go today.'

'Daphne isn't your friend,' said Gwendoline, a flare of jealously coming up in her again.

'She is,' said Mary-Lou, with such certainty that Gwendoline was annoyed.

'Baby!' said Gwendoline, scornfully. 'You're too silly even to see that Daphne only uses you because you can help her with her French. That's the only reason she puts up with you hanging round her. She's told me so.'

Mary-Lou stood looking at Gwendoline, the parcel in her hand. She felt suddenly very miserable. 'It's not true,' she said. 'You're making it up.'

'It *is* true!' said Gwendoline, spitefully. 'I tell you Daphne has said so herself to me heaps of times. What would a girl like Daphne want with a mouse like you! You're just useful to her, that's all, and if you weren't so jolly conceited you'd know it without being told!'

Mary-Lou felt as if it must be true. Gwendoline would never say such a thing so emphatically if it wasn't. She picked up the parcel, her mouth quivering, and turned to go.

'Mary-Lou! You don't mean to say you're going to bother with that parcel after what I've just told you!' called Gwendoline, in surprise. 'Don't be an idiot.'

'I'm taking it for Daphne because I'm *her* friend!' answered Mary-Lou, in a shaky voice. 'She may not be mine, but if I'm hers I'll still be willing to do things for her.'

'Stupid little donkey!' said Gwendoline to herself, and began to slam books back on to shelves and to make a terrific cloud of dust with the blackboard duster.

She didn't tell Daphne that Mary-Lou had gone off into the darkness with her parcel. She was feeling rather ashamed of having been so outspoken. Daphne might not like it. But after all it was nearly the end of the term, and there would be now no need for Mary-Lou to help Daphne. She would probably be glad to be rid of Mary-Lou when she no longer needed her help with her French.

Half-past seven came and the supper-bell rang. Girls poured out of the different rooms and went clattering down to the dining-room. 'Oooh! Coffee tonight for a change! And jammy buns and rolls and potted meat!'

They all sat down and helped themselves, whilst Miss Parker poured out big cups of coffee. She glanced round the table. 'Two empty chairs! Who's missing? Oh, Ellen, of course. Who's the other?'

'Mary-Lou,' said Sally. 'I saw her just after prep. She'll be along in a minute, Miss Parker.'

But five minutes, ten minutes went by and there was no sign of Mary-Lou. Miss Parker frowned.

'Surely she must have heard the bell. See if you can find her, Sally.'

Sally sped off and came back to report that Mary-Lou was nowhere to be found. By this time Gwendoline was in a great dilemma. She and she only knew where Mary-

Lou was. If she told, she would get Mary-Lou into trouble. Surely she would be back soon? Maybe she had had to wait at the post-office!

Then she suddenly remembered something. The post-office shut at seven! It wouldn't be any use Mary-Lou trying to post a parcel there, because it would be shut. Why hadn't she thought of that before? Then what had happened to Mary-Lou?

A cold hand seemed to creep round Gwendoline's heart and almost stop her breathing. Suppose—suppose that the wind had blown little Mary-Lou over the cliff? Suppose that even now she was lying on the rocks, dead or badly hurt! The thought was so terrible that Gwendoline couldn't swallow her morsel of bun and half-choked.

Daphne thumped her on the back. Gwendoline spoke to her in a low, urgent voice.

'Daphne! I must tell you something as soon after supper as possible. Come into one of the practice-rooms where we shall be alone.'

Daphne looked alarmed. She nodded. When supper was finished she led the way to one of the deserted practice-rooms and switched on the light. 'What's the matter?' she asked Gwendoline. 'You look like a ghost.'

'It's Mary-Lou. I know where she went,' said Gwendoline.

'Well, why on earth didn't you tell Miss Parker then?' asked Daphne, crossly. 'What *is* the matter, Gwen?'

'Daphne, she took your precious parcel to the post just after seven o'clock,' said Gwendoline. 'She took the coast road. Do you think anything's happened to her?'

Daphne took this in slowly. 'Took my parcel to the post? What*ever* for! At this time of night, too.'

'She went all soppy and said that although it meant her going out in the dark and the wind, she'd do it because **you** were her friend,' said Gwendoline.

'Why didn't you stop her, you idiot?' demanded
Daphne.

'I did try,' said Gwendoline. 'I even told her that you
were *not* her friend—you only found her useful for helping
you with your French, as you've often and often told me,
Daphne—and you'd think that would stop anyone from
going off into the dark on a windy night, wouldn't you, to
post a silly parcel?'

'And didn't it stop her?' said Daphne, in a queer sort
of voice.

'No. She just said that she would take it for you because
she was *your* friend,' said Gwendoline, rather scornfully.
'She said you might not be her friend, but she was yours,
and she'd still be willing to do things for you.'

Gwendoline was amazed to see tears suddenly glisten in
Daphne's eyes. Daphne never cried! 'What's up?' said
Gwendoline in surprise.

'Nothing that you'd understand,' said Daphne, blinking
the tears away savagely. 'Good heavens! Fancy going
out on a night like this and taking the coast road—just
because she wanted to take that parcel for me. And the
post-office would be shut too! Poor little Mary-Lou!
What can have happened to her?'

'Has she fallen over the cliff, do you think?' asked
Gwendoline.

Daphne went very white. 'No—no, don't say that!'
she said. 'You can't think how awful that would be. I'd
never, never forgive myself!'

'It wouldn't be *your* fault if she did,' said Gwendoline,
surprised at this outburst.

'It would, it would! You don't understand!' cried
Daphne. 'Oh, poor kind little Mary-Lou! And you sent
her out thinking I didn't like her—that I only just used her!
I *do* like her. I like her ten times better than I like you!
She's kind and generous and unselfish. I know I did use

her at first, and welcomed her just because she could help me—but I couldn't help getting fond of her. She just gives everything and asks nothing ! '

' But—you told me heaps of times you only put up with her because she was useful,' stammered Gwendoline, completely taken aback by all this, and looking very crestfallen indeed.

' I know I did ! I was beastly. It was the easiest thing to do, to keep you from bothering me and nagging me about Mary-Lou. Oh, I shall never, never get over it if anything has happened ! I'm going after her. I'm going to see if I can find her ! '

' You can't ! ' cried Gwendoline, in horror. ' Hark at the wind ! It's worse than ever ! '

' If Mary-Lou can go out into that wind to post a stupid parcel for me, surely *I* can go out into it to find her ! ' said Daphne, and a look came into her pretty, pale face that Gwendoline had never seen before—a sturdy, determined look that gave her face unexpected character.

' But, Daphne,' protested Gwendoline, feebly, and then stopped. Daphne had gone out of the little music-room like a whirlwind. She ran up to the dormy and got her mackintosh and sou-wester. She tore down to the cloakroom and put on her Wellingtons. Nobody saw her. Then out she went into the night, flashing on her torch to see her way.

It was a wild night, and the wind howled round fiercely. It took Daphne's breath away as she made her way to the coast road up on the cliff. Whatever would it be like there ! She would be almost blown away.

She flashed her torch here and there. There was nothing to be seen but a few bent bushes, dripping with rain.

She went a little farther and began to call loudly and desperately.

' Mary-Lou ! Mary-LOU ! Where are you ? '

The wind tore her words out of her mouth and flung them over the cliff. She called again, putting her hands up to her mouth. 'Mary-Lou! MARY-LOU! MARY-LOU!'

And surely that was a faint call in answer. 'Here! Here! Help me!'

19   A HEROINE!

DAPHNE stood quite still and listened. The cry came again on the wind, very faint. 'Here! Here!'

It seemed to come from somewhere in front. Daphne struggled on against the wind, and then came to a place where the cliff edge swung inwards. She followed the edge round cautiously, not daring to go too near, for the wind was so strong. Still, it seemed to be dying down a little now.

She suddenly heard Mary-Lou's voice much nearer. 'Help! Help!'

Daphne was afraid of being blown over the cliff if she went too near the edge. But the voice seemed to come from the edge somewhere. Daphne sat down on the wet ground, feeling that the wind would not then have so much power over her and began to edge herself forward, holding on the tufts of grass when she could.

She came to where the cliff had crumbled away a little, and made a series of ledges, going steeply down to the sea. She crawled to this place, lay flat down and shone her light over the broken cliff.

And there, a few feet below, was poor Mary-Lou, clinging

for dear life to a ledge, her white face upturned to the glare of the torch.

'Help!' she called again, feebly, seeing the torch. 'Oh, help me! I can't hold on much longer!'

Daphne was horrified. She could see that if Mary-Lou did leave go, she would hurtle down to the rocks a long way below. Her heart went cold at the thought. What could she do?

'I'm here, Mary-Lou!' she called. 'Hold on. I'll fetch help.'

'Oh—Daphne! Is it you! Don't go away, Daphne. I shall fall in a minute. Can't you do something?'

Daphne looked down at Mary-Lou. She felt that it would not be the slightest use leaving her and going for help for it was clear that Mary-Lou might leave go at any moment. No, she must think of something else and do it at once.

She thought of her mackintosh belt, and her tunic belt. If she tied those both together and let them down, Mary-Lou might hold them and drag herself up. But would they reach?

She undid her mackintosh belt and took off her tunic belt with fingers that fumbled exasperatingly. All the time she kept up a comforting flow of words to Mary-Lou.

'I'll save you, don't you worry! I'll soon have you up here! I'm making a rope with my belts and I'll let it down. Hold on, Mary-Lou, hold on, and I'll soon save you!'

Mary-Lou was comforted and held on. She had been so frightened when the gale took her and rolled her over and over to the edge of the cliff. How she had managed to hold on to the tufts of grass she didn't know. It had seemed ages and ages till she heard Daphne's voice. Now Daphne was here and would rescue her. Whatever Gwendoline had said, Daphne was her friend!

Daphne lay down flat again. She found a stout gorse

bush behind her and she pushed her legs under it till her feet found the sturdy root-stem growing out of the ground. Heedless of scratches and pricks, she wound her two feet firmly round the stem, so that she had a good hold with her legs and would not be likely to be pulled over the cliff by Mary-Lou.

A frantic voice suddenly came up to her. ' Daphne ! This tuft of grass is giving way ! I shall fall ! Quick, quick.'

Daphne hurriedly let down the rough rope, made of her two belts. Mary-Lou caught at it and looped the end firmly round her wrists. Daphne felt the pull at once.

' Are you all right ? ' she called, anxiously. ' You won't fall now, will you ? '

' No. I don't think so. My feet have got quite a firm hold,' called back Mary-Lou, much reassured by the belt round her wrists. ' I shan't pull you over, shall I, Daphne ?

' No. But I don't think I'm strong enough to pull you up ! ' said Daphne, in despair. ' And the belts might break and let you fall. I don't see that we can do anything but just hang on to each other till somebody finds us.'

' Oh, poor Daphne ! This is awful for you,' came back Mary-Lou's voice. ' I wish I'd never thought of taking that parcel.'

' It was kind of you,' said Daphne, not knowing how to get the words out. ' But you're always kind, Mary-Lou. And Mary-Lou, I'm your friend. You know that, don't you ? Gwen told me the beastly things she said. They're not true. I think the world of you, I do really. I've never been fond of anyone before.'

' Oh, I knew Gwen told me untruths, as soon as I heard your voice and knew you'd come to look for me,' said Mary-Lou, out of the darkness. ' I think you're a heroine, Daphne.'

' I'm not,' said Daphne. ' I'm a beastly person. You simply don't know how beastly.'

' This is a funny conversation to be having on a cliff-side in a stormy night, isn't it ? ' said Mary-Lou, trying to sound cheerful. ' Oh dear—I am so sorry to have caused all this trouble. Daphne, when will people come to look for us ? '

' Well, only Gwen knows I've come out,' said Daphne. ' If I don't come back soon, surely she will tell Nosey Parker, and they'll send out to look for us. I do hope she'll have the sense to tell someone.'

Gwendoline had. She had felt very worried indeed about first Mary-Lou and now Daphne. When Daphne had not come back after half an hour, Gwendoline had gone to Miss Parker. She told her where Mary-Lou had gone and that Daphne had gone to look for her.

' What! Out on the coast road at night! In this weather! What madness ! ' cried Miss Parker, and rushed off to Miss Grayling at once.

In two or three minutes a search-party was out with lanterns, ropes and flasks of hot cocoa. It was not long before the two girls were found. Miss Grayling gave an agonized exclamation as she saw them. ' They might both have been killed ! '

Daphne's arms were almost numb with strain when the search-party came up. They saw her lying flat on the ground, her legs curled tightly round the stem of the prickly bush, holding the two belts down the cliff-side—and there, at the other end, holding on for dear life, was Mary-Lou, the sea pounding away far below her.

A rope was let down to Mary-Lou, slipped right over her head, and tightened over arms and shoulders. Another one looped tightly round her waist. Daphne got up thankfully, her legs almost asleep, and Miss Parker caught hold of her. ' Steady now ! Hold on to me ! '

Mary-Lou was pulled up safely by a hefty gardener. She

lay on the ground, crying with relief.   The gardener undid
the ropes and lifted her up.   'I'll carry her,' he said.
'Give her a drink, Mam, she's freezing!'

Both girls felt glad of the hot cocoa.   Then, holding on
to Miss Parker, Daphne staggered back to school, followed
by the gardener carrying Mary-Lou, and then by the rest
of the party.

'Put both girls to bed,' Miss Grayling said to Matron.
'They've had a terrible experience.   I only hope they don't
get pneumonia now!   Daphne, you saved little Mary-
Lou's life, there's no doubt about that.   I am very proud
of you!'

Daphne said nothing at all, but, to Miss Grayling's
surprise, hung her head and turned away.   She had no
time to puzzle over this, but helped Matron to get Mary-
Lou undressed and into bed.   Both girls were soon in warm
beds, with hot food and drink inside them.   They each felt
extremely sleepy, and went off to sleep quite suddenly.

The second-formers were in bed, worried and sleepless.
Gwen had told them about Mary-Lou going off, and
Daphne following her to see if she could find her.   They
knew that a search-party had gone out.   All kinds of
horrible pictures came into their minds as they lay in bed
and listened to the wind.

They talked long after lights out.   Sally did not forbid
them.   This was not a usual night—it was a night of
anxiety, and talking helped.

Then, after a long time, they heard Miss Parker's quick
footsteps coming along the corridor.   News!   They all
sat up at once.

She switched on the light and looked round at the seven
waiting girls.   Then she told them the story of how Mary-
Lou and Daphne had been found, and how Daphne, by her
ingenious idea, had saved Mary-Lou.   She described how
she had laid herself down on the wet ground, her feet curled

round the gorse bush stem, and had held the belts down to Mary-Lou until help came.

'Daphne's a heroine!' cried Darrell. 'I never liked her—but, Miss Parker, she's been marvellous, hasn't she! She's a real heroine!'

'I think she is,' said Miss Parker. 'I did not guess that she had it in her. She's in bed now, in the San., but I think she'll soon be all right again. We'll give her three cheers and a clap when she comes back to class.'

She switched off the light and said good night. The girls talked excitedly for a few minutes more, thankful that they knew what had happened. Fancy Daphne turning out like that! And doing it for Mary-Lou! Why, Gwen had always said that Daphne only put up with Mary-Lou because she helped her with her French.

'Daphne must be fond of Mary-Lou,' said Darrell, voicing what everyone thought. 'I'm glad. I always thought it was mean to use Mary-Lou and not really like her.'

'I wonder what became of the parcel,' said Belinda 'Mary-Lou can't have posted it, because the post-office was shut. I bet nobody thought of the precious parcel.'

'We'll go and hunt for it tomorrow,' said Sally. 'I say—what a small dormy we are tonight—only seven of us. Ellen gone—and Daphne and Mary-Lou in the San. Well, thank goodness they're there and not out on the cliff.'

The wind rose to a gale again and howled round North Tower. The girls snuggled down closer into the beds. 'I do think Daphne was brave,' said Darrell, 'and I can't *imagine* how timid little Mary-Lou could possibly have dared to go out in this gale. *Mary-Lou* of all people.'

'People are queer,' said Irene. 'You simply never can tell what a person will do from one day to the next.'

'You never said a truer word!' chuckled Darrell. 'To-day you put your French grammar away in the games cup-board and tried to put your lacrosse stick into your desk—and goodness knows what you'll do tomorrow.'

20   AN ASTONISHING PARCEL

IT was difficult to do tests in the midst of so much excite-ment. The story of Mary-Lou and Daphne ran through the school and everyone talked about it. The two girls did not appear in school that day, because Matron was keeping them quiet. They neither of them seemed any the worse for their adventure.

Before afternoon school Darrell, Sally, Irene and Belinda set off up the cliff-path to look for the parcel. The wind had completely died down and it was a lovely day, one of Cornwall's best. The sky was as blue as a cornflower, and the sea picked up the colour and made the view a really beautiful one, as the girls walked up the coast-path.

'Look—that must be where Mary-Lou was blown over,' said Darrell, pointing to where the cliff had crumbled. 'And see—surely that's the gorse bush Daphne wound her legs round. Golly, she must have been scratched!'

The girls stood and looked at the place where Mary-Lou and Daphne had had their frightening adventure. Sally shivered, thinking of what it must have been like in the dark night, with the wind howling round and the sea pounding on the rocks below.

'It's horrid to think of,' she said. 'Come on—let's hunt

about for the parcel. Mary-Lou must have dropped it somewhere near here, I should think.'

They began to look. It was Darrell who found the parcel, lying wet and torn in the grass some little way off.

' I've got it ! ' she shouted, and ran to pick it up. ' Oh, it's all coming to pieces. The paper is pulpy, and the contents are coming out ! '

' Better take off the paper and carry the things inside home in our hands,' said Sally. So Darrell stripped off the wet, pulpy paper and shook out the contents. They fell on the grass.

They were rather queer. The girls looked at them, lying there. There were four purses of different sizes and shapes. There were three boxes, the kind that brooches or lockets are sold in by jewellers—little leather boxes with a catch you had to press to open them.

Darrell picked one up and pressed it. It shot open— and a little gold bar brooch gleamed inside. She looked at it, bewildered, then passed it to Sally.

' Isn't that Emily's brooch—the one she lost ? '

' It's got her name behind it if it is,' said Sally, in a sober voice. She took out the brooch and looked at the back of the little gold bar.

' Yes—it's Emily's,' she said. ' Her name is there.'

Sally opened another of the boxes. It contained a little gold necklace, plain and simple.

' Katie's ! ' said Irene at once. ' I've seen her wearing it ! Good gracious—how did these come to be in the parcel ? Is it the right parcel we've found ? '

Sally picked everything up from the grass. Her face looked very serious. ' It's the right parcel,' she said. ' Look—these purses belong to people we know. That's Gwen's. And that's Mary-Lou's. And that's surely Betty's.'

The four girls looked at one another in bewilderment.

They looked at the contents in bewilderment

'If this was the parcel that Mary-Lou was posting for Daphne, how was it Daphne put all these things into it?' said Sally, voicing what everyone was thinking.

'Could she have got them from Ellen?' said Darrell, puzzled. 'We all know Ellen must have taken them. Wherever did she get them from? Is she doing it to shield Ellen, or something?'

'We'll have to find out,' said Irene. 'Sally, we'd better take the parcel to Miss Grayling. We can't keep this to ourselves.'

'No, we can't,' said Sally. 'We'll go back at once.'

They went back, saying very little, puzzled and solemn. Here were the stolen things, the things they had accused Ellen of taking—Daphne had somehow got hold of them and for some extraordinary reason was sending them away—and Mary-Lou had almost lost her life in trying to post them, and had been rescued by Daphne! It was all most complicated.

'I think it's all very mysterious,' said Belinda. 'I can't make head or tail of it. It's a pity Ellen's been expelled, or we might go to her and show her what we've found.'

The girls had no idea that Ellen was still at Malory Towers. What with one rumour and another they were all firmly convinced she had been sent home!

The bell was ringing for afternoon school as they got in. They caught Miss Parker as she was going to the second form and asked her for permission to go and see Miss Grayling.

'We've found the parcel that Mary-Lou went to post and we think we ought to hand it over to Miss Grayling,' explained Sally.

'Very well. Don't be too long,' said Miss Parker, and went on her way. The four girls went to Miss Grayling's part of the buildings and knocked at her door.

'Come in!' said her low voice, and they opened the door

and went in.   She was alone.   She looked up in surprise
when she saw four girls.   Then she smiled, for she liked
all of them, even harum-scarum Belinda.

' Please, Miss Grayling, we found the parcel that Mary-
Lou went to post for Daphne,' said Sally, coming forward.
' And here are the things that were inside it.   The paper was
so wet that we had to take it off.'

She placed the purses and the boxes down on the Head
Mistress's desk.   Miss Grayling looked at them in surprise.
' Were *these* inside ! ' she said.   ' Are they all Daphne's
then ?   I understand that it was Daphne's parcel.'

There was an awkward pause.   ' Well, Miss Grayling,
they are things belonging to us girls,' said Sally, at last.
' We missed them at various times.   Some of the purses
had money in when they were taken.   They are empty
now.'

Miss Grayling suddenly looked quite different.   A stern
expression came into her eyes, and she sat up straight.

' You will have to explain a little better, Sally,' she said.
' Am I to understand that these were stolen at some time
from one or other of you this term ? '

' Yes, Miss Grayling,' said Sally, and the others nodded.

' You think Daphne took them ? ' said Miss Grayling,
after a pause.   The girls looked at one another.

' Well,' said Sally at last, ' we did think Ellen had taken
them, Miss Grayling.   We knew she had been expelled,
you see—and we thought . . .'

' Wait ! ' said Miss Grayling, in such a sharp tone that
the four girls jumped.   ' Ellen *expelled* !   Whatever do
you mean ?   She is in the San. under Matron's eye.   She
went to her two nights ago with a blinding headache, and
we are keeping her under observation to try to find out
what the matter is.'

The girls were absolutely taken aback.   Sally went
brilliant red.   She oughtn't to have believed those rumours !

But she had wanted to believe them, because she didn't like Ellen. The girls couldn't find a word to say.

Miss Grayling eyed them sharply. ' This is most extraordinary ! ' she said at last. ' I simply cannot understand it. What made you think Ellen should be expelled ? And why did you think she had taken these things ? She is surely not that type of girl at all. As you know, she won a scholarship here by means of very hard work and she came with a most excellent report as regards character from her last head mistress.'

' We—we thought she had taken them,' began Sally. ' At least, I said we ought not to accuse her till we had definite *proof*—but, but . . .'

' I see. You actually accused the unfortunate girl to her face, I suppose ? When was this ? '

' The evening before last, Miss Grayling,' said Sally, trying to avoid the Head Mistress's eyes, which had suddenly become gimlets, and were boring into her.

' The evening before last,' said Miss Grayling. ' Ah, that explains matters. It must have been because of that that Ellen got so upset, and was overcome by that fearful headache and went to Matron. And somehow you thought she had been expelled—goodness knows why—some silly rumour, I suppose, fostered by you because you wanted to believe it ! You may have done serious damage to an innocent girl.'

Darrell swallowed once or twice. She was remembering how she had attacked Ellen that night in the second-form room. Certainly Ellen had been cheating—but Darrell had called her a thief and said unforgivable things to her. She looked at Miss Grayling and knew that she must tell her what had happened between Ellen and herself. It was because of *that*, she felt sure, that Ellen had been ill that night. Oh dear—how things did begin to go wrong once you were silly yourself !

'Can I say a word to you alone, please, Miss Grayling,' said Darrell, desperately. 'It's something the others don't know about, but I think I'd better tell you.'

'Wait outside the door for a minute or two,' ordered Miss Grayling, nodding at Sally, Belinda and Irene. 'I haven't finished with you yet.'

They went outside and shut the door, feeling surprised. Whatever had Darrell got to tell Miss Grayling? She might at least have told them too!

Darrell poured out the story of how she had followed Ellen that night and caught her in the second-form room cupboard, clutching the test-papers in her hand.

'And I called her a cheat, which she was,' said Darrell, 'and I called her a thief, too, and told her I'd tell Sally in the morning and it would be reported and she would be expelled. And I suppose it worried her so much that she got that awful headache and went to Matron. And I never knew, and we all thought that somehow you must have found out she was a thief and had expelled her quietly, without making a fuss.'

'Well, really!' said Miss Grayling, when this out-pouring had come to an end. 'The things that go on in this school that nobody knows about! It's incredible. Do you actually mean to tell me, Darrell, that you and Ellen were fighting together on the floor of the second-form room in the middle of the night? That is not at all a thing to be proud of.'

'I know,' said Darrell. 'I'm awfully sorry about it now. But I just saw red, Miss Grayling—and lost my temper. I can't bear cheats.'

'It's very strange,' said Miss Grayling, thoughtfully. 'Ellen is a scholarship girl, and I have never known such a girl have any need to cheat. I can't believe that Ellen was cheating. If she was, there is some reason for it that must be found out. Don't any of you like Ellen, Darrell?'

Darrell hesitated. 'Well—she's so nervy and snappy and irritable, Miss Grayling. She snaps if we jerk the table, she shouts at us if we interrupt her reading. She's terribly bad-tempered. I think Jean likes her more than any of us do. She's been awfully patient with her.'

'I wish I'd known all this before,' said Miss Grayling. 'Now I know why Ellen was so upset when I suggested sending her home. I thought possibly she might feel better and happier at home—and she must have thought I was really meaning to expel her, because somebody had come to me and told me she was stealing or cheating. Poor Ellen. I think she has over-taxed that brain of hers and this is the result.'

Darrell stood silent. She felt that Miss Grayling was not very pleased with her. 'I'm sorry for what I did,' she said, trying to blink back the tears. 'I know I keep on and on saying I'll never lose my temper again or lose control of myself. You won't believe me any more.'

'I shall go on believing you and trusting you every single time,' said Miss Grayling, turning her deep-blue eyes on Darrell and smiling. 'And one day you'll be strong enough to keep your promise. Probably when you are in the sixth form! Now tell the others to come in again.'

They came in. Miss Grayling addressed them gravely. 'What Darrell told me I think it is better not to repeat to you for my own good reasons. I think she should not repeat it to you either. I will just say this—Ellen is not the thief, you may be absolutely certain of that.'

'Not the thief!' said Sally. 'But—we all thought she was—and Alicia accused her to her face . . . and . . .'

Sally had let Alicia's name slip without thinking. Miss Grayling drummed on her desk with a pencil. 'Oh—so Alicia did the accusing, did she ?' she said. 'Then she has something to feel very guilty about. I think that that public accusation brought Ellen's trouble to a head. Sally,

you are head-girl of the form.   I leave it to you to show
Alicia that a little more kindness and a little less hardness
would be very much more admired by me, by you and
everyone else.'

'Yes, Miss Grayling,' said Sally, feeling extremely guilty
herself.   'But Miss Grayling—who *was* the thief?'

'It couldn't possibly have been Daphne,' said Irene.
'Nobody who did what Daphne did last night could possibly
be so mean.   Why, Daphne's a heroine!   Everyone says
so!'

'And you think that if someone does a brave deed quite
suddenly, then he or she could never do a mean one?'
asked Miss Grayling.   'You are wrong, Irene.   We all
have good and bad in us, and we have to strive all the time
to make the good cancel out the bad.   We can never be
perfect—we all of us do mean or wrong things at times—
but we can at least make amends by trying to cancel out the
wrong by doing something worthy later on.   Daphne has
done quite a bit of cancelling, I think—but her heroic deed
doesn't mean that she can never do a small, mean one.'

'Is she the thief then?' asked Sally, incredulously.

'That is what I mean to find out,' said Miss Grayling.
'If she is, she shall tell you herself, and you shall judge her.
Now go back to your classroom.   I am going to see Daphne
in the San.   And by the way, Ellen could see someone
today.   What about Jean?   You said she liked Ellen more
than any of you did.   Tell her to go and see Ellen after tea
and be nice to her.'

'Can she tell her we know she's not the thief?' asked
Darrell, anxiously.   'And oh, Miss Grayling—could I see
her for a few minutes too, by myself?'

'Yes,' said Miss Grayling.   'But no more fighting,
Darrell, or Matron will deal very promptly with you indeed!'

DAPHNE, ELLEN—
AND MISS GRAYLING

MISS GRAYLING made her way to the San. She spoke to Matron, who nodded. ' Yes, Daphne is quite all right now. She has just got up.'

The Head Mistress told Matron to take Daphne into the next room, where they would be alone. Daphne went, helped along by Matron, and sat down in an arm-chair, wondering rather fearfully what the visit was about. Miss Grayling looked so serious.

' Daphne,' said the Head, ' these things were found in the parcel that Mary-Lou went to post for you. You had packed them up yourself. Where did you get them ? And why did you want to send them away ? '

She suddenly tipped the purses and the little boxes on to Daphne's knee. The girl stared at them in absolute horror. She went very pale and opened her mouth to speak. But no words came.

' Shall I tell you where you got them from ? ' said Miss Grayling. ' You took them out of desks and lockers and drawers. You spent the money, Daphne. You did, in fact, exactly what you have done in two other schools, which have quietly intimated to your parents that they would rather have you removed. But they did not tell your parents why.'

' How did you know ? ' whispered Daphne, her once pretty face white and haggard.

' It is the custom at Malory Towers to get a confidential report of any new girl's character from her previous head mistress,' said Miss Grayling. ' We do not, if we can help it, take girls of bad character, Daphne.'

'Why did you take me **then**?' asked Daphne, not daring to meet the Head's eyes.

'Because, Daphne, your last head mistress said that you were not *all* bad,' said Miss Grayling. 'She said that perhaps a fresh start in a fine school like this, with its traditions of service for others, for justice, kindliness and truthfulness, might help you to cancel out the bad and develop the good. And I like to give people a chance.'

'I see,' said Daphne. 'But I'm worse than you think, Miss Grayling. I haven't only stolen—I've told lies. I said I'd never been to another school before, because I was afraid the girls might get to know I'd been sent home twice from schools. I pretended my people were very rich. I— I had a photo on my dressing-table that wasn't my mother at all—it was a very grand picture of a beautiful woman ...'

'I know,' said Miss Grayling. 'The staff were warned about you, but not the girls. I have heard many things that made me sad, Daphne, made me think that you did not deserve the chance you had been given. Your greatest drawback is your prettiness—you want to make people admire you, you want to make them think you come of handsome, distinguished parents, from a wealthy home— you have to have envy and admiration, don't you? And because your parents are not as grand as you feel they ought to be, with you for a daughter, and cannot afford to give you as much pocket-money and pretty things as the others, you take what you want—you steal.'

'I'm no good,' said Daphne, and she looked down at her hands. 'I know that. I'm just no good.'

'And yet you have done a very brave thing,' said Miss Grayling. 'Look at me, please, Daphne. The girls admire you today—they call you a heroine. They want to cheer you and clap you. You have plenty of good in you!'

Daphne had raised her head and was looking at Miss Grayling. She flushed. 'I'm to blame for what happened

to Mary-Lou,' she said. ' When I heard that Ellen had
been expelled for stealing the things I had really stolen
myself, I was afraid. I was too much of a coward to own
up—but I thought if the empty purses and the boxes were
found, my finger-prints would be on them and I'd be found
out. So I thought I'd send them away by post, to a made-
up address. And Mary-Lou knew I was anxious to get the
parcel off and that's how she met her accident.'

' I see,' said Miss Grayling. ' I wondered why you sent
away the things, Daphne. It is a great mercy that you
found Mary-Lou when you did. Otherwise your foolishness and wrong-doing might have caused a great tragedy.'

' I suppose you will be sending me home, Miss Grayling,'
said Daphne, after a pause. ' My parents will have to know
why. They will guess there is some serious reason. They
don't pay my fees you know, they couldn't afford to. My
godmother does. If *she* knows about this, she will stop
paying for my education ; I shall have spoilt my whole life.
Am I to be sent away, Miss Grayling ? '

' I am going to let the girls decide that,' said Miss Grayling,
gravely. ' That is, if you are brave enough to let them,
Daphne. I want you to go to the second form and tell
them the whole story. Confess everything to them and
see what they say.'

'Oh, I can't,' said Daphne, and covered her face with her
hands. ' After all I've said—and boasted ! I can't ! '

' Well, you have the choice,' said Miss Grayling, getting
up. ' Either I send you home without any more ado—or
you put yourself in the hands of your school fellows. It is
a hard thing to do, but if you really want to make amends,
you will do it. You have some good in you. Now is your
chance to show it, even if it means being braver than you
were last night ! '

She left Daphne and went in to see Ellen. She sat down
by her bed. ' Ellen,' she said, ' Daphne is in great

trouble. The others will know soon and I have come to tell you myself. It has been discovered that it was she who took all that money and the jewellery that was missing.'

It took a moment for this to sink into Ellen's mind. Then she sat up. '*Daphne!* But the girls thought it was I who took them! They accused me. They'll never believe it was Daphne.'

'They will,' said Miss Grayling, 'because I rather think Daphne herself is going to tell them! And now, Ellen, tell me—what made you take those test-papers the other night? You are a scholarship girl with brains—you did not need to cheat.'

Ellen lay down again suddenly. She was overcome with shame. How did Miss Grayling know? Had Darrell told everyone then? Of course she had.

'Nobody knows except Darrell and myself,' said Miss Grayling. 'Darrell told me, but told no one else. So you need not worry. But I want to know why you did it. There is something you are worrying about, Ellen, and these headaches of yours won't go until you are at peace with yourself and have lost whatever worry it is you have.'

'I *did* need to cheat,' said Ellen, in a small voice. 'My brain wouldn't work any more. And I got these headaches. I knew I wouldn't even pass the tests—and the girls that night accused me of being a thief, which I wasn't—and I got all hopeless and thought that I might as well be a cheat if they all thought I was a thief!'

'I see,' said Miss Grayling. 'But why wouldn't your brain work any more?'

'I don't know,' said Ellen. 'Because I'd worked it a bit too hard, I expect, when I went in for the Scholarship. You see, Miss Grayling, I'm not really very brilliant. I get good results because I slog so—I go on and on, working and studying, where perhaps a real Scholarship girl can get better results with half the work. I worked all through the hols. too. I was tired when I got here—but I did so badly want to do well my first term.'

' Did it matter so much ? ' asked Miss Grayling, gently.

' Yes,' said Ellen. ' I didn't want to let my people down. They've had to pay out more than they can afford really for my uniform and things. They're so proud of me. I *must* do well. And now I've ruined everything.'

' Not quite ! ' said Miss Grayling, feeling very much relieved to find that simple overwork was at the root of Ellen's trouble, and worry about what her family would think. ' I shall write your parents a letter to tell them that you have worked very hard and done well, but that you are over-strained and must have a real holiday when it comes. By next term you will be quite fresh again, and you will have forgotten all this and be ready to rush up to the top of the form ! '

Ellen smiled at the Head, and the little worried cleft in her forehead disappeared like magic. ' Thank you,' she said gratefully. ' I'd like to say a lot more, but I can't.'

Miss Grayling popped in to have a word with Mary-Lou, and then went back to her own quarters. So many girls—so many problems—so much responsibility in putting things right, and getting the best out of every girl ! No wonder Miss Grayling had more grey hairs than she should have had.

22   DAPHNE OWNS UP.
THE END OF TERM

IMMEDIATELY after tea that day the second form were told by Miss Parker that they were to go to their common-room and wait there.

'Why?' asked Belinda, in surprise.

'You'll see,' said Miss Parker. 'Go along now. Someone is waiting there for you.'

They all went, and rushed pell-mell into the common-
room, wondering what the mystery was. Mary-Lou was
there, looking a little scared, wrapped in her dressing-gown.
Matron had carried her down.

And Daphne was there, fully dressed! The girls rushed
at her. 'Daphne! You're a heroine! Daphne! Well
done! You saved Mary-Lou's life!'

Daphne did not answer. She sat there and looked at
them, rather white in the face, and did not even smile.

'What's the matter?' asked Gwendoline.

'Sit down, all of you,' said Daphne. 'I've got something
to say. Then I shall go away and you won't see me again.'

'Good gracious! Why all this melodrama?' asked
Jean, disquieted by Daphne's tragic voice.

'Listen,' said Daphne. 'You've got to listen. I'm the
thief. I took those things. I've been sent away from two
schools already for much the same thing. Miss Grayling
knew that, but she wanted to give me another chance. So
I came here. I told you lies—especially Gwen. We
haven't a yacht. We haven't three or four cars. I told you
I'd never been to school before because I didn't want anyone to find out I'd been expelled. I hadn't enough money
to pay for some of the subs. Jean wanted, and how could
I say that, when you all thought my father was a millionaire?
So I took money and purses. And I took jewellery too,
because I like pretty things and haven't nearly enough
myself.'

She paused. The faces round her were shocked and
horrified. Gwendoline looked as if she was about to faint.
Her grand friend with her millionaire father! No wonder
Daphne had never asked her to stay for the holidays. It
was all lies.

'You all look shocked. I knew you would be. Miss Grayling said I was to come and confess to you myself, and you would judge me. I can see you judging me now. I don't blame you. I've judged myself, too, and I hate myself! I let you accuse Ellen wrongly, I let you . . .'

'And I fell into the trap and accused Ellen!' said Alicia, in a shamed voice. 'You are a beast, Daphne. You could have stopped me. I shall never forgive myself for doing that to poor old Ellen.'

There was a long pause. Then Sally spoke. 'Is that all, Daphne?'

'Isn't it enough?' said Daphne, bitterly. 'Perhaps you want to know why I got the wind up and sent away those things in a parcel, which poor Mary-Lou took for me. Well, when the rumour went round that Ellen was expelled for thieving, I was scared those purses and things might be discovered, with my finger-prints on. I know the police always look for prints. So I thought I'd better pack them up, put a false address on and send them away through the post. Then nobody would trace them to me. And because of that idiotic idea, Mary-Lou nearly got killed.'

'Yes—and because of that, you came out after me, and risked your own life for me!' said Mary-Lou's soft voice. She got up and went to Daphne. 'I don't care what the others say. I'll stick by you, Daphne. I don't want you to go. You won't ever take things again here now, I know. There's more good in you than bad.'

'Well, I'm sure I don't want to have anything more to do with her,' said Gwendoline, in a disgusted voice. 'If my mother knew . . .'

'Shut up, Gwendoline,' said Darrell. 'I'm sticking by Daphne too. I've done some pretty awful things this week myself, though I can't tell you what. And I think this—whatever wrong Daphne has done this term is cancelled out completely by her courage last night! We thought her deed was brave and noble then—and what she has just told us now doesn't make it any less brave or noble.'

'I agree with you,' said Sally. 'She's cancelled out her wrong with a right, as far as I'm concerned. And what's more, it wanted courage to come and face us all like this. You've got plenty of that, Daphne. If we stick by you and help you, will it make any difference to you ? I mean— will you stop any underhand ways and mean tricks ? '

'Do you mean that ? ' said Daphne, a sudden hope making her face shine. 'What about the others ? '

'I'm with Sally and Darrell,' said Jean.

'So am I,' said Belinda, and Irene nodded too. Emily thought for a moment and added her word as well.

'Yes, I'll agree,' she said. 'I think you've behaved terribly badly, Daphne—and terribly well too. At any rate you ought to have a chance to make good.'

'You, Alicia ? ' said Sally. Alicia had been very silent for the last few minutes. She was overcome with remorse about Ellen. She raised her eyes.

'It seems to me that I need to have a chance given to me to make good, as much as Daphne,' she said, shamefacedly. 'I've been worse than any of you.'

'You have been very hard and merciless, Alicia,' said Sally. 'You jeer at me for wanting to get proof before we accuse people, and for wanting to be fair and kind—but it's better in the end.'

'I know,' said Alicia. 'I do know that. I'm sorry. I've disliked you because you were head-girl instead of me this term, Sally. I've been a perfect idiot. I'm not the one to judge Daphne. I'll follow your lead, you may be sure.'

'Well, it seems as if it's only Gwendoline who is standing out,' said Sally, turning to the sulky-looking girl. 'Poor Gwendoline ! She's lost her grand friend and can't get over it. Well, we'll go and tell Miss Grayling that we are

all agreed on the matter except Gwendoline. We want to
give Daphne another chance, and we don't want her to go.'

'No, don't do that,' said Gwendoline, alarmed at the
thought of appearing small and mean to Miss Grayling.
'I agree too.'

'And you agree, Daphne?' said Sally, looking at the
quiet girl in the chair.

'Thank you, Sally. With all my heart,' said Daphne,
and turned her head away. It was a great moment in her
life—the forking of the ways. It was up to her to take the
right way and she knew it. If only she was strong enough
to !

A timid hand touched her arm. It was Mary-Lou.
'Come back to Matron now,' she said. 'She told us we
were to, as soon as the meeting was over. I'll help you
up the stairs.'

Daphne smiled for the first time, and this time it was
a real smile, a sincere one, not turned on for the sake of
being charming. 'You're the one that needs helping up !'
she said. 'Come on, or Matron will be hounding us out
of here.'

Jean went to see Ellen—a very different Ellen. Things
seemed to be clearing up magically. 'I feel miles better
now,' said Ellen. 'I'm not doing any more real lessons
this term, Jean, and no work at all in the hols. I shan't
snap and snarl any more either. I've lost that awful headache that made me so jumpy. It suddenly went after I'd
had a talk with Miss Grayling. It was most extraordinary.'

'You're lucky to be in bed just now,' said Jean. 'The
tests are simply awful. You should have seen the maths
one, Ellen. Honestly I could only do half the sums. But
the French one, set by Mam'zelle Dupont, was wizard.'

What with one thing and another, the week of tests passed
very quickly and then it was the last week of all. Mistresses
began to look harassed as the task of adding up marks,

correcting papers, making out reports, grew heavier and heavier. Mam'zelle Dupont worked herself up into a frenzy because she had lost her beautifully added-up marks list, and begged Miss Parker to do it for her again.

Miss Parker wouldn't. ' I've enough worries of my own,' she said. ' You're as bad as Belinda, Mam'zelle. She managed to answer a history test when all the rest of the class were doing a geography paper. Don't ask me how. That girl is the worst scatter-brain I ever saw in my life. How she got hold of a history paper when I had given out geography tests . . .'

' But why didn't she point out the mistake to you ? ' asked Mam'zelle, astonished.

' She said she didn't even *notice* that the questions were history ones,' groaned Miss Parker. ' These girls ! They will be the death of me. Thank goodness there are only two more days till the end of term ! '

Only two more days. But what hectic ones ! Packing things, looking for things, losing things, exchanging addresses, tidying cupboards, stacking books, cleaning paint-pots . . . all the thrilling little things that come at the end of term, and add to the excitement of going home.

' It's been a queer sort of term,' said Darrell to Sally. ' Don't you think so, Sally ? I'm not very pleased with some of the things I've done. You've been fine, though. You always are.'

' Rubbish ! ' said Sally. ' You don't know how many times I've hated Alicia for defying me. You don't know lots of things about me ! '

' I've enjoyed this term though,' said Darrell, remembering everything. ' It's been interesting. Ellen and her snappiness—and the way we all thought wrong things about her—and now it's all come right and she's quite different and she and Jean are as thick as thieves together ! '

' And then Daphne,' said Sally, the word ' thieves '

bringing her to mind. ' That was an extraordinary affair, wasn't it, Darrell ?   I'm glad we gave her a chance.   Isn't it funny the way she's dropped that silly Gwendoline Mary and taken Mary-Lou for her friend ? '

' Jolly good thing,' said Darrell.   ' Mary-Lou may be a timid little thing—but she's sound at heart.   And it's much better for her to have a friend of her own than go tagging after us all the time.   But I shall always like little Mary-Lou.'

' Gwendoline looks sour these days,' said Sally, nudging her friend as Gwendoline went by alone.   ' Nobody's darling now ! '

' Won't do her any harm,' said Darrell, hard-heartedly. ' She'll soon be Mother's darling and Miss Winter's darling, and have her bed made for her and everything done !   Dear darling Gwendoline Mary.   She didn't come very well out of the Daphne affair, did she ? '

' No, she didn't.   Perhaps she'll be better next term,' said Sally, doubtfully.   ' Oh, my goodness, what *is* Belinda doing ? '

Belinda shot by with a work-basket in her arms, from which trailed yards and yards of wool and cotton.   It wound itself round people's ankles and legs and at last forced her to stop.

' Get off my cottons ! ' she yelled indignantly.   ' You're holding me up ! '

' Oh, Belinda—you'll always be an idiot ! ' cried Darrell, unwinding some red wool from her right ankle.   ' Go away !   I'm getting a forest of cotton round me.   Belinda, don't forget to bring back a whole lot of funny sketches after the hols.'

' I will ! ' said Belinda, with a grin.   ' And what about Alicia thinking up a new trick for next term.   Hie, Alicia, we've thought of some holiday prep for you !   Make up some super tricks for next term, see ? '

' Right ! ' called Alicia.   ' I will.   You can bank on

that! Better than the "Oy!" on Mam'zelle's back, Darrell!'

'Oy! What is an Oy?' demanded Mam'zelle Dupont, bustling up. 'An "OY!" on my back? What is this you have done to me now?'

She screwed herself round, trying to see what an oy was, and the girls screamed with laughter.

'It's all right, Mam'zelle. It's not there now.'

'But what *is* an oy?' demanded Mam'zelle. 'I shall ask Miss Parker.'

But Miss Parker was not interested in Mam'zelle's 'oys'. She was only interested in getting the girls safely away on holiday. Then she could sit down and breathe in peace.

And at last they were really off. Cars swung into the drive. The train-girls went off singing. Belinda rushed frantically back for her suit-case, which she had as usual forgotten.

'Good-bye, Malory Towers!' yelled the girls. 'Good-bye, Potty! Good-bye, Nosey! Good-bye, Mam'zelle Oy!'

'They're gone,' said Mam'zelle. 'Ah, the dear, dear girls, how I love to see them come—and how I love to see them go! Miss Parker, you must tell me, please. What is this "Oy"? I have never heard of it.'

'Look it up in the dictionary,' said Miss Parker, as if she was speaking to her class. 'Four weeks of peace, blessed peace. I can't believe it!'

'They will soon be back, these bad girls,' said Mam'zelle. And she was right. They will!

THIRD YEAR AT MALORY TOWERS

Zerelda stood looking at the bustle

THIRD YEAR
AT MALORY TOWERS

by

ENID BLYTON

ILLUSTRATED BY
JENNY CHAPPLE

CONTENTS

DARRELL was busy helping her mother to pack her clothes to take back to boarding-school. Her little sister Felicity was watching, wishing that she too was going with Darrell.

'Cheer up, Felicity!' said Darrell. 'You'll be coming back with me in September. Won't she, Mother?'

'I hope so,' said her mother. 'Miss Grayling said she thought she would have room for her then. Oh, Darrell, surely you don't want all those books! They make your trunk so heavy.'

'Mother, I do!' said Darrell. 'And do let me take back my roller-skates. We're allowed to skate round the courtyard now. It's such fun.'

'All right,' said Mrs. Rivers. 'But it means unpacking half the trunk, because they must go at the bottom. Oh dear—did we mark your new bedroom slippers?'

'No!' groaned Darrell. 'Felicity, be a darling and mark them for me. Matron absolutely goes off the deep end if she finds anything not marked.'

Felicity darted off to get a pen. She was eleven and Darrell was fourteen. How she longed to go to Malory Towers too! According to Darrell it was the finest school in the kingdom!

'I wish we hadn't got to call for that new girl,' said Darrell, bent over her trunk. 'What's her name now, Mother? I keep forgetting it.'

'Zerelda,' said her mother. 'Zerelda Brass.'

'Golly!' said Darrell. 'Zerelda! Whatever will she be like?'

'Oh, all right, I expect,' said Mrs. Rivers. 'She's

American, you know. But her English grandmother has asked her over here for a year, and she's to go to Malory Towers. It's a marvel they were able to take her at short notice like that.'

'What's she like?' asked Darrell. 'Have you seen her?'

'No. Only a photograph,' said Mrs. Rivers. 'She looked about twenty there! But she's only fifteen, I think.'

'Fifteen! Then she won't be in my form,' said Darrell. 'She'll be in one higher up. Mother, isn't it a shame Sally's in quarantine for mumps? She'll be late coming back.'

Sally Hope was Darrell's best friend at school. Usually they arrived together at Malory Towers, for either Darrell's father or Sally's drove them down together in their cars. But this time Sally would be late because of the mumps quarantine.

'You'll have to write and tell her everything,' said Mrs. Rivers. 'Oh, thank you, Felicity—you've marked the slippers beautifully. Have you put in your bed-jacket, Darrell? Oh yes, there it is. Well, now we're really getting on. Where's the list? I'll just run down it and see if we have left anything out.'

'If Sally hadn't been in quarantine we wouldn't have had to call for Zerelda,' said Darrell. 'There wouldn't have been room. Mother, I have a feeling she will be awful. Whatever shall we talk about to her all the way down to Cornwall?'

'Good gracious—can't you talk about Malory Towers?' said her mother. 'You seem to be able to talk about it for hours on end at home.'

At last the packing was all done. Then there was the usual hunt for the key of the trunk, which always disappeared regularly each holiday.

'Have you signed my health certificate, Mother?' asked Darrell. 'Where is it? In my night-case? Right. I wonder if Irene will have got hers safely this term?'

Felicity giggled. She loved hearing about the harum-scarum Irene who always started off safely with her health certificate, and could never find it when she arrived.

Darrell's father was driving her mother and Darrell down to Malory Towers the next day. They had to start early, so all the packing was done the day before. All that Darrell had to do the next day was to go round the house and garden with Felicity and say good-bye to everything, even the hens!

'I shan't have to say good-bye to *you* in September, Felicity,' said Darrell. 'Well, good-bye, now, and just see you get on well in games this term, so that I can be proud of you when you come to Malory Towers!'

They were off at last, purring away down the road to the West Country. It was a lovely day in January, cold and sunny. Darrell pulled the rug round her. She was sitting alone at the back of the car. Her mother was in front. Soon they would come to Zerelda's house and then Darrell would have her at the back with her.

Zerelda lived in a big house about fifty miles along the way. Her grandmother had been a great friend of Mrs. Rivers' mother, and it was really Darrell's Granny that had asked Mrs. Rivers if she could fetch Zerelda and take her down to the school with Darrell.

'I think it would be so nice if she and Darrell could have a good long talk about the school,' said Darrell's Granny. 'Zerelda is sure to feel a bit queer, going to a school in a different country.'

But Darrell didn't feel very pleased about it. She was disappointed that they couldn't fetch Sally, her friend, and somehow she didn't like the sound of Zerelda. Was it the unusual name ? Or was it that she felt her mother didn't altogether like the sound of Zerelda either ? Anyway, they would soon see !

'Here's Notting,' said Mr. Rivers, seeing the name on a signpost. 'This is where we call for the American, isn't it ? '

'Yes,' said Mrs. Rivers, looking at a card in her hand. ' Turn to the right by the church. Go up the hill. Turn to the right again at the top and you will see a big white house. That's where Zerelda is living.'

They soon drew up at a big white house, almost a mansion. A butler opened the door. Then a smart, little old lady came running out, the friend of Darrell's Granny.

' This *is* kind of you ! ' she said. ' Zerelda ! Are you ready ? Here they are.'

No Zerelda appeared. Mrs. Rivers said they wouldn't come in and have coffee, as they wanted to be at the school before dark.

' If Zerelda is ready, we'll set off straight away,' said Mr. Rivers. He felt a little annoyed. Where was this Zerelda ? She ought to have been ready and waiting ! He went to the back of the car and got ready a strap for the luggage.

' Zerelda ! Come at once ! ' called her grandmother. She turned to the butler. ' Do you know where Miss Zerelda is ? Oh dear, where can she be ? '

It was some minutes before Zerelda appeared. And when she did arrive Darrell couldn't think that it *was* Zerelda ! She suddenly saw a tall, willowy person come down the stairs, with glinting hair the colour of brass, arranged in a big roll on the top of her head, with curls cascading over her shoulders.

Darrell stared. Who was this   She looked like somebody out of the films. And, good gracious, she had lipstick on surely ?

It couldn't be Zerelda. This girl looked about twenty. She came forward with a lazy smile.

'Oh! Zerelda! Where were you?' said her grandmother. 'You've kept us waiting.'

'Sorry,' drawled Zerelda. Her grandmother introduced her to the Rivers family. Mr. Rivers looked impatient. He hated to be kept waiting—and he didn't like the look of this Zerelda much!

Neither did Darrell. In fact, she felt quite alarmed. Zerelda must be seventeen or eighteen at least! Whatever would they talk about in the car?

'You'd better put on your school hat,' said her grandmother, handing it to Zerelda.

'What! Wear that terrible thing!' said Zerelda. 'Gee, Gran'ma, I never shall!'

Darrell didn't dare to say that she would certainly have to. She was quite tongue-tied. Zerelda seemed really grown-up to her. It wasn't only her looks, and the way she did her hair—it was her self-confident manner, and her grown-up way of talking.

She slid gracefully into the seat by Darrell. 'Now, Zerelda, you remember you're going to an English school, to learn a few English ways,' said her grandmother, at the window of the car. 'Oh dear, wipe that lipstick off your mouth. I've told you again and again it won't do here. You seem to think you're eighteen, but you're only a school-girl. Now mind you . . .'

Mr. Rivers, feeling that talk between Zerelda and her grandmother would probably go on for some time, put in his clutch and revved up the car. 'Good-bye!' said Mrs. Rivers, feeling that they might stay there for ever if she didn't firmly say good-bye.

The car moved off. Zerelda's grandmother was left still talking at top speed in the drive. Mr. Rivers heaved a sigh of relief, and looked at his wife out of the corner of his eye.

She looked back. Darrell caught the look and felt a little comforted. Daddy and Mother thought the same about Zerelda as she did!

'Have you got enough rug?' Darrell asked politely.

'Yes, thanks,' said Zerelda. There was a silence. Darrell racked her brains to think what to say.

'Would you like me to tell you something about Malory Towers?' she asked Zerelda at last.

'Go ahead, honey,' said Zerelda, rather sleepily. 'Spill the beans. What's our class-teacher like?'

'Well—you won't be in my class, because you're fifteen, aren't you?' said Darrell.

'Nearly sixteen,' said Zerelda, patting the big roll on the top of her head. 'No, I guess I won't be in your class. You're not very big are you?'

'I'm as big as anyone else in my form,' said Darrell, and she thought to herself that if she wore her hair in the same ridiculous way as Zerelda did, she too would look tall.

She began to talk about Malory Towers. It was her favourite subject, so her voice went on and on, telling about the great school with its four big towers, one at each end— the courtyard in the middle—the enormous pool in the rocks, filled by the sea each tide, where the girls bathed in the summer-time.

'And in each tower are the dormies where we sleep, and our common-rooms—the rooms we play about in, you know, when we're not in class,' said Darrell. 'Our house-mistress is Miss Potts. By the way, which tower are you in?'

There was no answer. Darrell looked in angry indignation at Zerelda. She was fast asleep! She hadn't heard a single word of all that Darrell had been telling her! *Well!*

DARRELL was so annoyed with Zerelda for falling asleep whilst she told her all about her beloved Malory Towers that she made up her mind not to say another word when Zerelda deigned to wake up.

She took a good look at the American girl. She was certainly very striking-looking, though her mane of hair was not really a very nice shade of gold. Darrell thought that Brass was a good surname for Zerelda. Her hair did look brassy! Darrell wondered if it had been dyed. But no, surely nobody would let her do that. Perhaps girls grew up more quickly in America though?

'It's a pity she's coming to Malory Towers,' thought Darrell, looking closely at Zerelda's beautifully powdered face, with its curling eye-lashes and rosy cheeks. 'She just won't fit. Though Gwendoline will love her, I expect! But Gwendoline Mary always does lose her silly heart to people like Zerelda!'

Mr. Rivers looked back at the sleeping Zerelda and gave Darrell a comradely grin. She smiled back. She wondered what Zerelda's father and mother could be like; she thought they must be pretty queer to have a daughter like Zerelda.

Then she gave herself a little shake. 'She may be quite nice really. It may just be because she comes from a country that lets its girls grow up sooner than ours do,' thought Darrell. She was a very fair and just girl and she made up her mind to give Zerelda a chance.

'Though thank goodness she'll be in a higher form, as she's nearly sixteen,' thought Darrell. 'I shan't see much

of her. I hope she's not in North Tower. Oh dear—
whatever would Miss Potts think of her if she was!'

She thought of the downright Miss Potts. She thought
of plump, sensible Matron who never stood any nonsense
from anyone. And she thought of the mistress who took
the third form, in which Darrell had already been for a
term.

'Miss Peters! Gracious! She'd have a fit if Zerelda
was in her form!' thought Darrell, seeing the mannish,
hearty-voiced Miss Peters in her mind's eye. 'It's really
almost a pity she won't be in my form. I'd love to see Miss
Peters deal with Zerelda!'

Darrell was tired when they at last reached Malory
Towers. They had stopped twice on the way for meals,
and Zerelda had awakened, and talked in a gracious, grown-
up manner to Mr. and Mrs. Rivers. Apparently she
thought England was 'just wunnerful'. She also thought
that she, Zerelda, could teach it a few things.

Mrs. Rivers was polite and friendly, as she always was
to everyone. Mr. Rivers, who had no patience with people
like Zerelda, talked to Darrell and ignored the American
girl.

'Say, isn't your father wunnerful?' said Zerelda to
Darrell, when they were speeding on their way again.
'Those great eyes of his—and the black beetling brows?
Wunnerful!'

Darrell wanted to giggle. She longed to tell her father
about his 'black beetling brows' but there was no chance.

'Tell me about this school of yours,' said Zerelda, sweetly,
thinking that Darrell was rather silent.

'I've told you already,' said Darrell, rather stiffly, 'but
you must have been bored because you went to sleep.'

'Say, isn't that just too bad?' said Zerelda, apologetically.

'There's no time to tell you anything, anyway,' said
Darrell, 'because here we are!' Her eyes shone as they

always did when they saw Malory Towers again for the
first time.

The car swept up to the front door. It always seemed
like the entrance to a castle, to Darrell. The big drive was
now crowded with cars, and girls of all ages were rushing
about, carrying bags and lacrosse sticks.

'Come on,' said Darrell, to Zerelda. 'Let's get out.
Golly, it's grand to be back! Hallo, Belinda! I say,
Irene, got your health certificate? Hallo, Jean. Heard
about Sally? She's in quarantine. Sickening, isn't it?'

Jean caught sight of Zerelda getting out of the car, and
stared as if she couldn't believe her eyes. Zerelda still had
no hat on, and her hair cascaded down her shoulders, and
the roll on top glinted in a ray of late sunshine.

'Golly—who's that? Some relation of yours?' said
Jean.

Darrell giggled. 'No, thank goodness. She's a new
girl!'

'No! My word, what does she think she's come to
Malory Towers for? To act in the films?'

Darrell darted here and there among her friends, happy
and excited. Her father undid the trunks, and the school
porter carried them in. Darrell caught sight of the label
on Zerelda's trunk. 'North Tower'.

'Blow! She's in our tower after all,' she thought.
'Hallo, Alicia! Had good hols.?'

Alicia came up, her bright eyes gleaming. 'Super!' she
said. 'My word—who's that?'

'New girl,' said Darrell. 'I know how you feel. I
couldn't take my eyes off her either when I first saw her.
Unbelievable, isn't she?'

'Look—there's our dear Gwendoline Mary having a weep
on Mother's shoulder as usual!' said Alicia, her attention
caught by the sight of Gwendoline's mother, who was
dabbing away tears as she said good-bye to Gwendoline.

' There's Miss Winter, Gwendoline's old governess, too,'
said Darrell. ' No wonder poor Gwen never gets any better
—always Mother's Darling Pet. We get some sense into
her in term-time, and then she loses it all again in the hols.'

Gwendoline caught sight of Zerelda and stared in surprise. A look of great admiration came over her face.
Alicia nudged Darrell.

' Gwendoline's going to worship Zerelda. Look ! Don't
you know that expression on her face ? Zerelda will have
at least one willing slave ! '

Gwendoline said something to her mother and her
governess. They both looked at Zerelda. But it was plain
that neither of them liked the look of her as much as Gwendoline did.

' Good-bye, darling,' said her mother, still dabbing her
eyes. ' Write to me heaps of times.'

But Gwendoline Mary was not paying much attention.
She was wondering if anyone was looking after Zerelda.
Could she possibly go up to her and offer to show her round ?
Then she saw that Darrell was with her. Darrell would
soon push her off if she went up, she knew.

Zerelda stood looking round at all the bustle and excitement. She was dressed in the same brown coat, brown
stockings and shoes as the others, and yet she managed to
look quite different. She didn't seem to notice the curious
glances thrown at her. Darrell, seeing her father and
mother about to go, rushed over to them to say good-
bye.

' It's so nice to see you plunging into everything so happily
as soon as you're back,' said her mother, pleased to see how
gladly everyone greeted Darrell. ' You are no longer one
of the smaller ones, Darrell—you seem quite big compared
to the first- and second-formers now ! '

' I should think so ! Babies ! ' said Darrell, with a laugh.
' Good-bye, darlings. I'll write on Sunday as usual. Give

Felicity my love and tell her Malory Towers is as nice as ever.'

The car moved off down the drive. Darrell waved till it was gone. Then she felt a punch on the back and turned to see Irene there. 'Darrell! Come along to Matron with me. I can't find my health certificate.'

'Irene! I don't believe you,' said Darrell. 'Yes, I'll come. Where's my night-case? Oh, there it is. Hie, Gwendoline, look out with that lacrosse stick of yours. That's twice you've tripped me up.'

Darrell suddenly remembered Zerelda. 'Oh golly! I've forgotten Zerelda. She's going to be in North Tower too. I'd better get her or she'll be feeling absolutely lost. I know how I felt when I came here first—everyone laughing and ragging and talking and I didn't know a soul!'

She set off towards Zerelda. But Zerelda did not look at all lost or bewildered. She looked thoroughly at home, with a tiny smile on her red mouth as if she was really rather amused by everything going on around her.

Before Darrell could reach her someone else spoke to Zerelda.

'Are you a new girl? I believe you are in North Tower. If you like to come with me I'll show you round a bit.'

'Gee, that's kind of you,' said Zerelda, in her slow drawl.

'Look,' said Darrell, in disgust. 'There's Gwendoline Mary all over her already! Trust *her*! She just adores anyone like Zerelda. Zerelda, come with us. We'll take you to Matron.'

'I'll look after her, Darrell,' said Gwendoline, turning her large pale-blue eyes on Darrell. 'You go and look for Sally.'

'Sally's not coming back yet,' said Darrell, 'she's in quarantine. I'll look after Zerelda. She came down with us.'

'You can *both* take me around,' said Zerelda, charmingly,

and smiled her slow smile at Gwendoline. Gwen slipped
her arm through Zerelda's and took her up the steps into
the hall.

Alicia grinned. 'Let's hope dear Gwen will take her off
our hands for good,' she said. 'But I suppose she'll be in
a much higher form. She looks about eighteen!'

The groans of Irene attracted their attention. 'Oh,
Irene! I simply don't believe you've lost your health
certificate again,' said Darrell. 'Nobody could possibly
lose it term after term as you do.'

'Well, I have,' said Irene. 'Do come to Matron now
and stand by me.'

So they all went to find Matron. Darrell and Alicia gave
up their health certificates. Matron looked at Irene.

'I've lost it, Matron,' said Irene. 'The worst of it is
I don't even remember having it today! I mean, I usually
remember Mother giving it to me, anyhow—but I don't
even remember that this time. My memory's getting worse
than ever.'

'Your mother came to see me not ten minutes ago,' said
Matron, 'and she gave me your certificate herself. Go
away, Irene, or you'll make me lose it too!'

Gwendoline brought Zerelda to Matron. Matron stared
as if she couldn't believe her eyes. 'Who's this? Oh—
Zerelda Brass. Yes, you're in North Tower. Is this your
health certificate? She's in your dormy, Gwendoline.
Take her there—and—er—get her ready to go down for a
meal.'

Darrell grinned at Alicia, and Alicia winked back. Matron
wouldn't be quite so polite about Zerelda tomorrow.

'Come on,' said Alicia. 'Let's go and unpack our night-
cases. I've heaps to tell you, Darrell!'

3 THE FIRST EVENING

'ANY more new girls coming, have you heard?' Darrell asked Alicia.

'Yes, one. Somebody called Wilhelmina,' said Alicia. 'She's coming tomorrow. One of my brothers knows one of *her* brothers. When he heard she was coming here, he whistled like anything and said, "Bill will wake you up all right!"'

'Who's Bill?' said Darrell.

'Wilhelmina, apparently,' said Alicia, taking the things out of her night-case. 'She's got seven brothers! Imagine it! *Seven!* And she's the only girl.'

'Golly!' said Darrell, trying to imagine what it would be like to have seven brothers. She had none. Alicia had three. But seven!

'I should think she's half a boy herself then,' said Darrell.

'Probably,' said Alicia. 'Blow, where's my toothbrush? I know I packed it.'

'Look—there's Mavis!' said Darrell. Alicia looked up. Mavis had been a new girl last term. She had not been a great success, because she was lazy and selfish. She had a beautiful voice, pure and sweet, but curiously deep—a most unusual voice that was being well trained.

Mavis was proud of her voice and proud of the career she was going to have. 'When I'm an opera-singer,' she was always saying, 'I shall sing in Milan. I shall sing in New York. When I'm an opera-singer, I shall . . .'

The others got very tired of hearing about Mavis's future career. But they were most impressed with her strong, deep voice, that could easily fill the great school hall. It was so rich and sweet that even the little ones listened in delight.

' But the worst of Mavis is that she thinks she's just perfect because she's got such a lovely voice,' Jean had complained a dozen times the term before. Jean was head-girl of the third form, and very blunt and forthright. ' She doesn't see that she's only just a schoolgirl, with duties to do, and work to get through, and games to play. She's always thinking of that voice of hers—and it's wonderful, we all know that. But what a pity to have a wonderful voice in such a poor sort of person ! '

Darrell hadn't liked Mavis. She looked at her now. She saw a discontented, conceited little face, with small dark eyes and a big mouth. Auburn hair was plaited into two thick braids.

' Mavis is all voice and vanity and nothing else,' she said to Alicia. ' I know that sounds horrid, but it's true.'

' Yes,' said Alicia, and paused to glance at Mavis too. ' And yet, Darrell, that girl will have a wonderful career with that voice of hers, you know. It's unique, and she'll have the whole world at her feet later on. The trouble is that she knows it now.'

' I wonder if Gwendoline will still go on fussing round her, now she's seen Zerelda ? ' said Darrell. Gwendoline, always ready to fawn round anyone gifted, rich or beautiful, had run round Mavis in a ridiculous way the term before. But then Gwendoline Mary never learnt that one should pick one's friends for quite different things. She was quite unable to see why Darrell liked Sally, or why Daphne liked little Mary-Lou, or why everyone liked honest, trustable Jean.

' Where's Betty ? ' asked Darrell. ' I haven't seen her yet.' Betty was Alicia's best friend, as clever and amusing as Alicia, and almost as sharp-tongued. She was not in North Tower, much to Alicia's sorrow. But Miss Grayling, the Head Mistress, did not intend to put the two girls into the same house. She was sorry they were friends, because they were too alike, and got each other into trouble continually because of their happy-go-lucky, don't-care ways.

'Betty's not coming back till half-term,' said Alicia, gloomily. 'She's got whooping-cough. Imagine it—six weeks before she can come back. She's only just started it. I heard yesterday.'

'Oh, I say—you'll miss her, won't you,' said Darrell. 'I shall miss Sally too.'

'Well, we'll just have to put up with each other, you and I, till Betty and Sally come back,' said Alicia. Darrell nodded. Alicia amused her. She was always fun to be with, and even when her tongue was sharpest, it was witty. Alicia was lucky. She had such good brains that she could play the fool all she liked and yet not lose her place in class.

'But if I do that, I slide down to the bottom at once,' thought Darrell. 'I've got quite good brains but I've got to use them all the time. Alicia's brains seem to work whether she uses them or not!'

Mary-Lou came up. She had grown a little taller, but she was still the same rather scared-looking girl. 'Hallo!' she said. 'Wherever did you pick Zerelda up, Darrell? I hear she came down with you. How old is she? Eighteen?'

'No. Nearly sixteen,' said Darrell. 'I suppose Gwendoline is sucking up to her already? Isn't she the limit? I say, what do you suppose Miss Potts will say when she sees Zerelda?'

Miss Potts was the house-mistress of North Tower, and, like Matron, not very good at putting up with nonsense of any sort. Most of the girls had been in her form, because she taught the bottom class. They liked her and respected her. A few girls, such as Gwendoline and Mavis, feared her, because she could be very sarcastic over airs and graces, or pretences of any sort.

Darrell felt rather lost without Sally there to laugh with and talk to. She was glad to walk downstairs with Alicia. Belinda came bouncing up.

' Where's Sally ? Darrell, I did some wizard sketching in the hols. I went to the circus, and I've got a whole book of circus sketches. You should just see the clowns ! '

' Show the book to us this evening,' said Darrell, eagerly. Everyone loved Belinda's clever sketches. She really had a gift for drawing, but, unlike Mavis, she was not forever thinking and talking of it, or of her future career. She was a jolly schoolgirl first and foremost, and an artist second.

' Seen Irene ? ' said Alicia. Belinda nodded. Irene was her friend, and the two were very well-matched. Irene was talented at music and maths, but a scatterbrain at everything else. Belinda was talented at drawing, quite fair at other lessons, and a scatterbrain almost as bad as Irene. The class had great fun with them.

' Seen Zerelda ? ' asked Darrell, with a grin. That was the question everyone asked that evening. ' Seen Zerelda ? ' No one had ever seen a girl quite like Zerelda before.

At supper that night there was a great noise. Everyone was excited. Mam'zelle Dupont beamed at the table of the third-formers of North Tower.

' You have had good holidays ? ' she enquired of everyone. ' You have been to the theatre and the pantomime and the circus ? Ah, you are all ready to work hard now and do some very very good translations for me ! *N'est ce pas ?* '

There was a groan from the girls round the table. ' No, Mam'zelle ! Don't let's do French translations this term. We've forgotten all our French ! '

Mam'zelle looked round the table for any new face. She
always made a point of being extra kind to new girls. She
suddenly caught sight of Zerelda and stared in amazement.
Zerelda had done her hair again, and her golden roll stood
out on top. Her lips were suspiciously red. Her cheeks
were far too pink.

' This girl, she is made up for the films ! ' said Mam'zelle
to herself. ' Oh, *là là* ! Why has she come here ? She
is not a young girl. She looks old—about twenty ! Why
has Miss Grayling taken her here ? She is not for Malory
Towers.'

Zerelda seemed quite at home. She ate her supper very
composedly. She was sitting next to Gwendoline, who was
trying to make her talk. But Zerelda was not like Mavis,
willing to talk for hours about herself. She answered
Gwendoline politely enough.

' Have you lived all your life in America ? Do you think
you'll like England ? ' persisted Gwendoline.

' I think England's just wunnerful,' said Zerelda, for the
sixth time. ' I think your little fields are wunnerful, and
your little old houses. I think the English people are
wunnerful too.'

' Wunnerful, isn't she ? ' said Alicia, under her breath to
Darrell. ' Just wunnerful.'

Everyone had to go early to bed on the first night, because
most of the girls had had long journeys down to Cornwall.
In fact, before supper was over there were many loud yawns
to be heard.

Zerelda was surprised when Gwendoline informed her
that they had to go to bed that night just about eight o'clock.
' Only just tonight though,' said Gwendoline. ' Tomorrow
the third-formers go at nine.'

' At *nine*,' said Zerelda, astonished. ' But in my country
we go when we like. I shall never go to sleep so
early.'

'Well, you slept in the car all right,' Darrell couldn't help saying. 'So you must be tired.'

They all went to the common-room after supper, chose their lockers, argued, switched on the wireless, switched it off again, yawned, poked the fire, teased Mary-Lou because she jumped when a spark flew out, and then sang a few songs.

Mavis's voice dominated the rest. It really was a most remarkable voice, deep and powerful. It seemed impossible that it should come from Mavis, who was not at all well-grown for her age. One by one the girls fell silent and listened. Mavis sang on. She loved the sound of her own voice.

'Wunnerful!' said Zerelda, clapping loudly when the song was ended. 'Ree-markable!'

Mavis looked pleased. 'When I'm an opera-singer,' she began.

Zerelda interrupted her. 'Oh, that's what you're going to be, is it? Gee, that's fine. *I'm* going in for films!'

'Films! What do you mean? A film-actress?' said Gwendoline Mary, her eyes wide.

'Yes. I act pretty well already,' said Zerelda, not very modestly. 'I'm always acting at home. I'm in our Dramatic Society, of course, and last year at college I acted Lady Macbeth in Shakespeare. Gee, that was . . .'

'Wunnerful!' said Alicia, Irene and Belinda all together. Zerelda laughed.

'I guess I don't say things the way you say them,' she said, good-naturedly.

'You'll have a chance to show how well you can act, this very term,' said Gwendoline, remembering something. 'Our form's got to act a play—"Romeo and Juliet". You could be Juliet.'

'That depends on Miss Hibbert,' said Daphne's voice at once. Daphne had already imagined herself in Juliet's part. 'Miss Hibbert's our English mistress, Zerelda, and . . .'

'Bed, girls,' said Miss Potts' voice at the door. 'Eight o'clock! Come along, everyone, or you'll never be up in the morning!'

4 ZERELDA GOES INTO THE FOURTH

IT was fun settling in the next day. The girls rushed into the third form classroom, which overlooked the courtyard and had a distant view of the sea.

'Zerelda's to go to the fourth form classroom,' said Jean, looking round for the American girl. 'She's not with us after all.'

'I didn't think I would be,' said Zerelda. 'I'm much older.'

Jean looked at her. 'Zerelda,' said Jean, 'I'd better give you a word of advice. Miss Williams, the fourth form mistress, won't like your hair-style—or your lipstick either. You'd better alter your hair and rub that awful stuff off your lips before you go to the fourth form. Anyway, they'll rag you like anything if you don't.'

'Why should I do what you tell me?' said Zerelda, on her dignity at once. She thought a great deal of her appearance and could not bear to have it remarked on by these proper little English girls.

'Well, I'm head-girl of this form,' said Jean. 'That's why I'm bothering to tell you. Just to save you getting into trouble.'

'But Zerelda's hair looks lovely,' said Gwendoline, who always resented having to have her own hair tied neatly, instead of in a golden sheet over her shoulders.

Nobody took the slightest notice of Gwendoline's bleating.

'Well, thanks all the same, Jean, but I'm not going to make myself into a little pig-tailed English schoolgirl,' said Zerelda, in her lazy, rather insolent drawl. 'I guess I couldn't look like you, anyway. Look at you all, plain as pie! You ought to let me have a try at making you up— I'd soon get you some looks!'

Daphne, who fancied herself as very pretty, laughed scornfully. 'Nobody wants to look a scarecrow like you! Honestly, if you could see yourself!'

'I have,' said Zerelda. 'I looked in the glass this morning!'

'When you're in Rome, you must do as Rome does,' said Jean, solemnly.

'But I'm not in Rome,' said Zerelda.

'No. It's a pity you aren't!' said Alicia. 'You'll wish you were in three minutes' time when Miss Williams catches sight of you. Go on into the classroom next door for goodness' sake. Miss Williams will be along in half a minute. So will our teacher, Miss Peters. She'd have a blue fit if she saw you.'

Zerelda grinned good-humouredly, and went off to find her classroom. As she got to the door Miss Williams came hurrying along to the fourth-formers. She and Zerelda met at the door.

Miss Williams had no idea that Zerelda was one of her form. The girl looked so grown-up. Miss Williams blinked once or twice, trying to remember who Zerelda was. Could she be one of the new assistant mistresses?

'Er—let me see now—you are Miss Miss—er . . . Miss
. . .' began Miss Williams.

'Zerelda,' said Zerelda, obligingly, thinking it was a queer thing if the mistresses all called the girls 'Miss'.

'Miss Zerelda,' said Miss Williams, still not realising anything. 'Did you want me, Miss Zerelda?'

Zerelda was rather astonished. 'Well—er—not exactly,' she said. 'I was told to come along to your class. I'm in the fourth form.'

'Good heavens!' said Miss Williams, weakly. 'Not—not one of the girls?'

'Yes, Miss Williams,' said Zerelda, thinking that the teacher was acting very queerly. 'Say, haven't I done right? Isn't this the classroom?'

'Yes,' said Miss Williams, recovering herself all at once. 'This is the fourth form room. But you can't come in like that. What's that thing you've got on the top of your head?'

Zerelda looked even more astonished. Had she got a hat on by mistake? She felt to see. No, there was no hat there.

'There's nothing on my head,' she said.

'Yes, there is. What's *this* thing?' said Miss Williams, patting the enormous roll of hair that Zerelda had pinned there in imitation of one of the film-stars.

'That? Oh, that's a bit of my hair,' said Zerelda, wondering if Miss Williams was a little mad. 'It really *is* my hair, Miss Williams. I've just rolled the front part up and pinned it.'

Miss Williams looked in silence at the roll of brassy-coloured hair and the cascades of curls down Zerelda's neck. She peered at the too-red lips. She even looked at the curling eye-lashes to make sure they were real and not stuck on.

'Well, Zerelda, I can't have you in my class like this,' she said, looking very prim and bird-like. 'Take down that roll of hair. Tie it all back. Clean your lips. Come back to the room in five minutes.'

And with that she disappeared into the form room and
the door was shut. Zerelda stared after her. She patted
the roll of hair on top. What was the matter with it ?
Didn't it make her look exactly like Lossie Laxton, the
film-star she admired most of all ?

Zerelda frowned. What a school ! Here were a whole
lot of girls, all growing up fast, and not one of them knew
how to do her hair, not one of them looked smart—' and I
bet they're all as stupid as owls ', said Zerelda, out loud.

She decided to go along and do something to her hair.
That prim and proper Miss Williams might say something
to the Head. Zerelda had been very much impressed with
Miss Grayling and the little talk she had had with her.
What had Miss Grayling said ? Something about learning
to be good-hearted and kind, sensible and trustable, good,
sound women the world could lean on. She had also said
that Zerelda might learn something from her stay in England
that would help her afterwards—and that Zerelda, if she was
sensible and understanding, might also teach the English
girls something.

' Well, I don't want to get the wrong side of Miss Grayling
from the word go,' thought Zerelda, as she went to find her
dormy. ' Where's this bedroom of ours ? I'll never find
my way about in this place.'

She found the dormy at last and went in to do her hair.
She looked at herself in the glass. She was very sad at
having to take down that beautiful roll of hair. It took her
ages to put it there each morning. But she unpinned it and
brushed it out. She divided it into two, and pinned it back,
then tied her mane of hair with a piece of ribbon so that
it no longer fell wildly over her shoulders.

At once she looked younger. She rubbed the red from
her lips. Then she looked at herself. ' You look plain and
drab now, Zerelda,' she said to herself. ' What would Pop
say ? He wouldn't know me ! '

But Zerelda didn't look plain and drab. She looked a young girl, with a natural, pleasant youthful face. She went slowly to find her classroom. She was not sure whether she had to knock at the door or not. Things seemed to be so different in an English school—more polite and proper than in an American school. She decided to knock.

'Come in!' called Miss Williams, impatiently. She had forgotten all about Zerelda. Zerelda went in. She now looked so completely different that Miss Williams didn't recognize her!

'What do you want?' she asked Zerelda. 'Have you come with a message?'

'No,' said Zerelda, puzzled. 'I'm in the fourth form, aren't I?'

'What's your name?' said Miss Williams, looking for her list of names.

Zerelda was now quite certain that Miss Williams was mad. 'I told you before,' she said. 'I'm Zerelda.'

'Oh, good gracious—so you are,' said Miss Williams, looking at her keenly. 'Well, who would have thought your hair would make such a difference! Come and sit down. That's your place over there.'

The fourth form were mystified and amused. They were all keen hard-working fifteen-year-olds, who were to work for their School Certificate that year.

'Let me see—how old are you, Zerelda?' said Miss Williams, trying to find Zerelda's name on her list.

'Nearly sixteen,' said Zerelda.

'Ah then—you will probably find the work of this form rather easy,' said Miss Williams. 'But as it's your first term in an English school, that's just as well. There will be many different things for you to learn.'

Zerelda looked round at the fourth-formers. She thought they looked too clever for words. How serious they were! She wished she was back in the third form with Alicia,

Darrell, Belinda and the rest.   They had all seemed so jolly
and care-free.

The third form were busy making out time-tables and lists
of duties.   Books were given out.   Miss Peters, tall, mannish, with very short hair and a deep voice, was in charge.
The girls liked her, but sometimes wished she would not
treat them as though they were boys.   She had a hearty
laugh, and a hearty manner.   In the holidays she rode
practically all the time, and was in charge of the riding-
teams on Saturday mornings at Malory Towers.

' I really wonder she doesn't come to class in riding-
breeches,' Alicia had said often enough to the third form,
making them giggle.   ' I'm sure she hates wearing a
skirt ! '

' Shall I put a set of books for the new girl, Wilhelmina
Robinson ? ' asked Jean, who was in charge of the books.
' When is she coming, Miss Peters ? '

' This morning, I believe,' said Miss Peters.   ' She and
her brothers have been in quarantine for something or other.
I think Miss Grayling said she would be arriving this
morning.   By car, I suppose.'

After Break the third form went to the sewing-room for
half an hour, and it was from there that they saw the arrival,
the quite astonishing arrival, of Wilhelmina Robinson.

They suddenly heard the clatter of horses' hooves outside
—a tremendous clatter.   Alicia went to the window at once,
wondering if there was a riding-lesson for anyone.   She
gave an exclamation.

' I say ! Just look here ! Whoever is it ? '

All the class crowded to the window.   Miss Donnelly,
the gentle, sweet-tempered sewing-mistress, protested
mildly.   ' Girls, girls ! What are you doing ? '

' Miss Donnelly, come and look,' said Alicia.   So she
went to the window.   She saw a girl on a big black horse,
and with her were seven boys, ranging in age from about

eight to eighteen, each of them on horseback ! There was a
great deal of laughter, and stamping and curveting and cries
of ' Whoa there ! '

' Golly ! It must be Wilhelmina ! ' said Darrell. ' And
her seven brothers ! Don't say that her brothers are coming
to Malory Towers too ! '

' Well ! What a way to arrive ! ' said Gwendoline Mary.
' Galloping up like that on horseback ! What a peculiar
family Wilhelmina's must be ! '

5   THE ARRIVAL OF WILHELMINA

UNFORTUNATELY the bell for the next class rang at
that moment and the third-formers could not see what
happened next. Would Miss Grayling come out to the
horse-riders ? How would Wilhelmina enter the Towers ?
Darrell imagined her riding up the steps and into the hall !

' Golly ! Fancy riding to school like that,' said Alicia.
' I suppose she's going to keep her horse here. One or
two girls do do that already. Bringing all her seven brothers
too ! What a girl ! '

Nobody had been able to see clearly what Wilhelmina
had looked like. In fact, it had been difficult to tell her
from the boys, as they had all been in riding-breeches.
The third-formers went to their classroom, discussing the
new arrival excitedly. Wilhelmina promised to be a
Somebody !

' I shall be scared of her,' said Mary-Lou.

' Don't be silly,' said Mavis, who was always very scornful

of Mary-Lou. 'Why should you be scared of her ? I just
hate tomboys, and I'm sure she's one. She'll think of
nothing but horses and dogs, and she'll smell of them too.
People always do when they're mad on animals.'

'Miss Peters doesn't,' said Darrell.

'Oh, Miss Peters !' said Mavis. 'I'll be glad when I'm
out of her class. She's too hearty for anything !'

Darrell laughed. Miss Peters was rather hearty and loud-
voiced. But she was a good sort, though not at all
sympathetic to people like Mavis. Neither had she much
patience with Alicia or Betty when they played any of
their idiotic tricks. In fact, she had looked with such
disfavour on tricks in class that poor Alicia and Betty had
almost given up playing any.

Wilhelmina didn't turn up in the classroom that morning,
but Jean found Matron waiting for her in the passage when
the third form went out to get ready for dinner. With
her was somebody who, except for the school tunic, looked
exactly like a boy !

'Jean,' said Matron, 'you're head-girl of the third,
aren't you ? Well, look after Wilhelmina for me, will
you, and take her down to dinner ? She couldn't come
yesterday because she wasn't out of quarantine. Here
you are, Wilhelmina—this is Jean, head-girl of your form.'

'Hallo,' said Wilhelmina and grinned a boyish grin that
showed big white teeth set very evenly. Jean looked at her
and liked her at once.

Wilhelmina had hair cropped almost as short as a boy's
It curled a little, which she hated. Her face was boyish
and square, with a tip-tilted nose, a big mouth, and big,
wide-set eyes of hazel-brown. She was covered with
freckles from forehead to firm little chin.

'Hallo,' said Jean. 'I saw you arrive—on horseback,
didn't you ?'

'Yes,' said Wilhelmina. 'My seven brothers came with

me. Mummy was awfully cross about that. She wanted me to go in the car with her and Daddy—but we got our horses and shot off before they started ! '

' Good gracious ! ' said Jean. ' Did you really ? Have you each got a horse ? '

' Yes. We've got big stables,' said Wilhelmina. ' Daddy keeps racehorses too. I say—I've never been to boarding-school before. Is it awful ? If it is I shall saddle Thunder and ride away.'

Jean stared at Wilhelmina and wondered if she meant all this. She decided that she didn't. She laughed and pulled Wilhelmina along to the cloakroom, because she had to wash ink off her hands before dinner. Miss Potts would be sure to spot them if she didn't !

' Malory Towers is a jolly fine school,' said Jean. ' You'll like it.'

' Shall I be able to ride Thunder each day ? ' asked Wilhelmina, staring round the big cloakroom where girls were chattering and laughing as they washed. ' I tell you, I wouldn't have come if they hadn't let me bring Thunder. I shall have to look after him too, even if it means missing some of my lessons. He would hate anyone else looking after him.'

' Haven't you ever been to school before ? ' asked Belinda, who had been listening to all this with interest.

' No. I shared the tutor that three of my brothers had,' said Wilhelmina. ' There wasn't a school near at all. We live miles out in the country. I expect I shall be at the bottom of the form.'

Belinda liked this outspoken girl. ' I bet you won't,' she said, and cast her eye round to see if Gwendoline was about. Yes, she was. ' Not while Gwendoline Mary is in the form, anyway ! '

' Don't be beastly,' said Gwendoline, cross at having fun poked at her in front of a new girl.

'It will all seem a bit queer to you at first,' said Jean. 'If
you've been even to a day school before it helps—but never
to have been to school at all—well, you're sure to feel a bit
strange, Wilhelmina.'

'I say—would you mind very much if I asked you
something?' said Wilhelmina, staring hard at Jean.

'What?' said Jean, wondering what was coming. The
others came round to listen. Wilhelmina looked round at
them all.

'Well,' she said, 'I've never in my life been called
Wilhelmina. Never. It's a frightful name. Everyone
calls me Bill. After all, people call William Bill for
short, don't they? So my brothers said they'd call me
Bill, short for Wilhelmina! If you all start calling me
Wilhelmina I shall be miserable. I shan't feel I'm
myself.'

In the usual way if a new girl asked for a nickname, she
would have been laughed at, or told to think again. Nick-
names were only given when people knew you well and
liked you. Gwendoline Mary opened her mouth to say
this but Belinda spoke first.

'Yes. We'll call you Bill. It suits you. Wilhelmina's
a nice name for some people, but not for you. You really
are a Bill. What do you say, Darrell—and Jean?'

'Yes,' they agreed at once. They couldn't help liking
this sturdy, freckled girl with her short hair and frank
smile. She *was* Bill. They couldn't possibly call her
anything else.

'Well, thanks awfully,' said Bill. 'Thanks *most* awfully.
Now I can forget I was ever christened Wilhelmina.'

Mavis and Gwendoline Mary looked as if they didn't
approve of this at all. Why should a new girl get a nickname at once, just because she wanted it? Daphne looked
disapproving too. How could any girl want a boy's name?
And how could anyone like to wear her hair as short as

Wilhelmina and get so many freckles? Why, Daphne couldn't bear it if she got so much as a single freckle!

Zerelda came into the cloakroom, her hair still done properly, without the big roll on the top of her head. Jean looked at her.

'Gracious, Zerelda! You do look different—about ten years younger! I bet Miss Williams was mad with you, wasn't she?'

'She was mad all right,' said Zerelda. 'Really queer, I mean! I'm quite scared of her. I'd rather have your Miss Peters. I say—who in the big wide world is this?'

She stood and stared in the utmost wonder at Bill, who looked back, quite unabashed. The two took in one another from top to toe.

'Are you a boy or a girl?' enquired Zerelda. 'Gee, I wouldn't know!'

'My name's Bill,' said Bill with a grin. 'Short for Wilhelmina. What's yours?'

'Zerelda. Short for nothing,' said Zerelda. 'Why do you wear your hair like that?'

'Because I couldn't bear to wear it like yours,' retorted Bill.

Zerelda stared at Bill again as if she really couldn't believe her eyes.

'I've never seen a girl like you before,' she said. 'Gee, you're wunnerful! Gee, I think all you English people are wunnerful!'

'Anyone would think you hadn't got an English mother,' said Darrell. 'You've lived with her all your life, haven't you? You always sound as if you have never met anyone English before.'

'My mother's as American as anyone,' said Zerelda. 'I don't know why she's gotten it into her head to send me to England. She's forgotten she was ever English. I'd like

to take you back to America with me, Bill. Why, nobody
would believe you were real, over there! Gee, you're
just . . .'

'WUNNERFUL!' chorused everyone, and Zerelda
laughed.

A bell rang. 'Dinner!' yelled Belinda. 'I'm starving.
Rotten breakfasts we get here!'

'Rotten!' agreed everyone. They had all eaten big
plates of porridge and milk, scrambled eggs, and toast and
marmalade, but it was always agreed that the food was
'rotten'—unless, of course, an outsider dared to criticize
the food, and then it suddenly became 'too wizard for
words'.

They tore down to the dining-room. Zerelda went to
sit with the third-formers, having put up rather a poor
show in the fourth form that morning, and feeling rather
small—but Miss Williams called her over.

'Zerelda! This is your table now. Let me look at
your hair.'

Zerelda submitted to Miss Williams' close examination,
glad that she had not put any red on her lips. How dare
Miss Williams treat her like a kid of six? She felt angry
and annoyed. But she soon cheered up when she saw the
steaming dishes of stew, surrounded with all kinds of
vegetables. Gee, she liked these English meals. They
were—no, not wunnerful—what was the word the others
used—yes, they were wizard!

Darrell wrote to Sally that night and told her about
Bill and Zerelda.

You'll like Bill (short for Wilhelmina), [she wrote]. All grins
and freckles and very short hair, mad on horses, has seven brothers
says just exactly what she thinks, and yet we don't mind a bit

She bit her pen and then went on.

But, oh my, *Zerelda*! She thinks she's going to be a film-star and says she's 'wunnerful' at acting. You should have seen the way she did her hair—and the way she made up her face! We thought we were going to have some fun with her and take her down a peg or two, but she's not in our form after all. She's nearly sixteen so she's gone into the fourth. I bet Miss Williams had a fit when she saw her walking into her classroom this morning. Sally, do hurry up and come back. Betty isn't back yet either, so Alicia and I are keeping each other company, but I'd so *much* rather have you. You steady me! Alicia doesn't. She makes me feel I'm going to do idiotic things. I hope I'll last out till you come back!

Somebody put their head in at the door. 'Hey, is Wilhelmina here? Matron wants her. Wilhelmina!'

Nobody stirred. 'Wilhelmina!' said the voice again. 'Hey, you, new girl! Aren't you Wilhelmina?'

Bill put down her book hastily. 'Golly, yes, so I am!' she said. 'I quite forgot. I really must tell Matron to call me Bill.'

She went out and everyone laughed. 'Good old Bill! I'd like to see Matron's face when she tells her to call her Bill!' said Belinda.

6 BILL AND THUNDER

AFTER a few days it seemed to Darrell as if she had been back at school for weeks. The world of home seemed very far away. She thought pityingly of her sister Felicity at her day school. Why, Felicity didn't even *guess* what it was like to be at a proper boarding-school, where you got up all together, had meals together, planned fun for every evening, and then all rushed off to bed together.

Wilhelmina, or Bill, had been rather silent those first two or three days. Darrell wondered if she was homesick. As a rule the happy, normal girls did not mope and pine— life was so full and so jolly at Malory Towers that there simply wasn't time for anything of that sort.

All the same, she thought Bill looked a bit serious. ' Not homesick, are you ? ' she asked, one morning when she was walking down one of the corridors with Bill.

' Oh no. I'm horse-sick ! ' said Bill, surprisingly. ' I keep on and on thinking of all our horses at home that I love so much—Beauty and Star and Blackie and Velvet and Midnight and Miss Muffet and Ladybird, and . . .'

' Good gracious ! However do you remember all those names ? ' said Darrell, in surprise.

' I couldn't possibly forget them,' said Bill, solemnly. ' I'm going to like Malory Towers, I know that, but I simply can't help missing all our horses, and the thunder of their hooves and the way they neigh and nuzzle—oh, you can't understand, Darrell. You'll think me silly, I know. You see, I and three of my brothers used to ride each morning to their tutor—four miles away—and we used to go out and saddle and bridle our horses—and then off we'd go, galloping over the hills.'

' Well, you couldn't do that all your life long,' said Darrell, sensibly. ' And anyway, you'll do it in the hols. again. You're lucky to have been able to bring Thunder with you here.'

' That's why I said I'd come to Malory Towers,' said Bill. ' Because I could bring Thunder. Oh dear, Darrell—it's been the week-end so far, when there weren't lessons—I'm just dreading to think what will happen when I have to go to classes and perhaps shan't see Thunder all day long. It's a pity Miss Peters wouldn't let him stand at the back of the classroom. He'd be as good as gold.'

Darrell gave a squeal of laughter. ' Oh, Bill—you're

mad! Golly, I'd love to have Thunder in the classroom too. I bet he'd neigh at Mam'zelle, and she'd teach him to whinny in French!'

'She wouldn't. She doesn't like horses. She told me so,' said Bill. 'She's scared of them. Imagine that, Darrell! I shouldn't have thought there was anyone in the world silly enough to be frightened of a horse.'

Most of the third-formers had been out to the stables to see Bill's wonderful horse. Actually he didn't seem very wonderful to Darrell, who didn't know a great deal about horses, but she did think he was lovely the way he welcomed Bill, whinnying in delight, pushing his big velvety nose into the crook of her arm, and showing her as plainly as possible that he adored every bit of his freckled little mistress.

Mavis, Gwendoline, Daphne and Mary-Lou would not go near him. He was a big black horse, and they all felt certain he would kick or bite. But the others loved him.

Zerelda was not scared of him, and she admired him very much. 'Gee, he's wunnerful,' she said. 'But what a pity you've got to get yourself up in those awful breeches to ride him, Wilhelmina.'

Bill scowled. She hated to be called by her full name. 'I suppose you'd ride him in flowing skirts, with your hair down to your waist—and rings on your fingers and bells on your toes!' she retorted. 'All the way to Banbury Cross.'

Zerelda didn't understand. She didn't know the old English nursery rhyme. She smiled her lazy smile at Bill.

'You're wunnerful when you scowl like that,' she said.

'Shut up,' said Bill, and turned away. She was puzzled by Zerelda and her grown-up ways—and even more puzzled by her good humour. Zerelda never seemed to take offence, no matter how much anyone laughed at her or even jeered, as Mavis did very often.

She made the others feel small and young and rather

stupid. They felt uncomfortable with her. She really did seem years older, and she deliberately used a grown-up manner, jeering gently at their clothes, their 'hair-do's' as she called them, their liking for getting hot and muddy at games, and their complete lack of interest in the lives and careers of film-stars.

But she was generous and kind, and never lost her temper, so it was difficult really to dislike her. Gwendoline, of course, adored her. She quite neglected Mavis for Zerelda, which annoyed that conceited young opera-singer immensely.

The first full week of school began on the next day, Monday. No more leniency from the mistresses, no more slacking from the girls, no more easy-going ways. 'Work, now, work for everyone!' said Miss Peters. 'It's not a very long term but you must work hard and show good results even if we are a week or two short.'

The third form did not have only the third form girls from North Tower but the third-formers from other towers too, so it was a fairly big form. The standard was high, and Miss Peters was strict.

Mavis had been in Miss Peters' black books the term before, because of her poor work. But as it had been her first term, she had not been too hard on her. But now she, like everyone else, was getting tired of Mavis's parrot-cry, ' when I'm an opera-singer ' and she was quite determined to make Mavis a good third-former, opera-singer or not.

' You'd better look out, Mavis,' said Gwendoline, catching a certain look in Miss Peters' eye that morning as she studied Mavis. ' I know that look! You'll have to work this term, and forget your voice for a bit! '

' When I want your advice I'll ask for it,' said Mavis. ' I'm not scared of our hearty Miss Peters, if you are! I'm not going to slave and make myself miserable at Malory Towers for Miss P. or anyone else. Waste *your* time, if you like—you'll never have a career, or be Somebody! '

Gwendoline was very hurt. Like many silly, weak people she had a great idea of herself, and was so continually spoilt at home that she really did think herself wonderful.

' If you're going to say things like that I shan't be friends with you,' she whispered.

' Go and tag round Zerelda then,' said Mavis, forgetting to whisper softly enough.

' Mavis ! That's enough whispering between you and Gwendoline,' said Miss Peters' loud voice. ' One more whisper and you can stay in at Break.'

Bill couldn't seem to settle down that first Monday morning at all. She stared out of the window. She seemed very far away. She paid no attention at all to what Miss Peters was saying.

' Wilhelmina ! ' said Miss Peters at last. ' Did you hear *any*thing of what I have just said ? '

Everyone turned to look at Bill, who still gazed out of the window, a dreamy expression on her small square face.

' *Wilhelmina !* ' said Miss Peters, sharply. ' I am speaking to you.'

Still Bill took no notice at all. To the girls' amusement and surprise she suddenly made a little crooning noise, as if she was quite by herself and there was nobody else in the room at all !

Miss Peters was astonished. The girls giggled. Darrell knew what Bill was doing. She had heard that funny little crooning noise before—it was the noise Bill made to Thunder, when he nuzzled against her shoulder !

' She must be pretending she's with Thunder ! ' thought Darrell. ' She's in the stables with him. She's not here at all.'

Miss Peters wondered if Wilhelmina was feeling all right. She spoke to her again. ' Wilhelmina, are you deaf ? What's the matter ? '

Gwendoline gave Bill a poke in the back and made her
jump. She looked round at Gwendoline crossly, annoyed
at being so rudely awakened from her pleasant day-dreams.
Gwendoline nodded violently towards Miss Peters.

'That'll do, Gwendoline,' said Miss Peters. 'Wilhelmina, will you kindly give me your attention. I've been
speaking to you for the last few minutes.'

'Oh, sorry! Have you really?' said Bill, apologetically.
'Perhaps you kept calling me Wilhelmina, though? If
you could call me Bill I should always answer. You
see . . .'

Miss Peters looked most disapproving. What an extraordinary girl!

'In future, Wilhelmina, please pay attention to all I say,
and I shall not need to address you by any name at all!'
she said. 'As for calling you Bill—please don't be
impertinent.'

Bill looked astonished. 'Oh, Miss Peters! I wasn't
being impertinent. I'm sorry I wasn't listening to you. I
was thinking about Thunder.'

'Thunder!' said Miss Peters, who had no idea that Bill
had a horse called Thunder. 'Why should you think about
thunder on a lovely sunny day like this? I think you are
being very silly.'

'But it's just the *day* to think of Thunder!' said Bill,
her eyes shining. 'Just think of Thunder, galloping over
the hills and . . .'

Everyone tried to suppress giggles. They knew perfectly well that Wilhelmina was talking about her horse, but
poor Miss Peters looked more impatient than ever.

'That's enough, Wilhelmina,' she said. 'We'll have no
more talk of thunder or lightning, or . . .'

'Oh, how did you know that my brother George's horse
was called Lightning?' said Bill in delight, honestly thinking
that Miss Peters was talking of horses.

But now Miss Peters felt certain that Wilhelmina was being silly and rather rude. She gazed at her coldly.

'Have you got your book open at page thirty-three?' she asked. 'I thought you hadn't! How do you think you are going to follow this lesson if you haven't even got the right page?'

Bill hastily found page thirty-three. She tried to put all thoughts of Thunder out of her mind. She made a soft clicking noise, and Alicia and Irene grinned at one another.

'Horse-mad!' whispered Alicia, and when Miss Peters' back was turned, Alicia rocked to and fro as if she was on a trotting horse, sending the class into fits.

Darrell hugged herself in delight. It was lovely to be back at school again, lovely to sit in class and work, and giggle and hear Miss Peters ticking off this person and that. She missed Sally very much, but Alicia was fun.

'I'll beg her to play one of her tricks,' thought Darrell. 'We haven't had any *real* fun in class for terms and terms!'

7   IN THE THIRD FORM COMMON-ROOM

IT was sunny but cold the first week or two of that Easter term. The girls squabbled over getting the seats by the radiator in the common-room. Gwendoline, Mavis and Daphne were the ones that complained most of the cold —but they were the ones who took as little exercise as they could, so of course they always got chilblains and colds.

Bill didn't seem to feel the cold at all. She was still tanned, although it was early in the year. Darrell and Alicia liked the cold, and they loved rushing out to play lacrosse in the afternoons.

They went out ten minutes before the others to practise catching. Gwendoline couldn't understand it, and she and Mavis became friends again in sympathizing with each other over the cold, and jeering at Alicia and Darrell for being so hardy.

Zerelda, of course, being a fourth-former, was now not very often able to be with any of the third-formers, so Gwendoline had had to give up any idea of being her best friend. Zerelda did not seem to be very happy in the fourth form, Darrell thought. She often came slipping into the third form common-room in the evening—saying she wanted to borrow a book or a gramophone record—and then stopping to talk to Darrell and the others.

' Got a special friend yet ? ' Darrell asked her one evening.

Zerelda twisted one of her curls carefully round her finger and then shook it back into its proper place.

' No,' she said. ' Stuck-up things, the fourth form ! They seem to think I don't pull my weight. And they think the end of the world has come because I don't want to try and get into the third match-team for lacrosse ! '

' Well, you're so tall, you could do well in the team,' said Darrell, considering her. ' You ought to be able to take some fine catches. Can you run ? '

' Run ! I don't *want* to run ! ' said Zerelda, astonished. ' As for that games captain—what's her name—Molly Ronaldson—well, I ask you, did you ever see such a girl ? Big as a horse and just about as clumsy ! Shouts and dances about on the field as if she had gone mad ! '

Darrell laughed. ' Molly Ronaldson is one of the finest games captains we've ever had. We've won more matches with her than ever before. She's got an absolute genius for

picking the right people for the match-teams. My goodness, if I could get into one of the teams I'd be so thrilled
I wouldn't be able to sleep at night.'

' Is that so ? ' said Zerelda, in her slow drawl, looking
quite astonished. ' Well, maybe I wouldn't sleep at night
if I had spots on my face like Gwendoline goes in for, or if
I broke one of my nails—but I'd not lose my beauty sleep
for any game in the world ! '

' You're a queer person, Zerelda,' said Darrell. She
looked at her earnestly. ' You're missing all the nicest
years of your life—I mean, you just won't let yourself
enjoy the things most English girls of your age enjoy. You
spend hours over your hair and your face and your nails,
when you could be having fun at lacrosse, or going for
walks, or even messing about in the gym.'

' Messing about in the gym ! That's another thing I
can't understand your liking ! ' said Zerelda. Gwendoline,
who had come up to join in the conversation, nodded her
head in agreement.

' I can't understand that either,' she said in a prim voice.
' It's a pity gym is compulsory, and games too. I wouldn't
bother much about them if they weren't.'

' Only because, dear Gwendoline, you're so jolly bad
at them that you make a fool of yourself every time you
go into the gym or on the games field,' said Alicia, maliciously. ' Zerelda's different. I bet she'd be good at them
—but she thinks that all that kind of thing is beneath her.'

Any other girl would have resented this, but Zerelda only
grinned. Gwendoline, however, flared up at the unkind
sneer at *her* games and gym performances, and scowled
angrily at Alicia.

' Nice little scowl you've got, Gwen,' said Belinda,
appearing suddenly with her sketch-book. ' Do you mind
if I draw you like that ? It's such a *lovely* scowl ! '

Gwendoline scowled still more and flounced away. She

knew Belinda's clever pencil and dreaded it ! She didn't
want her scowl to be drawn and passed round the common-
room, accompanied by delighted giggles. Belinda shut her
book and looked disappointed in rather an exaggerated
manner.

' Oh, she's gone ! And it was such a lovely scowl !
Never mind—I'll watch out for it and draw it another
time.'

' Beast ! ' said Gwendoline, under her breath and went
to sit by Mavis. She knew she would have to look out for
Belinda and her pencil now ! Once Belinda wanted to
draw something she didn't rest till she had done so !

' You'd better go back to the fourth form common-room
now,' said Jean to Zerelda. ' The fourth-formers won't
like it if you begin to live with us ! We're rather beneath
their notice, you know. And, after all, you *are* a fourth-
former, Zerelda.'

' I know. I wish I wasn't,' said Zerelda, getting up.

' Aren't the fourth form girls " wunnerful " then ? ' said
Alicia, with a grin.

Zerelda shrugged her shoulders and went out gracefully.
' If she'd think of something else besides her looks and the
way she's going to act, and being grown-up, and would put
herself out to play games decently and take some interest
in her work, the fourth form wouldn't make her feel out of
things,' said Jean, with her usual common sense. ' But
what's the good of telling Zerelda that ? She simply doesn't
belong to the school at all.'

Irene drifted in, looking for something. She hummed
a lively little tune. ' Tumty-ta-ti-tumty-ta-ti-too ! ' She
had just composed a gay dance, and was very pleased about
it. The girls looked at her and grinned at one another.

' Where are you off to at this time of the evening, Irene ? '
asked Alicia.

Irene looked surprised. ' Nowhere,' she said. ' I'm

just looking for my music-book. I want to write down my new tune. Tumty-ta-ti-tumty-ta-ti-too!'

'Yes, very nice,' said Alicia, approvingly. 'But why have you got your hat and cloak on if you aren't going anywhere?'

'Oh, good gracious, have I?' said Irene, in dismay. She looked down at her cloak and felt her hat on her head. 'Blow! When did I put these on? I did take them off, didn't I, when we came back from the walk this afternoon?'

'Well, you didn't have them on at tea-time or Miss Potts would have said something!' said Alicia. 'You really are a chump, Irene.'

'Oh, yes, I know now what must have happened,' said Irene, sitting down in a chair, still with hat and cloak on. 'I went up to get a clean pair of stockings—and I was thinking of my new tune—and I must have taken my hat out instead of my stockings, and put it on—and then put on my cloak too. Blow! Now I shall have to go and take them off and find my stockings—and I do want to write down that tune.'

'I'll take them up for you and find your stockings,' said Belinda, who knew that Irene wouldn't be able to do anything sensible till she had written down her tune.

'*Will* you? Angel!' said Irene, and pulled off her hat and cloak. Darrell laughed. Belinda was as much of a scatterbrain as Irene. It would be a wonder if she got as far as the cupboard to put away Irene's things—and ten to one that she wouldn't remember the stockings!

Belinda disappeared with the hat and cloak. Irene began to hum her tune again. Mavis sang it in her lovely rich voice.

'Fine!' said Irene, pleased. 'You make it sound twice as good, Mavis. One day I'll write a song for that voice of yours.'

'I'll sing it in New York,' said Mavis, graciously. 'And

that should make you famous, Irene, if *I* sing one of your songs ! When I'm an opera-singer, I . . .'

' When you're an opera-singer, Mavis, you'll be even more conceited than you are now,' said Alicia's sharp voice, ' which sounds impossible I know, but isn't.'

' Jean ! Can't you stop Alicia saying such beastly unfair things ? ' protested Mavis, red with annoyance. ' I'm *not* conceited. Can I help having a voice like mine ? It's a gift, and I shall make it a gift to the whole world too, when I'm grown up.'

' Alicia's tongue *is* getting a bit sharp,' said Jean, ' but you do rather ask for sharp things to be said to you, Mavis.'

Mavis was silent and cross. Gwendoline began to sympathize with her, for she too hated Alicia's hard hitting. Mary-Lou, darning a stocking in a corner, hoped that she would not come in for a flick of Alicia's tongue !

' Where's Belinda ? ' said Darrell. ' She's an awful long time getting those stockings for you, Irene.'

' So she is,' said Irene, who had now completely forgotten about her stockings. ' Blow ! If she doesn't bring them soon, I'll have to go and fetch them myself. I simply must put a clean pair on for supper.'

Mam'zelle came bustling in, tip-tapping on her small feet in their high-heeled shoes. She held a hat and cloak in her hand.

' Irene ! ' she said, reproachfully, ' these are yours ! Three times already have I cleared up your things from this place and that place. Now this time I have almost fallen down the stairs because of your hat and cloak ! '

Irene stared in surprise. ' But—where were they ? ' she asked.

' On the stairs—lying for me to fall over,' said Mam'zelle. ' I see them on the stairs as I come down, and I say to myself, " What is this ? Is it someone taken ill on the stairs ! " But no, it is Irene's cloak and hat once more.

I am very displeased with you, Irene. You will take an order-mark ! '

' Oh *no*, Mam'zelle ! ' said Irene, distressed. Order-marks counted against the whole form. ' Mam'zelle, I'm really very sorry.'

' One order-mark,' said Mam'zelle, and departed on her high heels.

' Blow Belinda ! ' said Irene. ' What possessed her to put them on the stairs ? '

Belinda came in at that moment. She was greeted by a volley of remarks. ' We've got an order-mark because of you, idiot ! What did you do with Irene's things ? Mam'zelle found them on the stairs ! '

' Golly ! ' said Belinda, dismayed. ' Yes, I remember. I was going up the stairs with them, and I dropped my pencil. I chucked the things down to find it—and must have forgotten all about them. I *am* sorry, Irene.'

' It's all right,' said Irene, solemnly putting on her hat and cloak. ' I'll take them up myself now—and I'll jolly well *wear* them so that *I* can't leave them lying about either ! '

She disappeared for a long time. The bell rang for supper. There was a general clearing-up, and the girls got ready to go to the dining-room.

' Where's Irene now ? ' said Jean, exasperated. ' Honestly she ought to be kept in a cage then we'd always know where she was ! '

' Here she is ! ' said Darrell, with a shout of laughter. ' Irene ! You've still got your hat and cloak on ! Oh, you'll make us die of laughing. Quick, Alicia, take them off her and rush upstairs with them. She'll get another order-mark if we don't look out.'

DURING the first two or three weeks of term poor Zerelda had a very bad time.   Although she was older even than the fourth-formers, and should therefore have found the work easy, she found, to her dismay, that she was far behind them in their standard of work !

It was a blow to Zerelda.   After all her posing, and grown-up ways, and her manner of appearing to look down on the others as young and silly, it was very humiliating to find that her maths, for instance, were nowhere near the standard of maths in the fourth form !

' Have you never done these sums before ? ' asked Miss Williams, in astonishment.   ' And what about algebra and geometry ?   You don't appear to understand the first thing about them, Zerelda.'

' We—we don't seem to do our lessons in America the same way as you do them here,' said Zerelda.   ' We don't bother so much.   I never liked algebra or geometry, so I didn't worry about them.'

Miss Williams looked most disapproving.   Was America really so slack in its teaching of children, or was it just that Zerelda was stupid ?

' It isn't only your maths,' she said at last.   ' It's almost everything, Zerelda.   Didn't you ever study grammar in your school ? '

Zerelda thought hard.   ' Maybe we did,' she said at last.   ' But I guess we didn't pay much attention to the teacher who taught grammar.   I guess we played about in her lessons.'

' And didn't you do any history ? ' said Miss Williams.

' I realize, of course, that the history you would take would
not be quite the same as ours—but Miss Carton, the history
mistress, tells me that you don't know a single thing even
about the history of your *own* country. America is a great
country. It seems a pity to know nothing of its wonderful
history.'

Zerelda looked troubled. She tried to think of something
her school had really worked at. What had she taken real
interest in ? Ah—there was the dramatic class !

' We did a lot of Shakespeare, Miss Williams,' she said.
' Gee ! I just loved your Shakespeare. He's wunnerful.
I did Lady Macbeth. You should have seen me trying to
wash the guilt off my hands.'

' Yes. I can quite imagine it,' said Miss Williams, drily.
' But there's a little more to education than being able to
act Lady Macbeth. Zerelda, you will have to work very
very hard to catch up the work of your form. I am willing
to give you extra coaching, if you would like it, and Mam'zelle,
who is very distressed at your French, says she also will
give you some of her free time.'

Zerelda was really alarmed. Gee, wasn't it enough to
have all these classes and games, and be expected to attend
each one and be serious over the work, without having to
do a whole lot of extra study ? She looked so very alarmed
that Miss Williams laughed.

' Well, Zerelda, I won't burden you with extra work
just yet, if you'll really make an effort and try to give your
attention to your school work and not—er—*quite* so much
attention to your face, shall we say—and nails—and hair ? '

Zerelda was annoyed. She was going to study to be a
famous film-star, so what was the use of all this algebra
and history stuff ? Just waste of time for a girl like her !
She had good brains, she knew she had—it was just that
American schools and English were so different. They had
different standards. Life was easier in America.

She looked down at her long, beautifully polished nails and well-kept hands. She felt that Miss Williams had shamed her and made her feel small. Zerelda couldn't bear that! She was better than any of these tough little English girls any day! They didn't know a thing really! So she looked stubborn and said nothing. Miss Williams gathered up her papers, thinking that Zerelda was really a very difficult girl.

'Well, that's all for now,' she said, briskly. 'I shall expect much better work from now on, Zerelda—and please do think of the other fourth-formers too. You know that returned work means an order-mark, which counts against the whole form. You have got far too many.'

Zerelda thought that order-marks were very silly. She wouldn't have minded at all getting twenty or thirty a week! But the other fourth-formers minded very much.

The head-girl, Lucy, spoke to Zerelda about it. 'Look here, Zerelda, can't you stop getting order-marks? There are two half-holidays given this term, but any form getting over forty order-marks has the holiday withheld. The form will be pretty wild if you make them miss their half-holiday, I can tell you!'

So, what with some serious talks from Miss Williams and some tickings-off from Lucy, and from Ellen, a serious, scholarship girl who had gone up from the third form into the fourth, and was very pleased about it, poor Zerelda had rather a bad time.

'There doesn't seem time to do anything!' she thought to herself, as she polished her nails that night. 'I simply must take care of my hair—and it takes ages to curl it properly and set it—and I can't let my complexion go—or my nails. I don't have a minute to myself. But I simply must do something about the work. For one thing, I feel as if I'm letting America down! I can't bear these English girls to be so much better at everything than I am!'

So Zerelda really did try with the work. But her pride would not let her cast off her posing and her grown-up ways. She no longer really looked down on the English girls, but she was still going to show them that she, Zerelda, was far, far above them in all the ways that mattered !

Zerelda had hoped that she would be able to show her ability for acting in the play the fourth form were going to perform. But, alas ! for her, it was a French play, and Zerelda's French did not please Mam'zelle at all.

' C'est terrible ! ' cried Mam'zelle Dupont, and the other Mam'zelle for once agreed with her. Both of them were astonished at Zerelda and her ways, and spent a few pleasant half-hours telling each other of ' Zerelda, cet enfant terrible,' that terrible girl.

When Zerelda had been awarded fifteen order-marks, had three lessons out of every six returned, and had one day given in no prep. at all because she said she couldn't do any of it, Miss Williams went to Miss Grayling.

' Zerelda Brass isn't up to the fourth form,' she told Miss Grayling. ' She's making them furious because of the order-marks she's getting. The trouble is they know what a lot of time she wastes over her appearance, and they think if she gave a bit more time to her work, it would be better all round. I've told her this myself, of course. I don't think she's a bad girl at all, Miss Grayling—only silly, and brought up with quite the wrong ideas. What are we to do ? '

' Do you think extra coaching would help ? ' asked Miss Grayling. ' She is nearly sixteen, you know. She ought to be well up to School Certificate standard. She had quite a good report from America.'

' No. I don't think extra coaching would help at all,' said Miss Grayling. ' It would worry her too much. She simply isn't up to the fourth form—and I really doubt if she's up to third form standard either ! The trouble is she's got such a great opinion of herself, and appears to look down on the others. They resent it.'

'Of course they do,' said Miss Grayling. 'And quite rightly.' She said nothing for a minute. She felt a little disappointed. She had hoped that the American girl would be good for the English girls, and that the English girls would help the American. But apparently it hadn't worked out that way.

'She must go down into the third form,' said Miss Grayling at last. 'I know it is a humiliation and that Zerelda will feel it a disgrace—but somehow I feel that won't do her any harm. Send her to me.'

'Thank you, Miss Grayling,' said Miss Williams, and went out, really relieved to think that Zerelda would no longer be her responsibility. She would now erase all those order-marks that Zerelda had unfortunately got for her form. They would be pleased. They were a good hard-working form, and Miss Williams was proud of them. She was glad to get rid of a girl who had brought them nothing but disgrace.

'But she's not really a *bad* girl,' thought Miss Williams, who was very fair-minded. 'She's just not up to standard in any way. She'll be better in the third form.'

She sent Zerelda down to Miss Grayling. Zerelda, who would have laughed at the thought of being scared of any teacher, when she first came to Malory Towers, actually found her heart thumping away hard as she went to find Miss Grayling in her pleasant drawing-room.

She went in and stood in front of the Head Mistress's desk. Miss Grayling put down her pen and looked at Zerelda, noting her brassy golden hair, done more neatly now, but still carefully set, her brilliantly polished nails, her carefully powdered face.

'Zerelda, I have sent for you because I think you are not up to the standard of the work in the fourth form,' said

Miss Grayling, going straight to the point, as she always did. Zerelda flushed bright red.

' I am sorry about this because you are really above their average age,' said Miss Grayling. ' But I think that it will be too difficult for you to cope with extra work, and also I am afraid that the fourth form, which is a School Certificate form, will not take kindly to quite so many order-marks as you have been producing for them.'

Zerelda blushed an even brighter scarlet, and was angry to feel herself going so red. What did she care about the silly fourth form ?

' Therefore I think you will do better if you go into the third form,' said Miss Grayling. ' They don't take life—or lessons—quite so seriously as they will when in the fourth form—so you should be happier there, and able to work better.'

Zerelda was shocked. To go down into a lower form ! What a disgrace ! True, she liked the third-formers, and didn't get on with the fourth form girls—but she didn't want to slide down a whole form ! Whatever would her people say—and her English grandmother would be amazed.

' Oh, Miss Grayling—gee, I wouldn't like that,' said Zerelda, in distress. She undid a button and did it up again, then undid it, not knowing what she did.

' Don't pull that button off, Zerelda,' said Miss Grayling. ' I think you'll soon settle down quite well in the third form. You can go there tomorrow. I will tell Miss Peters. Move all your things tonight.'

' But, Miss Grayling—don't make me do that ! ' begged Zerelda, feeling very small and disgraced, and not liking it at all. ' This is all new to me, this English school—and the work too. You see . . .'

' Yes, I quite see all that,' said Miss Grayling. ' It's partly because of that that I think life would be easier for you in the way of work, if you go into a lower form. I am convinced you will not get on at all in a higher form. But, Zerelda—don't slide down any further, will you ? You belong to a great country, and you are her only representative here. Be a good one if you can. And I think you can.'

This was the one thing that could touch Zerelda. Gee, she stood for America, didn't she ! She was living in England, but she was a bit of America. All right, she'd go down into the third form, she'd not even make a fuss. And if the girls teased her, she'd just show them she didn't care ! But—she would try to get on with the work all right. Certainly she wouldn't slide down any further !

' You may go, Zerelda,' said Miss Grayling, and Zerelda went. Miss Grayling watched her as she went gracefully out of the door. If only she could see herself as a proper little schoolgirl and not as Zerelda, the promising film-star, how nice she might be !

9   ON THE LACROSSE FIELD

MISS GRAYLING sent for Miss Peters and told her that Zerelda was to come into her form.

' That will be hard for her,' said Miss Peters. ' Not the work, I mean—though I don't think Zerelda will find even third form work easy—but the disgrace.'

Sometimes hard things are good for us,' said Miss Grayling, and Miss Peters nodded. After all, the girls didn't come to Malory Towers only to learn lessons in class —they came to learn other things too—to be just and fair, generous, brave, kind. Perhaps those things were even more important than the lessons!

'I don't know if you think it would be a good thing to say something to the third-formers before Zerelda appears in their classroom,' said Miss Grayling. 'You have one or two there—Gwendoline, for instance—who might not be very kind. A word or two beforehand might be as well.'

'Yes. Just as well,' said Miss Peters. 'Well, I don't expect an easy time with Zerelda, Miss Grayling. She's got such queer ideas about things—spends all her time on her appearance, you know—I've not much use for that kind of girl.'

'No,' said Miss Grayling, thinking that probably it would be good for Zerelda to have the hearty Miss Peters over her for a little while. 'Well—there's plenty of good in the girl—she seems very good-humoured, and I like her smile. Just say a few words to your form, but don't make a big thing of it.'

So, to the third form's intense surprise, Miss Peters said the 'few words' to them that afternoon in class.

'Oh, by the way,' she said, 'we are to have an addition to our form. Zerelda Brass is coming to us.'

Gwendoline drew in her breath sharply, and looked round with a triumphant expression. But she was not crowing over Zerelda's humiliation. She was delighted to think that the American girl would now be approachable—actually in her form, and in her common-room! Gwendoline could dance attendance on her all she pleased. She would be her friend.

Miss Peters read Gwendoline's face wrongly. 'Gwendoline! I hope you will not delight in another girl's inability to follow the work of a higher form. I think . .'

'Oh, Miss Peters!' said Gwendoline, a most hurt expression on her face, 'as if I would do anything of the sort.

I *like* Zerelda. I'm *glad* she'll be in our form. I shall welcome her.'

Miss Peters didn't know whether to believe this or not. She disliked and distrusted Gwendoline. She decided to give her the benefit of the doubt.

'It would be just as well not to discuss the matter with Zerelda if she would rather say nothing about it,' she said. She cast a sharp look at Alicia. She knew Alicia's sarcastic tongue. Alicia looked back at her. She didn't mean to jeer at Zerelda—but at the back of her sharp-witted mind she knew that Zerelda's disgrace would be a nice little weapon to taunt her with, if she gave herself too high-and-mighty airs.

After the afternoon class there was half an hour's lacrosse practice. The third-formers streamed out, Gwendoline last as usual, with Mavis running her close. They were the despair of the games mistress. All the girls began to talk about Zerelda.

'Golly! Fancy being chucked out of a form like that!' said Irene. 'Poor old Zerelda. I bet she feels awful.'

'I should think she feels too ashamed for anything,' said Mary-Lou. 'I know how I should feel. I shouldn't want to look anyone in the face again!'

'I bet the fourth form are glad,' said Jean. 'Ellen told me they had got more order-marks because of Zerelda than they've ever had before! Let's hope she doesn't present *us* with too many. We haven't done too badly so far—except when Irene and Belinda leave their brains behind!'

'I think we all ought to be very nice to Zerelda,' announced Gwendoline. 'I think we ought to show her we're glad she'll be in our form.'

Mavis looked at Gwendoline sourly. She knew quite well that once Zerelda appeared, she, Mavis, would lose Gwendoline's very fickle friendship. Nobody else had any time for Mavis. Gwendoline wasn't much of a friend, but at least she was somebody to talk with, and whisper to.

'Well,' said Darrell, 'Zerelda's got her faults, but she's jolly good-tempered and generous—and I vote we welcome her and show her we're glad to have her.'

So, feeling rather virtuous and generous-hearted, the third-formers made up their minds to be very nice to Zerelda, and ease her disgrace as much as they could. They pictured her slinking into their form room the next day, red in the face, hanging her head, almost in tears. Poor Zerelda! She would be glad of their welcome.

'Darrell! Darrell Rivers! Come over here and I'll give you some catches,' called the games mistress. Darrell ran up. She was a swift runner and loved lacrosse. How she longed to be in one of the match-teams. But it was hard for a third-former to be in a school team unless she was very big and strong.

'You catch well, Darrell!' called the games mistress. 'One of these days you'll get into a match-team. We could do with a good runner and catcher in the third match-team.'

Darrell glowed with pride. Oh! If only she *could* be in the match-team. How pleased her mother and father would be—and how she would boast to Felicity. 'I was in the match-team when we went to play Barchester. I was on the wing because I'm so fast. And I shot a goal!'

She pictured it all as she ran to take another catch. Suppose she practised very hard indeed every minute she could? Should she ask Molly Ronaldson for extra coaching? Molly always said she was willing to give the juniors any tips if they were keen enough to come and ask for them.

But Molly was seventeen and Darrell was only fourteen. Molly seemed a very high-up, distant, rather grand person to Darrell, who hadn't really a very high opinion of herself.

She saw Molly as she was going off the field, hot and

happy. She screwed up all her courage and went up to the big, sturdy girl shyly.

'Please, Molly—could I just ask you something? I do so want to be in one of the match-teams one day. Do you think there might be a *possible* chance if I do extra practice at catching—and—and if you could give me any tips?'

As red as a beetroot Darrell stared at Molly, the famous games captain. Molly laughed and clapped Darrell on the back.

'Good kid!' she said. 'I was only saying to Joan yesterday how you were coming on, and a spot of extra coaching would do you good. I'll send you the times I give extra practice to possible match-team players, and you can come along any of the times you're free.'

'Oh, *thank* you, Molly,' breathed Darrell, hardly able to speak for joy. 'I'll come every time I can.' She ran off, her face glowing. Molly had actually spoken to Joan about her! She had noticed her, had seen that she was coming on well. Darrell felt so happy that she leapt along like a deer, colliding with Mam'zelle round a corner, and almost knocking her over.

'Now, what is this behaviour?' said Mam'zelle, tottering on her high heels and clutching wildly at the wall. 'Darrell! What are you thinking of, to come round the corner like a wild beast?'

'Oh, Mam'zelle—*sorry*!' cried Darrell, happily. 'Honestly I didn't mean it. Oh, Mam'zelle, Molly Ronaldson is going to give me extra coaching at lacrosse. Think of it! I might be in the third match-team one day!'

Mam'zelle was just going to remark that not for anything would she rejoice at that big Molly giving Darrell coaching at that extraordinary game lacrosse, when she saw Darrell's shining eyes. She had a soft spot for Darrell, and she smiled at her.

Darrell ran straight into Mam'zelle

'I am very glad for you, *ma petite* !' she said. 'It is indeed a high honour. But do not go round the corner and knock your poor Mam'zelle over in this way again. You have made my heart go patter-pit !'

'Pitter-pat, you mean, Mam'zelle,' said Darrell, and ran off laughing.

She told the others what Molly had said. They were most impressed, all except those who disliked games. No one of the third form had ever been in a match-team, though one or two steady ones, such as Jean, had tried very hard. So had Sally.

'What with Bill rushing off to her horse every single minute, Irene rushing off to try out her new tune on the piano, Mavis trilling her voice, and now you, Darrell, racing off to practise catching from dawn to dusk, the third form will soon have a nice empty common-room,' said Alicia, a little jealous of Molly's notice of Darrell.

'Zerelda will be there to make up !' said Darrell. 'I don't expect she'll mind our company there—she was always slipping into our common-room till you stopped her, Jean.'

Zerelda came to the third form classroom the next day, carrying her pencil-box and paint-box, which she had forgotten to take to the form room the night before. She walked in looking quite unconcerned.

The third-formers immediately began to be nice. 'Here, Zerelda—wouldn't you rather have this desk till Sally comes back ?' said Darrell. 'It's got a nice position.'

'No, Zerelda. You come and sit by me,' said Gwendoline. 'I should like that.'

Alicia looked keenly at Zerelda. Zerelda looked exactly the same as ever ! She didn't hang her head, she didn't look upset, she wasn't even red in the face.

'I don't believe she cares a bit !' thought Alicia. But Zerelda did. She cared terribly. It was very hard indeed to walk into the classroom of a lower form, knowing that everyone had been told that she had been sent down.

She wished they wouldn't try and be kind to her like this. It was nice of them, but she hated to think they were being nice because they were sorry for her.

' Keep your chin up, Zerelda! ' she said to herself. ' You're American. Fly the Stars and Stripes! Make out you don't mind a bit.'

So, appearing quite unconcerned, she took the desk she had put her things in the night before, put in her pencil-box and paint-box, and began to look for the book she would need for the first lesson.

The third-formers felt a little indignant. They had so virtuously and generously decided to welcome Zerelda, and help her not to mind what they considered to be a great disgrace—and *she* didn't seem to mind at all. She was exactly the same as usual, speaking in her slow drawl, fluffing up her hair, appearing even more sure of herself than ever.

Darrell felt rather annoyed. She considered that Zerelda ought to have shown a little more feeling. She didn't stop to think that Zerelda might be putting on a show of bravery, and that was all. Underneath it all the girl was miserable, ashamed and feeling very small.

Miss Peters came in briskly as usual. Mary-Lou shut the door. Miss Peters swept keen eyes round the class. ' Sit ! ' she said, and they sat. That keen glance had taken in Zerelda—but Miss Peters saw what the others did not see —a rather panic-stricken heart under all Zerelda's brave show. A hand that shook slightly as she picked up a book —a voice that wasn't quite so steady as usual.

' She feels it all right,' thought Miss Peters. ' But she's not going to show it. Well, she's got plenty of pluck. Let's hope she'll learn that she's not so important a person as she thinks she is. If we got right down to the real

Zerelda, we might find somebody worth knowing! We *might*. I still don't know!'

The lesson began. Zerelda concentrated hard. She forgot her hair, her nails, her clothes. She really *worked* for about the first time in her life!

10   BILL AND MISS PETERS

MOST of the third-formers were now almost settled in to their term's work. Alicia, however, was restless, missing Betty and not finding that Darrell quite made up for her old friend. Darrell was steady and loyal and natural—but she hadn't Betty's witty tongue, nor her daredevil ways. Still she was better than anyone else. Alicia hoped that Sally wouldn't be back till Betty came!

Bill was restless too. Bill had got the idea that Thunder was pining for the other horses at home, and she was always disappearing to be with him.

'How you do coddle that horse!' said Alicia, in disgust. 'I wonder he puts up with it.'

Miss Peters was always pouncing on Bill for dreaming in class. Bill's standard of work was very uneven. She was brilliant at Latin, which she had taken continually with her brothers. She knew very little French, much to Mam'zelle's despair. She didn't know much maths because her brothers' tutor had devoted all his time to them at this subject and had not bothered much about her.

'He didn't think we did much maths in a girls' school, explained Bill. 'But I do know my tables, Miss Peters.

'I should hope so!' groaned Miss Peters. 'You will simply have to have extra coaching at maths, Wilhelmina.'

'Oh, I can't,' said Bill. 'I spend every minute of free time with Thunder.'

Miss Peters had known for some time now that Thunder was Bill's horse. She had seen him and admired him, much to Bill's delight. She had also marvelled at Bill's magnificent horsemanship. The girl rode as if she and her horse were one. She was never happier than when she was out riding with the others, galloping over the lovely country that lay behind Malory Towers.

But she was annoyed because she was only allowed to ride out with the others for company. She was not allowed to take Thunder out alone.

'But I do at home,' she protested loudly. 'I've gone off by myself every day for years and years and years. It's silly not to let me. What harm can I come to? I'm with Thunder all the time.'

'Yes, I know all that,' explained Miss Peters, patiently, for the twentieth time. 'But you are not at home now, you are at school, and you have to do as the others do, and keep their rules. We can't have one rule for you and one rule for them.'

'I don't see why not,' said Bill, obstinately. She often sounded rude, because she was so much in earnest, and Miss Peters sometimes lost patience with her.

'Well, you are not running this school, fortunately,' said Miss Peters. 'You must do as you are told. And, Wilhelmina, if you insist on being silly about these things, I shall forbid you to see Thunder for two or three days.'

Bill was dumbfounded. She stared at Miss Peters as if she couldn't believe her ears. She went red to the roots of her hair.

'But I couldn't *not* see Thunder,' said Bill, trying to speak patiently. 'You don't understand, Miss Peters.

Though you *ought* to understand because you're so fond of horses yourself.'

'I dare say,' said Miss Peters, equally patiently. 'But I'm not top-heavy about them, as you are—I mean, I don't think, dream, smell and ride horses every minute of the day and night as you do. Do be sensible, Wilhelmina. I'm putting up with quite a lot from you, you know, and it's time you pulled yourself together, and thought a little less of Thunder, and a little more of other things.'

But that was just what Bill couldn't do, as the other third-formers soon found out. She wouldn't go for extra practice at lacrosse. She wouldn't go for a nature walk. She wouldn't even take on any of her extra duties in the common-room, which everyone had to do in turn. She got Mary-Lou to do them for her instead.

Mary-Lou was so gentle and kindly that she would do anything for anybody. Jean was very cross when she found Mary-Lou doing the flowers in the common-room instead of Bill.

'Why are you doing this?' she demanded. 'You can see on the list it's Bill's week.'

'I know, Jean,' said Mary-Lou, scared at Jean's sharp tone. 'But Bill did so badly want to go and give Thunder an extra grooming today. He got so muddy yesterday.'

'I'm getting tired of Bill racing off to the stables, never joining in anything the third form does, and getting other people to do her duties,' said Jean. 'I shall talk to her about it.'

But she made no more impression on Bill than Miss Peters had done. Bill had spent her life with horses. She had, as Miss Peters said, thought, dreamt, smelt, groomed, ridden horses all her life, and she just didn't want to do anything else.

She would have been excellent at lacrosse if she had practised. She was magnificent at gym, daring, supple and with a wonderful sense of balance. The gym mistress was delighted with her, and sang her praises to everyone.

Bill could turn ' cart-wheels ' as easily as any clown in a circus, going over and over on hands and feet till the others were giddy with watching. She could fling herself in the air and turn a complete somersault. The gym mistress forbade anyone else to try and do it.

' You'll only damage yourselves,' she said. But nobody else really wanted to turn somersaults in the air !

Bill could also walk on her hands, and the others often made her perform to them in the evening when she could not go to the stables. Bill was good-natured and natural, and didn't get her head in the least turned by all the praise and acclamation given to her for her performances in gym or common-room.

Zerelda watched and marvelled. She could not imagine how any girl could want to do such extraordinary things. She thought Bill was decidedly mad, but she couldn't help liking her. In fact, most of the girls liked her very much indeed, though they were annoyed and exasperated when she wouldn't join in with them over anything.

Belinda did some beautiful drawings of Thunder. She was very good at drawing animals, and when Bill saw them she exclaimed in delight.

' Belinda ! They're simply marvellous ! Please, please give them to me ! '

' No,' said Belinda, tucking them away into her portfolio. ' I shall keep them with my collection of animal drawings.'

' Well,' Belinda, do some specially for *me*,' begged Bill. ' Oh, Belinda, you might. I'd have them all framed and stood on my dressing-table.'

' Gosh, Bill, you've got about six different photographs of horses there now,' said Belinda. ' You've no room for a picture of Thunder.'

' I have ! I should put him right at the very front,' said

Bill. ' Belinda, *will* you do me some drawings of Thunder ?
I'll do anything for you if you will.'

' Fibber ! ' said Belinda. ' The only person you'll do
anything for is Thunder. You wouldn't lift a finger to do
anything for Miss Peters or for anyone in the third form and
you know it.'

Bill looked taken aback. ' Am I really as bad as that ? '
she asked, anxiously. ' Is that what you all think of me ? '

' Of course,' said Belinda. ' Why, you don't even take
on your own duties. I heard Jean ticking you off for that
—but Mary-Lou's going on doing them just the same. So
you can't have a drawing of Thunder, my dear Bill, because
if you do you'll only go and stand and gaze devotedly at him
all the evening when you can't go to the stables, and that
will make us crosser than ever.'

Belinda paused to take breath. Bill looked as if she was
going to fly into a temper. Then her sense of fairness came
to her help.

' Yes. You're right, Belinda. I don't like you being
right, but you are,' she said, honestly. ' I probably *should*
keep flying upstairs to look at Thunder's picture if I had a
really good one. And I'm sorry about making Mary-Lou
do my duties after Jean had told me about it. I'll tell her
I'll do them all next week to make up.'

' Right,' said Belinda. ' I'll draw you a fine picture of
Thunder, with you on his back, if you like, if you keep
your word. But—I shall jolly well take it away if you start
being silly, because I'm only going to *lend* it to you till I
see if you'll keep your promise.'

Bill laughed. She liked Belinda. She liked Irene, too.
They both did the maddest, silliest things, but they were
fun, and you could always trust them to do the decent
thing. She longed for a picture of Thunder—she only had a
very bad photograph of him. Now she was going to get a
lovely drawing !

Jean quite thought that it was a belated result of her ticking-off that made Bill offer to do Mary-Lou's duties the next week. She was pleased.

Belinda kept her word and gave Bill a beautiful picture of Thunder, done in black charcoal, with Bill on his back in her riding-breeches and a yellow jersey. Bill was absolutely thrilled. She made Mary-Lou walk into the village with her to try to get it framed at once. She couldn't buy a frame there, so she took one of the horse-photographs out of its frame on her dressing-table and put Thunder's picture in it, neatly trimmed to fit.

Everyone admired it. 'Now you remember, Bill, it's not yours *yet*,' Belinda warned her. 'It's only lent. The very next time you dodge out of duties or third form activities you'll find that picture gone!'

But although Bill was better from that day in trying to do some of the things her form thought she ought to do, she still didn't get on very well with Miss Peters. She *would* sit and gaze out of the window, she *would* forget that her name was Wilhelmina, she would day-dream and not pay any attention to either Mam'zelle or Miss Peters.

Mam'zelle complained bitterly. 'This girl is not even polite! I say to her, "Wilhelmina, do not dream" and she does not even bother to hear me and answer. I say to her, "Wilhelmina, are you deaf?" and she still does not reply to me. Never, never will she learn any French— except for "*le cheval*"! Miss Peters, the only time I get that girl to turn round to face me is when I say suddenly the name of her horse. "Thunder!" I say, and she turns round at once. She is mad that girl. All English girls are mad, but she is the most mad.'

Miss Peters began to punish Bill in the way she resented and hated most. 'Here is a returned maths lesson,' she said to Bill. 'Do it please, and until you have brought it to me again you must not go to see Thunder.'

Or she would say, ' Wilhelmina, you have paid no attention in class this morning. You will not go to the stables at all today.'

Bill was angry and resentful—and disobedient ! She was not going to stop seeing Thunder for anyone in the world. Least of all for Miss Peters ! And so, to Jean's disgust, she ignored Miss Peters' punishments and slipped off to see Thunder whenever she liked.

Miss Peters did not even dream that Bill would disobey. ' One of these days she'll find out, Bill,' said Alicia. ' Then you'll be for it ! You really are an idiot.'

What with Bill and her horse, Zerelda and her ways, Irene and Belinda with their feather-brains, and Mavis and her opera-singing, Miss Peters considered that she had the most trying form in the school. ' And all from North Tower too ! ' thought Miss Peters. ' Really, I'm sorry for Miss Potts, their house-mistress. They must drive her mad ! Now I wonder when Wilhelmina is going to bring me that returned geography lesson. She won't go to see that horse of hers till she does ! '

But Miss Peters was wrong. At that very minute Bill was in the stable and Thunder was nuzzling into her hand for sugar !

11   ALICIA HAS A PARCEL

THE days flew by. It was still very cold and Gwendoline and Mavis complained bitterly, as they huddled near the fire in the common-room, or sat almost on top of the radiators.

Thunder was nuzzling into her hand for sugar

'You should rush about a bit more in gym or on the lacrosse field,' said Darrell, whose face was a rosy-pink with good health and happiness. She had gone out to the field every moment she could spare to have coaching from Molly. She was getting very good! She knew she was. Molly had praised her catching and said it was excellent.

Gwendoline looked at Darrell with her usual scowl. She really felt miserable in the cold weather, for she came from an overheated home and could not get used to the fresh-air atmosphere of school. It annoyed her to see Darrell without a single chilblain, and to watch her race out happily into the frosty air for her lacrosse practice.

Belinda came slipping up behind Gwendoline, who was quite unaware that she was scowling. Belinda's quick pencil set to work. Mavis nudged Gwen.

'Look out! Here's Belinda again!'

Gwen turned round quickly, trying to smooth the scowl off her face—but it was difficult to feel angry and yet not scowl!

'Go away, Belinda! I don't want you to draw me!' she said, peevishly. 'I wish you'd leave me alone. I hate the way you come slinking up—I call it really sly.'

'Oh no!' said Belinda. 'I'm just interested in you, that's all. You have such a *lovely* scowl—the ugliest in the whole school, I should think. Do, do scowl again, Gwen, and let me draw it.'

Gwen stopped herself from scowling, but it was a very great effort. Belinda grinned.

'Poor Gwendoline Mary—so annoyed, that it makes her want to scowl more fiercely than ever—but she won't! Well, never mind—I'll watch for the next time.'

She went away, and everyone laughed. Gwen's eyes filled with easy tears. She could always cry at any moment. How hateful Belinda was. Gwen thought she really must go and scowl at herself in the mirror, then she would see what was so unique about it. It probably was no worse a scowl than Mavis's or Bill's—but that horrid Belinda thought it was a fine way to tease her.

Darrell came in after her lacrosse practice, glowing and beaming. ' I say, girls ! What do you think ? I may be a reserve for the third match-team ! Only the third reserve —but it's something ! '

' What's a reserve ? ' asked Zerelda, thinking it must be something marvellous, judging by Darrell's shining eyes.

' Well—if three girls fall out from the next match-team, I'd take the place of the third one,' explained Darrell.

' Third reserves never play,' remarked Alicia. ' Everybody knows that. So don't hope too much, Darrell.'

' I'm not,' said Darrell. ' Alicia, I do wish you would get a bit of coaching too. Molly's fine—takes no end of trouble.'

' That fat, clumsy Molly ! ' murmured Zerelda, in her lazy drawl. ' Gee—I just can't bear to look at her ! '

It was silly of Zerelda to say things like that. It made Darrell and Jean and the rest of the keen lacrosse players annoyed. What did it matter what Molly looked like ? She was a splendid games captain, and had won more matches than had been won for years by Malory Towers !

' She may be fat, but she's not clumsy—she's a fast runner and very powerful,' said Darrell, stoutly.

' I'll say she is ! ' said Zerelda. ' I met her running down the stairs the other day, and I thought there was an earthquake coming. But it was only her great feet pounding on the stairs. You can keep your Mollies ! I don't want them. All brawn and no brains or charm ! '

' And you, I suppose, are all charm, and no brains ? ' said Alicia's smooth, malicious voice. ' How nice ! Well, America can keep her Zereldas. They're not much good here ! '

Zerelda flushed scarlet and bit her lip. The others

held their breath, expecting an outburst. But it didn't come.

'I guess I asked for that,' said Zerelda, stiffly, and she got up. She said no more, but went out of the room as gracefully as ever.

Nobody said anything. They felt uncomfortable. It wasn't right to taunt a girl when they had all decided to be nice to her—but on the other hand Zerelda was really very annoying and deserved to be ticked off.

'Where's Bill?' asked Darrell, to change the subject.

'Where do you suppose?' said Belinda. 'Giving Thunder titbits in the stable.'

'Well, I wish she wouldn't,' said Jean. 'It's absolutely flat disobedience, and she'll get into a terrific row if she's found out. I've argued with her and rowed her and told her to obey Miss Peters in case something worse happens —but she simply won't listen. I might as well talk to a stone wall.'

'She says Thunder isn't well,' said Mary-Lou.

'Imagination!' scoffed Alicia. 'She just says that so that she can go and see him without *too* guilty a conscience.'

'No. I am sure she really *does* think Thunder isn't well,' said Mary-Lou, in her gentle voice. 'She's very worried about him.'

'Well, why doesn't she ask Miss Peters to get the vet. to him?' said Irene.

'Because if she does Miss Peters will want to know how she knows he's not well,' explained Mary-Lou. 'And then the fat will be in the fire!'

'And there will be a sizzling noise and Miss Peters will go up in smoke!' said Belinda, taking out her pencil to draw Miss Peters going up in smoke.

Somebody put their head in at the common-room door. 'Hey there! Parcel post is in—and there's a parcel for you, Alicia.'

'Thanks,' said Alicia, and got up to go and get it. 'Hope it's some chocolates from my godmother. She usually sends me a box each term.'

She disappeared. Belinda finished her drawing and handed it round. Everyone yelled with laughter. Miss Peters was floating upwards, enveloped in smoke, and lightning was flashing from the smoke.

'Lovely!' said Darrell. 'I wish I could draw like you. I can't do anything like that! You're lucky, Belinda.'

'Yes, I am,' said Belinda, taking back her drawing, and adding a few more strokes. 'Don't know what I should do if I couldn't draw. I'd be miserable! Well, so would Irene be miserable if she couldn't have her music!'

'And I should be very very miserable without my voice,' said Mavis at once.

'Yes. You'd be ten times more miserable than either Irene or Belinda,' said Jean. 'And I'll tell you why. Because you just wouldn't be anything without your voice, Mavis! After all, Irene is good at maths, and she plays quite a good game of lacrosse, and she's always ready to have a bit of fun—like Belinda, who's pretty fair at everything besides being gifted at drawing. But you're nothing but a Voice! Take that away and I don't believe anyone would know you were here!'

'I can't help having a voice that overpowers the rest of me,' said Mavis, complacently. 'It's not my fault if I seem all Voice to you. When I'm an opera-singer I shall . . .'

This was the signal for everyone to begin talking at the tops of their voices. It didn't matter what they said, they just talked to drown Mavis's familiar parrot-cry. As they talked they laughed to see her annoyed face, its small dark eyes gleaming spitefully.

Well—she didn't care! Wait till she was a bit older —then she would show the others what a gift like hers meant. She would sweep the whole world to rapture over

her unique voice. Her family and her singing teachers
marvelled at her voice, and were never tired of predicting
a wonderful career. She could wait for that, even if it
meant putting up with commonplace people like the third-
formers !

Alicia came in with her parcel. 'It's not from my god-
mother,' she said, ' so don't crowd round me too hopefully.
It's from Sam.'

Sam was one of her brothers, a scamp if ever there was
one. The third-formers were never tired of hearing of his
escapades.

'Is it some sort of joke to play, do you think ? ' asked
Darrell, eagerly. 'Alicia, you haven't played a trick for
ages. I do hope it's a good one ! '

Alicia opened the parcel. Out fell a small box. Belinda
picked it up and looked at it. Something was written on
the lid.

'Sneeze, Boys, Sneeze ! '

'Whatever does it mean ? ' said Darrell, thrilled. ' Let's
open the box.'

'Well, look out then,' said Alicia, shaking out a letter
from her brother. ' Don't spill the contents. They may be
valuable ! '

Darrell opened the box. It was full of little white pellets,
round and flat, about half an inch in diameter. ' Whatever
are they ? ' said Darrell. ' And why the funny label on the
box—" Sneeze, Boys, Sneeze ! " '

Alicia was reading Sam's letter and chuckling. ' Listen
to this,' she said. ' Sam really is a scamp. These pellets
have been made by one of the boys in his form—he's a bit
of an inventor in his way. What you do is to put a pellet
on a shelf, damp it with a solution of salt water, and then
leave it. In half an hour it sends off a kind of vapour that
gets up people's noses and makes them sneeze terrifically ! '

Everyone laughed. ' Sam says he did it to his drawing

master,' said Alicia, chuckling again. 'And he sneezed forty-three times. The boys counted. What a joke!'

'Let's play it on Miss Peters!' said Darrell, thrilled. 'Oh, do let's!'

The idea of hearing the hearty Miss Peters sneezing forty-three times was very tempting. Alicia read Sam's letter to the end. 'He says on no account must we use more than one pellet at a time, because the effects are very bad if too much vapour gets up anyone's nose. And he says the pellet-vapour only floats out about four feet—so if we do play the trick on Miss Peters, she will start sneezing her head off—but we shan't sneeze at all!'

'It sounds an absolutely super trick,' said Darrell. '*Really* super! Alicia, we *must* play it. I should die of laughing to see Miss Peters sneezing like that. She has such a very terrifically loud sneeze—almost louder than anyone else's in the school.'

'Well—we mustn't begin to giggle too soon or giggle too much in case Miss Peters smells a rat,' said Alicia. 'Though I don't see how she can. After all, *she* will be the only one who sneezes.'

Everyone felt really thrilled. A trick on Miss Peters! Very few third-formers had ever dared to play jokes on her, for she was sharp, and so swift with punishment that usually nobody dared to annoy her too much. But this trick was surely foolproof!

'When can we play it? Tomorrow?' asked Darrell.

'No. Wait till we've got a test in maths or something,' said Alicia. 'Then, if Miss Peters sneezes too much, we shan't have the test!'

THE next excitement was that Sally came back! Darrell was overjoyed. She hugged Sally, and they both began to talk at once.

'It's good to be back! I did hate not coming at the beginning of the term!'

'Oh, Sally, I have missed you! There's lots to tell you.'

'You wrote awfully good letters. I'm longing to see Bill and Zerelda. Wasn't it a shame missing everything!'

Everyone was pleased to see Sally back—everyone that is, except Alicia. Alicia had got used to having Darrell for her companion and friend. Now she would have to share her with Sally—and she might not even be able to *share* her! Darrell might not want to bother with Alicia, with Sally back again.

So Alicia greeted Sally rather coolly, and made quite a show of being friendly with Darrell, hoping that Darrell would still want her for a friend. But Darrell forgot all about Alicia for a few days, she was so pleased that Sally was back.

There was so much news to exchange, so much to discuss. Sally marvelled at Zerelda and her ways, and heard two or three times all about how she had been taken from the fourth form and put into the third. She marvelled at Bill too and her prowess in the gym and on horseback. She thought Mavis and her voice were more difficult than ever to put up with. She was amused at the way Gwendoline followed Zerelda around and was not taken much notice of!

'Oh, Darrell—you don't *know* how good it is to be back again!' said Sally, happily. 'I kept on and on thinking of you all—working in class—joking with Mam'zelle Dupont, and being ticked off by Mam'zelle Rougier—and playing lacrosse, and having fun in the gym, and roasting chestnuts by the fire in the common-room. I was absolutely home-sick for school!'

'Well, now you're back again at last,' said Darrell. 'I chummed up with Alicia whilst you were away, Sally. Betty's in quarantine for whooping-cough and isn't back yet, so she was on her own and so was I.'

Sally didn't very much like the idea of Darrell being friends with Alicia. She felt jealousy creeping up in her. Jealousy was one of Sally's failings. She had conquered it for some time—but it came slipping into her heart again now when she saw how friendly Alicia was with Darrell. She didn't like it at all.

So Sally was as cool with Alicia as Alicia was cool with Sally, and Darrell was surprised and grieved about it. She had hoped that once Sally had settled in, she and Sally and Alicia might be companions till Betty came back. It didn't seem to Darrell to be quite fair to throw off Alicia entirely, as soon as Sally came back.

Darrell told Sally about Alicia's proposed trick. Sally didn't seem to think it a good trick to play at all!

'It's silly to play a trick like that on Miss Peters,' she said. 'For one thing, she'll guess it's a trick and will deal out awful punishments—and for another thing I don't much like those tricks that make people have sneezing fits. I think they're a bit dangerous.'

'Oh, Sally!' said Darrell, really disappointed. 'I thought you'd be so thrilled. Don't be so prim and solemn! I believe it's just because it's *Alicia's* trick you don't like it!'

Sally was hurt. 'All right—if you like to think things like that of me, you can,' she said. 'I suppose you think

I'm jealous of Alicia. Well, I'm not. I can quite see why you like her so much—jolly, witty, amusing—all the things I'm not!'

Now it was Darrell's turn to look hurt. 'You're silly, Sally,' she said. 'Yes, you are! You know you're my friend and I only went with Alicia and Alicia with me because you and Betty were away. Don't spoil things, Sally.'

'All right. I'll try not to,' said Sally, with an effort. But jealousy is a very hard thing to fight and an even harder thing to defeat. Try as she would Sally could not stop herself from being a little spiteful about Alicia, and she was so cool to her that Alicia, tickled to see her jealousy, began to play up to Darrell even more.

'Oh dear!' sighed Darrell to herself one afternoon as she ran out for a lacrosse practice, 'why is it that Alicia is always so *specially* nice to me in front of Sally—and why has Sally changed so much? She *is* jealous, I know—but does jealousy change people such a lot?'

Darrell wasn't at all jealous herself. It was not in her nature, so she couldn't really understand Sally's feelings. She saw both sides very clearly. Sally didn't like Alicia and wanted Darrell's entire friendship. Alicia didn't see why she should give up Darrell's companionship completely just because Sally had come back. Why not a threesome till Betty returned?

'Well, I shan't think about *either* of them!' said Darrell, as she caught the lacrosse ball very deftly, spun round and sent it cleanly and swiftly to another player. So she didn't bother about anything except giving her whole attention to the fun of running and catching and throwing.

Molly Ronaldson was really pleased with her. It was not only Darrell's swiftness and deftness that made her pleased, but the girl's keenness. She had never missed a practice, she had come out in the coldest weather and the bitterest winds. She was a Good Sport—and Molly Ronaldson had no higher praise for anyone than that.

' Darrell Rivers, count yourself as third reserve for the third match-team,' she said, as she went off the field with Darrell. ' I'll put the notice up on the board this evening. There's always a chance you might play in a match, so keep up your practice. In this term there's such a lot of illness and people often fall out by the dozen.'

' Oh, Molly—*thank* you ! ' said Darrell, finding it quite difficult to speak, she was so overcome. ' I won't let you down—I'll not miss a single practice, even if it snows ! I say, I do think it's super of you ! '

' No, it isn't really,' said Molly. ' I'm thinking of the *team*. You're good enough—so in you go—as reserve first, with a faint chance of playing in a match later on.'

Darrell rushed indoors, walking on air. Luckily she didn't collide with Mam'zelle round the corner this time. All she did was to bump into a bunch of fourth-formers, who scattered in alarm at her headlong rush.

' Darrell Rivers ! Are you mad ? ' said Lucy.

' No ! Well, perhaps I *am* a bit ! ' said Darrell. ' I'm third reserve for the third match-team ! Molly's just told me.'

' That's jolly good,' said Ellen. ' Congratulations ! Lucky thing ! I'll never be in any match-team, and I'm a fourth-former.'

Everyone seemed pleased and clapped Darrell on the back. She rushed to the third form common-room to break the news there. Most of the girls were there, sitting about, reading, playing games or sewing. They looked up as Darrell burst in.

' Here comes the hurricane ! ' said Alicia, with a grin. ' Shut the door, for goodness' sake, Darrell. There's an icy blast blowing round my legs already.'

Darrell slammed the door. ' Girls, I'm third reserve ! '
she announced. ' Molly's putting it up on the notice board
tonight.'

Alicia, who had been a little annoyed at Darrell's success
at lacrosse that term, made up her mind to be pleased about
it this time. It wouldn't do for her to be sour over this
and Sally to be sweet ! So she leapt up, thumped Darrell
on the back, and yelled congratulations as if there had never
before been anyone in the reserve.

She would hardly let Sally get near Darrell. Jean was
pleased too, and Irene and Belinda came round to marvel.
Even Mary-Lou added her bit, and Zerelda smiled and
looked pleased, though secretly she wondered how anyone
could possibly be so thrilled about such a peculiar thing.
Altogether it was quite a triumph for Darrell, and she basked
in the admiration with delight.

Sally was cross to see how pleased Alicia apparently was,
and how Darrell welcomed her delight. ' Oh dear ! ' she
thought, ' I am getting horrid ! I can't even make myself
say all the nice things to Darrell I'd like to say, just because
Alicia got there first ! '

Darrell was rather surprised that Sally didn't seem as
pleased as she had expected her to be. ' Aren't you glad,
Sally ? ' she asked anxiously. ' It's an honour for the third
form, you know. Do say you're pleased ! '

' Of course I'm pleased ! ' said Sally. ' It's—it's fine.
You've done jolly well, Darrell.'

But she didn't sound very whole-hearted about it and
Darrell felt faintly disappointed. Never mind ! Alicia was
thrilled—and so were the others. Perhaps Sally was still
feeling a bit out of things, having come back so late in
the term.

The next excitement was a notice put up on the board,
next to the notice about Darrell, to say that Miss Hibbert,
the English mistress, was going to start rehearsals for

'Romeo and Juliet'. All third-formers were to go to the art-room to be tried out for parts.

'Blow!' said Gwendoline, who didn't like Miss Hibbert because she had so often ticked her off for being affected and silly in her acting. 'I was hoping she had forgotten about the play. It's such a waste of time.'

'Oh *no*, it isn't,' said Zerelda, who had brightened up very much at the notice. 'Acting is marvellous! That's a thing I really *can* do. I did Lady Macbeth over in . . .'

'Yes, we know you did,' interrupted Daphne. 'We ought to know by now, anyway! You tell us often enough.'

'I suppose you fancy yourself in one of the chief parts, Daphne?' said Alicia. 'What a disappointment you'll get! Anyway, if Zerelda's so good, she'll play Juliet—if she can get rid of that American drawl!'

Zerelda looked alarmed. 'Do you think my way of speaking will stop me having a good part?' she asked.

'Well—I can't imagine Shakespeare's Juliet talking with a pronounced American accent,' said Alicia. 'Still—if you act the part well enough I don't see why you shouldn't get it!'

Zerelda had been rather subdued lately, but now she came to life again, with the hope of starring in 'Romeo and Juliet'! She paid a tremendous lot of attention to her appearance and spent as much time as she dared in front of her looking-glass. She also tried to get rid of her American drawl!

This amused the class very much. Zerelda had never made the slightest attempt before to speak in the English way and had laughed at the English accent and called it silly. Now she badgered everyone to tell her how to pronounce the words the way they did.

'Well, try to say "won*d*erful" with the D in the middle, instead of "wunnerful", for a start,' said Darrell. 'And say "twen*ty*-four" with the T in the middle, instead of

" *twenny*-four ". And couldn't you say " stop " instead of " starp " and " shop " instead of " sharp " ? Or can't you hear the difference ? '

Zerelda patiently tried to master the English way of speaking, much to Miss Peters' astonishment. She had felt quite pleased with Zerelda's efforts to keep up with the work of the form, but she was still annoyed with the girl's constant attention to her hair and appearance. Nor did she like Zerelda's still grown-up air, and her habit of appearing to look down on the others just because they were school-girls.

' Now I'll show them all ! ' thought Zerelda, studying the part of Juliet with great attention. ' Now they'll see what I mean when I say I'm going to be one of the greatest of all film-stars ! '

13   ZERELDA'S UNFORTUNATE REHEARSAL

MISS HIBBERT took a great deal of trouble in producing the school plays. She gave her time to each form in turn, and really achieved some excellent results. This term it was the third form's turn. They were to give the play towards the end of the term. They were thankful not to be doing French plays. Both the Mam'zelles took a hand in producing those, and as they had quite different ideas about acting, it was a little trying for the actors.

' Does Miss Hibbert choose the characters the first time ? ' asked Zerelda.

' Oh no—she tries us all out in almost every part several

times,' said Darrell. 'She does that for two reasons—she
says that in that way she really does find the right actor for
every part—and we all get to know every part of the play
and work better as a team.'

'Gee, that's wunnerful—I mean, won*der*ful,' said Zerelda.
'I've been studying Juliet's part. It's a lovely one. Would
you like to hear me do some of the lines ? '

'Well—I'm just going out to my lacrosse practice,' said
Darrell. 'Sorry! Look—ask Alicia. She's got nothing
to do this period.'

But Alicia was not going to admire Zerelda's Juliet. She
got up hastily. 'Sorry! I've got to go to a meeting,
Zerelda. But I'm sure you'd be just wunnerful! '

'I'll hear you, Zerelda,' said Gwendoline, glad of an
opportunity to please the American girl. 'Let's go into one
of the empty music-practice-rooms, where you won't be
disturbed. It will be lovely to see you act. I'm sure you
must be awfully good. As good as—what's the star you
like so much—oh yes, Lossie Laxton! '

'Well, maybe I'm not up to her standard yet,' said
Zerelda, fluffing up her hair in the way Lossie did on the
films. 'Okay, Gwen—we'll go to a practice-room.'

But they were all full, and music sounded from each of
them, with the exception of one at the end. Irene was
there, poring over a music score.

'I say, Irene,' said Gwen, going in, 'can you . . .'

'Go away,' said Irene, fiercely. 'I'm busy. Can't you
see ? '

'Well, you're not needing the piano, are you ? ' said
Zerelda. 'Can't you do your work, whatever it is, somewhere else ? '

'No, I can't. I shall want to try it out on the piano
in a minute,' said Irene. 'Go away. Interrupting me
like that ! '

Zerelda was surprised. She had never seen Irene so

annoyed before. But Gwendoline had. She knew that Irene could not bear to be disturbed when she was concentrating on her music, whether it was writing it out, or playing it on the piano.

'Come on,' she said to Zerelda. 'Let's go.'

'Yes. GO!' said Irene, with a desperate expression on her face. 'You've stopped me just when it was all coming beautifully. Blow you both!'

'Well, really, Irene, I do think you might let us use this room if you're only playing about with pencil and paper,' began Zerelda. 'I want to recite some lines of Juliet and . . .'

Then Irene went quite mad. She threw her music, her pencil and her music-case at the alarmed Zerelda. 'You're daft!' she shouted. 'Give up my music-hour for your silly acting! Oh yes, I know you're going to be a wonderful film-star, parading about in marvellous clothes, thinking of third-rate things if ever you *do* have a thought in your head—but what's all that compared to music! I tell you I'm . . .'

But Zerelda and Gwen did not wait to hear any more. They saw Irene looking round for something else to throw and as there was a vase of flowers on the little mantelpiece Gwen thought the sooner they went out of the room the better.

'*Well!*' said Zerelda. 'If that doesn't beat all! Irene's mad!'

'Not really,' said Gwen. 'It's only when she feels sort of inspired, and music comes welling up into her mind and she has to write it down. She's got the real artistic temperament, I suppose.'

'Well, so have I,' said Zerelda at once. 'But I don't go mad like that. I wouldn't have believed it of her.'

'She can't help it,' said Gwendoline. 'It's only when she's interrupted. Look—there's Lucy going out of one of the practice-rooms. We can have that one if we're quick ! '

They slipped into the room that Lucy had just left. Gwendoline sat down, ready to listen for hours if she could please Zerelda and make her feel really friendly towards her. Zerelda struck a lovesick attitude and began.

> ' Wilt thou be gone ? It is not yet near day ;
> It was the nightingale and not the lark,
> That pierced the fearful hollow of thine ear ;
> Nightly she sings on yon pomegranate-tree ;
> Believe me, love, it was the nightingale.'

Gwendoline listened with a rapt and admiring expression on her face. She had no idea at all whether Zerelda was good or not, but that made no difference to her praise.

' It's marvellous ! ' she said, when Zerelda at last stopped for breath. ' However have you learnt such a lot ? My goodness, you do act well. And you really look the part, Zerelda, with your hair and all.'

' Do I ? ' said Zerelda, pleased. She always enjoyed herself when she was acting. ' I know what I'll do. I'll shake my hair loose. And I'll wrap this tablecloth round me. No—it's not big enough. The curtain will do ! '

To Gwendoline's amusement Zerelda took down the blue curtain and swathed it round herself over her brown school tunic. She undid her brilliant hair and shook it all over her shoulders. She decided to put the tablecloth round her too. Ah—now she felt more like Juliet. Holding her hands out pathetically in front of her she began another speech. It sounded really a little queer because Zerelda tried very hard to speak in the English way but kept lapsing into her usual drawl, so that the whole effect was rather funny.

Gwendoline wanted to laugh but she knew how offended Zerelda would be. The American girl paraded up and

down, declaiming her speeches most dramatically, the blue
curtain dragging behind her like a train, her hair almost
hiding one eye.

Someone looked in. It was Bessie, a second-former.
She had come to practice. But seeing two third-formers
there, she fled. Then a fourth-former came. She was not
scared of third-formers, but was very much astonished to
see Zerelda and her strange raiment.

'I've got to practise,' she said, coming in. 'Clear
out.'

Zerelda stopped indignantly. 'Clear out yourself!' she
said. 'Gee, of all the nerve! Can't you see I'm
rehearsing?'

'No, I can't,' said the fourth-former. 'And wait
till a mistress sees you in that curtain—you'll be for it,
Zerelda Brass. Clear out now, both of you. I'm late
already.'

Zerelda decided to go all temperamental like Irene. She
caught up her book of Shakespeare's plays and threw it at
the fourth-former. Most unfortunately at that moment
Matron came by, and, as she always did, glanced into the
practice-rooms to see that each girl there was practising. She was filled with astonishment to see somebody
wearing a curtain and a tablecloth, with hair all over her
face, throwing a book at a girl about to sit down at the
piano.

She opened the door sharply, making everyone jump.
'What's all this? What are you doing? Oh, it's *you*,
Zerelda. What on earth have you got the curtain round
you for? Are you quite mad? And what has happened
to your hair? It looks a hundred times worse than usual.
Janet, get on with your practising. Gwendoline, you
shouldn't be here when a fourth-former is practising. As
for you, Zerelda, if I see any more tempers like that, I shall
report you to Miss Grayling! Throwing books at one

another indeed! A third-former too! You'll go down
into the first form if you behave like that!'

The girls couldn't get a word in, for Matron fired all
this off at top speed. She pushed Janet firmly down on the
stool, shooed Gwendoline out as if she was a hen, and took
Zerelda firmly by the shoulder.

'You'll just come with me and let me find out if you've
torn the cloth or the curtain,' she said. 'If you have
you'll sit down in my room under my eye and mend it.
And while I think of it—if you don't darn your stockings
better than you have been doing, I shall have to ask you to
come to me for darning lessons.'

Angry and embarrassed, poor Zerelda had to walk down
the corridor after Matron, trying to take the curtain and
cloth away from her shoulders and waist, and wishing she
could tie her hair back.

But Matron would give her no time to rearrange or tidy
herself. This stuck-up, affected American girl had annoyed
Matron so often—now Matron was getting a bit of her own
back! Let everyone see Zerelda in this rumpled, ridiculous
state!

And most unfortunately for Zerelda they met a whole
batch of giggling second-formers, who stared at Zerelda in
delighted amazement.

'What's she done? Where's Matron taking her?
Doesn't she look *awful*!' poor Zerelda heard the twelve-
year-olds say. She blushed miserably and looked round
for Gwen. But Gwen had gone. She knew Matron in
this mood, and she wasn't going to go near her if she could
help it!

They met Mam'zelle at the bend of the stairs, and Mam'-
zelle exclaimed in surprise. '*Tiens!* What is this?
Zerelda! Your hair!'

'Yes. I'm dealing with her, Mam'zelle,' said Matron
firmly. She and Mam'zelle were usually at war with one

another, so Matron did not stop to talk, but swept Zerelda along to her room at top speed, leaving Mam'zelle to gape and wonder.

Fortunately for Zerelda, Matron could find no damage done to either the tablecloth or the curtain. She was quite disappointed! She did Zerelda's hair for her herself, and Zerelda was so overcome by Matron's briskness and ability to talk without stopping that she submitted without saying a word.

Matron plaited Zerelda's hair into two fat plaits! Zerelda had never had her hair plaited in her life. She sat there, horror-struck. This awful school! Whatever would happen to her next?

'There,' said Matron, satisfied at last, tying the ends of the plaits with blue tape. She stepped back. 'Now you look a proper schoolgirl, Zerelda—and very sensible and nice too. Why you want to go about pretending you are twenty, I don't know.'

Zerelda got up weakly. She caught a glimpse of herself in the glass. How *awful*! Could that really be herself? Why, she looked a nobody—just like all the other English girls. She crept out of Matron's room and fled up to the dormy to try and put her hair right.

She met Miss Peters, who stared at her as if she didn't know her. Zerelda smiled a weak smile and tried to get by without a word.

'Well—*Zerelda*!' she heard Miss Peters say, as if she couldn't believe her eyes. Zerelda shot down the corridor, praying that she would not meet anyone else.

Gwendoline was in the dormy, and she too stared at Zerelda as if she was seeing a ghost.

'Did Matron do that to you?' she asked. 'Oh, Zerelda —you look like a real schoolgirl now—not a bit like yourself. Oh, I *must* tell the others that Matron plaited your hair.'

'If you dare to repeat such a thing I'll never speak to you

again ! ' said Zerelda, in such a fierce voice that Gwen was quite scared. She shook her hair free of the plaits. ' This horrible school ! I'll never forgive Matron, never ! '

14   BILL IS CAUGHT!

ALICIA had not been allowed to forget the sneezing trick. All the form begged her to do it—except Sally. Sally still said she thought it was a dangerous joke to play, but Alicia laughed at her.

' You only say that because it's *my* trick ! ' she said, knowing that Sally was jealous of her friendship with Darrell. ' If it was Irene's joke or Jean's you'd be thrilled.'

Jean was torn between her desire to see the trick played and her feeling that as head-girl she ought not to be too encouraging. Still, head-girls couldn't be too strict and prim—and she did badly want to see what would happen !

' There's to be a maths test next week,' said Alicia. ' That's the time to do it ! I bet we'll get out of the test all right. A-tish-oo ! '

Everyone laughed. Darrell hugged herself. Oh, school was such fun ! She enjoyed every single minute of it. She loved her work and her play, she loved the company of the chattering girls, she loved being third reserve—oh, everything was wonderful ! This was the nicest term she had ever had.

Then she saw Bill looking anything but happy. Poor Bill ! She was worried because Thunder was still not himself. Nobody else seemed to notice it—but Bill *knew*. Thunder wasn't just homesick, as she had thought at first.

He wasn't well. She was very worried about him—and the more worried she got, the less attention she paid to her work, and the crosser she made Miss Peters.

'Wilhelmina! Will you please pay attention! Wilhelmina! Will you repeat what I have just said? Wilhelmina, I will not have you in my class if you persist in looking out of the window and dreaming!' It was 'Wilhelmina! Wilhelmina!' all the time.

It was dreadful. Bill was really very miserable now, but she said very little unless anyone actually asked her about Thunder. She knew that Jean disapproved strongly of her continual disobedience. But she simply couldn't help it! She must, *must* see Thunder each day, especially just now.

Miss Peters was beginning to be puzzled over Bill. If the girl was so fond of her horse, why did she keep earning punishments forbidding her to see him? Miss Peters thought back a few days. Why, Bill couldn't have seen her beloved horse all the week. And yet she hadn't complained about it!

A suspicion came into Miss Peters' mind. Was Bill being disobedient? Surely not! Disobedience was not a thing that Miss Peters had to deal with very often. Girls rarely dared to disobey even her slightest word. She was noted for her good discipline.

She spoke about it to Miss Potts, who was in charge of North Tower. 'I'm puzzled about Wilhelmina, Miss Potts. I can't make her out. She is such a terrible dreamer, and yet she looks such a sensible, hard-headed little thing! Then, too, she seems so fond of that horse of hers—and yet although she knows I shall punish her by forbidding her to see him, she goes on being silly and getting punished! She can't have seen that horse of hers for a whole week now!'

Miss Potts looked startled. She frowned, trying to remember something clearly. 'Well—that's funny—I could swear I saw Wilhelmina in the stables yesterday when I went by. I looked in at the windows as I passed—and I'm almost certain it was Wilhelmina—standing beside a big black horse.'

' Yes—that would be Thunder,' said Miss Peters, grimly. ' The untrustworthy, disobedient little monkey! If I catch her disobeying I shall insist that the horse is sent back to her home. She can ride one of the school horses instead. I will not have her mooning all the morning over that horse, nice as he is—and being disobedient like that.'

Miss Peters was really very angry. She never could bear to be disobeyed. She went back to her room, feeling shocked and disappointed. She hadn't thought Wilhelmina would be so deceitful and untrustworthy. It just showed how little you knew about anyone!

Miss Peters felt more and more indignant about the whole thing as the day wore on. It so happened that she took the third form very little that day, as Miss Carton, the history mistress, Mam'zelle, Miss Linnie, the art mistress, and Mr. Young, the singing-master, each took the third form for a lesson. She had no chance of looking sharply at Bill to see if she looked guilty or not.

After dinner that morning there was about half an hour before afternoon school. This was a time when Bill very often slipped out to the stables. She usually went down the back stairs, out at a little side-door, and across to the stables by a path under the trees, so that, unless she was very unlucky, nobody would see her.

She slipped off to the stables as usual to see Thunder. He whinnied softly when he heard her footstep. She opened the big door and went inside. There was no one else there at all. Only the horses stamped and blew, glad of each other's company.

She went to Thunder's stall. He put his great black head into the crook of her arm and snuffled there happily. Bill stroked his velvety nose.

'Thunder, do you feel better? Let me look at your eyes. Oh, Thunder, they aren't as bright as they ought to be—and I don't like the feel of your coat. It should be much silkier. It's harsh. Thunder, what's wrong? Don't be ill, darling Thunder, I couldn't bear it.'

Thunder blew a little, and whinnied happily. He didn't feel well, certainly—but that didn't matter when Bill was with him. He could feel ill and yet be happy at the same time if she was with him.

Upstairs in North Tower, Miss Peters walked along the corridor. She meant to find Bill and have a straight talk with her. She went to the door of the third form common-room and looked in. Wilhelmina was not there!

'I want Wilhelmina,' said Miss Peters. 'Where is she?'

Everybody knew, of course. But nobody was going to tell. Darrell wondered if she could possibly slip out and warn Bill to come back quickly.

'Shall I go and find her for you?' she said.

'No. I'll find her,' said Miss Peters. 'Does anyone know where she is?'

Nobody answered. They all looked blank in a most irritating way. Miss Peters felt furious. She knew quite well that they all knew. Well, she couldn't expect them to sneak, if they thought Wilhelmina was somewhere she ought not to be—in the stables!

'I suppose she is in the stables,' said Miss Peters, grimly. She looked at Jean. 'You, as head-girl, Jean, ought to tell her not to be so foolish and dishonourable. You know I put everyone on their honour to obey any punishment I give.'

Jean went red and looked uncomfortable. It was all very well for Miss Peters to talk like that! Nobody could possibly make any impression on Bill if it meant that she would have to neglect Thunder!

'Stay here, all of you,' commanded Miss Peters, feeling

sure that one or other might rush off to the stables to warn
Bill if they got the chance. And Miss Peters meant to catch
Bill herself and stop this kind of thing for good and all.

'Oh, poor Bill!' groaned Darrell, when Miss Peters had
gone. 'Now she'll get into a fearful row! I say—I bet
Miss Peters has gone down the front stairs. If I race down
the back ones, I *might* get to the stables first and warn Bill.
I'll try!'

She didn't wait to hear what anyone had to say. She
shot out of the room, almost knocked down Matron outside,
raced down the corridor to the back stairs, went down them
two at a time, slid through the side-door and out under the
trees. She shot over to the stable door and squeezed
through it.

'Bill! Look out! Miss Peters is coming here!' she
hissed. She saw Bill's startled face beside Thunder's black
head.

Then she heard footsteps and groaned. 'It's too late—
you'll be caught. Can't you hide?'

Darrell shot under a pile of straw and lay there, her heart
beating wildly. Bill stood as if turned to stone, her freckled
face pale with fright. The door opened wide and Miss
Peters came in.

'Oh! So you *are* here, Wilhelmina!' she said, angrily.
'I suppose you have been systematically disobeying me the
whole week. I am really ashamed of you. You will never
settle down at school whilst you have Thunder here, I can
quite see that. He will have to be sent back home in a
horse-box.'

'No! Oh no, Miss Peters! Don't, don't do that!'
begged Bill, even her freckles going pale with anxiety. 'It's
only that Thunder's not well. He really isn't. If he was
well I'd obey you. But he needs me when he's not
well.'

'I'm not going to discuss the matter,' said Miss Peters,

Darrell and Bill tried to hide

coldly. 'You have heard what I said. I am not likely to change my mind after such a show of disobedience. Please go back to your common-room, Wilhelmina. I will tell you when I have made arrangements to send Thunder home and you can say good-bye to him till the holidays. It will probably be the day after tomorrow.'

Bill stood still, quite petrified. She couldn't make her legs move. Darrell couldn't see her, but she could imagine her very well indeed. Poor, poor Bill.

'Go, Wilhelmina,' said Miss Peters. 'At once please.'

And Bill went, her feet dragging. Darrell heard a smothered sob. Oh dear—what a pity she had to hide under this straw and couldn't go and comfort Bill. Never mind—Miss Peters would soon be going, and then Darrell could fly up to the common-room and sympathize warmly and heartily with Bill.

But Miss Peters didn't go. She waited till Bill had quite gone. Then she went over to Thunder and spoke to him in such a gentle voice that Darrell could hardly believe it was Miss Peters'! 'Well, old boy,' said Miss Peters, and Darrell heard the sound of her hand rubbing his coat. 'What's the matter with you? Don't feel well? Shall we get the vet to you? What's the matter with you, Thunder? Beautiful horse, aren't you? Best in the stables. What's up, old boy?'

Darrell could hardly believe her ears. She wriggled a little in the straw so that she could get a hole to peep through. Yes, there was Miss Peters, standing close to Thunder, and he was nuzzling her and whinnying in delight. Why, Miss Peters must love him! Of course, she was very fond of horses, Darrell knew that. But this was different somehow. She really seemed to love Thunder as if he was her own horse.

Miss Peters gave Thunder some sugar and he crunched it up. Then she went out of the stable and shut the door.

Darrell got out of the straw and shook herself   She went
to the door and listened.   Miss Peters had gone.   Good !

She opened the door and went out—and then she stood
still, thunderstruck.   Miss Peters *hadn't* gone !   She was
just outside, doing up her shoe-lace !   She looked up and
saw Darrell coming out of the stables.

She stood up, red with rage.   ' What were you doing in
there ? ' she demanded.   ' Were you there all the time I
was talking to Wilhelmina ?   You were in the common-
room when I left.   Did you actually dare to run down the
back stairs to warn Wilhelmina ? '

Darrell couldn't speak.   She nodded.   ' I shall deal with
you later,' said Miss Peters, hardly trusting herself to speak.
' What the third form is coming to I really do not know ! '

15   MAVIS HAS AN IDEA

BILL would not be comforted by Darrell or anyone else.
She hadn't gone to the common-room as Miss Peters had
told her to.   She had gone to the dormy and wept by herself.
Bill boasted that she never cried, but this time she did.   Her
seven brothers had taught her to be tough and boyish, and,
like a boy, she had scorned ever to shed a tear.

But she couldn't help it now.   When she appeared for
afternoon school the third-formers saw her red eyes and
came round her to comfort her.   But she pushed them
away.   Darrell was pushed away too, though Bill spoke a
few words to her, very gratefully.

' Thank you for coming to warn me.   It was decent of
you, Darrell.'

'Bill—it's a shame,' began Darrell. But Bill turned away.

'I can't talk about it,' she said. 'Please don't.'

So the third-formers gave it up, and looked at one another helplessly. You simply couldn't do anything with Bill if she didn't want you to. Darrell took her place in class that afternoon with much trepidation. She knew she would sooner or later be called to Miss Peters' room, and she wondered what would happen to her. Oh dear—and everything had been so lovely up till then. Now she had got herself into trouble, and she had only wanted to help poor Bill.

Miss Peters was in a grim mood that afternoon. She was looking out for anyone or anything that would feed her anger. But nobody, not even Mavis, Gwendoline or Zerelda, did anything to provoke her. Miss Peters was terrifying when she was like this. Her big, heavy face was red, her eyes flashed as they looked round the class, and her short hair seemed to cling more tightly to her head than usual !

All the third-formers felt miserable that evening, with Bill sitting like a figure of stone in a corner. It was Mavis who suddenly livened them up.

'I say,' she said, in a whisper, as if somebody was listening who shouldn't be there. 'I say ! Look here ! '

She held up a paper. On it was printed these words :

TALENT SPOTTING !

Have you a gift ? Can you play the piano well ? Can you draw ? Do you sing ?

Then bring your talent to the Grand Hall, Billington, on Saturday night, and let us SPOT your TALENT.

Big prizes—and a CHANCE to make your NAME !

TALENT SPOTTING !

The girls read it. 'Well, what about it ? ' said Alicia.

'Surely you are not thinking of being spotted for talent, Mavis?'

'Yes, but listen,' said Mavis, still in an urgent whisper, 'what about Irene going with her music—and Belinda with her drawing—and Zerelda with her acting—and me with my Voice? Think what prizes we would win!'

Everyone stared at Mavis scornfully. 'Mavis! As if we'd *ever* be allowed to go!' said Belinda. 'And besides, who wants to go to a fifth-rate affair like this? Talent spotting indeed! Just a silly show put on to amuse the people of Billington! And the prizes will probably be half-crowns! Don't be so silly.'

'But, Belinda—Zerelda—it's such a chance!' said Mavis, who had imagined herself standing on the platform and filling the hall with her lovely voice, being applauded to the echo and perhaps having her name in the papers. Poor, foolish Mavis. Her conceit blinded her to what the show really was—just a village affair got up for fun.

'Mavis, you're just too silly for words,' said Alicia, impatiently. 'Can you honestly see Miss Grayling allowing Malory Towers girls to go to a thing like this and make themselves cheap and idiotic? Do use your common-sense.'

'She can't. She hasn't got any,' said Daphne.

Mavis snatched the paper from Darrell, who was reading down it with a grin. 'All right,' she said. 'If you don't want a bit of fun, you needn't have it. I've a good mind to go on my own.'

'Don't be a fathead,' said Jean. 'Think of yourself standing up on a big platform, just a schoolgirl, singing to a crowded hall. It's ridiculous!'

But it didn't seem a ridiculous picture to Mavis. She could see it all very clearly. She could even hear the thunderous applause. She could see herself bowing time after time. It would be a little taste of what life would be like when she was an opera-singer!

She stuffed the notice into her pocket, wishing she hadn't said anything about it. But a little thought kept slipping into her mind, exciting her, making her restless.

'Suppose I go ? Nobody would miss me if I said I was going for an extra lesson in singing. They would just think Mr. Young was making up the lesson he missed last week.'

It was a very exciting thought. Today was Thursday. Mavis decided to think about it all Friday and make up her mind on Saturday. Yes, that was what she would do—then she could make her plans in good time if she decided to go !

She thought about it all day Friday. And Bill thought about Thunder. Neither of them dared to be too dreamy in class, but fortunately Miss Peters did not take the third-formers a great deal that day, having to take duty for another teacher who was ill. Mam'zelle came to take her place, and she was in a pleasant mood, very talkative, and not very observant. So Bill and Mavis were able to do a little dreaming in peace.

Bill had not dared to go to the stables again. She was hoping against hope that Miss Peters might change her mind and relent. Perhaps she would let Thunder stay after all. So she did not go near the stables, hoping that Miss Peters would tell her she was not going to be so harsh after all.

Miss Peters still had not said anything to Darrell. The girl wished she would get it over, scold her, punish her—but not keep it hanging over her like this. Perhaps that was part of Miss Peters' plan though to keep Darrell on tenter-hooks for a few days !

Saturday came. Mavis had made up her mind. She would go ! She would tell Miss Potts she had a singing-lesson. She often had extra singing at odd times, so Miss Potts would not think it at all queer. She would tell the girls that too. She wouldn't be back early enough for nine o'clock bedtime but she trusted the girls not to give her away. She would slip in up the back stairs.

So Mavis made her plans. She looked up the buses. She meant to catch the six o'clock bus. That would get her to Billington at seven. The show began at half-past. She could easily go into the hall and find out what she had to do.

She looked up the buses back. How long would the show last? About two hours, probably. There was a bus back at half-past nine—the last one. Goodness, it was late!

Mavis began to have a few qualms about her adventure. It was very, very late for her to come back alone in the dark all the way up the school drive from the bus-stop. Oh dear—would it be moonlight? She did hope so!

Bill came over to Darrell on Saturday morning. 'Darrell! Would you do something for me? I'm not going to go to the stables again unless I'm allowed to—just in case Miss Peters might change her mind about sending Thunder away—so would you *please*, Darrell, slip down there yourself and go to Thunder and see if he's all right?'

'Yes, of course,' said Darrell. 'He wasn't out with the other horses this morning. I saw them all go off, but Thunder wasn't there.'

'No, he wouldn't be,' said Bill. 'Nobody rides him but me. Do go, Darrell.'

Darrell went. It didn't matter *her* going in the least. She kicked herself for not having thought of it before. She could have gone yesterday for Bill too.

She went into the stables. All the horses were there. One of the grooms was there too, rubbing a horse down, whistling between his teeth as he did so.

''Morning, Miss,' he said.

'Good morning,' said Darrell. 'Where's Thunder? Is he all right?'

'He's over there in his stall, Miss,' said the groom, standing up. 'He doesn't seem too well. It's my opinion he's in for a bout of colic or something.'

Colic? That was tummy-ache, wasn't it, thought Darrell. Oh well, that wasn't anything very much. She went over to Thunder, who hung his head and looked miserable.

'He really doesn't seem very well, does he?' said Darrell, anxiously. 'Do you suppose he's missing his mistress? She's not been allowed to see him.'

'Well, he may be,' said the groom. 'But it's his insides are making him miserable, I guess. Have to have the vet to him if he doesn't pick up. But I did hear something about him being sent back home.'

Darrell said no more. She ran back to North Tower to find Bill, who was anxiously waiting for her.

'Thunder doesn't seem *very* well,' she said. 'But you needn't worry. The groom said it was only that he might be going to have a bout of colic. That's nothing, is it?'

Bill stared at her in horror. 'Colic! Why, it's one of the worst things a horse can have! Oh, Darrell, think what a big stomach a horse has and imagine him having an ache all over it. It's *agony*!'

'Oh—I didn't know,' said Darrell. 'But—surely it isn't as serious as all that, is it?'

'It is, it is,' said Bill, and tears came into her eyes. 'Oh, what shall I do? I *daren't* go to the stables in case I'm caught, and I might spoil Thunder's chance of not being sent home after all. Miss Peters hasn't said anything more to me about him going. Oh, what *shall* I do?'

'You can't do anything,' said Darrell. 'Really you can't. He'll be all right tomorrow. Don't you worry, Bill. Oh, blow—it's begun to pour with rain—just as I wanted to go and practise catching again.'

Bill turned away. Rain! What did *rain* matter! She sat down in a corner and began to worry hard. Colic!

One of her brothers' horses had had colic and had died. Suppose—suppose Thunder got very ill in the middle of the night—and nobody knew ?   The grooms did not sleep very near the stables.   *Nobody* would know.   And in the morning Thunder would be dead !

Whilst Bill tortured herself with these horrible thoughts, Mavis delighted herself with pleasant ones.   She had made all her plans.   She didn't care a bit if she was discovered after it was all over—by that time she could have been received with wonder and applause, and Malory Towers would praise her and admire her.

' How bold she is to do a thing like that ! ' they would say.   ' Just the kind of thing an opera-singer *would* do ! All fire and temperament and boldness !   Wonderful Mavis ! '

Nobody had any suspicion of Mavis's mad plans that night.   Miss Potts said nothing when she told her that she was to have an extra singing-lesson, and would be having her supper early to make time for it.   The girls took no notice either.   They were used to Mavis and her odd lessons at all times.

' It's all too easy for words ! ' thought Mavis, exultantly. ' I shall easily be able to catch the bus.   Nobody will guess a thing !   Whatever will the girls say when I come back tonight !   Well—they'll know I am something besides just a Voice ! '

She caught the bus easily.   It was pouring with rain, but she had her mackintosh with her.   She did not wear a hat in case somebody noticed the school-band, so her head was bare.   But as the bus stopped just by the Grand Hall at Billington, she wouldn't get her hair very wet.

The bus started off with a jolt.   Off to fame !   Off to applause !   Off to the Beginning of a Wonderful Career !

MISS POTTS noticed that Mavis was not at the supper-table. She was about to remark on it when she remembered that Mavis had told her something about an extra singing-lesson. She must have had supper early then, as she some-times did when Mr. Young came late. So Miss Potts said nothing.

The girls thought nothing of it either. They were used to Mavis and her continual extra voice-training now. They hardly missed her. As they often said, Mavis was really nothing but a Voice and a lot of conceit.

Bill was very silent and worried, and ate hardly anything. Warm-hearted Darrell felt sorry for her. She knew she was worrying about Thunder and not being able to go to him. She whispered to Bill.

'Shall I go and have a look at him for you after supper?'

Bill shook her head. 'No. I don't want to get you into trouble. Nobody's allowed in the stables when it's dark.'

No one said anything about Mavis not being in the common-room after supper. Alicia switched on the wireless. Belinda began to do a ridiculous dance. Zerelda got up and joined her. Everyone laughed. Zerelda could be really funny when she forgot her airs and graces.

She was pleased at the girls' applause. 'Shall I act a bit of "Romeo and Juliet" for you?' she asked, eagerly. 'I'm tired of waiting for that rehearsal with Miss Hibbert!'

'Yes, do, Zerelda!' said Gwen, at once. The others

were not so keen, but they sat back, prepared to be patient
for a little while.

Zerelda began. She struck a pose, lifted up her voice
and began to speak and act the part of Juliet, trying to talk
in the English way.

The result was so very comical that the girls roared with
laughter. They honestly thought that Zerelda was being
funny on purpose. Zerelda stopped and looked at them,
offended.

'What are you laughing at? This part is very tragic
and sad.'

Still the girls thought that Zerelda was being funny, and
they laughed again. 'Go on, Zerelda! This is priceless!'
said Darrell. 'I never knew you could be so comical.'

'I'm not being comical,' said Zerelda.

'Do go on,' begged Irene. 'Come on—I'll be Romeo.
We'll rag the whole thing.'

'I'm *not* ragging,' said Zerelda. 'I was playing the
part properly—as I thought it ought to be played.'

The girls looked at her in surprise. Did she really mean
it? Did she honestly think that kind of acting was good?
It was so bad that it was funny.

They didn't know what to say. They could, however,
quite well imagine what Miss Hibbert would say. She had
her own way of dealing with stage-struck people who thought
they could act. Zerelda was appalling. She flung her
hands about, made terrible faces which were supposed to be
tragic, and was altogether too dramatic for words.

'She can't act for toffee!' whispered Alicia to Darrell.
'What are we to say?'

Fortunately the door was opened at that moment and a
fourth-former came in to borrow a gramophone record.
Zerelda, offended with everyone, sat down in a chair and
took up a book. She hated everyone in the school! Why
had she ever come here? Not one of them thought

anything of her—and she was worth the whole lot put together.

When the bell rang at nine o'clock Mavis was not back. Jean noticed it at once. 'Where's Mavis ? I haven't seen her all evening.'

'She said she had a singing-lesson,' said Darrell. 'But what a long one it must have been ! Well, she'll come along when Mr. Young's finished with her, I suppose.'

'He's never as late as this,' said Jean, puzzled. 'I wonder if I ought to tell Miss Potts.'

'No, don't. She may be messing about somewhere, and you'll only get her into trouble,' said Belinda. 'She'll be up in the dormy probably.'

But she wasn't. The girls undressed and got into bed. Jean did not allow talking after lights out, so there was nothing said until Jean herself spoke.

'I say ! You don't think, do you, that that idiot of a Mavis has gone off to that talent spotting affair ? You know —the thing at Billington Grand Hall.'

There was a silence. Then Alicia spoke. 'I shouldn't be a bit surprised ! She's quite silly over her voice. She might think it was a wonderful chance to air it in public. She's always wanting to.'

'Well ! ' said Jean, angrily, 'she'll just *have* to be reported then. Honestly, she's the limit.'

'We can't do much just now,' said Darrell. 'She may be back at any minute. I forget what time the concert began. I expect she'd catch the half-past eight bus back and be here just after half-past nine. It must be nearly that now. You'll have to report her tomorrow morning, Jean—what a perfect idiot she must be, if she really *has* gone ! '

'What I'm afraid of,' said Jean, 'is that they might let her get up on the platform and sing—and, you know, she really has got such a wonderful voice that it would be bound to bring the house down—and that's just what Mavis would love—cheering and clapping and applause ! She'll be worse than ever if that happens—and she won't care a bit about being reported and punished.'

' Leave it till tomorrow morning,' said Darrell, sleepily. ' She'll be along soon. Tick her off then, Jean, and report her in the morning.'

Miss Potts heard the voices in the dormy and was surprised. She came to the door—but as she heard Jean's clear voice say ' Now, no more talking, girls ' at that moment, she did not open the door to scold. If she had, she would have switched on the light and noticed Mavis's empty bed. As it was, she went away at once.

The girls were tired. Jean tried to keep awake to tick off Mavis, but she couldn't. Her eyes closed and she fell fast asleep. So did everyone else—except Bill. Bill hadn't heard a word about Mavis. She was wrapped up in her own thoughts and they were very miserable ones. Thunder ! How are you getting on ? Have you missed me ? Bill talked to Thunder in her thoughts, and heard nothing else at all.

Darrell too was asleep. She had meant to have a last comforting whisper with Bill, who slept next to her, but she fell asleep before she could say the words. Only Bill was awake.

Mavis didn't come. Ten o'clock struck, and eleven. No Mavis. All the girls were asleep except Bill, and she didn't think about Mavis. Twelve o'clock struck. Bill counted the strokes.

' I can't go to sleep ! I simply can't ! I shall lie awake till the morning. If only I knew how Thunder is getting on ! If I knew he was all right, I'd be all right, too. But supposing he really has the colic ? '

She lay and thought for a few minutes. She remembered a window that overlooked the stables. If she went to it and opened it and leaned out, she might perhaps hear if Thunder was all right. A horse with colic makes a noise. She would hear that.

Bill got out of bed, and felt for her dressing-gown and slippers. She put them on. She groped her way to the door, bumping against Darrell's bed as she did so. Darrell woke up at once.

She thought it was Mavis coming back. She sat up and whispered loudly. 'Mavis!'

No answer. The door softly opened and shut. Somebody had gone out, not come in. Who was it?

Darrell got her torch and switched it on. The first thing she saw was Bill's empty bed. Was Bill ill? Or had she gone to the stables? Surely not, in the middle of a pouring wet night!

She went to the door and opened it. She thought she saw something a good distance down the corridor. She ran after the something.

Bill had gone to the window that overlooked the stables. She opened it, and Darrell heard her and went towards the sound. Bill leaned out of the window and listened.

Her heart went cold! From the stables came a groaning and a stamping. There was a horse in distress there, quite certainly. Bill knew it was Thunder. She felt sure it was. He had colic! He was in agony. He would die if somebody didn't help him!

She turned away from the window and jumped violently when Darrell put a hand on her shoulder. 'Bill! What are you doing?' whispered Darrell.

'Oh, Darrell—I was listening to see if any noise came from the stables over there—and there's a horse in pain. I'm sure it's Thunder. I must go to him! Oh, Darrell, please come with me. I might want help. Do, do help me.'

'All right,' said Darrell, unhappy to hear Bill's tearful

voice. 'I'll come. Come back and get on something warmer. It's pouring with rain. We can't go out in dressing-gowns.'

Bill didn't want to stop to put anything on, but Darrell made her. The two girls put on cardigans and tunics and mackintoshes. Then they slipped down the back stairs, went through the little side-door and ran across to the stables in the pouring rain.

Darrell could hear a horse groaning and stamping. Oh dear! It sounded awful. With trembling fingers Bill undid the stable door and went inside. There was a lantern standing in a corner, with a box of matches beside it. Her fingers trembled so much that she couldn't strike a match and Darrell had to light the lamp.

Both girls felt better when the light streamed out into the dark stable, that smelt of horses and hay. Bill made her way swiftly to Thunder's stall. Darrell followed with the lantern.

Thunder's eyes were big and frightened. He hung his head in misery. From his body came weird rumbling noises, like far-away thunder.

'Yes. He's got colic. He's bad. Darrell, oh, Darrell, we mustn't let him lie down. That would be fatal. We must walk him about all the time.'

'Walk him about? Where?' asked Darrell, in astonishment. 'In the stables?'

'No. Outside. It's the only thing to do, keep him walking so that he can't lie down. Look, he's trying to lie down now. Help me to stop him!'

But it is a very difficult thing to prevent a big horse from lying down if he wants to! Neither of the girls would have been able to stop him if Thunder had really made up his mind to lie down—but fortunately he decided to stand up a little longer and nuzzle against Bill. He was so very, very glad to see her!

Bill was crying bitterly. 'Oh, Thunder! What can I do for you? Don't lie down, Thunder. Don't lie down!'

'You ought to have the vet, Bill, oughtn't you?' said Darrell, anxiously. 'How can we get him?'

'Could you possibly ride over and fetch him?' said Bill, wiping her eyes with the back of her hand. 'You know where he lives—not far off, really.'

'No, I couldn't,' said Darrell. 'I don't ride well enough to get a horse and gallop off on a dark night. You go, Bill, and I'll stay with Thunder.'

'I can't leave him even for a *minute*!' said Bill. She seemed quite unable to think what to do. Darrell thought hard.

An idea came into her head. She touched Bill on the shoulder. 'Bill! Stay here and I'll get help somehow. Don't worry. I'll be back as soon as I can!'

17   A MIDNIGHT RIDE

DARRELL raced off into the rain. She had thought of something—but she didn't want to tell Bill what it was. Bill wouldn't like it. But still, it was the only sensible thing Darrell could think of.

She was going to wake up Miss Peters and tell her about Thunder! She remembered how she had heard Miss Peters talking to the horse, sympathizing with him, and she remembered, too, how Thunder had nuzzled happily against her. Surely Miss Peters would understand and come to their help?

She went indoors. She made her way to Miss Peters' room, stumbling through the dark corridors. She wondered if she had come to the right room. Yes, this must be it. She rapped at the door.

There was no answer. She rapped again. Still no answer. Miss Peters must sleep very, very soundly! In desperation Darrell opened the door and looked in. The room was in darkness. She felt for the light switch and put it on.

Miss Peters was lying humped up in bed, fast asleep. She slept very soundly indeed, and even a thunderstorm did not usually awaken her. Darrell went to the bed and put her hand on Miss Peters' shoulder.

Miss Peters awoke at once then. She sat up and stared at Darrell in amazement. 'What is it?' she said. 'What have you come to me for?'

Darrell would have gone to Miss Potts or Matron in the usual way—but this was something so unusual that the girl felt only Miss Peters could deal with it properly. She began to tell Miss Peters all about the trouble.

'It's Thunder. He's got colic and Bill's afraid he'll die if he lies down. Can you get the vet, Miss Peters?'

'Good gracious! Have you and Bill been out to the stables at this time of night?' said Miss Peters, looking at her clock, which showed half-past twelve. She sprang out of bed. She pulled on riding-breeches and jersey and riding-coat, for she had been riding that day with the school, and her things lay ready to hand.

'Yes,' said Darrell. 'But don't be angry, Miss Peters —we simply had to go when we heard Thunder in pain.'

'I'm not angry,' said Miss Peters. 'I was worried myself about Thunder today. I rang up the vet and he said he would come tomorrow. I'll come down with you and have a look at the horse myself.'

In a few minutes she was in the stables with Darrell.

Bill was amazed to see her, but very comforted when she saw how capably Miss Peters handled the distressed horse. Thunder whinnied to her and nuzzled against her shoulder. Miss Peters spoke to him gently, and Bill's heart warmed to her.

'Oh, Miss Peters—can we get the vet to come now? I'm so afraid Thunder will lie down and we won't be able to get him up again.'

Thunder's insides gave a most alarming rumble just then and he groaned in pain and fright. He seemed about to lie down, but Miss Peters took him out of his stall at once, and began to walk him up and down the stables. The other horses looked round, mildly surprised at all these unusual happenings. One or two whinnied to Miss Peters. They were very fond of her.

'Darrell! Go quickly and get sou'westers for yourself and Bill. Then take the horse into the yard and walk him round and round. I'll go and phone the vet and come back at once.'

Darrell flew off. She came back with the sou'westers. She had to put Bill's on for her, because Bill looked at the sou'wester as if she simply didn't know what it was!

'I'm going to phone now,' said Miss Peters. 'Walk him out, Bill.'

She went. She telephoned the vet's house. The sleepy voice of his housekeeper answered her. 'I'm sorry, Mam— but the vet has gone to Raglett's farm to a cow. He said he'd sleep there for the night. No, Mam—I'm afraid they're not on the telephone. You can't get the vet tonight. I'm sorry.'

Miss Peters put down the receiver. Couldn't get the vet! What was to be done? The horse needed medicine, and only the vet could bring it and make him drink it down. Miss Peters could see that Thunder's condition was serious. Something *must* be done!

She went out to the stables again. In the yard the two girls were walking Thunder round and round, the rain pouring down on them. She told them that the vet could not be reached. Bill groaned. She was in despair.

'He's at Raglett's farm,' said Miss Peters. 'That's about five miles off, on the Billington Road. I know what I'll do. I'll saddle one of the other horses and ride to the farm myself and get him. That would be the best thing.'

'What! In the dark and the rain?' said Darrell, hardly able to believe her ears.

'That's nothing,' said Miss Peters. 'Thunder is a lovely horse—I don't mind what I do for him.'

Bill's hand groped for Miss Peters' arm. She was sobbing. 'You *are* good!' she said. 'Thank you, Miss Peters. You are the kindest person I've ever known. Oh, if only you can get the vet!'

Miss Peters patted Bill's shoulder. 'I'll do my best. Don't worry, Bill!'

Darrell was struck with surprise. Miss Peters had called Bill Bill. Gracious! And she was going to ride for miles in the dark to fetch someone to help Thunder. She was a perfectly marvellous person! 'And to think I never even guessed it before!' marvelled Darrell, valiantly leading Thunder round the yard. 'People are awfully decent underneath.'

Miss Peters was soon galloping off into the night. The two girls took it in turns to lead Thunder round the yard. He seemed better when he was walking.

'Darrell—I do feel so awful now to remember all the horrid things I thought about Miss Peters,' said Bill, once. 'She's the decentest person I've ever met. Fancy riding off like that to get the vet. Darrell, I shall never be able to repay her. Shall I?'

'No. I don't suppose you will,' said Darrell. 'I think

she's fine. Golly—won't the girls be thrilled to hear about all this tomorrow!'

Miss Peters was riding fast through the night. The rain beat down on her but she didn't mind. She was an all-weather person, and thought nothing of rain, wind, snow or fog! She galloped off to Raglett's farm, and at last got to the gate that led up to the farm.

There was a light in one of the sheds. Miss Peters guessed the vet was there with the farmer, and the cow he had gone to tend. She rode up to the door, her horse's hooves making a loud noise in the night.

The farmer came to the door in surprise. Miss Peters hailed him in her loud, deep voice. 'Is the vet here? Can I speak to him?'

'He's in yonder,' said the farmer. Miss Peters dismounted and went into the shed. The vet was there, kneeling beside a cow. By the cow's side were two pretty little calves.

'Mr. Turnbull,' said Miss Peters, 'if you've finished here, could you possibly come to Malory Towers? That horse Thunder I told you about on the telephone this morning is in a bad way. Colic. He needs help.'

'Right,' said the vet, getting up. 'I've finished here, as it happens—much earlier than I thought. I'll come along now. I'll get my horse. Well, Raglett, that cow's fine now—and she's got two of the prettiest calves I ever saw!'

Presently the vet and Miss Peters were riding back over the road to Malory Towers. When they were half-way there Miss Peters' horse suddenly shied and reared.

'Hey there! Whoa! What's the matter?' cried Miss Peters—and at the same moment she saw something lying beside the road. It was a dark shape, hardly visible in the darkness of the night.

'Mr. Turnbull. Come here!' yelled Miss Peters. 'I

think there's somebody here. I hope they haven't been knocked down by a car and left helpless ! '

The vet had a powerful torch. He switched it on. The beam played over a huddled up bundle—a bundle with a mackintosh on !

' Good heavens ! It's a young girl ! ' said the vet. ' Is she hurt ? '

He picked the girl up. Miss Peters gave a loud and horrified exclamation. ' It's MAVIS ! Good gracious me ! Mavis ! Whatever is she doing lying out here in the dark at this time of night ? This is terrible ! '

' She's fainted from exhaustion I think,' said the vet. ' Doesn't seem to have any bones broken. Look, she's opening her eyes.'

Mavis looked up and saw Miss Peters. She began to cry weakly. ' They wouldn't let me sing. And I missed the last bus, and I've been walking all night in the rain.'

' What *is* she talking about ? ' said the vet. ' Look, she's wet through ! She'll get pneumonia unless we're pretty quick. I'll take her on my horse. Help me to lift her up.'

Amazed, horrified and distressed, Miss Peters helped to lift Mavis on to the vet's horse. He held the girl steady in front of him. Then off they went again, this time more slowly.

They came to Malory Towers. ' If Mavis can walk I'll take her straight in to Matron,' said Miss Peters. ' Oh dear, what a night ! You go to the stables, Mr. Turnbull. Darrell and Bill are walking Thunder in the yard.'

The vet disappeared in the direction of the stables. Miss Peters guided the exhausted Mavis into North Tower. She could hardly walk. Miss Peters half-dragged her up the stairs to Matron's room.

' It's Mavis! Good gracious me! '

Matron awoke and opened her door in surprise. She exclaimed in horror when she saw Mavis. 'What's all this? Where has she been? She's soaked through and shivering. Miss Peters, there's an electric blanket in that cupboard. Put it into the little bed over there, will you, and get the bed hot. And put my electric kettle on. Good gracious! What can have happened?'

'Goodness knows,' said Miss Peters, doing all the things she had been asked to do, whilst Matron quickly undressed Mavis, flinging her soaking clothes on the floor in her hurry to get her into a warm bed. It wasn't long before she was tucked up with two hot-water bottles, whilst Matron prepared some hot cocoa.

Mavis tried to tell her what had happened. She spoke in a poor croaking voice. 'I only went to Billington—to that talent spotting concert—but they said they couldn't let schoolgirls enter. I tried and tried to make them let me sing, but they wouldn't. And then I missed the last bus so I began to walk all the way home. But it rained and blew and I was so tired I fell down. And I couldn't get up again. So . . .'

'Now, don't talk any more,' said Matron, gently. 'You drink this cocoa and go to sleep. I'll be here in this other bed so you'll be all right.'

Miss Peters had slipped out of the room, murmuring something about seeing to a horse, much to Matron's surprise. She couldn't make out why Miss Peters was in riding things nor how it was that she had found Mavis on the road. Well, the main thing was to see to Mavis. She could find out the rest of the mystery afterwards.

Miss Peters went down to the others. Bill and Darrell had welcomed the vet with joy and relief. Thunder knew him and whinnied. It wasn't long before the vet had made him drink a huge draught of medicine. 'You've done well to keep him on his feet,' he told the two tired girls.

'Probably saved his life. Now—off you go to bed. I'll stay with him till morning. Miss Peters will help me. Off you go!'

18   NEXT MORNING

BILL hadn't wanted to leave Thunder, of course. But Miss Peters spoke to her firmly and gently. ' Now, Bill— you must leave matters to us. You know that we shall do our best for the horse, and now that he has had that draught he will be all right. We'll walk him as long as necessary. But you and Darrell have done your share and you are tired out. Be sensible, Bill, and do as you are told.'

' Yes, I will,' said Bill, unexpectedly. She took Miss Peters' hand in hers and held it tightly. ' Miss Peters—I can never repay you. Never. But I'll never forget to-night and all you did.'

Miss Peters patted Bill on the back. ' That's all right. I'm not asking for any repayment! I'm fond of Thunder, too, and I knew how you felt. I'm not sending him home, Bill. You shall keep him. I don't somehow think I shall ever have to punish you again by saying you mustn't see him.'

' You won't,' said Bill, her white face gleaming in the lamplight. ' I'll be your—your very best pupil from now on, Miss Peters!'

' Well—that will be a wonderful repayment,' said Miss Peters, smiling. ' Now do go, both of you. You look so pale and tired. You must both have breakfast in bed!'

' Oh no ! ' protested both girls. ' We couldn't bear it.'

' All right. I can't bear it either,' said Miss Peters. ' You can go to bed early instead ! Now, good night—or rather, good morning ! It's nearly three o'clock ! '

The two girls stumbled into North Tower, yawning. They hardly said a word to one another, they were so tired. But they were happy, and felt as if they had been friends for years ! Bill slid into bed. She whispered to Darrell.

' Darrell ! I know you're Sally's friend, so you can't be mine. But I'm yours for ever and ever. Just you remember that ! I'll pay you back some day for all you did tonight.'

' That's all right,' said Darrell, sleepily, and was asleep almost at once.

In the morning, what a to-do ! Darrell and Bill slept so soundly that not even the bell awoke them. When Jean pulled at them they shrugged away and cuddled down again, hardly waking.

' Darrell ! Bill ! I say, what's the matter with them both ! Wake up, you two, the bell's gone ages ago. Do wake up—we want to tell you something. Mavis isn't back ! Her bed is empty ! '

The rest of the girls were talking excitedly about Mavis's non-appearance. Jean was very worried. She felt that she ought to have reported the night before that Mavis had not come to bed with the rest of them. She was feeling very guilty.

' I must go to Miss Potts at once,' she said and she rushed off. But Miss Potts knew all about Mavis, for Matron had already reported to her. Miss Grayling knew, too. There had been a great upset about it. Mavis was now in the san. where sick girls were kept, and Sister, who looked after the san., was in charge of her. The doctor had been to see her already.

Jean listened to all this in amazement. ' Did Mavis—
did she go to Billington ? ' she asked.

' Oh ! So you know about that too,' said Miss Potts,
grimly. ' Funny sort of head-girl you are, Jean, not to
have reported that Mavis was not in the dormitory last night.
Very remiss of you. There are times when you have to
make a distinction between telling tales and reporting.
You know that. We might have saved Mavis from a serious
illness if we had learnt from you that she hadn't gone to bed.'

Jean went white. ' I fell asleep,' she said, miserably, ' I
was going to wait till the last bus came in—and if Mavis
didn't come in then I was going to come and report. But I
fell asleep.'

' A lame excuse,' said Miss Potts, who was angry with
herself for not having popped her head into the third form
dormy the night before, when she had heard talking. If
only she had !

' Can we see Mavis ? ' asked Jean.

' Certainly not,' said Miss Potts. ' She is seriously ill.
She got soaked through, and then lay for some time by the
roadside. She has bronchitis now—and we are hoping it
won't turn to anything worse. Her throat is terribly bad,
too—she can hardly whisper.'

Jean went back to the third form dormy feeling guilty and
alarmed. She found the third-formers gathered round
Darrell, listening excitedly to her tale of the night before.
Bill was not there. She had rushed off to the stables at
once, of course.

' Listen . . .' said Jean. But nobody listened. They
were all agape at Darrell's amazing tale. Jean found herself
listening, too.

' But—would you believe Miss Peters could be so utterly
decent ? ' said Belinda, in surprise. ' She was super !
How lucky that you fetched her, Darrell ! '

' It *was* a night ! ' said Darrell. ' Bill and I must have

walked miles and miles with Thunder round the yard.   I
wonder how he is this morning.'

Footsteps raced up the corridor to the dormy.   Bill burst
in, her face glowing.   'Darrell!   DARRELL!   He's all
right.   Right as rain, and eating his oats as if he couldn't
have enough.   The vet stayed with him till half-past seven,
and Miss Peters stayed till now.   She never went to bed
again!'

'Golly!   She's wonderful,' said Alicia, seeing Miss
Peters in an entirely new light.   'Bill, why didn't you and
Darrell wake us up, too!'

'We never thought of anything like that,' said Bill.
'We only thought of Thunder.   Darrell was marvellous,
too.   Oh, I feel so happy.   Thunder's all right.   He's not
going to be sent home.   Everything's fine.   And I shall
never, never forget what Miss Peters did last night.'

'You will!' said Alicia.   'You'll sit and look out of the
window and dream in class, just as you always do!'

'I shan't,' said Bill, earnestly.   'Don't tease me, Alicia.
I feel a bit queer though I feel so happy.   Now I know that
Miss Peters is so fond of Thunder—and he loves her, too,
fancy that!—I shall feel quite different about everything.
I might even let her ride him.'

Jean at last got a word in.   'Listen to *me* now!' she said,
and she told the third-formers about Mavis.   They listened
in horrified silence.   Darrell burst out at once.

'Gracious!   So Miss Peters didn't only save Thunder
last night—she saved Mavis, too.   But I say—fancy Mavis
trying to walk home all those miles in the dark by herself.
She's afraid of the dark, too.'

The girls were happy about Bill and Thunder, but upset
about Mavis.   They stood about in the dormy, talking,
forgetting all about breakfast.   Somebody came running up
the corridor.   It was Lucy of the fourth form.

'I *say*!   What are you all thinking of?   Aren't you

coming to breakfast ? The bell's gone long ago. Mam'zelle is absolutely furious ! '

' Oh dear ! Come on, everyone,' said Jean. ' I feel all in a whirl.'

The news about Thunder and about Mavis spread all through the school, and was the talk in every class from the bottom form to the top. Darrell and Bill had to tell the tale over and over again.

It was Sunday so there were no classes. In the school chapel, where the service was held, a prayer was said for Mavis. All the girls joined in it, for although few of them liked Mavis they were all sorry for her. The news went round that she was worse. Her parents had been sent for ! Oh dear, thought Jean, it was all her fault !

By the next morning, however, Mavis had taken a turn for the better. Thunder, too, was perfectly all right. Bill was thrilled. It seemed impossible that a horse in such pain as Thunder had been should be quite recovered the day after. How wonderful people like doctors and vets were !

The girls settled down to their classes on Monday, glad that Mavis was better. Jean especially was thankful. Perhaps she would soon be back in school. The whole matter would have blown over. Mavis would be given a talking to by Miss Grayling, but no punishment because she had punished herself enough. Everything would be all right.

Miss Peters had had a good rest on the Sunday, and was taking the third form as usual on Monday. When she came into the classroom, she had a surprise.

' Hurrah for Miss Peters ! ' cried Darrell's voice, and to the amazement of the forms on each side of the third form room, three hearty cheers rang out for Miss Peters. She couldn't help being pleased. She smiled pleasantly all round.

'Thank you,' she said. 'That was nice of you. Now
—open your books at page forty-one. Alicia, come up to
the blackboard, please.'

Darrell looked with interest at Bill several times that
morning. Bill didn't gaze out of the window once. She
paid great attention to every word that Miss Peters said.
She answered intelligently, and when it was her turn to
come up to the blackboard, she did extremely well.

'Very good, Bill,' said Miss Peters, and a gasp went
round the class. Miss Peters hadn't called her Wilhelmina
as she always did. She had called her Bill. Bill grinned
as she went back to her place. She looked a different
person.

Darrell admired her as she watched her in class after
class. Bill had made up her mind to do a thing and she
meant to do it. She *would* do it, too! Darrell thought that
it was quite possible for Bill to rise near the top of the class
once she had made up her mind to do it.

'I suppose that's what Daddy would call strength of
character,' thought Darrell. 'He's always saying that
strength of character is one of the greatest things anyone can
have because then they have courage and pluck and determination, no matter what difficulties come. Bill's got it.
I bet she won't dream, or gaze out of the window again,
or not bother with her work. She's going to repay Miss
Peters for Saturday night!'

Miss Peters knew that Bill meant to repay her for that,
too. She trusted Bill now. They understood one another,
which really wasn't very surprising, because they were very
much alike. Miss Peters was mannish, and Bill was boyish.
They both loved life out-of-doors and adored horses. They'
had disliked one another very much indeed—but now they
were going to be firm friends. That would be nice for
Bill.

'Darrell! Are you day-dreaming?' said Miss Peters'

voice. 'You don't seem to have written down anything
at all!'

Darrell jumped and went red. Gracious! Here she
was admiring Bill for being able to stop dreaming in class
—and she, Darrell, had fallen into the same fault herself!
She pulled herself together and began to write.

That afternoon Miss Hibbert was going to take the first
rehearsal of the play in the art-room. This was often used
for dramatic work because it had a small platform. Zerelda
was very much looking forward to the afternoon. She sat
in her place, murmuring some lines from 'Romeo and
Juliet' below her breath. Miss Peters saw her lips moving
and thought she was whispering to Gwen.

'Zerelda!' she said, sharply. 'What are you saying to
Gwendoline?'

'Nothing, Miss Peters,' said Zerelda, surprised.

'Well, what were you saying to yourself then?' demanded Miss Peters. 'Stand up when you answer me,
Zerelda.'

Zerelda stood up. She looked at Miss Peters and recited
dramatically what she had been murmuring to herself.

'Wilt thou be gone? It is not yet near day;
It was the nightingale and not . . .'

A volley of laughter from everyone in the class drowned
her voice. Miss Peters rapped sharply on her desk.

'Zerelda! I hope you don't really *mean* to be rude.
That's enough! We are doing geography, not Shakespeare.
Sit down and get on!'

AFTER the dinner hour that day the third-formers brought up the subject of Alicia's trick again.

'You know, Alicia—I don't somehow feel as if I want it played on Miss Peters now,' said Bill.

'Nor do I,' said Darrell.

'I don't want it played at all,' said Sally, stoutly.

'Well, you're the only one that doesn't,' said Alicia. 'So keep quiet. What does everyone else say?'

'*I* don't quite like to play it on Miss Peters now,' said Belinda. 'I feel like Bill and Darrell. You know—it seems a bit odd to give three cheers for somebody and then the very next day play a trick on them like that.'

'*I* shouldn't mind,' said Zerelda, who hadn't liked being ticked off in class that morning by Miss Peters. 'What's in a trick, anyway! Only a bit of fun. I guess it wouldn't matter at all.'

'I agree with Zerelda,' said Gwen's voice. 'Why shouldn't we? Don't you agree, Daphne?'

'I don't know,' said Daphne, who had been rather struck with Miss Peters' dramatic ride through the night. 'No—I think on the whole I'd rather play it on Mam'zelle—or Miss Carton, perhaps.'

'Well, I don't much care who we play it on,' said Alicia. 'Darrell and I will agree to what the majority say.'

'Darrell and you!' exclaimed Sally. 'What's Darrell got to do with it? It's *your* trick, not hers!'

'Oh, we've just been planning it out together that's all,' said Alicia, coolly, pleased to see Sally's jealousy flare up in public. Darrell went red. It was true she had enjoyed talking over the trick with Alicia—but she knew quite well that Alicia was only saying that to make Sally cross. Bother them both! Why couldn't they all be friends together? Never mind—Betty was coming back soon. Then perhaps Alicia would stop teasing Sally and Sally would stop being jealous and spiteful.

'Well—let's play the trick on Mam'zelle then,' said Irene. 'Mam'zelle's lovely to play tricks on. We haven't played one on her for terms and terms.'

'Right. Mam'zelle it shall be,' said Alicia. 'Do you agree, Darrell? We'll talk about the best time and so on together when we've got a minute to ourselves. It's time to go over to the art-room now.'

They all went off to the art-room, Sally looking glum. Alicia slipped her arm in Darrell's and bore her off as if she really was her best friend. Darrell glanced back at Sally and tried to take her arm away from Alicia. But Sally gave her such a sour look that Darrell was annoyed, and didn't go back to her after all.

Privately Darrell thought the hour of Shakespeare was a dreadful waste, because it was a fine sunny afternoon when a game of lacrosse could have been arranged. Still it would be fun to see Zerelda trying to impress Miss Hibbert.

Zerelda was excited. This was her great chance. If only she could bring it off—make Miss Hibbert say what a gift for acting she had. 'Zerelda, you're a born actress!' she would say to her. 'You have a great Gift. You must turn all your attention to building it up. You have the right appearance, too—striking, graceful, mature. It will make me very proud to teach you this year!'

Zerelda had done a little roll of hair on top of her head again—not so big a roll as before, certainly, but still a roll, pinned up to make her look older. Her hair was not tied back so tightly either. She had made up her face a little— put red on her lips, pink on her cheeks, and had smothered herself with powder. Her hands were white. Her nails were very long and highly polished. She hoped she looked a finished actress !

Miss Hibbert did not look at all like a producer of plays. She was neat, with a well-fitting coat and skirt, and her hair, slightly wavy, was brushed well back. She wore a pair of glasses with rather thick rims. She had a lovely speaking voice, very pleasant to listen to. She was very efficient, and knew exactly how to pick the right actor for the right part.

She looked over the girls as they came in. She knew Zerelda already because she had taken her for a few lessons in the fourth form. She looked in astonishment at Zerelda's make-up. Good gracious ! What did the girl think she was up to !

Miss Hibbert had absolutely no idea at all that Zerelda fancied herself as an actress or as a film-star. Nobody had told her. Perhaps if she had known, she might have been a little more patient, even a little kinder. But she didn't know.

There was a lot to get through. For one reason or another two rehearsals had been put off, and Miss Hibbert was feeling a little rushed for time. She handed out copies of the play and looked round the form.

' Now—has anyone acted in this play before ? '

Nobody had. Zerelda stepped forward and said a few words, trying to speak the English way. ' Please, Miss Hibbert, once I did Lady Macbeth in Shakespeare.'

' Oh,' said Miss Hibbert, gazing at Zerelda's hair. ' Zerelda, I don't like the way you do your hair. Don't come to my classes with that silly roll on top again.'

Zerelda went red and stepped back.

' Has anyone read the play ? ' Darrell and Mary-Lou put up their hands, and so did Zerelda.

' Does anyone know any of the parts ? Has anyone been

sufficiently interested to learn any of the speeches ? ' went on Miss Hibbert.

Zerelda stepped forward again. 'Please, Miss Hibbert, I know all Juliet's speeches, every one of them. I guess I could say them all, right now. It's a wunnerful part, Juliet's. I've been rehearsing it like mad.'

'Yes. She's awfully good as Juliet,' put in Gwendoline, and got a grateful smile from Zerelda.

'Very well. As you've taken the trouble to learn the part, you can take it this afternoon,' said Miss Hibbert. She looked round the class for a boyish third-former to take the part of Romeo. Her eye fell on Bill.

'You,' she said. 'What's your name—Wilhelmina—you can take the part of Romeo today. And you, Darrell, can be the nurse, and you . . .'

Quickly she fitted part after part. The girls looked at their copies of the play and prepared to read and act them.

'Not very inspired,' said Miss Hibbert, after the first few pages had been read. 'Turn to the part where Juliet comes on. Zerelda, are you ready ? '

Was she *ready* ? Why, she was waiting on tenterhooks to begin ! She was full of it ! She was Juliet to the life, poor, tragic Juliet.

Zerelda launched herself into the part. She declaimed her lines in a most dramatic manner, she flung herself about, she marched up and down, she threw her head back, imagining herself to be beautiful and most lovable.

'Stop, Zerelda,' said Miss Hibbert, amazed. But Zerelda did not stop. Heedless of the giggles of the class she ranted on. Irene gave one of her enormous snorts, and Miss Hibbert glared at her. She spoke loudly to Zerelda again.

'STOP, Zerelda ! '

Zerelda stopped and stared blankly at Miss Hibbert, surprised to see that she looked so furious.

'How dare you behave like that?' stormed Miss Hibbert.
'Sending the class into fits! Do you think that's the way
to behave in a Shakespeare class? They may think it
comical but I don't. Those are lovely lines you have been
saying—but you have completely spoilt them. And do you
really think it is clever to throw yourself about like that,
and toss your head? Don't you know that Juliet was
young and gentle and sweet? You are trying to make her
into some horrible affected film-star!'

Zerelda took in what the angry mistress was saying. She
could hardly believe it. She went rather white under the
pink on her cheeks.

'And why have you made yourself up like that?' demanded Miss Hibbert, roused to more anger by the giggles
of the rest of the form. 'I cannot tell you how horrible
you look with that stuff on your face. You would not dare
to go to Miss Peters' class like that. I'm not going to put
up with it. You may as well make up your mind, Zerelda,
that you will never be an actress. You simply haven't got
it in you. All that happens is that you make yourself really
vulgar. Now go and wash your face and do your hair
properly.'

Zerelda felt like a balloon that had been pricked. All her
confidence and pride oozed out of her. She crept to the
door and went out. Some of the girls felt sorry for her.

Rather subdued by this unusual outburst, the rest of the
form went on with the reading. Miss Hibbert, a little
sorry that she had been so very hard on Zerelda, handed
out a few words of praise. 'Alicia, you're good. Mary-
Lou, you have a nice voice if you could remember to hold
your head up when you speak your lines. Darrell, I can
see you are trying. Next time we will all take different
parts.'

'Miss Hibbert, had I better go and see what has happened to Zerelda?' asked Gwen, timidly. 'Miss Hibbert,

she really did think she had a gift for acting, you know. Aren't you going to let her be in the play at all ? '

' I may give her a very small part—where she can't throw herself about,' said Miss Hibbert. ' But certainly not a good part. It must be obvious even to you, Gwendoline, that Zerelda hasn't the faintest idea of acting, and never will have. Go and find her and tell her to come here to me. I want to talk to her. The class is now dismissed.'

The third-formers went out quietly. Poor Zerelda ! What would she do now ?

' Put a bold face on it, I expect,' said Alicia. ' Just as she did when she was sent down to the third form. She won't care ! She'll go on in just the same way, thinking the world of herself, and very little of anyone else ! '

Zerelda was found by Gwen in the cloakroom. She had washed her face quite clean and tied back her hair. But she had been too scared to go back to the art-room.

' Zerelda, Miss Hibbert wants you,' said Gwen. ' I'm sorry about that row. It's a shame.'

' *Can't* I act, Gwen ? ' said Zerelda, her lip quivering suddenly. Gwendoline hesitated.

' Well—you weren't very good really,' she said. ' You —you just seemed to be terribly funny. You might make a very good *comedian*, Zerelda.'

Zerelda said nothing but went off to the art-room. Even Gwen thought she couldn't act ! In fact, she was so bad that she became ridiculous. Zerelda was shocked and dismayed. She dreaded hearing what Miss Hibbert had to say.

But Miss Hibbert was unexpectedly kind. ' I hear that it is your ambition to be a great actress, Zerelda,' she said. ' Well, my dear, it is given to very few of us to be that. You haven't the gift—and you haven't another thing that all really fine actresses need.'

'What?' whispered Zerelda.

'Well, Zerelda, in order to be able to put yourself properly into some other character, you have to forget yourself entirely—forget your looks, your ambitions, your pride in acting, everything! And it takes a strong and understanding character to do that, someone without conceit or weakness of any sort—the finer the character of the actor, the better he can play any part. You are thinking of yourself too much. You were not Juliet being acted by Zerelda this afternoon—you were Zerelda all the time—and not a very nice Zerelda either!'

'Shan't I ever be any good at acting?' asked Zerelda, miserably.

'I don't think so,' said Miss Hibbert, gently. 'I can always tell at once those who have any gift for it. You have let your foolish worship and admiration of the film-stars blind you, Zerelda. Why not try to be your own self for a while? Stop all this posturing and pretending. Be like the others, a schoolgirl sent here to learn lessons and play games!'

'It's the only thing left for me to be,' said Zerelda, and a tear ran down her cheek.

'It's a very, very *nice* thing to be,' said Miss Hibbert. 'You try it and see! I wouldn't have been so hard on you if I'd known you had set your heart on being an actress. I thought you were just being ridiculous.'

Zerelda left the art-room, hardly knowing what to think. She had made herself ridiculous. She never, never wanted to act again! All she wanted to do was to sink into being a nobody, hoping that none of the others would notice her and tease her about that afternoon.

She joined the others at tea, slipping into her place unnoticed by the girls. Miss Potts looked at her and saw that she had been crying. 'Funny thing!' thought Miss Potts, 'it's the first time I've noticed it, but Zerelda is getting to look much more like the others now—a proper little schoolgirl. Perhaps Malory Towers is beginning to have an effect after all!'

20   THE TRICK!

ONE or two days slipped by. Mavis was still very ill and could not be seen, but it was known now that she was mending. Everyone was relieved. The girls sent in flowers and books, and Zerelda sent her a complicated American jigsaw.

Bill had quite recovered from her midnight adventure and so had Darrell. Miss Peters was delighted with the change in Bill's work. It was still uneven, but she knew that Bill was paying great attention and really trying hard. Zerelda, too, was working even better, and had actually asked Mam'zelle for extra coaching!

Zerelda had sorted things out in her mind. She had definitely given up the idea of becoming a film-actress. She didn't even want to *look* like one! She wanted to look as like the others as possible, and to make them forget how ridiculous she had been. She began to copy them in every way she could.

'Isn't Zerelda queer?' said Belinda to Irene. 'When she first came here she gave herself such airs and graces, and looked down on the whole lot of us—now she tries to copy us in everything—the way we speak, the way we do this and that—and seems to think we're just " wunnerful ! " '

'She's much nicer,' said Irene, trying out the rhythm of a tune on the table in front of her. 'Tum-tum-ti-tum. Yes, that's how it goes. I like Zerelda now, really I do.'

' Look—Gwendoline's scowling again ! ' said Belinda, in a whisper. ' I can get that scowl this time. Isn't it a beauty ! '

Gwen suddenly became aware of Belinda's intent glances. She straightened her face at once. ' If you've drawn me, I'll tear up the paper ! ' she said.

' Oh, *Gwen*—scowl half a minute more and I'll get it ! ' begged Belinda. But Gwen walked out of the room, putting the scowl on outside the door because she felt so annoyed with Belinda and her impish pencil.

' About that trick,' said Alicia, suddenly to Darrell. ' Shall we play it on Friday ? Mam'zelle was murmuring this morning something about a test then.'

' Oh *yes*. Let's ! ' said Darrell, thrilled. She saw Sally nearby, her face glum. ' Sally ! Do say you agree. It really will be funny—and quite harmless.'

' I've said already I'm not going to have anything to do with the trick,' said Sally. ' I think it's a silly trick, and might be dangerous. I can't see how anyone can sneeze and sneeze without feeling exhausted. Do it if you like— but just remember that I don't agree ! '

' Spoil-sport,' said Alicia, in a low voice to Darrell. Darrell sighed. She couldn't back out of the trick now just to please Sally—but she did hate it when Sally wouldn't be friends. Never mind—Betty would be coming back this week. On Friday perhaps ! Then Alicia wouldn't bother about her any more. Betty had been away for more than six weeks now—it was past half-term—but she had been sent away to the seaside, after her whooping-cough was over, because she had had it so badly. Good gracious—there were only three or four weeks to the end of the term ! How the time had flown. It was March now, and the early daffodils were blowing in the courtyard.

Alicia and Darrell made their plans. ' We'll put the little pellet, soaked in salt water, on the little ledge behind

Mam'zelle,' said Alicia. ' Let's see—who's on duty to get
the room ready on Friday ? Oh, I do believe it's you, isn't
it, Darrell ? That will be easy then. You can put the
pellet there yourself.'

' Yes, I will,' agreed Darrell, beginning to giggle at the
thought of Mam'zelle's surprise when she kept sneezing.

All the third-formers knew about the joke. Only Sally
disapproved. Jean didn't think there was any harm in it
at all, so she didn't draw back either. Everyone was thrilled
at the thought of Friday.

It came at last. Darrell slipped into the form room with
the little pellet and a sponge soaked in salt water. She set
the pellet on the ledge and squeezed a few drops of water
from the sponge over it. That was apparently all that was
needed to make it work.

The others came in to get ready for the class. They
raised their eye-brows at Darrell, and she nodded back,
smiling. They all took their places, ready for Mam'zelle.

She came in, beaming as usual. ' *Asseyez-vous, mes
enfants*. Today we have a great, great treat. It is a test ! '

Deep groans from the class.

' Silence ! ' hissed Mam'zelle. ' Do you want Miss Potts
to come and find out what is the meaning of this terrible
noise ? Now, I will write some questions on the blackboard, and you will answer them in your books.'

She turned to write on the blackboard, and got the first
whiff of the fine vapour, quite invisible, that was streaming
from the curious little pellet.

Mam'zelle felt a tickling in her nose, and felt about her
plump person for her handkerchief. ' Ah, where is it,
now ? I have a nose-tickle.'

' Your hanky's in your belt, Mam'zelle,' called Alicia,
hoping that Irene wasn't going to do one of her explosions
too soon. She already looked as if she was on the point of
bursting.

Mam'zelle also looked as if she was bursting. She snatched at her handkerchief and pressed it to her nose. But no handkerchief could choke down that colossal sneeze. Mam'zelle always did sneeze loudly at any time—but this time it sounded like an explosive shell!

'A-WHOOSH-OOOO! Dear me,' said Mam'zelle, patting her nose with her handkerchief. 'I'm sorry, girls, I could not help it.'

Irene had already bent down to hide her giggles under the desk. Alicia glanced at her in amused annoyance. Whatever would she do when Mam'zelle's second sneeze came along. Ah—it was coming. Mam'zelle was making a frantic grab for her handkerchief again.

'Oh, *là là*! Here is another snizz. I hope I do not get a cold. A-WHOOOSH-OOOOOOO!'

Irene exploded and so did Belinda. Mam'zelle, quite shaken by her enormous sneeze, glared at them both.

'Irene! Belinda! It is not kind to laugh at another's discom. . . . A-WHOOOSH-OO!'

But now even Alicia could not hide her laughter. Darrell leaned back weakly and tried to stop laughing because her side ached so much. Even Sally was smiling, though she tried hard not to.

'A-WHOOOSH-OOO!' sneezed Mam'zelle again. She reeled back to her chair, and mopped her forehead. 'Never have I snizzed like this before,' she said. 'It is unheard of that I snizz so much. A-WHOOOOOSH-OOOOOO!'

The last one was so terrific that it shook poor Mam'zelle right out of her chair. By now the whole class was in convulsions. Gwen was falling out of her chair. In another moment Irene would be rolling on the floor. Tears of laughter were pouring down the cheeks of half a dozen of the girls.

Mam'zelle sat staring at the blackboard wondering if the sneezing had finished. Perhaps the attack was over.

' A-tish-oo! ' sneezed poor Mam'zelle

She got up cautiously and went to the blackboard—but at once her nose began to tickle again and she put up her handkerchief. 'A—WHOOOOOOOOOSH-OOO!'

Mam'zelle sank down into her chair again. At this moment the door opened and Miss Potts looked in with a sheaf of papers. 'Oh, excuse me, Mam'zelle, but you left these . . .' she began, and then stopped short in surprise at seeing the whole form rolling about in helpless laughter. Whatever was happening?

She looked at Mam'zelle, and Mam'zelle looked back, trying to tell her what was happening. Another exploding sneeze nearly blew Miss Potts out of the door.

'A-WHOOOSH-OOOOOO!'

The class sobered up when they saw Miss Potts. They hoped she would go immediately—but she didn't. Rather alarmed at Mam'zelle's agonized expression, she went over to her. 'It is these snizzes——' Mam'zelle began to explain and was then overcome by another.

The vapour found its way to Miss Potts' nose. She was just about to open her mouth and speak when she too felt a sneeze coming. Her nose began to tickle and she felt for her handkerchief.

'A-TISH-OOO!' she sneezed, and Irene burst into one of her explosive laughs at once. Miss Potts glared at her.

'Irene! Do you think. . . . A-TISH-OOOO!'

'A-WHOOOOSH-OOOO!' from Mam'zelle. 'Miss Potts what is this snizzing? I cannot stop my snizzes—A-WHOOOSH-OO!'

Miss Potts sneezed three times without being able to get a word in between the sneezes. Then a sudden suspicion flashed into her mind. She looked at the giggling girls.

'Jean,' she said, 'you are head-girl of this form. Is this a trick? A-TISH-OO!'

Jean hesitated. How could she give the whole form away?

Mam'zelle saved her from further questioning. She sneezed such a mighty sneeze that she fell off her chair. She moaned. 'I am ill! I have never snizzed like this before. I am very ill. A-WHOOOOSH-OO.'

Really alarmed, Miss Potts, hindered by two or three sudden sneezes of her own, dragged Mam'zelle to her feet. 'Open the window,' she commanded Darrell. 'Fetch Matron. Mam'zelle certainly does look ill.'

In great alarm Darrell opened the window and Mary-Lou ran for Matron. Matron came, puzzled by Mary-Lou's breathless tale of Mam'zelle's sneezes. She saw Mam'zelle's pale face and took her arm to lead her away. The pellet-vapour overtook Matron also, and she did a very sudden sneeze indeed. Miss Potts also obliged with two more, and Mam'zelle prepared for yet another. Then Matron took Mam'zelle from the room, and Miss Potts followed, to make sure poor Mam'zelle was all right.

The girls, alarmed and frightened though they were, could not stop from laughing at the sight of the three adults sneezing in chorus together. 'You were nearly caught out with Miss Potts' question, Jean,' said Alicia. 'It was a narrow shave! Let's hope she doesn't ask it again.'

'I hope Mam'zelle isn't *really* knocked out,' said Darrell, anxiously. 'She did look rather awful. I think I'll quickly take that pellet and throw it out of the window before Miss Potts comes back and sees it!'

So she threw it out, being caught for a sneeze herself first. Then the form settled down to wait for someone to come back.

It was Miss Potts. 'Mam'zelle is not at all well,' she began, severely, handkerchief in hand in case she began to sneeze again. 'She has had to go to bed. She is quite exhausted. The strange—very strange—thing is, that as soon as we left this room not one of us had any wish to sneeze. Jean, will you please explain this to me. Or perhaps you, Alicia, would like to do so? I feel that you probably know more about it than anyone else.'

Alicia hardly knew what to say. Jean nudged her. 'Go on. You'll have to tell.'

So Alicia told. It didn't seem nearly such a funny idea when it was told stammeringly to a frowning Miss Potts.

'I see. One of your asinine tricks again. I should have thought that third-formers were above such childish things. Were you all in this, every one of you?'

'Sally wasn't,' said Darrell. 'She refused to agree. She was the only one who stood out.'

'Only one sensible person in the whole of the form!' said Miss Potts. 'Very well—with the exception of Sally, each of you will forfeit the next half-holiday, which is, I believe, on Thursday. You will also apologize to Mam'zelle and work twice as hard at your French for the rest of the term!'

21   MAVIS AND ZERELDA

IT was a sorry ending to what everyone had thought to be a very fine trick. 'I suppose that pellet had been made stronger than usual,' said Alicia, gloomily.

Sally didn't say 'I told you so' which was very good of her, Darrell thought. 'I shall give up the half-holiday just the same as you all do,' she told Darrell. 'I may have stood out against the trick, but I'm going to share the punishment, of course.'

'You're decent, Sally,' said Darrell, slipping her arm in

hers. 'Let's go downstairs and see if there's anything interesting on the notice-board. I believe there's a debate tonight we might go to—sixth-formers against fifth-formers, all arguing their heads off.'

They went to find the notice-board. One of the fourth-formers was also there, looking at it. It was Ellen. 'Hallo, Darrell!' she said. 'Congratulations!'

'What on?' asked Darrell, surprised.

'Well, look—you're playing for the third match-team next Thursday!' said Ellen. 'Three people have fallen out, ill—so all three reserves are playing—and you're one of them, aren't you?'

'Oh—how perfectly wizard!' cried Darrell. She capered round the hall—and then her face suddenly sobered. 'I say—will Miss Potts let me play next Thursday? That's the half-holiday, isn't it, except for match-players? Oh, Sally—do you think I shan't be able to play because we've all got to give up our half-holiday and work instead?'

'What *are* you talking about?' said Ellen, puzzled. Darrell told her.

'Goodness!' said Ellen. 'You won't be able to play then. You can't expect Potty to let you off a punishment in order to have a great treat like playing in a match-team.'

Darrell groaned. 'Oh—what simply awful bad luck! My first chance! And I've chucked it away. Oh, Sally, why didn't I back you up and stand aside with you, instead of going in with Alicia?'

It was a terrible blow to poor Darrell. She went about looking so miserable that Sally couldn't bear it. She went to Miss Potts' room and knocked at the door.

'Please, Miss Potts—Darrell is down to play in the third match-team next Thursday,' said Sally. 'And because of the trick today she's supposed to work on that day. She's terribly disappointed. You said I needn't give up the half-holiday because I didn't agree to the trick. Can I give it up, please, and let Darrell take it instead of me ?   Then she could play in the match.'

' A kind thought, Sally, but quite impossible,' said Miss Potts.   ' Darrell must take her punishment like the rest of the form.   It's her own fault if she misses her chance of playing in the match.'

Sally went away sadly.   She met Darrell and told her how she had tried to get her the half-holiday so that she might play in the team.   Darrell was touched.   ' Oh, Sally !   You really *are* a sport !   A proper friend !   Thank you.'

Sally smiled at her.   Her jealousy slid away suddenly. She knew she had been silly, but she wouldn't be any more. She linked her arm in Darrell's.

' I'll be glad when Betty's back and Alicia has her for company,' she said.

' So will I,' said Darrell, heartily.   ' It's annoying the way she keeps trying to make us into a threesome.   Don't let's, Sally.'

Sally was satisfied.   But how she wished she could give Darrell her half-holiday !   Poor Darrell—it was such a wonderful chance—one that might not come again for ages.

They met Sister and asked her for news of Mavis.   ' Much better,' said Sister.   ' Her *voice* has gone though.   She can only croak, poor Mavis.   She seems very miserable.   She can have a visitor tomorrow.   She's asked for Zerelda, so you might tell her she can go to see Mavis after tea.'

Darrell and Sally looked at each other in astonishment. Zerelda !   Whatever did Mavis want Zerelda for ?

Mavis was very unhappy.   She had been horrified when she found that her voice had gone.   She had only a croak that sounded quite unlike her own voice.   ' Oh, Sister— won't I ever be able to sing again ? ' she had asked, anxiously.

' Not for some time,' Sister had said.   ' Oh, yes, I expect it will come back all right, Mavis—but you have been very ill with throat and chest trouble, and you won't have to try and sing for a year or two. If you do, the specialist says you will damage your voice for ever, and will never be able to become a singer.'

Mavis let the tears slide down her cheeks without wiping them away. No Voice! No singing for a year or two—and perhaps not then. Why, she might not become an opera-singer after all. Throat trouble—chest trouble—they were the two things a singer must always guard against.

'It's my own fault! Why did I creep off in the rain that night?' wept poor Mavis. 'I thought it was a grand thing to do. The others didn't. Perhaps Zerelda would understand though—she's going to be a grand film-actress, and she understands how a singer or an actress longs to be recognized, aches for applause.'

So, when Sister told her she could have a visitor and asked her whom she would like, she chose Zerelda! She must tell Zerelda everything. Zerelda would understand and sympathize.

Zerelda was surprised, too, to be chosen. She hadn't liked Mavis very much. But she went to see her, taking some fruit, some sweets and a book that had just come for her from America. Zerelda was always generous.

She was shocked to see how thin Mavis looked. 'Sit down,' said Mavis, in a terrible croak.

'What's happened to your voice?' asked Zerelda, in alarm.

'I've lost it—perhaps for ever!' said Mavis, in a pathetic croak. 'Oh, Zerelda, I've been an idiot. I'm sure nobody would understand but you!'

In a series of pants and croaks she told Zerelda all the happenings of that Saturday night—and how they wouldn't even *let* her sing. 'So it was all for nothing. Oh, Zerelda,

what am I to do without my voice ? I shall die ! The
others have always told me that I'm nothing without my
voice, nothing at all.'

'Don't talk any more, Mavis,' said Sister, putting her
head in at the door. 'You talk instead, Zerelda.'

So Zerelda talked. What did she find to talk about ?
Ah, Zerelda suddenly found a bit of character and quite a
lot of wisdom. She had learnt quite a few things already
from her term at Malory Towers—she had especially learnt
from her failure at acting. And she told Mavis all she had
learnt.

It wasn't easy to tell what had happened in the Shakespeare
class—but when Zerelda saw how Mavis was drinking it all
in, paying her the very closest attention, she spared herself
nothing.

'So you see, Mavis,' she finished at last, 'I was much,
much worse than you. You really *had* a gift. I never
had ! You were proud of a real thing. I was vain of
something false, that didn't exist. I'm happier now I
know, though. After all, it *is* more sensible to be what we
really are, isn't it—schoolgirls—not future film-actresses
or opera-singers. You'll feel the same, too, when you've
thought about it. You can be *you* now you've lost your
voice for a bit.'

'Oh, Zerelda,' croaked Mavis, slipping her hand into
the American girl's, 'you don't know how you've helped
me. I was so terribly miserable. I didn't think anything
like this had ever happened to anyone before. And it's
happened to *you* as well as to me ! '

Zerelda said nothing. It had cost her a lot to make
such a confession to Mavis, of all people. But with all her
faults, Zerelda was generous-hearted, and she had quickly
seen how she, and she alone, could help Mavis.

Sister put her head in again. She was glad to see Mavis
looking so much happier. She came right in. 'Well,

you *have* done her good, Zerelda!' she said. 'She looks quite different. You're friends, I suppose?'

Mavis looked eagerly at Zerelda. 'Yes,' said Zerelda, firmly. 'We're friends.'

'Well, two minutes more and you must go,' said Sister and went out again.

'I'm going to make the others see that I wasn't only a Voice,' croaked Mavis. 'Zerelda, will you go on helping me? Will you be friends with me? I'm not much, I know—but you haven't got a friend, have you?'

'No,' said Zerelda, ashamed to say it. 'Well—I suppose I'm not much of a person either, Mavis. I'm just a no-account person—both of us are! We'll help each other. Now I must go. Good-bye! I'll come again tomorrow!'

22   THINGS GET STRAIGHTENED OUT

MAM'ZELLE soon recovered from her fit of 'snizzes', and returned to her teaching the next day. At first she had felt very angry when Miss Potts had explained to her that it was all because of some trick the girls had played.

But gradually her sense of humour came back to her and she found herself chuckling when she thought of Miss Potts and Matron also being caught by the trick and sneezing violently too.

'But I, I snizzed the greatest snizzes,' said Mam'zelle to herself. 'Aha—here is Mam'zelle Rougier. I will tell her of this trick.'

She told the prim, rather sour-faced Mam'zelle Rougier

who did not approve of tricks in any shape or form. She
was horrified.

'These English girls! Have you told Miss Grayling?
They should all be punished, every one.'

'Oh *no*—I haven't reported them to the Head,' said
Mam'zelle Dupont. 'I only do that for serious matters.'

'And you do not call this a serious matter!' cried Mam'-
zelle Rougier. 'You will overlook it, and not have the
girls punished at all! That Alicia—and the mad Irene and
the bad Belinda—it would do them good to have a hard
punishment.'

'Oh, they are all being punished,' said Mam'zelle,
hastily. 'They are to give up their half-holiday, and work
instead.'

'That is no real punishment!' said Mam'zelle Rougier.
'You are poor at discipline, Mam'zelle Dupont. I have
always said so.'

'Indeed, I am not!' cried Mam'zelle Dupont, annoyed.
'Have you no sense of humour? Do you not see the funny
side?'

'No, I do not,' said Mam'zelle Rougier, firmly. 'What
is this "funny side" that the English speak of so much?
It is not funny. You too know that it is not, Mam'zelle.'

The more that Mam'zelle Rougier talked like this the
more certain Mam'zelle Dupont was that the joke had been
funny. In the end she quite persuaded herself that she
had really entered into it and laughed with the girls.

She almost felt that she would like to remove the punishment Miss Potts had imposed. But Miss Potts would not
hear of it. 'Certainly not! Don't be weak, Mam'zelle.
We can't possibly let things like that pass.'

'Perhaps not,' said Mam'zelle, a sudden idea coming
into her head. 'The bad girls! They shall come to me
for the whole of Thursday afternoon, Miss Potts, and I will
make them WORK.'

' That's better,' said Miss Potts, approvingly. She found Mam'zelle very difficult at times. ' Keep them at it all the afternoon ! '

' I shall take them for a walk,' thought Mam'zelle. She hated walks herself, but she knew how much the girls loved them. But when Thursday afternoon came, it was such a pouring wet day that not only was no lacrosse match possible but no walk either.

Darrell saw a notice up on the board beside the list of players. ' MATCH CANCELLED. ANOTHER DATE WILL BE FIXED LATER.'

' Look at that ! ' she said to Sally. ' No match after all. How frightfully disappointed I'd have been if I'd been playing—and it was cancelled. I wonder if there's any hope of my playing on the next date it's arranged. I suppose the girls who are ill will be better by then, though.'

The girls went to their classroom that afternoon, to work, while all the other forms went down to the big hall to play mad games together, and to see a film afterwards on a big screen put up at the end of the hall.

Mam'zelle was waiting for them, a broad smile on her face. ' Poor children ! You have to work this afternoon because of my snizzes. You must learn some French dances. I have brought my gramophone and some records. I will teach you a fine country dance that all French children know.'

In surprise and glee the third-formers put back all the desks and chairs. They hoped Miss Potts would come by, or Miss Peters, and see what kind of work they were doing on their forfeited half-holiday ! What sport to see their faces if they looked into the room !

But Mam'zelle had made sure that both these mistresses would not come that way. Miss Peters had gone off for the afternoon. Miss Potts would be in the big hall with her first form. Mam'zelle was safe !

'The coast is bright!' said Mam'zelle, gleefully. The girls giggled.

'You mean, "the coast is *clear*",' said Jean.

'It is the same thing,' said Mam'zelle. 'Now—begin! Form a ring, please, and I will tell you what to sing as you go round to the music.'

It was a hilarious afternoon, and the third-formers enjoyed it very much. 'You're a sport, Mam'zelle,' said Darrell, warmly, at the end. 'A real sport.'

Mam'zelle beamed. She had never yet been able to understand exactly what a 'sport' was—she only knew it was very high praise, and she was pleased.

'You made me snizz—and I have made you pant!' she said, to the breathless girls. 'We are evens, are we not?'

'Quits, you mean,' said Jean, but Mam'zelle took no notice.

'I shall tell Miss Potts you have quite exhausted yourselves in your hard work this afternoon,' said Mam'zelle. 'Poor children—you will be so hungry for tea!'

Zerelda had enjoyed herself as much as anyone. In fact, she was very surprised to find how much she had enjoyed the whole afternoon. Why—a week ago she would have turned up her nose at such rowdiness, and would only have joined in languidly, pretending it was all beneath her.

'But I loved every minute!' thought Zerelda, tying her hair back firmly. It had come loose with the dancing. 'I must have been a frightful idiot before. No wonder the girls laughed at me.'

She saw her old self suddenly—posing, trying to be so grown-up, piling up her hair in Lossie Laxton's terrible style, looking down on all these jolly schoolgirls. She wouldn't bear to think of it.

'It's *fun* to be a proper schoolgirl,' she thought. 'Lovely to be just myself, instead of trying to be like Lossie. What an idiot I was—far worse than Mavis, who did at least have a *real* gift ! '

Mavis was getting on well. She looked forward immensely to Zerelda's visits. Many of the third-formers had been to see her now, but she looked forward to Zerelda's visits more than to anyone else's. She thought Zerelda was wonderful—wonderful to have learnt a lesson that she, Mavis, meant to try to learn, too.

It was a little comfort to Zerelda to feel that someone did think she was wonderful, even though she knew now that she wasn't. Now that Mavis had stopped talking about her voice and her marvellous future, she seemed a different kind of person—simpler, more natural, with a greater interest in other people.

' I'm never going to mention my voice again,' Mavis told Zerelda. ' I'm never going to say, " when I'm an opera-singer " again. Perhaps if I'm sensible and don't boast and don't think about my voice, it'll come back.'

' Oh, it'll come back, I expect,' said Zerelda, comfortingly. ' You did your best to get rid of it though ! Oh, Mavis—you're just like me—reduced to being a schoolgirl and nothing else. But, gee, you wouldn't believe how nice it is to belong to the others, to be just as they are, and not try to make out you're too wunnerful for words ! '

' Tell me about Mam'zelle and the sneezing again,' begged Mavis. ' You do make me laugh so. You're terribly funny when you tell things like that, Zerelda.'

Zerelda was. She could not act any part, but she could tell a story in a very humorous way, and keep everyone in fits of laughter. Privately Alicia thought that that was Zerelda's real gift, the ability to be really funny—but she wasn't going to say so ! She wasn't going to give Zerelda any chance of thinking herself ' wunnerful ' again !

The girls admired the way Zerelda gave her time so

generously to Mavis. They thought a good deal more of
her for taking Miss Hibbert's rather harsh ticking-off so
well, and for taking to heart all she had said.

'I didn't think she had it in her,' said Darrell to Sally.
'I really didn't. I thought she was just an inflated balloon
—and when Miss Hibbert pricked her, I thought she'd just
deflate and there'd be nothing. But there *is* something
after all. I like her now, don't you?'

'Well—I always did think she was very generous, and
I liked her good nature,' said Sally. 'But then I didn't
have such a dose of her silliness as you did—I didn't come
back to school till so late.'

'I'm glad Betty's back, aren't you?' said Darrell.
'Thank goodness! Now Alicia has got someone to go
round with, and she doesn't always want you and me to
make a threesome. I wish Bill had a friend. She's rather
one on her own.'

'Well—I don't mind making up a threesome with Bill
sometimes,' said Sally. 'Though Bill doesn't *really* need
a friend, you know, Darrell—honestly I think Thunder takes
the place of a friend with her.'

'Yes. He does,' said Darrell, remembering that dark
rainy night when she and Bill had walked Thunder round
and round the yard. 'But it would be nice for Bill if we
let her go with us sometimes. She's a sport.'

So Bill, to her delight, was often taken in tow by Darrell
and Sally. She thought the world of Darrell. 'One day
I'll repay her for that night,' thought Bill, a hundred times
a week. 'I'll never forget.'

She was very happy now. Thunder was quite well.
Darrell and Sally welcomed her. She was doing well in
class. And Miss Peters was Simply Grand!

Bill was a simple person, straightforward, natural and very
loyal. These things made a great appeal to Miss Peters,
who was much the same. So there grew up a real under-

standing between the form-mistress and Bill, delightful to them both.

'I'm so happy here,' said Bill to Darrell. 'I didn't want to come—but oh, I'm so *glad* I came!'

CHAPTER XXIII

23   A LOVELY END TO THE TERM!

THE term was coming to an end. Darrell as usual was torn in two over her feelings about this. 'I do so love going home—but I do so love being at Malory Towers!' she said to Sally.

'Well, you're lucky to have both worlds,' said Sally. 'So am I. I love being at home—but I love school, too. It's been a good term, hasn't it, Darrell?'

'Yes,' said Darrell. 'I've only had one bitter disappointment—and that was, that after all the practising I've done, and all the extra coaching I got, and the help that Molly gave me—I never played in the third match-team after all.'

'Did they play the match that was cancelled?' asked Sally.

'No. The other school hadn't a free date,' said Darrell. 'We break up next week—so there's no chance now. That's the only thing that has really spoilt the term a bit for me —and you being so late back, of course.'

'Isn't it a gorgeous afternoon?' said Sally, as they strolled out into the courtyard, and looked at the daffodils growing everywhere there, dancing in the March breeze. 'There's half an hour before dinner. What shall we do?'

'Let's go out to the lacrosse field,' said Darrell. 'It

will be lovely there. I feel restless after sitting still so
long. A bit of running and catching will do us good.'

Sally didn't really want to. She was not as good at
games that term as usual, because she had come back so
late. But she saw Darrell's eager face and put aside her
own wishes.

'All right. I'll get the sticks. You go and ask for a
ball,' she said. They met again on the field, and were
soon running and catching and passing.

They were the only ones there. Molly Ronaldson,
passing by, smiled to see Darrell out there again. What
a sticker she was! She really did stick to whatever she
made up her mind to do. Molly liked that kind of thing.

She called to Darrell. 'My goodness, you deserve to
play well, Darrell! Have you heard that we are playing
Barchester after all, next week—you know the match that
was cancelled the half-holiday Thursday? We thought
we wouldn't be able to fix it up again—but Barchester have
just let us know that they can play us next Thursday—the
day before we break up.'

'Oh, really?' said Darrell. 'Molly—any chance of
my being in the reserve three again? Do say yes!'

'Well, last time, apparently, you would have actually
played in the match, as all the reserves were to play,' said
Molly, 'but I heard that you played the fool, you and the
third form, and got the half-holiday forfeited. So you
wouldn't have been able to play after all.'

'Yes, that's true,' said Darrell. 'But I haven't played
the fool since. Put me in the reserve next Thursday,
Molly, please do. Not that I've much hope of playing in
the match this time, because everyone who was ill is all
right again!'

'True,' said Molly. 'Well, I shall be making a new list
of match-team players, and you may be in the reserve or
you may not. I'm making no promises! I'll come and

watch the third and fourth forms playing lacrosse on Monday afternoon. I shall only want a few players from them for the Barchester match, so it's up to you to do your best ! '

' Isn't Molly marvellous ! ' said Darrell to Sally, her face in a glow as Molly walked off.

' Well—I think she's very good as a games captain,' said Sally, who didn't get quite such wild enthusiasms as Darrell got. ' Anyway—you play well on Monday, when Molly's watching, and see if you can get in the reserve again, Darrell.'

So Darrell did. She was nimble and swift, she was deft at catching, unselfish in her passing, and very sure in her attack on goal. Molly was on the field, watching the various games being played there. She walked from one to another, sturdy, deliberate, her sharp eyes noting every good pass and swift rush.

That night the names of the girls in the third match-team were to be put up. The names of the reserve girls would be put below the team-list. Darrell hardly dared to go up to the notice-board and look to see if her name was in the reserve.

Surely it would be ! Surely she had been better than most of the fourth-formers, and certainly far better than any other third-former ! She glanced hopefully but fearfully at the names of the three reserves.

Hers wasn't there ! In real dismay Darrell read down the three reserve names again. No—her name was not there—not even as third reserve, which she had been before ! Molly hadn't thought her good enough to put her in the reserve this time. What a terrible disappointment.

Sally came running up. ' Darrell ! Is your name down ? Are you in the reserve ? '

Darrell shook her head. ' No,' she said. ' Not this time. Oh, Sally—I'm awfully disappointed.'

Sally was too. She slipped her arm through Darrell's. ' Bad luck, old thing. I *am* sorry.'

'Oh well—I'm as bad as Zerelda used to be—imagining I'm good enough at lacrosse to be in the reserve for the Barchester match,' said Darrell, her voice a little shaky. 'Serves me right!'

'It doesn't, it doesn't!' said Sally. 'You *ought* to be at least *first* reserve—yes, you ought, Darrell. You are *awfully* good—super—at lacrosse. And you've practised so hard, too.'

'Don't rub it in,' said Darrell, Sally's eager championship making her feel much worse. They went to the common-room together. Mavis was there with Zerelda, for the first time.

'Hallo, Mavis!' cried Sally, in surprise. 'I thought you weren't coming to join us again till tomorrow. I'm so glad you're back.'

'Welcome home again!' said Darrell, trying to forget her disappointment. 'I'm glad you're all right, Mavis. How do you feel?'

'Grand,' said Mavis, in her changed voice. She no longer had the deep, delightful voice she used to have. It was hoarse and had lost its lovely tone. The girls were used to it by now, but poor Mavis wasn't. She couldn't bear this horrid, creaky voice! But she had made up her mind not to grumble or complain. 'I'm glad to be back, too. Sister was awfully nice to me, and it's cosy over in the san.—but I did miss all the fun and noise of school.'

She coughed. 'Don't talk too much all at once,' said Zerelda. 'You know Sister put me in charge of you—and I've got to deliver you well and healthy up to Matron tonight, before you are allowed to sleep in our dormy again!'

'I'll be all right,' said Mavis. 'Darrell—are you in the reserve? Zerelda said you were sure to be. I'm looking forward to seeing a match again.'

'No. I'm not,' said Darrell, and turned away. Zerelda looked up, surprised and sorry.

'Gee, that's too bad,' she said, and then stopped as Sally frowned at her to stop her saying too much about it. Darrell was feeling it very much. She couldn't understand why Molly had left her out of the reserve this time. It didn't seem fair, after all she had said!

Darrell went out of the room. Sally didn't follow her, knowing that she wanted to be alone and get over her disappointment before she faced the rest of the form.

There came a clatter of feet down the corridor. The door burst open and the rest of the third form poured in. 'I say! Where's Darrell! My goodness, has she seen the notice-board?'

'Yes. She's frightfully disappointed,' said Sally. The beaming third-formers looked immensely surprised.

'Disappointed!' echoed Alicia. 'Why? She ought to be so bucked that she's doing a war-dance round the room!'

Now it was Sally's turn to be surprised. 'But why, you idiot? She's not even been put into the reserve this time!'

'No—she hasn't—because, idiot, she's in the team itself!' cried Alicia.

'Yes. Actually in the *team*!' said Bill, joyfully. 'Isn't it an honour?'

Sally gasped. 'Gracious! Darrell must just have looked at the names of the reserves—and not looked at the names in the *team* at all! How like her!'

'Where *is* she?' demanded Alicia, impatiently.

'Here she is!' yelled Belinda from the door. 'Darrell! Come here!'

Darrell came in, looking rather subdued. She gazed round in surprise at the excited third-formers. 'What's up?' she said.

'*You* are!' cried Irene, slapping her on the back. 'Up on the notice-board, silly! In the TEAM!'

Darrell didn't take it in.   The others all crowded round
her impatiently, talking at the tops of their voices.

' You're in the TEAM !   Don't you understand ? '

' Not in the reserve.   You're PLAYING on Thursday
against Barchester.'

' Look at her—quite dumb.   *Darrell !*   Do you mean to
say you only looked at the names in the reserve and not at
the names in the match-team itself ?   Well, of all the
donkeys ! '

Light suddenly dawned upon Darrell.   She seized Alicia's
wrists joyfully.   ' Alicia !   Do you mean it ?   I'm in the
TEAM !   Golly—I never thought of looking there.'

Then there was so much shouting and congratulating and
rejoicing that Matron came in to see whatever the noise was
about, and to find out how Mavis was standing it.

Mavis was standing it very well.   She was smacking
Darrell on the back and calling out ' Jolly good !   Jolly
good ! ' in a cracked but most determined voice.   Her
face shone with pleasure, just like the faces of the rest.

Matron went out again without being noticed.   She
smiled to herself.   ' All because someone's put into the
team ! ' she thought.   ' Well, well—what a thing it is to be
a schoolgirl ! '

It was a lovely thing to Darrell at that moment.   She
thought she had never been so happy in her life before—
just when she had felt so disappointed and miserable, too !
She was almost in tears when she saw the pleasure and
pride of the others.   ' Why, they must like me an awful
lot ! ' she thought, happily.   ' Oh, I *do* hope I play well on
Thursday.   If only we can beat Barchester !   We haven't
for a whole year.'

She could hardly wait till Thursday came—but it dawned
at last, sunny and clear—the ideal day for a match.   It was
a home match, and as it was the day before breaking up, all
girls who wished to could watch it.   Most of them turned

up to cheer the Barchester girls when they arrived in their coach.   Then they all streamed to the field to find seats on the wooden forms.

Darrell was nervous.   She was cross with herself for this, but she couldn't help it.   Molly came by, and grinned at her.   'Got stage-fright?   Wait till you're on the field— you'll soon forget it!'

Molly was right.   Once on the field, with her lacrosse stick in her hands, dancing about joyfully, all Darrell's nervousness went, and she was eager for the match to begin. She was on the wing.   She glanced at her opponent.   She was a big, sturdy girl.   Oh dear—probably she could run even faster than Darrell!

She certainly could run very fast and she was powerful too, getting the ball from Darrell nearly every time by tackling strongly and swiftly.

'Play up, Darrell!   Play up!' yelled the watching third-formers, every time Darrell got the ball and sped off with it.   'Oh, well passed!   Oh, well caught!   Play UP, Malory Towers!'

Goal to Barchester.   Goal to Malory Towers.   Half-time.   One all.   Slices of sour lemon being brought out on plates.   And here was Molly beside Darrell, talking to her earnestly.

'Darrell!   You're tiring the other girl out nicely.   She's good, but she gets winded more quickly than you do.   Watch your chance, tackle her next time she comes up, get the ball, pass to Catherine, run level, let her pass back to you and then SHOOT!   Do you hear?'

'Yes.   Yes, Molly,' said Darrell, almost swallowing her slice of lemon in her eagerness to take it all in.   'Yes—I think my opponent's tiring.   I can out-run her.   I'll do what you say if I can.   Tell Catherine.'

'I have,' said Molly.   'Now—there's the whistle. You're all doing well.   But I think it will have to be you who does a bit of shooting this half, Darrell. The others allow themselves to be tackled too easily. Good luck.'

Molly went off the field. A chorus went up from the watchers. 'PLAY—UP—Malory TOWERS! PLAY—UP—Malory TOWERS!'

And Malory Towers played up. Darrell and Catherine passed beautifully to one another, and Catherine shot. Two goals to Malory Towers! Then the Barchester team got going again. Second goal to them. Two all. Fifteen minutes to play. 'PLAY—UP—Malory TOWERS!'

Darrell felt the time slipping by. Two goals all—Malory Towers must shoot again before time was up. She took a fine pass, and ran with the ball in her lacrosse net. Her opponent tackled her. Darrell dodged her very neatly and sped down the field.

'Go it, DARRELL! SHOOT! SHOOT!' yelled everyone, but Darrell was too far from goal to do that. Instead, she sent the ball to Catherine, who, alas! muffed the catch, fell over, and let the enemy snatch it up from where it rolled on the ground. Then down the field rushed the Barchester wing, back towards the Malory Towers goal.

But there the goal-keeper stopped it valiantly. Hurrah! Saved again! Up the field came the ball again, and Darrell made a remarkable catch, leaping high in the air.

'Go it, DARRELL!' yelled the onlookers. Darrell ran towards the Barchester goal. Catherine kept level with her, watching carefully for a pass. When she was tackled Darrell passed the ball deftly to Catherine, making a lovely throw. Catherine caught it, but was tackled immediately. Out of the corner of her eye she saw Darrell, watching.

She threw. It was a clumsy throw, but Darrell ran to catch the ball. Once in her net she kept the ball there, dodging cleverly when she was tackled. A great cry came up from the onlookers.

'SHOOT! SHOOT! SHOOT!'

And Darrell shot. She threw the ball with all her might at the goal. The Barchester goal-keeper came out to stop it. The ball struck her pad, then struck the goal-post—and rolled to the back of the net.

'GOAL!' What a cry went up. 'Jolly good, Darrell! Fine shot! Hurrah! Three goals to two!'

Almost immediately the whistle blew for time. The two teams lined up and cheered one another. Darrell was trembling with excitement and joy. She had played in a match—she had shot the winning goal!

'Well played, young Darrell!' said Molly's voice. 'You did well. That was a very fine goal.'

Darrell went off to the big tea provided for the two match-teams, her heart singing. This was a great moment for her. The third-formers all crowded round her, clapping her on the shoulder, praising her, delighted that one of their own form should have shot the winning goal.

Darrell was very tired and very happy that evening. What would her father and mother and her sister Felicity say when she told them all this? Thank goodness she was seeing them tomorrow, and they would know. She could hardly wait to tell them!

All the third-formers shared in Darrell's delight. They cheered her when she came into the common-room, and she stood there blushing and embarrassed.

'Good old Darrell! So modest she didn't even think of looking in the team-list for her own name—and so marvellous that she shoots the winning goal!' cried Irene, and thumped Darrell on the back so hard that she coughed.

The last day came. All the packing was done, except for a few things that the car-girls were bundling into their cars at the last minute. Good-byes were said. Addresses were exchanged and immediately lost. Matron tried to find Belinda who had completely disappeared. Miss Potts tried to find Irene, who also seemed to have disappeared.

There was a tremendous noise and confusion, in the middle
of which seven boys appeared on seven horses in the drive
among the cars !

'Bill ! Good heavens ! Here are all your brothers
again !' yelled Darrell.   But Bill was getting Thunder from
the stables, and was not there.   She appeared a moment
later on her horse, and yelled with delight to see all her
brothers and their horses in the drive.

'You've come to fetch me ! Look at Thunder ! Isn't
he in good condition ? Get up, Thunder ! Oh, he's so
pleased to see you all.'

The train-girls went, and there was a little more peace.
Irene wandered round lamenting that someone had taken
her suit-case.   Gwen went round scowling because nobody
had yet come to fetch her, and she didn't want to be the last.
Belinda stalked her with an open sketch-book and pencil.

'Gwen ! It's my last chance ! Let me sketch that
scowl !'

Darrell laughed.   How like Belinda to do that when her
mother and father were waiting patiently in the car for her
outside !

Zerelda popped up to say good-bye.   How different she
looked now from when she came.   She wore her school
hat for one thing—a thing she had said she would never do !
'Good-bye,' she said.   'See you again next term.   It's
been wunnerful here.   I'm glad I came—and gee ! I'm glad
I'm coming back !'

'Good-bye !' croaked Mavis, waving to everyone as she
climbed into her car.   'See you next term.'

Bill galloped off with her brothers, calling a mad good-bye.
Mam'zelle Dupont watched her go in amazement.   'In
France such a thing could not happen !' she declared.
'That Bill !   I think at home she must let her horse sleep
with her in a corner of her bedroom !'

Darrell giggled.   Belinda came by with a wooden box

of bath salts she had suddenly remembered leaving in the bathroom. She collided with Mam'zelle and the box fell to the floor.

A green powder covered the hall, and a green cloud rose up into the air, with a very strong smell.

'Now, Belinda, I . . .' began Mam'zelle, and then paused with her mouth wide open. She felt frantically about her plump person for her handkerchief. Just as Miss Potts came up with Miss Peters, Mam'zelle sneezed. It was one of her best efforts.

'A—WHOOOOOSH-OOOOOOO!'

'Good gracious!' said Miss Potts, startled. 'I never knew anyone sn . . .'

'A-Whooooooo——' began Mam'zelle again and Miss Potts ran for shelter.

Darrell and Sally giggled helplessly. They remembered the afternoon of the Trick. Darrell suddenly picked up somebody's umbrella and opened it.

'Now sneeze, Mam'zelle!' she cried, holding the umbrella over Miss Potts and Miss Peters. 'I'll protect everyone!'

Darrell's mother, coming up the steps in search of her, was amazed to see this sight. Darrell flung away the umbrella joyfully and sprang at her mother. 'Oh, here you are. I thought you were never coming! Sally, are you ready? Good-bye, Mam'zelle, good-bye, Potty, good-bye, Miss P., good-bye, Matron. See you all next term! This has been a SUPER term!'

'Good-bye!' said Matron. 'Be good.'

'Good-bye,' said Miss Potts and Miss Peters together. 'Remember your holiday reading!'

'A-Whoooosh-ooooo!' said Mam'zelle, and ran forward to wave. Gwen just saved her from falling over the open umbrella.

The car drove off. Darrell waved frantically till they

were out of the front gates. Then she leaned back contentedly and began.

'Mother! Daddy! What DO you think? I played in the third match-team yesterday against Barchester School—and I shot the winning goal. Mother, I . . .'

Sally listened contentedly. Good old Darrell! She had had a lovely term and enjoyed it. She was sorry it was over. But there would be the summer term—and the autumn term—and the winter term—oh, terms and terms and terms!

'Here's the last glimpse of Malory Towers, Darrell,' said Sally, suddenly. Darrell opened the window and leaned out.

'I'll soon be back, Malory Towers!' she called 'Goodbye for a little while. I'll soon be back!'

UPPER FOURTH AT MALORY TOWERS

' Let's slip off by ourselves,' said June

UPPER FOURTH
AT MALORY TOWERS

by

ENID BLYTON

ILLUSTRATED BY
JENNY CHAPPLE

CONTENTS

1 DARRELL GOES BACK TO SCHOOL WITH FELICITY

DARRELL RIVERS was very excited. It was the day to return to Malory Towers, her boarding-school—and this time she was taking her young sister Felicity with her.

Felicity stood on the front steps beside her fifteen-year old sister, dressed in the same brown and orange uniform, feeling excited, too. She was almost thirteen, and should have gone to Malory Towers two terms before, but she had been ill and had to stay at home.

Now it was the summer term, and she was to go with Darrell at last. She had heard so much about her sister's school—the fun they had there, the classrooms overlooking the sea, the four towers in which the two hundred and fifty girls slept, the great swimming-pool hollowed out of the rocks on the shore . . . there was no end to the things that Darrell had told her.

'It's a good thing we're going by train this time, not by car,' said Darrell. 'You'll travel down with the girls then, and get to know some of them. Sally's going by train, too.'

Sally was Darrell's best friend, and had been ever since her first term at Malory Towers almost four years ago.

'I hope I get a friend like Sally,' said Felicity, nervously. 'I'm shyer than you, Darrell. I'm sure I shall never pluck up enough courage to speak to anyone! And if Miss Potts gets cross with me I shall sink through the floor!'

Miss Potts was the first-form mistress, and also the house mistress for North Tower, the tower to which Darrell belonged, and to which her young sister would go, too.

'Oh, you needn't be afraid of Potty,' said Darrell, with a laugh, quite forgetting how scared *she* had been of her when she was in the first form. 'Dear old Potty—she's a good sort.'

Their father's car drew up at the front door, and the two girls ran down the steps. Mr. Rivers looked at them and smiled.

'*Both* off this time!' he said. 'Well, I remember quite well Darrell going off alone for the first time almost four years ago. She was twelve then—now you're fifteen, aren't you, Darrell!'

'Yes,' said Darrell, getting into the car with Felicity. 'And I remember you saying to me, "You'll get a lot out of Malory Towers—see that you put a lot back!" '

'Daddy's said that to me, too,' said Felicity. 'I'm jolly lucky to have an older sister to show me round—though honestly I feel as if I know every corner of Malory Towers already.'

'Now, where's Mother?' said her father, and he hooted the horn. 'Really, this is a dreadful family to collect. If your mother appears in good time, one of you girls is missing, and if you girls are here, your mother is not! We shall miss the train if we don't look out!'

Usually they went all the way down to Cornwall to Malory Towers by car, but this time it was impossible, so Mr. Rivers was driving them up to London and seeing them off in the school-train. Felicity had sometimes been to see her sister off by train, and had felt scared of all the girls chattering and laughing on the platform—now this time she was actually going to be one of them! She hugged her tennis-racket to her and thought joyfully of the coming term.

Mrs. Rivers came running down the steps, looking very pretty in a simple grey suit with a little blue blouse. Darrell and Felicity looked at her proudly. Parents mattered a lot when you were at boarding-school! Everyone wanted to be proud of the way their fathers and mothers looked and spoke and behaved. It was dreadful if a mother came in a silly hat, or if a father came looking very untidy.

'My dear, we were *just* going without you,' said Mr. Rivers. 'Now—have we really got everything? Last time we got five miles on the way and then you said you'd forgotten Darrell's night-case.'

'Yes, we've got everything, Daddy,' said Darrell. 'I've checked every single thing—night-cases, with brush-and-comb, tooth-brush and paste, night-things, health certificate, everything! Tennis-rackets to carry, and bowler hats for riding! We can't pack those, they're too awkward.'

Felicity glanced round to see if her new bowler hat was there, too. She felt very proud of it. She had only had a jockey-cap before.

They set off in the car to drive to London. Felicity's heart sank a little as her home disappeared from view. Three whole months before she would see it again! Then she cheered up as Darrell began chatting about the girls.

'I hope Bill will arrive with all her seven brothers on horseback,' she said. 'It's such a sight to see them all galloping up the school drive. Bill was supposed to come in her parents' car the first term she came, but she slipped off, got her horse, Thunder, and came with all her brothers on their horses, too!'

'Bill's real name is Wilhemina, isn't it?' said Felicity, remembering. 'Do even the mistresses call her Bill?'

'Some of them,' said Darrell. 'Not the Head, of course. And Miss Williams, our fourth-form mistress doesn't either. She's a bit starchy—very prim and proper, but I like her now. I didn't at first.'

It didn't seem long before they were all on the station platform, finding their way between hosts of excited girls to a North Tower carriage. Felicity felt shy and nervous. Oh, dear—so many girls, and they all knew one another, and she didn't know anyone. Oh, yes, she did—there was Sally, Darrell's friend, coming towards her, smiling.

'Hallo, Darrell, hallo, Felicity—so you're really coming to Malory Towers at last. Jolly good! Wish I was coming for the first time too, so that I would have years and years of it in front of me, like you. You don't know how lucky you are!'

'I remember someone saying that to *me* on my first day,' said Darrell. 'I was twelve then—now I'm going on for sixteen. Gosh, how old!'

'Yes—and don't forget we'll feel jolly old before this term's out!' said a familiar voice behind Darrell. 'We've all got to work for School Certificate! My hair will be quite grey by the end of term!'

'Hallo, Alicia!' said Darrell, warmly. 'Did you have good hols? Look, this is my young sister, Felicity. She's a new girl this term.'

'Is she really?' said Alicia. 'Well, I must find my cousin then. She's a new girl this term, too. Now where is she? I've lost her twice already!'

She disappeared, and Sally and Darrell laughed. They were sure that Alicia wouldn't bother much about any new-girl cousin! However, she appeared again almost at once bringing with her a twelve-year-old girl, very like her.

'This is June,' she said. 'You might as well make friends with Felicity, June, because you'll see plenty of her this term and for a good many years to come! Though whether Felicity will *want* to see much of you after she knows you well is very doubtful!'

Darrell looked at Alicia to see whether she meant this or not. You never knew with sharp-tongued Alicia! June looked all right, and had a very determined chin and mouth. A bit domineering, Darrell thought—but being in the bottom form of the school didn't give you much chance for that kind of thing. The older girls just sat on you hard if you didn't keep your place.

'Look!' said Alicia, nudging Darrell and Sally. 'There's Gwendoline Mary—come by train instead of car—and staging the same old scene as ever!'

Felicity and June turned to see. They saw a fair-haired girl with large, pale blue eyes, saying good-bye to her mother and her old governess. It was a very sentimental farewell, and a lot of sniffing was going on.

'Gwendoline always does that,' said Alicia in disgust. 'At her age, too! You can forgive a first-former going away from home for the first time—but a fifteen-year-old, no!'

'Well, it doesn't last long,' said Sally. 'Gwendoline won't even bother to remember to wave to her mother, I'm sure, once she gets into the carriage.'

Sally's mother was talking to Darrell's parents. There were no tears or protestations there! Darrell was thankful that her mother and father were so sensible. She looked at Felicity, and was pleased to see her young sister looking interested and happy.

More girls came up and surrounded Darrell and the others. 'Hallo! Had good hols? I say, is this your young sister? Has she got a temper like yours, Darrell?'

This was from Irene, harum-scarum as usual, her night-case coming undone, and her coat lacking a button already.

'Well—Felicity *has* got a temper,' said Darrell, with a laugh. 'All our family have. I don't expect Felicity will show hers much though. She'll be too shy her first term.'

'I don't know about that!' said Sally, slyly. 'I seem to remember *you* going off the deep end properly in your first term, Darrell! Who sent me flying to the ground that first-half-term—and who gave dear Gwendoline some very hearty slaps in the swimming-pool?'

'Oh, dear—yes, I was dreadful,' said Darrell, and she blushed. 'Really awful. I'm sure Felicity will never do anything like that.'

'My cousin's got a bit of a temper, too,' said Alicia, with

a grin. 'She's only got brothers, and you should hear them shout and yell at one another when they disagree.'

'Here's Miss Potts,' said Sally, as the first-form mistress came up with a list in her hand. 'Hallo, Miss Potts, have you collected everyone?'

'Yes, I think so,' said Miss Potts, 'except Irene. Oh, there you are, Irene. I suppose it didn't occur to you to come and report your arrival to me? Thank goodness Belinda is going by car. That's one less scatterbrain to see to. Now, you'd better get into your carriages. There are only four more minutes to go.'

There was a scramble into the carriages. Sally and Darrell pulled Felicity into theirs. 'The new girls are supposed to go with Potty in her carriage,' said Darrell, 'but we'll let you come in ours. Good-bye, Mother, good-bye, Daddy! We'll write on Sunday and tell you all the news.'

'Good-bye!' said Felicity, in rather a small voice. 'Thanks for lovely hols.'

'Thank goodness we haven't got Gwendoline in our carriage,' said Alicia. 'We are at least spared the history of all her uninteresting family, and what happened to them last hols. Even her dogs are uninteresting!'

Everyone laughed. The guard blew his whistle. Doors slammed, and the train moved off slowly. Parents and girls waved madly. Darrell sank back into her seat.

'Off to Malory Towers again!' she said, joyfully. 'Good old Malory Towers!'

THE journey was a very long one, but the train arrived at the station for Malory Towers at last. Out poured the girls, complete with night-cases and rackets, and rushed to find good seats in the school coaches that took the train-girls on the last part of their journey.

Felicity was tired and excited. Darrell, didn't seem in the least tired, but she was certainly excited. 'Now we shall see the school, and all the rest of the girls,' she said to Felicity, happily. 'Watch for the first glimpse of it when I tell you.'

And so Felicity had the same first glimpse that Darrell had had four years back. She saw a large castle-like building of grey stone rising high on a hill. Beyond was the deep blue Cornish sea, but that was now hidden by the cliff on which Malory Towers stood. Four towers stood at the corners of the building, and Felicity's eyes brightened as she thought of sleeping in one of the towers. She would be in North Tower with Darrell—and it had the best view of the sea! She was very lucky.

'It's lovely,' said Felicity to Darrell, and Darrell was pleased. It was going to be nice to have her sister at school with her. She felt sure that Felicity would be a great success.

Girls who had already arrived by car stood about the drive ready to welcome the train-girls. There were shrieks and squeals of delight as the coaches drove up to the magnificent front entrance, and swarms of girls ran to help down their friends.

'Hallo, Belinda!' shouted Irene, climbing down and leaving behind her night-case. 'Done any decent sketching?'

'Darrell!' called a shy-looking fifteen-year-old. 'Sally! Alicia!'

'Hallo, Mary-Lou! Anyone put a spider down your neck these hols?' cried Alicia. 'Seen Betty?'

Betty was Alicia's friend, as witty as she was, and as mischievous. She came up and banged Alicia on the back.

'Here I am! You're jolly late—the train must have been even later than usual.'

'There's Mavis,' cried Sally. 'And Daphne—and I say, hallo there, Jean. Seen Bill anywhere?'

'Yes. She came on Thunder as usual and she's in the stable with him,' said Jean, the quiet, shrewd Scots girl, who was now no longer in the same form as Darrell, but was going up. 'She came with the groom, because all her brothers went back to school before we did this term. A very tame arrival!'

Felicity stood unheeded in the general rush and excitement. She hoped that Darrell wouldn't entirely forget her. Alicia had completely forgotten about her cousin June. That youngster now came up to Felicity and grinned. 'Our elders are making a fine noise, aren't they?' she said. 'We're small fry to them. Let's slip off by ourselves, shall we, and make them look for us when they deign to remember we're here?'

'Oh, no,' said Felicity, but June pulled her arm and dragged her away. 'Yes, come on. I know we're supposed to go to Matron and give in our health certificate and our term's pocket-money. We'll go and find her on our own.'

'But Darrell won't like . . .' began Felicity, as she was led firmly away by June.

So it was that when Darrell looked round for her young sister, she was nowhere to be seen!

'Where's Felicity?' she said. 'Blow! What's happened to her? I know how awful you feel when you're new, and I wanted to take her under my wing for a bit. Where in the world has she gone?'

'Don't worry,' said Alicia, unfeelingly. 'I'm not bothering about young June. She can look after herself all right, if I

know anything about that young lady. She's got all the cheek
in the world!'

'Well, but Felicity hasn't,' said Darrell. 'Dash it, where
has she gone? She was here a minute ago.'

'Anyone seen my night-case?' came Irene's voice in a
mournful wail.

Nobody had. 'You must have left it in your coach seat,'
suggested Darrell, knowing Irene's scatter-brain ways. Irene
darted off after the coaches, which were now making their
way slowly down the drive. 'Hie, hie!' she yelled. 'Wait a
bit!'

'What *is* Irene doing?' said Miss Potts, crossly. 'Irene, come
back and stop shouting.'

But Irene had stopped a coach and was climbing up into
the one she had ridden in to the school. Miss Potts gaped.
Did Irene think she was going home again? She did such
mad things that anything was likely with Irene.

But Irene found her night-case, waved it wildly in the air
to show the others she had found it, and climbed down again
to the drive. She ran back, grinning.

'Got it!' she said, and stood it firmly down on the ground
—too firmly, because it at once burst open and everything
fell out.

'Oh, *Irene*—why does every case you possess always do
that?' said Darrell, helping her to pick everything up.

'I can't imagine,' said Irene, stuffing everything in
higgledy-piggledy. 'I have a bad effect on them, I suppose.
Come on, let's go and find Matron.'

'I haven't found Felicity yet,' said Darrell, beginning to
look worried. 'She can't have gone off with anyone because
she doesn't *know* anyone.'

'Well, anyhow, let's go to Matron and hand in our health
certificates and money, and ask if she's seen Felicity,' said
Sally. 'The drive's pretty well empty now—she's obviously
not here.'

So they trailed off to Matron, who had been dealing most efficiently with dozens of girls, health certificates and pocket-money for an hour or more. Darrell was pleased to see her—kindly, bustling, starched and competent.

'Hallo, Darrell! Well, Alicia, turned up again like a bad penny, I see!'

'Mother says you always used to say that to *her* when she came back each term,' said Alicia, with a grin.

'Yes. She was a bad lot,' said Matron, smiling. 'Not nearly as bad as you, though, Alicia. We'll have to have a talk about "How to Darn" this term, by the way. Don't forget. Aha, Irene, there you are at last. Got your health certificate?'

It was a standing joke that Irene's health certificate always got lost if Irene was given it to bring to Matron. But the last few terms Irene's mother had sent the certificate by post, so it had always arrived safely on the morning of the day that school began.

Irene looked alarmed. Then she smiled. 'You're pulling my leg, Matron,' she said. 'It's come by post as usual.'

'But it hasn't,' said Matron. 'That's the whole point. Plenty of post for me this morning—but no health certificate. It's probably in your night-case, Irene. Go and unpack it and look.'

Darrell was looking round for Felicity, but still she couldn't see her. She really felt very worried and rather cross. Why hadn't Felicity done as she was told, and kept close by her, so that she couldn't lose her in the crowd of girls?

'Matron,' she said, 'you haven't by any chance seen my little sister, have you?'

'Yes,' said Matron. 'She was here a few minutes ago, and handed in her health certificate. She said you had her money. Nice to have her here, Darrell.'

Darrell was astonished. Felicity had actually gone to Matron and given in her own certificate without waiting to be taken! It didn't seem like Felicity at all—she was so shy.

'Where's she gone now?' she wondered out loud.

'She's gone to have a look at her dormy,' said Matron, and turned to deal with Belinda, who seemed to have lost all her money and was turning out her pockets in despair. 'Belinda! I vow and declare that I'll ask Miss Grayling to put you and Irene into another Tower next term. If I have to deal with you two much more I shall go raving mad. Sally, go and see if Irene has found her health certificate yet.'

Sally went off to find Irene in the dormy, and Darrell went off to find Felicity. Sally found Irene sitting mournfully on her bed, the contents of her night-case strewn on the eiderdown—but there was no health certificate there.

'Oh, Irene—you really are a mutt,' said Sally, rummaging round and shaking out the legs of Irene's pyjamas just in case she had put the precious piece of paper there. 'I thought your mother always posted the certificate now.'

'She *does*,' groaned Irene. 'She never fails. She's marvellous like that.'

'Well, all I can say is that she must have given it to *you* to post this time!' said Sally. 'And you must have forgotten.'

A sudden light spread over Irene's humorous face. She slapped Sally on the back. 'Sally, you've got it!' she said. 'That's just what happened! Mother *did* give it to me to post, and I forgot.'

'Well, where did you put it? Left it on your bedroom table at home, I suppose?' said Sally, half-impatient.

'No. I didn't,' said Irene, triumphantly. 'I put it into the lining of my hat, so that I shouldn't lose it on the way to the post—but when I got to the post-office, I just bought some stamps and walked home again. So the certificate should be in my hat-lining still. In fact, I'm sure it is because now I come to think of it, my hat felt jolly uncomfortable all day long '

It took some time to find Irene's hat, which had rolled under the next bed—but to Irene's joy the envelope with the certificate in was actually still under the lining. She shot off to Matron joyfully with it.

'I put it in my hat to remember to post it,' she explained, 'but I forgot, so it came with me today still in my hat.'

Matron didn't understand a word of this, but dismissed it all as part of Irene's usual irresponsibility, and thankfully took the certificate before Irene could possibly lose it again.

'Did Darrell find her young sister?' she asked Irene.

But Irene didn't know. 'I'll go and find out,' she said, and wandered off again.

Darrell *had* found Felicity. She had found her in the dormy of the first form, with June and several others. June was talking away to everyone as if she was a third-termer, and Felicity was standing by shyly, listening.

'Felicity!' said Darrell, going up to her. 'Why didn't you wait for me? Whatever made you go and find Matron by yourself? You knew I was going!'

'Oh, *I* took her,' said June. 'I thought she might as well come with me. We're both new. I knew Alicia wouldn't bother herself with me, and I didn't think you'd want to bother yourself with Felicity. We've given in our certificates, but you've got to give in Felicity's money.'

'I know that,' said Darrell, very much on her dignity. What cheek of this new first-former to talk to her like that! She turned to Felicity.

'I do think you might have waited,' she said. 'I wanted to show you your dormy and everything.'

3   THE FIRST EVENING

DARRELL went back to her own dormy to unpack her
night-things, feeling puzzled and cross. She had so much
looked forward to taking Felicity round and showing her
her dormy, her bed and every single thing. How *could* her
young sister have gone off with June and not waited for her?

'Did you find Felicity?' asked Alicia.

'Yes,' said Darrell, shortly. 'She'd gone off with that
cousin of yours—what's her name—June. It struck me as
rather extraordinary. You'd think these youngsters would
wait for us to take them round a bit. I know I'd have been
glad to have a sister or a cousin here, the first term *I* came.'

'Oh, June can stand on her own feet very well,' said Alicia.
'She's a hard and determined little monkey. She'll always
find things out for herself—and as for taking her under my
wing, I wouldn't dream of putting anyone so prickly and
uncomfortable there! Wait till you hear her argue! She can
talk the hind leg off a donkey.'

'I don't like the sound of her much,' said Darrell, hoping
that June wouldn't take Felicity under *her* wing. Surely
Felicity wouldn't like anyone like June!

'No. She's a bit brazen,' said Alicia. 'We all are! Fault of
my family, you know.'

Darrell looked at Alicia. She didn't sound as if she minded
it being a fault—in fact she spoke rather as if she were proud
of it. Certainly Alicia was sharp-tongued and hard, though
her years at Malory Towers had done a great deal to soften
her. The trouble was that Alicia's brains and health were too
good! She could always beat anyone else if she wanted to,

without any effort at all—and Darrell didn't think she had ever had even a chilblain or a headache in her life. So she was always very scornful of illness or weakness in any form, as well as contemptuous of stupidity.

Darrell determined to see as much of Felicity as she could. She wasn't going to have her taken in tow by any brazen cousin of Alicia's. Felicity was young and shy, and more easily led than Darrell. Darrell felt quite fiercely protective towards her, as she thought of the cheeky, determined young June.

They all unpacked their night-cases and set out their things for the night. Their trunks, most of them sent on in advance, would not be unpacked till the next day. Darrell looked round her dormy, glad to be back.

It was a nice dormy, with a lovely view of the sea, which was as deep blue as a delphinium that evening. Far away the girls could hear the faint plash-plash of waves on the rocks. Darrell thought joyfully of the lovely swimming-pool, and her heart lifted in delight at the thought of the summer term stretching before her—nicest term in the year!

The beds stood in a row along the dormy, each with its own coloured eiderdown. At the ends of the dormy were hot and cold water taps and basins.

Irene was splashing in one basin, removing the dust of the journey. She always arrived dirtier than anyone else. No one would ever guess that the scatter-brain was a perfect genius at music and maths, and quite good at her other lessons too! Everyone liked Irene, and everyone laughed at her.

She was humming a tune now as she washed. 'Tumty-tooty-tumpty-tooty, ta, ta, ta!'

'Oh, Irene—don't say we're going to have that tune for weeks,' groaned Gwendoline, who always complained that Irene's continual humming and singing got on her nerves.

Irene took no notice at all, which maddened Gwendoline, who loved to be in the limelight if she possibly could.

'*Irene*,' she began, but at that moment the door opened and in came two new girls, ushered by Matron.

'Girls—here are the Batten twins,' she said in her genial voice. 'Connie—and Ruth. They are fourth-formers and will be in this dormy. Look after them, Sally and Darrell, will you?'

The girls stood up to look at the twins. Their first thought was—how unalike for twins!

Connie was bigger, fatter, sturdier and bolder-looking than Ruth, who was a good deal smaller, and rather shy-looking. Connie smiled broadly and nodded to everyone. Ruth hardly raised her head to look round, and as soon as she could she stood a little way behind her sister.

'Hallo, twins!' said Alicia. 'Welcome to the best dormy in the school! Those must be your beds up there—the two empty ones together.'

'Got your night-cases?' said Darrell. 'Good. Well, if you'd like to unpack them now, you can. Supper will be ready soon. The bell will go any minute.'

'Hope it's good,' said Connie, with a comradely grin. 'I'm frightfully hungry. It's ages since we had tea.'

'Yes—we get a wizard supper the first evening,' said Sally. 'I can smell it now!'

Connie and Ruth put their noses in the air and sniffed hungrily.

'The Bisto twins!' said Alicia, hitting the nail right on the head as usual. Everyone laughed.

'Come on,' said Connie to Ruth. 'Let's hurry. I've got the keys. Here they are.'

She undid both bags and dragged out everything quickly. Ruth picked up a few things and looked round rather help-lessly.

'Here. These must be our drawers, next to our beds,' said Connie, and began to put away all the things most efficiently. She took the washing-things to the basin and called Ruth.

'Come on, Ruth. We'd better wash. I'm filthy!' Ruth went

to join her, and just as they were towelling themselves dry, the supper-bell went. There was a loud chorus of joy.

'Hurrah! I hope there's a smashing supper. I could do with roast duck, green peas, new potatoes, treacle pudding and lots of cheese,' said Belinda, making everyone's mouth water.

'What a hope!' said Darrell.

But all the same there was a most delicious supper that first night—cold ham and tomatoes, great bowls of salad, potatoes roasted in their jackets, cold apple pie and cream, and biscuits and butter for those who wanted it. Big jugs of icy-cold lemonade stood along the table.

'My word!' said Connie to Ruth. 'If this is the kind of food we get here, we'll be lucky! Much better than the other school we went to!'

'I hate to undeceive you,' said Alicia, 'but I feel I *must* warn you that first-night and last-night suppers are the *only* good ones you'll get in any term. We're supposed to be jolly hungry after our long journeys to Cornwall—hence this spread. Tomorrow night, twins, you'll have bread and dripping and cocoa.'

As usual Alicia was exaggerating, and the twins looked rather alarmed. Darrell looked round for Felicity. Where was she? She couldn't have her at the Upper Fourth table, of course, but she hoped she would be near enough to say a word to.

She was too far away to speak to—and she was next to that nasty little June! June was talking to her animatedly, and Felicity was listening, enthralled.

Alicia saw Darrell looking across at Felicity and June. 'They've soon settled in!' she said to Darrell. 'Look at young Felicity listening to June. You should hear the tales June can tell of her family! They're all madcaps, like mine.'

Darrell remembered how interesting and amusing Alicia could be when she produced one of her endless yarns about her happy-go-lucky, mischievous family. She supposed that

June was the same—but all the same she felt rather hurt that Felicity should apparently need her so little.

'Well, if she thinks she can get on by herself, all right!' thought Darrell. 'I suppose it's best for her really—though I can't help feeling a bit disappointed. I suppose that horrid little June will find out everything she needs to know and show Felicity the swimming-pool, the gardens, the stables, and all the things I'd planned to show her.'

Felicity badly wanted to go to Darrell after supper and ask her a few things, but as soon as she said she was going, June pulled her back.

'You mustn't!' said June. 'Don't you know how the older ones hate having young sisters and cousins tagging after them? Everyone will be bored with us if we go tailing after Alicia and Darrell. In fact, Alicia told me I'd jolly well better look after myself, because first-formers were such small fry we weren't even worth taking notice of!'

'How horrid of her,' said Felicity. 'Darrell's not like that.'

'They all are, the big ones,' said June in a grown-up voice. 'And why *should* they be bothered with us? We've got to learn to stand on our own feet, haven't we? No—you wait till your sister comes over to you. If she doesn't, you'll know she doesn't want to be bothered—and if she does, well don't make her feel you're dependent on her and want taking under her wing. She'll respect you much more if you stand on your own feet. She looks as if she stood on her own all right!'

'She does,' said Felicity. 'Yes, perhaps you're right, June. I've often heard Darrell speak scornfully of people who can't stand on their own feet, or make up their own minds. After all—most new girls haven't got sisters to see to them. I suppose I shouldn't expect mine to nurse me, just because I've come to a new school.'

June looked at her so approvingly that Felicity couldn't help feeling pleased. 'I'm glad you're not a softy,' said June.

'I was afraid you might be. Hallo—here comes Darrell after all. Now, don't weep on her shoulder.'

'As if I should!' said Felicity, indignantly. She smiled at Darrell as she came over.

'Hallo, Felicity. Getting on all right?' said Darrell, kindly. 'Want any help or advice with anything?'

'Thanks awfully, Darrell—but I'm getting on fine,' said Felicity, wishing all the same that she might ask Darrell a few things.

'Like to come and see the swimming-pool?' said Darrell. 'We might just have time.'

Darrell had forgotten that the first-formers had to go to bed almost immediately after supper on the first night. But June knew it. She answered for Felicity.

'We've got to go to bed, so Felicity won't be able to see it tonight,' she said, coolly. 'We planned to go down tomorrow before breakfast. The tide will be in then. I've asked.'

'I was speaking to Felicity, not to you,' said Darrell, in the haughty tones of a fourth-former. 'Don't get too big for your boots, June, or you'll be sat on.' She turned to Felicity and spoke rather coldly.

'Well, I'm glad you're settling down, Felicity. Sorry you're not in my dormy, but only fourth-formers are there, of course.'

A bell rang loudly. 'Our bedtime bell,' said June, who appeared to know everything. 'We'd better go. I'll look after Felicity for you, Darrell.'

And with that the irrepressible June linked her arm in Felicity's and dragged her off. Darrell was boiling with rage. She gazed angrily after the two girls, and was only slightly mollified when Felicity turned round and gave her a sweet and rather apologetic smile.

'The brazen cheek of that little pest of a June!' thought Darrell. 'I've never wanted to slap anyone so much in my life.'

4   ALL TOGETHER AGAIN

GOING to bed on the first night was always fun, especially in the summer term, because then the windows were wide open, daylight was still bright, and the view was glorious.

It was lovely to be with so many girls again too, to discuss the holidays, and to wonder what the term would bring forth.

'School Cert. to be taken this term,' groaned Daphne. 'How simply horrible. I've been coached for it all the hols, but I don't feel I know much even now.'

'Miss Williams will keep our noses to the grindstone this term,' said Alicia, dolefully.

'Well, *you* don't need to mind,' said Bill. She had spoken very little so far, and the others had left her alone. They knew she got, not homesick, but 'horse-sick' as she called it, the first night or two back at school. She was passionately attached to all the horses owned by her parents and her seven brothers, and missed them terribly at first.

Alicia looked at her. 'Why don't I need to mind?' she said. 'I mind just as much as you do!'

'Well, I mean you don't really need to work, Alicia,' said Bill. 'You seem to learn things without bothering. I've been coached in the hols, too, and it was an awful nuisance just when I was wanting to ride with my brothers. I jolly well had to work, though. I bet *you* weren't coached in the hols.'

'Mavis, are *you* going in for School Cert.?' asked Darrell. Mavis had been very ill the year before, and had lost her voice. It had been a magnificent voice, but her illness had ruined it. She had always said she was going to be an opera singer, but nobody ever heard her mention it now. In fact, most of the girls had even forgotten that Mavis had had a wonderful voice.

'I'm going in all right,' said Mavis. 'But I shan't get through! I feel like a jelly when I think of it. By the way— did you know my voice is getting right again?'

There was a pause whilst the girls remembered Mavis's lost voice. 'Gosh! Is it really?' said Sally. 'Good for you, Mavis! Fancy being able to sing again.'

'I mayn't sing much,' said Mavis. 'But I shall know this term, I expect, if my voice will ever be worth training again.'

'Good luck to you, Mavis,' said Darrell. She remembered that when Mavis had had her wonderful voice they had all thought the girl was a Voice and nothing else at all—just a little nobody without an ounce of character. But now Mavis had plenty of character, and it was quite difficult to remember her Voice.

'I wonder if she'll go back to being a Voice and nothing else,' thought Darrell. 'No—I don't think she will. She deserves to get her voice back again. She's never complained about it, or pitied herself.'

'I say!' said Mary-Lou's voice, 'who's this bed for, at my end of the room? There are nobody's things here.'

The girls counted themselves and then the beds. 'Yes— that bed's over,' said Darrell. 'Well, it wouldn't have been put up if it hadn't been going to be used. There must be another new girl coming.'

'We'll ask tomorrow,' said Alicia, yawning. 'How are you getting on, twins? All right?'

The two new girls answered politely. 'Fine, thank you.' They had washed, cleaned their teeth, brushed their hair, and were already in bed. Darrell had been amused to see that Connie had looked after Ruth as if she had been a younger sister, turning down her bed for her, and even brushing her hair!

She looked at them as they lay in bed, their faces turned

sleepily towards her. Connie's face was plump and round,
and her thick hair was quite straight. She had a bold look
about her—'sort of pushful' thought Darrell. The other twin,
Ruth, had a small heart-shaped face, and her hair, corn-
coloured as Connie's, was wavy.

'Good night,' said Darrell, and grinned. They grinned
back. Darrell thought she was going to like them. She wished
they had been absolutely alike though—that would have
been fun! But they were really very unalike indeed.

One by one the girls got yawning into bed and snuggled
down. Most of them threw their eiderdowns off, because the
May night was warm. Gwendoline kept hers on. She always
liked heaps of coverings, and nobody had ever persuaded
her to go without her quilt in the summer.

Miss Potts looked in. Some of the girls were already
asleep. 'No more talking,' said Miss Potts, softly. A few
grunts were made in reply. Nobody wanted to talk now.

Darrell wondered suddenly if Felicity was all right. She
hoped she wasn't homesick. She wouldn't have time to be if
June was in the next bed, talking away! What an unpleasant
child! thought Darrell. And the cheek she had! It was past
believing.

When the bell rang for getting up the next morning, there
was a chorus of groans and moans. Nobody stirred out of
bed.

'Well—we *must* get up!' said Darrell at last. 'Come on,
everybody! Gracious, look at Gwendoline—still fast asleep!'

Darrell winked at Sally. Gwendoline was not fast asleep,
but she meant to have a few more minutes' snooze.

'She'll be late,' said Sally. 'Can't let her get into trouble
her very first morning. Better squeeze a cold sponge over her,
Darrell!'

This remark, made regularly about twenty times every
term, always had the desired effect. Gwendoline opened her
eyes indignantly, and sat up. 'Don't you dare to squeeze that

sponge over me,' she began angrily. 'This beastly getting up early! Why, at home '. . .'

'Why, at home "We don't get up till eight o'clock," ' chanted some of the girls, and laughed. They knew Gwendoline Mary's complaints by heart now.

'Did your old governess make her darling's bed for her?' asked Alicia. 'Did she tie her bib on her in the morning? Did she feed her sweet Gwendoline Mary out of a silver spoon?'

Gwendoline had had to put up with Alicia's malicious teasing for many terms now, but she had never got used to it. The easy tears came to her eyes, and she turned her head away.

'Shut up, Alicia,' said Darrell. 'Don't start on her too soon!'

Alicia nudged Sally, and nodded towards the twins. Connie was making Ruth's bed for her!

'I can do that,' protested Ruth, but Connie pushed her aside. 'I've time, Ruth. You're slow at things like this. I always did it for you at our other school, and I can go on doing it here.' She looked round at the others, and saw them watching her.

'Any objection?' she asked, rather belligerently.

'Dear me no,' said Alicia in her smooth voice. 'You can do mine for me, as well, if you like! I'm slow at things like that, too!'

Connie didn't think this remark was worth answering. She went on making Ruth's bed. Ruth was standing by, looking rather helpless.

'What school did you come from?' asked Darrell, speaking to Ruth. But before the girl could answer, Connie had replied.

'We went to Abbey School, in Yorkshire. It was nice—but not as nice as this one's going to be!'

That pleased the fourth-formers. 'Did you play hockey or

' Don't you dare squeeze that sponge over me! '

lacrosse at your other school?' asked Sally, addressing her question to Ruth.

'Hockey,' said Connie, answering again. 'I liked hockey—but I want to play lacrosse, too.'

'Will *you* like lacrosse, do you think?' asked Sally, addressing her question once more to Ruth, wondering if she had a tongue.

And once again Connie answered: 'Oh, Ruth always likes what *I* like! She'll love lacrosse!'

Sally was just about to ask if Ruth ever said a word for herself, when the breakfast-bell rang. The girls hastily looked round the dormy to see if any clothes had been left about, and Alicia hurriedly pulled her quilt straight. Gwendoline was last as usual, moaning about a lost hair-grip. But then Gwen always had a moan! Nobody took much notice of that!

Darrell looked anxiously for Felicity as the girls filed into the big dining-room, all the North Tower girls together. South Tower girls fed in the South Tower, East in the East and so on. Each tower was like a separate boarding-house, with its own common-rooms, dining-rooms and dormies. The classrooms were in the long buildings that joined tower to tower, and so were such special rooms as the lab., the art-room and the sewing-room. The magnificent gym was there, too.

Felicity came in, looking neat and tidy. Miss Potts, seeing her come in, thought how very like she was to Darrell four years ago, when she also had come timidly into the dining-room for her first breakfast.

In front of Felicity was June, looking as if she was at least a third-termer, instead of a new girl on her first morning. She looked about chirpily, nodded at Alicia, who did her best not to see, grinned at Darrell, who stared stonily back, and spoke amiably to Mam'zelle Dupont, who was at the head of the first-form table. The second form were also there, and Darrell and Alicia had the satisfaction of seeing two second-formers push June roughly back when she attempted to sit somewhere near the head of the table.

But nothing daunted June. She merely sat down somewhere else, and said something to Felicity, who grinned uneasily. 'Something cheeky, I bet,' thought Darrell to herself. 'Well, her form will put her in her place pretty soon—and she'll come up against the second form, too. There are some tough kids in the second—they won't stand much nonsense from a pest like June!'

Felicity smiled at Darrell, who smiled back warmly, forgetting for the moment that Felicity had probably gone to see the swimming-pool before breakfast without her. She hoped her little sister would do well in the class tests that day and prove that she was up to standard.

Sally suddenly remembered the empty bed in her dormy, and she spoke to Miss Potts.

'Miss Potts! There's an extra bed in our dormy. Do you know whose it is? We're all back.'

'Oh, yes,' said Miss Potts. 'Let me see—there's one more new girl coming today—what's her name now—Clarissa something—yes, Clarissa Carter. That reminds me—there's a letter for her already. Here it is, Sally—put it up on her dressing-table for her, will you?'

Gwendoline took the letter to pass it down the table. She glanced at it, and then looked again. The letter was addressed to 'The Honourable Clarissa Carter '.

'The *Honourable* Clarissa Carter!' thought Gwendoline, delighted. 'If only she'd be my friend! I'll look after her when she comes. I'll do all I can!'

Gwendoline was a little snob, always hanging round those who were rich, beautiful or gifted. Alicia grinned as she saw the girl's face. 'Gwendoline's going all out for the Honourable Clarissa,' she thought. 'Now we shall see some fun!'

5   AN INTERESTING MORNING

THE Upper Fourth were taken by Miss Williams, a scholarly, prim mistress, whose gentleness did not mean any lack of discipline. As a rule the Upper Fourth were a good lot, responsible and hard-working—but this year Miss Williams had sometimes had trouble with her form. There were such a lot of scatter-brains in it!

'Still, I think they will all get through the School Cert.,' thought Miss Williams. 'They are none of them *really* stupid, except Gwendoline. Daphne is much better since she has had regular coaching in the holidays. Mavis has picked up wonderfully. So has Bill. And though little Mary-Lou is quite sure she will fail, she is quite certain to pass!'

Her form did not only consist of the North Tower girls, but of the fourth-formers from the other towers. Betty Hill, Alicia's friend, was one of these. She was as quick-tongued as Alicia, but not as quick-brained. She came from West Tower, and Alicia and she had often groaned because the authorities were so hard-hearted that they would not let Betty join Alicia in North Tower!

Miss Grayling, the Headmistress, had once asked Miss Potts, North Tower's house-mistress, if she should change Betty Hill over to North Tower, as Betty's parents had actually written to ask if she would.

'I can manage Alicia alone,' said Miss Potts, 'or even Betty alone—but to have those two together in one house would be quite impossible. I should never have a moment's peace—and neither would Mam'zelle.'

'I agree with you,' said Miss Grayling. So a letter was sent to Mr. and Mrs. Hill regretting that it was impossible to find room for Betty in North Tower. Still, Alicia and Betty managed to be very firm friends indeed, although they were in different towers, meeting in class each day, arranging walks and expeditions together—and planning various wicked and amusing jokes and tricks.

The North Tower fourth-formers went eagerly to their classroom after Prayers. They wanted to choose their desks, and to sort out their things, to look out of the window, clean the blackboard, and do the hundred and one things they had done together so often before.

The twins stood and waited till the other girls had chosen their desks. They knew enough not to choose till then. By that time, of course, there were very few desks left—only those for two East Tower girls who were still not back, and for Clarissa Carter, and for themselves.

'We'll sit together, of course,' said Connie, and put her books and Ruth's on two adjoining desks. They were, alas, in the hated front row, but naturally all the other rows had been taken, the back row going first. It was the only row really safe enough for whispering, or for passing a note or two.

Darrell looked out of the window, and wondered if Felicity had been to see Miss Grayling yet. She must ask her, when she saw her at Break. Miss Grayling saw all the new girls together, and what she said to them always impressed them, and made them determine to do their very best. Darrell remembered clearly how impressed she had been, and how she had made up her mind to be one of the worth-while people of the world.

'I wonder who will be head-girl this term,' said Alicia, interrupting Darrell's thoughts. 'Jean's gone up, so she won't be. Well—I bet *I* shan't be! I never have, and I don't expect I ever will. The Grayling doesn't trust me!'

'I expect Sally will be,' said Darrell. 'She was head of the second when we were in that form, and a jolly good head she made—though as far as I remember, you didn't approve at all, Alicia!'

'No, I didn't,' said Alicia, candidly. 'I thought *I* ought to be head. But I've got rid of silly ideas like that now. I see that I'm not fitted to be head of anything—I just don't care enough.'

Part of this was just bravado, but quite a bit of it was truth. Alicia *didn't* care enough! Things were so easy for her that she had never had to try hard for anything, and so she didn't care. 'If she had to work jolly hard at lessons, as I have to do,' thought Darrell, 'she'd care all right! We value the things we have to work hard for. Alicia does things too easily.'

Gwendoline had chosen a seat in the front row! Everyone was most astonished. Alicia eyed her wonderingly. Could she be sucking up to Miss Williams? No, nobody in the world could do that. Miss Williams simply wouldn't notice it! Then what was the reason for Gwendoline's curious choice.

'Well, of *course*!' said Alicia, suddenly, and everyone gazed at her in surprise.

'Of course *what*?' said Betty.

'I've just thought why dear Gwendoline has chosen that front seat,' said Alicia, maliciously. 'At first I thought she'd gone out of her senses, but now I know!'

Gwendoline scowled at her. She was really afraid of Alicia's sly tongue, and she thought it quite likely that Alicia *had* hit on the correct reason.

But Alicia did not enlighten the class just then. She smiled sarcastically at Gwendoline and said, 'Dear Gwen, I won't give you away—you really have a very *Honourable* reason for your choice, haven't you?'

Nobody could imagine what she meant, not even Betty—but Gwendoline knew! She had chosen a front desk because she knew that the Honourable Clarissa Carter would have to have one there, too—and it would be a very good thing to be next to her and help her!

She flushed red and said nothing, but busied herself with her books. Miss Williams came in at that moment and Gwen rushed to hold the door.

The first day of school was always 'nice and messy' as Belinda called it. No proper lessons were done, but tests were given out, principally to check up on the standard of any new girls. Time-tables were made out with much groaning. Irene always gave hers up in despair. Although she was so good and neat at both maths and music, she was hopeless at a simple thing like making out her own time-table from the big class one.

It usually ended in Belinda doing it for her, but as Belinda wasn't much better, Irene was in a perpetual muddle over her time-table, appearing in the wrong classroom at the wrong time, expecting to have a maths lesson in the sewing-room, or a sewing-lesson in the lab.! All the mistresses had long ago given up expecting either Irene or Belinda to be sane and sensible in ordinary matters.

Irene, with her great gift for music, and Belinda, with her equally fine gift for drawing, seemed to become four-year-olds when they had to tackle ordinary everyday things. It was nothing for Irene to appear at breakfast-time without her stockings, or for Belinda to lose, most inexplicably, every school book she possessed. The girls loved them for their amusing ways, and admired them for their gifts.

Everyone was busy with something or other that first morning. Darrell made out a list of classroom duties—filling up the ink-pots, doing the classroom flowers, keeping the blackboard clean, giving out necessary stationery and so on. Each of the class had to take on a week's duty, together with another girl, during the term.

Just before Break Miss Williams told the girls to tidy up their desks. 'I have something to say to you,' she said. 'It will only take about two minutes, but it is something that I am sure you all want to know!'

'She's going to say who's to be head-girl this term!' whispered Sally to Darrell. 'Look at Gwendoline! See the look she's put on her face. She really thinks *she* might be!'

It was true. Gwendoline always hoped she might be head of the form, and had enough conceit to think she would make a very good one. Just as regularly she was disappointed, and always would be. Spoilt, selfish girls make poor heads, and no teacher in her senses would ever choose Gwendoline Mary!

'I think probably most of you will know that Jean, who passed School Cert. last year, has gone up into the next form,' said Miss Williams. 'She does not need to work with the School Cert. form this term. She was head-girl of the Upper Fourth, and now that she has gone, we must have another.'

She paused, and looked round the listening class. 'I have discussed the matter with Miss Grayling, Miss Potts, Mam'-zelles Dupont and Rougier,' said Miss Williams. 'We are all agreed that we would like to try Darrell Rivers as head-girl.'

Darrell flushed bright red and her heart beat fast. Everyone clapped and cheered, even Gwendoline, who always dreaded that Alicia might conceivably be chosen one day!.

'I am quite sure, Darrell, that our choice is right,' said Miss Williams, smiling her gentle smile at the blushing Darrell. 'I cannot think for one moment that you would do anything to make us regret our choice.'

'No, Miss Williams, I won't,' said Darrell, fervently. She wished she could go and tell her parents this very minute. Head-girl of the Upper Fourth! She had always wanted to be head of something, and this was the first time her chance had come. She would be the very best head-girl the form had ever had.

What would Felicity say? It would be a grand thing for Felicity to be able to say 'my sister, of course, is head of the Upper Fourth!' Felicity would be proud and pleased.

Darrell rushed off at Break to find Felicity and tell her. But again she had disappeared. How absolutely *maddening*! Darrell only had a few minutes. She rushed round and about and at last found Felicity in the Courtyard, with June. The Courtyard was the space that lay inside the hollow oblong of the building that made up Malory Towers. It was very sheltered, and here everything was very early indeed. It was now gay with tulips, rhododendrons and lupins, and very lovely to see.

But Darrell didn't see the flowers that morning. She rushed at Felicity.

'Felicity! I've got good news for you—I've been made head-girl of the Upper Fourth!'

'Oh, Darrell! How super!' said Felicity. 'I'm *awfully* glad. Oh, Darrell, I must tell you—I saw Miss Grayling this morning, and she said to me and all the other new girls, exactly the same things that she said to you, when *you* first came. She was grand!'

Darrell's mind took her back to her own first morning— standing opposite Miss Grayling in her pleasant drawing- room, hearing her talk gravely to the listening girls. She heard the Headmistress's voice.

'One day you will leave school, and go out into the world as young women. You should take with you a good under- standing of many things, and a willingness to accept re- sponsibility and show yourselves as women to be loved and trusted. I do not count as our successes those who have won scholarships and passed exams, though these are good things to do. I count as our successes those who learn to be good- hearted and kind, sensible and trustable, good sound women the world can lean on.'

Yes, Darrell remembered those long-ago words, and was very very glad she was beginning to be one of the successes —for had she not been chosen as head-girl that very day, head of the Upper Fourth, the School Cert. form!

'Yes. Miss Grayling's grand,' she said to Felicity.

'And *you're* grand, too!' said Felicity, proudly, to Darrell. 'It's *lovely* to have a head-girl for a sister!'

6   CLARISSA ARRIVES

GWENDOLINE was keeping a good look-out for the coming of the last new Upper Fourth girl, Clarissa. She was about the only girl in the form who had no special friend, and she could see that it wouldn't be much good trying to make friends with the twins, because they would only want each other.

'Anyway I don't like the look of them much,' thought Gwendoline. 'They'll probably go all out for games and gym and walks. Why aren't there any nice *feminine* girls here— ones who like to talk and read quietly, and not always go pounding about the lacrosse field or splash in that horrible pool!'

Poor lazy Gwendoline! She didn't enjoy any of the things that gave the others such fun and pleasure. She hated any-thing that made her run about, and she detested the cold water of the pool.

Daphne and Mary-Lou didn't like the pool either, but they enjoyed tennis and walks. Neither of them went riding because they were terrified of horses. Bill, who now rode every day on Thunder before breakfast, scorned Daphne, Mary-Lou and Gwendoline because they wouldn't even offer Thunder a lump of sugar and screamed if he so much as stamped on the ground. She and Darrell and the new twins arranged an evening ride twice a week together, and Miss Peters, the third-form mistress, and Bill's great friend came with them. They all enjoyed those rides on the cliffs immensely.

Felicity was not allowed to go with them because she was only a first-former. To Darrell's annoyance she learnt that the only other good rider in the first form was June, so once again it seemed as if Felicity and June were to be companions and enjoy something together.

'It'll end in Felicity having to make June her friend,' thought Darrell. 'Oh, dear—it's an awful pity I don't like June. Felicity likes Sally so much. We ought to like each other's friends. The mere *thought* of having June to stay with us in any holidays makes me squirm!'

The North Tower Upper Fourth girls paired off very well —except for Gwendoline. Sally always went with Darrell, of course. Irene and Belinda, the two clever madcaps, were inseparable, and very bad for each other. Alicia was the only one who had a friend from another Tower, and she and Betty were staunch friends.

Daphne and Mary-Lou were friends, and Mavis hung on to them when she could. They liked her and did not mind being a threesome sometimes. Bill had no special friend, but she didn't want one. Thunder was hers. Bill was better with boys than with girls, because, having seven brothers she understood boys and not girls. She might have been a boy herself in the way she acted. She was the only fourth-former who chose to learn carpentry from Mr. Sutton, and did not in the least mind going with the first- and second-formers who enjoyed his teaching so much. She had already produced a pipe for her father, a ship for her youngest brother, and a bowl-stand for her mother, and was as proud of these as any of the good embroiderers were of their cushions, or the weavers of their scarves.

So it was really only Gwendoline who had no one to go

with, no one to ask her for her company on a walk, no one to giggle with in a corner. She pretended not to mind, but she did mind, very much. But perhaps now she would have her chance when the Honourable Clarissa came. How pleased her mother would be if she had a really nice friend!

Gwendoline ran her mind back over the friends she had tried to make. There was Mary-Lou—stupid little Mary-Lou! There was Daphne, who had seemed to be so very friendly one term, and then had suddenly become friends with Mary-Lou! There was Mavis, who had had such a wonderful voice and was going to be an opera singer. Gwendoline would have liked such a grand person for a friend in after life.

But Mavis had fallen ill and lost her voice, and Gwendoline didn't want her any more. Then there had been Zerelda, the American girl who had now left—but she had had no time for Gwendoline!

Gwendoline thought mournfully of all these failures. She didn't for one moment think that her lack of friends was her own fault. It was just the horridness of the other girls! If only, only, only she could find somebody like herself—somebody who had never been to school before coming to Malory Towers, who had only had a governess, who didn't play games and somebody who had wealthy parents who would ask her to go and stay in the holidays!

So Gwendoline waited in hopes for Clarissa's arrival. She imagined a beautiful girl with lovely clothes, arriving in a magnificent car—the Honourable Clarissa! '*My* friend,' thought Gwendoline, and she imagined herself at half-term saying to her mother and Miss Winter, her old governess, 'Mother, I want you to meet the Honourable Clarissa Carter, my best friend!'

She did not tell any of the girls these thoughts. She knew the words they would use to her if they guessed what she was

planning—snob, hypocrite, fraud! Sucking up to somebody!
Just like dear Gwendoline Mary!

Clarissa did not arrive till tea-time. Gwendoline was
sitting at table with the others, so she did not see her until
the Headmistress suddenly appeared with a strange girl.

Gwendoline looked up without much interest. The girl was
small and undersized-looking—a second-former perhaps.
She wore glasses with thick lenses, and had a wire round
her teeth to keep them back. Her only beauty seemed to be
her hair, which was thick and wavy, and a lovely auburn
colour. Gwendoline took another slice of bread-and-butter
and looked for the jam.

The new girl was so nervous that she was actually trembling! Darrell noticed this and was sorry for her. She too
had felt like trembling when she first came, and had faced so
many girls she didn't know—and here was a poor creature
who really *was* trembling!

To Darrell's surprise Miss Grayling brought the girl up
to the Upper Fourth table. Mam'zelle Dupont was taking
tea and sat at the head.

'Oh, Mam'zelle,' said Miss Grayling, 'here is Clarissa
Carter, the last new girl for the Upper Fourth. Can you find
a seat for her and give her some tea? Then perhaps your
head-girl can look after her when tea is finished.'

Gwendoline almost dropped her bread-and-butter in surprise. Goodness, she had nearly missed her chance! Could
this small, ugly girl really be Clarissa? It was, so she must
hurry up and put her plan into action.

There was a space beside Gwendoline and she stood up
in such a hurry that she almost knocked over Daphne's cup
of tea. 'Clarissa can sit by me,' she said. 'There is room here.'

Clarissa, only too glad to sit down and hide herself, sank
gladly into the place beside Gwendoline. Alicia nudged Darrell. 'Got going quickly, hasn't she?' she whispered, and
Darrell chuckled.

Gwendoline was at her very sweetest. 'Sickly-sweet' was the name given by Alicia to this particular form of friendliness shown by Gwendoline. She leant towards Clarissa and smiled in a most friendly way.

'Welcome to Malory Towers! I expect you are tired and hungry. Have some bread-and-butter.'

'I don't think I could eat any, thank you,' said Clarissa, almost sick with nervousness. 'Thank you all the same.'

'Oh, you must have *some*thing!' said Gwendoline and took a piece of bread-and-butter. 'I'll put some jam on it for you. It's apricot—very nice for a wonder.'

Clarissa didn't dare to object. She sat huddled up as if she wanted to make herself as small and unnoticeable as possible. She nibbled at the bread-and-butter, but couldn't seem to eat more than a bit of it.

Gwendoline chattered away, thinking how good and sweet she must seem to the others, putting this nervous new girl at her ease in such a friendly manner. But only Mam'zelle was deceived.

'The dear kind Gwendoline,' she thought. 'Ah, she is a stupid child at her French, but see how charming she is to this poor plain girl, who shakes with nerves.'

'Sucking up,' said everyone else round the table. They said nothing to Clarissa, feeling that it was enough for the new girl to cope with Gwen, without having to deal with anyone else as well. Mary-Lou liked the look of Clarissa, in spite of her thick glasses and wire round her front teeth—but then Mary-Lou always felt friendly towards anyone as timid as herself! They were about the only people she wasn't afraid of.

After tea Mam'zelle spoke to Darrell. 'Darrell, you will take care of Clarissa, *n'est-ce pas*? She will feel strange at first, *la pauvre petite!*'

'Mam'zelle, I'm awfully sorry, but I've got to go to a meeting of all the head-girls of the forms,' said Darrell. 'It's in five minutes' time. Perhaps Sally—or Belinda—or . . .'

'*I'll* look after her,' said Gwendoline, promptly, thrilled that Darrell had to go to a meeting. 'I'll show her round. I'll be very pleased to.'

She gave Clarissa a beaming smile that startled the new girl and made everyone else feel slightly sick. She slipped her arm through Clarissa's. 'Come along,' she said, in the sort of voice one uses to a very small child. 'Where's your night-case? I'll show you the dormy. You've got a very nice place in it.'

She went off with Clarissa, and everyone made faces and grinned. 'Trust our Gwendoline Mary to show a bit of determination over things like this,' said Alicia. 'What a nasty little snob! Honestly, I don't think Gwendoline has altered one bit for the better since she came to Malory Towers!'

'I think you're right,' said Darrell, considering the matter with her head on one side. 'It's really rather queer—I would have thought that being even a few terms here would have made everyone better in some way—and Gwen has been here years—but she's just the same sly, mean, lazy little sucker-up!'

'How has it made *you* better, Darrell?' said Alicia, teasingly. 'I can't say I've noticed much difference in *you*!'

'She was decent to start with,' said Sally, loyally.

'Anyway, I've conquered my hot temper,' said Darrell. 'I haven't flown out in a rage for terms and terms—you know I haven't. That's one thing Malory Towers has done for me.'

'Don't boast too soon,' said Alicia, grinning. 'I've seen a glint in your eye lately, Darrell—aha, yes I have! You be careful.'

Darrell was about to deny this stoutly, when she stopped herself, and felt her cheeks going red. Yes—she *had* felt her eyes 'glinting', as Alicia used to call it, when she spoke to that pest of a June. Well, she could 'glint' surely, couldn't she? There was nothing wrong in that—so long as she didn't lose her temper, and she certainly wasn't going to do *that*!

'I'll "glint" at you in a minute, Alicia,' she said, with a laugh. 'A head-girl "glint" too—so just you be careful what you say!'

THE Upper Fourth soon began to settle down to its work. Miss Williams was a fine teacher, and was quite determined to have excellent results in the School Certificate exam. Mam'zelle Dupont and Mam'zelle Rougier both taught the Upper Fourth, but though actually Mam'zelle Rougier was the better teacher, plump little Mam'zelle Dupont got better results because she was friendly and had a great sense of humour. The girls worked better for her than for the other Mam'zelle.

This term there was an armed truce between the two French mistresses. The English mistresses regarded them with great amusement, never knowing from one term to the next whether the two Frenchwomen would be bosom friends, bitter enemies, or dignified rivals.

Miss Carton, the history mistress, knew that the School Certificate form was well up to standard except for miseries like Gwendoline, who didn't even know the Kings of England and couldn't see that they mattered anyhow. She used her sarcastic tongue on Gwendoline a good deal these days, to try and whip her into some show of work, and Gwen hated her.

The girls grumbled because they had to work so hard in that lovely summer term. 'Just when we want to go swimming, and play tennis, and laze about in the flowery courtyard, we've got to stew at our books,' said Alicia. 'I shall take my prep out into the open air tonight. I bet Miss Williams would let us.'

Surprisingly Miss Williams said yes. She knew that she

could trust most of the Upper Fourth not to play about when they were supposed to be working, and she thought that Darrell was a strong enough head-girl to keep everyone up to the mark if necessary. So out they went after tea, and took cushions to sit on, in the evening sun.

Gwendoline didn't want to go. She was the only one, of course. 'You really seem to *loathe* the open air,' said Darrell, in surprise. 'Come on out—a bit more fresh air and exercise would take off some of your fat and get rid of those spots on your nose.'

'Don't make personal remarks,' said Gwendoline, nose in air. 'You're as bad as Alicia—and everyone knows she's been dragged up, not brought up!'

Clarissa, who was with her, looked at Gwendoline in surprise. Gwen had been so sweet and gracious to her that it was quite a shock to hear her make a remark like this. Gwen was quick to see the look, and slipped her arm through Clarissa's.

'If *you're* taking your prep out, I'll take mine, of course,' she said. 'But let's sit away from the sun. I hate getting freckled.'

Betty saw Alicia sitting out in the courtyard and came to join her. Darrell frowned. Now there would be nonsense and giggling and no work done. Belinda and Irene began to listen to the joke that Betty was telling Alicia, and Irene gave one of her sudden explosive snorts when it was finished. Everyone looked up, startled.

'Oh, I say, that's super!' roared Irene. 'Here, Betty, tell the others.'

Darrell looked up. She was head-girl of the form, and she must stop this, she knew. She spoke out at once.

'Betty, stop gassing. Alicia, you know jolly well we're supposed to be doing our prep.'

'Don't talk to me as if I was a first-former,' said Alicia, nettled at Darrell's sharp tone.

'Well, I shall, if you behave like one,' said Darrell.

'She's glinting, Alicia—look out, she's glinting!' said Irene, with a giggle. Everyone looked at Darrell and smiled. Darrell certainly had a 'glint' in her eye.

'I'm not glinting,' she said. 'Don't be idiotic.'

'I glint, thou glintest, he glints, *she* glints!' chanted Betty. 'We glint, you glint, they glint!'

'Shut up, Betty, and go away,' said Darrell, feeling angry. 'You don't belong to our prep. Go and join your own.'

'I've done it, Miss Glint,' said Betty. 'Shall I help you with yours?'

To Darrell's horror, she felt the old familiar surge of anger creeping over her. She clenched her fists and spoke sharply to Betty again.

'You heard what I said. Clear out, or I'll take the whole of this prep back indoors.'

Betty looked angry, but Alicia nudged her. 'Go on. She's on the boil already. I'll meet you after we've done prep.'

Betty went, whistling. Darrell bent her red face over her book. Had she been too dictatorial? But what were you to do with someone like Betty?

Nobody said anything more, and prep went peacefully on, accompanied by one or two groans from Irene and deep sighs from Gwendoline. Clarissa sat beside her, working slowly. Gwen copied whatever she could. Nobody could cure her of this habit, it seemed!

After an hour Miss Williams came into the courtyard, pleased to see the North Tower Upper Fourth working so peacefully and well.

'Time's up,' she said. 'And I've a message from your games mistress. The pool is just right now for bathing, so you can all go down there for half an hour, as you had to miss your bathe yesterday.'

'Hurrah!' said Irene, and threw her book into the air. It went into the nearby pool, and had to be retrieved very hurriedly. 'Idiot!' said Belinda, almost falling in herself as she tried to fish out the book. 'I suppose you think that's *your* history book you're drowning. Well, it isn't—it's mine.'

'Have we all *got* to go?' Gwendoline asked Miss Williams, pathetically. 'I've been working so hard. I don't feel like swimming.'

'Dear me—can you actually *swim* yet, Gwendoline?' said Miss Williams, with an air of surprise. Everyone knew that Gwendoline could still only flap a few strokes in the water and then go under with a scream.

'Oh, we don't *all* need to go, do we?' said Mary-Lou, who could swim, but still didn't like the water much. Neither did Daphne, and she added her pleas to the others.

'You're all going,' said Miss Williams. 'You are having to work very hard, and these little relaxations are good for you. Go and change at once.'

Thrilled at the thought of an unexpected evening bathe, Darrell, Sally and Alicia rushed to the changing-room. Darrell had forgotten her annoyance with Alicia, but Alicia hadn't. Alicia bore malice, which was a pity. So she was rather cool to Darrell, who, most unfortunately for Alicia, didn't notice the coolness at all. The others followed, chattering and laughing, with a rather mournful tail composed of Gwen, Daphne and Mary-Lou. Clarissa came to watch. She was not allowed to swim or to play tennis because she had a weak heart.

'Lucky thing!' said Gwendoline, getting into her bathing-suit. 'No swimming, no tennis—I wish *I* had a weak heart.'

'What a wicked thing to say,' said Darrell, really shocked. 'To wish yourself a thing like that! It must be simply horrible to keep on and on having to take care of yourself, and think, "I mustn't do this, I mustn't do that." '

'It *is* horrible,' said Clarissa, in her small shy voice. 'If it hadn't been for my heart I'd not have been taught at home —I'd have come to school like any other girl. It's got much better lately though, and that's why I was allowed to come at *last*.'

This was a long speech for Clarissa to make. Usually she was quite tongue-tied. As it was, she went red as she spoke, and when she had finished she hung her head and tried to get behind Gwendoline.

'Poor old Clarissa,' said Gwendoline, sympathetically. 'You mustn't do too much, you know. Would you know if you *had* done too much?'

'Oh, yes. My heart begins to flutter inside me—as if I had a bird there or something,' said Clarissa. 'It's awful. It makes me want to lie down and pant.'

'Really?' said Gwendoline, pulling her towel-wrap round her. 'Well, you know, Clarissa, I shouldn't be a bit surprised if *I* hadn't a weak heart, too, that nobody knows about. If I try to swim for long I get absolutely panicky—and after a hot game of tennis my heart pumps like a piston. It's really painful.'

'Nice to hear you *have* a heart,' said Alicia, in her smoothest voice. 'Where do you keep it?'

Gwendoline tossed her head and went off with Clarissa. 'Beast, isn't she?' her voice floated back to the others. 'I can't bear her. Nobody likes her really.'

Alicia chuckled. 'I'd love to know what sort of poisonous nonsense Gwendoline Mary is pouring into poor Clarissa's ears,' she said. 'I don't think we ought to let Gwendoline take complete charge of her like this. It's not fair. You ought to do something about it, Darrell. Why don't you?'

Darrell did not like this direct attack. She suddenly realized that Alicia was right—she ought to have made certain that Gwen didn't take such utter and complete charge of the rather weak little Clarissa. She would get all the wrong ideas in her very first term—and the ideas you had at the beginning were apt to stick!

'All right,' she said, in a rather snappy tone. 'Give me a chance! Clarissa has only been here a few days.'

Splash! In went Gwendoline

'My dear Darrell, you're glinting again,' said Alicia, with a laugh that provoked Darrell even more. She took hold of herself hastily. Really, she was getting quite touchy!

It was fun down at the pool. The good swimmers had races, of course. Mary-Lou bobbed up and down in the shallow end, swimming a few strokes every now and again. She always got in quickly, even though she hated the water. Daphne was in, too, shivering as usual, but bobbing beside Mary-Lou, hoping that Darrell wouldn't make her join in the racing. Mavis was swimming slowly. She had got over her dislike of the water, but had to be careful not to over-swim, or play too much tennis because of her illness the year before.

Only Gwendoline still stood shivering on the brink. Alicia, Sally and Darrell longed to push her in, but it was too much fag to get out of the pool.

'If Gwen doesn't get in soon, she won't get in at all,' said Alicia. 'Order her in, Darrell! Go on, put that glint in your eye, and give one of your orders!'

But not even Darrell's shouts persuaded poor Gwendoline to do more than wet her toes. She had got hot sitting in the courtyard and now the pool felt icy-cold. Ooooh!

It was Clarissa who made her get in. She came running up to stand beside Gwendoline, slid on a slimy patch of rock, bumped hard into Gwendoline, and knocked her straight into the water!

Splash! In went Gwendoline with a terrible yell of fright. The girls clutched at one another and laughed till they cried. 'Look at poor Clarissa's face,' wept Darrell. 'She's simply horrified!'

'Who did that?' demanded a furiously angry Gwendoline, bobbing up, and spitting out water. 'Beasts, all of you!'

WHEN Gwendoline heard that it was Clarissa who had pushed her in, she didn't believe it. She made her way over to where an apologetic Clarissa was standing.

'Who pushed me in, Clarissa?' she demanded. 'They keep saying it was *you*, the idiots! As if you'd do a thing like that!'

'Oh, Gwendoline. I'm so very sorry but actually it *was* me,' said Clarissa, quite distressed. 'I slipped and fell, and bumped against you—and in you went. Of *course* I wouldn't have done it on purpose! I'm most terribly sorry about it!'

'Oh, that's all right then,' said Gwendoline, pleased to see such a very apologetic Clarissa. 'It did give me an awful shock, of course—and I hurt my foot against the bottom of the pool—but still, it was an accident.'

Clarissa was more apologetic still, which was balm to Gwendoline's wounded feelings. She liked to have the Honourable Clarissa apologizing so humbly. She made up her mind to be very sweet and forgiving, and then Clarissa would think more than ever what a nice friend she was for anyone to have.

But the others spoilt it all. They would keep coming up and yelling 'Jolly good push!' to Clarissa, and 'Well done, Clarissa—you got her in nicely!' and 'I say, Clarissa, that was a fine shove. Do it again!'

'But I *didn't* push her,' protested Clarissa, time and time again. 'You know I didn't.'

'Never seen such a good shove in my life!' said Alicia, and really, Gwendoline began to be quite doubtful as to whether Clarissa really *had* meant to push her or not! Then unfortunately Clarissa suddenly saw the funny side of all the shouted remarks and began to laugh helplessly. This made Gwen really cross, and she was so huffy with Clarissa, that in great alarm, Clarissa began to apologize all over again.

'Look at the twins,' said Alicia to Sally. Sally looked and laughed. Connie was carefully rubbing Ruth dry, and Ruth was standing patiently, waiting for her sister to finish.

'Why doesn't Connie leave her alone?' said Sally. 'Ruth can do everything for herself—but Connie always makes out she can't. She's too domineering for words!'

'And she's not nearly so good as Ruth is at lessons,' said Alicia. 'Ruth helps her every night, or she would never do the work. She's far behind Ruth.'

'And yet she domineers over her the whole time!' said Darrell, joining in. 'I hate to see it—and I hate to see Ruth putting up with it, too.'

'Speak to her about it,' said Alicia at once. 'Head-girl, aren't you?'

Darrell bit her lip. Why did Alicia keep on and on twitting her like this? She thought that perhaps it was partly envy—Alicia knew she would not really make a good head-girl herself, and envied those who were, and tried to make them uncomfortable. She, Darrell, ought not to take any notice, but she couldn't help feeling annoyed about it.

'You've got a lot on hand now, haven't you,' went on Alicia, rubbing herself dry. 'Looking after young Felicity—seeing that Clarissa doesn't get too much poison from dear Gwendoline, trying to buck up Ruth a bit, and make her stand up for herself—ticking off Betty when she spoils our prep.'

Darrell felt herself beginning to boil again. Then a cool hand was laid on her shoulder, and she heard Sally's calm voice. 'Everything in good time! It's a pity to rush things and spoil them—isn't it, Darrell? You can't put things right all at once.'

Darrell heaved a sigh of relief. That was what *she* ought to have said—in a nice calm voice! Thank goodness Sally had said it for her!

She gave Sally a grateful smile. She determined to look up Felicity a bit more, and try to prise her away from that objectionable June. She would put one of the others on to Clarissa to offset Gwendoline's influence—and she would certainly have a few quiet words with Ruth, and tell her not to let Connie make such a baby of her.

'Why,' thought Darrell, 'it's quite absurd—whenever any of us speak to Ruth, Connie always answers for her. I really wonder she doesn't answer for her in class, too!'

It was quite true that Ruth hardly ever answered for herself. Alicia might say to her, 'Ruth, can you lend me that French dicky for a moment,' but it would be Connie who said, 'Yes, here's the dictionary—catch!'

And Sally might say, 'Ruth, don't you want a new ruler —yours is broken,' but it would be Connie who answered, 'No, thanks, Sally, she can use mine.'

It was annoying, too, to see how Connie always walked a little in front of Ruth, always offered an explanation of anything before her twin could say a word, always did any asking necessary. Hadn't Ruth got a soul of her own—or was she just a weak echo or shadow of her stronger twin?

It was a puzzle. Darrell decided to speak to Ruth the next day, and she found a good chance when both of them were washing painting-jars in the cloakroom.

'How do you like Malory Towers, Ruth?' she asked, wondering if Ruth would be able to answer, if Connie wasn't there!

'I like it,' said Ruth.

'I hope you're happy here,' said Darrell, wondering how to lead up to what she really wanted to say. There was a pause. Then Ruth answered politely.

'Yes, thank you.'

She didn't sound happy at all, Darrell thought! Why

ever not? She was well up to the standard of work, she was
good at all games, there was nothing dislikeable about her
—and the summer term was fun! She ought to be very happy
indeed!

'Er—Ruth,' said Darrell, thinking desperately that Sally
would be much better at this kind of thing than she was,
'—er—we think that you let yourself be—er—well *nursed* a
bit too much by Connie. Couldn't you—er—well, stand on
your own feet a bit more? I mean . . .'

'I know what you mean all right,' said Ruth, in a funny
fierce voice. 'If anyone knows what you mean, *I* do!'

Darrell thought that Ruth was hurt and angry. She tried
again. 'Of course I know you're twins—and twins are always
so close to one another, and—and attached—so I quite
understand Connie being so fond of you, and . . .'

'You don't understand anything at all,' said Ruth. 'Talk
to Connie if you like, but you won't alter things one tiny bit!'

And with that she walked out stiffly, carrying her pile of
clean paint-jars. Darrell was left by herself in the cloakroom,
puzzled and rather cross.

'It's not going to be any good to talk to Connie, I'm sure,'
thought Darrell, rinsing out the last of the jars. 'She'd be as
fierce as Ruth. She's ruining Ruth! But if Ruth *wants* to be
ruined, and made just a meek shadow of Connie, well, let
her! I can't see that I can stop her!'

She took her pile of paint-jars away, and made up her
mind that that particular difficulty could not be put right.
'You can't drag twins away from each other if they've always
been together and feel like one person,' she decided. 'Why,
some twins know when the other is in pain or ill, even if they
are far apart. It's no good putting those two against me.
They must do as they like!'

The next thing to do was to ferret out Felicity, and see
how she was getting on. She ought to be more or less settled
down now. Perhaps she had made some more friends. If

only she had others as well as June, it wouldn't matter so much—but Darrell felt that the strong-minded June would cling like a leech to someone like Felicity, if Felicity had no other friend at all!

So she found Felicity in Break, and asked her to come for a walk with her that evening. Felicity looked pleased. To go for a walk with the head-girl of the Upper Fourth was a great honour.

'Oh, yes—I'd love to come,' she said. 'I don't think June's fixed anything for tonight.'

'What does it matter if she has?' said Darrell, impatiently. 'You can put her off, surely? I haven't seen anything of you lately.'

'I like Miss Potts,' said Felicity, changing the subject as she often did when Darrell got impatient. 'I'm still a bit scared of her—but my work's a bit in advance of the form, really, Darrell, so I can sit back and take things easy this first term! Rather nice!'

'Yes. Jolly nice,' agreed Darrell. 'That's what comes of going to a good prep school—you always find you're in advance of the lowest form work when you go to a public school—but if you go to a rotten prep school, it takes years to catch up! Er—how is June in her work?'

'Brilliant—when she likes!' said Felicity, with a grin. 'She's awfully good fun—frightfully funny, you know. Rather like Alicia, I should think.'

'*Too* like Alicia,' Darrell thought to herself, remembering how wonderful she had thought Alicia in *her* first term at Malory Towers. 'Isn't there anyone else you like, Felicity?' she asked her sister.

'Oh, yes—I like most of my form,' said Felicity. 'They don't seem to like June much, though, and sit on her hard. But she's like indiarubber, bounces up again. There's one girl I like awfully—her name's Susan. She's been here two terms.'

'Susan! Yes, she's fine,' said Darrell. 'Plays lacrosse awfully well for a kid—and she's good at gym, too. I remember seeing her in a gym display last term.'

'Yes. She's good at games,' agreed Felicity. 'But June says Susan's too pi for words—won't do anything she shouldn't, and she thinks she's dull, too.'

'She would!' said Darrell. 'Well, I'm glad you like Susan. Why don't you make a threesome—you and June and Susan? I don't think June's a good person to have for an only friend.'

'Why, you don't even know her!' said Felicity in surprise. 'Anyway, *she* wouldn't want Susan in a threesome!'

A bell rang in the distance. 'Well, see you this evening,' said Darrell. 'We'll go on the cliffs—but don't you go and bring June, mind! I want you to myself!'

'Right,' said Felicity, looking pleased.

But alas, that evening a meeting was called of all the School Certificate girls, and Darrell had to go to it. She wondered if she could possibly squeeze time in for even a short walk with Felicity. No, she couldn't—she had that essay to do as well.

She sent a message to her sister by a second-former. 'Hey, Felicity,' said the second-former, 'compliments from Head-Girl Darrell Rivers, and she says she can't take baby sister for a walky-walk tonight!'

Felicity stared at her indignantly. 'You know jolly well she didn't say that!' she said. 'What *did* she say?'

'Just that,' said the cheeky second-former, and strolled off.

Felicity translated the message correctly and was disappointed.

'Darrell can't go for a walk tonight,' she told June. 'I suppose she's got a meeting or something.'

'I bet she hasn't,' said that young lady, scornfully. 'I tell you, these fourth-formers, like Alicia and Darrell, don't *want* to be bothered with us—and we jolly well won't go bothering them! Come on—we'll go for a walk together!'

DARRELL forgot about Clarissa for a day or two, because for some reason the days suddenly became very full up indeed. Head-girls seemed to have quite a lot of duties Darrell hadn't thought of, and there was such a lot of prep to do this term.

Gwendoline now had Clarissa very firmly attached to her side. She sat next to her in class, and offered to help her whenever she could—but this usually ended, not in Gwen helping Clarissa, but the other way round!

Their beds were next to each other's at night, for Gwendoline had persuaded soft-hearted Mary-Lou to change beds with her, so that she might be next to Clarissa.

'She's never been to school before, you see, Mary-Lou,' she said, 'and as I hadn't either, before I came here, I do understand how she feels. It's at night you feel things worst. I'd like to be near her just to say a few words till she settles down properly.'

Mary-Lou thought it was extraordinary of Gwendoline to develop such a kind heart all of a sudden, but she felt that it ought to be encouraged anyway—so she changed beds, and to Darrell's annoyance one night, there was Gwendoline next to Clarissa, whispering away like anything.

'Who told you you could change beds?' she demanded.

'Mary-Lou,' said Gwendoline, in a meek voice.

'But—why in the world did you ask *Mary-Lou?*' said Darrell. 'I'm the one to ask, surely.'

'No. Because it was Mary-Lou's bed I wanted to change over, Darrell,' explained Gwen, still in a meek voice. She saw that Darrell was annoyed, and decided to offer to change back again. Then surely Darrell would say all right, keep next to Clarissa!

'But, of course, if you'd rather I didn't sleep next to Clarissa—though I only wanted to *help* her——' said Gwendoline, in a martyr-like voice.

'Oh, stay there,' said Darrell, who could never bear it when Gwendoline put on her martyr-act. So Gwendoline, rejoicing inwardly, did stay there, and was able to whisper what she thought were comforting words to Clarissa at night. She was too far away from Darrell's bed to be heard—and in any case Darrell, usually tired out with work and games, slept very quickly, and heard nothing.

Clarissa thought Gwendoline was really the kindest girl she had ever met—not that she had met many, however! Feeling lonely and strange, she had welcomed Gwendoline's friendliness eagerly. She had listened to endless tales about Gwendoline's uninteresting family, who all seemed to be 'wonderful' according to Gwen, and yet appeared to the listening Clarissa to be uniformly dull!

She said very little about her own family, though Gwendoline questioned her as much as she dared, longing to hear of Rolls Royces and yachts and mansions. But Clarissa merely spoke of their little country house, and their 'car'—not even 'cars', thought the disappointed Gwendoline.

As Clarissa had a weak heart, and did no games or gym, she hadn't much chance to get together with the other girls. She either had to rest at these times, or merely go to watch, which she found rather boring. So she looked forward eagerly to the times she could be with Gwendoline, who was practically her only companion.

That is, till Darrell really took the matter in hand! Seeing Gwendoline's fair head and Clarissa's auburn one bent together over a jigsaw puzzle one fine evening, when everyone should have been out of doors, she made up her mind that something really must be done!

She went to Mavis. After all, Mavis had no real friend, she just made a threesome with Daphne and Mary-Lou. She could quite well spare some of her time for Clarissa.

'Mavis,' said Darrell, 'we think that Clarissa is seeing a bit too much of darling Gwendoline Mary. Will you try and get Clarissa to yourself a bit and talk to her?'

Mavis was surprised and pleased. 'Yes, of course, Darrell,' she said. 'I'd love to.' Secretly she thought that the small, bespectacled Clarissa was quite well paired off with Gwendoline—but if Darrell thought otherwise, then it must be so! So obediently she went to try to prise Clarissa away from the close-clinging Gwen.

'Come down to the pool with me, Clarissa,' she said, smiling pleasantly. 'I'm not bathing today—but we'll go and watch the others. They want someone to throw in pennies for them to dive for.'

Clarissa got up at once. Gwendoline frowned. 'Oh, Clarissa —you can't go just yet.'

'Why? We've nothing much to do,' said Clarissa, surprised. 'You come, too.'

'No. I feel rather tired,' said Gwendoline, untruthfully, hoping that Clarissa would stay with her. But she didn't. She went off with Mavis, rather flattered at having been asked by her. Clarissa had not much opinion of herself. She thought herself dull and plain and uninteresting, and indeed she certainly appeared so to most of the girls!

Darrell beamed at Mavis. Good old Mavis! She was doing her best, thought Darrell, pleased. But poor Clarissa didn't have much of a time with Gwendoline afterwards!

Gwendoline was rather cold, and gave her very short, cool answers when she returned from the pool. Clarissa was puzzled.

'I say—you didn't really mind my going off with Mavis for a bit, did you?' she said at last.

Gwendoline spoke solemnly. 'Clarissa, you don't know as

much about Mavis as I do. She's not the sort of girl your family would like you to be friends with. Do you know what she did last year? She heard of a talent-spotting competition in a town near here—you know, a very *common* show with perfectly dreadful people in it—and she actually went off by herself to sing in the show!'

Clarissa was truly horrified, partly because she knew that she herself would never have had the courage even to think of such a thing.

'What happened?' she said. 'Tell me.'

'Well—Mavis missed the last bus home,' said Gwendoline, still very solemn. 'And Miss Peters found her lying by the road about three o'clock in the morning. After that she was terribly ill, and lost her voice. She thought she had a wonderful voice before that, you know—though I can't say *I* ever thought much of it—and so it was a very good punishment for her to lose it.'

'Poor Mavis,' said Clarissa.

'Well, personally I think she ought to have been expelled,' said Gwendoline. 'I've only told you this, Clarissa, because I want you to see that Mavis isn't really the kind of person to make friends with—that is if you were thinking of it.'

'Oh no, I wasn't,' said Clarissa, hastily. 'I only just went down to the pool with her, Gwen. I won't even do that if you don't want me to.'

Poor weak Clarissa had said just what Gwendoline hoped she would say, and the next time that Mavis came to ask her to go for a short walk with her, she refused.

'Don't bother Clarissa,' said Gwendoline. 'She really doesn't want you hanging round her.'

The indignant Mavis walked away and reported to Darrell that *she* wasn't going to bother about that silly little Clarissa any more! She had better find someone else. What about Daphne?

Daphne came by at that moment and heard her name. In a fit of annoyance Darrell told her that Mavis had been rebuffed by Clarissa, and that Mavis had suggested that she, Daphne, should have a try. What about it?

'I don't mind having a shot—just to spoil darling Gwendoline Mary's fun,' said Daphne with a grin. So she tried her hand at Clarissa, too, only to be met with excuses and evasions. Gwendoline had quite a bit to tell Clarissa about Daphne, too!

'You see, Clarissa,' said Gwendoline, 'Daphne isn't really *fit* to be at a school like this. You mustn't repeat what I tell you—but a year or two ago Daphne was found out to be a thief!'

Clarissa stared at Gwendoline in horror. 'I don't believe it,' she said.

'Well, just as you like,' said Gwen. 'But she *was* a thief—she stole purses and money and brooches—and this wasn't the only school she'd stolen at, either. When it was found out, Miss Grayling made her come into our common-room, and confess everything to us—and we had to decide whether or not she should be expelled. It's as true as I'm standing here!'

Clarissa was quite pale. She looked across the courtyard to where Daphne was laughing with Mary-Lou. She couldn't believe it—and yet Gwendoline would never, never dare to tell such a lie as that.

'And—did you all say that—you didn't want her expelled?' she said at last.

'Well, *I* was the first to say she should have a chance and I'd stick by her,' said Gwen, untruthfully, for it had been little Mary-Lou who had said that, not Gwen. 'So she was kept on—but as you can see, Clarissa, she wouldn't be a really *nice* friend to have, would she? You'd never feel you could trust her.'

'No. I suppose not,' said Clarissa. 'Oh, dear—I hate thinking nasty things about Mavis and Daphne like this. I hope there are no more nasty tales to tell.'

'Did you ever hear how Darrell slapped me about a dozen times in the swimming-pool, for nothing at all?' said Gwen, who had never forgotten or forgiven this episode. 'I had a bad leg for ages after that. And you know that girl in the fifth —Ellen? Well, she tried to get hold of the exam papers and cheat by looking at the questions, the night before the exam! She did, really.'

'Don't,' said Clarissa, beginning to think that Malory Towers was a nest of cheats, thieves and idiots.

'And even Bill, that everyone thinks such a lot of, was in awful disgrace last year, through continual deceit and disobedience,' went on the poisonous voice in Clarissa's ear. 'Do you know, Miss Peters had to threaten to send Bill's horse, Thunder, away to her home, because she was so disobedient?'

'I don't want to hear any more,' said Clarissa, unhappily. 'I really don't.'

'Well, it's all true,' said Gwendoline, forgetting her own record of deceit and unkindness, and not even realizing how she had distorted the facts, so that though most of them were capable of simple and kindly explanations, she had presented them as pictures of real badness.

Darrell came up, determined to get Clarissa away from Gwendoline's everlasting whispering. 'Hey, Clarissa,' she called, in a jolly voice. 'You're just the person I'm looking for! Come and help me to pick some flowers for our classroom, will you?'

Clarissa sat as if rooted to the spot. 'Come on!' called Darrell, impatiently. 'I shan't bite you—or even slap you!'

'Oh, dear!' thought Clarissa, getting up slowly, and remembering Gwen's tale of the dozen slaps Darrell had given her, 'I hope she *doesn't* go for me!'

'Has dear Gwendoline been regaling you with tales of our

dark, dreadful deeds?' said Darrell, and then, as she saw
Clarissa go red, she knew that she had hit the nail on the head.

'Bother Gwendoline!' she thought. 'She really is a poisonous
little snake!'

10   A DAY OFF!

THREE or four weeks went by. The School Certificate girls
worked very hard indeed, and some of them began to look
rather pale. Miss Williams decided it was time to slack off for
a bit.

'Go for an all-day picnic,' she suggested. 'Go to Langley
Hill and enjoy yourselves.'

Langley Hill was a favourite spot for picnics. It was a
lovely walk there, along the cliff, and from the top there was
a magnificent view of the countryside and the sea.

'Oh thanks, Miss Williams! That would be super!' said
Darrell.

'Smashing!' said Alicia, which was the favourite adjective
of all the first-formers at the moment, often ridiculed by the
older girls.

'Langley Hill,' said Clarissa. 'Why, that's where my old
nurse lives!'

'Write and ask her if we could go and have tea with her,'
said Gwendoline, who didn't like what she called 'waspy
picnics' at all. 'It would be nice for her to see you.'

'You always think of such kind things, Gwendoline,' said
Clarissa. 'I certainly will write. She will get us a wizard tea,
I know. She's a marvellous cook.'

So she wrote to her old nurse, who lived at the foot of

Langley Hill. ('Thank goodness we shan't have to walk all the way up the hill with the others!' thought Gwendoline, thankfully. 'I really am getting very clever!')

Old Mrs. Lucy wrote back at once. 'We're to go to her for tea,' said Clarissa. 'She says she'll have a real spread. What fun!'

'We'd better ask permission,' said Gwendoline, suddenly thinking that Darrell might prove obstinate if the idea was suddenly sprung on her on the day of the picnic. 'Go and ask Miss Williams, Clarissa.'

'Oh no—you go,' said Clarissa, who was always scared of asking any mistress anything. But Gwendoline knew better than to ask a favour of Miss Williams. Miss Williams saw right through Gwendoline, and might say 'No' just on principle, if Gwen went to ask her a favour! She didn't trust Gwendoline any farther than she could see her.

So Clarissa had to go—and with many stammerings and stutterings she at last came out with what she wanted to ask—and handed over her old nurse's invitation.

'Yes. You can go there for tea, so long as you take another girl with you,' said Miss Williams, thinking what an unattractive child Clarissa was, with her thick-lensed glasses and the wire round her teeth. She couldn't help looking so plain, of course—but that dreadful hang-dog expression she always wore made it worse!

The day of the picnic dawned bright and clear, and promised to be lovely and hot.

'A whole day off!' rejoiced Darrell. 'And such a day, too! I vote we take our bathing-things and bathe at the foot of Langley Hill. There's a cove there.'

'You'll have to take your lunch with you, but you can have your tea at the little tea-place on top of the hill,' said Miss Williams. 'I've asked the kitchen staff to let you go and help them cut sandwiches and cakes to take with you. Be off with you now—and come back ready to work twice as hard!'

They clattered off, and in half an hour were streaming up the cliff-path on their way to Langley Hill, each girl carrying her share of the lunch.

'I should think we've got far too much,' said Mavis.

'*Do* you? I don't think we've got enough!' said Darrell, astonished. 'But then, my idea of a good picnic lunch is probably twice the size of yours, Mavis! You're a poor eater.'

Gwendoline and Clarissa panted along a good way behind the others. Darrell called to them to hurry up. She was annoyed to see the two together again after all her efforts to separate them.

'Clarissa gets a bad heart if she hurries,' called Gwendoline, reproachfully. 'You know that, Darrell.'

'Oh, Gwen—I hardly ever feel my heart this term,' said Clarissa. 'I believe I'm almost cured! I can easily hurry.'

'Well,' said Gwendoline, solemnly, 'I'm just a *bit* worried about *my* heart, Clarissa. It does funny things lately. Sort of flutters like a bird, you know.'

Clarissa looked alarmed. 'Oh, Gwen—that's just what mine used to do. You'll have to be careful. Oughtn't you to see a doctor?'

'Oh no, I don't think so,' said Gwen, bravely. 'I hate going to Matron about anything. She makes such a fuss. And she's quite likely not to believe what I say. She's very hard, you know.'

Clarissa had been to Matron once or twice, and had thought her very kind and understanding. She didn't know that Gwendoline had tried to stuff Matron up with all kinds of tales, term after term, whenever she wanted to get out of anything strenuous, and that Matron now consistently disbelieved anything that Gwendoline had to say. She merely handed out large doses of very disgusting medicine, no matter what Gwen complained of. In fact, Alicia said that she kept a special large bottle labelled 'Medicine for Gwen' on the top shelf of her cupboard, a specially nasty concoction made up specially for malingerers!

'Look at Connie,' said Gwen, as they gradually came nearer to the others. 'Carrying Ruth's bag for her as well as her own! How can Ruth put up with it?'

'Well, they're twins,' said Clarissa. 'I expect they like to do things for each other. Let's catch them up and talk to them.'

But the conversation as usual was carried on by Connie, not by Ruth!

'What a heavenly day for a picnic!' said Clarissa, looking at Ruth.

'Beautiful,' said Connie, and began to talk about the food in the bags she carried.

Gwen spoke to Ruth. 'Did you find the pencil you lost— that silver one?' she asked.

Connie answered for her as usual. 'Oh yes—it was at the back of her desk after all.'

'Ruth, look at that butterfly!' said Clarissa, determined to make Ruth speak. 'Whatever is it?'

'It's a fritillary, pearl-bordered,' answered Connie, before Ruth had even got a look at the lovely thing. Then Gwen and Clarissa gave it up. You just couldn't get Ruth to speak before Connie got her word in.

They had the picnic in sight of Langley Hill, because they were much too hungry to wait till they had climbed up to the top. Gwendoline was very thankful. She was already puffing and blowing.

'You're too fat, that's what the matter with you, Gwendoline,' said Alicia, unsympathetically. 'Gosh, what a wonderful scowl you've put on now—one of your best. A real snooty scowl!'

Belinda overheard and rolled over to be nearer to them. She gazed at Gwendoline, and felt all over herself for her small sketchbook, which was always somewhere about her person.

'Yes—it's a peach of a scowl,' she said, 'a smasher! Hold it, Gwen, hold it! I *must* add it to my collection!'

Clarissa, Ruth and Connie looked surprised. 'A collection of *scowls?*' said Connie. 'I never heard of *that* before!'

'Yes, I've got a nice little bookful of all Gwendoline's different scowls,' said Belinda. 'The one that goes like this' —and she pulled a dreadful face—'and this one—and this one you must have seen hundreds of times!' She pulled a variety of faces, and everyone roared. Belinda could be very funny when she liked.

'Oh quick—Gwen is scowling again!' she said, and flipped open her little book. 'You know, one term I stalked Gwen the whole time, waiting for her scowls, but she got wise to me the next term, and I hardly collected a single one. I'll show you my collection when I get back if you like, Clarissa.'

'Er—well—I don't know if Gwen would like it,' she began.

'Of course she wouldn't,' said Belinda. Her quick pencil moved over the paper. She tore off the page and gave it to Clarissa.

'There you are—there's your darling Gwendoline Mary,' she said. Clarissa gasped. Yes—it was Gwen to the life—and looking most unpleasant, too! Wicked Belinda—her malicious pencil could catch anyone's expression and pin it down on paper immediately.

Clarissa didn't know what in the world to do with the paper—tear it up and offend Belinda—or keep it and offend Gwendoline. Fortunately the wind solved the problem for her by suddenly whipping it out of her fingers and tossing it over the hedge. She was very relieved.

It was a lovely picnic. There were sandwiches of all kinds, buns, biscuits and slices of fruit cake. The girls ate every single thing and then lazed in the sun. Darrell reluctantly decided at three o'clock that if they were going to have tea at the top of Langley Hill, and bathe afterwards, they had better go now.

'Hold it, Gwen. I must add it to my collection.'

'Oh, Darrell—Clarissa and I have been given permission by Miss Williams to go and have tea with Clarissa's old nurse, Mrs. Lucy, who lives at the foot of the hill,' said Gwendoline, in the polite voice she used when she knew she was saying something that the other person was going to object to.

'Well! This is the first I've heard of it!' said Darrell. 'Why ever couldn't you say so before? I suppose it's *true*? You're not saying this just to get out of climbing Langley Hill and bathing afterwards?'

'Of course not,' said Gwendoline, with enormous dignity. 'Ask Clarissa!'

Clarissa, feeling rather nervous of Darrell, produced the invitation from Mrs. Lucy. 'All right,' said Darrell, tossing it back. '*How* like you, Gwen, to get out of a climb and a bathe! Jolly clever, aren't you!'

Gwendoline did not deign to reply, but looked at Clarissa as if to say 'What a head-girl! Disbelieving us like that!'

The girls left Gwen and Clarissa and went to climb the great hill. The two left behind sprawled on the grass contentedly. 'I'm just as pleased not to climb that hill, anyway,' said Gwen. 'This hot afternoon, too! I wish them joy of it!'

They sat a little longer, then Gwen decided that she was being bitten by something. She always decided this when she wanted to make a move indoors! So they set off to find Mrs. Lucy's cottage, and arrived about a quarter-past four.

The old lady was waiting. She ran out to greet Clarissa, and petted her as if she was a small child. Then she saw Gwendoline, and appeared to be most astonished that there were no other girls besides.

'But I've got tea for twenty!' she said. 'I thought the whole *class* was coming, Miss Clarissa dear! Oh my, what shall we do? Can you go after the others and fetch them?'

'YOU go after them, Gwen,' said Clarissa, urgently. 'I daren't tear up that steep hill. They'll be half-way up by now.'

'No, indeed, Miss Clarissa, I wouldn't dream of *you* racing up that hill, and you only just recovering from that bad heart of yours,' said Mrs. Lucy at once. 'I meant this other girl to go.'

Gwendoline was certainly not going to go chasing up Langley Hill in the hot sun, to fetch back people she disliked to enjoy a fine tea. Let them go without!

She pulled rather a long face. 'I will go, of course,' she said, 'but I think there's something a bit wrong with *my* heart, too—it flutters, you know, when I've done something rather energetic. It makes me feel I simply must lie down.'

'Oh dear—that's how I used to feel!' cried Clarissa, sympathetically. 'I forgot you spoke about your heart today, Gwen. Well, it can't be helped. We can't get the others back here to tea.'

'What a pity,' mourned Mrs. Lucy, and took them inside her dear little cottage. Set on a table inside was a most marvellous home-made tea!

There were tongue sandwiches with lettuce, hard-boiled eggs to eat with bread-and-butter, great chunks of new-made cream cheese, potted meat, ripe tomatoes grown in Mrs. Lucy's brother's greenhouse, gingerbread cake fresh from the oven, shortbread, a great fruit cake with almonds crowding the top, biscuits of all kinds and six jam sandwiches!

'Gracious!' said Gwen and Clarissa, in awe. 'What a spread!'

'Nurse, it's too marvellous for words,' said Clarissa. 'But oh dear, what a waste! And such an expense, too!'

'Oh now, you needn't think about that,' said Mrs. Lucy at once. 'Your sister came to see me yesterday, her that's married, and she gave some money to spend on getting a good spread for you all. So here it is—and only the two of you to eat it. Well, certainly, Miss Clarissa, you did give me to understand in your letter that the whole class were coming.'

'No, Nurse—I said the whole of our form from North Tower were coming for a picnic and could we (that's Gwen and I) come and have tea with you,' explained Clarissa. 'I suppose you thought that 'we' meant the whole lot. I'm so very sorry.'

'Sit you down and eat,' said Mrs. Lucy. But even with such a wonderful spread the two girls could not eat very much after their very good lunch. Gwen looked at the masses of food in despair.

And then Mrs. Lucy had a brainwave.

'Don't you have midnight feasts or anything like that at your school?' she said to Clarissa. 'I remember your sister, her that's married, used to tell of them when *she* went to boarding-school.'

'A midnight feast!' said Gwen, remembering the one or two she had enjoyed at Malory Towers. 'My *word*—that's a *super* idea, Mrs. Lucy! Could we really have the food for that?'

'Of course you can. Then it will get to the hungry mouths it was made for,' said old Mrs. Lucy, her eyes twinkling at the two girls. 'But how will you take it?'

Clarissa and Gwen considered. There was far too much for them to carry by themselves. They would simply *have* to have help. Clarissa was very excited. A midnight feast! She had read of such things—and now she was going to join in one—and provide the food, too!

'I know,' said Gwen, suddenly. 'We have to meet Darrell

and the others at half-past five, at the end of the lane down there—the one that leads up from the cove. We will bring some of the girls back here to help to carry the stuff!'

'Good idea,' agreed Clarissa, her eyes shining behind their thick glasses. So, just before half-past five by Mrs. Lucy's clock, Gwen and Clarissa slipped along to the end of the lane to meet the others.

But only two were there—and very cross the two were. They were Alicia and Belinda.

'Well! Do you know it's a quarter to six, and we've jolly well been waiting for you two for twenty minutes!' began Alicia indignantly. 'The others have gone on. We've had to wait behind. Haven't you got watches?'

'No,' said Gwendoline. 'I'm so sorry. I'm afraid Mrs. Lucy's clock must have been slow.'

'Well, for goodness' sake, put your best foot forward now,' grumbled Alicia.

But Gwen caught at her arm.

'Wait a bit, Alicia. We want you and Belinda to come back to Mrs. Lucy's cottage with us. It isn't far.'

Alicia and Belinda stared in exasperation at Gwen. Rapidly she told them about the feast, and all the food left over—and how Mrs. Lucy had offered it to them for a midnight feast.

A grin appeared on Alicia's face, and a wicked look on Belinda's. A midnight feast! That would be a fine end to a very nice day. All that food, too! It simply couldn't be wasted.

'Well, it would certainly be a sin to let all that wonderful food go stale,' said Alicia, cheerfully. 'I quite see you couldn't allow that. And I'm sure we could all do with a feast tonight, after our walking, climbing and bathing. We'll go back and help you carry the stuff.'

No more was said about being late. The four of them went quickly back to Mrs. Lucy's cottage. She had packed it up as best she could in net bags and baskets. The girls exclaimed in delight and thanked her heartily.

'We'll bring back the baskets and bags as soon as we can,' promised Clarissa. 'My, what a load we've got!'

They had indeed. It was all the four could do to lug it back to Malory Towers. Sally was waiting for them as they came down the cliff-path. 'Whatever *have* you been doing?' she asked. 'Darrell's in an awful wax, thinking you'd got lost or something. She was just about to go and report that you'd all fallen over the cliff!'

Alicia laughed. 'Take a look at this basket,' she said. 'And this bag! Clarissa's old nurse gave us the whole lot for a midnight feast!'

'Golly!' said Sally, thrilled. 'How super! You'd better hide the things somewhere. We don't want Potty or Mam'zelle finding them.'

'Where shall we put them?' wondered Alicia. 'And where shall we have the feast? It would be better to have it out-of-doors tonight, it's so hot. I know! Let's have it down by the pool. We might even have a midnight swim!'

This sounded absolutely grand. 'You go and tell Darrell we're safe,' said Alicia, 'and we four will slip down to the pool, and hide these things in the cubby-holes there where we keep the life-belts and things.'

Sally sped off, and Gwen, Clarissa, Alicia and Belinda swiftly made their way down to the pool. The tide was out— but at midnight it would be in again, and they could splash about in the pool, and have their feast with the waves running over their toes. The moon was full, too—everything was just right!

Alicia packed the food into a cubby-hole and shut the door. Then she and the others went up the cliff-path, but half-way up Alicia remembered that she hadn't locked the door of the cubby-hole she had used.

'Blow!' she said. 'I suppose I'd better, in case anyone goes snooping round. You go on, you three—and I'll come as soon as I've locked up.'

She went down and locked the cubby-hole, slipping the key into her pocket. She heard footsteps near her as she pocketed the key and turned round hastily.

Thank goodness it was only Betty, her West Tower friend! 'Hallo! What are *you* doing here?' said Betty.

Alicia grinned and told her about the hoard of food. 'Why don't you ask *me* to come along?' said Betty. 'Any objection?'

'No. It's just that Darrell mightn't like it,' said Alicia, hesitating. 'You know that we aren't supposed to leave our towers and join up together at night. That's always been a very strict rule.'

'Well—is there anything to stop me from looking out of my dormy window, hearing something going on at the pool, and coming along to see what it is?' said Betty, with her wicked grin. 'Then I don't see how you can prevent everyone from saying, "Come along and join us." '

'Yes—that's a wizard idea,' said Alicia. 'You do that. Then nobody will know I told you! I'll call out, "Come and join us," and that will make everyone else join in—and Darrell won't be able to say no!'

'Right,' said Betty, and chuckled. 'I could do with a spree like this, couldn't you? Where did you go today? Langley Hill? We went to Longbottom, and had some good fun. I say—I suppose I couldn't bring one or two more West Tower girls with me, I suppose, could I? After all, it's not like being *invited* if we just pop along to see what the noise is. No one will ever know.'

'All right. Bring Eileen and Winnie,' said Alicia. 'They'll enjoy it. But for goodness' sake don't say I told you, or Darrell will blow my head off! She's taking her head-girl duties very, very seriously!'

'She would!' said Betty, and laughed. 'Well, see you tonight—and mind you're *very* surprised when we appear!'

She sped off and Alicia went to join the others. 'Whatever made you so long?' demanded Belinda. 'We thought you must have thrown a fit and fallen into the pool. You'll be late for supper now if you aren't quick.'

'Have you told Darrell about the food and the midnight feast?' asked Alicia.

'Yes,' said Belinda. 'She looked a bit doubtful at first, and then when we reminded her that the great Fifth had had one last term, she laughed and said, "All right! A feast it shall be then!"'

'Good for Darrell,' said Alicia, pleased. 'Did you suggest that down by the pool would be a good place?'

'Yes. She agreed that it would,' said Belinda. 'So we're all set!'

The Upper Fourth winked at one another so continually that supper-time that Mam'zelle, who was taking the supper-table, looked down at her person several times to see if she had forgotten some article of apparel. Had she lost a few buttons? Was her belt crooked? Was her hair coming down? Then why did these bad girls wink and wink?

But it was nothing to do with Mam'zelle or her clothing or hair—it was just that the girls were thrilled and excited, full of giggles and nudges and winks, enough to drive any mistress to distraction.

Mam'zelle was indulgent. 'They are excited after their picnic,' she thought. 'Ah, how well they will sleep tonight!'

But Mam'zelle was wrong. They didn't intend to sleep at all well that night!

'FOR goodness' sake don't let Potty or Mam'zelle guess
there's anything planned for tonight,' said Darrell to the
others after supper. 'I saw Mam'zelle looking very sus-
picious. Come into the common-room now, and we'll arrange
the details. How gorgeous to have so much food given to us
—Clarissa, many thanks!'

Clarissa blushed, but was too nervous to say anything. She
was delighted to think that she could provide a feast for the
others.

They all went to the common-room and sat about to discuss their plans. 'It's such a terrifically hot evening that it
really will be lovely down by the pool,' said Sally. 'There
won't have to be any of the usual screeching or yelling though
—sounds carry so at night, and although the pool is right
down on the rocks, it's quite possible to hear noises from
there if the wind is right.'

Alicia was pleased to hear Sally say this. It would make it
seem natural for Betty and Eileen and Winnie to come and
say they had heard sounds from the pool.

'I and Sally will keep awake tonight,' planned Darrell.
'Then when we hear the clock strike twelve, we will wake you
all, and you can get into dressing-gowns and bring your
bathing-things. We'd better fetch them from the changing-
rooms now, or else we may wake up one of the staff, if we
rummage about late at night.'

'Is all the food safely down by the pool?' asked Bill, who
was very much looking forward to this adventure. It was the
first time she had ever been to a midnight feast!

'Yes. Safely locked in the cubby-hole on the left,' said Alicia. 'I've got the key.'

'We'll have a bathe first and then we'll feast,' said Darrell. 'It's a pity we haven't anything exciting to drink.'

'I bet if I went and asked old Cookie for some lemonade, she'd leave us some ready,' said Irene, who was a great favourite with the kitchen staff.

'Good. You go then,' said Darrell. 'Ask her to make two big jugfuls, and stand them on the cold larder floor. We'll fetch them when we're ready.'

Irene sped off. Then Alicia was sent with Mavis to fetch the bathing-things from the changing-room. Everyone began to feel tremendously excited. Clarissa could hardly keep still.

'I wish I hadn't had so much supper,' said Gwendoline. 'I'm sure I shan't feel hungry by midnight.'

'Serves you right for being a pig,' said Belinda. 'You had five tomatoes at supper. I counted!'

'A pity you hadn't anything better to do,' said Gwendoline, trying to be sarcastic.

'Oh, it's wonderful to watch your nice little ways,' said Belinda, lazily. 'No wonder you're getting so fat, the way you gobble everything at meals. Dear me, what a wonderful drawing I could make of you as a nice fat little piggy-wig with blue eyes and a ribbon on your tail.'

Everyone roared. 'Do, do!' begged Sally. Gwendoline began to scowl, saw Belinda looking at her, and hastily straightened her face. She wished she hadn't tried to be sarcastic to Belinda. She always came off badly if she did!

Alicia and Mavis came back, giggling, with the bathing-things. 'Anyone spot you?' asked Darrell, anxiously.

'I don't think so. That pestiferous young cousin of mine, June, was somewhere about, but I don't think she'd spot anything was up,' said Alicia. 'I heard her whistling somewhere, when we were in the changing-room.'

Irene came back from the kitchen, grinning all over her

face. 'I found Cookie, and she was all alone,' she said. 'She'll have two thumping big jugs of lemonade ready for us on the floor of the larder, any time after eleven o'clock tonight. The staff go to bed then, so she says any time after that will be safe for us to get it. Whoops!'

'This is going to be super,' said Alicia. 'What exactly did you say the food was, Clarissa?'

Clarissa explained, with Gwen prompting her proudly. Gwen really felt as if she had provided half the feast herself, and she basked in Clarissa's reflected glory.

'Did you ever have midnight feasts at your last school, Ruth?' asked Darrell, seeing that Ruth looked as excited as the others.

Connie answered for her as usual. 'No. We tried once, but we got caught—and my word we did get a wigging from the Head.'

'I asked Ruth, not you,' said Darrell, annoyed with Connie. 'Don't keep butting in. Let Ruth answer for herself.' She turned to Ruth again.

'Was your last head very strict?' she asked. Connie opened her mouth to answer for Ruth again, caught the glint in Darrell's eye, and shut it.

Ruth actually answered, after waiting for a moment for Connie. 'Well,' she said, 'I think probably *you* would call her very strict. You see. . . .'

'Oh, not *very* strict, Ruth,' interrupted Connie. 'Don't you remember how nice she was over . . .'

'I'M ASKING RUTH,' said Darrell, exasperated.

What would have happened next the form would dearly have loved to know—but there came an interruption that changed the subject. Matron popped her head in and said she wanted Gwendoline.

'Oh, *why*, Matron?' wailed Gwendoline. 'What haven't I done now that I ought to have done? Why do you want me?'

'Just a little matter of darning,' said Matron.

'But I've *done* the beastly darning you told me to,' said Gwen, indignantly.

'Well then—shall we say a little matter of *un*picking and *re*-darning?' said Matron, aggravatingly. The girls grinned. They had seen Gwen's last effort at darning a pair of navy-blue knickers with grey wool, and had wondered if Matron would notice.

Gwendoline had to get up and go, grumbling under her breath. 'I could do her darning for her,' suggested Clarissa to Darrell. 'I don't play games or do gym—I've plenty of time.'

'Don't you dare!' said Darrell at once. 'You help her too much as it is—she's always copying from you.'

Clarissa looked shocked. 'Oh—she doesn't *copy*,' she said loyally, going red at the idea of her daring to argue with Darrell.

'Don't be such a mutt,' said Alicia, bluntly. 'Gwendoline's a turnip-head—and she's always picked other people's brains and always will. Take off your rose-coloured glasses and see Gwen through your proper eyes, my dear Clarissa!'

Thinking that Alicia really *meant* her to take off her glasses for some reason, Clarissa removed her spectacles most obediently! The girls were about to laugh loudly, when Darrell bent forward in surprise.

'Clarissa! You've got real green eyes! I've never seen proper green eyes before! You must be related to the pixy-folk—people with green eyes always are!'

Everyone roared—but on looking closely at Clarissa's eyes, they saw that they were indeed a lovely clear green, that somehow went remarkably well with her wavy auburn hair.

'My word—I wish I had stunning eyes like that,' said Alicia enviously. 'They're marvellous. How sickening that you've got to wear glasses.'

'Oh, it's only for a time,' said Clarissa, putting them on again, looking rather shy but pleased at Alicia's admiration.

'I'm glad you like my green eyes! Gwendoline thinks it's awful to have green eyes like a cat.'

'If all cats have green eyes, then our dear Gwendoline certainly ought to have them,' said Belinda at once.

Clarissa looked distressed.

'Oh, but Gwendoline has been very kind to me,' she began, and then everyone shushed her. Gwen was coming in at the door, scowling, holding a pair of games knickers and a pair of games stockings in her hands.

'I do think Matron's an absolute *beast*,' she began. 'I spent *hours* darning these last week—and now I've got to unpick all my darns and re-do them.'

'Well, don't darn navy knickers with grey wool, or red stockings with navy wool this time,' said Alicia. 'Anyone would think you were colour-blind.'

Clarissa longed to help Gwen, but after Darrell's remark she didn't like to offer, and Gwen certainly didn't dare to ask for help. The girls sat about, yawning, trying to read, longing for bed because they really felt tired. But not too tired to wake up at twelve and have a bathe and a feast.

They didn't take long getting into bed that night. Even slow Gwendoline was quick. Irene was the quickest of the lot, much to Darrell's surprise. But it was discovered that she had absentmindedly got into bed half-undressed, so out she had to get again.

The bathing-things were stacked in someone's cupboard, waiting. Dressing-gowns and slippers were set ready on the ends of each bed.

'Sorry for you, Darrell, and you, too, Sally, having to keep awake till twelve!' said Irene, yawning. 'Good night, all—see you in a little while!'

Sally said she would keep awake for the first hour, and then wake Darrell, who would keep awake till twelve. Then each would get a little rest.

Sally valiantly kept awake, and then shook Darrell, who

slept in the next bed. Darrell was so sound asleep that she could hardly open her eyes. But she did at last, and then decided she had better get out of bed and walk up and down a little, or she might fall off to sleep again—and then there would be no feast, for she was quite certain no-one else would be awake at twelve!

At last she heard the clock at the top of the Tower striking twelve. Good. Midnight at last! She woke up Sally and then the two of them woke everyone else up. Gwendoline was the hardest to wake—she always was. Darrell debated whether or not to leave her, as she seemed determined not to wake—but decided that Clarissa might be upset—and after all, it was Clarissa's feast!

They all put on dressing-gowns and slippers. They got their bathing-things out of the cupboard and sent Irene and Belinda for the jugs of lemonade. The dormy was full of giggles and whisperings and shushings. Everybody was now wide awake and very excited.

'Come on—we'll go down to the side-door, out into the garden, and through the gate to the cliff-path down to the pool,' whispered Darrell. 'And for GOODNESS' sake don't fall down the stairs or do anything idiotic.'

It wasn't long before they were down by the pool, which was gleaming in the moonlight, and looked too tempting for words. Irene and Belinda had the jugs of lemonade.

'Let's get out the food and have a look at it,' said Sally. 'I'm longing to see it!'

'Alicia! Where's the key of the cubby-hole?' said Darrell.

'Blow!' said Alicia. 'I've left it in my tunic pocket. I'll skip back and get it. Won't be half a minute!'

ALICIA ran up the cliff-path, annoyed with herself for forgetting the key. She slipped in at the side-door of the Tower and went up the stairs. As she went along the landing where the first-form dormy was, she saw a little white figure in the passage, looking out of the landing window.

'Must be a first-former!' thought Alicia. 'What's she out this time of night for? Little monkey!'

She walked softly up to the small person looking out of the window and grasped her by the shoulder. There was a loud gasp.

'Sh!' said Alicia. 'Good gracious, it's *you*, June! What are you doing out here at midnight?'

'Well, what are *you*?' said June, cheekily.

Alicia shook her. 'None of your cheek,' she said. 'Have you forgotten the trouncing I gave you last summer hols for cheeking me and Betty, when you came to stay with me?'

'No. I haven't forgotten,' said June, vengefully. 'And I never shall. You were a beast. I'd have split on you if I hadn't been scared. Spanking me with a hair-brush as if I was six!'

'Served you jolly well right,' said Alicia. 'And you know what would have happened if you *had* split—Sam and the others would have trounced you, too!'

'I know,' said June, angrily. She was scared of Alicia's brothers. 'You wait, though. I'll get even with you some time!'

Alicia snorted scornfully. 'You could do with another spanking, I see,' she said. 'Now—you clear off to bed. You know you're not supposed to be out of your dormy at night.'

'I saw you all go off with bathing-things tonight,' said

June, slyly. 'I guessed you were up to something, you fourth-formers, when I spotted you and somebody else getting bathing-dresses in the changing-room tonight. You thought I didn't see you, but I did.'

How Alicia longed for a hair-brush to spank June with—but she dared not even raise her voice!

'Clear off to bed,' she ordered, her voice shaking with rage.

'Are you having a midnight feast, too?' persisted June, not moving. 'I saw Irene and Belinda with jugs of lemonade.'

'Nasty little spy,' said Alicia, and gave June a sharp push. 'What we fourth-formers do is none of your business. Go to bed!'

June resisted Alicia's hand, and her voice grew dangerous. 'Does Potty know about your feast?' she asked. 'Or Mam'-zelle? I say, Alicia, wouldn't it be rotten luck on you if somebody told on you?'

Alicia gasped. Could June really be threatening to go and wake one of the staff, and so spoil all their plans? She couldn't believe that anyone would be so sneaky.

'Alicia, let me come and join the feast,' begged June. 'Please do.'

'No,' said Alicia, shortly, and then, not trusting herself to say any more, she left June standing by the window and went off in search of the key to the cubby-hole. She was so angry that she could hardly get the key out of her tunic pocket. To be cheeked like that by a first-former—her own cousin! To be threatened by a little pip-squeak like that! Alicia really hated June at that moment.

She found the key and rushed back to the pool with it. She said nothing about meeting June. The others were already in the water, enjoying themselves.

'Pity the moon's gone in,' said Darrell to Sally. 'Gosh, it *has* clouded up, hasn't it? Is that Alicia back? Hey, Alicia, what a time you've been. Got the key?'

'Yes, I'm unlocking the cubby-hole,' called back Alicia. 'Clarissa is here. She'll help me to get out the things. Pity it's so dark now—the moon's gone.'

Suddenly, from the western sky, there came an ominous growl—thunder! Blow, blow, blow!

'Sounds like a storm,' said Darrell. 'I thought there might be one soon, it's so terrifically hot today. I say, Alicia, do you think we ought to begin the feast now, in case the storm comes on?'

'Yes,' said Alicia. 'Ah, here's the moon again, thank goodness!'

The girls clambered out of the water and dried themselves. As they stood there, laughing and talking, Darrell suddenly saw three figures coming down the cliff-path from the school. Her heart stood still. Were they mistresses who had heard them?

It was Betty, of course, with Eileen and Winnie. The three of them stopped short at the pool and appeared to be extremely astonished to see such a gathering of the Upper Fourth.

'I say! Whatever are you doing?' said Betty. 'We *thought* we heard a noise from the pool! It made us think that a bathe would be nice this hot night.'

'We're going to have a feast!' came Alicia's voice. 'You'd better join us.'

'Yes, do—we've got plenty,' said Irene, and the others called out the same. Even Darrell welcomed them, too, for it never once occurred to her that Betty had heard about the feast already and had come in the hope of joining them.

Neither did it occur to her that there was a strict rule that girls from one tower were never to leave their own towers at night to meet anyone from another. She just didn't think about it at all.

They all sat down to enjoy the feast. The thunder rumbled again, this time much nearer. A flash of lightning lit up the sky. The moon went behind an enormous cloud and was seen no more that night.

Worst of all, great drops of rain began to fall, plopping down on the rocks and causing great dismay.

'Oh dear—we'll have to go in,' said Darrell. 'We'll be soaked through, and it won't be any fun at all sitting and eating in the rain. Come on—collect the food and we'll go back.'

Betty nudged Alicia. 'Shall *we* come?' she whispered.

'Yes. Try it,' whispered back Alicia. 'Darrell hasn't said you're not to.'

So everyone, including Betty, Eileen and Winnie from West Tower, gathered up the food hurriedly, and stumbled up the cliff-path in the dark.

'Where shall we take the food?' panted Darrell to Sally. 'Can't have it in our common-room because it's got no curtains and the light would shine out.'

'What about the first-form common-room?' asked Sally. 'That's not near any staff-room, and the windows can't be seen from any other part.'

'Yes. Good idea,' said Darrell, and the word went round that the feast was to be held in the first-form common-room.

Soon they were all in there. Darrell shut the door carefully and put a mat across the bottom so that not a crack of light could be seen.

The girls sat about on the floor, a little damped by the sudden storm that had spoilt their plans. The thunder crashed and the lightning gleamed. Mary-Lou looked alarmed, and Gwen went quite white. Neither of them liked storms.

'Hope Thunder's all right,' said Bill, tucking into a tongue sandwich. Her horse was always her first thought.

'I should think . . .' began Alicia, when she stopped dead. Everyone sat still. Darrell put up her finger for silence.

There came a little knocking at the door. Tap-tap-tap-tap! Tap-tap-tap-tap!

Darrell felt scared. Who in the world was there? And why knock? She made another sign for everyone to keep absolutely still.

The knocking went on. Tap-tap-tap. This time it was a little louder.

Still the girls said nothing and kept quite silent. The knocking came again, sounding much too loud in the night.

'Oh dear!' thought Darrell, 'if it gets any louder, someone will hear, and the cat will be out of the bag!'

Gwendoline and Mary-Lou were quite terrified of this strange knocking. They clutched each other, as white as a sheet.

'Come in,' said Darrell, at last, in a low voice, when there was a pause in the knocking.

The door opened slowly, and the girls stared at it, wondering what was coming. In walked June—and behind her, rather scared, was Felicity!

'June!' said Alicia, fiercely.

'*Felicity!*' gasped Darrell, hardly believing her eyes.

June stared round as if in surprise.

'Oh,' she said, 'it's you, is it! Felicity and I simply *couldn't* get to sleep because of the storm, and we came to the landing window to watch it. And we found these on the ground!'

She held up three hard-boiled eggs! 'We were awfully surprised. Then we heard a bit of a noise in here and we wondered who was in our common-room—and we thought whoever it was must be having a good old feast—so we came to bring you your lost hard-boiled eggs.'

There was a silence after this speech. Alicia was boiling! She knew that June had watched them coming back because of the storm—had seen them going into the first-form common-room—and had been delighted to find the dropped eggs and bring them along as an excuse to join the party!

'Oh,' said Darrell, hardly knowing what to say. 'Thanks. Yes—we're having a feast. Er . . .'

'Why did you use our common-room?' asked June, innocently, and she broke the shell off one of the eggs. 'Of course,
it's an honour for us first-formers to have you Upper Fourth
using our room for a feast. I say—this egg's super! I didn't
mean to nibble it, though. So sorry.'

'Oh, finish it if you like,' said Darrell, not finding anything
else to say.

'Thanks,' said June, and gave one to Felicity, who began
to eat hers, too.

It ended, of course, in the two of them joining in the feast,
though Darrell really felt very uncomfortable about it. Also,
for the first time she realized that the three girls from West
Tower were still there, in North Tower where they had no
business to be! Still, how could she turn them out now? She
couldn't very well say, 'Look here, you must scram! I know
we said join the feast when we were down by the pool—but
we can't have you with us now.' It sounded too silly for
words.

Darrell did not enjoy the feast at all. She wanted to send
June and Felicity away, but it seemed mean to do that when
the feasters were using their common-room, and June had
brought back the eggs. Also she felt that Alicia might not
like her to send June away. Little did she know that Alicia
was meditating all kinds of dire punishments for the irrepressible June. Oh dear—the lovely time they had planned
seemed to have gone wrong somehow.

And then it went even more wrong! Footsteps were heard
overhead.

'DID you hear that?' whispered Sally. 'Someone is coming! Quick, gather everything up, and let's go!'

The girls grabbed everything near, and Darrell caught up the brush by the fireplace and swept the crumbs under a couch. She put out the light and opened the door. All was dark in the passage outside. There seemed to be nobody there. Who could have been walking about overhead? That was where the first-form dormy was.

June and Felicity were scared now. They shot away at once. Betty, Eileen and Winnie disappeared to the stairs, running down them to the side-door. They could then slip round to their own tower. The others, led by Darrell, went cautiously upstairs to find their own dormy.

A slight cough from somewhere near, a familiar and unmistakable cough, brought them to a stop. They stood, hardly daring to breathe, at the top of the stairs. 'That was Potty's cough,' thought Darrell. 'Oh blow—did she hear us making a row? But we really were quite quiet!'

She hoped and hoped that Betty and the other two West Tower girls had got safely to their own dormy without being caught. It really was counted quite a serious offence for girls of one tower to meet girls in another tower at night. For one thing there was no way to get from one tower to another under cover. The girls had to go outside to reach any other tower.

What could Potty be doing? Where was she? The girls stood frozen to the ground, waiting for the sign to move on.

'She's in the third-form dormy,' whispered Darrell, at

last. 'Perhaps somebody is ill there. I think we had better make a dash for it, really. We can't stand here for hours.'

'Right. The next time the thunder comes, we'll run for it,' said Sally, in a low voice. The word was passed along, and the girls waited anxiously for the thunder. The lightning flashed first, showing up the crouching line of girls very clearly—and then the thunder came.

It was a good long, rumbling crash, and any sound the girls made in scampering along to their dormy was completely deadened. They fell into bed thankfully, each girl stuffing what she carried into the bottom of her cupboard, wet bathing-suits and all.

No Miss Potts appeared, and the girls began to breathe more freely. Somebody *must* have been taken ill in the third-form dormy. Potty still seemed to be there. At last the Upper Fourth heard the soft closing of the third-form dormy, and Miss Potts' footsteps going quietly off to her own room.

'Had we better take the lemonade jugs down to the kitchen now?' whispered Irene.

'No. We won't risk any more creeping about tonight,' said Darrell. 'You must take them down before breakfast, as soon as the staff have gone into the dining-room, even though it makes you a bit late. And we'll clear out all the food left over before *we* go down, and hide it somewhere till we can get rid of it. *What* a pity that beastly storm came!'

The girls slept like logs that night, and could hardly wake up in the morning. Gwen and Belinda had to be literally *dragged* out of bed! Irene shot down to the kitchen with the empty jugs. All the rest of the food was hastily put into a bag and dumped into an odd cupboard in the landing. Then, looking demure and innocent, the fourth-formers went down to breakfast.

Felicity grinned at Darrell. She had enjoyed the escapade last night. But June did not grin at Alicia. Alicia's face was very grim, and June felt uncomfortable.

At Break Alicia went to find Hilda, the head-girl of the first form. Hilda was surprised and flattered.

'Hilda,' said Alicia, 'I am very displeased with June's behaviour. She is getting quite unbearable, and we fourth-formers are not going to stand it. Either you must put her in her place, or we shall. It would be much better for you to do it.'

'Oh, Alicia, I'm so sorry,' said Hilda. 'We *have* tried to put her in her place, but she keeps saying you'll give us no end of a wigging if we don't give her a chance. But we've given her lots of chances.'

'I bet you have,' said Alicia, grimly. 'Now, I don't know how *you* deal with your erring form-members, Hilda—we had various very good ways when *I* was a first-former—but please do *some*thing—and tell her I told you to!'

'Right. We will,' said Hilda, thankful that she had got authority to deal with that bumptious, brazen, conceited new girl, June! A week of being sent to Coventry would soon bring June to heel—she loved talking and gossiping, and it would be a hard punishment for her. Hilda went off to call a form meeting about the matter, feeling very important.

June was angry and shocked to hear the verdict of her form —to be sent to Coventry for a week. She felt humiliated, too —and how angry she was with Alicia for giving Hilda the necessary authority! Alicia was quite within her rights to do this. When a member of a lower form aroused the anger or scorn of a higher form, the head-girl of the offender's form was told to deal with the matter. And so Hilda dealt with it faithfully and promptly, and if she felt very pleased to do it, that was June's fault, and not hers. June was certainly a thorn in the side of all the old girls in the first form. It was quite unheard of for any new girl to behave so boldly.

Felicity found that she too had to give her promise not to speak to June. Oh dear—that would be very awkward —but she owed more loyalty to her form than to June. So she gave her promise in a low voice, not daring to look at the red-faced June.

That evening Felicity came to Darrell, looking worried. 'Darrell, please may I speak to you? Something rather awful has happened. Those crumbs we left in the common-room last night, under the couch, were found this morning, and so were two sandwiches. And Potty tackled Hilda and asked her if she'd been having a midnight feast there last night. Potty said she thought she heard something, but by the time she came out of the third-form dormy, where somebody was ill, and went to look in the common-room, it was empty.'

'Gosh,' said Darrell. Then her face cleared. 'Well, what's it matter? Hilda must have been asleep last night, and can't have known anything about it.'

'She *was* asleep—and she told Potty she didn't know a thing about any feast, and that the first form certainly hadn't been out of the dormy last night,' said Felicity. 'Some of them woke up in that storm, but nobody missed me or June, apparently.'

'Well, why worry then?' said Darrell. 'You shouldn't have come along with June last night, you know, Felicity. I was awfully surprised and not at all pleased to see you. You really ought to be careful your very first term.'

'I know,' said Felicity. 'I sort of get carried along by June. Honestly I can't help it, Darrell—she makes me laugh so much and she's so bold and daring. She's been sent to Coventry now, and she's as mad as anything. She knows it's all because of Alicia and she vows she'll get even with her. She will, too.'

'Felicity—do chuck June,' begged Darrell. 'She's no good as a friend. She's a little beast, really. Alicia has told me all about her.'

But Felicity was obstinate and she shook her head. 'No. I like June and I want to stick by her. She's not a little beast. She's fun.'

Darrell let Felicity go, feeling impatient with her little sister. Anyway, thank goodness Potty hadn't found out anything. She must be jolly puzzled about the crumbs and the sandwiches!

It seemed as if the whole affair would settle down—and then a bomb-shell came! Felicity came to Darrell again, the next day, looking very harassed indeed.

'Darrell! I must speak to you in private.'

'Good gracious! What's up now?' said Darrell, taking Felicity to a corner of the courtyard.

'It's June. I don't understand her. She says she's going to go to Potty and own up that she was at the midnight feast,' said Felicity. 'She says I ought to go and own up, too.'

Darrell stared at Felicity in exasperation. These first-formers! 'But if she goes and does that, it's as good as sneaking on *us*,' said Darrell, furiously. 'Where's this little pest now?'

'In one of the music-rooms practising,' said Felicity, alarmed at Darrell's fury. 'She's in Coventry, you know, so I can't speak to her. She sent me a note. Whatever am I to do, Darrell? If she goes to own up, I'll *have* to go, too, or Potty and the rest will think I'm an awful coward.'

'I'll go and talk to June,' said Darrell, and went straight off to the music-room, where the girls practised daily. She found June and burst into the room so angrily that the first-former jumped.

'Look here, June, what's behind this sudden piousness of yours—wanting to go and "own up"—when there's no need for anything of the sort?' cried Darrell, angrily. 'You know you'd get the Upper Fourth into trouble if you go and split.'

'I shan't split,' said June, calmly, playing a little scale up and down the piano. 'I shall simply own up I was at THE feast—but I shan't say whose feast. I—er—want to get it off my conscience.'

'You're a little hypocrite!' said Darrell. 'Stop playing that scale and listen to me.'

June played another little scale, a mocking smile on her face. Darrell nearly burst with rage. She slapped June's hand off the piano, and turned her round roughly to face her.

'Stop it,' said June. 'I've had enough of that kind of thing from my dear cousin Alicia!'

At the mention of Alicia's name, something clicked into place in Darrell's mind, and she knew at once what was behind June's pious idea of 'owning up'. She wanted to get even with Alicia. She would like to get her into trouble—and Darrell too—and everyone in the Upper Fourth—to revenge herself on Alicia's order to Hilda to deal with her.

'You *are* a double-faced little wretch, aren't you?' said Darrell, scornfully. 'You know jolly well if you "own up"—pooh!—that Potty will make enquiries and *I* shall have to own up to the spree in the pool, and the feast afterwards.'

'Oh—worse than that!' said June, in her infuriatingly impudent voice. 'Girls from another tower were there—or was I mistaken?'

'Do you mean to say you'd split on Betty and the others, too,' said Darrell, taking a deep breath, 'just to get even with Alicia?'

'Oh—not *split*—or even *sneak*,' said June, beginning to play the maddening scale again. 'Surely I can own up—and Betty's name can—er—just *slip* out, as it were.'

At the thought of June sneaking on everyone, under the cover of being a good little girl and 'owning up', Darrell really saw red. Her temper went completely, and she found herself pulling the wretched June off the piano-stool and shaking her violently.

A voice made her stop suddenly.

'DARRELL! Whatever *are* you doing?'

Darrell lost her temper

DARRELL stared wildly round. Miss Potts stood at the door, a picture of absolute amazement. Darrell couldn't think of a word to say. June actually had the audacity to reseat herself on the piano-stool and play a soft chord.

'June!' said Miss Potts, and the tone of her voice made the first-former almost jump out of her skin.

'Come with me, Darrell,' said Miss Potts. 'And you, too, June.'

They followed her to her room, where Mam'zelle was correcting papers. She gazed in surprise at Miss Potts' grim face, and at the faces of the two girls.

'*Tiens!*' said Mam'zelle, gathering up her papers quickly, and beginning to scuttle out of her room. 'I will go. I will not intrude, Miss Potts.'

Miss Potts didn't appear to have noticed Mam'zelle at all. She sat down in her chair and looked sternly at Darrell and June.

'What were you two doing?'

Darrell swallowed hard. She was already ashamed of herself. Oh dear—head-girl—and she had lost her temper like that! 'Miss Potts—June has something to say to you,' she said at last.

'What have you to say?' enquired Miss Potts, turning her cold eyes on June.

'Well, Miss Potts—I just wanted to own up that I had been to a midnight feast,' said June.

'Hilda said that there had been no midnight feast,' said Miss Potts, beginning to tap on the table with her pencil, always a danger-sign with her.

'I know. It wasn't a first-form affair,' said June smoothly.

'I gather from Darrell's face that it was a fourth-form affair,' said Miss Potts.

Darrell nodded miserably. 'Just the fourth-formers and you, June, I suppose?' said Miss Potts.

'Well—there were a few others,' said June, pretending to hesitate. 'One from my form as well as me. I won't mention her name.'

'Felicity was there,' said Darrell. 'But I take responsibility for that. She didn't mean to come. And Miss Potts—Betty Hill, and Eileen and Winnie were there, too.'

There was a silence. Miss Potts looked very grim.

'Girls from another tower?' she said. 'I think you know the rule about that, don't you, Darrell? And what could you have been thinking about to invite two first-formers as well? Of course—Felicity is your sister—but surely . . .'

'I didn't invite her,' said Darrell. 'And—well—I didn't exactly invite the West Tower girls either.'

'Don't let's quibble and make excuses,' said Miss Potts, impatiently. 'That isn't like you, Darrell. I imagine you were quarrelling with June because she wanted to own up?'

Darrell couldn't trust herself to speak. She nodded. 'I'm sorry I behaved like that,' she said, humbly. 'I thought I'd conquered my temper, but I haven't. I'm sorry I shook you, June.'

June was a little taken-about at this apology, and looked uneasy. But she was very cock-a-whoop and pleased with herself. She was in Potty's good books for 'owning up', she had got Darrell into trouble, and Alicia would get into trouble too and all the others—and she, June, would get off scot-free!

'You can go, June,' said Miss Potts, suddenly. 'I'm not sure I've got to the bottom of all this yet. Darrell had no right to use violence to you—but as she never loses her temper now unless something very serious makes her angry, I am inclined to take your "owning-up" with a pinch of salt.

You may be sure I shall find out whether you are to be praised or blamed!'

June shot out of the room, scared. Miss Potts looked gravely at Darrell. 'Darrell, you know that you will have to bear the responsibility for allowing girls from another tower into your tower at night, don't you?' she said. 'And I cannot possibly pass over your behaviour to June in the music-room. Whatever provocation you had does not excuse what you did.'

'I know,' said Darrell, miserably. 'I'm not a good head-girl, Miss Potts. I'd better resign.'

'Well—either you must resign, or you will have to be demoted,' said Miss Potts, sadly. 'Sally must be head for the time being—till we consider you can take the responsibility again. If you can't control yourself, Darrell, you certainly can't control others.'

The news soon flew through the school. 'Darrell Rivers has resigned as head-girl! Did you know? There has been a most awful row—something about a midnight feast, and she actually asked girls from another tower—and first-formers as well. Gosh! Fancy *Darrell Rivers* getting into disgrace!'

Felicity heard the news and was filled with the utmost horror. She went straight to June, quite forgetting that she was still in Coventry.

'Did you go and split?' she asked, sharply. 'What has happened?'

Full of glee at all that had happened, June told Felicity the whole thing from beginning to end. 'That will teach the fourth-formers to have a down on me and get me sent to Coventry,' she said. 'I've paid Alicia back nicely—and my word, you should have seen Darrell's face when she was shaking me, and Miss Potts came in and saw her. I'm glad she's not head-girl of her form any longer. Serves her right!'

Felicity could hardly believe her ears. She was trembling, shivering all over. June noticed it with surprise.

'What's the matter?' she said. 'You're my friend, aren't you?'

'I was. But have you forgotten that Darrell is my sister?' said Felicity, in a choking voice. June stared at her blankly. In her glee at being top-dog she *had* completely and utterly forgotten that Darrell was Felicity's sister.

'I feel like Darrell—I could shake you and slap you, you horrid, two-faced beast!' cried Felicity. 'As it is, I'm going to Hilda to tell her every single thing you've told me—that's not sneaking—that's reporting something almost too bad to be true! Ugh! You ought to be expelled. How could I *ever* have wanted you for my friend!'

And so the friendship between Felicity and June came to a most abrupt end, and was never renewed again. Susan was hunted out by Felicity and gave her the comfort she needed. June kicked herself for forgetting that Darrell was Felicity's sister; but the damage was done. Felicity had seen June in her true colours—and she didn't like them at all!

The fourth form were horrified at all that had happened. One and all they stood by poor Darrell, even Gwendoline coming to offer a few words of sympathy.

But Gwen's sympathy was, as usual, only on the surface. Immediately after she had been to tell Darrell how sorry she was, she was confiding to Clarissa that she really wasn't surprised that Darrell was in disgrace.

'I told you how she slapped me, didn't I,' she said. 'And she pushed Sally over once. It'll do her good to be humiliated like this. I never did like Darrell.'

Clarissa looked at Gwendoline with a sudden feeling of dislike. 'Why do you say this when you have just told her you're sorry, and that you'd do anything you could to put things right?' she said. 'I think you're beastly, Gwen.'

And to Gwen's unutterable surprise, the meek, weak Clarissa turned her back on her and walked away! It had cost her a great deal to say this to Gwen, and she was crying as she walked away.

She bumped into Bill, off to ride on Thunder. 'Here, look where you're going, Clarissa. I say, you're crying. Whatever's up?' said Bill, in surprise.

'Nothing,' said Clarissa, not wanting to say anything against Gwen.

Bill only knew one cure for unhappiness—riding a horse! She offered the cure to Clarissa now.

'Come for a ride. It's heavenly out now. You said you were allowed to ride if you wanted to. There's a horse free, I know. Miss Peters is coming, too. She's grand.'

Another time Clarissa would have said no, because it was difficult for her to make up her mind to begin anything fresh, and she had not yet ridden at Malory Towers, although she had been told that she could. But now, touched by Bill's blunt kindliness, and feeling that she wanted to get right away from Gwendoline, she nodded her head.

'All right. I'll change into my jodhpurs quickly. Wait for me.'

And in fifteen minutes' time, to Gwendoline's enormous surprise, Miss Peters, Bill—and *Clarissa* swept past her on the cliff, riding fast, shouting to one another as they went. *Clarissa!* Well! She hadn't even known that Clarissa had riding things with her. And there she was, off with that awful Bill and that even more awful Miss Peters! Gwendoline really couldn't understand it at all.

Sally was made temporary head-girl. 'I shall really *share* it with you,' she told the subdued Darrell. 'I shall come and ask you everything and take your advice—and I bet it won't be long before you're made head-girl once more. Miss Grayling told me twice I was only temporary.'

Darrell had written to her parents and told them the bad news. They would be sorry and upset, but they had to know. 'I thought I must tell you before you come to see me and

Felicity at half-term,' wrote Darrell. 'Please don't say any-thing about it when you see me, will you, because I shall howl! Anyway, dears, one good thing has come out of all this—Felicity's not friends any more with the horridest girl in her form, but with one of the nicest—Susan, that you saw at the gym display last term.'

Darrell had been very touched by the sympathy given to her by her form. The twins had been very nice, she thought, even though Ruth, as usual, had not said a word,—everything had been said by Connie. And as for Clarissa, she had been almost in tears when she came to Darrell.

'I believe Clarissa's awfully nice, when you can get under her meekness and shyness,' said Darrell to Sally. '*What* a pity she has to wear those glasses! Didn't you think she looked beautiful when she took them off the other day—those deep green eyes, like water in a pool.'

Sally laughed. 'You sound quite poetical,' she said. 'Yes, I like Clarissa now. Gwen doesn't quite know what to think about Clarissa going off riding with Bill, does she? I never knew Clarissa was so fond of horses! She and Bill gabble like anything about all the horses they have ever known—and Gwendoline looks on like a dying duck in a thunderstorm, trying to get a word in.'

'Half-term next week,' said Darrell. 'Oh, Sally, I never dreamt when I was feeling so proud of being made head-girl that I'd lose my position before even half-term came. I'm a terrible failure!'

'Well—plenty of people would like to be the kind of failure *you* are!' said Sally, loyally. 'You may be a failure at the moment—but you're a very *fine* failure, Darrell! You're a lot better than some people who think they're a success.'

HALF-TERM would soon be coming! The school was giving all kinds of displays—an exhibition tennis match played by four of the crack school players—a swimming and diving display—and a dancing display in the middle of the great courtyard.

'And after that,' said Daphne, gloomily, 'after that—the School Cert. exam! I feel awfully depressed whenever I think of it.'

'Think how light-hearted you'll be afterwards!' said Belinda.

'Yes—like you feel after going to the dentist,' said Clarissa. 'You get all gloomy beforehand and then after you've been you feel awfully happy.'

Everyone laughed. They knew that Clarissa had had bad times at the dentist, and they knew that she hated the wire round her front teeth, put there to keep them back. She was hoping she could have it off before long.

'Once I've got rid of that wire and my glasses you won't know me!' she said, and shook back her mass of auburn hair.

She had been riding quite a bit with Bill, and Gwendoline had felt rather out of things. Clarissa rode extremely well, and could apparently manage any horse in the school stables—and had actually been permitted to try Thunder!

Gwendoline found the everlasting horse conversation between the two very trying indeed.

'I once rode a horse who ran away with me and jumped over a hedge before I had even learnt how to jump!' Clarissa would begin.

And then Bill would go on. 'Did you really? I bet you stuck on all right. Did I ever tell you about Marvel, my brother Tom's horse?'

Then would follow a long story about Marvel. At the end Gwendoline would try to get a word in.

'I say—Clarissa, do you know where we are going for this afternoon's walk?'

'Not yet,' Clarissa would say. 'Well, Bill, I simply must tell you about my father's old horse that lived to be over thirty. He . . .'

And so the horsy conversation would go on, till Gwendoline felt she could scream. Horses! Horrible great snorting stamping creatures! How she wished Clarissa had never gone out for that first ride with Bill.

Gwendoline was beginning to be very much afraid of the coming exam. She was backward in her lessons, and because of her habit of picking other people's brains, and of copying their work, her own brains worked very badly when she had to think out something for herself. The exam paper had to be done with her own brains—she couldn't copy anyone's work then—and indeed Gwen knew perfectly well that Miss Williams would see to it that she, Gwendoline, would be seated much too far away from anyone else to copy!

She worried about the exam. She felt uncomfortably that she might possibly be the only person to fail—and what a disgrace and humiliation that would be! Her father would have a lot of hurtful remarks to make, and her mother would cry, and her old governess would look mournful, and say it was all her fault, she ought to have taught Gwen better when she was small. Oh dear—why did these beastly exams matter?

Gwendoline seriously considered the possibility of trying to see the papers beforehand—but that was silly, she knew. They were always locked up. She did not think to herself, 'I am *wrong* to think of such a thing,' she merely thought,

'I am silly to think there would be a chance of seeing them.'

Could she be ill? Could she complain of a sore throat and headache? No—Matron simply *never* believed her. She would take her temperature and say, 'My dear Gwendoline, you are suffering from inflammation of the imagination as usual,' and give her that perfectly horrible medicine.

She thought of Clarissa's weak heart with envy. To have something like that—that prevented you from playing those awful games, and from swimming and climbing up hills— now that was something really worth while having—something sensible. Unfortunately, though, it didn't let you off lessons.

Gwendoline thought about weak hearts for a while, and gradually a plan began to unfold itself in her mind. What about putting it round that her heart was troubling her? She put her hand to where she thought her heart was, and assumed an agonized expression. What should she say? 'Oh, my heart —it's fluttering again! I do wish it wouldn't. It makes me feel so queer. Oh, why did I run up those stairs so fast!'

The more she thought about this idea, the better it seemed. Next week was half-term. If she could work up this weak heart business well enough, perhaps her parents would be told, and they would be alarmed and take her away home. Then she would miss School Cert., which began not long after!

Gwendoline's heart began to beat fast as she thought out this little plan. In fact, she felt a little alarmed, feeling it beat so fast with excitement. Suppose she really *had* got one? No— it was only that she was feeling excited about this clever and wonderful idea of hers.

So, little by little, Gwen began to put it about that she didn't feel very well. 'Oh, nothing much,' she told Clarissa and Bill. '*You'll* know what I feel like, Clarissa—my heart sort of *flutters*! Oh, why did I run up the stairs so fast?'

Clarissa was sympathetic. She knew how absolutely sickening a weak heart was. 'Don't you think you ought to tell Miss Williams, or Miss Potts?' she said, quite anxiously. 'Or Matron?'

'No,' said Gwendoline, putting on a pathetically brave face. 'I don't want to make a fuss. Besides, you know, it's School Cert. soon. I mustn't miss that.'

If Alicia, Sally or Darrell had been anywhere near, they would have yelled with laughter at all this, but Bill and Clarissa didn't. They listened quite seriously.

'Well, *I* think you ought to say something about it,' said Clarissa. 'If you'd had to go through what *I've* had to—lie up for weeks on end, not do a thing, give up all the riding and swimming I loved—you'd not run any risk of playing about with a groggy heart.'

Gwendoline took to running up the stairs when she saw any of the Upper Fourth at the top. Then, when she came to the landing, she would put her hand to her left side, droop over the banisters and groan.

'Got a stitch?' Alicia would say, unsympathetically. 'Bend down and touch your toes, Gwendoline. Oh—I forgot—you're too fat to do that, aren't you?'

On the other hand Mary-Lou might say, 'Oh, Gwen, what's the matter? Is it your heart again? You really ought to have something done about it!'

Gwen did not perform in front of either Miss Williams or Miss Potts. She had a feeling that her performance would not go down very well. But she tried it on with Mam'zelle, who could always be taken in.

Mam'zelle was quite alarmed one morning to find Gwen sitting on the top stair near her room, her hand pressed to her heart, groaning.

'*Ma petite! Q'avez vous?* What is the matter?' she cried. 'You have hurt yourself? Where?'

'It's—it's all right, Mam'zelle,' panted Gwendoline. 'It's

—it's nothing—just this awful heart of mine. When I run or do anything energetic—it seems to go all funny!'

'You have the palpitations! You are anæmic then!' cried Mam'zelle. 'Me, I once suffered in this way when I was fifteen! You shall come with me to Matron, and she shall give you some good, good medicine to make your blood rich and red.'

Gwendoline didn't want her blood made 'rich and red' by Matron. It was the last thing in the world she wanted! She got up hastily and smiled weakly at Mam'zelle.

'It's over now! I'm quite all right. It's not anæmia, Mam-zelle—I've never been anæmic. It's just my silly heart. It's—er—it's a weakness in our family, I'm afraid.'

This was quite untrue, but Gwendoline added it because she thought it might convince Mam'zelle it was her heart and not her blood that was wrong! Mam'zelle was very sympathetic, and told Gwen she had better not play tennis that afternoon.

Gwendoline was delighted—but on thinking it over she regretfully decided that she had better play, because she wouldn't possibly be able to convince Sally that her heart had played her up again. Sally just simply didn't believe in Gwen's weak heart. So she played. Mam'zelle saw her and was surprised.

'The brave Gwendoline!' she thought. 'She plays even though she knows it may bring on the palpitations again! Ah, these English girls, they have the courage and the pluck!'

Gwendoline laid a few more plans. She would bring Mam'zelle up to her parents at half-term, and leave her to talk to them. She was certain that sooner or later Mam'zelle would speak about her heart—and then she, Gwen, would be anxiously questioned by her mother—and if she played her cards well, she would be taken home at once by a very anxious and frightened mother!

Gwen did not stop to think of the pain and anxiety she

would give to her parents by her stupid pretence. She
wanted to get out of doing the exam, and she didn't mind
how she did it. She was quite unscrupulous, and very clever
when she badly wanted her own way.

'I'm certain Mother will take me home,' she thought. 'I
really don't think I need bother about swotting up for the
exam. It will be a waste of time if I don't take it. Look at all
the others—groaning and moaning every evening, mugging
up Latin and French and maths and history and the rest!
Well—*I* shan't!'

And, to the surprise of everyone, Gwendoline suddenly
stopped working hard, and slacked!

'Aren't you afraid of doing frightfully bad papers?' asked
Mavis, who was rather afraid of this herself, and was working
very hard indeed.

'I shall do my best,' said Gwendoline. 'I can't do more.
It's this beastly heart of mine, you know—it does play me up
so, if I work too hard.'

Mavis didn't believe in this heart of Gwendoline's, but she
was really puzzled to know why the girl was so silly as to
waste her time, when she ought to be putting in some good
hard work preparing for the exam.

But, surprisingly enough, it was Connie who put her finger
on the right spot! She had a great scorn for the weak, in-
effectual Gwendoline. She was a domineering, strong-minded
girl herself, and she could not bear Gwendoline's moaning
and grumbling. For some reason or other Connie had been
touchy and irritable for the last week or two, and her bad
temper suddenly flared out one evening at Gwen.

Gwendoline had come into the common-room and flopped
down in a chair. Everyone was swotting hard for the exam
as usual, their heads bent over their books.

'I really must *not* carry heavy things again,' began Gwendoline, in her peevish voice. Nobody took any notice except
to frown.

'I've had to help Potty with the books in the library,' went on Gwen. 'Great heavy piles! It's set my heart fluttering like anything!'

'Shut up,' said Connie. 'We're working.'

'Well, there's no need for you to be rude,' said Gwen, with dignity. 'If you had a heart like mine . . .'

And then Connie exploded. She got up and went to stand over the astonished Gwendoline.

'You haven't *got* a heart, weak or otherwise! You're a big bundle of pretence! You're making it all up to get out of School Cert. *I* can see through you! That's why you're not working, isn't it—because you're banking on your heart letting you out, in some way or other you've planned! Well, let me tell you this—I don't care tuppence whether you do School Cert. or not, or whether you work or not—but I *do* care about my own work! And so do the others. So SHUT UP about your silly heart, and keep away from us with your moanings and groanings till School Cert. is over!'

With that Connie went back to her seat, glowering. Everyone was startled—too startled to say a word. They all felt that what Connie said was true.

'You hateful, cruel thing!' said Gwendoline in a trembling voice. 'I hope you fail! And you will, too—see if you don't! You only get decent marks because you're always cribbing from Ruth. We all know that! She'll pass and you won't! I think you're a beast!'

She burst into tears, got up and went out of the room, banging the door so violently that Mam'zelle and Miss Potts, working in their room not far away, wondered whatever was happening.

The girls looked at one another. Alicia made a face. 'Well, I expect Connie's right—though you were a bit brutal, weren't you, Connie?'

'No more brutal than you sometimes are,' said Connie, rather sulkily. 'Anyway, let's get to work again. Some of us are not like you, Alicia—skating lightly over every subject and doing everything well, without bothering. You don't understand how hard some of us find our work. Let's get on.'

There was silence in the room as the girls worked away, reading, making notes, learning by heart. Only Clarissa and Mary-Lou were really troubled about Gwen. Clarissa still believed in her weak heart, and Mary-Lou was always sorry for anyone who cried.

As for Gwendoline, her tears were not tears of sorrow, but of rage. That horrible Connie! If only she could get back at her for her unkind words. How Gwendoline hoped that Connie hadn't spoilt her beautiful plan!

17   HALF-TERM AT LAST

HALF-TERM came at last. It was a really lovely day, with bright sunshine and a nice breeze. The kitchen staff worked with a will to produce masses of good things for the grand School Tea. All the girls were excited about seeing their people.

Gwendoline had quite thought that Clarissa's people were coming, and had planned to introduce them to her mother and father. Then she suddenly heard Bill and Clarissa planning a picnic together on the half-term Saturday!

'Two of my brothers have their half-term at the same time,' said Bill, 'so they're coming with Mother and Daddy. We'll take our lunch up to the top of Langley Hill, shall we, and bathe in the cove afterwards, before we come back to the Tennis Exhibition.'

Gwen listened in astonishment. 'But what will Clarissa's father and mother say to that?' she said. 'Won't they want Clarissa to themselves?'

'They can't come on the Saturday, worse luck,' said Clarissa. 'They may be able to come over on Sunday though —at least, Mother might be able to, even if Daddy can't. They're dreadfully busy people, you know.'

'So I've asked Clarissa to come with us,' said Bill. 'My family will bring enough lunch for twice as many as we'll be, so we'll have a good time!'

Gwen was jealous. Why, she could have had Clarissa spend the day with *her*, if she'd known.

'Well! You might have told *me* your people couldn't come on Saturday,' she said. 'You know how much I should have liked you to spend your time with *my* people.'

Clarissa looked embarrassed. She had purposely not told Gwen, because she had so much wanted to go with Bill and her brothers—all nice horsy people! But she couldn't explain that to Gwen. So, to make up for her remissness she was extra nice to her, and promised to go and speak to Gwen's people when they arrived.

'You might just *mention* my heart to them,' said Gwendoline. 'I don't really like to make a fuss about it myself— but *you* could just say something, Clarissa.'

'Of course I will,' said Clarissa, who still believed in Gwen's weak heart. 'I think something ought to be done about it.'

So, on half-term Saturday, Clarissa was led up to Mrs. Lacy, Gwendoline's mother, and Miss Winter, her gentle and scared-looking old governess. Her father was not there.

Mrs. Lacy was talking to another mother. Clarissa sat down on the grass with Gwendoline, waiting till she had finished. Darrell's mother was near, and Darrell introduced her to Clarissa.

Soon she heard Gwen talking to her mother and Miss

Winter. 'Well, dear,' said her mother, fondly, 'and what has my darling Gwendoline been doing this term? Are you in the exhibition tennis?'

'Well, no, Mother,' said Gwendoline. 'I was almost chosen —but it was decided only to have girls from the fifth and the sixth.'

'How stupid!' said Miss Winter, feeling that Gwen would certainly have been better than any fifth- or sixth-form girl.

'What about your swimming, Gwen?' asked her mother. 'You said in one of your letters that you had won a back-stroke swimming race and I *did* think that was clever. Back-stroke is *so* difficult. I remember I could never do it at school because the water kept going over my face.'

Clarissa couldn't help hearing this conversation, though she was talking to Mrs. Rivers, Darrell's mother. She was horrified. Whatever did Gwen mean by all this?

'No, I'm not swimming today,' said Gwen. 'There's a lot of jealousy, you know, Mother—often the good ones aren't given a proper chance. Still, I don't really mind. I can *dive* almost better than anyone now.'

As Gwen always fell flat on her stomach, hitting the water with a terrific smack whenever she was made to dive, this was distinctly funny—or would have been to Darrell, Sally or Alicia. But it wasn't funny to Clarissa. It was shocking. What terrible lies—real thumping lies! However could Gwen say such things? She was very thankful that she was going out with blunt, straightforward Bill instead of having to be with Gwen and her silly, credulous mother. She saw very clearly why Gwen was as she was—this mother of hers had spoilt her, idolized her, believed every word she said—it was she—and probably that pathetic little governess too—who had made Gwendoline into the silly, conceited, untrust-worthy girl she was!

Clarissa felt that she really could *not* go and speak to Gwen's mother, after hearing all Gwen's untruths. She couldn't! Clarissa was meek, and weak in many ways, but she was straight and truthful. She was really shocked now.

She got up to slip away before Gwen could see she was going. But Gwen did see, and pulled her down again, so that she had to smile and say 'How-do-you-do?' to Gwen's mother and governess.

'I mustn't stop, I'm afraid,' said Clarissa, hurriedly. 'Bill's people have come and I mustn't keep them waiting.'

Gwendoline looked at her meaningly. Clarissa knew what that look meant. 'Say something about my heart.' But alas, she found that she no longer believed in Gwendoline's heart. She was sure that the girl had lied about that now, just as she had lied about the other things a few minutes back.

'And are *you* in the tennis or swimming exhibitions?' asked Mrs. Lacy, her large, pale blue eyes, so like Gwen's, looking down at Clarissa's small face.

'No, I'm not, I'm afraid,' said Clarissa.

'You see, *poor* Clarissa has a weak heart,' said Gwen, hastily, seeing a very good opening indeed here for Clarissa to bring up the subject of Gwen's own heart. But Clarissa didn't say a word.

'Poor child,' said Mrs. Lacy. 'What a dreadful affliction for a young girl. Now Gwen has always had such a *strong* heart, I'm glad to say. And doesn't she look well now—so plump and bonny.'

Gwen looked at Clarissa in desperation. This was all wrong! She gave her a sharp nudge. But still Clarissa didn't mention Gwen's weak heart! Gwen glared at her angrily.

Clarissa was now tongue-tied. She sat there, red in the face, her eyes blinking behind their thick glasses, wondering how in the world to get away from Gwen and her silly mother.

Bill came to her rescue with a shout. 'Clarissa! I say, can you come? We're ready!'

'I must go,' said Clarissa, nervously, and got up gladly. 'Good-bye, Mrs. Lacy.'

'But, Clarissa!' called Gwendoline after her, dismayed and angry that Clarissa hadn't done what she had said she would do.

'*Who* did you say that girl was?' said Mrs. Lacy. 'I didn't catch the name.'

'It's Clarissa Carter,' said Gwen, sulkily. 'Why did she have to rush off like that? Rude, I call it!'

'A most unattractive child,' said Mrs. Lacy. 'Very plain indeed. No manners either. Gwendoline, I do hope she isn't a friend of yours.'

'Oh *no*, Mother!' said Gwendoline, making up her mind that after Clarissa's failure to help her that morning she would never be friendly with her again! 'I don't like her at all. Very plain, as you say—almost ugly—and undergrown, too. Not at all clever, and rather unpopular.'

'I should think so!' said Miss Winter. 'She must have been very badly brought up. When I compare her with Gwendoline—well!'

Gwendoline basked in their approval. She kept a sharp watch for Mam'zelle. Mam'zelle was her only hope now!

The day went by very fast. The tennis exhibition was loudly applauded, and the swimming and diving were exclaimed at in wonder, even the fathers admiring the crisp clean strokes of the fast swimmers, and the beautiful diving.

Afterwards the dancing display was held in the amphitheatre of grass in the centre of the great courtyard. Mothers and fathers sat on the stone ledges surrounding the big circle, looking for their own girls as they came tripping in, dressed in floating tulle of different colours—and each parent, of course, felt certain that her own child was quite the nicest there!

Clarissa came back after her picnic lunch with Bill and her family. She did not go near Gwen, and would not even look in her direction in case she was beckoned over. But Gwen made no sign—she had Finished with Clarissa, the horrid little two-faced thing.

Most unfortunately for Gwendoline, Mam'zelle kept quite out of reach the whole day. She was busy helping the dancing mistress, dressing the girls, arranging their tulle skirts and wings, thoroughly enjoying herself. Gwendoline had to comfort herself by thinking that she would find it easy to get Mam'zelle the next day. She would ask Mam'zelle to show her mother and Miss Winter the beautiful bedspread she was making. Mam'zelle would certainly love to do that—she was very proud of her bedspread!

'I wish this day wasn't over,' sighed Darrell that night. 'It was lovely—and what a smashing tea!'

She was happy because her mother and father hadn't said a word about her not being head-girl any longer—but each of them had managed to convey to her that they understood all about it, and were backing her valiantly—her father by an extra hard hug, and her mother by linking her arm in Darrell's and holding it very hard as she walked round the Towers with her.

Felicity, of course, was mad with joy to see her parents again. 'I love Malory Towers!' she kept saying. 'Thank you for sending me here, Mummy and Daddy. I simply LOVE it!'

18   BEFORE THE EXAM

THE next day the girls expected most of their parents again, and could go out with them the whole day long. Clarissa stood at the window, looking out eagerly.

Gwendoline saw her. 'I suppose she's looking for her mother,' she thought. 'Horrid thing. I shan't even speak to her!'

She saw Clarissa suddenly wave in delight. Then she ran from the room and disappeared down the stairs. Gwen looked out to see what her mother was like—and if the car was a grand one.

To her surprise she saw an old Austin in the drive, and out of it stepped a most ordinary-looking woman. She had on a neat blue suit with a white blouse, and a scarf tied round her grey hair. She wore glasses, and had rather large feet in very sensible looking shoes.

'Well! I don't think much of Clarissa's mother—*or* her car!' thought Gwen to herself. 'Why, the car hasn't even been *cleaned*! And fancy arriving with a scarf tied round her head! My mother would never dream of doing that!'

She thought of her own mother with her large flowery hats, her flowery dresses, her flowery parasol, her floating scarves and strings of pearls. She would be ashamed of any-one like Clarissa's mother. She turned away, a sneer on her face, glad that she no longer meant to have Clarrisa for a friend.

'What a *lovely* sneer!' said an aggravating voice, and Gwen saw Belinda whipping out her pencil. 'Hold it, Gwen, hold it!'

Gwen made a noise like a dog growling, and went out of the room. Now she must find Mam'zelle and tell her that her mother wanted to see the beautiful bedspread. This went down very well indeed, and Mam'zelle hurried to get it to show 'that nice kind Mrs. Lacy'!

Every single girl was out for the whole day, either with her own parents or with someone else's. Miss Grayling was glad that the half-term came just before the School Certificate exam, so that the hard-worked girls might have a little time off to enjoy themselves. They really were working very hard,

Miss Williams reported. Except Gwendoline Lacy, of course. *There* was an unsatisfactory girl for you!

By seven o'clock everyone was back—except Gwendoline!

'Where's our dear Gwendoline?' asked Alicia, looking round the supper-table. Nobody knew. Then Mam'zelle, looking rather solemn, enlightened them.

'Poor Gwendoline—she has been taken home because of her bad heart,' said Mam'zelle. 'She has the palpitations so bad, poor, poor child. And will you believe it, when I told Mrs. Lacy—ah, the poor woman—about Gwendoline's affliction, she said that the dear, brave child had not complained to her, or said a single word. *Vraiment,* this poor child is to be admired!'

The girls digested this startling information in astonishment. They looked at one another. 'So Gwen's pulled it off after all,' said Sally. 'She'll miss the exam!'

Mam'zelle overheard. 'Yes, she will miss the exam—and how upset she was. "No, Mother," she said, so bravely, "I cannot go home with you—I must do the exam. I did not tell you of my trouble because I could not bear to miss the exam!" That is what she said. With my own ears I heard her.'

The Upper Fourth felt sick. What a sham! How hateful of Gwendoline to upset her mother like that! And she had got her way after all and would miss the exam. Clever, deceitful, sly Gwendoline!

'You were right, Connie,' said Alicia. '*How* right! Mam'zelle, what's going to happen to our darling Gwendoline Mary then? Isn't she coming back this term? *That* would be too good to be true!'

'I don't know,' said Mam'zelle. 'I know nuzzings more. I am glad I was able to tell Mrs. Lacy. Just to think that if I had not taken my bedspread to show her, she would never have known.'

'I suppose *Gwen* asked you to take the bedspread?' said

Connie. 'And I suppose one of her palpitations came on whilst you were there, Mam'zelle?'

'I do not understand why you talk in this sneering way, Connie,' said Mam'zelle, surprised. 'You must not be hard. You must have sympathy.'

The girls made various rude noises, which surprised Mam'zelle very much. Why these poohs and pahs and pullings of faces? No, no, that was not kind! Mam'zelle pursed up her lips and said no more.

'Well,' said Darrell, in the dormy that night, 'Gwen's got away with it all right—but fancy Mam'zelle falling for all that. Mam'zelle Rougier wouldn't. She sees right through Gwendoline—just like Miss Williams does!'

'All the same—she's lucky, getting out of the exam,' groaned Belinda. 'Wish *I* could! It's going to be awful to swot and swot all this week, after such a lovely half-term. And then—next Monday the exam! I'm surprised you can't all hear my heart going down with a plop into my bedroom slippers!'

It was very hard to swot in such lovely weather. Alicia longed for a game of tennis. Darrell longed for the swimming-pool. Clarissa longed to go and laze in the flowery courtyard and watch the goldfish jumping. Belinda wanted to go out sketching. Irene became plagued with an enchanting tune that begged to be put down on paper—but poor Irene had to turn her back firmly on the lilting melody, and do pages and pages of French translation.

There was a lot of touchiness and irritability that week. The twins were on edge, especially Ruth, though she had less to fear in the exam than Connie, who was not nearly so well up to standard. Irene was touchy because she wanted to get at her beloved music and couldn't. Darrell was irritable because she was too hot. Mavis was hot and bothered because she thought she was going to have a sore throat—just as her voice seemed about to get right too!

Only Alicia seemed really cheerful and don't-carish, and this attitude infuriated the others at times. Alicia was always the one to finish her work first and go off to swim. She could do her work and whistle an irritating little tune all the time, which nearly drove the others frantic. She laughed at their earnest faces, and their heartfelt groans.

'It's not worth all this amount of misery,' she would say. 'It's only School Cert. Cheer up, Connie—don't look like a dying duck over that French.'

Connie flared up as she had done to Gwendoline. She banged her book down on the table and shouted. 'Be quiet! Just because things are easy for you to learn, you sneer at others who aren't so lucky! Wait till you have a bad headache and have to learn pages of French poetry. Wait till your mind goes fuzzy because you're tired and want to sleep, and you know you mustn't. Wait till you have a bad night and have to think of things to say in a composition. Then you won't be quite so hard and don't-carish and sneering, and you'll shut up that awful whistling, too!'

Alicia was startled. She opened her mouth to retaliate, but Sally spoke first.

'Connie doesn't really mean all that,' she said in her quiet calm voice. 'We're all over-working and we're irritable and touchy. We'll be all right when the exam is over. After all, it's an important exam for us, and we're all taking it seriously and doing our best. Let's not squabble and quarrel when we want to save ourselves up for next week.'

Darrell looked at Sally in admiration. How did she always know the right thing to say? She had certainly poured oil on the troubled waters very successfully, because Connie spoke up at once.

'I'm sorry I said all that, Alicia. I *am* over-working and I'm touchy.'

'It's all right,' said Alicia, rather taken aback by this swift apology. 'Sorry about my whistling—and if anyone wants any help, they've only got to ask me. I'll share these envied brains of mine with anyone!'

After this there was peace. Alicia shut her book quietly and crept out. The others worked on in silence. Would they ever, ever know all they ought to know for the exam? Why hadn't they swotted more during the year? Why hadn't they done this and that and the other! In fact their thoughts were almost exactly the same as every other exam-class's thoughts the week before the exam!

The week went by, and the girls worked more and more feverishly. Miss Williams forbade any work to be done on the Sunday before the exam, and there were deep groans.

And then came a surprise. Gwendoline arrived back at Malory Towers!

She came back on the Saturday, just before supper, looking subdued and tearful. She had a short interview with Miss Grayling, and then was sent to join the others, who had just gone in to their supper.

'Why, GWEN!' said Mavis, in astonishment, seeing her first. 'We thought you weren't coming back.'

'Ah, here is Gwendoline back again,' said Mam'zelle. 'And how is the poor heart?'

'All right, thank you,' mumbled Gwen, slipping into her seat, and trying to look as if she was not there.

The girls saw that she had been crying and tried not to look at her. They knew how horrid it was to have people looking at red eyes.

'Jolly lucky you'll be, next week,' said Sally, trying to make light conversation. 'Whilst we're all answering exam papers, you'll be lazing away in the courtyard, doing what you like!'

There was a little pause. 'I've got to go in for the exam,' said Gwen, in a choking voice. 'That's why they've sent me back. It's too *bad*.'

To the girls' dismay Gwendoline's tears began to fall fast

into her plate of salad. They looked uncomfortably at one another. Whatever had happened?

'Better not say any more,' whispered Darrell. 'Don't take any notice of her. Poor Gwen!'

19   THE EXAM WEEK

NOBODY ever knew what exactly had happened to Gwen. She was much too hurt and ashamed to tell anyone the story. So she said nothing, but went about subdued and red-eyed the whole week-end.

Everything had gone so well at first! Her frightened mother had taken her straight home, after Mam'zelle had mentioned Gwen's strange heart flutterings and palpitations. She had made her lie down and rest, and she and Miss Winter had fussed over her like a hen with one chick. Gwendoline had loved every minute, and had at once produced the languid ways and the feeble voice of the invalid.

She was rather pleased to know that her father was away and not likely to be back at all that week. By that time Gwen hoped she would be established as a semi-invalid, would miss all the exam, and might then gradually get better, once the exam danger was over.

The doctor came and listened solemnly to Gwen's mother's frightened explanations. 'I'm *so* afraid it's her heart that's wrong, Doctor,' she said. 'The games are *very* strenuous at school, you know.'

The doctor examined Gwen carefully. 'Well, I can't find

anything wrong,' he said. 'Nothing that a week's rest won't put right, anyway. She's a bit fat, isn't she—she could do with a bit of dieting, I should think.'

'Oh, but Doctor—there *must* be something wrong with the child's heart,' insisted Mrs. Lacy. 'Miss Winter and I have been very troubled to see how she loses her breath, and can hardly get up to the top stair when she goes to her bedroom.'

'Well—why not get another opinion then?' said the doctor. 'I should like you to satisfy yourself about Gwendoline.'

'I'll take her to a specialist,' said Mrs. Lacy, at once. 'Can you recommend one, Doctor?'

The doctor could and did, and on Wednesday the languid invalid was carefully driven up to London to see the specialist recommended. He took one quick glance at Gwendoline and sized her up at once.

He examined her very carefully indeed, with so many 'hm's' and 'ha's' that Gwendoline began to feel frightened. Surely she hadn't *really* got something the matter with her? She would die if she had!

The specialist had a short talk with Mrs. Lacy alone. 'I will think over this, and will write to your doctor full details and let him know the result of my considerations. In the meantime, don't worry,' he said.

On Friday the doctor got a letter from the specialist, and it made him smile. There was nothing wrong with Gwendoline's heart, of course, in fact nothing wrong anywhere at all, except that she was too fat, and needed very much more exercise. 'Games, and more games, gym, walks, no rich food, no sweets, plenty of hard work, and no thinking about herself at all!' wrote the specialist. 'She's just a little humbug! Swimming especially would be good for her. It would take some fat off her tummy!'

The doctor had to paraphrase all this considerably, of course, when he telephoned the news to Mrs. Lacy that there was nothing the matter with Gwen. 'I should send her back to school at once,' he said. 'It's not good for the girl to lie about like this.'

Gwen was angry and miserable when she heard all this. She laid her hand to her heart as if it pained her. 'Oh, Mother!' she said. 'I'll go back if you say so—but give me one more week—I feel so much better for the rest.'

Mrs. Lacy promised Gwen that she should not go back for another week or more. Gwen was satisfied. So long as she missed the exam she didn't mind!

Then her father arrived home, anxious because of his wife's letters and telephone calls about Gwen. Gwen lay on the couch and gave him a pathetic smile. He kissed her, and enquired anxiously what the specialist had said.

'What! *Nothing* wrong,' he said in astonishment. 'I'll go round and see the doctor. I'd like to see the specialist's letter myself. I shall feel more satisfied then.'

And so it came about that Gwen's father actually read the candid letter—saw that Gwen was called a 'little humbug' —knew very clearly indeed that once more his daughter had tried a little deception—a cruel deception, that had caused her parents much anxiety—and all because she had merely wanted to get out of working for the exam.

What he said to Gwendoline the girl never forgot. He was angry and scornful and bitter—and at the end he was sad. 'You are my only child,' he said. 'I want to love you and be proud of you, like all parents. Why do you make it so hard for me to be proud of you, and to love you, Gwendoline? You have made your mother ill with this, and you have made me angry and disgusted—and very sad.'

'I won't do it again,' sobbed Gwendoline, terrified and ashamed.

'You must go back to school tomorrow,' said her father.

'Oh no, Daddy! I can't! It's the exam,' wailed Gwendoline. 'I haven't done any work for it.'

'I don't care. Go in for it just the same, fail and be humili-

ated,' said her father. 'You have brought it all on yourself.
I am telephoning to Miss Grayling to apologize for taking
you away, and to give her the specialist's instructions—games,
more games, gym, walks—and most of all, swimming!'

Swimming! The one thing Gwen detested most of all. She
dissolved into tears again and wept the whole of the evening
and the whole of the way down to Cornwall the next day.
What had she done to herself? She hadn't been so clever
after all! It had all ended in her having to take the exam without working for it, and in having to go in for games more
than ever—and probably bathe every single day in that nasty
cold pool! Poor Gwen. People do often bring punishment on
themselves for foolishness—but not often to the extent that
Gwendoline did.

The exam began. Everyone was jittery—even Alicia,
curiously enough. Day after day the work went on, whilst
the bright July sun shone in through the open windows, and
the bees hummed enticingly outside. The girls were glad to
rush off to the swimming-pool after tea each day—then back
again they went to swot up for the next day's exam.

Something curious had happened to Alicia. She didn't
understand it. The first day she sat and looked at the questions, feeling sure they would be easy for her. So they were.
But she found that she could not collect her thoughts
properly. She put her hand up to her head. Surely she wasn't
beginning a headache!

She struggled with the questions—yes, *struggled*—a thing
the quick-witted, never-at-a-loss Alicia had hardly ever done
before! She looked round at the others, puzzled—goodness,
how could they write so quickly? What had happened to her?

Alicia had seldom known a day's illness. She was strong
and healthy and clever. She really could not imagine why
this exam was so difficult. She could not go to sleep at night,
but lay tossing and turning. Had she been over-working?
No—surely not—the others had worked far harder than she

had, and had envied her for not having to swot so much. Well, WHAT was it then?

'Gosh,' thought Alicia, trying to find a cool place on her pillow, 'I know what it must feel like now, to have slow brains like Daphne, or a poor memory like Gwendoline. I can't remember a thing—and if I try, my brains won't work. They feel as if they want oiling!'

The others noticed that Alicia was rather quiet and subdued that week, but as they all felt rather like that, they said nothing. Quite a few of them went about looking very worried. Ruth looked white and drawn, Connie looked anxious, Gwendoline looked miserable, Daphne was almost in tears over the French—what a collection they were, thought Miss Williams—just like every other School Certificate form she had ever known, when exams were on. Never mind—it would be all behind them next week, and they would be in the highest spirits!

She glanced at one or two of the papers when they were collected. Darrell was doing fine! Gwendoline would be lucky if she got quarter marks! Mary-Lou was unexpectedly good. Connie's was poor—Ruth's was not good either. How strange! Ruth was usually well up to standard! It was doubtful if she would pass, if she completed the rest of her papers badly. And Alicia! Whatever in the world had happened to *her*! Bad writing—silly mistakes—good gracious, was Alicia playing the fool?

But Alicia wasn't. She couldn't help it. Something had happened to her that week and she was frightened now. 'It must be a punishment to me for always laughing and sneering at people who aren't as quick and clever as I am,' she thought, in dismay. 'My brains have gone woolly and slow and stupid, like Gwen's and Daphne's. I can't remember a thing. How horrible! I'm trying so hard, too, that my head feels as if it's bursting. Is this what the others feel sometimes, when I laugh at them for looking so serious over their work?

It's horrible, horrible, horrible! If only my brains would come back properly! I'm frightened!'

'Is anything the matter, Alicia?' said Darrell, on the last day of the exam. 'You look all out.'

Alicia never complained, no matter what went wrong with her. 'No,' she said. 'I'm all right. It's just the exam.'

She sat next to Darrell for the exam. At the end of the last paper, Darrell heard a slight noise. She looked up and gave a cry. Alicia had fallen forward over her papers!

'Miss Williams! Alicia's fainted!' she called. Matron was called, and as soon as Alicia came round again, looking bemused and strange, she was taken to the san. Matron undressed her—and cried out in surprise.

'You've got *measles*, Alicia! Just *look* at this rash—I never saw anything like it in my life! Didn't you notice it before?'

'Well—yes—but I thought it was just a heat-rash,' said Alicia, trying to smile. 'Oh, Matron—I'm so glad it's only measles. I thought—I really thought my brains had gone this week. I felt as if I was going potty, and I was awfully frightened.'

Alicia felt so thankful when she got in to bed and rested her aching head against the cool pillow. She felt ill, but happy. It was only measles she had had that awful week! It wasn't that her brains had really gone woolly and stupid—it wasn't a punishment sent to her for sneering at the others who were slower than herself—it was just—measles.

And with that Alicia fell asleep and her temperature began to go down. She felt much better when she awoke. Her brains felt better, too!

'I'm afraid you'll have no visitors or company this week, Alicia,' said Sister, who was in charge of the san. Matron had now departed back to school. 'Just your own thoughts!'

Yes—just her own thoughts. Thankfulness that she wasn't going to be slow and stupid after all—shame that she had been so full of sneers and sarcastic remarks to others not so clever as herself—sadness because she knew she must have done terrible papers, and would surely fail. She would have to take School Cert. all over again! Blow!

'Well,' thought Alicia, her brains really at work again, as her strong and healthy body began to throw off the disease, 'well—I'd better learn my lesson—I shan't be so beastly hard again. But I honestly didn't know what it was like to have slow brains. Now I do. It's awful. Fancy having them all your life and knowing you can't alter them. I'll never sneer at others again. Never. At least, not if I can remember it. It's a frightful habit with me now!'

It was indeed. Alicia was going to find it very hard indeed to alter herself—but still, she had taken the first important step—she had realized that there was something to alter! She would never be quite so hard again.

The exams were over at last! The girls went quite mad and the mistresses let them! The swimming-pool was noisy and full, the tennis courts were monopolized by the Upper Fourth, the kitchen staff were begged for ice-creams and iced lemonade at every hour of the day—or so it seemed! Girls went about singing, and even sour-faced Mam'zelle Rougier smiled to see them so happy after the exam.

Gwendoline wasn't very happy, of course. Miss Grayling had taken her father's instructions seriously, and Gwen was having more games, more walks—and more swimming than she had ever had before. But it was no good complaining or grumbling. She had brought it all on herself—it was nobody's fault but her own!

'NOW we can have a good time for the rest of the term,' said Darrell, pleased. 'No more swotting—no more long preps even, because Miss Williams says we've done enough. We'll enjoy ourselves!'

'It ought to be a nice peaceful end of term, with no horrid happenings,' said Sally. 'When Alicia comes back, it will be nicer still.'

Sally was wrong when she said there ought to be a nice peaceful end of term, with no horrid happenings—because the very next day the Connie Affair began.

It began with quite small things—a missing rubber—an essay spoilt because a page was missing, apparently torn out —a lace gone from one of Connie's shoes.

Nobody took any notice at first—things always *were* missing anyhow and turned up in the most ridiculous places—and pages did get torn out of books, and laces had a curious habit of disappearing.

But the Connie Affair didn't end there. Connie was always in trouble about something! 'Now my French poetry book has gone!' she complained. 'Now my cotton has gone out of my work-basket.' Now this and now that!

'But, Connie—how is it that so many things happen to you lately?' said Darrell, puzzled. 'I don't understand it. It's almost as if somebody was plaguing you—but who could it be? Not one of us would do silly, idiotic things like this—sort of first-form spite!'

Connie shook her head. 'I can't think who's doing it,' she said. 'I suppose it *is* someone. It can't be a series of accidents —there's too many of them.'

'What do *you* think about it, Ruth?' asked Darrell—but
Connie answered first.

'Oh, Ruth can't think who does it, either. It's very upset-
ting for her, because twins are always so fond of one another.
She's sweet, too—keeps on giving me her things when I lose
mine.'

'Well, it's certainly most extraordinary,' said Darrell. 'I'm
very sorry about it, it's a horrid thing to happen in the
fourth form!'

The girls talked about the Connie Affair, as they called
it, and puzzled about it. One or two of them looked at Gwendoline, wondering if she had anything to do with it.

'Don't you remember how Connie flared out at Gwen and
put her finger on Gwen's weak spot—when she was putting
over that nonsense about her heart?' said Daphne. 'And you
know—Gwen *has* done these nasty tricks before. Don't you
remember? She did them to Mary-Lou when we were in the
second form.'

'Give a dog a bad name and hang him,' quoted Darrell.
'Just because Gwen did once do things like this, and got a
bad name for it, doesn't mean we ought to accuse her of the
same thing now. For goodness' sake wait a bit before we
decide anything.'

'There speaks a head-girl,' said Irene.

Darrell flushed. 'I'm not head-girl,' she said. 'Wish I was.
But seriously, it really is jolly queer, all this business. The
things are so very *silly*, too—Connie's ink-pot was stuffed up
with blotting-paper this morning, did you know?'

'Well!' said Belinda. 'How petty!'

'Yes—most of the things are petty and spiteful and quite
futile,' said Darrell. 'You don't suppose they'll get any
worse, do you? I mean—stop being petty and get harm-
ful?'

'Let's hope not,' said Mavis. 'Here are the twins. Hallo,
Connie—anything more to report?'

'Yes—somebody's cut my racket handle,' she said, and showed it to them. 'Just where I grip it! Mean, isn't it.'

'You can use mine, Connie. I told you,' said Ruth, who was looking very distressed. 'You can use anything of mine.'

'I know, Ruth—but supposing your things get messed up, too?' said Connie. 'I'd hate that.'

'It's all very, very queer,' said Irene, and hummed a new melody she had just composed. 'Tooty-tooty-tee!'

Mavis sang to it—'It's all—very—queer! It's all—very—queer!'

'I say!' said Darrell. 'Your voice is coming back! That's just how you *used* to sing, Mavis! It is, really.'

'Yes, I know,' said Mavis, her face red with pleasure. 'I've tried it out when I've been alone—though that's not often here!—and *I* thought it had come back, too. Let me sing a song for you, and you can all tell me if you think I've got my voice back!'

She sang a song that the lower school had been learning. 'Who is Sylvia, what is she?' The girls listened spellbound. Yes—there was no doubt about it, Mavis's lovely low, powerful voice had come back again—better than ever. And this time it was owned by a Somebody, not a Nobody, as it had been before!

'We shall once again hear you saying, "When I'm an opera singer and sing in Rome and New York and . . ."' began Darrell. But Mavis shook her head.

'No, you won't. You know you won't. I'm not like that now. Or am I? Do say I'm not!'

'You're not, you're not!' said everyone, anxious to reassure a girl they all liked.

Darrell clapped her on the back.

'I'm *so* glad, Mavis. That almost makes up for this horrid Connie Affair. You'll be able to have singing lessons again next term.'

For a day or two it seemed as if the Connie Affair was at an end. Connie did not report any more strange happenings. Then she came to the common-room almost in tears.

'Look!' she said, and held up her riding-whip. It was one she had won at a jumping competition and was very, very proud of.

The girls looked. Someone had gashed the whip all the way down, so that in places it was almost cut through. 'I had it out riding this afternoon,' said Connie, in a trembling voice. 'I came home and took my horse to the stable . . .'

'You took two horses,' said Bill. 'Yours and Ruth's, too. I saw you.'

'I took the horses to the stable,' said Connie, 'and left my whip there. When I went back to look for it, I found it like this!'

'Anyone in the stables?' said Darrell.

'No. Nobody at all. Bill had been there, of course, and June and Felicity had, too—and I and Ruth. Nobody else,' said Connie.

'Well, *one* of those must have done it,' said Darrell. 'But honestly I can't believe any of them *did*. Ruth and Bill certainly wouldn't. My sister Felicity wouldn't even think of such a thing. And I feel pretty certain June wouldn't either, much as I dislike that cheeky little brat.'

'Anyway, both the first-formers had gone by the time I'd stabled the horses,' said Connie. 'You didn't see them when we left, did you, Ruth?'

'No,' said Ruth.

'Did you notice anyone else at *all*, when you were grooming your horse, Ruth?' asked Darrell, puzzled.

'She didn't even groom her horse,' Connie answered for her. 'I always do that. She stood there, looking at all the other horses, and would have seen anyone slinking round.'

Everyone was puzzled. Ruth went out of the room and came back with her own whip, a very fine one. 'You're to have this, Connie,' she said. 'I'm so upset about all these things happening. I insist on your taking my whip!'

'No, no,' said Connie. 'I don't mind taking things like rubbers and shoe-laces—but not your beautiful whip.'

That evening Darrell was alone with Bill. She was worried and puzzled. 'Bill,' she said, 'are you *sure* there was nobody else in the stable but you and the twins this afternoon? I suppose—er—well, Gwendoline wasn't there, was she?'

'No,' said Bill.

'I hated to ask that,' said Darrell, 'but it *is* just the kind of thing Gwen would do.'

'It's her own fault if we think things like that of her,' said Bill.

'Why does Connie groom Ruth's horse for her?' asked Darrell. 'Is Ruth so lazy? She's always letting Connie do things!'

'No. She's not lazy,' said Bill. 'She's just queer, I think—a shadow of Connie! Well, I must go and give Thunder a lump of sugar, Darrell. See you later.'

She went out and left Darrell thinking hard. A curious idea had come to her mind. She fitted one thing into another, like a jigsaw puzzle—she remembered all the unkind things that had been done to Connie, and she remembered also all the kind things that Ruth had done to try and put right the unkind things. She remembered also a queer look she had seen on Ruth's face that evening, when Connie had refused Ruth's whip.

'A kind of frightened, half-angry look,' thought Darrell. 'Just as if she'd apologized to Connie, and the apology had been refused.'

And then something clicked in her mind and she suddenly saw who the spiteful person might be that played all these petty tricks on Connie.

'What am I to do about it?' wondered Darrell. 'I can't tell anyone in case I'm wrong. It's got to be stopped. And I'm half afraid of going and tackling anyone to get it stopped. But I must! It's serious.'

She got up and went in search of Ruth. Yes, it was Ruth she wanted, and Ruth she must tackle!

21   DARRELL PUTS THINGS RIGHT

WHERE was Ruth? She wasn't in the common-room or the dormy or the classroom. Where could she be?

'Anyone seen Ruth?' asked Darrell, when she met any girls in her search. Nobody had. But at last a second-former said she thought she had seen Ruth going into the gardeners' shed by the stables.

Darrell sped off to look. She came to the shed, where the gardeners kept their tools, and stopped outside the door to try and think what she was to say.

As she stood there, she heard a curious sound. Somebody was certainly in the shed—and the sound was like a kind of groan. Darrell pushed open the door quietly and looked in.

Ruth was there, right at the back, sitting on some sacks. In her hand she held the cut and broken riding-whip, which she had obviously been trying to mend.

She didn't see Darrell at first. She put her hand over her face and made another sound—either a groan or a sob, Darrell didn't know which.

'Ruth,' said Darrell, going in. 'Ruth! What's the matter?'

Ruth leapt up in fright. When she saw it was Darrell she sat down on the sacks again, and turned her face away, still holding the broken whip.

'Ruth,' said Darrell, going right up to the girl, 'why did you spoil that lovely whip of Connie's?'

Ruth looked up quickly, amazement and dismay on her face. 'What do you mean?' she said. 'I didn't spoil it! Who said I did? Who said so? Did Connie?'

'No. Nobody said so. But I know you did,' said Darrell. 'And it was you who did all the other horrid things, wasn't it?—took this and that, hid things, and broke things, anything you could get hold of that belonged to Connie.'

'Don't tell anyone,' begged Ruth, clasping Darrell's hand tightly. 'Please don't. I won't do it again, ever.'

'But Ruth—why did you *do* it?' asked Darrell, very puzzled. 'Anyone would think that you hated your twin!'

Ruth slapped the broken whip against the sacks. She looked sulky. 'I *do* hate her!' she said. 'I always have done—but oh, Darrell, I love her, too!'

Darrell listened to this in surprise. 'But you can't love a person and hate them at the same time,' she said, at last.

'You can,' said Ruth, fiercely. 'You *can*, Darrell. I love Connie because she's my twin—and hate her because—because—oh, I can't tell you.'

Darrell looked for a long time at Ruth's bent head, and saw the tears rolling off her cheeks. 'I think I know why you hate Connie,' she said at last. 'Isn't it because she's so domineering—always answering for you, doing things for you that you'd rather do yourself—pushing herself in front of you—as if she was at least two years older?'

'Yes,' said Ruth, rubbing her wet cheeks. 'I never get a chance to say what *I* think. Connie always gets in first. Of course, I know she must have a better brain than I have, but . . .'

'She hasn't,' said Darrell, at once. 'Actually she ought to be in the lower fourth, not in the upper. I heard Miss Williams say so. They only put her with you in the upper class because you were twins, and your mother said you wouldn't like to be separated. Connie only keeps up with the form because you help her so much!'

There was a silence. Darrell thought about everything all over again. How very queer this was! Then a question arose in her mind and she asked Ruth at once.

'Ruth—why did you *suddenly* begin to be so beastly to Connie? You never were before, so far as I noticed. It all seemed quite sudden.'

'I can't tell you,' said Ruth. 'But oh—I'm so miserable about it.'

'Well, if *you* won't tell me, I shall go and ask Connie,' said Darrell, getting up. 'Something's gone awfully wrong, Ruth, and I don't know if I can put it right, but I'm going to have a jolly good try.'

'Don't go to Connie,' begged Ruth. 'I don't want you to tell her it was me that was so beastly all the time. And oh, Darrell, I was so *sorry* for Connie, too, when I saw how upset she was at losing her things. It's dreadful to hate somebody and make them unhappy, and then to know you love them, and try to comfort them!'

'I suppose that's why you kept giving Connie your own things,' said Darrell, sitting down on a tub. 'Queer business, this! First you hate your twin and do something to upset her, like spoiling the riding-whip she loved—and then you love her and are sorry—and come to give her your own riding-whip! I could see you were upset when she didn't take it.'

'Darrell—I *will* tell you why I hated Connie so much lately,' said Ruth, suddenly, wiping her eyes with her hands. 'I feel I've got to tell someone. Well—it was something awful.'

'Whatever was it?' said Darrell, curiously.

'You see—Connie adores me, and likes to protect me and do everything for me,' began Ruth. 'And so far we have always been in the same class together. But Connie was afraid she would fail in School Cert. and felt sure I would pass.'

'So you would,' said Darrell. 'And Connie would certainly fail!'

'Well—Connie thought that if she failed and I passed, I'd go up into the lower fifth next term, and she would have to stay down in the Upper Fourth and take the exam again another term,' went on Ruth. 'And that would mean she wouldn't be with me any more. So she asked me to do a bad paper, so that I would fail, too—and then we could still be together!'

Darrell was so astonished at this extraordinary statement that she couldn't say a single word. At last she found her tongue.

'*Ruth!* how wicked! To make you fail and feel humiliated when you could so easily pass! She *can't* love you.'

'Oh, but she does—too much!' said Ruth. 'Anyway, I said I *would* do a bad paper—somehow I just can't help doing what Connie wants, even if it's something horrid like that—so I *did* do a bad paper—and then afterwards I hated Connie so much for making me do it that I did all these horrible things to her!'

Poor Ruth put her face in her hands and began to sob. Darrell went and sat on the sacks beside her and put her strong comforting arm round Ruth's shoulders.

'I see,' she said. 'It's all very peculiar and extraordinary, but somehow quite understandable. It's because you're twins, I expect. Connie should have been your elder sister, then it wouldn't have mattered! You could have loved each other like ordinary sisters do, and you'd have been in different forms, and things would have been all right. Cheer up, Ruth. It's all been frightening and horrible to you, but honestly I can see quite well how it all happened.'

Ruth looked up, comforted by Darrell's simple explanation. She pushed her hair back and sniffed.

'Darrell, please, please don't tell Connie I did all those things,' she said. 'I'm awfully sorry now that I did. She wouldn't understand, and she'd be awfully upset and unhappy. I couldn't bear that.'

'Yes—but you can't go on like this—being bossed by Connie, and being just an echo for her,' said Darrell, sensibly. 'I don't see any way of stopping it except for us to tell her. I'll come with you if you like.'

But Ruth began to sob so much when Darrell suggested this that Darrell had to give up the idea. A distant bell sounded and she got up. 'You'd better go and bathe your eyes,' she said kindly. 'I'll try and think of some way to put things right without telling Connie—but it's going to be difficult!'

Ruth went off, sniffing, but much comforted. Darrell rubbed her nose hard, as she often did when she was puzzled. 'There's only one thing to do!' she said. 'And that's to tell Miss Williams. *Something's* got to be done!'

So that evening, after supper, Miss Williams was astonished to find Darrell at her door, asking for an interview. She wondered if Darrell had come to beg to have her position as head-girl restored to her. But it wasn't that.

Darrell poured out the strange story of the twins. Miss Williams listened in the greatest amazement. The things that could go on in a school, that nobody knew about, even though the girls concerned were under her nose all day long!

'So, you see, Miss Williams,' finished Darrell, 'if Ruth can't bear Connie to be told, everything is as bad as before! They'll both fail the exam, they'll both stay down in the Upper Fourth, instead of going up next term, and poor Ruth will go on being domineered over, and will hate and love Connie at the same time. It must be horrible.'

'Very horrible,' thought Miss Williams, horrified. 'And very dangerous. Things like this often lead to something very serious later on.' She did not say this to Darrell, who sat earnestly watching her, waiting for some advice.

'Darrell, I think it was very clever of you to find this out,' said Miss Williams, at last. 'And you have acted very wisely all through. I do really feel very pleased with you.'

Darrell went red and looked pleased. 'Can you think how to put things right?' she asked. 'Oh, Miss Williams, *wasn't* it a pity that Ruth did a bad exam paper! If she hadn't, things would have got right of themselves—the twins would have been in different forms.'

'Darrell,' said Miss Williams after a pause, 'what I am going to say now is between you and me. I glanced at all the exam papers before sending them up—and Ruth didn't do quite as bad a one as she thought! In fact, I feel pretty certain she will scrape through.'

'Oh *good*!' said Darrell, delighted. 'I never thought of that. So they'll be in different forms next term after all, then!'

'I think so,' said Miss Williams. 'That will give Ruth a chance to stand on her own feet and develop a personality of her own, instead of being Connie's shadow—and Connie will have to stop domineering over her—it will all disappear naturally and gradually, which is the best thing that could happen, in this curious case.'

'Won't Connie know anything then?' asked Darrell. 'Won't she have to be told?'

'That will be Ruth's business, and no concern of anyone else's,' said Miss Williams. 'Some day, when the right time comes, she may choose to confess to Connie—and perhaps they will even laugh at it all. Keep an eye on Ruth for me, will you, Darrell, for the rest of the term? You're in her confidence now and I shall trust you to see that nothing else goes wrong between the twins.'

'Oh, I will,' said Darrell, pleased to be asked this. 'I'd love to. I like Ruth.'

'And Darrell—I shall make you head-girl again in two days' time,' said Miss Williams. 'And this time I shall be very, very proud of you!'

22   'PING!'

EVERYONE was delighted when Miss Williams announced in her quiet voice, two days later, that Darrell was once more to be head-girl of the form. 'Thank you for taking on the position temporarily,' she said to Sally. 'But I am now convinced that Darrell deserves to be promoted again.'

'Why, Darrell? Why has Miss Williams put you back as head this week?' asked Belinda and the others, after class. But Darrell didn't tell them, of course. Miss Williams hadn't actually said that it was because of her trying to put right the affair of the twins—but she knew that it was. She had really acted like a responsible head-girl then.

No more spiteful things were done to Connie, and gradually the Connie Affair, as it was called, was forgotten. Ruth seemed to forget her dislike and resentment, and was very sweet to Connie. 'Next term,' thought Darrell, 'things will be quite all right—they'll be in different forms, and Ruth can go ahead with her good brains, and Connie can work at her own pace and keep her hands off Ruth.'

The term was slipping away fast now. Alicia was better, and fortunately no one else had caught measles from her. Most of the Upper Fourth had already had them, which was fortunate. Alicia groaned because she felt sure she had failed —and would have to take the School Certificate all over again.

She was to come back to school a week before Breaking-Up. The girls were very pleased. They had all missed Alicia's quickness and sense of fun. Gwendoline was perhaps the only one who didn't want her back. Poor Gwen—she had already lost some of her fat, through having to play so much tennis and go for so many walks, and swim—or try to—each day! But she certainly looked healthier, and her spots were rapidly going.

Clarissa amazed the class one day by coming back from a visit to the dentist and the occulist looking completely different! 'I haven't got to wear glasses *any* more!' she announced. 'And that awful wire's been taken from my front teeth. Do you recognize me, girls?'

'Hardly!' said Darrell, and Belinda got out her pencil to make a sketch of this different and most attractive Clarissa!

She stood laughing in front of them—her deep green eyes flashing round, and her white teeth no longer spoilt by an ugly wire. Her wavy auburn hair suited her eyes, and she looked unusual and somehow distinguished.

'You'll be a beauty one day, Clarissa,' said Belinda, her artist's eye seeing Clarissa at twenty-one, lovely and unusual in her colouring. 'Well, well—talk about an ugly duckling turning into a swan!'

Clarissa was now fast friends with Bill, much to the girls' amusement. Nobody had ever thought that the boyish Bill, who seemed only to care for her horse Thunder, and for Miss Peters (but a good way behind Thunder!) would make a friend in her form. But she had, and the two chattered continually together, always about horses, and rode whenever they could. Gwendoline didn't care. Since she had seen Clarissa going off at half-term with the dowdy-looking elderly woman in the old Austin car, she had taken no further interest in her.

Gwendoline wanted a grand friend, not somebody ordinary, whose people didn't even clean their old car when they came at half-term! So Gwen was once more alone, with no one to talk or giggle with, no one to call her friend.

'We ought to do something to celebrate Alicia coming back,' said Belinda. 'She's coming tomorrow.'

'Yes! Let's do something,' said Darrell, at once.

'Something mad and bad,' said Betty, who was in the courtyard with the others.

'A trick!' said Irene. 'We haven't played a trick for two whole terms. Think of it! What are we coming to? We must be getting old and staid.'

'Yes, let's play a trick,' said Sally. 'After all, the exams are over, and we worked jolly hard—we deserve a really good laugh!'

'What trick shall we play?' asked Mavis. 'Betty, didn't you bring anything back this term? Last term you brought back that awful spider that could dangle from the ceiling like a real one—but we never got a chance of using it. Gosh, I'd like to have seen Mam'zelle's face if we had managed to let it down over her desk!'

Everyone giggled. 'I didn't bring it back with me this term,' said Betty, regretfully. 'I stayed with Alicia in the hols and one of her brothers bagged it. But I tell you what I *have* got!'

'What?' asked everyone, getting thrilled.

'I haven't tried them yet,' said Betty. 'They're awfully queer things. They're little grey pellets, quite flat. One side is sticky, and you stick it to the ceiling.'

'What happens?' asked Irene.

'You have to dab each pellet with some kind of liquid,' said Betty, trying to remember. 'At least, I *think* that's right— and then, according to the instructions, a queer bubble detaches itself slowly from the pellet, floats downwards, and suddenly pops—and makes a pinging sound.'

Everyone listened in delight. '*Betty!* It's too marvellous for words!' said Irene, thrilled. 'Let's play the trick tomorrow, to celebrate Alicia's coming back. We'll have to get the step-ladder to put some of the pellets on the ceiling. Let's do it when Mam'zelle takes us. She's always fun to play tricks on.'

So, with much secrecy, the step-ladder was hidden in the cupboard outside the Upper Fourth classroom, and just before morning school, three flat grey pellets were quickly fixed to the ceiling, where, quite miraculously, so it seemed to the girls, they stuck very tightly indeed, and could hardly be seen at all.

Betty brushed each one over quickly with the liquid from a small bottle sent with the pellets. Then the ladder was bundled into the cupboard again, just as Mam'zelle's high heels were heard tip-tapping down the corridor. Daphne flew to hold the door open, and the others stood ready in their places.

'*Merci*, Daphne,' said Mam'zelle, briskly. 'Ah, Alicia—it is very, very good to see you back. You have had a bad time with your measle?'

'Well, actually I didn't mind my measle very much, after the first day,' said Alicia, with a grin. She was looking very well now.

'It is good that no one got the measle from you,' said Mam'zelle, sitting down at her desk.

'I had a measle last year,' said Irene, and this was the signal for everyone to talk about when they had a measle, too. Mam'zelle had to bring the talk to an end, because it showed signs of getting very boisterous.

'We will have no more measly talk,' she said, firmly, and wondered why the girls laughed so much at this.

They took quick, surreptitious glances at the ceiling every now and again, longing to see the new trick at work. Alicia had heard all about it, of course, and was thrilled with their novel way of celebrating her return. She had suggested that everyone should pretend they could not see the bubbles, or hear the 'ping' when they exploded.

Betty stuck some pellets to the ceiling

'Mam'zelle will think she's gone crackers,' she said. 'I know I should if I saw bubbles that pinged round me when nobody else did!'

'Today I go through the questions that you answered on the exam paper,' said Mam'zelle, smiling round. 'You will tell me what you put and I will say if it was good or no.'

'Oh *no*, Mam'zelle,' protested Alicia. 'We had to do the exam—let's forget it now it's over. Anyway, I did such a frightful paper, I've failed, I know. I can't bear to think of the exam questions now.'

Irene nudged Belinda. One of the grey pellets was beginning its performance. A small grey bubble was beginning to form up on the ceiling. It grew a little bigger, became heavy enough to detach itself, and floated gently down into the air. All three pellets had been placed just above the big desk belonging to Miss Williams, where Mam'zelle was now sitting.

With bated breath the girls watched the bubble slowly descend. It looked as if it was about to fall on Mam'zelle's head, decided not to, and skirted round her hair, near her left ear. When it got there, it burst suddenly, and a curious sharp, very metallic 'ping' sounded.

Mam'zelle almost jumped out of her skin. '*Tiens!*' she said. '*Qu'est ce que c'est que ça!* What was that!'

'What was what, Mam'zelle?' asked Sally, innocently.

'A ping—*comme ça!*' said Mam'zelle, and pinged again. 'Ping! Did you not hear a ping, Sally?'

'A ping? What exactly do you mean, Mam'zelle?' asked Sally, putting on a puzzled look that made Darrell want to cry with laughter. 'You don't mean a *pong*, do you?'

'Perhaps she means a ping-pong,' suggested Irene, and began to giggle. So did Mavis. Darrell frowned at them.

'I sit here, and suddenly in my ear there comes a *ping!*' said Mam'zelle. 'I feel it on my ear.'

'Oh, I thought you meant you *heard* it,' said Sally.

BY this time, of course, the girls were almost helpless with laughter. Tears were pouring down Darrell's cheeks and Sally was holding her sides, aching with laughter. Irene appeared to be choking and Alicia and Betty were holding on to each other helplessly.

Mam'zelle rushed to Miss Williams. She was taking a class in the second form, and was amazed at Mam'zelle's sudden entrance.

'Miss Williams! I beg you to come with me to your classroom,' Mam'zelle besought the astonished Miss Williams. 'It goes "ping" and it goes "pong"—right in my ears—yes, and down by my foot.'

Miss Williams looked astounded. Was Mam'zelle off her head? What was all this ping and pong business? The second form began to giggle.

'Mam'zelle, what exactly do you mean?' asked Miss Williams, rather crossly. 'Be more explicit.'

'In your classroom there are pings and pongs,' said Mam'zelle again. 'The girls do not hear them, but I do. And I, I do not like it. Miss Williams, come, *je vous prie!*'

As it looked as if Mam'zelle was about to go down on her knees, Miss Williams got up hurriedly and went with her to the Upper Fourth. The girls had recovered a little and were on the watch to see who might be coming. One or two more bubbles had floated down and burst with sharp pings, and another was just about to descend.

'Sssst! It's Miss Williams,' said Mavis, suddenly, from the door. 'Straighten your faces.'

With difficulty the girls pulled their faces straight, and stood up as Miss Williams entered with Mam'zelle.

'What is all this?' asked Miss Williams, impatiently. 'What is it that Mam'zelle is complaining of? I can't make head or tail of it.'

'It is a ping,' wailed Mam'zelle, beginning to despair of making Miss Williams understand.

'I think Mam'zelle has noises in her ears,' said Alicia, politely. 'She hears pings and pongs, she says.'

A bubble fell near Mam'zelle and burst. 'Ping!'

Mam'zelle jumped violently and dug Miss Williams unexpectedly in the ribs with her finger. 'There it comes again. Ping, it said!'

'Don't poke me like that, Mam'zelle,' said Miss Williams, coldly, whereupon another bubble burst, and yet another, and two pings sounded almost together. Miss Williams began to look puzzled.

'I go,' said Mam'zelle, and took a step towards the door. 'I go. There is something ABOMINABLE in this room!'

Miss Williams firmly pulled Mam'zelle back. 'Mam'zelle, be sensible. I heard the noise, too. I cannot imagine why the girls do not hear it.'

The girls suddenly decided they had better hear the next ping—so, when it came, they all called out together.

'Ping! I heard it, I heard it!'

'Silence,' said Miss Williams, and the girls stopped at once—just in time for a bubble to descend on Mam'zelle's nose and explode with an extra loud ping.

Mam'zelle shrieked. 'It was a bobble! I saw a bobble and it went ping.'

Miss Williams began to think that Mam'zelle really must be mad this morning. What was this 'bobble' now?

And then Miss Williams herself saw a 'bobble' as Mam'zelle called it. The bubble sailed right past her nose, and she gasped. It pinged beautifully on the desk and disappeared.

Miss Williams looked silently up at the ceiling. Her sharp eyes saw the three flat pellets there—and saw a bubble forming slowly on one. She looked back at the class, which, trying not to laugh, but not succeeding very well, gazed back innocently at her.

Miss Williams' lips twitched. She didn't know what the girls had done, nor exactly what the trick consisted of—but she couldn't help feeling that it was very ingenious—yes, and very funny, too, especially when played on someone like poor Mam'zelle Dupont, who could always be relied on to take fright at anything unusual.

'Mam'zelle, take your class out into the courtyard to finish the lesson,' she said. 'There will be no pings there. And if I were you I would give the housemaid instructions to take a broom and sweep the ceiling before you next take a class in this room.'

This last suggestion reduced Mam'zelle to a state of such astonishment that she could only stand and stare after Miss Williams' departing figure. Sweep the *ceiling*! Was Miss Williams in her right mind?

The class began to giggle again at Mam'zelle's astounded face—and then as another ping sounded Mam'zelle plunged for the door. '*Allons!* We go to the courtyard,' she said. 'We have been much disturbed. Come now, we will leave behind these bad pings and pongs and go to do some work.'

The story of the pellets and their pings flew through the school and made every girl gasp and laugh. There were so many visitors to the Upper Fourth form room that Miss Williams grew quite cross.

She stood a broom by the door. 'Anyone else who comes can sweep the ceiling six times,' she said. 'And let me tell you, it's not as easy as it looks!'

'Oh—that *has* done me good,' said Alicia that night. 'I've never laughed so much in my life. Mam'zelle's face when that first bubble pinged! I nearly died!'

'Miss Williams was rather a sport about it, wasn't she?' said Darrell. 'She spotted the trick all right, and wanted to laugh. I saw her lips twitching. I'll be sorry to leave her form and go into the fifth.'

'Yes—next term most of us will be up in the fifth,' said Sally. 'Goodness, how queer it will seem to be so far up the school.'

'I've liked this term,' said Darrell, 'although it had its horrid bits—like when I lost my place as head-girl.'

'I was glad when you got it back again,' said Ruth, speaking suddenly on her own, as she had done several times lately. She looked affectionately at Darrell. She had had a great admiration for her ever since Darrell had put things right for her—and had not told Connie. Miss Williams had quite casually told Ruth that although she had been disappointed in her exam paper, she thought probably she had passed all right—and that if Connie didn't, she hoped Ruth wouldn't very much mind her twin being left down in the fourth, whilst she, Ruth, went up into the fifth.

So it looked as if things would be better next term. Connie would soon get over the separation, and, after all, they would continually see each other in the dormy and at meal-times.

The last few days of the term flew by. The Breaking-Up day seemed to come all at once. The usual pandemonium broke out. Mistresses began to feel as if they were slowly going mad as girls whirled past them, shouting and calling, and trunks were hurled about, night-cases lost, rackets strewn all over the place, and an incessant noise raged in every tower.

The train-girls went off first, and were loudly cheered as the coaches moved off down the drive. 'Write to us! See you next term! Be good if you can! Hurrah!'

Darrell went to find Felicity, who seemed to be continually disappearing. She found her exchanging addresses with

Susan. June had gone with the train-girls, and Darrell had noticed that Felicity had not even bothered to wave good-bye to her. So *that* friendship was finished with. Good! Darrell still thought of June with dislike, but now that her little sister was no longer dragged around by June, but was standing on her own feet, she had lost the desire to slap June hard!

'Felicity! As soon as I find you and stand you by the front door, you disappear again,' said Darrell. 'Daddy will be here soon with the car. For goodness' sake come with me and don't leave me again. Where's your bowler hat? You've got to take it home with you in case you go riding in the hols.'

'It was here a minute ago,' said Felicity, looking round. 'Oh no, look—that pest of a Katie has got it—what an ass she looks—her head's miles too big for it. Katie! KATIE! Give me my BOWLER!'

'Felicity! Is there any *need* to yell like that?' said Miss Potts as she hurried by, almost deafened.

'Oh, Potty, I haven't said good-bye to you, Potty!' yelled Felicity. Darrell felt quite shocked to hear Felicity call her form-mistress Potty.

'Felicity!' she said. 'Don't call her that.'

'Well! You told me that everyone was allowed to on the last day of term,' said Felicity. 'POTTY!'

Belinda came by with Irene's music-case. 'Anyone seen Irene? She wants her music-case and I've just found it.'

She disappeared and Irene came along, groaning. 'Where's my wretched music? I put it down for a moment and some idiot has gone off with it.'

'Belinda's got it. Hey, Belinda, BELINDA!'

Mam'zelle came walking by with her fingers in her ears and an agonized expression on her face. 'These girls! They have gone mad! I am in an asylum. Why do I teach mad girls? Oh this noise, it goes through my head.'

'Mam'zelle! MAM'ZELLE! Good-bye. My car's come.'

'*Au revoir*, Mam'zelle. I say, is she deaf?'

'Hurrah! There's our car. Come on, Irene.'

Clarissa came by, excitement making her green eyes gleam. She looked very pretty. 'Mother's come,' she shouted to Bill. 'Come and see her. She wants to know if you can come and stay with me in the hols. Bill, come and see my mother!'

Gwendoline went out at the same time as Bill and Clarissa. Drawn up by the great flight of steps was a magnificent Bentley car, gleaming and shining. Leaning out was a charming auburn-haired woman, beautifully dressed. A most distinguished-looking man sat beside her.

'Mother!' shrieked Clarissa. 'You've come at last. This is Bill. You said you'd ask her to stay in the hols!'

Gwendoline gaped in amazement to see this gleaming car, and such parents—parents to be really proud of! But—how could they be Clarissa's? Hadn't Gwen seen her dowdy grey-haired mother come and fetch her one Sunday at half-term, in an old Austin car?

'Good-bye, Gwen,' said Clarissa, seeing her standing near, but she did not offer to introduce the girl to her mother.

'I thought that was your mother who came to take you out at half-term,' said Gwen, unable to stop herself from looking surprised.

'Oh no—that was my dear old governess,' said Clarissa, getting into the car. 'Mother couldn't come, so Miss Cherry popped over in her old car to take me out instead. Fancy thinking she was my *mother*!'

Gwen's car was just behind, and Mrs. Lacy was looking out and waving.

'Gwen! How are you? Oh, you *do* look well! Who was that pretty, attractive child that just went away in the beautiful Bentley. Is she in your form?'

'Yes,' said Gwen, kissing her mother.

'Oh, I *do* hope she is a friend of yours,' said her mother. 'Just the kind of girl I'd like.'

'You saw her at half-term,' said Gwen, sulkily. 'And you *didn't* like her. That's Clarissa Carter.'

Darrell and Felicity looked at each other and giggled. How sorry Gwen must be that she didn't get Clarissa's friendship! As it was, it was Bill who was going to spend most of the holidays with Clarissa, and not Gwen. Poor Gwen as usual wouldn't be asked anywhere.

'There's our car!' cried Felicity suddenly. She caught Mam'zelle round the waist. 'Good-bye, dear Mam'zelle. See you next term!'

'Ah, dear child!' said Mam'zelle, quite overcome at Felicity's sudden hug. She kissed her soundly on each cheek and everyone grinned at Felicity's startled expression.

'Good-bye!' cried Darrell, waving to the rest of the girls. 'See you in September. Look out, Belinda, you're treading on somebody's bowler!'

'It's mine, it's mine,' shrieked Felicity, in anguish. 'Take your great foot off it, Belinda.'

'You teach your young sister to be polite to her elders!' called Belinda, as Darrell and Felicity went headlong down the steps, almost knocking over poor Matron.

'Good-bye, Matron! Good-bye, Miss Williams! Good-bye, Potty! Hallo, Mother! Daddy, you look fine! Hurrah, hurrah, it's holidays!'

And into the car piled the two girls, shouting, laughing, happy and completely mad. They leaned out of the window.

'Good-bye! Happy hols! See you soon again! Good old Malory Towers—we'll come back in September!'